Sherwood

By Parke Godwin

Sherwood
The Snake Oil Wars
Waiting for the Galactic Bus
A Truce with Time
The Last Rainbow
Beloved Exile
Firelord
A Memory of Lions
Darker Places

With Marvin Kaye

A Cold Blue Light
Wintermind
The Masters of Solitude

Collected Short Stories

The Fire When It Comes

Anthology (Editor)

Invitation to Camelot

Play

Cold Journey in the Dark (One Act)

Sherwood

Parke Godwin

WILLIAM MORROW AND COMPANY, INC.
New York

It is the policy of William Morrow and Company, Inc., and its imprints and affiliates, recognizing the importance of preserving what has been written, to print the books we publish on acid-free paper, and we exert our best efforts to that end.

Library of Congress Cataloging-in-Publication Data

Godwin, Parke.
    Sherwood / by Parke Godwin.
      p. cm.
    ISBN 0-688-05264-9
    1. Robin Hood (Legendary character)—Fiction. I. Title.
    PS3557.O316S5 1991
    813'.54—dc20   90-28565
                                                          CIP

Printed in the United States of America

First Edition

1 2 3 4 5 6 7 8 9 10

BOOK DESIGN BY PAUL CHEVANNES

To Persia Woolley

Acknowledgments

Rather than list the many excellent standard texts researched in writing *Sherwood*, I will simply mention those that provided the clearest insight into England of the late eleventh century, such as *William the Conqueror*, by David C. Douglas, and *William Rufus*, by Frank Barlow. In addition, there was the indispensable *1066: The Year of the Conquest*, by David Howarth, whose lucid discussion of the principal historical characters, such as Harold and William, was enormously helpful. Dorothy Hartley's *Lost Country Life* became one of my bibles, along with Richard Marquiss's charming *In the Season of the Year: A Diary of the Nottinghamshire Countryside and Its Wildlife*. I am also much indebted to Edmund Burke's handbook, *Archery*.

For Marian's spoken charms in love and healing, I must thank Gail Duff's *Country Wisdom*. For the tale of the merchant and the angel on pages 203–205, I can give no reference. The plot kernel, the angel writing *inasmuch* on the sinner's forehead, was heard on a 1930s radio broadcast. What title and by whom escape me after fifty-odd years, but I claim no originality beyond the setting and adaptation.

I must thank a number of professional people, some of them personal friends, who went out of their way to aid me with specific research:

Dr. David Roffe, F.S.A., of Leicester, England, who commented on and sent me pages of *Domesday Book* relevant to the royal manor at Grantham.

Cheryl Kedwards, of Toronto, for specific pagan May Day rites.

Judith Tarr, author and equestrian, for expert advice on breeds and care of horses—and, with another author-friend, Susan Shwartz, for cheering me on.

Jean-Daniel Breque, translator, for help in French phrasing.

Many, many thanks to Morgan Llywelyn, who suspended work on her own book *Druids* to guide me through five marvelous days in Ireland en route to Sherwood.

Most of all, to Persia Woolley, who took much valuable time from writing her own *Guinevere: The Legend in Autumn* to put the bulk of this manuscript on disc when an injury made typing impossible for me. Her help and suggestions have been such that *Sherwood* could not have been completed as soon or nearly as well without her. "Thanks" is a pale word, Persia.

Special thanks to my agent, Merilee Heifetz, for being in my corner all the way on this.

Finally, Samcat, the tortoiseshell feline who graciously agreed to serve as model for Perdu, providing she didn't have to do any scenes with dogs. An ironclad cat contract has kept me honest.

Contents

BOOK I

Oak and Iron

1

ROBIN LISTENED TO the forest.

His disgrace was plain. Ten years old, always sure he knew every thicket and path in Sherwood, and look at him. Not only lost the doe's trail Will Scatloch said a blind man could follow, now he was lost himself. Robin felt angry and foolish and afraid.

The red doe was moving north. This late in summer she'd be with her fawn and would not stray far for water until sunset and then no farther than she must. But this one had wandered long and far. Perhaps her fawn had died. Once he picked up her trail over a bare muddy patch. Later the birds found it for him, pecking after the fat grubs turned up in leaf mold by her small hooves. That led him on, so absorbed in the stalk he forgot which way or how far he'd come. The oaks here were strange, the beeches too, older and more massive, sunlight feebler, shadows deep and chill. Nothing for it, Sherwood was bigger than even he could imagine, and dumb-as-bread Robin was lost for the first time in his life.

He couldn't just admit failure to Will Scatloch, didn't know the way back in any event. That frightened Robin more than anything. Ten this year, nigh to being a man, most of his life spent in this forest. His earliest memories were of this green silence that had always meant safety until today; of his father's folk a-Maying or flower-decked for Midsummer Eve when the soft gloaming scarce deepened toward dark before morning glowed bright. Every glade and footpath were known to him. He *thought* they were. . . .

13

What hour now? The bell at Blidworth church rang Nones long ago, it seemed. Closer to Vespers now by the paling light. Gloomy and dark here, the bracken tall and lush, wood blewits fanning here and there out of the earth like fantastical faerie thrones, fair as violets, poisonous as toadstool—

There was a sudden furious thrashing in the nearby thicket. Robin froze: from the sound of it, a beast large enough not to care how much noise it made. The deep grunting and snuffling scared him even more. A wild boar. Robin dropped silently, a Lincoln-dark smudge in the lighter green of the bracken. For endless moments the grunting and crashing—then, finally, the boar lumbered away beyond earshot. Rising when he could no longer hear its passage through the thickets, Robin gave himself pallid congratulations. He didn't manage that one too badly. Nothing timid about a boar. Will said that once in Wales he'd seen a boar charge straight at a huntsman's spear and run it clear through him in his red fury to kill the man. This was not the moment to test such a point.

He took up the red deer's north-leading trail and for a little time forgot his own problem in concentration. Not a young one, this doe. She'd learned every lesson the forest teaches its own from birth. She must know he was following, might be watching him now. Odd—Robin did feel that hackling of the short hairs on his neck, the animal awareness of eyes fixed on him.

Then a new sound removed all doubt and skipped a beat of his heart —a weird, wailing, inhuman sound rising up like a mad spirit from the forest. A *near* voice, eerie-howling in a jolting singsong chant and under it the muffled thumping of impossibly huge feet coming yet nearer, hastening to make short work of Robin Aelredson. The hoarse voice grew in volume, terrifying. *Jesus defend me,* Robin prayed, *that ent Will Scatloch.* Not a human man at all. The boy's mind blazed bright with terror. Of all nightmares, this one was to be most feared.

Robin Goodfellow—him, Puck-Robin, lord of the forest himself, and none more rightly afeared than a boy nicknamed after him by a mother (who should have known better) tucking him into bed one summer night when he fought sleep and wanted to stay up in the hall.

"No, to sleep, Puck-Robin," Maud whispered, kissing him firmly goodnight for the second time, "or I'll bar your door with rowan that you devil me no more."

His mother might think him the very Devil now and again, but she would never name him such; to name the Devil was to bring him sure, but Robin Goodfellow was a different, dangerous matter, ruling the forest as he lordly pleased. He piped to the animals and bade them dance, taught wild songs to the char-burners, dried up the cow's udder or soured the milk if the deywoman displeased him. Forest and wild heath, high as the treetops, low as the mole's burrow, all belonged to Great Robin who came now to punish a boy for taking his feared name in vain. Shivering in the chill shadows, the smaller and very mortal Robin's courage deserted him. *I swear by Saint Grimbald, Mum meant no harm, nor did I. Surely you would not harm me.*

No, that wouldn't hold any more water than a sieve. On Saint Grimbald's very day, not a month gone, didn't he waylay his own father, Thane Aelred, on the cart track to Papplewick, leaping from the thicket to demand ransom in Robin Goodfellow's great name? A guilty usurper and Goodfellow would know him one.

Robin's heart coated thicker with ice as the wailing chant grew to frenzy. The ominous *thump-thump* seemed louder, closer. Robin quailed. He crossed himself hastily, wishing he'd been more honest at his last confession, but no help now. In the next breath, the Forest Lord would burst out of the brambles for his vengeance, ten feet high and all horns, man body on hairy goat legs, red eyes burning into his rightful prey. *"Niddering* boy, you dare take my name?"

"No, I swear," Robin whimpered through chattering teeth. "I'm only poor Edward Aelredson, foolish servant of my lord's lowest thrall. . . ."

Sensibly, Robin abandoned the argument and bolted, running from stark fear, forgetting the doe or that he was lost, let his legs churn him on through vast dark naves of ancient beeches, through glossy birch ghost-white in twilight where the sun never reached, toward a place of sudden, blessed light. He broke out of the trees' shadow, bounded across a narrow brook and fell gasping on a soft carpet of tussock grass. When a little of his breath came back, Robin dared to look up and around him. No, by the light it wasn't late as he thought, but his fear had a more somber hue now. He'd outrun Goodfellow, but now he was more lost than ever, far from Denby, felt like he'd run miles. This oak-ringed clearing was strange to him. The truth wrenched at him: There were hundreds of like clearings, and he might weary-wander from one falsely beckoning place of light to another and never find the way home. His mother would worry and Da would search. A lamp would be alight for him each night at dusk forever, prayers said in hope and then despair, while poor Robin grew old in the clutch of Sherwood, the vines crawled up his legs and out his sleeves and grass rooted between his toes, and not even birds would know him from the lord whose name he stole—

"No," Robin muttered, common sense coming back with his wind. "Half a moment now."

Witless indeed, forgetting Will Scatloch's first lesson: Read what the forest told you. Robin raised his head, not so frightened now. Stretched out like this, belly to the earth, he felt the great beating heart of the forest under him. In this hush where the song of a single bird would be startling, he felt that throbbing soft as the pulse in his ear when he drifted safe to sleep in his own bed. Curiosity overcame the rest of his fear. At the other end of the clearing, across the brown grass lavender-smudged with heather, there was a small hut of wattle and thatch. Between him and the hut, apart from the great oaks that rounded this open space, a younger oak grew. Robin stood up and glanced back at the small rill gurgling past him. The water must come from the place called Holy Pool. He'd never seen the pool, but the stream ran from it past Denby steading and on down to Blidworth dale. He only had to follow it home.

Nowt to fear then. What a dunce he was to run from the mere thought of old Goodfellow, who might not even be real. No thane held north Sherwood but Aelred, none but Edward Aelredson would hold it after. The assurance sank deep in Robin, routing fear. Old Goodfellow was only a tale, Denby real and solid to hand, firm underfoot, writ down as Da's royal grant in the rolls at Nottingham.

And by God I know my way home.

He stood looking down at the brook with new confidence, a gawky boy with a tangle of chestnut hair, homespun trews worn and muddy at the knee, wash-faded Lincoln tunic out at the elbow for all the patient patching, always boy-dirty no matter how soon after the grim duty of the bath, weather-tanned skin and mild blue eyes in which an outlander or Briton like Will Scatloch might already discern the peculiarly English complacency that stemmed from unquestioned right of place. The boy stretched out again to drink from the swift-moving trickle, scooping up the water with a brown hand—and again felt that eyes were on him. No forest phantom—no, the raw voice that bolted him like a coward was only an old charcoal burner jumping up and down on his clamped-down cords of wood and singing daft because char-burners seemed to be born with half a wit. The eyes on his back now were closer but somehow didn't fill him with fear. He drank his fill before rising.

Whoever you are, this place is mine. You can't fright me on my own land.

Robin rolled over on one arm. He might have laughed from relief but something stilled the urge.

Serene and majestic, the doe stood well out into the clearing near the young oak. From her silvered muzzle Robin knew she had survived many winters, but they hadn't dimmed the alertness in those dark, liquid eyes. Not age at all in the proud lines of her but something like forever. Though downwind of him, when his human scent alone should have warned her off, she didn't move. She was not afraid of him, aware but unconcerned, as if, like him, she knew her rights in this place might be shared but never surrendered.

A twig snapped somewhere near; someone laughed. The doe sprang away like a loosed arrow into the thickets beyond the clearing. With a rush of relief, Robin recognized his father's voice. Good, then: Da and Will coming to fetch him. But no, that wouldn't do. He wouldn't be led home like a baby when he wasn't lost at all. Quick and quiet as the doe, Robin melted back into the brush, made himself part of it as the two figures appeared through the trees. Robin grinned. Not Will at all, but Aelred and Mum Maud herself. Truly, in what single breath had he been lost when he never left home?

Robin's father was tall but not bulky, and fairer than his son who took to Maud's coloring. Forestwise as Will, Aelred should have felt someone watching him, but just now his attention was all for the small, slim woman on his arm. They paused at the brook, speaking in low tones. Da just picked her up light as straw, and Robin heard her squeal of pleased outrage—"Aelred, stop!"—as he bounced her once or twice for fun and sprang over the brook to plump her down in the grass. Maud sat up, swatting at him lightly but laughing. Robin never thought of Aelred apart from Maud, never separated the boundless feeling for them from the safety he took for granted—Aelred in the great carved chair at table, Maud always on his left—nearest the heart, she said.

Once Minna the cook had told Robin a story about his parents while he munched fresh oatcakes in the kitchen house. Mum was from northern Mercia where, comely as she was, she'd caught the eye and fancy of Earl Leofric's cousin. This cousin complained bitterly to King Edward when fair *Hlaefdige* Maud turned him down flat as a flagstone to marry Thane Aelred. This was how Robin learned that Denby was a royal grant, not from the earl. As for Mum choosing Da, that was only good sense. Robin couldn't see why Minna went on so over something plain as the oatcake he munched.

Robin followed the couple with his eyes, once more the forestwise hunter. A fine joke to tell on Da at supper tonight. His parents strolled to the young oak, arms about each other. Maud touched the tree tenderly,

the way she sometimes ran her fingers through Robin's hair, but now—
he couldn't tell why—the gesture evoked a strange sensation in his chest.
Then Maud did something stranger yet, undid her yellow linen veil which
Robin had never seen her do in the daytime before. She drew the ivory
combs and gold pins and shook out her hair thick about her shoulders,
the same color as Robin's.

The boy's lip curled with embarrassment: Here was his own mum
acting like a girl and his sensible da just as bad, kissing her hair and then
her mouth. Dumb as bread, the pair of them, going on like this in a way
Robin didn't understand. They held on to each other by the tree, very
close, whispering. Maud glanced back at the tumbledown hut, giggling
like a little girl with a delicious secret.

What they did then was even more mystifying: put their left hands
palm to palm, and, joined so, to the trunk of the young oak. Aelred
looked up at the sky, most like reading the hour by the light as farmers
did. Robin's parents strolled slowly back into the forest the way they had
come.

On second thought—he couldn't say just why—Robin wouldn't tell
this joke at table after all. Instead, he'd backtrack and stalk Will Scatloch
and teach *him* a thing or two. Tomorrow for that; now he'd best be off
home himself. He felt hungry and Minna the cook promised clotted cream
to his blackberries at supp—

The arm encircled his neck from behind, gentle but imprisoning. The
Welsh lilt at his ear was soft as a rustle of leaves. "Well, what have you
learned today?"

"Jesus, Will!" Robin twisted away, glaring at the young man re-
proachfully, to hide his naked surprise and knowing ruefully how flaming
useless it would be to stalk Will Scatloch without getting caught himself.
Will was twenty or a little more, close as he himself could reckon, brought
back prisoner from the border fighting three years ago. Despite the leather
slave collar he wore, Will's word was law in north Sherwood next to
Aelred's who shrewdly perceived the difference between one more
ploughman and a born forester. Curly hair black as sin and a peculiar set
to his eyes, as if from that skewed advantage Will saw the world differently from other men. Slightly built, shorter than the bow he bent like a
wizard, Will Scatloch in his faded green tunic and trews looked like a
swatch of the forest itself.

"Even on your own land, mind to look about you."

Will spoke an odd-sounding English. There was something sad about
his lightest remark, a tinge of humor about the most serious, yet from

the first Robin responded to that voice as animals to the sound of trusted masters. "Did the birds mark the doe's trail?"

"Aye, they did. I found a marten's track, too," Robin enlarged. "Heard him first."

"There's lying," Will clucked. "You're deaf as a post."

"Who's deaf?"

"Did you hear me clump up behind you loud enough to be heard in Nottingham? Come on, then. Your lady mother will be wanting you in the hall."

"Not a whit," Robin denied. "She was just here with my da."

Will looked out into the clearing. Robin couldn't read his expression. "Where, then?"

"There by the little oak. What's that hut, Will? I never saw it before."

"Boy-*bach*." A sly grin punctuated Will's thoughtful silence. "If we had to live in the little of Sherwood you've seen, we'd be piled high as turves at drying."

Robin wouldn't be put off. "They went all strangely to the tree and Mum took off her veil like a silly girl and—"

Will pushed him firmly out of the thicket toward the brook, one arm about the boy's shoulder. "Your da will tell you on a day that will come. It is an old story and worth the telling."

There was that *someday* again. Everything would happen on a *someday* that never came, like the longbow Will promised him. "When can I have my bow?"

The forester handed Robin his arrow quiver to carry. "Did I not say the staves are cut? A good bow takes long seasoning like a boy."

Robin made a plaintive sound. Will said good yew bowstaves needed three or four years seasoning, which was forever at Denby where seasons meandered after one another like clouds across the sky, and nothing happened one year to the next. He'd be too flaming old to bend the bow when he got it. "I did track the doe, Will."

"Did you now?"

"Well," Robin admitted in a rush of confidence, "more like she found me. Very strange."

"How strange? What was the manner of it?"

Robin slipped the quiver over his shoulder, batting idly at the head of a tall weed as he trudged by Will's side. "I was drinking from the rill, and of a sudden I *knew,* that clear and sharp, that someone was watching me. And there was the doe by the single oak, bold as you please. As if . . . she knew me."

They walked on. Will seemed impressed somehow but said nothing for a space. "Do you know the way home then?"

They were following the stream which ambled now through a wide meadow. Robin suddenly spurted ahead of Will, running from pure energy and good spirits out into the soft afternoon sunlight. In the middle of the meadow, he whirled about to Will Scatloch, arms wide, arrogant, daring life to come and happen.

"Of *course* I can find it!" he sang out. "You just follow me."

Speak of strange. When Will Scatloch turned his mind to that moment later, he remembered Robin there in sunlight, hair burnished with that glow—but the boy's face was shadowed somehow where no shadow should be. Will never thought himself to have the Sight gift given to so many of his blood, but there *was* a darkening over Robin's face as if God had frowned across the sun.

On the same summer day in Normandy, another boy was learning his own very different world. Where Robin's was gold, Ralf Fitz-Gerald's world was iron. Throughout their lives, circling each other, this profound difference made them natural opposites and enemies: Robin had and Ralf wanted.

Pah! *Jesu merde—*

Ralf Fitz-Gerald spat blood, cursing with a facility beyond his fourteen years. Sitting to one side of the practice field watching the other squires-to-be working at sword and shield, his tongue gingerly explored the raw gum where two back teeth were pulled yesterday because he had parried too slowly with a wearied shield arm. The blunt sword was heavy enough to break off the teeth, and his jaw was one purpled mound of misery, swollen from where the ungentle surgeon had dug out the broken roots. There'd been a poultice of mulberry juice and a few drops of pain-killing clove oil afterward, then strong boiled chamomile to help him sleep. That helped a little, but not this morning. Ralf watched the sword practice, easing himself into a more comfortable position on the bench where the weight of the chain mail and scale-armor coat didn't gall his shoulders so much. He'd been let off the first hour of practice, but the merciless serjeant would be calling him out soon to take his place with the others.

Le droit . . . la gauche . . . garde, fou, gardez! Encore! Hour after hour until muscles didn't ache and the sword became part of iron wrist and arm. Ralf set his aching jaw. He might spit blood all day but would not complain or even wince. The other boys would laugh at him, especially Turold. Ralf glared balefully at Turold working with sword and shield, bigger than himself and similarly right-handed. More often than not, now that Ralf had a chance to watch him from the side, Turold let his shield drop slightly when he swung. A common mistake that killed more vavasors than the pox. Ralf had worked the harder on his left arm, always choosing the heaviest shield to work with. Turold still cracked his teeth yesterday. Today would tell a different tale.

Squire training was better than the years he spent as a page in the household of the Vicomte de Gavnay, though he was fortunate to get that. His father held a small castle at Le Thiel that guarded a main road between Normandy and Maine. A father with three sons and four daughters, hard put to foster the legitimate boys to greater houses, let alone Ralf who was a last, late fling with a village girl. The boy accepted that as he dealt with the broken teeth. The world was full of bastards; that was the way of things. His father did what conscience and circumstance allowed: took him at eight years from his stoic mother, who now had five younger children to feed, and presented him to Vicomte de Gavnay for a fostered page—

"My lord, this boy has my name. I recognize him."

—Ralf Fitz-Gerald, hopefully to progress from page to squire to knighthood.

From which he might reach anything. When one has nothing, having is important.

As a page he ran between kitchen and high table, fetched and carried, learned what little Latin and letters he needed from the vicomte's chaplain, as much of polite manners as he could absorb from *la vicomtesse*. Women of rank were treated a certain way, no matter how poor. Women of his mother's station were not included in the principle; yet somehow, like dawn between night and day, he had been given the chance to brighten and increase. At ten, Ralf knew without framing the words for it, that he would not go back; at twelve, as boys' time is measured, he'd half forgotten any other life. The ladies had called him a pretty child, now they spoke of a handsome boy. It meant nothing to him. To be a knight, a vavasor, was the only pride worth bearing. There was always war somewhere. If not at home, knights hired out for pay and adventure, young ones for experience. This reduced competition. Clumsy vavasors didn't last long. Good ones rose in the favor of Duke William, but always in war which was a part of life like hearing Mass or air to breathe.

"*Venez*, Ralf."

The bulky serjeant waved him to take his place in line. No more ease

today. Ralf took up the long, tapering shield and trudged toward the line
of boys. He wanted to go back to bed and lie there like a wounded animal,
but the serjeant wouldn't let him. *He* wouldn't let him. Ralf spat a gob
of blood, trying to make it look casual, and took his place opposite the
grinning Turold. The grin was all Ralf could see under the conical helmet
with its nose guard down. The grin was enough.

Turold mock-saluted him with his sword. "How's your jaw, *bébé?*"

Ralf shrugged and lifted his shield into proper guard. *"N'importe.*
You were lucky." He set his feet, balanced on them, alert, pain locked
tight in a small closet of his mind. He would not be slow again. Turold
had bad habits as a swordsman. When he lowered his shield—

"Le droit!"

His jaw throbbed. There was always pain, always war. Life was war.

"La gauche!"

There were those who fought, those who prayed—*you are slow,
Turold*—and those on the bottom who served their betters. The weak
served the strong who protected them. A good balance: God willed it so.
Just be one of the strong, elevated even as priests above common men.
Priests urged mercy on that account. Let them give it, then. Their office,
not Ralf's. Life was not mercy.

He was faster than yesterday. He would be faster still tomorrow. God
willed him to the sword as the priest to his altar. War was a continual
din over Normandy, near or far but always somewhere, small wars between bickering lords waiting out the weekly Truce of God in order to
have three days of glory and plunder, or not waiting at all. And always
talk now of Duke William's claim to England on King Edward's death.
William was a hard man, they said, but if he won England, there would
be estates and titles for the taking. Though heir to Normandy at seven,
William was a bastard like Ralf. No one called the duke such to his face
now. No one even remembered the fact aloud, but the bastard had won
over them all. So might another. The best would go to the strongest.

"Allez!"

At the serjeant's bawled command, the drill became free combat. Ralf
stepped back, concentrating fiercely. He crouched before the bigger Turold, hot under the heavy coat of iron scales, sweat stinging his eyes. Not
a heavy frame, but one already beginning to bulk in the shoulders and
already evincing the first scars of his station on arms and chest, and in
the dark eyes already a schooled hunger that knew if it wanted, it must
first take.

Turold hovered, showing off, spinning the heavy sword. "Remember what I did yesterday, *bébé?*"

I remember nothing else.

Turold lashed out with an overhand chop at Ralf's head. Easily blocked this time. Now the fool tried the same again.

"Hé là!" Ralf's shield came up flat overhead as his sword lashed out too quickly to be deflected, connecting with Turold's helmet hard enough to dent the iron. Turold dropped his sword. His eyes went dull, lost focus. He sank to his knees, pawing the helmet from his head. Ralf was rewarded with a gratifying splotch of blood in the tousled hair.

"Good, Ralf." The serjeant strolled over to buffet his shoulder; even that hurt his jaw. "The rest of you crippled geldings, you see that head chop? That's the way it's done. Surgeon! One more for you."

Ralf glowered down at Turold clutching his bleeding skull. His own jaw ached cruelly. "Does it hurt, *bébé?* So do I. I hope I broke your buggering skull."

The year Robin was sixteen, the year's ploughing, planting, and sheep-shearing came as always at their appointed time, but the far world beyond Denby and Sherwood seemed to shake with the tread of distant giants. The comet lit their sky at Eastertide and all men, high or low, pondered what it portended for England, though Denby and Blidworth village didn't stay the Maying for all of that. Old King Edward was dead and Harold Godwineson crowned almost at his funeral. More talk of Normans in the hall this last winter and spring, and then King Harold's call for the fighting men from all the earldoms to join him at Sandwich. Robin's father went with the shire fyrd, and with him a number of Denby men, including Wystan Fuller, husband of Minna the cook, and the big blacksmith John Littlerede.

This year, then, Robin had to oversee Denby's holdings, the planting, and collection of rents for the spring quarter. Just as well Little John was gone with Aelred; he was always on about his rents being too high in addition to the farriering he owed in kind to Denby. Robin took it on himself once to tell John a thing or two, and tart enough. Old Ethelwold the steward said he might have managed John as his father did, without ruffling the man's feathers.

"John's not the smoothest temper in the shire, Edward, and even less with his wife and children dead of the pox."

"But he *knows* I'm right, doesn't he?"

"Then you don't have to lord it, do you?"

A Briton from Gwent (it galled him to be called wild Welsh), Will Scatloch spent the most time with his lord's son in the forest and most clearly saw the truth. The boy always had the English look to him, a mildness that grew to complacency, occasionally to arrogance, but deep-rooted in a sense of place and God-given right. There's Saxon, Will pinned it down in his thoughts and often aloud to his wife Angharad. "It is different from us they are. We think of our place in the whole, this world and the Land of the Young to come. A Saxon sees what's his and to hell with the rest. Nay, love, and if we didn't come from Gwent, and ourselves standing here to tell him, mind, Robin would scarce believe the place was there. He's been to Grantham and Nottingham, not a step beyond, so there the world ends."

Not arrogance, but Will was right. The world ended at the far edge of what Robin knew: Nottingham goose fair, the market at Grantham. More familiarly home and the tread and tasks of each season and at the heart of it all the forest, remembered earlier than setting one foot before the other. This year past his bones fulfilled the promise of outsized hands and feet, shooting him up toward his father's height, not brawny but lithe, with the tendency of his people toward furious activity punctuated by long indolence. He liked his ale, tolerated church when Lady Maud insisted, picturing God as a patriarchal archetype of King Harold, and took his bow-hunting with a passion Will Scatloch would save for music or storytelling by the fire.

And yet . . . this year Robin often stopped in the middle of the task at hand in the field or forest or grooving an arrow to set its feather flights, and on the clearest of days thought or imagined he heard the sound of distant thunder.

Da's been gone most of this year. A strange time, what with comets and crownings and Normans claiming our king's a usurper, and nowt feeling as it should.

Three years now since Will made his first bow and showed him how to press it, but only this last twelvemonth or less before he felt the weapon part of his arm. Will had taught him to bend the bow not by pulling the string, but pressing his whole body forward into stance and draw. Not easy, though once learned, the method took advantage of the whole strength of a man's back and shoulders rather than putting all the strain on the shooting arm. The result was greater range and accuracy, more endurance over a day of shooting.

Shooting by instinct was the devil's own way until Robin learned to estimate distance without thinking in numbered paces. The draw was higher, anchored at the shooter's jaw rather than his shoulder. That took forever, it seemed, his aim getting worse, not better, but once he learned to *feel* distance, his arrows were never far off the small targets—but never close enough for Will, of course.

"There, Will. By Saint Wulfram, not a hand's width off."

"And no less, by Saint David."

"Well . . . close."

"Close for an Englishman."

"Well, what, then?"

"You're only on it once, Robin. Feel it with the whole of you. Don't hurry." That was true enough. When Will shot, the draw, stance, and loose were one fluid motion that only looked careless. "Be at the center, taking all the time you need."

"I did everything right, I swear."

"Right is it?" Will pulled the errant shaft from the turf. "The deer of Sherwood stand yet in no peril."

This September day he felt right. He paced away from the willow wand Will set upright in the meadow grass. As he paced, Robin listened to the first hint of autumn in the north wind—not cold yet, but you could feel it coming. The wind burned on his face and Robin read its force, nocking the arrow as he walked.

"Far enough," Will commanded, distant behind him. "Mark your wind."

No need; he knew the wind sure as the shoes on his feet. Nevertheless, he plucked up a handful of grass and let it fall from shoulder height.

"Now!"

Robin turned in a smooth motion. The mild eyes went a little sharper as they found the target, as the body stanced, drew, and loosed. The arrow sang through crisp September air—

Sure as a hawk stoops, swift as Da will fall on the Normans if they come. North wind all month, they'll never cross the Channel against it, and even if they do, there's Da and the king and every good lord and fyrd-man in England waiting for them. There, shaft, fly, stoop, and don't dare miss—

"Good, Rob!"

When he trotted back to Will, the little Welshman was kneeling by the arrow imbedded in the ground. The pile had driven in not a finger's width from the wand. Will's swart face creased with a broad grin. "Now the deer of Sherwood can beware of you."

As he unbraced his bow, Robin heard someone calling him in the distance; the voice came through the trees along the path to the hall. "Sounds like Much."

Much it was, the burly young miller, churning along the path toward them. Then the big bay mare galloped past him and into the meadow. Lady Maud calling to Robin and waving. She checked the mare to an easy trot, pleasurably flustered with her tidings. A few strands of chestnut hair had escaped her veil. One didn't think of one's mother as "pretty," Robin thought, but if there was any one feature he visualized thinking of Maud, that was the eyes. They were dark and deep-set, heavy-lidded. You might think of them as made for sorrowing but for the marvelous life in them—sparkling now, radiant as she reined in the mare. "Much couldn't wait when he heard the news, nor could I."

"What news, Mother?"

"Your father's coming home."

"Robin!" Much panted up to them, winded. "Little . . . Little John's back not this half hour gone—"

"Aelred sent him ahead," Maud punctuated. Yes, she was positively alight; Robin never knew a woman whom happiness could so ignite.

Flaxen-haired Much was a little older than Robin and stockier and would not be slighted of his office. "John said—wait, I'm that winded —to tell you the levies are all disbanded."

"But the mare needed a run anyway." Maud reined the horse about as it tossed against the bit. She rode well enough, but not often. "In two weeks, so Aelred said."

"Nay, ten days, lady," Much corrected with respect. "He'll ride through the night not to miss harvest."

"We will feast," Maud promised, and Robin suspected her as incapable as the mare of remaining still. "All of Denby must come. Robin, I'm off to Blidworth to tell Father Beorn and the folk." She touched her heels to the mare's flank and cantered away toward the eastward vale and the church atop the far hill, cloak billowing out, throwing the excitement over her shoulder. "There's so much to do! Your father mustn't think we've gone slack without him. . . ."

So there it was, Robin knew with a surge of joy and eagerness to be at it. God in His heaven, Da in the hall, the world set to rights. He turned back to Will and Much. "High time the king let them go. They must have eaten Kent bare for miles around."

And not a lord or freeman but needed to see to harvest and hog-slaughtering for winter. The Normans wouldn't come this late in the year, good weather all but gone and God's own north wind blowing against them.

"Robin," Much wondered, "all this talk of Normans. What are they, then?"

"I don't know. Foreigners 'cross Channel. Nowt to do with us."

Time to forget them and get on with what mattered. Robin's mind turned already to details his father would need to know. Fields, grain, tithes, and rents, what animals they could husband through the winter, which to be butchered and salted. Salt on hand, turf for cooking fires— all the vital things that must be timely looked to or go without. Neglect your dearest love before the land. The consequences were lighter. "What day is it, then?"

"I never know for sure." Much scratched in his long tow hair. "Near Saint Matthew's."

"Eight days hence," said Will Scatloch. "Father Beorn said so at Mass this morning—where Aelredson should have been were he good Christian."

"Then today's the twelfth." Robin draped a long arm around the little bowman's shoulder. "In good time, good weather, and Father's coming home!"

Did he, then? It was Will Scatloch's Welsh-sad way to wonder years after that last peaceful autumn of sixty-six. *Earls, thanes, churls like Much or slave like me: When you think on it, none of us ever came home again.*

Robin loped toward Denby with Much and himself on either side and never knew next month would be the end of his world. *Who would know that better than Britons, Angharad and myself? Listen to the songs, how all the great ones are promised to come again. Arthur and his combrogi sleep in a cave to be roused again in time of need.*

Even the English, without a drop of the Blood or a note of music in them, would deny Harold's death at Hastings and wait for him to return.

. . . No. Glorious as the songs might be when they stir the blood like whiskey—I am that long and far from my people in a colder place. The sun goes down, Robin, the lord keeps his bargain with the land, but only Christ will come again.

Robin stopped at the edge of the meadow, ear cocked. "Listen."

Much heard nothing. "What?"

"I thought I heard . . . the air's different."

Will sniffed: The crisp air had softened. "The wind's changed."

"So it has," Robin said, glad for the extra good days at harvesting. Still, he wouldn't have expected a south wind in the middle of September.

2

THROUGHOUT AUGUST AND well into September, Duke William's armada waited at Dives for a south wind that perversely refused to blow. Vanes pointed north day after day while good campaigning weather wasted away. The duke's vavasors wondered if the Easter comet was read amiss, not victory but disaster. At last, on the twelfth of September, the wind veered south and the ships were launched for the invasion of England.

When the craft were far out of Dives bent for the Wessex coast, the southerly breeze veered suddenly and stiffened into a dangerous beam wind from the west that scattered the laden craft. Through that first dark night they could neither turn back nor make headway north. Hardened warriors on land, they were crowded and seasick amid plunging, terrified horses. They could only founder or make shore wherever possible. Many drowned, others deserted, hordes remained unaccounted for. The greatest armada since Troy had run fifty miles against a demon gale only to wash back onto their own beaches.

The small village of St. Valery at the mouth of the Somme looked like a gnat shouldering a crow, a vast dumping ground above the harbor shallows thick-lined with ships, the crescent of the harbor crusted with supplies—casks of wine, bread, bundles of arrows and lances, extra mail coats, shovels and axes for sappers, salted meat, square timber stacks twice the height of a man of ready-made sections for castles on the English shore that might as well be distant as Troy now for all William would see of it.

Reined under William's bit, his lords muttered darkly. He was the strongest duke in France. No other man could collect or hold together so many men or command them not to pillage for supplies. More and more inclined to read the Easter comet's omen as ill: Harold mig¹ be a usurper of the duke's right to England, but the invasion was doomed not to be. Too much was lost at sea, good men, fine horses, and gear. The pope might be for William, but was God? A month at Dives, the wasted try against a south wind that only flirted and lured before scattering their craft. Day after day here at St. Valery with the wind still against them. What omen plainer?

The Vicomte de Gavnay did more than mutter. He could use reckless knights when needed, though he preferred the level-headed ones like Fitz-Gerald. De Gavnay was a far-seeing man, more given than most vavasors to reflection.

"If we go, we go now or resupply by any means. Send young Fitz-Gerald to me. Duke or no, William must hatch his eggs or get off the nest."

Among the thousands teeming about the beach, no messenger needed to search long for Duke William, easily the tallest man among them, a massive figure stalking the water's edge in a rusty black tunic with frugal gold embroidery under a red cloak generously cut to hide his stomach. William's thirty-eight years had never allowed for indolence or vanity, a fiercely energetic man who ran to paunch since early manhood and human enough to minimize it with subtle tailoring. More than that, like a humbling caveat from God, the red hair was thinning now.

Harold's, of course, is not. Wouldn't you know it? the Duke remembered sourly. *I will hate being bald.* He spent the pettiness on the surf in a glare black as his garment. The tide was coming in. Useles. with the wind ever mocking him from the north. Tomorrow was the twenty-seventh, Saint Michael's Day. No more good weather to count on even if they took ship this hour. The commanders would be at him again to strip the near countryside for supplies and provender. His reasoned refusal would be the same as yesterday. Harold had awaited their coming all summer and must be waiting still. Most of these knights had joined the venture for profit. If it failed, if they must limp back to a Normandy picked clean, that would be goad enough for another revolt in the spring.

In his rapt pacing, he came finally to his own ship, the *Mora,* high prow beached, much of its seventy-foot length beginning to tilt gently in the rising tide. William's hard, freckled fist rapped softly against the planks. For the tenth time since morning Mass, he glanced up at the weathervane pole high over the beach. Still northerly—what else?—but falling off now to mock him even more.

He thought with warmth of Matilda and the children. His duchess was the shrewdest and most trustworthy friend he had.

I wish you were here, Mora. I feel like a foolish gull on this beach, waiting out the weather and the will of God while both blow cold against me. You know what follows if we must abandon the venture. We make concerted war on the long-haired lords of England or my own make war on me. I lead or I lose.

Simple as that. Norman vavasors would come to heel only so long as he proved stronger. By comparison, the pack loyalty of wolves was more reliable. William had a sure instinct for men; so many of them had been trying to kill him since he was seven. Small wonder his teeth and wits grew sharp. In his rage he could give way to any cruelty; cooled, he thought more clearly than most.

As he leaned against the planks of the *Mora*, not even his duchess could have perceived William's mood. Forged in adversity, his mind was complex and contradictory, reactionary and touched with genius, cowed by Christian guilt and utterly fearless—audacious, ruthless, quick to scent opportunity, as quick to reckon the cost. At the moment, he recalled mistakes not to be repeated. An error to speak abroad of Edward's promise of the English throne. Frail cousin Edward blew hot and cold. One should have waited, measured him and his English more carefully, especially Harold. A bad mistake to underestimate a man whose easy charm lulled William into trust.

You were gulled too, Mora: We thought him softer. Capable but not hard enough for a crown. No sooner back in England than he forswore his oath to help my rightful cause, marching in state to Westminster even as Edward's casket was sealed. One hears the high and low cheered him alike. . . .

Was that God's will? If he was wrong in God's sight, if his claim to England was false, then God should say so. Since Dives, William began to fear the contrary winds were God's disapproval, and he knew his men felt as much.

I cringe before no man but I fear eternal suffering. Only Mora knows how I sweat of nights with that. Your honored oath would have spared me that, Harold. Your guilt's red as mine, yours the punishment.

The duke's hard mouth was a tight curl of disgust at the thought. Harold at Judgment. What hazard that plausible Saxon couldn't talk his way into Paradise? While honest William . . . alas.

He came out of his thoughts to notice the plainly dressed knight waiting respectfully for his attention. The fellow looked young to be belted, not tall but big in the shoulders and well muscled. "What is it?"

"Ralf Fitz-Gerald, sire. The Vicomte de Gavnay sends a request."

"Another request? Supplies?"

"Yes, my lord."

And subtle de Gavnay sent the youngest and least likely to offend his duke. "How old are you, boy?"

"Twenty, sir. Knighted this spring."

"You look younger." Still, William noted, there was a familiar look in the eyes: hungry for repute as himself at that age, probably no fool. "What says de Gavnay?"

"Wishes permission to forage for more supplies from the town and close farms; that we must pack them in from much greater distances now, by my lord duke's command, so he is hard put to keep his knights from taking what they want from Saint Valery."

"I don't care. Tell him no. Again."

"Yes, lord. The vicomte sends as well this final tally of our losses in mounts since Dives." The young knight proffered a short roll of parchment. William didn't read well, but the numbers were discouragingly high. "There must be a better way to ship horses."

"With my lord's permission, out of Dives they were tethered too close together, and incorrectly."

"I hear the Turks tie down the head and all four legs."

Ralf shook his head. "From what little I know of Turks, sire, a good horse has more sense. Tied so he can't move, a stallion doesn't know what to expect. He'll go mad with fear." Ralf produced a scrap of vellum from the scrip at his belt, smudged and often erased, but the diagrams were precise. To William they appeared painstaking, so many horses tethered just so, interspersed by so many experienced handlers.

"To embark as many as my lord will need, this is the surest way."

"Fitz-Gerald? Your father was late castellan of Le Thiel?"

"He was, sire. As to being my father," Ralf shrugged, "more or less. By bed, not blessing. Rest his soul nonetheless."

Finding them so seldom, William valued realists. He read much in the eloquent shrug. "Tell the vicomte my orders stand."

"My lord." The young knight bowed his head and wheeled away to his waiting horse. William measured the quick obedience and other aspects of Fitz-Gerald: young but not callow. Despite the slightly awkward gait of one who spent more time in the saddle than afoot, there were years of sword and shield work in the powerful shoulders. Purposeful eyes. Watchful. Probably spoke much less than he thought. "Wait."

Ralf halted and turned. "Sir?"

"You didn't ask why I refused de Gavnay."

"No, my lord. I know why."

"Do you indeed?"

"If the duke said to strip this town of every pig, chicken, or egg, I would do so. But profit abroad hardly begins with folly at home. God keep my lord."

William saluted the boy casually. For every hundred vavasors out of the chaos of Normandy while he was a hunted heir to the duchy, two or three learned more than to grab for themselves. Perhaps one had the rare ability to hold men to him through loyalty rather than force or fear. This Fitz-Gerald might well be that one if he lived.

William's nose caught the change before his eye.

The air—the smell was different. Dryer, warmer. He glanced at the weathervane, hardly daring to hope. The vane quivered and swung around to point firmly and at last south. The Duke took a deep, sufficing breath of the quickening breeze.

Yes. Now. By God's face, *now*. His voice carried far along the beach to other men who smelled the change and knew what it could mean. "The wind! Look! God *is* with us. To ship! We *go*!"

They had the wind, the tide, and a full, fair day for the crossing. "Sire Ralf!"

The knight swung his horse around. "My lord?"

"Are you for a place in my England?"

"Yes, sire. As God wills and my duke commands."

Suddenly William felt marvelous, almost as young as the waiting youth. "Then back to my lord de Gavnay," he roared on a wave of exultance, "and tell him to catch this tide or have no more of our venture than my boot up his backside. God willing, I will see you on Romney shore."

William splashed through the rising shallows, grasped the gunwale, and hauled himself aboard his ship to stand huge in the high prow where all could see him. "To ship, all of you!"

Through the frantic bustle, the porters forming human chains to pass the vital supplies to ship, the knights striding to take their horses, archers, and pikemen raggedly squaring into their companies, great Flemish horses lumbering up the gangplanks—the tall duke stood erect on the high-canted deck. Then he knelt and crossed himself. *Lord, I could not stir beyond Your will anymore than my ship without the wind. You who willed me duke will yet see me king.*

He commended into God's hands the safety of his wife and children, then rose to see the human tide lifting like the waters, running or trudging laden toward the endless line of ships. The freshening south wind carried their hoarse chant—

Deus vult! Deus vult!

God wills it. England was to be his after all.

Odd, though—a pause amid all the forward thrust of him now, later an ironic afterthought. The only man he ever misjudged was the only Englishman he ever admired.

On October 14, at Hastings, the duke defeated Harold's army to become William the First of England, though he spent four years bringing Saxons to heel. Not one man, not Harold alone he misread, but an entire breed. They were not a herd people, earthy but not easily led, loving their own patch of ground without concern for their like in the nearest shire or hundred. Northumbria was foreign to Mercia, the south and west to both. Thane Aelred of Denby went to Hastings with Harold, survived and submitted when he had to, only to rise and fight again, but never enough like him, never enough to turn the balance. England writhed for four long years.

"Stupid, obstinate," William despaired. "Must I kill one half of them to teach the rest?"

He must. The insular English, like Aelred and his son Edward, were slow or unable to comprehend the *concept* of defeat. In the summer of 1069, the north rose for the last time, native desperation against William's exhausted patience. With a new insurrection to quell and always the threat of revolt at home, William left Northumbria a gutted charnel heap. Vavasors like Ralf Fitz-Gerald had orders to leave no house unburned, no male alive over the age of twelve. York had rebelled and killed their Norman lords; Chester would surely follow. Common men and their farmer thanes for the most part, but the best foot soldiers in Europe as Ralf learned at Hastings where he buried two out of every three knights in his squadron. Not against cavalry; the Saxon nobles fought on foot, but for the first time, Normans faced the battle-ax, swung by men big as their own Viking ancestors.

Four years will change the face of a war. There was something else now, something new. The archers: To Normans, the bow was hunting sport; to Saxon foresters, it was a way of life. The English bowmen strangely absent at Hastings reappeared at York in the winter of 1070. Men in green wool and leather jerkins, poachers and outlaws who fed their families on the king's deer, led by thanes burned out, paupered for taxes, outlawed now themselves. Wielders of a coward's weapon, the Normans called them, with no niceties of honor about unseating a knight by killing his noble and very expensive horse. Lethal in a line, invisible in the forest or sudden, thick fogs. If one saw them, one was close enough to die. You cut the goose-feathered arrow from dead friends without ever seeing the sniper. By the winter of 1070, vavasors called them *les grises plumes*. Greyfeathers.

By that winter, knights like Ralf Fitz-Gerald, following William to recapture York, no longer looked too young. Neither did Robin of Denby, mere hours ahead of him at a tiny village called Tadcaster on the River Wharfe.

Time was vital, time for the mixed English, Dane, and Scot forces to consolidate at York—except that Saxons didn't trust mercenary Danes, King Malcolm's Scots trusted neither, and Norman cavalry could move faster than any of them thought possible. The English levies force-marched toward York through grey winter drizzle with William close behind. Short of walled York, pitched battle would be folly; they could only slow and harass.

One Norman column was moving north from Lincoln along Ermine Street. A second from Manchester traveled more slowly, harrowing the countryside and collecting supplies in a lengthening wagon train. This group, approaching River Wharfe, was too tempting to pass up. So said soft-spoken Aelred of Denby after questioning one of their scouts.

"My lords." Aelred glanced at the leaden sky. "The weather is with us, we know the country, and Leofwine here has found the place."

Aelred smoothed a muddy patch at his feet, the focus of shaggy, fur-cloaked men from Mercia and the northern marches—hulking men with yet the Norse build and blood. The scout, Leofwine of Brandeshal, was son to one of their thanes.

Aelred squatted to map the wet earth with a dagger point: a straight line for the Roman road, a curving snake for the River Wharfe crossing it at Tadcaster. The supply train would ford Wharfe in no more than two hours. Aelred spoke to the young scout. "Here, Leof, give them the sweet of it."

Leofwine hunkered down over the rough map. His startling blue eyes had an odd set to them, Aelred thought. *Sane as any of us but he doesn't look it.* The huge young man was like someone from old times, one of the berserkers who followed Ida or even Cerdic, with his hair tied back in long braids and that disturbingly intense glare.

"The ford here," he pointed with the dagger. "Roman work, lined with stone, the water's less than a foot deep, fifty paces bank to bank. Maybe ten wagons, but the riders in front keep getting too far ahead of them." When Leofwine smiled, he reminded Aelred of a contented wolf. "There's a full company of archers back there. One of 'em—one of the best, quick as a fox—he thinks we can hit the wagons from both banks while they're fording. That'll cloud their sunshine summ'at."

The warlords weighed the odds. Some thought they had too few archers as it stood, men needed at York. Others opined they wouldn't lose many if they hit and ran fast enough; in any case the gain would outweigh the loss. With some reluctance, Aelred agreed on that point. Leofwine dashed their objections, pointing to the mud at their feet.

"Frozen yesterday. Now it's thawed and there's fog coming in."

At Tadcaster, he said, the road sloped down to the ford, then up again. The fog would lie thickest on the river. Kill the lead oxen first, as many of the others as they could, jam up the ford. Every dead draft animal meant time spent to find another. The odds were with them.

"Yes," Aelred said.

The order was given. Leofwine, on his stolen Flemish gelding, would carry it back. He was putting foot to stirrup when Aelred caught him up. "Wait."

"Not much time, Thane."

"My son is with those archers."

"Whose isn't, then? I've got a half-brother gone to Ely with Hereward." Leather groaned under his weight as Leofwine hoisted himself to saddle.

"Tell my son—" To be careful, to do what he must but not foolishly. To remember what Will taught him. "He is Edward of Denby. Say I will greet him at Micklegate in York."

Leofwine's bleak northern visage lighted up. "Y'mean Robin?"

"Yes." Aelred's heart warmed. He grasped the bridle. "You know him?"

Leofwine roared his delight: Normans to kill and a small world after all. "Robin o' Sherwood's your son? Why, Robin it was saw the column first, saw the ford and lit up like a horn lamp with the plan." He swallowed Aelred's hand in a huge ham fist. "He'll show the Bastard some mischief, mark. God love you, sir: Were he not your son, I'd swear Robin's an outlaw born."

Robin lay next to Leofwine in the overgrown verge, twenty paces from the river ford. His plan and Leof's instinct for Northumbrian weather proved a potent mix. The whole company was keen for the venture. Men wouldn't be hard to hit even in fog like this, so long as you could see the shape of them. Nevertheless, Robin's mouth was dry and he needed to relieve himself again. Ridiculous: He just did.

Leofwine rumbled, "Hear anything?"

"No. Keep your voice down."

Eadwig's archers were in place, more on the south bank. They'd let the first cavalry and foot pass, then throw themselves across the road. The advance riders, turning to engage, would be cut off by Eadwig's twenty men assigned to their specific welfare. Robin tested the honed dagger blade on a thumb. It had to be sharp as Will's wit. He and Leof were to cut the throats of the lead oxen. That would slow things right enough. From where he lay, hidden from the road by fog and gorse, he could barely see the ford. The fog was pale grey, even smelled grey, like leaf mold and bird lime.

Robin cocked his head. "Listen."

Faint and distorted by mist, the rising rumble of iron-shod hooves on the road. Now the jingle and clink of harness and armor. Robin tried to wet his lips with a tongue gone thick and dry. He had to kill men today, might be killed himself. Da said the worst time was now, the waiting just before. Don't waste it, he said: Think what's to do, nothing else. What first, then next.

The sounds were nearer, became splashings as the first riders began to ford the shallows. Now the thing was begun, some of the tenseness left Robin. He flexed his shoulders under the dirty sheepskin jerkin and counted his arrows for the third time, knowing each like separate children in a family. This one flew true, that one had less reliable spin in flight. The best were grouped together for first need, the ones he'd made and fletched himself.

If they hit the lead team just before it reached the near bank, three or four wagons would be caught in the shallows. He thought of that—*keep thinking on that, not the ball of sick in your stomach.*

The advance riders and first foot soldiers clopped and trudged by their hiding place, the nearest briefly defined before they blurred away into fog. So many of them, Robin knew, and always more coming. He wondered if they'd been to Denby on the way here, God rot them. Except for taxes, they hadn't bothered Sherwood much, but you never knew what they'd do next. Normans didn't think like proper men.

"Unnatural," he said aloud.

Leofwine glanced at him. "Who?"

"Them. Unnatural lords. You'd think they wouldn't want to be so long from home. Things go slack."

He saw the glint of puzzled amusement in Leofwine's frosty eyes. *Right enough, I'm a farmer like my da and grandsire.* Leof's blood had been lords on Tees River since the old kingdom of Deira; more than five hundred years, he said. Besides Brandeshal, Denby was barely begun, a mere three generations. Yet for every year of that, and back to Alfred's time, Robin's kin had worked better land than Leofwine ever saw. "I wonder if they're good farmers, the Franks."

Leofwine kept his attention on the road. "They don't work the land, their blood's not in it. They just light and gobble like crows and fly away when there's nowt left. They don't know what owning means. They just take."

Leofwine's profile was heavy and bleak to Robin, the face of a moor-bred man. Brandeshal fought the Danes when they first came up Tees, fought the Scots, even their own earls sometimes. Hard enough himself to think of Norman overlords in Nottingham. For Leofwine, impossible.

The big northerner mused, "To think of the times I've cursed the fog that kept me from hunting." Then, more alert: "They're thinning out. Go, Rob."

Robin rose to a crouch and padded back through the verge toward the treeline, careful to make no noise. Fog phantoms became oak and birch sheltering small groups of men in dark green. Eadwig led this detail, a squat powerful Wessexman with the drawl of Somerset.

"Is it time, then?"

"Almost. Come on."

Eadwig slipped one leg between bow and string to brace the weapon. He caught up his quiver. "Get set, boyos. I'll be back."

Robin moved back out of the trees, Eadwig close behind him.

Ralf and Turold were among the last of the escort to clear the ford as the first wagons started across. Ralf felt the restiveness in his mount. The stallion snorted nervously, nostrils sending mist-distorted signals to his brain, but clear alarm: creatures he didn't know.

Turold first heard the clamor in the rear, not sudden noise but a rising babble and splashing at the ford and farther back the shouting of the rear guard: *Why the stop? What's the let up there?* Then the clear sound of a knight's horn sounding distress. Turold wheeled first, spurring his horse back to the ford, Ralf and eight others close behind him.

The first arrows sang close by his head; Ralf crouched forward behind his shield, seeing the ghostly figures across the road. His sword slashed at the nearest as he plunged through them. The horse stumbled, then reared as two Greyfeathers loomed in front of it. Well trained, at a touch of Ralf's knee, the stallion lashed out with fore hooves, then kicked at the marauders behind. Ralf heard Turold cursing: a high, angry sound as his old opponent from the training school dashed down into the shallows, spitting tags of prayer and obscenity—

The heavy horses churned the shallows of the ford about the stalled wagons. Ralf fought shadows, caught a fleeting glimpse of a slim figure stock still before him, the straight line of the longbow bent before the arrow smashed through his shield an inch from the wrist. Wagons asprawl of the fording, all the oxen dead. Blood-smell mixed with mist and made the stallion hard to manage as Ralf dodged and scythed at elusive, half-seen targets. One rebel lost his footing and went down in the water. Ralf trampled over him. The horse screamed and stumbled again, almost went down.

Then, suddenly as they came, the shadows were gone and the calling voices were all Norman. The horse lurched, favoring one foreleg. Ralf dismounted, feeling the icy water shock his feet and ankles and someone calling his name.

"Ralf Fitz-Gerald, where are you?"

The Greyfeather he trampled into the stones of the ford had slashed the stallion's off foreleg. Crippled him, the beggar.

"Ralf—"

Ah, fermez . . . Ralf leaned his forehead against the suffering animal's neck. His feet numbed in the freezing water, but he stroked the stallion's neck with sorrowing tenderness. Another of the best to be put down. *You would not want to live by half anymore than I would.*

He started to lead the limping horse toward the south bank where, dimly, the rear guard milled about the rear wagons. Here and there men called for help in the weak, shocked voice of the wounded. Some in English.

"Ralf, over here."

"Who's that?"

"Oderic." The voice, barely deepened from boyhood, sounded tight and queer.

"What is it? My horse is hamstrung. Are you hurt?"

"No, I—it's Turold."

Ralf led the stallion close to the south bank, then with a gentle slap at its rump, waded back through the shallows toward Oderic beside the wagon. The youth leaned over something propped against a heavy wagon wheel.

For Ralf ever after, this was the indelible image of Tadcaster: Oderic's face a pale circle in the cowl of his mail and Turold's body sprawled against the wheel, identifiable only by his surcoat. Someone had cut his throat neatly; that was the least of it. He couldn't have felt much of the rest. From the center of his forehead, the entire scalp had been ripped away.

Oderic made a queasy sound. Ralf snapped at him: "If you're going to be sick, do it downstream." He bent over, dashing cold water at his cheeks. He fervently wanted to be sick himself, but stomachs got used to everything like the rest of a man.

Trudging toward York with his company, Robin felt he could lie down in cold water and sleep for a year. If he could forget the ford. Too vividly he remembered Leofwine of Brandeshal screaming at the body of the Frank knight as he cut away the scalp and hair. Weeping Jesus, what a sound. Robin tried not to think on those he killed himself. Some of them must have been English. They tried to spare those. Some couldn't be helped. A safer sorrow was the waste of good oxen. Then he was too tired to regret anything. Maybe he'd do worse than Leofwine if Denby was at stake, though even home receded beyond the narrowing circle of his fatigue. No rest short of York with William so close behind. Say what you would about Normans, they moved faster, organized quicker than Saxons, that was one lesson learned.

The white limestone walls of York were two miles ahead when the order passed down the files to run. The men lurched forward in a clumsy jog, like a string of puppets, Robin staggering with them, too dulled to wonder about the smoke rising from a city supposed to be theirs.

The archers tramped into York through the arch of Micklegate Bar, into noise, confusion, and smoke dirtying the sky over the north of the city. Falling out with the others along Toft Green, Robin saw a steady stream of citizens hurrying north along Micklegate, bundles on their backs or hauling wagons piled high with the entire contents of dwellings. He dropped down next to Eadwig on the turf; it felt like a featherbed and himself melting into it. "Where's Leof?"

"Ah, then." Eadwig yawned, answering as if each word weighed ten stone. "He and his great Norman horse are nosing out William."

"Doesn't he ever tire out?"

"Doesn't believe in it," Eadwig slurred, near sleep himself. "Mark, he'll kill that horse."

At least they might have some meat. Beyond that wish—when Robin could think of it—he saw too few men on the south wall, all of them English. "Where's the Danes?"

Disorganized, the lot: sparse defense, scared people milling through the streets—and three fresh heads impaled high over the bar, two of them with reddish hair too long for a Norman. Robin's eyes closed by themselves as he melted back onto the turf, weightless, already drifting toward sleep. . . .

A boot nudged him. "Robin."

Bleary-eyed, he saw the foot first, then the broad head of the battle-ax, the shield. The mild face of Aelred smiling down at him. Robin leaped up, forgetting stiffness. "Da!"

"Well met, boy." They embraced and Aelred searched his son's face; perhaps with older wisdom, he read what Tadcaster had written there. "Not a hurt taken?"

"No, I just need . . . Father, what's wrong here? Where's the rest of our host?"

Aelred glanced bitterly at the severed heads over the bar. "There's two of them. The crop-head is the former knight-commander of York keep. The others are Scots."

"Malcolm's Scots? They're on our side."

"They were. Caught them looting the Minster library last night."

None of it made sense to Robin. His incomprehension was ragged with fatigue. "Library? There's nothing there but books."

"They fired it anyway; out of disappointment, I guess. Stupid sheep." To his son Aelred looked hardly rested himself, the long winter robe and cloak sodden and colorless with wear and mud. He could not have reached York more than twelve hours ago, little or no sleep since. "Son Edward, never trust a Scot. They're different blood from us; they can't think right." Aelred shouldered the heavy ax. "You might as well know the worst, then. We're alone."

Eadwig opened his eyes at that and sat up. "What's that, Thane?"

"One of Morcar's men is in command. If you can find him."

Eadwig stared up at the thane. "But the Dane—?"

"Bought off by William. Swein Estrithson's pulled them all back to the ships. When the Scots heard that, they grabbed what they could and most went last night." Aelred's unshaven jaw tightened with disgust. "What's left our carls are hanging for thieves."

From crowded, panic-surging Micklegate, something heavy crashed and splintered on cobblestones; from somewhere else the high-pitched scream of a frightened woman. Eadwig rose, shouldering his bow and quiver. "Better find some food, then. No use to fight hungry." He lurched away toward the street.

Aelred studied his son. "Get your feet wet at Tadcaster?"

"It went well, Da."

They stood on the green below the walls amid an acre of supine or prostrate men, some already asleep around them, smoke darkening the sky over Old Minster. "I wonder how things go at Denby," Aelred mused.

"Mother and Ethelwold have the hall well in hand and Will the forest."

"Well, then."

Home was better to think of than now. With one third of their expected strength, a few hundred archers and foot, the city retaken by English must be defended against a vengeful king coming with superior numbers of pikemen, cavalry, and siege engines. Only a little time before the walls would be breached. After that . . .

There it was. Nothing to say. Robin was glad of the shouts from the wall and the rider who galloped through the bar on a horse lathered and spent, leaping from the saddle to roar his impatience at all York.

"What's this? Who's about? Where's a *hlaford,* for Christ's sake!"

Robin and Aelred pushed through the hurrying crowd toward the blond-braided young giant clumsily brushing mud from his trews. The Norman scalp still hung from his broad belt. Robin grasped the man's big bear-paw. "Leof: about time you got here."

"Greetings, Thane Aelred. Rob." Leofwine's scowl vanished. "Well, we've Denby to count on, any road. Where are Swein's men? Drunk, I suppose."

Robin grated, "Don't hold your breath till you see them."

In few words, Aelred gave the scout the situation: The city's panic he could see for himself. Leofwine cast one black gleam of forlorn contempt at the walls. "If I'm to die, I'd rather at Brandeshal than here. Danes. . . ."

Eloquence in the single word. Brandeshal had fought them for nigh three hundred years before marrying those who stayed. As much Dane blood flowed in Aelred and Robin, though none of them would boast it today.

"William's not an hour behind me," was Leof's blunt estimate. "Two columns, one west of the river. Like as not they'll hit the west wall too."

"At least we slowed them at Wharfe." Saying it, Robin tasted the futility.

"Ah, what of that?" Leofwine growled. "Supplied or not, Bastard's comin'." He hauled himself back into the saddle. "Thane Aelred, if York's lost, I have to meet them with my father on Tees. They can't ask me to stay here."

Aelred just nodded. "I know that."

"Damn." Leofwine swabbed over his eyes, wiping at the fatigue. "Until then, I could find much less honor than to stand with you."

"God with you," Aelred took his hand.

They watched after Leofwine pushing his horse through the herds of humanity surging along Micklegate. Once more Aelred took up his ax and shield. They might have been standing in a field at home, Robin thought, his father looking as he did when too-early cold or rain wasted the yield: more than the crop, the labor and sweat lost and the thin, hard winter ahead.

"We almost did it," Aelred whispered to the walls and winter air. "Hold York, we held the north. We could have—"

Could have put an impassable bar across England, Robin knew. Could have fought and held out until William ran out of knights and fat horses and flaming well went home. Could have won. Let Swein Estrithson tell of that in his meadhall, and try to paint over his shame. Robin hardly had words for the truth in him, except that there were things you didn't sell. As for William, let him look on Aelred and know what he couldn't buy.

Defeat did not go with his father. Unthinkable: a man who tended Sherwood and his own easily as walking, who stretched the king's law to protect his folk. Who fined or more rarely flogged poachers whom sterner lords would have broken and turned out to beg. A man who commanded respect without raising his voice. Values unmeasurable in silver, laws never put to parchment, but *there,* solid as the white stone of these walls for all of that.

Someone over the bar shouted: "Here they come!"

"I must arm, Robin." Aelred encircled his son's shoulder with a hard arm as Eadwig jogged toward them, a bundle of arrows under each arm.

"Hey, coom, Rob. We're for the west wall."

"Good-bye, Father. I'll be back."

But Aelred held onto him a moment longer. "Listen, boy. What Leofwine said. About going home."

"Aye, Da. So will we."

Aelred's eyes held a darker truth. "Be sure you get to Denby."

"We both will, no fear."

"You'll know your time. You know the forests. Stay to them. Don't wait on me," Aelred hammered in the command, however soft his voice. "Get home."

The city as good as lost around them; yet to Aelred there were matters more important. "You know the bargain as well."

Robin knew it clear as the scar on Aelred's shield hand. "Aye, sir."

Then Eadwig threw him a bundle of arrows, anxious to be gone. "Rob!"

"Aye, coming. God keep you, Father."

Past Bootham Bar, running along the west rampart with the thin-stretched line of his company, Robin saw the devastated Old Minster at close hand: St. Peter's Church undamaged, but the library aflame, the exodus pouring out of Monk Gate toward the heath beyond. In the open square in front of St. Peter's a hasty gallows had been erected, an island in the surging river of humanity. They milled about it as one chained-and-noosed man after another was prodded up the ladder. Robin heard their brief, vindicated roar as the executioner tipped the ladder and called for the next condemned, and those nearest the gallows remembered the Normans and surged on toward Monk Gate.

When the long snake of the Norman column began to deploy in front of him, Robin slipped the leather shooting tab over the first three fingers of his right hand, Eadwig thonging it firmly about the wrist for him. Robin marked the sun: behind his right shoulder. The glare would be in William's eyes when he attacked. Good enough.

He chewed a chunk of mutton, watched the enemy come on, saw them only as enemies and not—not possibly—the future they were.

3

M ARIAN'S FEET WERE numbed misery; she'd been walking forever. The lines of homeless men and women teeming the Roman road to Doncaster grew larger by the hour as more carts and walkers joined it—frightened farmers peering from the trees before daring to come out, wary of Normans. Only then the man and wife and their grubby children might drag the cart onto the road. The rain had fallen all morning, a chill February drizzle that sooner or later got through the thickest wool. For hours nothing in Marian's awareness but the dull grinding of wheels and shuffling feet. No one talked; there was nothing to talk about. They were all like her, she guessed: burned out or driven off, steadings aflame and stock dead, come out of hiding only when the Frank knights were gone.

Marian hated the foreigners who did this and then called her kind stubborn or sullen. What else? *Go through our land like plague, burn out a life's work, kill my parents, then you goddamned foreigners want me to say thanks and love you?*

She was sixteen; they'd burned a part of her too. In another year she might have settled back in Tadcaster with a good husband of her own. Her mother, Godifigu, had worked this last year with her to lay away the fine linens and wool against that day. Up in smoke, the lot. Not the loss, but her mother's work, the love and care just . . . trampled down. When she thought of Godifigu stitching by candle or rush light, the plying needle a dear punctuation to soft, rambling gossip, she didn't know whether to cry or kill someone.

45

Her mother's body was charred black, barely recognizable by the bits of wool and shoe. They dumped her father in the pigsty.

The procession on the road grew longer as more and more people and wagons joined them. The northern sky was streaked far as one could see with smoke. A few like herself walked alone, most were old folk or very young. More women than men. Oxen that might have pulled the carts fed ravens now or were taken by the Normans, and twice now the short-haired horsemen had halted them, searching for able-bodied men or escaped soldiers from York.

The people about Marian kept their eyes on the road, patient oxen themselves. She might have been the first to see the man crouching among the trees in his muddy green, almost invisible when still. He took his time measuring the bedraggled lot of them before breaking into the open verge. From the man's labored gait, Marian couldn't tell whether he was merely exhausted, hunger-weak, or halt, or all three, but the bow he carried was his death warrant if the Normans caught him.

The archer reached the road a little forward of her. She couldn't see much of his face under the raveled hood, just streaked dirt and a scraggle of beard. He shouldered his way through the procession, moving on toward the woods to the south, hastened and encouraged by those behind: Hurry, lad. God bless—

"Horse! Look, the Normans!"

Holy Mary, not again. Marian turned to see the five mailed riders break out of the forest not far from where she first saw the fugitive. One of them cantered after him, the other four came on toward the miserable folk creeping along the road.

Something took Marian then, twisted her mouth in a snarl. *What are you wanting now? Someone over teething age to kill?* One of them searched her yesterday, the dirty pig, smelling of garlic and wine and horse sweat, putting his paws all over her. That was what she wouldn't suffer again; *that* turned her off the road hardly thinking where to go, but faster and faster, running toward the trees to the south, her ragged shoe soles catching in tangled grass. She could see the archer running and the Norman after him in full gallop now, drawing his sword. *Run!* He'd never escape, too far to cover, the rider already leaning out of the saddle to slash—

Done—no: The Saxon staggered but didn't go down. He spun wide and about, swinging his bow at the horse's head. The animal reared, startled, while the rider fought to keep his seat. Marian's legs churned her toward the forest. They wouldn't come after a woman, would they?

Not one woman. Somewhere close she heard the heavy drumming of hooves and dove into wet thicket—lay panting, unable to tell if the pounding was hooves or her own heart.

She lay still a long time.

When Marian dared to look about, the road was deserted. No foreigners, none of her own folk in sight. She glanced at the grey sky: going three by the light and dark soon. She could skirt the road into Doncaster; she wouldn't risk being pawed again. Her shoes were ruined and had to be resewn before she went much farther. Her linen undershift was sodden to the knees and so filthy the embroidered hem, stitched by her mother only last month, was past praying for. Marian started to walk, veering farther into the wood. For sure at Doncaster she might find a church for shelter, perhaps something to eat. Now that fear ebbed, she was fiercely hungry again, but the barley and bread in her wallet had to last.

Not a hundred paces before she found the Norman. The fear jolted her stomach, though she should have known. Overhead through the tree-tops, black against lead-colored cloud, the ravens were gathering. Smart birds, they always knew when something was dead or close to it.

The knight was very dead, sprawled in a clump of fern, not a big man but bulky with iron, ring mail from shoulders to boots, a heavy coat of iron scales over it all, sword belt twisted under him in the fall. He lay on his back, astonished eyes wide open like his mouth, as if he were saying *Oh!* to the long grey-feathered arrow centered in his chest. A small black beetle browsed near his mouth.

"Get his knife."

Marian's heart missed another beat; if she were frighted once more today, she'd not live out her span. The voice spoke again, in English with the northern sound like her own.

"Go on, get his knife. I've lost mine."

"Show yourself," she quavered. "If you be Christian man—"

"Ah, shut up, you'll wake the flamin' dead." The voice wheezed, the sound of a man rising painfully. The thicket parted in front of her and the archer emerged. Close, Marian saw how young he was under the hood and dirty beard, obviously in pain, shoving the hood back to reveal matted chestnut hair. "You're from back north?" he grunted.

"T-Tadcaster." Marian hardly felt safer with him than the Normans; he looked as dangerous.

"I've been there."

"You're the one he chased, then."

He nodded. "Been waiting them out."

"I thought he got you at first."

As he moved past her toward the body, Marian saw the stain on the sheepskin just below his left shoulder. Not deep, she guessed, but he'd lost blood. Clumsily he tried to retrieve the heavy dagger from under the dead vavasor.

"Here," she said. "I'll get it."

"That's my last arrow. I won't leave it in the likes of him."

With difficulty he loosened the dead man's sword belt and mail coat, favoring his shoulder, then tried to cut at the canvas under the iron scales, wincing with every movement. The questing beetle had found a home in the Norman's right eye. Marian always wondered at the plucked-chicken way they barbered themselves. They'd always have colds in England: no beard or mustache, the hair cut short above the ears, with long bangs covering the forehead. "Don't like hair, then, do they?"

"They think it's vanity except to cover their front, an insult to God." The archer struggled with the knife. "Burn out women and children but devil if they'll miss a Mass."

He was having a bad time of it and the shoulder bleeding again. Marian reached for the dagger. "Let me."

"Get away."

"You're mucking it proper." So he was. The wound must hurt him something fierce, though he wouldn't show it. Finally with a hiss of impatience, he passed the blade to her. "Almost through; just a little more."

Marian sawed vigorously. He'd never have managed at his rate. She cut away the last of the canvas and pried the mail rings apart beneath, exposing the padded tunic. "He's an old one."

"Just been here a while," he told her. "The careless ones don't last. Pity the horse ran off."

Careless just this once chasing him, the knight got slowed by thicket long enough for the archer to brace bow and get off his remaining shaft. He'd tried to catch the horse but it bolted.

When Marian had cut open the padded coat around the wound, he tried to take the knife back. "You won't want to finish this."

"Na, I'll do it."

"I've not much time. They'll be looking for this boyo."

"I can do it quicker. I did our pigs at Martinmas." Marian met his eyes, meaning it. "Small difference." She dug the knife deep into the wound, trying not to feel disgust. Small difference, but still. . . .

The archer watched her with added respect. "You're from a steading, then?"

Marian plied the knife firmly. "Near two good hides and pasture up Tadcaster. Finest sheep in the shire . . . there." The arrow pile came clotted from the wound. The archer wiped it carefully as a newborn babe, inspecting its set.

"Thanks, girl."

"You're bleeding. I've a few simples."

"No time." He looked up at the circling ravens. Two were descending, flapping down to the forest floor to wait. "Normans know what the birds mean. We should go farther into the wood. They don't like to follow in there. You have anything to eat?"

"Some bread and barley, bit of comfrey and willowbark."

"Come on."

Marian hung back; he wasn't the foreigner who squeezed her breasts roughly, but all men were the same on that account. Perhaps the knife in her hand helped him read the thought. His smile was a pale grimace.

"I couldn't do you ill now if I wanted to. What's your name?"

"Godifigu Marian."

"Marian . . . that's a good name. Edward of Denby." He wove a little on his feet, clearly near the end of his stamina. "My folk call me Robin. I hope my da got home. . . .

Marian didn't hear much hope in the sound of him. He walked away into the forest. After a moment of indecision, she followed after.

Hurt or not, Robin set a pace that had Marian panting. He moved as surely through the forest as she would about her father's house, halting only when the last light, filtering through oak and silver birch, was almost gone. "We can chance a fire now, but keep it small."

"Nowt to burn," Marian looked about. "Wood's wet as me."

He pointed to a rotted log. "Inside's dry. Cut from the inside."

The wound must be hurting more, since he talked less. Marian used the dagger to cut chips from the inside of the log, kindling with flint, steel, and dried bracken from her small wallet. She felt better with the cheery little flame, more like home and the rightness of things. No soft town woman, she knew how to make do with little and no wasting. Her wallet held essentials: needle and thread, a length of clean linen, a small leather boiling bag, half a pound of barley, and an end of stale bread. She made a rack of green sticks to hold the boiling bag of water, setting the bread atop the bag to freshen in steam. Across the fire, the man who called himself Robin stared at nothing.

"How is it?" she asked.

She had to speak twice. In the firelight, his face was haggard under the grime. The red-rimmed eyes came back from a far place. "What?"

"Take some of the bread. I'll put a poultice to your shoulder."

Sicker than hungry, he chewed the bread without relish. She cut off a patch of clean linen and covered it with the steaming comfrey leaves. Under his outer clothing, the remnant of linen shirt was well stitched but far past washing now. Marian pulled it over his head while he fretted about the lost horse.

"Didn't have to bolt, stupid nag."

"Shouldn't wonder, the smell of you. When was it you last bathed?"

He didn't remember. "Stop nattering, just do it." He jerked when the hot poultice touched the wound. "*Jesus.*"

"Lie still."

"What else would I do?" he ground through his teeth. "Tie it round and be done."

Men: They hated to show anything hurt. Less sharply she asked, "How'd you dodge out when the Normans came?"

Securing the bandage, Marian's hands were gentler than her voice. "My mother sent me to call the pigs. I was away when the Normans came. Why do they burn everything?"

"An army's like a household, got to eat. Willy Bastard cleaned our cupboard, there's the end."

The bastard king was well named, Marian cursed to herself. Let him burn in hell ten lifetimes for each of her parents, the same for every slaughtered sheep and stolen goose, most for her kitten Biddy they must have killed for sheer meanness. "I'll help you on with your shirt."

"Let be; I'll do it."

"I'll brew some tea."

He only nodded, slipping away into his own silence. When the willowbark was ready, they shared her one small wooden cup. Marian stared into the fire. "There was a battle at Wharfe. Nigh the ford."

"Yes."

"Couldn't see much with the fog."

"The tea's good." Robin looked up at her. "Well you thought to provide yourself."

"So should you have. For the walking."

"Walking?" He handed her the cup with wan disgust. "First three days I did nowt but run . . . where will you go?"

Marian didn't know. Perhaps Doncaster for a start.

"Doncaster's full of Franks."

Where then? Marian wondered forlornly. *Some church that might still have a Saxon priest. I'm a parish orphan now if ever one was left on charity's doorstep.*

Even in sleep Robin was still at York.

Stakes! We need more stakes!

So many of them, so few of us. They came over the walls and crashed through Bootham Bar too sparsely manned to stop them. You could only run east through the narrow, twisting streets, past St. Mary's Church toward the high mound and fire-gutted remains of the Norman keep, and still their horsemen flanked you easily. And there you turned for a last fight with River Fosse at your back and thanes like Father somehow forging discipline out of the rout.

The last he saw of Aelred, his father was forming with other lords and carls into the familiar shield wall. The remaining archers on their left and right behind as many sharpened stakes as they could anchor in time.

Get sweating, get those stakes in. Move!

The cold, helpless fear you might suppress but couldn't conquer as the iron behemoth of horses and men formed; the feel of them shaking the earth as they came down at you, faster and faster, the ground shaking under your feet and the thunder—

Draw and loose, draw and loose—men and horse weren't hard to hit when you were Scatloch-skilled to pin a darting hare, but so many of them and always more. Robin went a little mad, felt the lunacy like Leof's at Tadcaster course white-hot through his body, briefly erasing terror. They were running out of arrows; someone would soon have to retrieve what they could. He and Eadwig, standing shoulder to shoulder, made huge wagers on each shot, keeping a feverishly precise tally of who was ahead. A hundred pounds on this one, five hundred on the next. Eadwig owed Robin a thousand in silver, now two thousand—

Robin, fall out. Bring up more shafts. Run, lad.

He ran, weeping Jesus, he ran for the last bundles of arrows as if the Devil lashed him on, hearing even then the deep, paralyzing roar of that last charge. Some hit the archers, but most slammed into the shield wall that couldn't hold, couldn't hold, couldn't hold—

Father!

There was no line anymore, no anything.

He remembered in his dream and long after—he quit then. Between one breath and the next, he just gave up, all strength and courage drained away. He dropped the bundled shafts. His shoulders sagged, tears coming. Something stopped them, a hand or a voice like Will Scatloch's slapped the defeat so hard across its whimpering face that Robin's shoulders, drooping in surrender, shot square again.

Get home.

The knights weren't satisfied to break the shield wall but went at the bodies until there was nothing but red. Robin swam Fosse, skirting to the south, wet and half-frozen. From where he hid, he saw the end of it, the whole city burning, men digging a vast common pit for the rebel dead.

Shivering. Denying: Father got away for sure. He'll be home before you are, waiting with Mother. He got away like me and Eadwig.

No. Eadwig's dead.

Then the weary dream repeated like a dull song-round. Draw and loose again as that wall of iron and horses thundered closer and closer. *More shafts! We can't hold them—*

He'd sweated in his sleep despite the cold. When Robin woke he felt depleted but not as sick, and the girl Marian was boiling barley over the built-up fire, stropping the dagger on a slab of bracket fungus. A farm girl right enough, long fingers certain at whatever task she set them to.

With some chance he'd live out the day, Robin had time to study her over his barley: fair complected and her cheeks narrow, the whole set of her face clean and sharp as a vixen fox's. Up Tadcaster the folk were mostly Dane blood. She looked that but for the surprising brown eyes that warmed the whole. Her hair hung loose, greasy and dull now, though a rainwater wash would see it gold. Quiet too, there was a blessing. Worn out like this, he couldn't hold with chatter. At home, Will's wife Angharad nattered all day, whatever her mood, until Lady Maud politely told her to put a stopper in it.

In short, blunt snatches while she sewed at her shoes, Marian told him of her family. Her father was—had been—a free sokeman. There'd been a younger sister who died in her first year and was buried in the churchyard not a furlong from Wharfe ford. One other boy didn't live past his first week. Nothing unusual to Robin. His mother had lost two herself the same way. Infants didn't have much chance, weren't really counted in the family until they'd lasted the first year.

Close to two hides of land, Marian said, and cottars who paid her father in kind, and more often than not there were ten or more about the long table, though hardly ever any folk from outside. A good life; she couldn't remember being hungry ever. The things she described were familiar to Robin, a smaller Denby. At her age, he reckoned, she would be close to wedding, and her da'd not strain much to provide dowry in oxen or even silver, perhaps a few strips of arable laid on.

She was his own kind. Her tongue, as his, softened the middle of words and chopped off the endings back in her throat . . . and where in hell was she to go now?

Well, he had worries of his own. He and Aelred had been too long from home. Now there was seed-corn to riddle, arable to plow, and the lambing. When he mentioned these things to Marian, she just nodded. Her year turned as his, marked by the same unchanging tasks that needed no listing.

"Can you walk?" she asked him.

"Have to, don't I?" He tried to laugh as he rose; it sounded weak as a cough. "You're still for Doncaster?"

Marian shouldered her wallet. "Some place without Normans."

"Where's that?" The words came out harder than Robin meant them. "They're halfway to Chester now. I thank you for the food and the help, but I'm for Sherwood."

She just looked at him, accepting it. "Well, then."

No, she shouldn't have to go it alone. He had no energy to obstruct the urge. "It's a safe place, girl. You're welcome at Denby if you want to come."

Marian didn't move, didn't yet trust him that much, he guessed. Robin could think of no more to say, just walked away through the stand of silver birch. When he turned back at some distance, she hadn't moved. "Damn it, woman, do you come or stay? I can't wait on you."

Robin went on, telling himself he wouldn't look back again, much as he wanted her to come. Finally he had to. Marian was following him, long legs striding to catch up.

4

$\mathcal{H}$AIMO THE SQUIRE blew on cold fingers, gave the saddle cinch a final tug and turned to Ralf. "Ready, sir?"

Muffled in a heavy cloak against the cold, Ralf hobbled on frostbitten feet to mount. Never such a country for the Devil's own weather. Chester would be the final push. They crept westward across the long mountain spine of England, over moss and limestone outcrop, contending with bitter cold, threatened mutiny, and now deserters. Ralf's former lord, Vicomte de Gavnay, was missing this morning when the rest left their tents to face sudden, inexplicable fog. Not surprising that the vicomte left, nor the five vavasors who defected with him. But where could the fools go in midwinter with fog, dangerous patches of mire, and Greyfeathers prowling their flanks like wolves?

The king's orders were reasonable considering his short temper of late. "Bring them back, Fitz-Gerald. Tell the vicomte, if he refuses he may as well live at sea. His lands will be forfeit and himself dead if he sets foot in Normandy."

William was no more given to idle threats than easy trust. If he must, the man who left Northumbria an open grave would shovel de Gavnay into it without hesitation.

Ralf watched Haimo mount, only a few paces away but blurred by fog. The squire was his own age, he guessed. That wasn't young if you'd lasted since Hastings where veterans were made in minutes. This last year old friends, even old enemies like Turold, had gone down. As for horses, he lost count of the good Flemish mounts cut out from under him. If Saxons weren't used to fighting cavalry, vavasors had never faced a phalanx of battle-axes. As the longbow to the peasant, the ax was the natural weapon of English lords, part of them, balanced in their hand like the sword in his own, idly tossed and spun like a toy at any odd moment, until the heft became instinctive. The small ax in a lord's belt was his badge of rank. The awkward little throwing ax looked ridiculous until it flew at you.

To hell with that: Think now, think today. De Gavnay.

"They can't have got far," Haimo reasoned. "Which way, sir?"

The other search parties were fanned out west and south. "East. The way we came."

"There's the bogs," Haimo worried. "Best we take care."

The bogs were a severe danger. Very like, the deserters hadn't counted on the sudden fog. Who would this time of year, this high in the mountains? Everything was backward here. William strove for an unnatural kingdom where neither land nor men followed nature, where lords took pride in honorless pursuits like husbandry, and serfs became warriors in minutes.

They walked the horses along the barely visible trail of yesterday's wagon ruts. Riding at his knee, Haimo winced. "My feet . . . Jesus help me if I have to walk much today. Damn those deserters."

War brought out such differences, Ralf knew, who could be counted on and who not, neither forgotten by zealous William. The vicomte was one of those men who gave orders more readily than he accepted them. A man who couldn't obey should not command, title or ancient name be damned.

"Don't get ahead of me, Haimo."

The tents were vanished behind them; only a few yards of moss and barren limestone visible behind and to the front now. The fog wrapped them closer. Ralf felt eerily that he'd slipped into limbo, that beyond this blanketing mist no world existed anywhere. His bay stallion was a poor replacement for the one crippled at Wharfe but had a good flare to its nostrils. He trusted that for scenting trouble before it fell on them. *Fool, de Gavnay. If I don't get you, the bogs or the Greyfeathers will.*

The bay tossed its head, snorting; at the same time Ralf heard the sounds and reined short. Somewhere in the fog a horse screamed in mortal terror. Ralf thought he heard a man's cry. "There. Off to the right."

Haimo said it flatly. "The bogs."

More cries now, close or far, they couldn't be sure with the distortion of fog, but men and horses were in dire condition. Strangely unreal to Ralf: the thick cocoon of mist that covered all of the visible world, and that sound of human and animal terror gradually thinning like horns desisting one by one from alarm, the silence following a palpable void.

"Dismount." Ralf did it. "Go slowly."

"What use, sir? Sinkholes everywhere. We will only make two more gone."

Ralf cupped hands to his mouth. "Hallo! Who's there?"

After a moment a strong voice came out of the fog. "Over here."

They moved forward, leading the horses cautiously. Ralf took one step, then another, probing with his sword—suddenly lurched off balance as the world went out from under him. "Haimo!" Instinct closed his fingers tight around the reins. The mire already sucked at his thighs. Haimo hooked strong arms under Ralf's shoulders, snapping at the bay:

"Back. *Va, va,* back!"

Between horse and squire, Ralf was hauled back to firmer ground, cursing, pawing mud from boots and mail. *Merde,* what a misbegotten place. Nothing stayed dry. The sword cleaned and greased last night already flushed with a patina of wet rust. He'd be a futile hour again tonight picking this muck out of the mail. Thank God for Haimo and a quick horse, it was better than dead. "*Merci,* Haimo."

"Take care." The squire took a deep breath of damp air. "That was too near."

Ralf got up, calling again. "*Hallo! Qui va là?* Whose man are you?"

The voice came again, calm enough or merely resigned. "God's man, I hope, and apparently still the king's. Ralf?"

"Vicomte?"

"Over here, Sire Fitz-Gerald."

De Gavnay guided them with his voice. A half-dozen creeping paces showed them dim motion in the mist, a sword brandished in a gauntleted fist.

"My lord."

The older man sheathed the sword and sat down, regarding his captors without expression. He removed his helmet, scratched at the short salt-and-pepper hair. "Good day, Ralf. One assumes I am to return with you?"

"Yes, my lord. Your men?"

"You did not hear?"

"Was that—?"

"Where you almost went." De Gavnay dropped his eyes to the moss between his splayed feet. "Swallowed as we will be."

"We must go back."

The vicomte didn't move but spoke out of a vast weariness. "We're not supposed to be here, Ralf. Why else does God allow us to lose our way in fog where there should be none or sink in mire that was solid earth yesterday?"

Zut, that was the man for you: philosophizing in a fog. "Come sir," Ralf prompted. "Your horse?"

The seated man only waved vaguely. "Didn't you hear? Just luck I didn't—God's mercy, they were in it before I—I couldn't help them at all."

"I know. It is quick. Come back with us, my lord." Ralf waited; still de Gavnay made no move to rise. "I would not wish to relieve you of your sword."

"Why not?" The vicomte stood up, loosed the sword belt and handed it to Ralf, who twinged with embarrassment.

"You knighted me, my lord. I have respect, but the king—"

"Ah, yes. The king." The older man's fatigue seemed more than physical. "William Bastard has victory and the crown, but if they are beaten—if they were beaten four years ago, why are they still fighting?" He clapped his gloved hands together. "That is what I have been thinking of. The *why* behind it all. Purposes larger than William's. I tell you, Ralf. And you, Squire Haimo: I am not a religious man, but God has shown me we will not conquer here."

The heart's gone out of you. You are not strong enough for this. Ralf handed the bay's reins to Haimo. "Lead the way. Take care. Go exactly as we came."

The squire led off with the two horses, his lords following. Progress was painfully slow; only when they saw the faint outline of limestone slabs did Ralf relax, muttering to de Gavnay, "What's this talk of God and defeat? We win everywhere."

"At every turn," de Gavnay conceded. "But still—"

"When the last of them go down or bend knee, my lord, there will be honors for all of us. Lands."

The vicomte gave Ralf a sidewise smirk. "Even when you were my page, you had the look of purpose. We all came for profit, vavasor. Yet, in York, after we took the city, I confessed and was shriven." He paused, reexamining some thought, then went on in that colorless voice. "Then

I went to bed. I rarely dream since we came here. I drink myself to sleep.''

"We all do." Ralf kept his eyes on the horses ahead of them. "If the water's not tainted, they poison it ahead of us."

The vicomte went on doggedly. "I dreamed that night. In my dream, the same confessor came and said that William and all of us would be swallowed as this mire devoured my men."

To Ralf, the man was talking rot. "A dream of a priest is not God's voice."

"But God's symbol and what omen stronger? If we are so victorious, why don't the Saxons *know* they are finished?"

"They'll learn. They'll accept it, soon or late."

"*Sans doute*. They are a reasonable folk. Except when they're not."

Ralf dug deep for his own conviction. "They fly in the face of God. The pope himself has blessed this venture."

Ex cathedra sanction did not appear to assure de Gavnay. "You know how odd dreams are. I understood the priest. He was Norman, but I knew he was speaking English."

Ralf was tired of this nonsense. Their problem was more immediate. In the few moments he'd given his attention to de Gavnay, he'd lost the squire and the horses; they were no longer visible. "Haimo, you're too far ahead. I can't see you."

He waited for an answer: only the sound of invisible hooves shying about. "Haimo . . . ?"

The vicomte halted, one arm on Ralf's. "*Écoutez.*"

"I hear nothing."

"Listen."

Instinct had been Ralf's savior since Hastings, along with Jesus. Not the wet cold made his skin crawl now. He dropped to his knees with de Gavnay. The horses were near, not wandering off. Their audible malaise was specific. They caught alien scents. Inch by inch, the two men crept forward over the sopping moss until, only a few feet away but barely visible, they saw the body of Haimo. He lay on his back, the long arrow protruding from his throat.

"That's what I heard." De Gavnay motioned for his sword belt and drew the blade.

Ralf strained for any sound or movement in the coiling fog. The dryness in his mouth was familiar enough by now to be ignored; even continual fear became ordinary. He thought of de Gavnay's foolish dream, more affected than he cared to admit. Victory was the king's, death was personal. *Maybe Death will come for me today. He has let me go a long time.*

Before his kind sailed from Norway into the Seine and accepted the White Christ, a man believed in the Norns, who spun out and cut the measure of his fate. Come down to that, three or four generations was scant time to forget Odin. His grandfather, baptized or not, believed warriors were given to know Death in whatever shape he came to summon them. *Lord God, I do not turn from You to old Odin. I do not blaspheme, but give me to see my death that I may cry my coming only to You. Amen.*

Enough of that. He wasn't dead yet. Ralf swallowed to moisten his mouth and jerked himself back to wariness. There might be one Saxon out there or half a dozen.

De Gavnay noted in a whisper: "Had to be close to see Haimo."

Ralf remembered the slim archer at Wharfe ford. "They don't need to see much."

Which included the two of them. They lay in the damp moss, waiting out the Greyfeathers, waiting to die if that was the way of it. As always, the fear wore away to anger.

"I can respect the men who stand up to fight us," Ralf hissed. "Greyfeathers are lice."

"And lice are damnably single-minded," his companion noted. "Keep down."

Time passed. They could hear the horses snuffling about somewhere close if invisible. The mist eddied away after a time before a freshening wind. De Gavnay, who might be pondering on his dream as prophecy, had the look of a man faced with the inconceivable and wholly accepting it.

5

THEY WERE GIVEN shelter at a small church in Tickhill. The Saxon priest said they were fortunate; there'd be a Norman in his place next week. He found serviceable shoes for Marian, an old cloak for Robin, and a bit of cheese and bread to travel on. As a matter of course, the priest heard their confessions before blessing them on their way. Marian's sins made more sense to him than Robin's, mostly those of omission, missed devotions, and the abuse of God's name in connection with Normans. Forgivable. As for the forester lad—

He seemed distracted beyond common sins, not that he'd had leisure of late for all that many. This winter had seen his first war and himself farther from home than ever before. The world was bigger than he guessed. He'd taken the lives of faceless men but thought little on that. He hoped Aelred escaped from York and *tried* not to think on that. No, he hadn't forgotten God's place in the lives of men.

"It's me I can't find." Through the lattice of the confessional, the priest heard the young voice go husky and tight. "I feel like I'm in a dark place, no light at all, and all of me's scattered and I'm reaching about for bits and ends of something to know at least by the feel. But they're gone."

"We're in the right. God won't let us lose."

Finally to the root, the close things. Denby knew one way, one law. The Normans would come there eventually. He couldn't just bow down to foreigners, but what could he fight with? The pact with his folk, the lord's bargain with the land, how much could he save of the one life he knew?

"If Da's dead, then I am thane and have to be the law and not half the man he was. He said after Hastings, when we were losing everywhere, that we hadn't forgotten how to fight, just how to hate. Well, I've remembered right enough. I hate them, Father . . . and I'm terribly afraid."

The priest was silenced by his own honesty. Rome gave William a holy banner and approved this rape of a country. By such token those who opposed William opposed the temporal authority of Christ. An Englishman could break inside between such impossible choices. *What am I first then?* The priest scourged his soul again as he'd done since Hastings. *God's man or English?*

"Go in peace, Edward," the priest bade him. "I can't absolve you of what taints my soul as well. I hate them too."

Robin had never hated before. If the emotion sickened, at least it gave him the strength to keep going. He had the simple shortsightedness of youth for balm. They hadn't lost. Couldn't lose.

South of Tickhill, the country grew more familiar, but Robin kept a wary eye for foreign horsemen. The forests were lusher than at home, Marian noticed, meadows and cultivated lands far better and more carefully tended.

"Must be that fine in summer."

"You'll see," Robin promised as they trudged along. "Bad years now and again, but that's anywhere." His father's land was the best in Nottinghamshire. The hall was built by his grandsire Brihtnoth in a time of relative peace, no stockade but just a low stone wall about the steading. A barn big as the hall, chicken house, a sty, and good wattled hut for the pigs. "And a fine kitchen house," Robin painted it for himself as well as Marian as they passed out of forest into open meadow. "There's always water kept boiling for one thing or another. And a dovecote."

"Doves." Marian's mouth watered; she tasted them with the word. They'd eaten the last of their food the evening before.

"Good, aren't they? Doesn't take a trice to dress a brace of 'em on a spit with fresh basil leaves." Robin scratched under one arm, remembering another advantage never considered luxury until he'd left it. "And a bath house: great round tubs for sinking down and soaking, sweet herbs laid on."

He called to mind everything of home he could remember until he must have right bent the girl's ear. Better that than fear and uncertainty.

"Five more miles, there's an old oak: Roman Oak they call it, been there that long, that's the end of Mansfield's park. After that is Denby land."

Marian was tired and hungry, but not bored. She knew Robin's tale now. Lords at home were remote from her; she never saw them, just their reeves when they came on business. Lordling or not, Robin seemed little different from her, gave the same importance as she to familiar things. Hardly older than her, some of him grown, some still boy, but all forester, sharp-eyed as a kestrel hawk.

"Stay, girl!"

The sudden halt at the meadow's edge jarred Marian. "What?"

"There. See them?"

She strained her eyes to see the tiny, distant movement: far, but coming swiftly on. "Franks."

They melted back into the trees, unmoving as the Normans came near enough to be heard, close enough as they clattered by for the fugitives to see the trussed hens or haunch of pig hanging from a saddle.

Marian said it in a cold whisper. "Who'd they burn out for that, then?"

Robin only gave silent thanks they weren't for Denby or from it.

Rain set in before they passed Roman Oak onto Denby, and waxed to a downpour. In late afternoon they climbed steadily over ground shadowed with ancient oak, silent carpeted with soft mulch, until they reached the last gentle ridge before meadow. Just across the meadow was the hall.

"There." Robin pointed. "Across the vale, that's Blidworth church."

Across the meadow, splashing through a stream that curved round the steading wall and tumbled toward the vale; then they stood at the gates of Denby. Robin breathed deep of the home air. He took an ancient hunting horn from the gatepost and blew four notes—short, long, short, long—then leaned against the post, rain spattering over his face, grinning at his bedraggled companion.

"In the old days you blew this horn to let them know you weren't an enemy." He spoke with an old-fashioned formality. "You are welcome, Marian."

"Thank you." Marian's teeth chattered; she was soaked through, miserable as a wet cat. "God's truth, I've forgot what warm and dry feel like."

"You'll have it now." Robin sniffed at the air. "Warmth in it, smell? Good if it soaks in proper." He opened the gate and waved Marian in.

They hadn't taken many steps toward the hall when the instinct that read
the rain said something wasn't right. Even on a rainy day there should
be more movement, a livelier feel to the steading—snuffle of pigs, clucking hens, Minna the cook or Angharad bustling between kitchen house
and hall. Someone was home; smoke rose from the hall. Then a door
opened from one of the small bowers.

God love him, it's Will. I'm home.

"Robin! Angharad, love, it's Robin!"

And out of their house came Will Scatloch followed by a pretty woman
slight and dark as himself, both of them surrounding Robin with hugs
and a torrent of welcome liberally laced with Welsh.

"Och, come *home,* is it?"

"And that thin," Angharad pitied.

"And that dirty," Will roared, holding his old pupil at arm's length.
"The sight of you, boyo! We should have a harper in the hall this night."

Angharad peered at Marian. "And who's this now?"

For the moment, Robin only asked quietly, "Where's my father?"
From their silence, he gleaned more answer than he wanted. "Where is
the thane?"

Will only shook his head and looked aside. "We hoped he might be
with you."

True then. Robin stared at the trodden mud by his foot. He *did* see
Aelred's shield in that pile by the burial pit. Known for weeks, all that
time a stone sinking in water. Now he touched bottom. They mustn't see
how little he was prepared.

"Well, then. I'll see my mother in the hall."

"And the Lady Judith," Angharad added.

"This time of year?" Robin puzzled. "How's that?"

Not exactly visiting, he was told. Fled out of Mercia before the king's
vengeance, there was the truth and the pity of it, her family dead, hall
burned and nowhere to go but to her kin, to Lady Maud.

Robin felt colder than the day itself. "What's happened here, Will?
Something, I can feel it."

His father's forester looked as cold with disgust. "Bloody Normans,
that's what."

His worst fears were confirmed. "I saw some of them this morning.
Did they hurt anyone? Did they—?"

"Na, 'twas weeks gone," Will reassured him, "but they were foraging
on the way north. Precious little they left us."

"Thieves!" spat Angharad. "Great clods in iron and mud all over kitchen and hall. Not a horse left in the stable, nor a pig, nor any of the salt winter meat. The dovecote's cleaned out, the same for Blidworth.'' This with a glance at Marian: little left over for hospitality.

Defeat had not been left in distant York but stood here at his elbow, gloating with a Norman face in the chill rain. Robin would think of that anon. ''Let's get out of the rain.''

''I'll see to some supper, sir. There's a great good pot of soup.'' Angharad scampered away, holding her skirts out of the mud then stopped short. ''No, and bless me, where is my mind?'' Back the other way then. ''I must tell mistress you're here. Welcome you home, sir.''

Robin drew Marian close to make a third in their somber group. ''Will, this is Marian of Tadcaster.''

''Give you good day.'' Will nodded. ''It's not been too bad for the folk, Robin. Men like Wystan, some others. I looked the other way in the matter of poaching. You'll be speaking to them about that.''

Robin led Marian the last few steps to the hall and pushed the door in: The fire pit blazed up, holy Jerusalem in the center of the world, its warmth a beacon. An old man in a long red robe and Phrygian cap was throwing a split log on the fire. He hurried down the hall to Robin swiftly as stiff limbs and winter damp would allow. ''Edward. Thrice welcome home.''

Robin flung his arms around the old steward. ''Ethelwold, my good friend.''

''You are well? You took no hurt?''

''None to speak of. This is Marian of Tadcaster who saved my life not many days past.''

Ethelwold inclined his head to Marian and led her to the fire. ''Come and get dry, child.''

''Ethelwold has been steward at Denby since my father bore the ax.''

''Thank you, sir.'' Marian bathed in the delicious warmth that wrapped itself about fatigue and already made her drowsy. Robin and the older man spoke in low tones.

''What of the thane, Robin?''

''He couldn't come.''

They understood each other. ''Men have passed through,'' Ethelwold told him. ''They said York was lost, though not easily won. We prayed daily for you.''

''There's always next year, Ethelwold. What did the foreigners leave us?''

Not much, the steward warranted with a sigh. He and Will went to see all the folk after the Normans moved on. With careful husbanding none would starve but the year would be thin without a good crop season.

The thought hovered between them: brave intent to fight next year, but what new host and whence, when every landowner would struggle just to make ends meet?

"My son." Lady Maud stood in the doorway, a cloak thrown hastily about her. She passed it to waiting Angharad and moved to meet Robin, holding out arms he eagerly came into.

"Mother . . . thanks to God the *nithings* did nowt but steal."

Maud looked up at him searchingly. "Where is your father?"

Angharad didn't tell her then; that was his place. Robin would rather be whipped. "At York, Mum."

"At—?" An instant before question became bright horror in Maud's eyes, the visage of a cry without sound. Robin felt her form, pressed to his, go tense then swell with a shuddering breath. "I see."

She was dry-eyed but suddenly busy, as if courtesy could fill unfillable void. "Who is this you have brought with you?"

Robin admired Marian then, the natural good manners of her as she curtsied to his mother. "Marian Elfricsdaughter of Tadcaster. *Hlaefdige,* I am sorry to ask hospitality at such a time."

"None of that," Robin hushed her. She'd seen the livid pain in his mother and respected it. In few words he told of his wound from the Norman vavasor and Marian's timely help. Not to mention the food she shared. "Don't speak of hospitality; it's only your due."

"You are most welcome, Marian." Maud touched her hand. "Angharad, look in my chest, bring something dry for our guest. The red kirtle has always been a bit large for me. And tell Wystan to heat the tubs. My Puck-Robin came home dirty as a hog in a wallow."

"Ah, Mum, there was no time for washing."

"There is now, so look to it." Maud was composed now and in charge, though her voice trembled. All the steading knew of Robin's return now and trooped into the hall—Will Scatloch, Minna the cook and her husband, Wystan, cottar-stablers called from home to clean out the empty horse stalls. Maud issued a flurry of instructions: They would sup early, let Minna see to it; one must take the news to Blidworth church for Father Beorn and Tuck.

"But first," Lady Maud decided, "we will give thanks where thanks most are due."

* * *

Kneeling with the household, Marian already knew more of Denby than would be plain to a casual male visitor. Lady Maud tended a tidy house. By and large, that was. The rushes strewn over the plank floor wanted changing, the scenting rosemary faint. If she stayed any time at all, she must make herself useful.

Still—these folks *had*, always had, you could feel that in their manner. At least Robin had blood to come home to, something steady and unchangeable like Lady Maud. *You can hear that when she prays.*

"Almighty God, we thank Thee for the safe return of my son."

"Amen."

"I will send new candles and alms to Blidworth church," Maud pledged, "and ask chantry prayer for my husband Aelred each month until Easter a year, and once each year on this date, that our sorrow be seen no greater than our gratitude."

"Truly," Ethelwold chorused.

"We also give thanks again that our kinswoman Judith comes to us without harm."

"For which His handservant thanks Him evermore."

The new voice was lower and more musical than Maud's, smoothed with the sound of book-learning. Marian turned her bowed head slightly to see the striking young woman standing at the door a moment before she knelt. The voice and stance, the weathered but expensive clothes, all indicated to Marian someone more used to giving commands than gratitude. Young perhaps, but she even knelt like a mother superior. Someone had mentioned a woman come to visit . . . Judith, wasn't it?

Bowed over clasped hands, Lady Maud's head came up, no longer submissive but defiant. "And as Christ is our Shepherd, rid us of this foreign usurper who stole our throne, our land, and the very food from our board."

"A-*men*," sang out Will Scatloch.

"Jesu witness," Angharad seconded softly but no less fervently.

"And the Norman priests," from Robin kneeling next to Marian.

There's honest prayer, she thought, remembering the kind man turned out of his tiny parish at Tickhill.

"And the false Bishop of Rome," Robin ground out, "who gave his blessing to these thieves. May he sicken and die."

"Cousin," Judith reprimanded him, "do not offend God in the act of prayer. You curse the Vicar of Christ."

"Well, cousin, when His Holiness remembers that office, I'll clepe him so. When he takes money to bless a thief, that's what I call him."

"Edward, you are arrogant."

"Arrogant or honest?"

"Hush, both of you," Maud intervened. "We are praying."

"No, Mother. Before God, when such men speak for Christ, we'll need more than prayer."

Right enough, Marian concurred wholeheartedly. Her feminine instincts were partially eased concerning Judith: a cousin, then. How close? Was there some understanding between them?

Well, speak of blessings, supper was prompt, plain but plentiful. At Maud's signal, the folk divided naturally between the high and low tables that ran along the north and south walls. When Marian made to join the servants, Robin guided her firmly to one end of the family table. Maud took her place in one of the two ornate, high-backed chairs of state. From old habit, Robin took that to the right of his father's, but his mother stayed him.

"Take your place, Edward."

Her meaning was clear. With obvious reluctance, Robin sat down in the thane's chair. Maud said a short grace. Judith followed with a prayer in Latin with the fluency of a bishop, and the supper of bread and barley-mushroom soup was served. Marian tried not to make noise as she ate, ravenous enough to swallow twice as fast and pray for more.

Ethelwold was on her left. To Marian, his age made him seem remote. *Until he looks at you and you can see the kindness. And I like Robin's mother. As for Judith, there's a right lord's lady. She makes me feel I should eat in the kitchen house behind the stove. Proper nun, then, couldn't half pray in Latin.*

"Steward? Sir?" she whispered timidly. "Where did the lady learn holy language?"

"Part of her schooling," the old man answered politely. "At Bayeux."

That must be a far place, beyond London or Winchester.

"Oversea in France," said Ethelwold. "Lady Judith was early drawn to the Church." In time, as these things went, she might have been an abbess. "Ah, well." The steward sat back with a sigh. "Nothing is what it was. Tell me of your own, then. I know Tadcaster."

"They burned us out, sir."

"Oh. Like so many others." Ethelwold laid a dry hand on Marian's. "Your family?"

"Gone."

"Eat then. May it well become you. Whatever else, there's plenty of soup."

Marian devoured her grateful fill, content with the buzzing talk from both tables. She didn't want to talk about her folk and Ethelwold didn't press. From him she learned (with some comfort) that Judith was kin on Lady Maud's side, daughter to a Mercian thane. Through her mother she also claimed blood ties to the old royal house of England—something complicated; the steward couldn't recall at the moment but it linked her as well with William of Normandy. Earl Edwin of Mercia was dead, killed by his own followers, as men said. For Judith's family, the Normans fell on the hall like locusts, parents and servants dead, holdings burned, and herself escaped with no more than the clothes on her back.

Ent that a bleeding shame? Marian spared as much sympathy as one woman could for another far more poised and beautiful, a mudlark's pity for the lost tailfeather of a peacock. *At least she made off in a clean shift, nor did she have to bury what the Normans left of her parents and little Biddy, my cat.*

"The lady was apt when the Normans came," Ethelwold told her. "She speaks Frank better than their knights." And then he left the hall on an errand from Lady Maud. Now there was more news from Will Scatloch: The Normans had raised one of those quick-built wooden castles at Nottingham—that close, mind—and would levy a new tax this year.

"Another geld?" Robin slammed down his spoon. "Steal from us and tax us for the privilege?"

"And they've brought rabbits to south Sherwood," Will attested. "Small hares they are, beasts of warren. But my lord knows how to snare them, so he does."

Deftly put, Will's meaning drew laughter from both tables: There was more than one way to lime a Norman. Marian decided she liked Will Scatloch even if he was Welsh—a sunny, cheerful man in his thirties (she guessed) with a wife to match. Angharad fussed with voluble patience at her two small sons who used the lower table more for mischief and squabbling than supper. Marian had never seen slaves in Northumbria. Though Will's respect for Robin was evident and Robin's as to a near-equal, both Will and his wife wore slave collars, owned by Denby house and hold.

Much was deep-dyed in these people. Like Lady Maud who'd lost a husband and a life, though you'd never know it to see her now, cool as Judith. There were differences between this life and her own at Tadcaster,

Marian learned. Let William at his whim raise them up or turn them out to beg, this family lived a certain way. A body felt Denby wouldn't change if the world fell apart clean up to its gate . . . but now Ethelwold returned with those articles he was sent for.

At his arrival, the hall quieted around Marian. Spoons were laid aside. The steward placed his bundle before Robin: a folded cloak of fine black-dyed wool, a small gilded ceremonial ax, and a golden cruciform brooch inlaid with red enamel.

But for the sputter and lick of flame about the logs, the hall was very still. Robin's brown hand rested on the cloak. What he spoke was clearly a formal declaration.

"At York, Aelred Brihtnothson stood with the host. Even when Scots and Danes fled, when the city was lost, the shield wall stood firm. The Normans will remember that wall."

Robin rose and placed the cloak about his shoulders. Maud fastened it with the great brooch.

"You have spoken of the thane who was my husband," his mother said for all to hear. "What of the thane who is my son?"

For Marian's part, he might have said much about Tadcaster alone. He did not. "I stood with the bowmen as my father bade me." No more. The fighting and running like a hunted animal, the painful wound, all the footsore miles to get here—of that, nothing at all. Robin thrust the gilt ax in his belt.

"I take up what is mine."

Judith raised her cup to him. "Hail, Thane."

And there, Marian came to realize through all that followed, was the key that opened the door to Robin of Denby. She suspected the hardness in him was new, laid over an old ease. These people did not readily share their feelings. He said *mine* and gathered to him his reality, pretending the burden was light when he staggered under it, pretending Normans didn't exist. That, reflected Marian of Tadcaster, was like denying the air that you still must breathe.

6

THE ANCIENT PORT city of Chester, northwestern entrance to England on the banks of River Dee, was as strategically vital to William as the recapture of York. With Chester as garrison and supply base, a chain of forts could be maintained along the Welsh marches to keep the Britons effectively plugged up in their mountains. Chester was not the last English resistance; there was Hereward's stand to come in the impenetrable fens around Ely. Hereward inspired and drew Saxons to him, but Ely was a contained infection. If William couldn't get in, Hereward could not get out. Chester had to be taken and held now. Without the base on Dee, William did not rule in the west.

For this reason the king force-marched his vavasors across the Pennines through winter. The complacent English with their outdated notions of war never considered the impossible whereas William demanded and achieved it as a matter of course. He reached Chester before the dilatory English were even close, entered with no resistance from the frightened citizens, and considered his next move. By his order no standards were flown on the red sandstone walls, no mark of occupation visible. Possibly the English didn't know they were late. Now, while they were nowhere in sight, the final stroke was prepared.

"My lords," William presented the plan to his Norman counts, "our horse will deploy to the south and remain hidden. Two scouts will stalk the English, cavalry to move on their signal. Here on the walls we will avoid detection until the last possible moment. When the English awake, they'll be too late as usual, caught between our walls and the cavalry.''

The king's logic was sound: Why fight a defensive and inconclusive battle against a foe who would only retire to fight again, when the royal forces could finish them today?

What William liked about the plan was its English origin. *Les grises plumes* had used this tactic to ambush his wagons at Tadcaster. The concept of poetic justice would not occur to the Norman conqueror, but he relished basting the gander in sauce prepared for the goose. One of the very survivors of that raid had proposed the ruse—Sire Ralf Fitz-Gerald—did the lords recall him?

Some few vaguely recalled a shabby vavasor who looked as if he'd been born in his battered mail.

"A competent man," said William, "with a loyalty and diligence I recommend to all of you. I would present him but at the moment Sire Ralf is hunting the enemy. To your charges, my lords.''

Good to be out of iron if only for a few hours. Ralf and Fulque de Granville wore plain wool homespun for the reconnaisance, carried no weapons but swords, nothing to slow down fast horses. Wrapped in hooded dun cloaks, they'd been probing for the English since first light on Welsh-Sarb mares too small for war but fast and durable. Some of the approaching enemy would be mounted. If discovered and pursued, the scouts relied on speed to get away. Meanwhile, their observation post was a wooded hill with a good view of Watling Street for several miles, the most logical approach to Chester.

Early March and still wet winter. Fulque shivered beneath his cloak. "Such a country. All the colors of the world in summer, but now it's hard to believe there ever were any.''

Fulque was given to musings like that at odd moments. He was one of those few, like Ralf, who'd lasted from the beginning, a man of mixed Norman and Breton blood who understood the Welsh jabber of these border peasants and sometimes sounded like one, though all Norman in the saddle.

Ralf suggested, "Perhaps one of us should nose down the road a mile or so." The English couldn't be far off now. If they planned to attack today, they'd not have camped more than ten miles from Chester last night and been on the march before light. Rarely any sun to gauge time by these winter days. One learned to estimate by feel as the peasants did.

"There." Fulque narrowed his eyes at the movement so distant it looked like part of the road itself squirming where Watling Street rounded a curve of low hill. The tiny surge fattened, became the head of a long worm writhing into view around the distant bend. Became ranks of men trudging on toward Chester, flanked by their few mounted lords. The long-legged English always amused Ralf to see them ride; astride the small native horses, their feet nigh dragged on the ground. Few horses, Ralf estimated. They wouldn't be used in battle anyway. No archers he could make out.

The column blurred in his sight; he rubbed at his eyes. Since they occupied Chester, he hadn't felt right at all. The blood sang too loudly in his ears and even by a warm fire he was always cold.

"Ralf?"

". . . uh? *Qu'est-ce que c'est?*"

Fulque peered at him with concern. "Are you deaf?"

"What did you say?"

"I said who rides to Chester and who to the squadrons?"

"Oh." Ralf had to push his mind through what would have been clear a month ago. Reporting back to William was the softer job: perhaps a bit of rest, hot food, and a chance to dry off. The other got cold bread and pork, cold riding, and a battle at the end. Huddled under the dripping trees, both of them wanted the ride to Chester and were frank about it. Unlike the new young bachelor knights who came this year and missed the worst of it, neither Ralf nor Fulque glowed with the prospect of heroism before dinner.

They decided the usual way. Ralf took an English silver penny from the purse at his belt, faced with the likeness of King Edward and backed with a cross. "Name it, face or cross."

He flipped the coin, caught and covered it on his left wrist. Tongue in cheek, Fulque de Granville considered his choice. "Cross."

Cross it was. "Your mother was a fey, Fulque. You have unnatural luck."

"Not at all." Fulque untethered his mare and mounted. "I am very religious. See you in the city. Good luck."

Good luck. Ralf cast one more hard-bitten glance at the long snake of men moving on Chester. His luck was failing like his health, going ragged around the edges, wearing thin. He trotted the mare for a hundred yards through the woods, broke out onto heath and kicked her into a gallop toward the waiting squadrons a mile beyond.

* * *

Vision that blurred in and out of focus frequently, a persistent twitch in his eyelids and muscles, but Ralf, waiting with the second wave of horse, saw it all, saw it end. Of the outcome there was no question from the beginning. Once more the fatal inability of English to organize rapidly had been their undoing. The host was small, no more than seven hundred, mostly ax and spear men. Many who should have strengthened their force were dead at York or simply gone home to the spring ploughing. Doomed from the outset. On the banks of Dee there was a weird, silent, drawn-out hush when the English knew it, and all before a blow was struck.

When the English approached the timber bridge across Dee, the hidden watchers within the walls and the cavalry concealed by the quarry to the south, saw a single rider push ahead to inspect the crossing and the apparently unmanned walls.

Now he sees the section cut out of the bridge, Ralf thought. *Now he wonders about the walls: Are they really empty?*

After a few moments, the rider turned and rejoined the main force. Now.

The first wave of horse broke into a gallop, the second only fifty yards behind. *How long before they see us?* Ralf wondered. *How long before the men on the walls show themselves?*

Soon enough. There in the grey noon light were the defenders close-packed on the south wall and the first element of cavalry already ranging across the road, blocking retreat as Ralf's wave swung in behind them. Cut off, the English reacted not in panic but as purposeful ants in a colony, forming into the familiar square, thanes and carls the tough outer shell, the more lightly armed fyrd-men within.

Then from the timber and turf revetment that formed the south wall of Chester's defenses issued more cavalry and foot troops to deploy along the opposite bank of the river. To Ralf, the scene and the deliberate, doom-ridden hush were eerie. The English were finished before starting; they had to know it.

The wind blew, scudding ripples over the narrow Dee.

Ralf set his tapered shield and soothed the restive bay stallion with crooning sounds. In the moments before the first charge, in the unnatural silence, the random images were clear and long remembered: the large wart of sandstone near the south end of Dee Bridge, where someone long ago had carved the goddess Minerva into living rock. The English scout paused by it before reporting back. *Did you pray to her?* Not likely; these people didn't trust anything or anyone not of themselves. Ralf thought he saw Fulque de Granville's shield in the line across the river. He noted a few dappled grey gulls, unconcerned with destiny, scavenging dead fish on the near bank, a cormorant diving for fresher fare—and two white swans gliding serenely downstream west of the bridge. Fulque said they mated for life. Rare foolish thought to envy a brace of swans, but they had a better chance of seeing tomorrow than the English, who had turned their backs on the far shore and simply waited for the inevitable charge, shields resting by their feet while the pitifully few archers arrayed on their flanks without any protecting stakes, sticking arrows in the earth before them with the preoccupied care of cobblers at a bench. Two of the bowmen casually strolled to the south end of the bridge. As if clout-shooting in a peaceful meadow, one of them bent into his weapon and, with one shaft, gauged wind and distance between himself and the Norman crossbowmen ranged below the walls.

Then nothing moved. Time stopped. Only the sound of the wind blowing cold over Dee.

They should surrender, Ralf thought, but probably won't. Reasonable men, de Gavnay said, except when they're not.

The first wave of horse moved forward at a walk, then Ralf's line. Within bowshot now if the archers wanted to fly a few, though it would be a thin rain. The word muttered back from the riders in front. *"Préparez!"*

Both lines halted. Ralf hefted his heavy spear, finding the right balance, feeling both lines around him bunched like muscle to spring.

Then one of the thanes in the first English rank dropped his shield and stalked out a dozen paces toward the poised lines of horse. He stood alone, the great ax resting on his shoulder. Negligently, he removed his helmet and scratched vigorously at long brown hair.

He's laughing, Ralf realized. Not in scorn or bravado; rather the man seemed amused by the foregone absurdity of the position and his chances. With no haste at all, he turned and strolled back toward his ranks. Without breaking stride, the thane looked over his shoulder and casually invited the Normans with a sweep of his arm.

In the two lines of horse, spears were raised, swords drawn. Concentrated, Ralf felt the blood shoot through him, no longer cold—

"DEUS VULT!"

God wills it.

"GILLELMO VULT!"

William wills it.

The first line rumbled forward, gathering speed. Ralf saw the heavy spears jut from the waiting shield wall. He was moving now with his own line, head low and forward, taking best advantage of his shield. That wall could open quickly enough to finish any man who fell. The first shock buckled but didn't break them. Ralf guided the stallion with knee and thigh, trusting the animal's trained obedience under him. Even the best mounts wouldn't crash a nettle-wall of spears unless they felt no hesitation in the rider.

Nearer; almost on them . . .

Ralf braced himself, aware as always in this instant before collision of being both mortal and terribly alive. Feeling the keen, cold wind in his lungs and the clouded light over all of them. At the last moment he snapped erect in the stirrups—seeing it all, seeing nothing—and flung the spear with a curse like a prayer.

He came alive and unhurt out of Chester with his usual dull astonishment. One had to add Divine Will to luck; he'd begun to feel his continued survival sheer presumption on God's indulgence. God had to be with you. Lamentably, He was elsewhere the day Ralf's luck ran out. Predictable: Something was wrong this spring. He was exhausted, a hacked blade with no edge left, who fought when he must and drank to fallen friends, trying at first not to remember their faces, then not able to. Fatigue was the traitor. In a world of wet cold and sharp iron, he yearned for the smallest relief of warmth and softness, a place to go home. A week, even a day. Any scullion knew the most dangerous tool to hand was a dull knife. Dulled vavasors made mistakes, dropped their guard.

With Chester secure, sites for the marcher forts must be selected before King William retired to Winchester. Dangerous work with remnants of the vanquished rebel force lurking in the forests. Inexplicable men they were, deeming it valiant to stand and die if necessary, just as honorable but shrewder to run and fight another day. Their women were as practical; you took your life in your hands bedding them. Some were available for pay, some for patriotism. The former were full of pox, the latter might poison your wine or cut your throat while you slept.

The day Ralf's luck ran dry, two of their scouts had sighted a handful of Greyfeathers running for a nearby spur of wood, a peninsula of trees perhaps a mile long, half a mile through, jutting into open heath. Only one scout made it back to Ralf's party, a young knight named Rollo, fresh out of Bayeux.

With Fulque de Granville, Rollo, and three crossbowmen as young as the new knight, Ralf left the road to run the rebels to ground. Crossbows would give them some range at least in a fight. At less than fifty paces, they hit harder than longbows.

They found the arrow-shot scout near the spur of forest. Ravens were already busy about the corpse and had to be chased off. Kneeling by the body with Fulque, Ralf cautioned Rollo, "Look sharp. You're new here. If the Greyfeathers are in there, you'll never know what killed you anymore than this one did."

Fulque ran an appraising finger along the arrow shaft. On this island men cut them to the length of their own arm precisely as a tailor cut a nobleman's tunic. "Too long for Welsh."

"What of that?" Rollo scoffed, impatient for action. "Let's after them."

"I said look sharp. Watch the woods," Ralf snapped.

Rollo looked all of a very young twenty. "What difference the arrow, long or short? They'll get away."

"You might live longer," Ralf said. "If the notion appeals."

The arrow's length was significant. They were on the Powys border. If the sighted bowmen were Welsh, they'd be moving west into the mountains by now. If English, they wouldn't readily go where Powys tribesmen would kill them as quickly as Normans; more likely they'd bear east or south.

"Or they could be waiting us out in the woods," Fulque ventured for Ralf's ears alone. "Do you feel valorous today?"

"No," said Ralf with utter conviction. They understood each other. If someone had to enter the woods, better the new ones than them. After four years and the war all but done, this would be a ridiculous time to die. "You've got a crossbow. We'll go around."

He gave his orders to Rollo: Take the three bowmen and flush them out. Fulque and he would wait in the heath beyond the spur. "Go in on foot, Rollo. The horses will only make you a richer target. If they can kill you and grab the horse, they'll ride it home and use it for ploughing."

"Plough with *my* Flemish?" Rollo's expression reflected the profanation. He was the son of a count. The breeding, the dear expense, and long training of a war stallion, not to mention the mutual trust and affection that grew between man and such a companion, made him worth far more than a villageful of peasants. "My horse would kill any villein who tried that."

"Tell the Saxons. *Hélas,* if not to the plough, then to the carving board. They are an unsentimental folk."

"I'll kill those pigs."

"*Bonne chance,*" Fulque waved them on.

Rollo was eager and pleased as he cantered away with his detail. Arrogant as Taillefer at Hastings, Ralf remembered: riding out alone before Harold's lines, tossing his sword high while he bawled out some silly doggerel. Ralf's half-smirk faded to cold pity as he looked after the four. The next thought came out with surprising candor. "*Bon Dieu,* it's time we stopped dying here."

"Prudent thought, *ami,*" Fulque observed. "We must bring that to the king's attention. *Allons.*"

Prudent indeed. Just so much wine in a jug, and that day Ralf's ran dry. He was riding the heath behind Fulque, the spur of forest to their right. Alert for movement among the trees, he failed to see that Fulque had drifted too close to them. Distantly just then, too far to be sure, Ralf thought he heard Rollo shouting—

A brief moment, eyes turned back toward the sound, he didn't see the man in faded green rise up at the tree line, caught only Fulque's hoarse warning—"*Couvrez,* Ralf!—then sudden, searing pain as the long arrow went through his scale-iron surcoat and the mail legging beneath, pinning his leg to the saddle. The stallion screamed, staggered, and went over on its left side, crushing Ralf's other leg against something hard.

Sangre du Christ, he wouldn't think it possible if he hadn't seen it before. The damned arrow went clean through iron, mail, leg, thick leather saddle and half killed his horse.

"Fulque . . . help me."

Eyes already glazing with shock, Ralf saw his comrade wheel about, then jerk and topple from his horse as he took the second arrow in his back. Frightened, Fulque's horse skittered away in a wide circle, then bolted back in the direction from which they'd come. Ralf lay helpless, wincing with each spasm of the stricken animal to which he was nailed neat as crucified Jesus. After the first wave of sickness passed, he was aware of silence and sudden thirst. The jolt of a wound always did that. *Think. Help yourself. You don't want to die today.*

He fumbled for his dagger to cut off the arrow shaft; perhaps he could lift himself free. His left leg was a different problem, sufficient unto its time. It hurt as much as the right leg, could be broken. "Fulque. . . ."

No answer. Stupid to call out, Fulque was gone. Stupid indeed after his warnings to Rollo, to lie here himself like a piece of beef *en brochette.* Should have seen it coming months ago when he started dropping or knocking things over. Clumsy . . . *merde.*

Ralf sawed with shaking hand at the shaft. A movement lifted his eyes—then he died sure as Fulque but saw it coming, knew he was already dead despite the foolish breathing. Over the twisting horizon of the wounded horse's shoulder and his pinned leg, the man in green came into view. He halted by the stallion's jerking head, leaning on his bow, and regarded Ralf with mild but utterly merciless eyes. A big man with a dirty, straw-colored beard. Under the ragged hood and dirt, Ralf saw only that scraggle of beard and the pale eyes looking at him like God's last glance at someone damned. His loose trousers, gartered at the ankles with hemp, were filthy and tattered, torn above one knee to show a brown linen bandage black with old blood.

I asked God that I might see Death coming. This is when you die, not from the blow. He'd never given quarter himself; why should the Saxon? Ralf crossed himself, glaring up at the Greyfeather with the last of defiance and English lame as himself. "Come on . . . be quick."

Stupid bravado. The stolid archer just stood there, his face shadowed by the hood. He lifted his head to observe the sky. Something like expression lit the colorless eyes, not fierce or vindictive but detached as a ploughman taking note of weather. The bearded lips curved with something like pleasure.

Breathing shallowly, Ralf felt tiny needles of cold sweat prickle his forehead under the mail cowl. The wounds and the pain, not fear. Death had already taken him. "Do not . . ." he gasped with his scant English, "do not you know how it is done?"

The archer only drew his own knife, caught the horse by one ear and expertly slit its throat. For a moment he watched the blood spurt, then pool, steaming from the dying animal's neck. Unhurriedly, he wiped the blade clean on a tuft of grass and walked away toward the forest.

Dull with shock now, Ralf was aware only of his jerky breath visible in the chill air and the weakening convulsions of the horse. Pain faded. He stared up at a sky the color of slate and saw now what the Saxon had left him to. Not dead, no part of death at all, not yet with so much of dying yet to come. The scavenger ravens—first one, then another wheeling overhead . . . three . . . four, circles against low clouds, not slow and searching but tight and purposeful. They settled around Fulque immediately, but as more of the damned things collected, they began to take interest in him and the horse. Five of them now. They'd gorge until they could barely fly. One of them, in no hurry, cocked its head at Ralf from the horse's shoulder.

They were very efficient, going at the dead horse through the soft eyes and open throat wound. More of the birds settled down about him. Cursing feebly, Ralf slashed at them with his knife. He managed to draw his sword and used that, but with diminishing effect. There was intelligence of a sort in their eyes, black and hard as polished coal. They merely flapped away beyond reach and settled down again. Waiting. No longer resigned, terror swelled like a cold bubble in Ralf as he flailed the sword until his arm ached. They hardly moved away now, used to the motion and knowing its range.

That was how Rollo found him, the sword a lead weight almost too heavy to lift, dull-eyed, spitting weak curses. Shock had passed, pain returned, and he was colder than ever before in his life.

"We'll cut you free, Ralf."

When he could focus on Rollo's face, the younger knight looked pale, leached of his arrogance. But then, Ralf noted dimly, one of his bowmen was tied across his horse, the stub of an arrow shaft in his back. Rollo had some luck; perhaps he'd last awhile.

"*Pardi,* but you look terrible, Ralf."

"So do you. Now you know why I said take care, *hé?*"

"Give me your dagger. You are lucky."

"Oh, yes." Ralf's teeth chattered with a deep cold that froze from his guts outward. "G-God . . . did not wish me to die today—"

"Got to break off this buggering shaft."

"—perhaps tomorrow. *Get those filthy birds off my friend.*"

"Lie still."

Inconceivably living still, but some things were stamped deep in Ralf as face and cross on the sides of a coin. Not the black birds, not black at all, but an impassive peasant face gazing at him, then leaving him to slow death or a quicker one at his own hand and the eternal punishment meted to suicides. A devil who let him see his end coming slowly, every moment of it. For Ralf Fitz-Gerald, who once sent a half-pagan prayer to God that he might see his end in time to prepare, Death was a silent man with a face like a wind-scoured wall. Death was a man in green.

7

$\mathcal{N}$ow that she could expect at least one good meal a day, Marian felt
the world back in place and turning smoothly. By law Denby was responsible for her now, not that they made much of that. Robin seemed
pleased; as for Maud, on the day when Marian should have left, the
hlaefdige just let her work as deywoman, seeing to the new calves, which
was no work at all, the way she loved them. . . .

So I guess I'm to stay and that glad of it, as Angharad would say.
She's a droll one, she and Will and their two boys running up and down
the steading. Angharad said she was bought as a wife for Will by Robin's
father and a good thing they got on in all the important ways because
they fight six days to the week over the rest. They're the first Welsh I
ever saw: take to heart so much that we let go by. Both of them thick
as bread when they're drunk, throwing pots and curses at one another
until I swear their bower shakes with it all. Angharad told me they always
fight and then make love and it's all right again. Slaves, aye, but I'll
hazard they weren't half so well off at home, wherever that was.

How they love to make pictures and music with words, like when
Angharad chid Will for getting drunk without her, and he protested such
was not the case. "Drunk is it? I'm not drunk until I can't hold onto a
blade of grass to keep from falling off the world." Now, that's far gone,
but then I've never drunk Welsh whiskey. More potent than a harming
spell from a *wicca* woman, Robin says, but beer for me. Still, I like them

both and their snuffly little boys. Sometimes in the hall, even if supper's just bread and lentils, the fire is cozy and Will and Angharad are like two extra candles at table, a little less shadow from worry and taxes and the big, black lump of what's coming. They're bright colors. We're darker; we're greys and browns to their reds and blues. They show what they feel, we cover it up. Like Robin the day we came home. He spoke of his father at York, scant of himself. And Lady Maud, she's a dear one but she'd fair burn to death before mentioning the flame.

Oh, but I've seen the fire get to her, just a little but enough to show the woman plain. When Minna the cook sent me to ask her about something, Angharad met me at the door to the lady's bower. No, I mightn't come in just then, but I saw past her, saw Maud all slumped in her chair by the fire. That was morning and she'd been up all night with Angharad's youngest who was croupy and feverish. Just the side of her face, but the tears were shining in the firelight. I saw the loss of her husband she wouldn't show to anyone else. Don't know but what I wouldn't keep such to myself as well, like waiting to wash my undershift in private.

Lady Judith, then—thought she looked down on me at first, though it's only how she looks at the world, what with years in a convent oversea. Each night after supper she reads from the big Bible and never stumbles over the words. A scholar, that one; you can hear in the words how she feels about them, like a nun at prayer. Could have been an abbess . . . but I don't know. Ethelwold can say what he likes, but there's that about Judith that won't shut out the world as a proper nun would. Since I've helped to comb and brush her out—fine and black that hair is, with rich ivory combs from York with goldwork to them—ah, well, sheer waste to put such a woman in a convent, and Lady Judith doesn't half know it. So here she sits at Denby, run out of her life as me out of mine, part religious and the rest plain woman looking for a husband like me. The difference is, I've found where to look and she hasn't, but then mine's closer. Would it be all that book-learning makes her look older? If that's what reading brings, I'll have nowt of it, thanks the same.

This Denby is its own world entire—the hall, Blidworth village, the fields and forests around. The land's better than up home, grass sweeter, cows fatter. At least the goddamned Normans left us the cows (and penance yet *again* to do for taking the Lord's name in vain, just cause or none). There's parts of the near forest where the oldest trees bend together like the nave of a church. Not so holy as Father Beorn's church at Blidworth. It was good to stay and talk with him when I went with Lady Maud's gift of candles. A fine, straight man. There's priests and priests. Robin says Beorn was carl to the Earl of Northumbria before he took orders, and when he walks with the swing of those shoulders, you can believe Beorn wore mail and hefted ax long before he put on a priest's robe. Not caught in the middle of wanting like Judith. Beorn was one thing once, another now, and no mucking about. And fat Tuck, his sexton, who wanted once to be a priest himself, so the talk goes. Not that one; he's so much of everything else, there's not the room for holiness. Beorn's at God's beck every minute, but Tuck says, "Aye, Lord, in a minute," and gets on with this world first.

Speak of a world, will you *look* at this day? Like a morning-gift of gold to a bride. You expect spring to come sure as Sunday, but then you step out the door like this and you have the promise firm in your nose and eye, cows lowing and the *wup-wup* of the few silly chickens the foreigners left us; and all of it fresh and early as morning dew on an apple. Let the sun put a kirtle of soft gold on such a day and watch God turn its head with compliments.

Good folk here and no mistake. I feel comfortable with them. Like Wystan the fuller, washing clothes in the stream like there was war between him and them, and Will Scatloch laughs: *Listen to Wystan the Wash. Drub-drub-slap-curse-drub . . .* but a contented cursing. And John Littlerede, the smith at Blidworth. Little? Right enough, God took two ordinary men or maybe three and said, "I'll make a great clout of a man just for the fun." Banging away at the forge, shaggy as an unsheared sheep, all sweat and sparks singeing the red hair on his chest where the apron doesn't cover it. The village joke and pride for his size: Never go a journey round Little John without food or water, it's days. And that full of opinions, always sure he's in the right. Robin says he was to Hastings with Thane Aelred and Wystan and never lets a body forget that. Or himself, mayhap. John watches me when I pass the forge, he does. Poor man, his wife three years dead and he's not much past thirty, so for sure there's more than a king and a battle he can't forget, with the children gone into the ground from pox along with the wife. I don't mind his looking after me, just that I have no answer for him.

It is a world here, all I'd ever want—as now with this puzzled suckling calf, still so new that how to feed is a coil to him. *Come, I'll show you.* A world like music, summ'at, with Lady Maud and Ethelwold keeping strict time along with Wystan's drubbing and John's great hammer, and the bell from Blidworth church across the dale. Will and Angharad, they're the song itself that might be a little too wild for all the beauty. Birds and chicks and children for the tiny, high pipes. . . .

And him.

Robin in the middle of it all, working in the fields, the smell of dirt on his hands, the good rank smell of earth ready for new seed as I am for a man. He's the clear horn sounding high over the lot, minding this place just as Lady Maud sits by the slave-child's bed through a sickness, looking after things, both of them. No fear if the world falls down: Get on with it, tend to business. With the world as it is, what else can we do?

If he asked the question I see in John's eyes, there'd be answer right enough, there's that much alike we are. I've not spoken of that to Father Beorn. Natural wishing and wanting's no sin, and I pray often enough, mostly here in the barn with the calves. When the ash blooms, I'll find just the right leaf, with an even number of leaflets, and put it under my pillow. . . .

Even ash, even ash, I pluck thee/This night that my own true love I'll see/Neither in rich nor in his rare/But in the clothes he every day wear.

That will bring a clear dream of the future, never fails. Pray God take no offense if I help His will along just a little. Pray God let me stay here with Robin and I'll not weep for the loss of kin or land. There's a strange thought, then: losing all only to find more. That's a woman's thought, right enough. I must be growing up. Even ash, even ash, I pluck thee. . . .

So Marian perched on the milking stool, patiently teaching the newborn to feed itself. They didn't always naturally take to the teat. She gave her milk-moistened finger to the baby mouth, then let it drink milk from her cupped hand. When the calf had the gist of it, Marian tilted the pail, holding it high enough that the calf knew it must keep its head raised to feed. Finger to hand to pail to teat and no more problem.

"There you have it." Marian stroked the calf's skinny flank. Soon as the dear was weaned, the sooner fresh milk, butter, and cheese for the family.

"Lord Robin!"

Now who was that? Marian went to the open barn door and peered about.

"Lord Robin, quick!"

Wystan by the sound of him and running hard, not going round to the gate but dashing straight across the north meadow. He floundered across the stream, vaulted the stone wall, wet to the thighs. Marian hallooed him. "*Hoch,* Wystan, what is it?"

Wystan jittered this way and that, agitated, bow in hand. "God-a-mercy, where's the thane?"

Marian waved him west. "To the fields since sunup. What's the matter?"

Wystan bolted away toward the fields, trailing behind him one sufficing word.

"Normans!"

Robin was overseeing the ponderous business of turning the team of eight oxen and heavy, wheeled plow with Much and Anlaf the cooper when he spied Wystan churning toward them, quiver bouncing on his back, and Will Scatloch wondered: "Now why is the Wash hunting today and not a word to either of us?"

Robin didn't know but instinct tightened his gut. Wystan stumbled to a gasping half before Robin. "Normans, Thane. Coming through Sherwood from the north."

"To Blidworth?"

"To Denby."

"Easy on, catch some breath," Robin steadied him. "How many?"

The fuller counted two knights and four of their followers. "Those half-knights they always have."

"Squires. Armed?"

"Every one, God rust them tight."

Robin spun about to his forester. "You with me, Will. Wystan, get to Blidworth and fetch Little John fast as you can. Tell them all to lock their doors tight. Go on."

"Give me to breathe," Wystan protested. "I've been running since I saw them."

"I'd give you a horse if I could. You're not an old man. You'd nip off fast enough poaching my deer. Go on, hop it."

Not old, but not spring green anymore, Wystan sucked in a deep breath and trotted off on the mile trek to Blidworth.

Jogging toward the hall, Robin paced himself to let Will keep up. Wystan was an incorrigible poacher, but no matter today if he spied the Normans out in time. They could state their business at the gate, long enough in England to know the meaning of hearth right and the perils of ignoring it. They would not enter his gate. Robin wondered at his very determination, as if his actions followed a pattern woven long ago. So they did. Beaten and beaten again from Hastings to York, where they shoveled Aelred into a common pit with other brave men; Norman crows, who stripped Denby on their way to that unequal combat, leaving barely enough to see his folk to harvest. . . .

"Judith, I need you."

He strode into the hall, where Maud and his cousin were trying to calm Minna and Angharad. Will's wife had started like a bird at Wystan's news, twittering in Welsh; Lady Maud and Judith come from sewing to assure them both that the world wouldn't end because of a few strangers. Robin's mother might be as apprehensive as her women, he knew, but she smothered that tight between clasped hands. "Robin, how is it?"

"Normans, Mum, but only six. Keep your women in the hall. Where's Marian?"

"In the barn." Maud met her son's eyes levelly. Robin saw something there that matched his own mood. "What will you do?"

"That's up to them." He took the throwing ax from Will, tossed it once and jammed the weapon into his belt. "Judith, I'll need you to speak Frank for me."

She was reluctant. "Surely you will not provoke them."

"They don't enter here."

"Edward." Judith pulled away from his grip that already propelled her to the door. "Look at you, look at your forester. Armed and begging for trouble like alms."

"Don't dally now."

"Have we not lost enough, cousin? Haven't *you*?"

"Judith, you heard the thane." Maud's composure was an iron lid clamped tight over something that glowed hot beneath. "Angharad has just tidied and scented the rushes with my last sachet of sweet herbs, and you know these Normans always smell of horse."

"Maud, for the love of—"

"I am not disposed to be gracious to the men who made me widow. Not here, Judith. Not today."

Robin was waiting before the closed gate when the six riders in mail forded the stream and halted before him. Ready and waiting—Judith at his side, Little John close on the other with a heavy sledge resting on his shoulder, Will and Wystan wide on both flanks, arrows nocked. Robin measured the two knights. They couldn't misread his intentions. One was John's age or even older, he guessed; more weary experience than haughtiness there. The young one had a long red scar on his cheek, newer even than his obvious arrogance. Aelred said they did a lot of praying all night long before the duke tapped them with a sword and made them knights, and then the fools thought themselves and their flaming fat horses half holy.

Robin had learned how to hate well enough at York. The emotion suffused natural fear. He felt like a bent bow, ready to loose. "Ask their business, Judith."

The older knight spoke at some length in a courteous tone. Judith nodded. "They are on the king's service, riding to Grantham. They have traveled long from Chester and ask hospitality until tomorrow."

From Chester. No rumor then but truth. Carters from Edwinstowe said they'd heard the city had fallen.

"Tell them no. Their kind's been here before and picked us clean. We have no hospitality to give."

Judith translated, watering it down considerably from the careful sound of her in that throaty Frank. Suddenly, the young knight broke in sharply. To Robin's English ear, accustomed to meaning conveyed as much by inflection as word, the peremptory insolence was plain, nor did he miss the warning glare the other knight shot at his juvenile companion. As for Judith, the look she gave the blabberer would have frosted a warm July. She pointedly excluded him from the parley.

"One at least has manners," she told Robin. "He says they are tired and hungry and ask only the night's lodging in our hall."

Robin hooked a thumb in his belt near the long-headed ax. "Marian?"

From where she stood at the barn door, alert as the rest of them: *"Ja, Thegn?"*

"Draw these bastards a bucket from the well. Judith, they may water the horses in the stream yonder."

The water was duly brought and offered to the knights with Marian's noncommittal "May it well become you." The scarred young knight jabbered again, evidently unused to tact or even caution. Judith merely ignored him, but Robin found that difficult.

"What did he say, cousin?"

"Naught, he's a fool."

"I don't like the sound of him."

"He needs gentling," John offered. "If I'd a mouth like that, my da would've strapped some manners into me, right enough."

Wystan's fingers twitched on his bowstring. "No regard for a lady's ear. Think he was raised in a sty."

"Robin," Judith mediated, "this—boy demands to speak with the lord of the hall."

"He does." Robin elaborately tapped his chest. Plain enough. "Is he dim?"

"He doesn't believe you, not with mud up to your knees."

Robin shifted his gaze to the alert squires as Marian passed the bucket to the young knight. His own men were calm as rock but for Little John's fingers drumming on the hammer haft. "Inside the gate, Marian. Judith, they may have hospitality if they can pay for it."

She dutifully relayed and heard the answer. As one might expect, they were not pleased. "They take it ill from the king's bound subjects—"

John said it in a low, lethal voice. "Our king is dead."

"Steady on," Robin murmured.

"—but they can pay in silver."

"I have no doubt. What parish poor box did they rob to get it? Denby takes its rents in kind, tell them. Two horses."

Judith implored in a low voice, "Edward, this is not good sense."

Robin only pointed to the young knight's handsome grey. "And this one of them."

"There's dear," Will chortled.

"And since my mother objects to the smell of horse in a clean hall, they'd have to put up in the stable."

To this, the older man's reaction was in his eyes. He was for going on, but the puppy was a different matter. He rattled off a rapid stream of invective, spat in the bucket, and dashed it to the ground at Robin's feet.

Little John casually shifted his balance. "D'you think we've insulted him, then?"

"Bluster, no more." Judith's even features tightened with apprehension. "I don't understand all of it."

"Give me the drift, Judith."

"Well, discounting the coarse terms and coarser suggestions, he says you are no true lord but a Saxon peasant to sell what should be offered or what they could as easily take."

Robin smiled amiably at the young Norman. "Price a bit high?"

"He says his horse is better bred than yourself; that lords do not go afoot. Nor does the son of the Count of the Vexin sleep in a stable."

"Why not?" Robin countered. "It was good enough for Jesus."

"Edward," Judith caught at his elbow. "This boy is barely into his spurs. These people are not of the same blood as their churls. They see you no better than your men."

"I had no time to dress." Robin's expression was utterly blank. Watching him, the outlanders might have thought his mild blue eyes a little sleepy. "I think that's enough. Go inside the gate, Judith."

"Edward, I pray you think of your mother."

"Now." Without tensing or raising his voice, Robin knew how it would be. Something deep stirred in him. If his cousin knew these foreigners, the years since Hastings had not left him or his father ignorant. Judith herself said there was no law in Normandy but that of William, nothing writ down that a man could take to court. They were like their horses, governed only by a strong rider. Thirty years past, despite personal inclinations, Aelred stood with earl and king against Godwine because of oath and loyalty. Thirty years ago, knights like these were trying to kill William before he could grow up, only so the strongest of them could take his place. Robin learned that much from his father. Law and right were never that simple, not just a question of whose hand held the sword, but these men would never understand that.

His eye flicked to John: If they took him for a like peasant, no coil there. All men fought and some were lucky enough to rise like grandsire Brihtnoth. That didn't stop John from arguing his rights to Robin who could at least understand what the man was saying. These foreign knights had looked down so long from the back of a horse, they couldn't see the ground anymore.

Robin stepped close to the young knight's grey. "Want to see how fast I can set you afoot?"

The ax whipped from his belt and sank deep in the grey's skull. The big animal dropped like a house, too fast for the astonished vavasor to more than clear the stirrups before he hit the ground and sprawled unceremoniously with a yelp of astonishment. In the next instant, Will despatched the older knight's horse with one shaft. Little John, with a roar of pure joy, brained one of the squires' stallions with his hammer. The sound made Robin wince involuntarily, like the cracking of a huge walnut. Cursing, the boy-knight bounded up, far past caution, drawing his sword—

"No!" The other vavasor shot him a command meant for the squires as well. Prudent counsel: Robin's ax was cocked for any target, Will and Wystan ready to loose at more than mounts.

"Well struck, John," Wystan crowed. "There's a mite back for Hastings."

"Not enough." John quivered, starting for the nearest of his enemies, hammer raised, but Robin stepped in front of him.

"Hold, John."

"I was to Hastings with your father—"

"I said *enough*."

"They butchered Harold's body, didn't they, Wystan?"

"John." A tall man himself, Robin had to look up to meet the black-smith's eyes; he found there the same baffled, clouded murder that made him drink deep of nights himself.

John barely saw him. "Get away. . . ."

"As you were loyal to Aelred and to me." Robin didn't move, dared not, though John could have broken him in two. "Let be."

Now the thing was done, Robin felt the coiled violence go slack in him. He snapped his arm out at the foreigners. "Out. Clear *out,* the lot of you. Judith, let them stay clear of Blidworth, that's mine too."

Seething and grumbling, riding double with their squires, the two Normans departed, the young one throwing his last sentiments over a shoulder far less bruised than his dignity.

"He says the king will hear of this," said Judith with small surprise. "There was little need for this."

"Judith, I'm sick of need. I fought them—"

"And won of course," she countered with cool irony. "And thus will they depart England presently."

More collected now; perhaps he did go too far, and wise to stop John for a start. Robin was already thinking on what must come next, what his father would do. "Wystan, tell the kitchen they'll butcher today. Some for salting, some for feast. John?"

The smith looked more amenable now than a moment past, sledge resting on the ground, sane at least. "Aye, *hlaeford?*"

"Tell Father Beorn and Tuck, all my tenants will feast at Denby tonight; that this night I take up the coronet and renew all fealties. We hold hall moot."

John's attention drifted away to Marian perched on the wall and ob-viously relishing the Norman rout. "Thane, if there's to be moot, there's a matter I would speak of."

No time for that now. "Ethelwold will hear it." Robin clapped the big man on his rock-hard arm and jumped the wall with Will close behind. Judith was waiting, nothing but reproval in the slow shaking of her veiled head.

"Mad, Edward."

"That's as it may be."

His cousin resembled Maud; as much life in her eyes but lying deeper, smokier. "I would not see Denby wiped away as my father's house was.

These men said more than I told you. They go to Grantham to prepare a residence for Queen Matilda.''

Which meant that, soon or late, the king would come to Denby. Judith touched her cousin's cheek in deep concern. "Puck-Robin, the old days are gone. They know many ways to hinder a man or a house. Break your fist, break your heart against them—no matter. They are reality, at least of the secular kind. Only the Church is eternal. You will learn.''

Looking after Judith, Robin wanted to deny her truth but could not. These foreigners were a stone too huge to break, a stone descending on him. Nevertheless, he forced a reckless grin for Marian's sake. "Did you see that puffed-up pricket when he went on his arse? The one that spat in your bucket?''

"Wish he'd drunk from it,'' Marian said, "for I spat in it first. But I was frightened.''

"Oh—'' Robin would have brushed it off, made some careless answer, but somehow that wouldn't do for this girl anymore than Maud. She always seemed to look closer at him than anyone ever had, close enough to know bluster or the smallest lie. His smirk faded to honesty. "Me too. Then I saw John about to start a proper war. One of us had to keep some wits about him.''

At the courtyard well, Marian rinsed out the bucket, fastidiously cleaning it of Norman, welcoming the sight of Anlaf's oxen dragging the last of the dead horses toward the kitchen where Minna and Wystan were already at the butchering. Will Scatloch strolled to the well and dippered cool water from Marian's bucket.

"At least there's fresh meat to the table tonight,'' he relished.

"Will, why does Lady Judith think Robin did wrong?''

He considered the question and answered with another. "Do you?''

"Not me, Will Scatloch.''

"I could not be saying rightly. The lady's not country folk like us.''

"That's true enough.''

Will squinted at Marian. "Before the foreigners came, did you go much beyond home?''

"Not far. Twice a year to the fair at Newton. Once to York.''

"Alike for Robin.'' Will unbraced his bow in one practiced motion. "The best natural archer in Britain, I'm bound, but wasn't I years teaching him? You couldn't tell that boyo he was ever wrong.'' Will drank again, wiping his mouth on the back of his hand. "He's like you, lass. He knows this place. *His* place. Beyond that the truth of it is, he's thick as John.''

8

ROBIN WAS NOT too thick to know the peril in his situation. He moved speedily to conclude the formalities of his inheritance. Tonight he must greet all his people, make sure the most distant crofter knew him, even the children, aware of the same question in them that nagged at him. Did they have a competent thane or not? To that end this night's feast, frenzied activity in Minna's kitchen, Ethelwold, Maud, and Judith opening chests and shaking out the long-folded finery, the arrival by oxcart of a great barrel of ale from the Queen's Rest in Blidworth, part of Ceolred the taverner's duties in kind, furnished to Denby at each hall moot.

Following the cart by twos and fours, by family groups along the narrow forest tracks or across the dale from Blidworth trooped the folk who now paid their rents and trusted their future to Edward Aelredson. An informal parade trudged behind Father Beorn's aging mare and Tuck's mule, the only four-legged beasts on Denby land not hitched to a plow this spring.

Like Papplewick and Edwinstowe, Blidworth remembered when more Dane than English was spoken along the sickle-curve of its one road. The fresh water that sustained it rose in the forest to the north of Denby steading, called Holy Pool for reasons not even Father Beorn could remember, though no one thought bad memory cause to change the name. From Holy Pool, the rill tumbled past Denby down to the grain mill, meandered past John Littlerede's smithy and under the rickety bridge that connected Robin's hall with his village. Up the hill, then, past John's

91

house and smithy, one saw first Anlaf's small house and his cooperage with the wattle hut where he seasoned out his barrel staves. Beyond that lay the Queen's Rest, where old Queen Edith once made it her occasional custom to break her journeys from Mansfield to her own estate at Grantham. Occasion depended on whether or not she was speaking to Aelred and Maud, who did not share her loyalty to the Norman cause.

The scraggle of huts that was Blidworth forked the hill like a saddle with Blidworth church at its crown, built in stone with small, high windows no less than fourteen feet above the ground and too small for a Dane to squeeze through, since raiding churches was their early habit. The church's stone tower had been refuge for the village in the old, dangerous days, accessible only from inside the nave, with small round-topped windows for light. The herringbone or intertwined-rope designs cut into the foundation stones were interspersed here and there with older runes, and in Beorn's churchyard were bones interred between spear and sword and covered with the owner's shield. Some of them had come to raid, fought against Alfred or shrugged off his ultimate victory and settled down to stay. Dry-dust wives lying beside them had left offerings at Holy Pool to a saint of the new religion barely understood, whose mangled British name they couldn't remember anymore than Beorn or Tuck could now.

Blidworth was a going village before Robin's grandfather first hunted in Sherwood with King Canute—and *there* was a tale to tell over a cup or three, full of magic about a certain glade, a tree, and a woman who might have been completely human or not entirely . . . as those things went. A tale that showed the kind of thanes Sherwood bred. First there was Brihtnoth, the king's carl, all soldier at first and rarely in Sherwood, but he settled down soon enough. Something about the light that he always loved, a softness and a peace. His son Aelred never left Denby unless called by crown or earl. The mellow sunlight of Nottinghamshire that lured Brihtnoth warmed his son from birth. He made a good marriage, folk said—

Married up, Aelred did, you only have to look at Lady Maud to see that. Well, that's only shrewd business. Being content with the lot you're born to is all very well for some, despite what a bishop might preach of a Sunday, but if we Saxons hadn't an eye for profit and improvement, there wouldn't be an England fat enough for Willy Bastard to rob, say I, and Sherwood the heart of it, like the best cut of loin from a hog fed on acorns.

Aelred, bless his memory, was not one of those lords who nodded in once a year to collect his rents or just sent his steward. His grandfather had been no more than a freeman, a sokeman farmer of no more than one hide of land. Their line had three generations in title now, counting Robin, and if you counted Bastard as a king. Blidworth had its own inconsistent snobbery: On the one hand they could boast of three thanes in royal service, on the other men who knew the land and crops as well as their tenants. This made for a good balance, they felt. As for Robin, he was the second to be born on the land, might have been born in Sherwood itself, tagging after Will Scatloch since he could walk, with bracken and heather caught in his shoes before he learned to wipe his nose, that one. They all knew the boy but weren't yet sure of the man. They would gather this night at Denby to see how he carried himself, hear what he said in his cup and without it, and note the difference. They weren't wild Welsh, didn't let liquor take them into wild boast or fancy and for good reason. What a man said or promised drunk he was held to sober, though by the time the last of them straggled through Denby's gate, all knew they would feast on Norman horse and were delighted. Like all village people, they hoped the Normans wouldn't come too close, wouldn't change their lives that much. Like his father before him, Robin knew this before greeting the first of them in his courtyard.

When the spring dusk deepened enough for torches to make a difference, Ethelwold announced the feast ready. A great eager sigh of appetite then as they milled and jostled through the hall door to take their places. Beside the two long tables, trestles had been set up to either side of the fire pit where choice sections of the windfall horses revolved on a spit, turned by Minna and Wystan. As this was a solemn meet with legal matters to pass, Denby kept precise state. The first cup of ale was drawn from the barrel by Judith and presented to Father Beorn, the next to Robin by his mother. Marian and Angharad bustled about, carving, filling and serving platters. Dressed in his finest scarlet linen, Robin presented the cheer to the hall at large. For however long Denby could keep Normans away, this was his place, from roaring fire to smoke-blackened rafters and the hides of land around; from the munching, bellowing farmers and their wives turned out in Easter-best yellow-dyed veil, to family and priest, these were his people. At the low table Tuck swilled, gulped, and belched in enormous good spirits, waiting his turn at Little John who arm-wrestled all comers to quick defeat—until Tuck bared his oak-limb of an arm to the shoulder and slammed his challenging elbow on the board—"Now, by God, try you 'gainst a better man!"—and forced John's huge fist down onto the table with a thump and roar of triumph. "Did you mark *that,* Lord Robin?"

"Well tried, Sexton."

"Let's feast every week on the generous Normans."

Not that horse meat would ever replace venison, boar, or even chicken at a civilized table, but Maud approved her son's principle with an iron righteousness. Judith, after chewing long and swallowing daintily, laid her knife aside and refused more when Marian brought a fresh serving. "No, thank you. This beast did not die in a state of composure."

"The cutting and chewing will wear you out," Marian agreed in sympathy, "but Minna says salting will help and then slicing it thin as bacon."

"Let us hope." Judith turned to the barley soup.

When the eating slowed to a buzzing contentment and the children shrieked about the table in a game of tag, Robin descended from his place, caught Angharad's eldest, and firmly deposited him by his mother. "Play time's done, boy. Time to be a man and listen to business."

The trestles were removed and the thane's great chair placed at the center of the hall. Ethelwold struck with his staff three times on the floor planks. The ceremony began with Father Beorn's blessing on all and their proceeding. Still lean and fit at forty-odd, Beorn always had, for Robin, the aspect of an aging hawk. Lately though, there was an element of bafflement in the priest, as if the hawk didn't know where to hunt anymore. Not that far to look for the cause: For all the ceremony of investment, Robin couldn't be that sure of his land or title under this foreign king; for all his blessing, would Beorn have a church hereafter, with Norman priests and bishops moving in on every hand?

"Edward Aelredson," Beorn asked formally, "do you accept the holding of Denby?"

"I do."

Tuck came forward with a small silver reliquary containing their church's one treasure, a lock of the hair of Saint Dunstan. Beorn took the reliquary and held it out to Robin who placed his right hand on it.

"Do you swear by these most holy objects that you will keep faith with each householder of Denby in house, field, and forest as Aelred did, charging no man unduly but in accordance with the custom and writ of Nottinghamshire?"

Maud waited with the gold coronet. Robin wondered if Beorn knew the half of what he took on himself or all of what he swore by. "By Holy Church, I so swear."

The priest settled the gold circlet on Robin's head. It was warm from the fire and his mother's hands but felt heavy. "I have sworn to keep the laws as my father did. Now let every householder come forward and make pact with me."

The swearing was done in order of precedence. First Beorn for the church. Ethelwold read from the roll, its parchment browning with age. "Blidworth church and its livings. . . ."

For Lady Maud, Robin merely ratified the land settled as dowry when she married Aelred. "It's me who should kneel to you, Mum."

"Not anymore, Puck-Robin," she murmured for his ear alone. "You take up the bargain for us all."

In her turn Judith received his formal kiss with dignity, along with a stipulated amount of Robin's own land for her maintenance. "I thank you, cousin."

Robin sensed her gratitude somewhat strained: How it must gall Judith to accept charity from someone she always regarded as a poor country relative, no matter how freely given. More than that, responsibility for Judith's welfare now meant settling a dowry when she married. Beautiful as his cousin was, what man of her station would want a land-poor wife? Old widow Gudrun who helped Minna in the kitchen could be more easily married off.

On through the freeholders until Robin's mouth grew dry with the repeated pledge and his palms sweaty from clasping so many hands.

"John Litterede, smith. Rents in kind: tithings to Blidworth church. Farriering to Denby on need throughout the year and repair to the thane's plows and wagons. Three furlongs arable . . . Wystan the fuller . . . Anlaf the cooper . . ."

Through the half-free churls like Much who worked the mill, finally to the slaves. "Gwylm Scatloch, thrall, and his wife, Angharad, same. One bower at Denby. Duties as forester to the thane, the services of his wife to Lady Maud. Allowances of lentils and available greens twice a year. One acre of arable—"

—Until Robin yearned for more ale to wet his dry throat, though that wouldn't do until the last of them had knelt and knew their rights and place at Denby, even to the older women like Gudrun, widowed years gone. For these Robin added a touch of personal warmth to the warranties. "What you had before you shall have so long as I am thane. Ethelwold, who remains?"

"Marian of Tadcaster."

So she did. "Call her."

Though Marian had worked furiously all afternoon in the kitchen, she'd turned herself out well to serve the tables tonight, hair washed and shining. The new tow kirtle with its red wool piping made her very fetching. She was born free; by law she had the right of her own inheritance, little or nothing as it might be now. She could leave Denby, marry when and whom she pleased. Robin took her hands between his in the customary manner. "Do you accept me as your lord under law?"

"My lord, I do."

In all things, he hoped. "Then you are now of Denby. Your rents will be in services as my steward will inscribe on the roll."

Robin gave her the symbolic kiss—more tenderly and held a little longer than with the others—and pressed two silver pennies into Marian's hand, betokening her right to bequeath her property without let to her children.

"My lord, you are generous."

Their heads were close together; no one saw Robin's wink. "That knight you cut my arrow from, he was generous." Marian would understand. You always turned out a dead Norman's purse. Whatever English money you found he likely stole, so it was only justice and thrift. "That's all, Ethelwold?"

The steward rolled up the parchment. "All, Thane."

"Good. Marian, bring me more ale. My throat's parched with all this talk."

"And wipe your face," she suggested, rising. "You're all over sweat."

Robin raised his freshly filled cup to the tables. "May it well become you! God willing, we will have a good harvest. Now, although the Normans have provided supper tonight"—he waited through their appreciative laughter—"you all know the times are yet lean. The reliefs due me on my father's death are suspended until each man's harvest is in."

"God save our lord," sang out Wystan, mellow with food and ale.

"Save him from you," Will Scatloch sallied back at him. "You've had more of his grace than his grace should grace you with."

"Well said, Will. Forest rights, then. Red does are carrying fawns and the roe deer soon to rut. No does will be taken. Will and I will be looking sharp to this. And no red pricket yearlings, mind. On Will's permission or mine, each householder may take one great buck until we call an end—and trust me, we will keep tally. You, Wystan!''

The summons caught the fuller with a mouthful of horsemeat. ''Me, sir?''

''You.'' Robin spoke amiably though meaning it. ''Were it not for honest Minna for a wife, you'd be up before me four days out of God's seven for poaching.''

So he would, Robin thought; say so now and let be, as Da would do. Doubtless Wystan confessed scrupulously to their priest, and never meat went into Wystan's pease porridge at home without a bit to the church, Tuck swore, or some to a needy friend, or a portion to Denby's kitchen through Minna's conscience or caution. Robin handed his gold coronet to Ethelwold. ''And now let's finish the barrel.''

The formalities dissolved quickly in buzzing gossip at the tables. Robin sat old Ethelwold in the great chair. The steward had been on his feet throughout the ceremony and found it good to sit down and accept a cup from the new thane's hand. ''Robin, there's a matter I nigh forgot what with all else tonight. Littlerede there.''

''Oh?'' Robin glanced carelessly at Little John drinking his ale, quite at ease but marking them both well. The man did mention some business. ''Not his rents again. They're fair and he's just pacted to them.''

''Not that. The man has made a marriage bid,'' Ethelwold said as Lady Maud joined them to hear his last words.

''So I heard,'' Maud nodded with a spark of mischief Robin didn't comprehend.

''That's more than I have, Mum.'' Robin looked from one to the other. ''What woman, then?''

''Marian, dear.''

''What?'' Suddenly Robin felt off balance, rushed too fast and against his will. Nobody, it seemed, told him anything. ''Well, I thank you both for sharing the news. Does he indeed?'' Startled enough to blurt his first reaction. ''Tell him no. Tell him I . . . can't consider it tonight.''

''They're both free,'' Maud reminded her son—of that and perhaps other things. ''Your permission is formality.''

True, he would merely arrange the terms on either side as a broker, but why didn't people discuss these things with him to begin with? Robin cast beleaguered eyes at Marian and up to the rafter beams. ''God's mercy, Mum. Bit sudden, ent it?''

Maud's smile illustrated more than it spoke. ''To none but you.''

"He's pestered me these last two weeks," said Ethelwold.

"Oh?"

"True, Robin, but you had so much more of weight to think about."
Ethelwold elided the rest with an eloquent shrug.

"I see," Robin fumed quietly. "Now it's out and I'm supposed to
say bring on the flower chaplets, let's off to Blidworth church for a grand
wedding."

"John gave our steward to understand this was an offer of affection."
Maud looked after Marian who was clearing the high tables. "A fair
offer for a fair girl."

"Well, yes." Robin felt unaccountably constricted. "Yes, she's that,
but—"

"And ripe for wedding," Maud added lightly enough. "In such a
case, your father would decide very quickly." Her point deftly made,
Lady Maud signaled Angharad to attend her and left the hall with
Judith.

Robin worried back and forth about the dark courtyard, stumbling now
and again over cottars settling down for the night under wagons or posing
riddles to each other over the last of the ale. These were the overspill
from the hall where, as in the barn and stable, every sleeping space was
already jammed. At length Robin's preoccupied pacing brought him to
a spot along the north wall where he brooded on burdens and tried to
think as his father would, of one fact weighed against another. If William
built a residence at Grantham, he'd be hunting in Sherwood, surely
coming to Denby. A brave move in the sight of Robin's householders to
chase off the Norman knights and feast on their horses, but he'd get the
bill for that, not them. If his embattled pride allowed, Robin could easily
see now the difference between courage and folly. At the moment, privately, he regretted his action.

They will come again and what can I do? Very brave to pact with my
people when we could all be turned out tomorrow; when I don't know
if I own the land anymore but have to go on each day as if nothing was
changed. Then Mum and Ethelwold pull *this* out of their sleeves, John's
"bid of affection." A surprise to none but me? I can believe that what
with the gossips nattering over their spinning, and likely even Will and
Angharad discussing the terms. And can't I just hear Judith urging the
suit to Maud—though not to me, of course, I can wait on them chewing
it over from now until damn all—"*It's a perfectly good match, dear*

Maud. She's of his sort, there's one less mouth to feed, and he is not too old for her. . . ."

Devil he's not. John's past thirty, a flaming ancient. No denying he's a good man, a strong man. Save Will, none better to stand with me today. A good honorable man—but somehow I don't reckon him a wise one. He would have killed more than horse today if I hadn't stopped him, and God knows where I found the least of Da's wisdom to do that.

Weeping Jesus, as if there ent enough to decide between one sun and the next. The world is moving too fast for me to catch hold of it. No sooner had the feel of this place in my hand when the foreigners came. When was there time after that, with holding Denby together and then off at war, to think of women and marriage? The world's turned upside down. At York and Tadcaster, I marched with men Da would've hanged for thieves, some of them. Since last autumn the difference between me and them has been no more than which of us got caught. What time for anything but staying alive?

Did John speak to Marian? If he did, why didn't she? . . .

Is it that she wants him too?

No, she's more like to me than him, we both know that. Didn't she look fair tonight, with her hair all spilling like gold from a hoard. I never thought a woman would make me hurt just to look at her, not just for wanting her but for so much more.

Mayhap they have talked of it together. Mayhap more than talked. She did tarry by him tonight for longer than needed. And the woman is free. . . .

I'm John's proper lord and as good a man as he, even if he was to Hastings and that. But he's had a wife and knows women's ways and wouldn't be long finding the right words to say to Marian who has a mind of her own. He's ahead of me there. If he's bestirring himself, I'd best be putting in my own word.

And say what, then? "You'd be safer John's wife than lady in my hall, safer to bear his children in more peace than I or mine are like to know." Not sweet but the plain truth.

Marian, listen to me. I know the men who follow this William, I've fought them. They're the thunder we've heard just over the hill, the cloud at noon that shadows and chills us. If I marry you, you'll live in that shadow until they're gone, and who knows when that will be, or if you'd see that day as wife or widow? Greater than us are dead, Marian, our church going Frankish, earls in prison or following at Bastard's heel, collared and chained like dancing bears.

This much for surety: Even if Judith is right and the Church is all that matters because it makes all folk one in God, I think God cut the Channel to make us an island folk, a people apart and better than Normans, come to that. You can see they're not too quick-minded; been here four years and hardly one can speak proper English.

Yet Judith was wise to urge caution with them, and I a fool not to heed. All I could see then, all I could remember was Aelred at York, when he told me we had to stand alone. How I loved him then. Even understood him. Someone had to stand, not just for York, but for *us,* for . . . I don't know what. Mayhap that's the price we pay for being an island folk with our own ways. Danes are merchants when they're not thieves; William bought off their *nithing* little prince quick enough, and Scots are pure shit who'll turn on anyone outside their own blood. So we stood alone, as Leofwine's family most like did at Brandeshal when their turn came, poor souls. Da knew he'd never get out of York alive, only that I must.

I wish I knew what Da would do now. He didn't live to see the problems I'll have. That's why the words for Marian get mixed up with all the others. Should a man go courting with his head on the block? Nay, he should not.

On the other hand, ere his head came off, he could say he made a shift for the girl, shot one good arrow at the clout.

Caution from here on, then. Caution when the foreigners come back. Caution that we can keep a little of our own, being little folk as we are. William will come, sure as winter. If a tame bear is what he wants, what will keep Denby whole, I'll bend knee and call him king, no mind how it sticks in my throat, until I can see a way out for us.

The coronet was that heavy when Beorn set it on my brow, as if it came with all this worry stuffed inside.

Judith said their churls are different blood from them. There's the difference between them and us, the peg to hang my argument on. I *know* my folk. From Grandfather down to me, we've kept a balance between crown and plain folk, and if we took a little here, we gave as much there, had to, since men like John could always take a grievance to hundred court with a fair chance of winning.

If I can make my folk understand why we have to bend that we won't break.

If I can make William understand that I'm pledged to folk and land, not just a rabble of lords; that the peace he wants means caring down as well as up. I'm bound to try, but we can't expect too much of a foreigner without laws or proper upbringing; like preaching gospel to geese.

Oh, but it's a wicked maze to blunder through, no way out and no way back.

9

Now AND HENCEFORWARD to be in William's grip, Chester was still a Saxon city, sprawling beyond the original Roman walls but following the legion plan of a square. Draw a cross within that square to join the four cardinal points of the compass and one has the design of Chester: a legion fortress, later an access for Viking raiders, then a rich Saxon port for the foreign trade that anchored at Water Gate.

Those few merchant sailors with an urge to pray might stop at St. Peter's, nearest their anchorage. If they turned into North Gate they had another chance to observe their religious obligations at St. Werburgh's Minster which, under a *custos* of twelve priests and assorted lay brothers, had dominated the spiritual life of Chester for a hundred and fifty years. Hard by North Gate, the Minster infirmary was a byword with traveling merchants and sailors. If one got mauled in a tavern fight, the brothers could patch you as well as any. If the injury looked to be fatal, your friends could fetch a priest in minutes. Early mornings and evenings a convalescent like Ralf Fitz-Gerald could hear the workmen going to and from work on the new castle going up by Bridge Gate, and every few hours the Minster bell sounding the offices of daily prayer.

How good it was to sleep clean and dry, soft linen smoothing the welts and bruises stamped into his skin by a life in iron. Good to sleep at all when the fever let him. One wounded leg and a fractured bone in the other had shattered the dam of Ralf's tough constitution, and then everything—bad food, exhaustion, ague, the old water-sickness—burst forth to founder him. The Norman surgeon muttered with pity over the battered lump of Ralf: not just the wounds but everything else. Four years of everything else.

"By the Face of God, man, you would not drive a serf as you have driven yourself."

For reply, Ralf only rasped, "That's why they're serfs."

The dour, red-faced English lay brothers who tended his recovery were urged to diligence in tending him and told that King William took a special interest in this patient. If hereafter he died from any but the most obviously natural causes, those responsible would follow with bare time to shrive the murder from their souls. *That*, Normans thought, would keep the sheep in the fold.

For more satirical reasons, the brothers compared their conquerors to sheep in return. Only a sheep could manage to look haughty and stupid at the same time. But they took prudent care of Ralf Fitz-Gerald. He would walk with crutches for weeks, then a cane. The fever might return at any time, always waiting its chance, never to be entirely cast out. There were times, sodden in his sweat and misery, when he wept not from pain or sadness, but simply too weak to hold back the tears.

His legs itched fiercely as they mended. Still too weak to be impatient, Ralf occasionally glanced, but without yearning, at his gear and mail rusting on their rack. Spring at last turned warmer and a little less damp, overcast as ever, and this day Ralf felt strong enough to try the crutches provided him. For the first time, he was bed-weary, but by carelessness or petty intent, the last brother to attend him had left the wine on a table by the door. Clumsy and still without strength, Ralf managed to stand straight on the crutches and start a labored passage to the table. Much farther than he thought. The false energy deserted him halfway. To hell with the wine; Ralf decided he only wanted to lie down and sleep. He hovered, wobbling in the middle of the stone floor when the door swung wide on the massive figure of King William.

"What in all good reason are you doing out of bed?"

"My liege." Ralf's voice sounded reedy, frail. "I was just . . . trying to fetch some wine." The king just stared at the pitiful rag of him. Ralf felt idiotically compelled to offer explanation. "I never drink water anymore."

"Get back in bed." As much brusque command as concern, William set the wine by the bed and turned to see Ralf tottering on the unfamiliar crutches, about to collapse. The king simply caught him up lightly and deposited him on the cot, adjusting the blankets as he studied the pale knight.

Always weighing us, Ralf thought, always testing, trusting as little as he needs, like a moneyer biting gold to prove its worth.

William had lost girth this last hard winter, though his gold-trimmed black tunic still imperfectly concealed the tendency to paunch, and the skull-capped red bangs fell more sparsely over his forehead. Wanly, Ralf wondered if there were anywhere left in his own punished bones for the hardiest vanity. The brothers shaved him dutifully; he couldn't remember his last glimpse in a mirror. "My liege . . . honors me to come."

William poured wine into a wooden goblet and passed it to Ralf. "How does it go? One hears you were a master of craft in the matter of Grey-feathers before one of them got you."

"Not so wise as Fulque de Granville." Ralf crossed himself listlessly. "God rest his soul."

"Amen. I've set chantry priests to assure that rest."

"That is good. . . ." Ralf trailed off as his feeble attention lost focus, but the king snatched it back.

"Your former lord de Gavnay does well, too. Considering."

"For all his faults—I grew up in his fosterage—he is not an evil man."

William grunted skeptically. "For myself, I see him well past contrition but yet a league from good intent. Would you trust him? If you were a king?"

One did not dissemble to this man, this strength. "No, my lord."

"He is on a very short tether. I'll keep no hound nor horse nor man I can't trust. He impressed me at York. I had for a time considered him for a barony in the north. On better thought I gave the fief to Eustace de Neuville. Do you know why?"

Such men as himself should never assume the king's motives. "I don't know, my lord."

"Baron Eustace knows his place," William said simply. The lesson was clear to Ralf, as if it needed repetition by now. Like strong drink, ambition became a man better as disciplined taste than indulgence. "As for *le vicomte,* men do not desert me twice. I prefer my friends close and enemies even closer. He will be at my beck for some time." Abruptly William brushed the subject aside with the negligence it now deserved. "And you? You have lands at . . . ?"

"None, my liege."

William sat on the edge of the bed, careful not to disturb Ralf's limbs. "A vavasor of proven courage, loyalty and"—he gestured at Ralf's gear and armor—"entirely portable estate."

"Truly," Ralf admitted, "I am a poor bachelor knight without so much as a good horse to my name."

The king rose again, restless as always. "Do you miss your kin?"

Honestly Ralf did not. He could barely remember them. He would by now look down on his mother's peasant brood; his father's would look down on him. Both facts were equidistant and painless. "We were never close. They may all be dead now."

William smiled down at him with a sudden rush of confidence. "I miss my children, Ralf. You should marry. Bachelor knights have their place, but a family . . ."

The intimacy surprised Ralf. *He means it.* This obsessively private man who rationed his trust like a miser, who bestrode the Channel, duke on one shore and king on the other—difficult for Ralf to imagine this man relaxing with a wife or dandling children on his knee. For himself the thought of marriage might not be new though dusty from lack of use in four years when he'd been settled as the wind.

William stared out of the window toward North Gate. "The border castles will be up before summer. The war is over, and I could use some peace myself. My seneschal has found a fair place at Grantham for my queen. No more than a day east of Nottingham and fine hunting. The forest is huge."

"Sherwood, my lord. We put up the castle at Nottingham before joining your grace in the north."

"Long may it stand," William commented dryly. "Longer than its intended castellan who went down at York." William turned back to the man in the bed. "The post is yours now. Collection of all revenues for Nottingham city and shire. For yourself, the livings of southern Sherwood, authority over the whole."

Dulled by sickness, Ralf could only stare at the huge man by the window. Comprehension was ragged these days. Sometimes when people spoke, he heard the words while meaning blurred and he saw only grey sky dirtied with carrion birds, and against that sky a man with a face like death.

Fool; he'd missed what the king was saying.

"—northern forest lies within an English honor called Denfield—no, Denby—who held it of King Edward. Long ago, Edward told me this forest was the best hunting in England. Now, this Englishman at Denby."

William left the window to loom over Ralf again. "There are too few like you whom I can trust, and far fewer English. I can't replace every shirttail thane in this island—cannot yet, you understand. But you will hold my warrant as crown officer in Sherwood. You will give this Saxon to understand that he holds his lands at my pleasure. Any more trouble from him—"

Ralf's dry lips moved thickly. He wet them with wine. "Sire?"

"Eh, what?"

"Pardon, I do not follow you."

William barked at him: "What, are you dense?"

"Does my liege honor me with a *vicomté?*"

"I did not say so." William's smile was small and cool. "Ambition stirs already?"

"No, my king, not beyond loyalty, I swear."

"Not too quickly, Ralf." Softly uttered but a clear warning. "I know you loyal. Nourish that virtue and urge this Denby to emulation."

With the wine and fatigue, Ralf already felt his awareness melting toward sleep, but one word of William's snagged on memory. "There was some trouble?"

William shrugged. "More insult than injury. My commission to appraise Grantham. They asked hospitality. Denby refused them. Edward Aelredson. Remember his name."

"Ayl—?"

"Aelredson. His cousin was there, a woman who speaks Frank, more luck. There might have been worse done without her to mediate. As it is, Aelredson and his men killed three horses to emphasize their refusal. A popinjay," William ground out, "a *boy,* as I heard it, no older than Rollo who came fuming to me with the matter. He didn't believe the fellow was lord at all, thought him a farm lout. Fortunately, Rollo was not senior knight of the commission."

Nevertheless he was son to the Count of Vexin whose lands lay between Normandy and those of the Franks, vital enough to cost William reparation in several horses beside the time and trouble that might better have been spent on more pressing matters. Not to mention the smoothing of Rollo's ruffled feathers. Such incidents would not reoccur.

"Your warrant will make you Denby's suzerain," the king instructed his new officer. "He pays his taxes to you. Let him live, but not too well. Let him stand, but not too straight. The English have always flouted forest law, but now those forests are mine—and you are my arm, Sire Fitz-Gerald."

Ralf understood completely. Men like this boy-lord were to be kept poor and bent.

"Be faithful in this charge, Ralf. Treachery may bring gain but never strength. Faithful men I will prefer to a dozen counts."

The king did not yet invest him as vicomte, but on second thought, that the dull Saxons would better comprehend his authority in their own language and custom, Ralf would take up his new honors as *scir-gerefa,* Lord High Sheriff of Nottingham.

BOOK II

Angel, Write on Us

10

W HEN ROBIN ENTERED his mother's bower, Maud was vigorously shaking wrinkles from a length of saffron-yellow linen. "I hope my son can spare me a few moments."

"Wanted to speak with you any road, Mum."

"No need to go to Midsummer Eve looking like a lout."

Robin dismissed the notion with a grimace. "Scant time for that this year."

"Indeed? Come here."

"What's this?" he grumbled as Maud draped the linen expertly over his shoulder, her lips pursed in calculation. "If you've a mind for sewing, I'd have you make it in blue."

"My blue is out," Maud said, pulling here and tucking there at the cloth. "No more until Grantham fair. I can do the hem and sleeve with the piping I've left. Yellow is a good color for you." Maud stooped, turning the material at his ankle. "Be still, I'm measuring. What had you to speak of? Now how can a body keep you in trews?" She despaired of the ragged, muddy garment. "Half muck and the rest hole. Yes, what is it?"

"Well, I'm trying to tell you."

"Don't fidget—there, that will do it." Maud took her son's hand to stand up. "To it, then. What?"

Robin plunged. "Well, it's about marriage."

"Judith? Yes, I've thought on that." Maud laid the linen on her bed.

"We could manage a small dowry with some of my land, a bit of yours and the rents with them. Not much, I know."

"Uh." Robin glanced vaguely about him. "You're sure there's no blue linen?"

"My solemn word," Maud sighed. "Now as to your cousin—"

"I was thinking of Marian."

He expected some surprise; to his own, Maud merely settled herself on the comfortable backed bench with his father's best blue linen robe hanging behind it on the usual peg, ready for the owner as the day he left. "I know."

In such situations Robin was no quicker than any man, just a little slow. "In truth I was—uh?"

"Marian." A hint of amusement curled the corners of his mother's lips. "The blacksmith's bid must be considered."

"I'm not talking about John. For a start, I mean."

Maud received that with equal serenity. "Oh?"

"I'll be marrying her myself." Robin hurried on before his mother could say anything, though she hardly seemed inclined to interrupt. "I didn't want Judith about when we talked. I know what she'll say."

"Has said."

"Nor Ethelwold, nor even Father Beorn—" Robin stopped and blinked; beyond one slightly elevated eyebrow, his mother appeared anything but startled by his revelation. "What? Who said?"

"Robin, you look positively bewildered." Maud raised her clasped hands and let them fall again in her lap. "Ethelwold knows. Accordingly, he delayed the whole matter of Littlerede. Father Beorn knows, and of course Judith."

Robin felt considerable wind gone out of his sail. "And thinks it mad, right?"

"You know Judith. For all her education, she is Elswith's daughter and still that young. Yes, you do look a bit confused."

He would settle for that description. "Just wondering, then. Between the lot of you, have you told the priest when he should speak the banns?"

"Oh, go along." Maud went to gather up the linen again.

"I ent even asked her yet."

"That is a good place to start," his mother advised. "You will find Marian in the wool room and the day wasting."

Was that all? Robin felt slighted off, wanting her to say more, that she approved and would at least consider the rightness of the matter. At the moment Maud seemed unusually absorbed in cloth. "I do think it's right, Mum. I want you to think so too."

Maud looked over her shoulder, quite serious. "I knew that much the day you brought her here. She's young and strong and no one's fool." She paused, silent, with the linen in her arms and her back to Robin. He saw her hand go out to caress the blue robe on its peg in a gesture that might have lingered had she not cut it short. "Denby is a special place. Sometimes I think a magic place. Some plants will grow here, some not."

Maud fell silent again. She didn't turn to him. Robin felt he was being politely dismissed or forgotten, still he hovered in the doorway, wanting her to put some seal on his decision and not sure how to ask. "I suppose I wanted to say that I love her, Mum."

"Yes," Maud said so softly he almost missed it. "Take some care to find her a kitten."

Yes, that would be meet, but where? Minna's kitchen tabby was still a formidable mouser but far past littering. "I'll be to Blidworth for one."

Maud took down the blue robe, folding it carefully over the yellow linen in the crook of her arm. "You know how she talks of her Biddy."

"Yes. I do cherish her, Mum."

"I know. I heard you."

Settled then. Robin felt better. "I've always fancied that robe of Da's. Might I have it?"

Her look was his answer: *Not yet. This is mine.* "In time. Marian said the yellow would better go with your eyes."

When he left his mother, Robin made straight for the wool room of the barn. The matter was thought out, discussed and decided. No dawdling then, get on with it, and any uncertainty—he'd never been about serious courting before, after all—would be consumed in direct action. So much for his forthrightness; for his sincerity, Robin's mind worked just then on the availability of kittens in Blidworth.

Will Scatloch was at the well, filling a goat-stomach waterbag. There was an open leather wallet beside his bow and quiver, filled with bread and cheese.

"Will, where are you off to?"

"South Sherwood." Will stoppered the bag and tied it at his belt. "The char-burners see everything, look you, and not always daft. There's parkers from Nottingham inside our boundaries."

Was that trouble? Will seemed to be carrying more arrows than usual in his quiver, but Denby's marker stones were on record in Nottingham. "What great matter is it?"

"They wore a new livery. That means a new sheriff," Will concluded. "Worth a look. Will you be coming?"

No, Will could more than handle that, while Robin's bent was toward the wool room and Marian. "Not today. Take Wystan, he bends a fair bow."

"And fairly often," Will agreed dryly. "The Wash has had good measure of your bounty and can spare a day guarding it. I want to see these new liveries from Nottingham."

"Will? Who . . . ?"

Will observed his lord with a dark, canny eye. Robin did not seem to be entirely present. "Who what?"

"Who in Blidworth has kittens?"

Will bent to gather up his kit. "Better ask of a passing cat. It's parkers I spoke of."

Robin just shook his head. "Women."

"Aye," Will said, puzzled even further. "And what of them?"

"I think I'll be scholar at Whitby before I understand women."

There's prophecy, Will reflected, collecting his gear. He went to fetch Wystan for the journey.

Soft days like this were the worst for Maud. Mellow, drowsy days between delicate spring and the warmth of deep summer when young people walked out together all night long with midsummer close and the gloaming magical, and a spate of marrying to come in July. On such days trivialities were like willowbark to a headache; they kept the sharpest pain at a distance, but what simple for her soul?

Like flax wound on a distaff, her mind turned on the same unacceptable fact that must be accepted. She never saw Aelred dead, just—gone, not there, her future cut off by a great, keen blade. Incomplete, unfinished. Requiem said, mourning without a wake, absence aching like the pain some warriors could still feel in an amputated limb.

It was my right to see my lover's body, to kiss his lips and say farewell, see him into the earth and know he is gone. For that lack, it is not Aelred who haunts this bower but my dead self hungering.

Yes, there would be enough blue piping for Robin's robe if she skimped here and there.

Angharad, fetch the sewing box. . . .

On long midsummer nights, still glowing with the sun, even after years of marriage there were times when they hardly slept at all but made love until the ghost-light became day—slowly, relishing the splendor of it, whispering and laughing while they rested at how stern and aloof volatile young Angharad thought them. Such velvet nights were the sweet, painful worst in memory, the fragrance of Sherwood a heaviness on her heart.

Fitting to remember the kitten for Marian. The girl loved as naturally as she would give birth with God's blessing. Others like Judith held life at arm's length before accepting it, if ever.

And some are like Lazarus, walking about closer to death than life, not knowing why but expected to be grateful for the gift of another day.

The leper's known by his yellow robe and bell, the beggar by rags and his whining plea for alms, the halt by his crutch. Those with scrofula lie up by the king's gate to receive his healing touch. Like any trade, affliction has its stall and sign, if I could find a device for mine. My sores do not show—Beorn, Angharad, try to understand that—nor my rags from a shining life, nor would one guess how halt I am.

I will give Robin his father's blue robe, but . . . not yet, son. Not while I can still smell his body in it, imagine the warmth of his arms under the sleeve; not while I can still hold it in my cold bed, wrap it about his pillow and not yet feel futile. Not while my body still fits to what is gone and this little left of him.

Elswith could never fathom why I turned down the earl's cousin. Pompous young man with waxed mustaches and his bangs fussy-curled with tongs. But rich enough, Elswith said, considering I was just a carl's daughter. God give you gentle rest, sister, you were always more for climbing the family tree than I was, passing on to Judith that something-by-marriage kinship with the royal line of Ethelred, like a poor end of thread hanging from a silken sleeve.

That night in the earl's hall, sister and I sat in the gallery gossiping about the men at the long tables below. Elswith was already betrothed to that too-handsome Dane who gave Judith her looks, but just as excited over the bid made for me. . . .

Maud, you little silly, he's looked up to you with every breath. At least wave to him.

Elswith, who is that there?

Him? That's Thane Somebody from Sherwood. The one in blue? That's his son—

—who had glanced up to me more often than the bidding cousin, but I saw something in his eyes that I must answer, that we never lost. I found more happiness in this forest place than ever my sister did at court. Sweet Christ, it is the happiness, like the dull ghost-pain in the womb after the child stillborn, physical, palpable as that. I am traitor even to Robin, wishing him away that he won't see me bleed. Go, go for God's sake. Get married, take the girl and leave me be. Leave me to silence, all of you.

I've heard that in the desert lands along the spice routes a man shows his wealth by how fat his wives become. "Look! See how I can afford to feed them." I'm told they are as public with their grief and let others measure the depths of their loss by the number of mourners hired to wail. I thought the custom vulgar and faintly ridiculous. Now I could envy such mourning, ready-cut and run up like a flag. No, I'm not bred to the habit. Sorrow is not worn to be seen anymore than my undershift. I cannot keen like Angharad's hill kind. Pity: Such a letting might drain the wound.

Dear Ethelwold, saying I've grown too silent, do you think it is for lack of a scream? The pillow I hug of nights, I've woken to find it wet with tears, and weep sometimes in front of Angharad when there's too much to be held back. She understands—she tries—with her hands and hot tea ready, poor little thing with her prattle that grates where it would soothe while I bite back the scream. *How easy it is for you, woman, with your man safe and close in bed at night. Get out, get out before I let myself hate you for that.*

We do not show our wounds here. When Robin held me and told me, the blade went in and twisted, and I fell dead as Aelred though none saw me die. When I rose like Lazarus, my soul measured its loss like this linen and fixed the price to the last penny of *wergild.*

Odd to find that hating, so new to me, wears so well. Vengeance? Not so foreign a fury after all; she may board this year at my table until my price is paid in my own coin. For the rest, it's well that God did not give us the open, easily read faces of Angharad's blood, or her nature that must speak its heart *now* or burst. A cold blessing, no doubt. Even Father Beorn would run from the murder in me now. . . .

Yes, Angharad, that is splendid work. You were always nimbler with a needle than I—*Woman, stop your mouth, for God's sake. Can't you see me dying, you wretched little—*

Dear God, stop the pain.

You won't? Then leave it on the forge of me and all silent-screaming widows in England who will have more than the comfort of Your only begotten in this loss. Is it that You cannot understand us any better than William's Normans, used to one way and no other? One might gather as much. We came late to You, but read our hearts. Read our laws. Everything has a value and must be paid for. Judas suffered guilt over Jesus, but our Loki slew Baldur and slept well, I hear—

What? Yes, Angharad. Tea would be lovely now. Ask Lady Judith to join us, and I'll get on with the needle while you're gone.

Robin found Marian working in the wool room with Gudrun, the floor ankle-deep in last week's sheared fleeces which Gudrun laid one by one on a long table, rolled and carefully tied. The small room reeked of lanolin boiled from the fleeces yesterday. Cooled now, the grease floated in brownish blobs that Marian skimmed and strained into a clay pot.

"Give you good morning, Gudrun." Robin greeted the old woman with elaborately casual cheer, fingering the fleece she was rolling, inspecting the yield in Marian's pot. "No such thing as too much good oil."

Gudrun winked at Marian. "Our thane's in a passing good mood today."

Robin felt uncomfortable. Sheep oil was a lame gambit to open a courting. "Well, oil's important."

"Plenty on it," Marian assured him.

To it: He took her arm. "Come out to the well. There's that I'd speak of."

Outside, Robin found he could look anywhere but at Marian. He dippered a drink he didn't want from the well and offered it to her while judging the soft cumulus clouds dreaming past high noon overhead. "Looks to be a fine day."

"For all manner of things," Marian agreed. "What shall we speak of?"

"I was pondering on . . . uh . . . Little John."

"He's a large pondering."

"Well." Robin leaned back against the lip of the well, arms folded, ready to take a very large bull by the horns. "This marriage bid he's made. Have y'come to any agreement?"

"Aye, we have that."

"Oh." In Robin's stricken imagination, Marian took an agonizing amount of time to roll the thought this way and that like dough for baking. Here in the warm June sunlight, he was sharply aware of her strong, lank body under the dun linen, from the movement of her shoulders to the bare feet brown-stained with grease, and how much he wanted her, and would she please, for God's sake, speak to the point.

"We have some agreement," she said coolly. "John thinks I would make a good wife. I think he's a wonder at smithing. Has he spoken to you?"

Damn it, there was a clergy-careful answer that told him nothing. *I ask her straight out, she answers riddle.* Once more his chin jutted to the sky. "I'd know what answer you gave him."

So soft as to be barely audible, "None. Robin."

They stood close together in the warm sun. A few scouting bees passed them by sensing honeysuckle close.

Robin tried a different tack. "Now, if you were at home, being free and that, your da would've managed it. But it is my place here, just as I must make provision for Judith. Just . . . ."

Marian's eyes danced over him. "Just what, then?"

Robin stirred restlessly; there were complex sentiments to convey. "Before the war, before the foreigners came, this was a happy place. From my grandfather's time dowry wasn't the most important part. My mother passed up a rich man to marry Aelred and nary day's regret." He took a deep breath and committed to a frontal attack. "John's a good man, but I've thought on it."

"As a lord should," Marian prompted sweetly.

"I've thought long on it—as I said, mind."

"Aye, as you said."

"There's none but you I'd have beside me in my hall."

He shot a quick sidewise glance at her, not sure how she was taking this or if he was making the best case for his heart that would be lark to her now, not the plain robin he was. Marian leaned against the well, long legs crossed and arms folded perhaps in sly imitation of his male stance. Suddenly she giggled. "Well, you went all around your barn to say it, Robin. And what of dowry?"

He could look at her then; something in her voice opened a door. "God's body, who's talkin' dowry?"

"I've nowt but my two silver pence."

"Ah, shut up."

Marian laughed aloud. "That was the first thing you said to me when we met in the forest."

"Well, am I a poet with a harp? Don't you know what I'm trying to say? More than dowry or that I'd be a good and proper husband to you, it's—"

She turned quickly with a stilling finger on his lips. "Don't, it would be bad luck." She was serious, frowning under a shadow of real fear. "Don't, Robin. I know what you're saying and what I'd say. Be that to me and I to you, but don't say it yet."

There was confusion for a man: a woman who said yes with all but the word. "I've been days coming to it, like climbing a steep hill. I would say it."

"Please. Not yet. I'm not that . . . brave." Not shy but troubled by a cloud she hadn't guessed was there. All her life love came easily, love for all things she gathered close and cared for—her parents and the animals they husbanded, little Biddy to whom she once whispered all her secrets. Then in one day the foreigners swept them all away like crumbs from a table. If to name the Devil was to bring him, to name this happiness might endanger it, tempt a thieving fate to snatch it away. Robin knew his losses, Marian knew her own. "Please?"

"But you're saying you will marry me?"

"I gave John no answer because I would have no one else on Denby but you."

"Good. This is a good thing for both of us." Robin tried to sound sober and sensible, but he couldn't manage that, not as marvelous as he felt. "Go to the kitchen; tell Minna to put us some food for walking."

"Where do we go?" Marian wondered. She had to inquire of his receding back as Robin loped toward the gate.

"Is that a way to plight a troth, arguing with your bridegroom?"

"I'd best start with your mum's needle," she hooted after him. "The knee's gone out of your trews and the seat bare enough to blush at, and from now on, it's my place to mend you."

"Kitchen!" he roared back in enormous good spirits. "We've a long way."

For all she wouldn't say or let him speak, Robin knew in that exultant moment that she was happy as summer itself, scampering for the kitchen, long legs shearing gracefully over the muddy patches.

"And much to see!" he sang out after her. Then he waited for her by the gate, a little dizzied with his joy. Not much of that about lately. Willy Bastard won the war, but he couldn't take this away, not by a long bowshot.

Good or bad news traveled Sherwood swift as a martin from house to barn. Minna devined most of it from the hectic flush in Marian's cheek before the girl bubbled the tidings over the food she was wrapping. In less time than tepid porridge took to cool, Minna told Gudrun who passed the tidings to Blidworth village. Ethelwold, resting by the stove, gave Minna a told-you-so nod. Angharad, brewing tea for Lady Maud, allowed it was the best news she'd heard since the promise of Arthur's return.

"Grand," she said over and over. "Just passing *grand.*"

"Oh, yes." Ethelwold covered a small yawn. "They will have healthy children. Get on with the tea, Angharad."

She stuck out her tongue behind the steward's back and trotted away to Maud's bower, tea and tidings steaming alike, and so she served both to Maud and Judith. "What do you think of that, now? He's asked her."

Waiting for huzzahs, Angharad was bleakly disappointed. Where she boiled with the news, they weren't even surprised.

"Oh?" Judith took up her tea, sipping daintily. "Then I expect they'll speak the banns this Sunday."

Maud said only, "I suppose, yes. Thank you, Angharad; that will be all. Let the brew steep longer next time."

No fathoming Saxons at all. Bursting, Angharad stared from one to the other. "Suppose? It is glorious!"

Her mistress gave her a tiny nod and smile over the teacup. "Yes, quite."

Could a body take the measure of that? Angharad puzzled through the soft bee-buzzing afternoon. Born and raised in cold water, the whole of them. First banns a-Sunday, that will be all and steep the tea longer next time. *Dyw!*

By Angharad's Celtic lights, there was a definite want of color to the Saxon soul and no more song than a sow could sing.

They took the forest path toward Edwinstowe. Passing a honeysuckle bush, Marian broke off a twig and stuck it in Robin's belt. "For courting luck."

"You've already said yes."

"I could change my mind," she teased airily. "Take me for wife but not for granted."

As if he would. As if he could. Robin kicked himself for a clod who might learn tact from a boar hog.

"Robin, look: bluebells." Marian knelt over the flowers like found treasure. They were passing through a patch of half-cleared wood bordering open heath. Little John had worked many extra hours this spring to claim this acre as bookland. Robin decided then and there to reckon it John's at Midsummer when new-cleared land was recorded. He would be telling the man himself about Marian's choice, that was only fitting. He would try to do it in kindness and friendship. Poor, unlucky John: There was a darkness on the man since Hastings, darker since the loss of his family. *But there it is. I'm happier this day than ever in my life. Like summer roses on the old high table, she's beauty in the middle of my plain life. I'd give John anything else now, anything but her.*

"Before they cut the trees and let the sun in, I'm bound there wasn't a bell to be seen." Marian plucked one of the blossom by its fat stem and wound it in Robin's hair. "Now you're a proper bridegroom. You'd think they were dead or not there at all, but it's a miracle what will grow with just a little sun."

Walking on, they heard the bell from Blidworth church. Father Beorn on the bell rope. The tones peeled the hour's office easy and even-spaced across the dale, where Tuck's arm clamored you to it. They stopped to eat near the brook from Holy Pool, Marian laying out the food on her spread apron. She took off her veil and shook out the long hair dulled now with sheep oil, scratching vigorously at her scalp. "Wants scrubbing."

Robin munched on a chicken joint, enjoying her unconsciously graceful preening. "Set you a riddle you can't answer."

"Oh-ho, not in your lifetime." Her father had been a great riddler of winter nights. "None I haven't heard or can't answer."

"Bet that last egg?"

"Done. Riddle me, Aelredson."

Robin set on with a sly grin. "I am very strong with a fiery red point, but I die shuddering in release. Behind me is the man who brought me to this desperate state—"

"Ah, you're naught!" Marian threw a handful of grass at him. "That's a man's root going into a woman."

"You think so, do you?"

"Fine bawdy riddle for a bride who ent brided yet."

"Wrong! It's a burning arrow."

"Oh, for sure." Most riddles had double meanings and this the plainest of all. " 'An arrow,' says the innocent lad. Or a hot poker dipped in water. Aye, and Jesus was born in Tadcaster. Why don't you just say you want to top me?"

He fair choked on his chicken. "Now who said a word—?"

"No mind; set me another."

"Wystan ought swill out your mouth with the week's wash." Still, he wasn't all that innocent. The sight of her, half reclining, cheek on her palm, with the long curve of her body under the gown and the wondrous lines they drew in his longing, and where in the world could he weave words into a riddle for how he needed Marian?

Watching him, she was taken with a sudden fit of giggles. "Men, roosters, and boars, you're all the same. I've said yes, so you think: Right, let's get on with the bedding."

"Weeping Jesus, I thought no such—"

"Because I'm a maid, do I have to be bloody stupid? Don't be wroth, Robin, just a bit of fun. Set your riddle."

She wronged him to think he was set on that course before all others; on the other hand, he couldn't say the notion was entirely absent. He was irritated because she took it all so lightly. "Mark: I am beauty crafted for killing, most dangerous when I curve as in a smile. When I bend, poison shoots from my belly. Imprisoned, I grow longer when my master releases me—"

"I have you!" Marian held up his longbow. " 'And I serve no man unstrung.' Last egg is mine!"

Robin gave it over. "You're too quick for me."

She broke the boiled egg into two halves, head bent over them, suddenly quite serious. "They'll want nigh half of every single egg, the foreigners."

"We'll manage."

"How, Rob?"

"Because we must."

"Doesn't seem right." Her head was lowered over the food in her hands, but the voice was level. "We will show them a proper hall."

He gripped her hand and knew from the answering squeeze that he'd done more in the touching than any words could. Sad and afraid and yet full of joy, Robin wondered if Aelred felt so when he brought Maud to see what Marian must know today. Marian would more than try; she'd show the Normans what proper was. He was tender lifting her to her feet, retrieving her veil and apron. "No fear, girl. Not a bit of it."

Now he could kiss her; the best answer he could make for both of them. Her mouth was honest as the rest of her, the warmth of her tongue searching his, admitting the fear along with the desire for him. He held her close a moment, wishing he had the ease with women Will had imparted with the bow and forest.

Marian murmured against his shoulder, "I am afraid. For all of us."

"Come on," he said softly. "Not far now." A little weight was gone from his back now. At least he didn't have to be frightened all alone.

Marian picked up the longbow, caressing the dark, smooth wood. "Did Aelred leave you this?"

"No." Robin was amused at the notion, explaining the custom as they walked on. Only ax or sword were fit to be passed from thane to son. The bow was for hunting and sport, not war honor.

"You fought with it," Marian remembered.

"Just fell out that way. Keeping Sherwood is our crown service. Will taught me the bow along with the forest." Some good lads there were who bent a fine bow at Tadcaster and York, but a place in the shield wall must be earned by rank and service. "You could say I'm halfway between honor and ordinary."

As they left the Edwinstowe path and turned eastward, Marian began to have some sense of Denby's holding. They must be near the northern extent of Robin's land. He stopped finally, head cocked to one side. "Hear that?"

Hear what? "Not a sound."

"Listen. Still yourself down. There's always something to hear."

With hard concentration, Marian caught the barely audible sound of running water.

"The rill from Holy Pool," Robin told her. "Starts just north of here."

A little farther on they came to the brook itself. Just beyond lay the oval-shaped clearing formed by bordering oaks; one much younger than the others stood out in the clearing with a small forester's hut nearby.

"Robin, what house is that?"

"Don't know. No one does." Some old char-burner's long ago, or perhaps a monk praying his thorny way to sainthood through solitude. The wattle hut was there when Robin's grandfather first stumbled into the clearing years ago.

"The hall is only the head, Marian. This is the heart of Denby."

Robin jumped the rill and sat down on the tussock grass, inviting Marian beside him. She was glad to rest, weaving a chaplet from green heather sprigs while Robin began to find the words to tell her of this clearing. "You must understand this place. Mum was book-learned but she came to it out of love. I think women understand these things quicker than men."

Truly, he considered, the tale should be writ down. Will Scatloch said no, that such should only be sung by a proper bard, but then how could a body keep the story straight with all the natural human forgetting and exaggerating a pack of Welsh would bring to it? "I was ten when I found this place . . ."

As he spun out the tale, Marian saw with a woman's sight why this clearing was as much a part of his marriage proposal as the asking or any dowry. This *was* his offering to her in dower.

Robin's great-grandfather had been a sokeman farmer of Southwell, a freeholder like Marian's, but his son Brihtnoth took service as a soldier in King Canute's household in the days when England and Denmark were one kingdom. In time Canute made Brihtnoth a thane of five hides with Blidworth village part of his holding. Carl-service was to be thanked for his advancement, but Brihtnoth was a farmer born and always fancied working his own land someday.

Sherwood was wilder then, fewer paths trodden from one village to another, and the game running thick. One autumn day when his new hall was yet a-building, Brihtnoth went out alone to hunt. In a little while he sighted a doe. Naturally, he couldn't take her in rut season, but as does went at this time of year, with her hock glands sending scent-signals, there would be one or two bucks bound to follow her.

"I've hunted red deer since I was twelve," Robin said in a voice that recalled more frustrated than fruitful stalks. "There ent any female, human or animal, more contrary than a doe leading on a buck. Between chasing and fighting and then keeping the does he's won, a buck gets nowt of rest or much to eat."

"Here." Marian placed the finished heather chaplet on his head. "A crown for my lord."

"Do you mark what I'm telling you, girl?"

"As to the good father at Mass."

"This is a mickle matter."

"I know." She brushed his cheek with her lips. "Tell me."

Well, then, the doe led Brihtnoth a merry chase, showing herself, doubling back and nipping off again this way and that until she led him to this clearing. Most strange, Brihtnoth realized, not a buck had he sighted the whole day. When she showed herself—"There, by the hut"—Brihtnoth just fell down to rest and drink from the stream. He was run out and too tired to be hungry, and he said to the doe, "Fair enough, woman. You go your way and I'll mine." When Brihtnoth rose from drinking, though he'd not heard the doe make off, she was gone and just where she'd been was the most beautiful woman a man could find in a year of looking.

Marian made a warding sign behind her back. "Was she of the Good Neighbors, then?"

Who could say? Denby was of divided opinion to the present day. She might have been a *weird* or *wicca* woman or just a girl of Blidworth village and real as butter. Real or magic, her name was Guntrada, she was Dane and that lovely, and Brihtnoth was a strapping young thane who needed a wife in order to pass on his lands to an heir.

"Guntrada was my grandmother," Robin said, "and it is plain fact that she asked after the marrying that they spend their first night in this old hut."

When Brihtnoth asked why, with their bower at Denby new and ready, Guntrada said, "I bring you great dowry, husband, and I will ask a morning-gift of my own devising."

So they passed their wedding night in the hut. Brihtnoth was so well pleased with Guntrada that a fitting gift of gold was the least he could give her in the morning. He bent over her; her hair, red as the doe's pelt, all tumbled on the pillow, and knew he would grant whatever Guntrada wished.

Winding a bit of grass around her finger, Marian commented slyly, "That's a good time for asking."

As the tale went, Guntrada wound her arms about his neck like supple vine around the trunk of a tree, and named her morning-gift. Their mingled blood in the earth. For what they took, they must give something back. Then she led Brihtnoth out of the hut to a tiny sapling oak barely a hand's span out of the ground, two brave leaves spread out to catch the sun. Guntrada took Brihtnoth's hunting knife and drew blood from her hand, some from his. Drop by mingled drop the blood fell on the new leaves. That was the beginning of Denby's bargain with the land, perhaps not so holy as the Church might wish, but no less a consecration.

Almost finished. Robin ducked his head, wondering if Marian understood beyond the words of the tale to the truth of it. Like the bread and wine at Communion, he believed without having to fathom the mystery at the ritual's heart. "Aelred and Maud spent their wedding night here. I want us to do the same."

Marian was looking up at the oval of sky framed in the oaks. "We will, Robin."

Good, then. She knew that much and would reconcile the rest in time. "Not really against what Father Beorn preaches. Just that we don't forget where all this comes from. Magic or hard work, who can tell, year in and out we have the best harvests in the shire."

There: Clearest meaning was simplest told, but he needn't add his own tale of finding the doe when he was a boy, since he'd never told that to any but Will who thought the matter best kept secret. Robin didn't hold with most of the old ways, being practical farmer and baptized Christian, but no one should argue with abundance. Heathen or not, the tradition worked more for good than ill.

Nor need he worry about Marian's understanding, deeper than his own in this and aware of the bargain implied even in the common sense of sewing and turning clover in wearied earth after taking the barley out of it. Her own father and all men made the same bargain. Who could demand of the earth without good care in return? Christian as Robin, country-born to country thrift, Marian would not discard old wisdom any sooner than she would throw out a perfectly good gown just because she had a newer one.

The blood, she knew, was no more than symbol for the heart and spirit that must go into working land as her own parents put theirs year by year into Tadcaster earth. Maud had made the bargain: Often, helping her at some task by daylight or candle, Marian had seen the thin white scar on the heel of Maud's left hand.

"We'll make the bargain together, Robin. Was that what you wanted me to know?"

He took the heather crown from his own head and centered it on the gold of hers. "Yes."

They lay back in the grass, Marian snuggled into Robin's shoulder. The forest was even quieter now around them, the soft rustling of the nearby rill a peaceful sound to lull her to sleep. Marian captured Robin's hand where it stroked at her hair and cupped it gently over her breast in a smaller understanding. Time drifted by them like the clouds overhead.

"One riddle I can't answer," Robin murmured. "How to pay our taxes. That's a witting Da didn't leave me."

For the time Marian was content to drowse in his arms and wonder sleepily at the curious pattern of chance in her life. If the foreigners hadn't torn out her life by the roots, she might have said the ash charm at home for less of a husband. Plucked from her own soil, blown on the wind to take root again and deeper in a place no *wicca* woman could have foretold.

Still . . . the night she said the charm, she dreamed of a man all in black and gold, which was most odd. The dream should show her future husband in everyday clothes. Robin didn't own such finery and never wore black. She couldn't recall any face on the man. Dreams were very unreliable that way. Any road, now that she was plighted, wouldn't it be stupid to turn her eyes from what she had to some stranger in black? God forbid, he might even be a priest.

Vespers had rung a good half hour since when Robin and Marian turned into Denby gate. Happy enough, Robin might have blurted his betrothal to anyone within earshot, but nary man, woman, chick, nor child was stirring.

"They must all be in the hall," he guessed as they walked hand in hand toward it. "Yes, I hear 'em."

Impossible not to hear as they drew closer: a gabble of voices topped by the high squealing of children excited just to be excited. When they entered the hall, the entire household was there but no preparations had been made for supper, or rather they appeared to have been interrupted. Gudrun waited in the far entrance with a bowl of salt. The rest stood about in agitated clumps of conference, Will's sons jiggling about the edges. Gwaun, the youngest, darted down the hall toward Robin with his brother Eddain in raucous pursuit.

"Thane!" little Gwaun piped. "There's news. My father says—"

Angharad fetched Gwaun up firmly by one ear, exasperated. "Did I not say quiet? You'll get a hiding, you will."

"What is it?" Marian didn't like the intuition like a sudden shadow on her happiness.

"Normans!" Eddain shrilled. "Sheriff, king, and all."

Robin tried to quell them. "Peace, both of you. Angharad, what's this now?"

She bobbed her head to him while wrestling Gwaun to order. "My husband has the telling of it, sir."

Will waited with the family and Ethelwold near the fire pit. To one side, Wystan looked worried and Minna worse. Gwaun struggled against his mother's restraint. "But it's Normans coming *here!*"

"Hey, mind your mum." Robin leveled a warning finger. "She'll smack you silly. Be still, boy."

Of all the times for more trouble when he wanted to present Marian to his family for the bride she would be. There were merry plans to make, glad things to be done for a change this lean year—but none of his folk seemed primed for gaiety now. Robin looked from his mother to Judith and his steward. "Who's to be hanged? What's this of Normans?"

Maud only gestured to Will Scatloch. "Give account, man."

"We met with those liveried men from Nottingham," Will nodded to Wystan, still carrying his bow and quiver. "The new sheriff's men right enough."

"And caught them in the act," Wystan said with dark relish. "Pulling down my lord's boundary stones."

"We stopped them," said Will, "but they said no mind, the new boundary's a mile north of the old, if you please."

"In a pig's—by what right?" Robin spat. "Those boundaries have been known in Nottingham since Brihtnoth was thane."

"The new sheriff is a Norman knight," Judith explained quietly. "Sire Ralf Fitz-Gerald. You might have expected as much."

"Fitz what? What kind of Christian name is that?"

"A common enough prefix in Normandy," she shrugged. "Someone's son out of wedlock but recognized by his father."

Robin seethed; in all the years of Denby, no one, crown or common, had questioned the limits of their land. "At least they named him for what he is. I'll be seeing this Fitz-whoever."

Will agreed gravely. "You will that, Thane. That's the rest and the worst of it. He's coming here presently with the king."

"And the queen with her appanage," Judith took it up. "A royal progress, most like, a large party as these things go. Household, officers, knights, the lot." Which meant, beside the enormous inconvenience of a totally disrupted hall just scraping by until the new crops came in, that William more than likely meant to call Robin to account for the insulted knights. "The word is they journey to Grantham. The king will pause to put you in his pocket. That is how these things are done, Edward."

"I see." Robin looked at his bride-to-be. Of all the days to hear such news. Clinging to his arm, Marian's clouded expression mirrored his own suddenly chilled mood. Damn William and damn to hell all Normans. They'd been happy for a few hours, forgetting all else in the confidence that they could manage anything because they were in love. More than Marian to think of: blood kin, family, or servants, they were all his to be cared for. Robin felt the great, shadowy weight of this William already bowing him down. He looked around at all of them, one by one, and forced a cocky grin. "William and his Fitz? All I can say is, there's two right bastards with no sense of occasion. I would have none of you frighted by this. I will do what must be done." Gently he urged Marian forward to his family. "Mother, Judith. All of you. Marian is to be my lady wife."

"I know. I have been happy for that already." In the way Maud embraced her, Marian felt as if she'd come home. "You will be my daughter, Godifigu Marian, and I bless you."

Judith was as gracious with a kiss, calling Marian cousin, which now she would be, though with the blessing, Marian read a surfeit of tired knowledge in Judith's dark eyes. Ethelwold and the men surrounded Robin with a babble of congratulations, but Angharad said it best for all of them—worried for her own but happy for this while keeping a firm hold on her squirming sons. "Bless us!" she sang out, her delighted seal on it all. "Bless all in this house!"

And save us from what's coming, Robin prayed. "Minna, Gudrun: Foreigners comin' are just that and no more. Get on with supper."

11

O

NCE BEYOND THE boundary tree called Roman Oak, the royal party
was on Denby land. Still physically ill, Ralf Fitz-Gerald rode behind
William, Queen Matilda, their young daughter Adelaide, and Earl
Waltheof. The son of honored old Earl Siward, Waltheof was the last
of the high English lords to retain his titles and land. He rode at tiny
Matilda's side, charming her as usual. The new sheriff of Nottingham
felt the earl, barely his elder, charmed far too easily to be sincere.
Though Ralf could personally attest to the suppleness of Waltheof's
loyalties, this pliant disposition had won the earl the rich manor of
Mansfield as a gift from William. Ralf glowered at the earl's scarlet-
cloaked back. Whether or not William trusted Waltheof, he must certainly need him.

The royal appanage clopped and rumbled along the cart track, a com-
plement of mounted knights before and behind, foot soldiers, the household officers of treasury and seal, panterers, musicians, huntsmen,
wagons laden with bedding and other comforts—all descending on little
Denby like falcons on a sparrow. This forest lord would have his wings
clipped and know his authority in Sherwood henceforth second to Ralf's.

This helped to offset Ralf's illness and the fatigue of riding. He was
still far out of fighting condition. When he rose that morning at Mansfield, he felt chilled, the first familiar sign of relapse. To ride in this
condition was minor misery. To fight thus had been hell. When the
water-sickness took Ralf's entire squadron at Dover, they still had to

ride all day and sometimes fight while their bowels loosened and fouled them every few minutes, in the worst cases.

Now there were compensations. Since Chester, Ralf had moved in ever-higher circles of favor and comfort. He glanced at the ridiculously small figure of Queen Matilda laughing now at some clever sally of Waltheof's. Ralf's liking and respect for the queen were unforced: surely the smallest woman in Europe married to one of the largest men, but sturdy as a mule. Matilda had borne nine children since the age of nineteen, the youngest but two years since, and then she had risen from confinement to cross the Channel for her coronation at London. The dear lady deserved a respite. Small chance of that, so the word went. William was a ferociously faithful husband with unflagging energies.

The cart track led now through vast arcades of ancient beech and oak that might have been growing when Caesar came. Someone forward passed word back to the king that hunting would be unusually fine sport here.

And living, Ralf yearned from the pallor of his illness. When England was at last secure, a man could find peace in such a forest, where the iron world passed by on tiptoe not to disturb this vast, verdant slumber. To live in such a place, leagues from ambition; to sit by a fire in the evening with a woman speaking in a voice like a soft lute of small and wonderful nothings—but there was the world for you. Men born with few advantages must make the most of what came their way. Still, there were gentler blessings one might wish—

Gardez!

Lulled by fever and the peace about him, Ralf snapped erect with the familiar warning in his gut. The bay stallion tugged at his bridle with a confirming snort, ears twitching. Ralf turned in the saddle to see the rear guard plodding along, oblivious. The knot in his stomach squeezed tighter. Then he chided the fear. If there were Greyfeathers about, some of the king's men would be dead now. Yet he'd survived on such instinct and almost died the day he ignored it for one instant. Ralf trotted the bay forward to William's side.

"Sire, take care. My lord can call me a fool, but—"

Even as Ralf spoke, the two foresters slid silently out of a thicket only a few paces away. The dark one had the look of the Welsh border. The younger man had the same impervious expression once bent on Ralf under a grey sky before leaving him to the carrion birds. The longbow this one carried, the faded green trews, the whole line of the man proclaimed him Greyfeather. He saluted Earl Waltheof.

"Hoch, Earl."

"Hoch, Thegn." Waltheof conversed briefly with the bearded, sun-brown man, then flowed into Franc. *"Mon roi,* allow me to present the very man you seek: Edward, Thane of Denby. He welcomes your majesties to Sherwood. Though he fears his hospitality insufficient to royal company, his gate is open to you."

"Indeed?" William surveyed the drably clad young man, who met him eye for eye in cool inspection. "So this is the lord for whose ill manners I had to placate the Count of Vexin. He looks innocent enough, but then did not Saint Gregory call Saxon children angels?"

"He did, my lord. In a tiresome pun on their Anglian birth."

"You criticize a saint, Waltheof?" Matilda chided.

The earl evaded silkenly. "Madam, we are told that wit is no kin to holiness. Let it not demean me to suggest that holiness is no warranty of wit."

True, Ralf agreed silently as the thane's impenetrable glance rested on him: They all look like angels when young. Then they grew up and you saw nothing in their faces, even when they killed you. The merciless or the mad never looked fierce, merely blank.

No sooner had the royal party swarmed over Denby—to the strained courtesy of Maud and the muttered imprecations of Ethelwold—when William roared his spirited intention to hunt forthwith in his new forest. He called for a boar spear, and the chase moved out of the courtyard in a roil of shouting knights, huntsmen beaters, and baying hounds. Robin and Will in their wake were appalled by this thunderous manner of hunting.

"Glory to God, they sound like a war," Will whistled. "The game's in Scotland by now."

Robin's folk had strict orders to stay out of the forest today. With all the noise, a boar would be the only creature mean enough to brave this king. Robin privately wished good fortune to the quarry. Boar was mortally dangerous game for any man less than skilled with a heavy spear or who quailed for one heartbeat at the crucial moment. Common to lose hounds in such a hunt, not unusual for men to be slashed or even gutted by the maddened beast that knew neither caution nor fear. Robin prayed William would flush a boar from the angriest corner of hell.

No luck there. He had to admire the cold courage of this king. When he took his stand in an open spot, hounds baying about the thicket where the boar had gone to ground, the beaters flushed William's prize directly toward him, twenty stone of razor-tusked, hurtling death.

"Clear all!" the king bellowed. "My game." Men scattered in every direction as the king crouched alone in the boar's path.

Robin knew the hot, churning ferocity and strength of the boar and the speed so many hunters underestimated in the last moment before they died. William planted his feet and crouched forward behind the leveled spear. The boar took it high in the shoulder, screaming rage and momentum driving the point clear through and out one tough, bristling flank, going for his own kill even as his life gushed out.

William struggled with the still deadly mass twice his own bulk. *"Les chiens!"*

The loosed hounds howled in to rip out the boar's throat, but still it fought with a high-pitched squealing fury until William pinned it to the earth, kicking at the blood-maddened dogs. "Bring the bread!"

One huntsman darted forward with a bag of stale bread while another thrust his own spear through the boar's heart. Between them they sopped the bread in blood to lure the dogs away from the carcass. While the game was trussed on poles for carrying, William strolled to Robin, wiping his red-spattered hands on a towel provided by Earl Waltheof.

"My good earl, tell Edward we bring our own feast tonight. Lest he worry about his village, my men know they will answer to me for any disturbance. As he will himself in breaking my laws."

Robin could only relay noncommital thanks through Waltheof, while William observed him with a trace of ironic humor. "You Saxons are always astonished to find that I am a civilized king. I treasure civil peace, Thane. At your age, I saw so little of it. We will speak again before supper."

C'est toute de belle, Maman!

Queen Matilda bent her thoughts with rueful tenderness on her eldest daughter, who had just tripped off to explore Denby's quaint timber hall. Adelaide at thirteen had been in England less than a month. She found "belle Don-bee" fascinating and exotic. Matilda found it merely English and uncomfortable. But then lavish conceits, to be awash with passion for a face, a song, or a dream—such fancies went with being thirteen, did they not?

The queen sat alone in Lady Maud's bower, relishing a rare and blessed moment of privacy. She rested on a cushion added to the oaken chair to ease the ravages wrought on her lower back by riding, gratified that Lady Maud had a passable glass mirror, since her own had been broken jolting over the ruts from Mansfield. The widow appeared to have few other luxuries, plain as she was silent. One heard her husband died at York. From Lady Judith's few comments, Matilda gathered Maud's was a marriage of deep and lasting affection. *We have that in common, if nothing else.* Very likely the blue robe hanging on its peg had belonged to her husband. The whole ambience of this spotless chamber was more that of a place shared by lovers than a widow's arid solitude.

Bending to the mirror, Matilda dabbed egg white into the deepening lines about her eyes. This Maud must be of her own age; time had been kinder to the Saxon woman, who had obviously led a more tranquil existence until her husband's death. *So many more lines in the last two years since Henry was born. The egg will not rout them all.*

The Welsh slave woman with the unpronounceable name had regarded her with awed deference and would have removed every iron object from the bower had not Judith told her the measures were unnecessary. The woman appeared unconvinced but knelt to Matilda and sidled out.

The queen was completely at sea. "What was all that about iron?"

"She believes you are of the fey folk," Judith explained. "Among Angharad's people, feys are carefully respected but cannot approach or touch iron, she tells me. To leave any in this chamber would be insult to you, she thinks, and liable to bring retribution on the house."

"Me a fey?" Matilda found that amusing. "*La.* No doubt because I am so small."

Fey she was not. Though less than four and a half feet tall, William's consort had been sturdy enough since youth to carry power and heavy burdens without strain. Daughter to the Count of Flanders, cousin to King Philip of France, she had been her husband's very effective regent-duchess in Normandy, always aware of the unstable elements both of them juggled from day to day. She trusted and loved more readily than William, not to a fault, but affection came easier to Matilda. She had not suffered her husband's brutal childhood.

She and Gilly had invested wisely: Cecily to the Church, Adelaide now betrothed to Alfonso of León. One hoped he would not prove a royal clod. Spaniards always turned the simplest aspects of life into enormous difficulty, but the alliance would be valuable. If Alfonso bored her, Adelaide could go early and alone to bed.

Matilda took up her brush, making mental note to advise Adelaide on the royal virtues of modesty and reserve. The child had prattled a good half hour at that blond girl—Marianne?—while Lady Judith translated patiently. Matilda remembered that the maid was attractive in a country way, though Judith was much more of a beauty. Nevertheless, Adelaide must learn to be gracious at some remove.

God's mercy, I am tired.

This evening would be strained at best. She would call the English women to attend her beforehand, that she know them better. Denby was a small problem inside the larger knot of a hostile country, which was itself only the hinge pin of larger concerns and dangers. Malcolm of Scotland was harrowing Northumbria again, the Danish fleet still raided the eastern shores when opportunity allowed. Gilly must be ever watchful of jealous vassals at home, and cousin Philip at Paris was happy to have Normandy harried elsewhere and unable to vex him personally.

But the skilled mason laid one brick at a time with equal care to each. Philip was oversea, the English here and now. Hold tight the rein and know the breed, Gilly always said. This Matilda could do, employing her own considerable skills in statecraft. Her husband had a fine instinct for competent men, but had his blind spots as well. A little feminine wisdom might carry them farther than good horses.

The queen sent for the women of Denby.

Maud was in her hall when the queen's summons reached her. She was informed that supper would be taken in the courtyard. The high table with the two great chairs would be reserved for the royal family, high nobles, and Lady Judith as a courtesy to young Adelaide. The thane's family would share the low table with William's knights. Maud might have expected such an arrangement; still, it caught her emotionally unprepared. Beyond King Edward's consort Edith, no woman had ever usurped the inviolable symbol of her place, always sitting as Maud's guest. Now the midget queen politely commandeered her chair and her presence. Maud was not a profane woman, but now she was inspired.

"Niece, in over twenty *years*—"

"I know, Aunt Maud. Be patient. All things end."

"That's true. Even plagues."

The hall was suffocating. Added to the heat of summer, sweating Frankish cooks jabbered at each other over the fire pit and the boar they were basting. Marian scrubbed diligently at one end of the age-blackened high table. Minna worked at the other while comparing Normans to barn rats under her breath. Every woman of Denby, from Maud to old Gudrun muttering in the kitchen, suffered the torn-up and scattered frustration of habit-grooved lives suddenly and enormously disrupted.

Marian came down the hall at Maud's summons, rubbing a bit of crushed tansy over her hands. For all the chaos, Maud read the girl clearly: She was young and resilient. The foreigners would be gone tomorrow, and then she'd marry her Robin. "You must get used to being called lady yourself now. Not so easy, you find?"

"Not this week it ent." Marian pushed a stray wisp of gold back beneath her veil. The headpiece was donned clean and crisp that morning but going limp in the heat. "Lord, that child Adelaide! Natter, natter. Weren't for Judith, I wouldn't know what the girl was on about."

"Nor I." Maud glowered at the Frankish cooks. "Not a word."

"Really?" Judith remembered differently. "Mother said you had twice her ear for Frank and Latin."

Maud deflected the compliment. "Elswith always exaggerated my gifts, at least until I married Aelred. She always felt I wed beneath her. You must be my ears and tongue." Distractedly Maud watched six of the king's husky male servants juggle the high table off the dais. "I will *not* give place at table. If I must, then neither I nor Marian nor Ethelwold will sit at all. Tonight there is more honor in standing." Maud slipped her arms through Judith's and Marian's. "Come, let us wait on the royal abbreviation."

Knowing graciousness often more efficient than force, Matilda fulsomely praised Maud's bower and regretted the temporary inconvenience. She arranged the informal audience with the care of an artist in mosaic: the two Frankish women behind her chair, ready to freshen her coiffure, herself composed and absolutely still so that the least movement of hand or eye would register. Such were the subtler tools of power.

Shrewdly, Matilda let the three women remain kneeling a little longer than necessary before acknowledging them. She could not have found three more representative examples of English womanhood. Judith was of the class Matilda knew best, the overeducated last bloom of Saxon aristocracy. No matter her scholarship, Judith's outlook would be as silk-lined and cosmopolitan as Matilda's own. Maud? What Germans would call a "good burgher's wife." Excellent manners worn smooth with time. Composed, always knew what to do with her hands, courteous beyond fault, but distant.

Oh, but the maid, Marianne. *There* was a broad flourish of happiness a child could read. The quality brimmed, shone from the girl, the kind of spiritual burnish that attracted stray animals as well as men. *Charmante.* No wonder Adelaide was drawn to her. Yes, these three would be her English touchstones to prove the rest.

"Ladies, please sit. I thought we might take some cool tea while the women fuss over me. Judith, I must say that what England lacks in weather, it gains in the loveliness of its daughters. Does Adelaide tell me aright that *jolie* Marianne is to be married?"

"To Thane Edward, *ma reine*," Judith affirmed. "As soon as possible."

"That is no doubt why she is so radiant." Matilda took the girl's hand in her own. "My warmest wishes for happiness." At least the bumpkin thane was not climbing the social ladder through marriage, the queen surmised. Couldn't afford to in any case. Tidier this way, kept him at home. The children would come quickly and often enough to take at least some of his mind off making trouble—an idle supposition Matilda later found to be her first misreading of the native mind. "Jehanne, fetch my jewel case."

From the case, Matilda chose an amethyst ring set in silver and fitted it to astonished Marian's finger. *Hands like leather. An ox like her country lord. They'll bear legions between them.* "There, Marianne. This once belonged to a vicomtess."

The girl emitted a little squeak of pleasure, showing the ring for Judith and Maud to admire, followed by an effusion of shire dialect in thanks.

"She wonders how the queen could part with such a treasure," Judith said. "Such things are heirlooms, passed from mothers to daughters. It is too great a gift."

Matilda shushed the gratitude. "No, it is nothing. It belonged to a very small vicomtess." Even smaller now, she recalled. *La Vicomtesse de Gavnay* had parted with much more than jewelry through her husband's unreliable loyalties. "Judith, you will be near me at supper, Waltheof will translate for the king. Lady Maud and Marianne will be directly opposite at the other table."

"Madame, by your leave," Judith modified with a glance at her taciturn aunt. "Lady Maud and Marian will not sit with the men but will serve the tables and give the health and try to please your royal presence in every way proper."

Matilda wondered if the matter was quite one of propriety. "Not sit in their own house?"

English women did not sit at table when men spoke of state business. "It is not done, madame."

"I see." The Norman queen hoped she saw, able to read nothing in Maud's demurely downcast gaze. A courteous modesty or a profound disdain, one could not say at all. Ralf Fitz-Gerald called them brick walls. The image was apt.

Just before supper Robin was summoned by William with a courtesy bare and brusque enough to brook no delay. His own bower confiscated by the ailing sheriff and several other officers, Robin changed clothes in the barn, put on the new robe his mother had made for him, and set the gold coronet on his head. If he must kneel to this foreigner, at least he would look like Aelred's son.

The courtyard bustled with cooks, bakers, and servants coming and going about the laden tables. The king lounged mountainously against the well with Waltheof for company, wiping his hands and face on a towel, ruddy complexion further reddened by the late sun. Robin knelt to him, warily assuming the king's purpose went beyond the social.

"*Bon soir*, Edward. I have been to Mass in your little church and just washing up. Your people make marvelous soap."

"My lord may take some as a gift," Robin offered, regretting that Waltheof must translate for him. "We have plenty of soap, if little else."

William absorbed the double-edged comment with a shrewd appraisal of the young man. "Your language is very difficult. Like an old house with too many dark corners where meaning is often mislaid." The royal tone darkened to a shade less congenial. "You have met my sheriff? You will respond to his authority in better grace than you did to my other knights when they called here. That will not happen again, Denby."

Waltheof devined Robin's discomfort. "Just say yes, that will avoid much awkwardness."

"I understand, my lord king."

"So." That granted, William turned affable again. "You hold your lands directly from me, and thus you will render and receive them tonight. Forests are my personal property. You will be accountable through Sire Ralf at Nottingham. Any offense to him is one to me, you comprehend?"

To his credit, Robin glimmered with the beginnings of a diplomat. "I well mark the king's meaning."

Done, then. William beamed, clapping Robin on the shoulder. "I am glad. Until supper. By the way, your steward complained to mine about the moving of boundary stones."

"I meant to speak of that, my lord. Surely my boundaries have never been disputed."

William shrugged it off. "Common mistake. Consider it corrected. I will speak to Sire Ralf, who will be as reasonable as yourself, I have no doubt. Just heed my laws and keep my peace among your people. The less trouble you are to me"—the king held up both broad hands—"*bien*, one washes the other, does it not?"

William strode away. Robin relaxed vastly, blowing out his cheeks. "Lets me know where I stand, don't he?"

Waltheof knew that for a fact and longer than the thane. "He takes one firmly by the wrist and need not twist for you to feel helpless. You did well."

"Well?" Robin blurted honestly. "Give in or go down. We have to live."

The earl's expression altered slightly. "So we do, Robin. May I call you that? I heard your lady mother use the name with affection."

Robin felt flattered by the earl's solicitude. Though young himself, Waltheof had about him the glitter, barbering, and tailoring of fabulous and distant courts. Robin's father followed him without question in the uprising. "My lord, how did you fare after York? You were one of our leaders. We thought Bastard would hang you for sure."

"It is convenient to speak more than one language. I am useful to William." The earl moved closer to Robin, lowering his voice. "In some ways the king is more practical than we, in others far less so. This is a strange country to him, men like you stranger still. More than he dares admit, he needs Englishmen around him. Thus he may prune the tree but will not cut it down entire. For myself, I try to save what I can of England."

"God strengthen you in that," Robin prayed sincerely. "He trusts you enough to enlarge your estates."

"Trust?" Waltheof threw a hard glance across the courtyard at William joking with a knot of young vavasors. "You saw him in the chase today. As William's passions, so his policies. He is the hunter. For the time we must follow at his heels"—he patted the scarlet breast of his own short Norman tunic—"and in his livery, as it were. The honors he bestows are like the sops he threw to the dogs today, merely stale bread to be eaten at heel."

The earl's easy manner evoked Robin's confidence. He admired the effortless expression of the man's sinuous mind. "Nay, but did you hear him? The forest's his own personal property."

"They were so under our own kings."

"But think on it if you will. England is more forest than field by any road you take. That is a mickle lot of land for one man to call his own."

"One part in five," Waltheof estimated.

Robin glared at the Normans scurrying about his little courtyard, troubled by an emerging and possibly dangerous conviction. "That ent right, my lord."

"It is reality."

Robin knew only the truth to which he had been born. So many folk lived in and by the forest, no laws could work without thought to their number and welfare. He wrestled with another truth for which he'd never needed words. "I just don't know. Common law must come from common sense."

The earl only smiled—a little sadly, Robin thought. "Our magnificent native delusion."

Robin didn't know what a delusion was, but plunged ahead. "When your father Siward gave his voice in the Witan to Edward as king; when you gave yours to Harold, did you leave your common sense outside? I think you did not. Yet, I must swear fealty to this king without my yea or nay in the matter."

"As you said, you have to live."

"But there's the point. Doesn't he swear to me as well? I have to make him understand what my folk need. Does he think a man will starve before he breaks a law? Will you help me?" he beseeched Waltheof. "Help me make it clear to William that his idea of law will never work here, not without some thought to the men who must bend to it. You must help me, my lord. Words are easy for you."

Earnest, hemmed in, tongue-tied before educated men, Robin felt something vast but inarticulate stir in his soul. Father, Son, Holy Ghost. Kings, lords, and commons: the eternal significance of three in thought, prayer, or magic. He thrust his mind out like an unsure hand, groping for familiar, three-sided reality and found no trinity but, inexplicably, a square. A fourth side without definition or even a name. Both William and Robin were illiterate, but what the Englishman innately understood as good politics would forever elude the greatest ruler of his day and the sons who succeeded him.

12

UNTIL TODAY, MARIAN had never seen Normans at close hand, unless dead or a threat. She had a perverse curiosity about the knights swaggering about the courtyard with their picked-chicken tonsures and hairless faces, the haughty court officials and Frankish servants crawling over Denby like fleas on a dog.

"Just men," Angharad humphed as they walked toward the hall. "Big lumps tracking dirt in Lady's hall, and won't it be weeks before things are set to rights? Show me your ring again—oh, there's rich!"

"*Allo, Marianne. Ici!*" Adelaide waved frantically from the hall entrance. "Come!"

The heat of the hall struck Marian in a torrid wave. The cooks still sweated at roasting the boar over the fire pit. Adelaide bent solicitously over a dark young knight in a gold-embroidered black robe hunched on the edge of the bare dais and holding a cup in both hands as if he feared to drop it.

He's the one been made Sheriff of Nottingham.

As Marian approached, the man's eyes lifted to her.

That he was obviously ill was her second thought; for the first, something in Marian stopped dead and gasped *oh*. She would never, even years later, be able to say why. Perhaps the glamour of an opposite or the instinct of a bee for the right flower. Quite often the most practical woman's life could date from such an *oh*, unforgettable as a star falling across an autumn sky at the very moment one made a secret wish: strange beauty from a far place. For the space of a breath, before Marian saw the bright glaze of fever, the man's eyes held hers and, for that moment, Robin was utterly forgotten. Adelaide had to speak twice to her.

"*Marianne, s'il vous plaît*, you will be so kind as to bring of some hot water for Sire Ralf?"

The dregs in his cup appeared to be willowbark mixed with an herb Marian didn't know. She was on an errand for the queen and passed the cup to Angharad. "You fetch it, dear. I must get back."

Marian passed on through the hall. Somehow, as women felt such things, she knew the man's eyes were following her. She was some way across the courtyard when Angharad came fluttering after her. "Marian, you must come again quick."

This day had been impossible since cockcrow. "What is it, y'mad woman? Minna has hot water in the kitchen."

"No, he's collapsed."

"Who?"

"Fell down, just now he did, right there in the hall, shaking all over, and may it not be some hellish matter as plague?"

Angharad turned and dashed back into the hall, Marian hurrying behind.

Two hastily recruited grooms carried Ralf to Robin's bower. Judith was summoned, since her schooling included the making of ordinary medicines. Adelaide hovered at the foot of the sickbed, eager to be part and tell what she knew. The good sheriff was talking to her, she said, and then was suddenly overcome by his malady, for in truth, he had been ill for days.

Judith touched the backs of her fingers to the flushed, dry forehead. "Burning up. What was he drinking?"

Willowbark and chamomile, Adelaide reported, a bit of honey added in hot water. "He was just asking for more."

"Those are the best," Judith judged briskly. "We must break this fever. Get him covered up."

Marian had trusted methods of her own where fever was concerned. "Angharad, bring me some thread and some violets from the patch across the brook, a dozen will do."

Angharad scurried out of the sickroom, lamenting in Welsh the ills fallen like sleet on Denby.

"Judith, let's get him undressed; he'll rest the better."

"Then we must call back the grooms." To Marian's surprise, Judith actually blushed. "Meeter for men to do that than ourselves."

Shy one, ent you? Aye, he's a man and a handsome one, and we both know it. "Only a man; likely doesn't know we're here, he's that sick."

"He may die whatever we do," Judith worried. "The fever's too high."

The violets would tell Marian that much. "I'll tend him. Can you be quick with the medicine?" She wrestled the robe off Ralf. "Now through that sleeve with your arm, boyo—"

Judith left the bower to concoct the medicine. Marian got the linen shirt over the sick man's head and bent to cover him with the blanket. The sight of his mauled upper body wrenched a gasp of pity from her. He had been in the same war as Robin, but so much longer, so much the worse for it. Robin's body was smooth yet, brown from the fields and healthy. This man was broader in the shoulders, muscles standing out in ridges from hard stomach to bull chest. Robin said these men lived in iron. This one was iron himself. But all the rest of it. . . .

His skin was not brown but dead white with no health to it, deep-welted from armor worn days on end over years, crisscrossed with old white scars and newer ones still red that puckered the skin like snags in cloth. There were odd lumps under some of the wounds and deep indentations beneath others that might have been broken bones. So many of them.

If this was the enemy who slaughtered her folk, Marian saw now what the man paid for it. She had spent her life helping animals and crops to grow and could deeply mourn the death of a small cat, rage at the injustice of pain inflicted on any helpless thing. Covering the carnage of Ralf Fitz-Gerald with the blanket, Marian could almost forgive the man—but then Angharad was back with her thread and a clutch of violets, keeping her wary distance from the stricken Norman.

"Is it plague that he has?"

"Don't be a dunce." Marian bit off a length of the thread. "You know the look of plague."

Angharad backed to the door, not convinced. "Could it spread to my boys?"

"No, just an ague. Go along, love. Ta."

Marian crossed herself when Angharad was gone, not that sure herself what she dealt with. The sick man muttered and tossed like one in a bad dream. Marian remembered only one charm against sickness, one her mother swore by for menstrual cramps. Since the charm invoked Jesus, its potency would not be amiss for this poor wreck of a foreigner.

"The ague is painless/Mary was sinless when she bore Jesus/Let the ague go away in the name of Jesus."

Marian crossed herself and wound the threaded violets into a bracelet which she secured about the man's right wrist. Wrist and hand were scarred as the rest of him. The wilting of the delicate petals against his skin, quick or slowly, would tell her the degree of fever. Nothing now but to wait. Marian cooled his forehead with a wet compress, repeating her charm in a whisper.

As she leaned close over him, his eyes opened. The power of the man bunched under her like sudden violence in the earth itself, the instinctive gathering of an animal whose survival depended on alertness. Then his eyes focused on her. He relaxed, running his tongue over fever-dried lips.

"Easy, man," Marian soothed, working the wet cloth over his face. "Easy."

He mumbled something.

"Don't go on at me in Frank now, I've had enough of that."

"It is of nothing, the fever," he croaked in a queer, liquid-sounding English. "Come and go. I have seen you this day. You are called Marianne."

She was surprised that he knew her name but more by the strange and pleasing manner in which he pronounced it, drawing out the throaty sound like music. A different sort of man altogether from her Robin. Not much older except for the eyes, the rest of him beautiful enough in his foreign way to have been made by the Devil to tempt a girl whose mind wasn't firmly in the right place and her first banns already spoken in the church.

"Your simple is in the making," she told him crisply.

He said her name again before the shaking took him. "Marianne."

Maud would present the cheer to their royal guests, then serve the tables with Marian. Ethelwold stood as cup bearer behind Edward's chair, Will Scatloch at his master's side to do instant bidding. Little Denby had in all likelihood not held such pointed state with their own kings.

Seated between Matilda and Adelaide, Judith observed the scene about her with an educated eye. Her experience bestrode the Channel, aware of opposed motivations, finding one inexorable and the other hopeless. There sat her cousin at the low table, aloof as his mother and steward amid rowdy vavasors. Across from him at the high table sat William.

Though servants scurried between them continually, the tense energy of opposition between them, like opponents in an arena, never blurred. Judith could feel it.

Waltheof was on the king's right. Next to him was the royal chaplain, Gillelmo of Poitiers. Judith was grateful for the distance between herself and the chaplain; the obsequious cleric had mired her in conversation too long that afternoon. She winced at Poitiers' Latin in the offertory prayer before supper began: the letter of the holy language but hardly its majesty. Poitiers' ambition vaulted the walls of his limitations. He had been at some length confessing to her his determination to record the life of William as the first truly great ruler of England, would not Lady Judith agree? She sidestepped with practiced humility. Such matters could hardly be judged by women—the reply of a sheep-wit, but the chaplain seemed pleased. Such mediocrities easily were.

So far supper had proceeded with no undue awkwardness. Aunt Maud was decorum itself, presenting the first cup to William while Waltheof explained the native custom. Marian set the second in front of Queen Matilda. After serving the king, Maud pointedly passed over the rest of William's high officers, setting the next draft of ale before her son.

"May it well become you."

Then she met the king eye for eye, as if to say, *There, that is the way it is done at Denby. I will lose no sleep if you find it not to your liking.*

Over the uproarious gabble from both tables, goose-bone pipes and tabors squealed and pounded through "The Feast of Canute." Maud and Marian served with faultless courtesy. Cousin Edward, who would normally chat with Ethelwold over a common dish, thrust the cup over his shoulder to be ceremoniously refilled by his old steward and, insofar as possible, ignored the rabble of knights around him.

The Sheriff of Nottingham was too ill to dine; a pity to Judith, who found him the most attractive man in the royal retinue. Unlike the bluff vavasors jibing at Edward for his long hair and old-fashioned clothes, Fitz-Gerald impressed Judith as mannerly and grave beyond his years. Of course the garrulous Adelaide was only too ready to publish the man's condition. He was but *demi-noblesse,* if Judith took her meaning, her father's creature in all respects. Until Papa noted him, the man had no more than his horse and armor. Judith acknowledged the intelligence without comment. She was only a hapless creature herself now, poor as a lean cow in a sacked byre, remembering plenty and knowing it gone.

My poor family. We are the past, my dears. These gobbling, belching

*vavasors are the present. Yet God is good to you, Puck-Robin. The best
you could hope for is all you want. Your Marian is lovely and that's a
blessing. Will it be so simple for me?*

It was Judith's melancholy gift to see so much and both sides too
clearly. Her cousin had eaten little and drunk less, clearly girding himself
for the bleak business to come. At last, when the servants and hounds
lolled about the courtyard, torpid with food themselves, the king's offi-
cious little steward Tancarville knocked on the high table for attention.

"Edward of Denby, are you prepared to swear fealty for your lands
and receive them from your rightful lord?"

Robin rose in his place. "I am ready."

"Let you come forward," Tancarville directed.

Robin held his place. "But an oath between lord and man is an agreement which neither should make without clear understanding of the
terms."

William frowned across the tables. "One thought such agreement was
reached this afternoon. You find some impediment?"

As Robin began to speak, Waltheof relayed instantly in Frank, shading Robin's blunt words toward the most respectful construction, sometimes having to veer away from literal meaning, since Robin's assertions,
plain enough to an English subject, might well be incomprehensible to
a Norman.

"There's the letter of forest law, but the spirit as well. Even a bee
which flies in a straight line will go around a tree in its way rather than
bash into it. In the same way, men following the straight line of the law
often have to make such allowance. We brook no poachers on crown
land. . . ."

But over the years Denby found they must temper the law and pass
on some of their hunting rights to tenants. This practice was more good
sense than benevolence, for surely the king could not hunt every royal
preserve in every season. When animals of chase and warren grew so
numerous that the forest couldn't feed them, they ravaged crops and
became a pestilence to farmers. Since the game was far more than Denby's
table could consume, carefully regulated hunting by commons was only
good husbandry. Thus lord, folk, and land throve alike, while neither
King Canute nor his successor, Edward, ever had cause to complain of
poor hunting or lax justice in Sherwood.

Judith applauded silently: a very clear argument and no less than truth.
King Canute got on well with Robin's grandfather, who could match him
horn for horn in ale and better him in Welsh whiskey. They were old

campaigners together. Canute gave Brihtnoth his head in local matters. According to Maud, Aelred had more of a problem. King Edward's vindictiveness, glossed over by his clerical apologists, was too well known in northern Sherwood. His piety had little of compassion and neither extended to hunting, for which Edward had the enthusiasm of his Norman upbringing. When he hunted on Aelred's land, the thane always ordered his tenants to stay clear of the forest—to no avail on one dolorous occasion.

The king's party caught one of Aelred's cottars red-handed with a freshly killed buck. Edward was furious and demanded Aelred punish the man with mutilation then and there. Normally Aelred would have tempered the punishment to fit the circumstances. Appealing to the king that it was a lean year for crops availed nothing. Aelred had no choice but to carry out the sentence and cut off the poacher's right hand.

Not the punishment itself—as Aelred recounted the incident—but the indecent, gleeful satisfaction on Edward's ascetic face as he watched the poor man writhe on the ground, pawing at the blood-spurting stump of his wrist before they cauterized and bound it up. Later Aelred washed his hands continually and still felt them unclean. Maud said he was livid: the gentlest man alive gone sick with rage, pungently describing his royal lord in terms Maud wouldn't have thought him to know. Fragile, capricious Edward, beloved of the Church for his celibacy yet cruel enough to relish the agony of a man helpless as a limed bird and call it righteousness. Most agile and paradoxical man who could hold himself so high above human frailty and so far beneath contempt. Robin was fourteen then and saw with his own eyes what his father was forced to do, saw what the doing cost him. That memory surely added urgency now to his words.

"My lord king must know there are more differences in the conditions of men here than in his own country. Each of mine is pacted to me and I to him in the rights and duties of his station. Some have no rights but those we give them; others have many by their own inheritance or purchased by rents in kind or through their own labor, as in the clearing of bookland. These rights are writ down in the rolls of the forest courts at Nottingham and Papplewick."

Throughout Robin's earnest recital of these facts, basic to Englishmen as their catechism, Judith saw the reactions of the Norman vavasors go from incomprehension to boredom, and then to open scorn. They guffawed and mouthed farting noises at the thane, who proudly ignored them. No, Judith knew: Such men could not be expected to see his reasons. They were vassals themselves; they had survived by being the fittest, always jealous of their own rights but hardly those of Frankish serfs. Robin's realities were alien to them. Those who conquered and took against those who held and nurtured.

Even little Adelaide, dipping a bit of bread in a sauce bowl, wondered to Judith: "That peculiar man, what *is* he talking about?"

If William was puzzled or amused, he gave no sign of either, listening intently until he cut Robin off with a gesture of impatience. "Lord Edward, you have spoken of your realities, as you call them. Now I will speak of mine. First, your tenants of whatever former condition are no longer free but bound to the land. I bid you consider that; if the change galls some, certainly it relieves others such as your own slaves, who may see more equality in my truth than yours. Secondly, my officers have assessed your holdings at"—William studied a scrap of parchment proffered by his steward—"ten pounds in silver, the tax on which is payable now."

Ten pounds! Judith needed no computation to realize the enormous disparity. She saw Maud freeze in her place. Ethelwold, by his reaction, might be going into a seizure.

Robin faltered, his dismay audible. "With respect, my lord, there is only one way your men could arrive at such a geld."

The steward Tancarville interrupted, bristling: "You imply error?"

"No, but—"

"Perhaps dishonesty in the officers of the king's treasury?"

Robin shook his head vigorously. "What need of dishonesty when they account my woodland at the full value of ploughed arable?"

William corrected him bluntly. "*My* land."

"Unlawful!" Ethelwold burst out, slamming his beaker of ale on the board. "Unjust!"

"Ethelwold," Robin cautioned him. "It is my place to speak here."

"I *will* speak, Thane," the old steward thundered in a voice longer accustomed to command than his young lord. "My lord king, I have a steward's proper competence and know well the laws of taxation. Never in England under the very worst of our kings was forest taxed as arable."

"Thane Edward," Waltheof reproved with his leavening of light charm, "you should school your servant. He presumes on his place."

Judith saw Robin stiffen at this slight to Ethelwold and knew as well that he needed the earl just now. She laughed aloud, rising in her place to turn attention to her. *"Mon roi puissant,"* she trilled, "this is amusing. Ethelwold is no servant but a worthy officer of this holding. If he presumes, the earl forgets. When his own father Siward vanquished Macbeth, Ethelwold stood high among his carls and nigh to a thane's wergild himself. Waltheof was a mere boy then and no doubt presuming mightily himself."

"Lady," Waltheof chuckled, bowing his head to her. "I yield to truth and your better memory."

Do that. Judith returned his salutation and resumed her seat. *If we are beaten, must we lick the whip?*

William shot a squelching glance at Judith. "I had not finished. Lord Edward, your lands are so assessed. What my sheriff collects will depend on how well you keep the law in my forest. My steward will read the legal rights of your serfs. You will allow these and no more."

Tancarville read from another writ, pronouncing in a sharp, monotonous voice the hard dimensions of an impossible future. Robin's "serfs" would be allowed free pasturage for cattle and sheep and to loose their swine in Sherwood for acorns and beechmast. They had the right to fallen deadwood, so much per householder, but no cutting of live trees whatsoever on pain of mutilation for the first offense, death for the second. No hunting at all in Sherwood beyond Robin's own rights of chase which he would no longer allow to any serf.

"For fear of bad example," the king commented, "of which there has already been far too much through your laxity."

Clearly dismayed at these unlivable terms, Robin persisted doggedly. If no wood was cut, more peat would have to be carted in from Lincoln and Ely since Sherwood had no bogs. Deadwood alone would hardly be sufficient against the cold months. No cutting of trees meant no more bookland, less crops where more were needed.

"I speak of ancient customs, my lord, customs based on common sense. Does the king sweep them *all* away?"

A buzz of astonishment around the tables that spread even to the Norman servants. William took some wine before answering in a voice level but iron. "Denby, you cannot know how your countrymen weary me with this quibbling. The law, it is me. I am the law. Do you presume to teach me that which I am by God's will?"

Robin dropped his eyes to the table before him. "I do not, sir."

"Then surely you will agree that a king's right to rule derives from that will?"

Robin hesitated. Judith saw something war behind his eyes between foreign law and his native instinct. "All men testify to that, sir, but—"

"But what, Thane?" William pressed the point. "What? I am most curious."

"But . . . the right does not bespeak the manner."

Tancarville exploded: "Impertinence!"

"No, by your leave." Robin held up a warding hand. "Let my lord suppose I am husband to an erring wife. God's will decrees the wife is servant to the husband and subject to his will, so it is my right and duty to chasten her. But this is a good wife—"

Standing unobserved at the end of the high table, Marian blew an encouraging kiss to Robin.

"—more obedient than not and careful in keeping my house. If, in the fear that she go a mile in error, I break her bones for going an inch, where does it profit my house? Then as the husband, so the lord, so even the ploughman who does not kill his ox for eating a little more fodder then's put out for him."

Well turned, Edward. Judith would not have credited her cousin with skill in debate, futile though his efforts were. She saw the ax poised over him; he was the ox for killing today. Swear unqualified fealty to William and he forswore all his life had taught him was right, but what choice? *Do it, Edward. Survival is not always dishonor.*

William took the tax roll from his steward and perused it before addressing Robin. "You tread a fine line between your 'common sense' and what I would deem outright resistance. Are you now prepared to swear fealty to me for your lands?"

In a flat, lifeless voice: "I am."

The king rose, followed by Poitiers the chaplain, and took a position between the tables. When Poitiers lifted the coronet from his head, Robin had to be reminded to kneel, which he did with such barely disguised distaste, the obeisance looked forced and awkward.

"Your cousin is so maladroit, Judith," Adelaide tittered. "Does he not know how to kneel?"

For a moment Judith prayed for a miracle: the earth to yawn beneath Adelaide and swallow her on the instant. "It is like taking exercise, *chérie*. If seldom practiced, there is a certain stiffness."

Haltingly, prompted in the foreign form of the oath by the chaplain, Robin swore his fealty. "I, Edward Aelredson, purpose to become your man and promise by Holy Church that from this time forward, I will be faithful to William, King of the English, and will maintain my homage toward him entirely against every man."

Looming hugely over him, William took the coronet from Poitiers.

"And I swear to hold with you so you keep my laws." He resettled the circlet on Robin's head. "Rise, Thane Edward, and hold these lands for me."

The king kissed Robin on the cheek, sealing the oath. To Judith's mind, he did it as well as Judas ever could.

She could not bring herself to quit the table after Matilda retired, grateful that the queen did not require her presence. Judith felt her place just now was here. Singly and in groups the officers and knights swaggered away from the tables until there were left only those of Judith's family. Robin stood bleak and alone on the spot where he had sworn to the king. Ethelwold, seated at last, slumped beyond fatigue, his dignity a cold mask over disgust. Tight-lipped Maud busied herself in wrapping broken meats for the poor of Blidworth with Marian assisting her. None of them looked at one another, no one spoke. To one side of the low table, Will Scatloch drank whiskey with the riveted intensity of earnest prayer. An excellent idea; Judith poured herself another cup of wine.

I told Edward the matter would come to this. He only reared and tossed like a stallion fighting the bridle. Now they've gelded him, though he argued well before bending. Yes, Adelaide, he did that clumsily. Pride is not supple.

My God, I feel for all my blood this day. But thank you, William, for showing me clearly that I am not of your kind. You know so little of us. Sleep lightly, Conqueror. I know my blood. Don't push us too far. Tell your queen, who studies to know us, that she saw our heart today: antique, unadorned, but unbreakable. This is our *place you have stolen. There's that in us, and let the Church call it heresy, that will deny our land is anyone's to parcel out by any will including the Divine. Deem it a failing of our uniquely secular mind.*

Poor Puck-Robin's doomed, but at least his fate is clear. Where's mine beyond a new need for humility? I was fifteen the year before they came, writing home from Caen conceited accounts of my accomplishments and how even wise Lanfranc made so much of me. Hardly a thought to marriage then; if that had been an issue, I assumed it would come as one more plum taken with little effort.

But now you're marked-down goods at the marriage fair, Judy girl: overeducated, underfit, and poor. Nothing to sell but a mind and this ridiculous, transient form. A good merchant should go where the trade thrives, though I never considered marriage with one of their kind. Never until today.

So ill he could not rise for supper. There is a silence in him, a stillness. One senses where he has been and come through. I will look in on him later. Bargain-priced goods should have a place at the front of the stall. For now, I'll finish the wine to wash away the bad taste of their power and our helplessness. To help me sleep. And William Bastard, King of the English, Duke of Normandy, and whatever else you steal from now unto death—may God efficiently damn you to everlasting hell.

King William had finished his prayers and maneuvered his heavy bulk into the too-narrow bed. He did not anticipate good rest. English beds were no better than English cooking, sturdy necessities never refined to pleasures. Such were always a problem on progress. He tended to thrash about in sleep, forever rolling over on tiny Matilda.

A long day, but William was hardly composed for sleep. His soul was shriven, but his secular politics still niggled at him. Young Denby might be one drop in a downpour, but in his annoying, hair-splitting manner symbolized the whole English problem. By the single candle's light William poured a cup of hot chamomile from the jug on the bedside table, which he and Mora always shared before sleep.

Propped up on her pillows, Matilda yawned over the tea. "Gilly, stop mumbling."

"I'm not."

"Don't say that. I know you. You'll mumble and grind your teeth and toss all night and shove your monstrous elbows in my ribs and I won't get a wink of sleep."

"Just thinking . . . and I'm tired." William sipped some of the pallid tea, wondering why they made a bedtime habit of chamomile when he always found the stuff faintly insipid. "You must be as well."

Matilda sighed like a little girl. "Exhausted."

"God willing, we can rest a few days at Grantham." No longer, surely. He must be in Lincoln soon, Normandy thereafter.

"Gilly, you *are* grinding your teeth. Go to sleep or you'll be an absolute beast tomorrow. What is it?"

"Did you mark Denby before he finally condescended to swear?"

"He has a certain—I hesitate to call it charm. One hears his grandfather was little more than a peasant in mail."

"No, that's not it." To William more a disturbing similarity. At his coronation in London, Aldred, Archbishop of York, held up the whole proceeding with the same legalistic haggling. "The damned Saxon flatly refused to put the crown on my head until I swore a separate oath to rule as well as the best of their own kings. Listening to Denby, the old mule came to mind.''

''Proud boy.'' Matilda shifted to nestle close to her husband. ''And . . . I begin to sense that pride has different colors for them. *Dieu*, my feet are cold.''

William felt her small and very chill feet slip between his heavy legs for warmth. Another of England's endearments: Even in summer Matilda usually had to wear wool bedsocks, but they'd been mislaid at Nottingham. He massaged her feet gently under the covers, enjoying her gratitude. ''Best of their kings, indeed. How do I know who was best or why? Hard enough to understand their impossible language.''

''I thought of that,'' Matilda murmured against his shoulder. ''These women of Denby. . . .'' The queen giggled softly. ''Marianne: Now there's rustic for you, but I like the girl. As for Maud—*bien*, I did not expect them to sing our praises. But Judith is like one of us. She will teach the others to me. I wish them to attend me at Grantham.''

William couldn't see the advantage. ''You have women enough already.''

''For your own reasons, Gilly, and good ones they are, too. The point of that impossible tax was to keep the pup in line, not so? What better way to understand them if his ladies are close to me? It's not as if we were just visiting. We are a new power in possession of a very ancient one and we know nothing of them.''

''There's the meat of it.'' William shifted heavily to face Matilda on the pillow. Her hands were cold as her feet; he pressed them to his lips. ''Did you hear that upstart? One can't take this, one can't take that. 'It is the custom, my lord. It is only common sense.' Just like that rheumy old steward of his and the archbishop. Lawyers! Every one of them. Can you imagine our barons arguing a point of law?''

Matilda could not. ''Not to save their lives.''

''There's the point again,'' William grumbled, rolling over on his back. ''Pride and stupidity in our own nobles is a navigational constant like the North Star. It is easy to stay one step ahead of them. But here is different. Men like this Denby sit on my stomach and won't digest any more than tonight's supper.''

''You ate too much. You always stuff when you're restless. That's got your humors confused. Take some more chamomile.''

''I don't want any more chamomile,'' William growled. ''You say it helps me sleep, but it never does and I don't like the taste.''

''Blow out the candle then.''

They settled down in the darkness, Matilda warm at last in his arms.
"He impressed me, Mora."

"Who?"

"Denby. What bothers me is, I'm not sure how."

God had made every man to stay in his place, gave human society a
balance. Should the legs of a chair be free to break with the seat and
high back and just wander away? Perverse! Waltheof was easier to understand, born to power, ready to pay the going price to keep it, thoroughly predictable. But what did men like Denby want that could be so
easily devined? Something about the young man twinged William like
cold water on a diseased tooth.

*His ignorance or God's sign to me that, just as I turned his mother
out of her bed tonight, I am the usurper after all?*

His chaplain salved his conscience often enough and said he was not.
Rome herself said as much. King Edward's widow Edith, Harold's own
sister, was strongest in support of William and first to welcome him in
London. Still his dreams were troubled and dark portents reared in the
slightest occurrence. He paid with an agony of scruples. He had even
sent a message to Harold the night before Hastings, willing to accept the
result of single combat. Let God decide the right between them. Harold's
answer was the thousands waiting on the ridge north of Hastings, the
long, deep line of Englishmen. There was no turning back then.

After the battle they found only one of Harold's flags, the Dragon of
Wessex, which had once been the symbol of his earldom. Of his battle
standard, the Fighting Man, there was no trace. A richly embroidered
banner set with precious stones and known to every man on both sides.
Not the sort of prize men would overlook. The lost flag troubled William.
He would have destroyed both so that nothing remained of Harold.

*Why did you take the crown? The Church was with me. You knew that
you and every man who followed you would be excommunicated.*

Was Harold so sure of his right that he flew in the very face of God?

And if he did, from what inconceivable source did such unthinkable
right derive?

William stared up into the darkness, listening to the soft breathing of
his sleeping wife. How easily Mora slept when she had the chance, an
art he must acquire.

No doubt Thane Edward slept as soundly, the young were given that.
If the boy only knew how few real troubles he had.

13

*F*ROM THE PORCH of his church, Father Beorn could see all of Blidworth down the east slope, the dale to the west and the forest dreaming around it all in the July sun as if peace were a reality and a song measured to the steady clang of John Littlerede's hammer on his forge. The mill stood idle. Now where was young Much this morning? Across the dale at Denby, folk were at the first of the thane's haying. Two women carried small bundles along the path from the hall toward his church: That would be Judith and Marian with new candles from Lady Maud. Beorn looked forward to Judith's visits. The girl had a good mind and a fine wit for seasoning, if a little too aware of both.

Head still shawled from the confessional, the taverner's daughter bobbed homeward down the west hill toward the Queen's Rest. A good strapping girl, Freda, though no better behaved than Beorn could expect. Well, tavern customers hardly looked to her for moral guidance. Now and then the priest found it necessary to reiterate his lecture on fornication. Freda warmed a bed now and then, most lately John Littlerede's as the gossip went. Where Father Beorn could not condone, at least he understood. John was a widower, lonely and lately rejected by Marian, and sins of the flesh were like weeds in a sewn field. A total absence would be ideal; more realistically, Beorn strove to keep them at a minimum.

Three years ago when she was fifteen, the name Freda uttered in confession called for sterner measures. Her contrition was sincere but matter-of-fact, Robin's a bit smug. The boy was quite pleased with himself. Nothing good could come of that. Beorn laid down the law to both on the spiritual and practical dangers of fornication. He explained bluntly to Freda that no matter how generous Denby was to its folk, any child she bore Robin would be just another parish brat, don't look for him to legitimize the get when he'd be making a proper marriage elsewhere. Freda listened, respectful but barely chastened. Her da would beat her if he knew, but he did that anyway and she was used to it.

Robin got a worse blistering. "Wipe that silly smirk off your face. You're about as repentant as a fox in a henhouse. It is Freda I am thinking of. When you take advantage of a girl in my parish, you'll answer to me, by God."

Beorn could not violate the secrecy of confession, but his circumspect advice to Robin's father must have been effective; that particular weed never sprouted again. Sometimes Robin and Freda passed a word after Mass or at the tavern. Sometimes she looked after him as he strode home across the dale. The matter faded for Robin as these things did for young men. With stolid good sense, Freda accepted the news of his betrothal as she did the Norman soldiery recently battened on Blidworth. She got on with her life, short-changed them in the tavern when they were drunk enough not to notice, and gave thanks that the bastards were restrained beyond arrogance by their stern king. Like the rest of Blidworth, Freda gaped sullenly at King William when he came to Mass and filched what she could from his retainers.

Still, she was a sturdy young thing with a blush in her plump cheeks and hair halfway between red and gold like autumn leaves. She would bear strong children to the right man, so why not John Littlerede? Alcuin the beekeeper or young Much were closer to Freda's age but lacked steadiness as yet. Beorn would speak to John—tactfully, touching lightly about the fringes of the subject so John might guess at the center himself. He was not a man to be alone, having—Beorn wouldn't call it a mean streak—a tendency to brood over things not as easily shaped in his mind as the iron on his anvil. Part of the man never came back from Hastings, more died when his family was taken, leaving him like Job, asking reasons of God. So went the world, but even God might admit John was owed good fortune in arrears. Meanwhile, Father Beorn would broach the subject of Freda in such a way that John might think the notion his own.

Judith and Marian had passed the cooper's house and the tavern, coming up the rise now toward his church. In the morning's warmth both had dressed without veils. Immodest perhaps, but there were two beautiful women for the sun to shine upon. Black and gold, one glossy, the other throwing the sun's own burnish back to heaven, and Marian waving gaily—

"Give you good day, Father!"

"And you, Marian. Are those our new candles?"

"Dipped two days ago," Judith called.

"And look!" Marian scooped into her sack, bringing forth a fat bunch of new radishes. "Small and tender. Angharad knows how you love them."

"You must thank her for me."

"Thank us," Judith corrected. "We pulled them."

"You know how fast radishes grow," Marian brimmed, flushed from the uphill walk. "This year so fast that when Angharad planted them, she swore she had to jump back out of their way."

Beorn took their bundles. "And how's the thane this day?"

"Oh, just terrible," Marian sputtered. "Out haying, trying to be three places at once and nothing going right. He sent to the mill for Much: The lad's nowhere about. Sent for Wystan: nowhere to be found."

"I wondered about the mill," Beorn mused, inviting them into the church. "You can set the new candles, Marian, and perhaps Judith will compare a passage in Romans with me. I sometimes have difficulty in making Paul's meaning clear to Blidworth."

"At your bidding, Father."

"You are more the scholar, I fear."

"Is it not the servant who best knows her master's kitchen?"

"Stuff, girl," Beorn chuckled, not at all taken in. "Your modesty is like your veil: worn out of habit, but you'll leave it off quickly enough to show the beauty God gave you."

Beorn glanced away to spare himself Judith's blush, which he privately thought rather practiced—and so saw the tiny figure emerge from the forest to the south, bow in hand, loping downhill into the dale. Much the miller: *So that's where the layabout's been.* A fine day might tempt a man to idleness, but that was no excuse to neglect his work or his lord's need. Beorn would be giving that one a word or two.

Marian lingered behind the priest and Judith, hating to be indoors at all in summer. She saw Much running fast as his legs could churn toward the brook just as Little John came out of the smithy with buckets yoked across his broad back. He set down the yoke and was filling the buckets from the rill when Much pounded up and threw himself belly down to drink from the stream, splashing water over his face. Only a moment, then he sprang up again. By the look of him, Much had been running hard for some time. The two men were too distant to hear, but John must have said something. Much only shook his head vehemently, swept his arm back toward the forest, then ran on northward along the dale toward Holy Pool.

From John's plain agitation, the matter was nothing good. The blacksmith took a few strides after Much, then paused, scratching at his beard. Abruptly, he took the hill toward the church in long strides.

"Give y'good day, John," Marian greeted him. "What's the matter with Much?"

John barely halted by her. "It's bad," he spat bluntly. "Bad as can be. Where's the priest?"

John was already lunging toward the porch. Marian hurried after, cradling her sack of candles. She pattered down the nave in John's wake to Father Beorn who bent over the lectern with Judith, studying the open Testament. John genuflected hastily. "Father!"

"Aye, man, what is it?"

"Trouble, the worst. Much has fled into Sherwood. He's afraid."

And well he might be from the tale. Wystan had spied out the home thickets of some roe deer, and neither he nor Much could resist taking one. Though well inside Robin's land, there were sheriff's men nosing about. The two of them were seen and had to leave their kill and run—Wystan for Denby to throw himself on the mercy and protection of the thane. As for Much—

"I don't know," John worried. "Somewhere to hide. Thane will have to answer, he can't 'scape it." The big smith swayed this way and that, clearly wanting to vent his frustration in curses but mindful of his surroundings and company. "Gah! We don't have enough trouble? The Normans will be on us like flies."

Beorn tried to think: Certainly Robin would need cool-headed counsel. "Those fools. What they've done without meaning any harm."

"Pray for us, Father," John said grimly. Then to Marian who knew too well what this trouble could mean: "Well, girl. I thought as things are I'd wish you happiness."

She pressed his hand. "Thank you, John."

"Ah, thanks for what? There'll be little peace or happiness for any of us now. Wystan's my best friend, but curse me if he hasn't done for us good this time."

"Plain truth, Thane. That man there's one of them."

By the fire pit the two foresters in scarlet and blue livery waited for a release Robin would not give. "We thought you might tell us where to find the other man."

"How in hell would I know?" Robin shot back, furious. "You think I just sit here waiting for my folk to break the law?" Hardly: he'd been in the fields since first light, caked with dust, sweat-sticky in the ruin of an old shirt hanging loose over ragged linen trousers. They had the good luck of dry weather for haying; he and every available worker were bent to get the fodder in before rain—and now this. Robin couldn't bring himself to look at hangdog Wystan for fear he might physically hurt the little fuller. "You're sheriff's men. Why are you patrolling my land?"

The question was folly and Robin knew it, a delaying intimidation. Fitz-Gerald's liveries had authority anywhere in Sherwood now. These two were English and honestly sympathized with the lord's position, but they had caught the poachers. The third of their party was a Norman, worse luck, and ran hotfoot back to Fitz-Gerald. Nothing for it, they had their duty and families of their own to think of.

A grim scene: Wystan with Will at his elbow like a jailer, Minna hovering tensely at the end of the hall. Maud sat at the high table, half turned away from this fresh impossibility added to the burden on their lives, knowing like her son that it must be dealt with, but momentarily at a loss for means to cope. Robin paced up and down, trying to regain control of what was clearly out of his hands now, more frightened for Wystan and all of them than he dared show.

"My man won't surrender to you. I'll bring them both to Nottingham."

"Sir, we'll have to take this one."

"You'll take nowt!" The force in Robin's denial stopped the two men short. "I will bring them and be there to see decent justice done."

"No, lord," Wystan begged, terrified. "Let you punish me here."

"Shut up." Will prodded him ungently. "You've done enough this day."

"Go back to the sheriff," Robin directed. "Say that I'll deliver them in three days."

The foresters exchanged doubtful glanced. "Sir," the younger one ventured, "the matter would fare best if you gave us this one now."

"Would it indeed?" Lady Maud turned on him, disgust and frustration evident as her son's. "If you were our men, would you not want the same protection? Lord Edward has pledged to bring them; that is enough. Minna—there, dear, it will be well—give these men something to refresh them. In the kitchen," she added with with pointed emphasis.

The middle-aged forester was a pleasant-featured man who clearly disliked the whole business himself. "These are bad times, Thane. Not like the old days when your father and the sheriff could always see through to agreement in such matters. This Fitz-Gerald—well, he's not bad as some of them, if you know what I mean, but he can be hard."

Robin vividly remembered the black-clad figure, ravaged but tough as fire-hardened ash. No, he would not underestimate Ralf Fitz-Gerald. "Three days. Minna, do as your mistress bids and get them a meal."

Better that Minna didn't see this. When she reluctantly led the foresters from the hall, Robin turned at last on Wystan. "Do you know what you've done?"

Miserable and frightened, Wystan just bored his eyes into the floor. "No, lord. Just a roe it was, plenty on 'em now, and you said each householder—"

"You've had that and more!" Will Scatloch burst out, unable to keep silent. "You think we're stupid that we don't know how much you've taken?"

Robin felt a clear doom descending on all of them, torn between the need to save Wystan and the urge to break his neck. "Where's Much? You're for Nottingham, both of you."

"No, please." Wystan fell on his knees. "I beg you, lord. Do what you will, but—"

"I can't. Don't you understand anything? Where's the miller?"

"Bloody dim." Will Scatloch felt sour with fear and a helplessness heavy as Robin's. "You know what will happen if we don't give you up."

"He's a dog that can't learn," Robin ground out. "Wystan, I'm no longer the law here."

That was not the evidence of Wystan's small lifetime. "You are, my lord. Your father was."

Robin jerked the man to his feet. "Up!"

"Your father was a kind man," Wystan quavered.

"Too kind." Maud rose from the table, implacable. "You stole as nimbly from Aelred in his time. You are guilty as Cain. Were it a matter of flogging, we would do it."

"So I would, by God," Robin vowed. "I wish I could flay you, cut off a hand, send you barefoot to Canterbury for penance, may God damn you, but I *can't.*"

Behind his own fear, the abject sight of Wystan made Robin want to weep in pity and understanding of the man: born on Denby, fought for all of them with Aelred. Now, for an empty word like *justice* Aelred's son denied him the only place where justice held any meaning for Wystan. There had always been Denby, always would be. The fuller's mind could not conceive of its loss, or that king and sheriff leaned so close over them all that their shadows covered everything.

"When I took up the ax and coronet, I took all your lives in these hands and swore to protect you." So Robin would, whatever that called for. He would argue with this sheriff—plead, deny, and delay, even perjure himself. If the two hadn't run away, he might have said they were hunting for him. He still might make the sheriff believe that. Something. *Anything.* "What can be done I'll do, but I won't throw the lot of us in the fire to save you."

Searching Robin's face for mercy or any relenting, Wystan saw only sad resolution. He appealed to Lady Maud. "Speak for me, lady, I've served your family all my life—"

Robin grabbed him suddenly, shaking the little man back and forth savagely. "Why did you do this to me? *Why?* We're burning, you fool, and you—Christ!" He shoved Wystan so hard that the man sprawled on the floor. Robin checked a violent urge to kick him senseless. "Don't talk of service now, not to me. Where is Much?"

"On my faith, lord, I don't know."

"You'd better know, you've killed us all."

"I swear I don't," Wystan cringed. "I never meant—"

"Will, get him out of my sight." Of course he never: never meant, never thought. "Before I kill him."

"Come on, mun: Out with you." Will led the culprit toward the door, but Robin halted them.

"Hear me, Wystan. We go to Nottingham in three days. You bolt like Much did and you're the sheriff's to do with as he will."

When they were alone, neither Robin nor Maud moved. Besieged, Robin sank wearily onto a bench at the low table. When he looked at his mother, he could muster no hope to lighten the moment.

"Jesus, Mum."

Maud folded her hands on the table. "Your father painted the bargain oak on his shield because that is the truth we live by. We endure. Whatever that takes."

"I hate this."

"I know."

"But I meant it. We have to live, have to . . . endure." Too restive now to sit, Robin got up, pacing the hall. "Have I been too easy on them as the king said? I try to govern my lands as Da did, tried to strike a balance between what they need and what has to be. Damn him, Wystan *is* loyal. He's family to me like Will and Angharad and the rest. A faithful, stupid hound I can't whip out of killing chickens. He just feels the pain but can't see why."

"I just don't know." Slumped in her high chair, Maud gave it up. "I just—why won't they leave us *alone?*"

Robin heard the ragged catch in her voice. His mother would contend and cope as she always did, he knew that. In a few minutes she would be Lady Maud again, but in this small private moment shared only between the two of them, she bent low under the weight of it all. Robin went to his mother and took her hands.

"Now you must leave tears to me," he whispered. "I was the one to be married a-Sunday."

"God-a-mercy," Maud gasped, halfway to tears when he reminded her. "I forgot. Well." She sat erect from long habit and took a steadying breath. "Marian will understand. And I must see that Minna does. If I can."

They both knew there was no easy road to that. Maud left the table to kneel by the fire pit, beckoning Robin to join her. They crossed themselves.

"Almighty Father, we who are Thy servants ask for strength to succor those who serve us. Let Thy hand be on my son's shoulder . . ."

Robin echoed the prayer with all his heart, hearing a deeper counterpoint beneath the Christian orison. If his blood must go into the tree, let it not be now when the sun shone brightly and Marian loved him. She was as magic to his life as Guntrada was to Brihtnoth when he first saw her by the oak.

". . . and protect our house and all those given into our care. Amen."

Robin crossed himself again. "Amen."

14

RALF WOKE TO the morning noises of Nottingham beyond the open
window. He blinked up at the rafters to pierce the wine fog of the night
before, then turned his head to look at the sleeping Saxon woman. Time
to get her up and out, work to do. Denby was charged to appear with
the felons today.

He had felt stronger this last fortnight once the fever passed. The
malady might return at any time for months or even years. That was
the price he paid to be the tail of William's conquering comet, like the
abcesses some vavasors suffered from sitting wet saddles year in and out.
One could be in worse condition than his. Death was worse: When one
had been close to it so often, each breathing moment was profit.

He'd overslept; the sun was well up. Ralf stretched and rolled over to
look without interest at the woman. As English whores went, she wasn't
the worst, more efficient than affectionate, but with a cowlike good nature.
He'd chosen her for looks more than appetite. She reminded him—

He remembered jolting out of blood-boiling dreams and someone bending over him, touching him, and his whole body clenched like a fist until
he found her face in the fever-haze and saw no danger there, only concern.
Strange the things a man couldn't forget, one face out of so many, a
look that didn't fade but grew brighter in memory.

Marianne. No, the damned English pronounced that backside-to like
everything else: *Marian.*

The woman snorted and opened flat brown eyes. No, not the same at

163

all. Ralf took her for the night because when he'd drunk enough she resembled the girl at Denby, the same incongruous coloring between eyes and hair. In morning light the illusion vanished. Beyond the rutting, he hadn't found what he sought. The woman was older than she looked last night, but whoring aged one quicker than war. Her features were coarser than Marian's, not nearly so well defined, the hair not gold but only dull yellow going stiff with dirt, the ineffable quality not there at all. She spoke a smattering of Frank lame as the three-legged kitten mooning round-eyed at Ralf last night from a pocket of the woman's apron; the damned thing tumbled furiously about the floor while she gave Ralf what he paid for. Now the kitten circled about on the blanket at his feet, wanting to be noticed and fed. Ugly little bugger: dark brown with ragged patches of tan and one white spot under its chin. The kitten had been born with one of its forelegs no more than a stump. The hind legs were already stronger to compensate. Now it sprang off the bed to chase a dust ball stirred by breeze. One absurd bit of fluff chasing another: Perhaps de Gavnay might have found philosophy in that.

The woman yawned.

"Time to go home," Ralf told her curtly. "There is business."

"Oh, not yet." She tried to cuddle to him. Her breath was sour with last night's wine. Ralf pushed her away. "*Vitement*. Out." He swung his legs to the floor and caught up the crippled kitten, greeting it nose to nose. "*Hé, chat, ça va?* Have you hunger?"

"Always hungry, that one," the woman muttered, slithering into her clothes. "Don't know why I picked her up. Not like there's milk and that to spare. Should have left the damned thing lost." She jammed her stubby feet into battered shoes. "Want to buy her?"

"Will lose," Ralf conjugated to the scrawny ball of fur. "Losing . . . lost. *Un chat perdu.*"

The woman watched him with eyes hard as calluses. "What about it, then?"

"About what?"

"You want to buy her?"

"You can have my boot if you don't get out of here." Ralf rummaged the purse tucked carefully into one of his shoes last night. With Saxon whores you didn't leave money lying about in plain sight. He threw her a silver penny, heard her gasp of surprise. An enormous price for an alley cat, but he could afford some indulgence now; that pleased him a little.

"That's a fair trade," the woman decided.

"More than fair." Ralf twisted around to her with a cynical grin. "Find enough strays, you could be rich. *Va t'en.*"

"Ta, then." The woman adjusted her soiled veil. Beyond good wine and poor light, Ralf wondered how he'd ever fancied a likeness to Marian. "You want me to come back tonight?"

"No."

She only shrugged; return or not meant little to her. Ralf heard her stump across the floor and the door closing behind her. He padded naked to the window, holding the kitten against his chest. A breeze off River Trent brought him the pungent reek of Nottingham, acrid with urine and dung and the stink from the tannery, all mixed with the redolence of cooked fish, mutton, and pork. Beyond the town the new keep hulked on its mound, commanding all. Ralf had wisely chosen for his own the residence of the former sheriff. That worthy had disdained service to a Norman king and gone with other dispossessed Saxons to serve the emperor at Constantinople. The house was spacious, built with Danish cunning in timberwork, two-storied with ample cellars and kitchen plus outbuildings. The hall was larger and certainly more cheerful than the small, bleak stone castle at Le Thiel managed by Ralf's father, not that Ralf had seen that much of the gloomy hall until the castellan suffered an attack of paternal conscience. The Nottingham keep was as cheerless beside being cramped and dirty, no more than a barracks and stable. Ralf preferred this clean, light place for living as well as his crown business.

The kitten mewed against his chest, separating the smell of fresh food from the effluvium of garbage and offal. Ralf buried his face in the furry little head. "Yes, Perdu. I am lost like you, but food is not so scarce in my house as some other things. We will see what we can find."

Her plaintive *mrrrow* stated that Perdu was clearly bent on breakfast. "I know," Ralf murmured into her fur. "We are both sad, sick little bastards but very hard to kill."

Denby should arrive about noon with the two felons—should if he knew his own best interests. For all of that, Ralf envied the man. Did Denby know how rich he was, born and bred in a forest like a vast church, in peace and silence like the balm of salvation itself? And about to know even more happiness with such a woman. Where did one find luck like that unless you were born with it? Marian wasn't as beautiful as the thane's cousin, or not in the same way. The treasure of Marian was that she seemed so much a part of that blessed peace, and somehow the thought of her echoed in a part of Ralf too long empty.

Years I've fought for a space to live in. Now the touch of one girl mopping my forehead shows me how little life I have to fill it. They tell me wise men see large meanings in small events. I have not one living creature to love but you, cat. It is a beginning.

No, too early in the day for such melancholy: to business. Today Thane Edward and his whole shire would know they bent to one law and that was William's in the person of Ralf Fitz-Gerald. The two poachers were nothing, the example all. Père Huger and his clerks had been diligent and thorough in preparation. The trial would be a mere formality.

The three of them had walked hours from Denby since the sun came up, stopping but once to rest and eat. Robin had the countryman's distrust of any large town, especially one crawling with foreigners whose horses crowded you to one side of the narrow street where offal and waste of every sort were thrown from windows to run downhill in rivulets if the street inclined that way, or just collect in fly-swarming bogs if it didn't.

They didn't talk much on the journey. Walking between Robin and Will, Wystan asked only that he not be bound like a prisoner. "Let me go as a man, my lord."

Robin had no intention of binding a man he'd known all his life. This whole business was shabby enough. Wystan walked free between himself and Will through teeming Nottingham, stood straight when they knocked and stated their business and entered the great hall where Norman soldiers manacled his hands and feet. Then they waited, the indifferent soldiers lounging idle along both walls. Not the most even this day, Robin's temper was further thinned by the delay. They shifted from one foot to the other before the high table on its dais at the head of the hall.

Three more men entered at length. Robin recognized two of them, the English foresters who'd come to Denby. He vented his silent contempt on them: not their wish, my lord, never theirs. Just plain men with families. Weeping Jesus, was that what made men into dogs? Where did men begin to lose honor? Not always in one throw, then, but one easier choice at a time until one day a man couldn't remember where it went or how. Someone at York had made the same easy choice and sold them out.

The third man in the sheriff's livery Robin took to be the wee manny who ran to Fitz-Gerald with the damning tale. At length a beefy priest clumped down the wooden steps from the upper storey and went to the high table. He set down a large leather folio from which he extracted several parchment writs, laying them out before him. He was slightly deformed, his right shoulder bunched and twisted through some violent dislocation and carried higher than the left. The man's clerical tonsure seemed new, the hair not yet trained to it. To Robin, he had more the look of a knight than a priest, scowling at Wystan before settling heavily in a chair.

They waited on. Two doves fluttered in through a high window, whirred about in the shadowed rafters, then flew out again. Wystan followed their passage.

"Lord Robin, did I ever tell you about Hastings?"

No less than a hundred times, but now the coming trial cast its own baleful but clear light over Wystan. Minna's shiftless husband, the wry joke of Denby and Blidworth, for whom complete honesty was just too far to reach. Robin regarded him now in profile, hair and beard like dull straw, slightly protruding but expressive blue eyes, a cast of expression changeable as April sky, flashing ever between candor and sly connivance. The face of a man who'd most like slip under heaven's fence to poach God's own forest. But somehow not a weak face. Robin had never thought of Wystan and dignity in the same breath. Now the coupling came naturally. Wystan's gaze followed the doves to an envied freedom. *Da never belittled the man. He always came at life sideways, but mostly did the best he could, I guess.*

"I tell you," Wystan declared in a voice low but firm, "I was better at Hastings with a borrowed ax than many carls in a lifetime. Lord Aelred said so, did he not, Will Scatloch?"

"He did that and often," Will confirmed.

Wystan sucked his lower lip under yellow teeth and seemed to do a private accounting that satisfied him. "I did my share."

"Watch out," Will said. "Here comes the Fitz-Gerald."

There was a general shuffling to attention among the soldiers as the sheriff descended the stairs and limped to the dais. Robin marked his favoring of the right leg. Such a man would be easy to track in Sherwood if one were hunting sheriffs.

"No, lord," Wystan said to Robin in sad reproof. "You should not have brought me here."

The priest laid aside the writ he was perusing and spoke in heavily accented English, "Who stands for the villein thief?"

"I do." Robin stepped forward. "And don't call him thief. He's not yet convicted."

"Let the witnesses come forward."

The three foresters moved closer to the dais, standing in a line.

"Père Huger now reads the charge." Fitz-Gerald's English was lame as his leg but Robin was surprised he spoke it at all. Most Normans considered it beneath them. The priest barked out the indictment in a peremptory manner more suited to the war-camp than court of law or altar: The accused and one other man were seen in Sherwood on said date in the illegal taking of a roe deer but fled to escape apprehension.

Fitz-Gerald addressed Robin directly. "Thane Edward, where is the other thief?"

"Accused," Robin corrected stubbornly. "Lord Sheriff, you call him thief after you find him guilty, not before."

"Where is he, Denby?"

"I don't know. I haven't found him yet." Nor would Robin before knowing what sort of justice to expect. "He may have quit the shire."

"You are the king's tenant," Huger reminded him. "That you find no fault in this proceeding, here is a copy of the English laws of forest and chase under which the villeins are charged."

One of the soldiers brought the writ to Robin. The parchment was new and the ink fresh. The writ might have been copied only a few days ago. No matter, they'd given him an opening and he leaped at it. "If Wystan is accused under English law, then by that law I will stand as his compurgator." He raised his right hand. "I swear by the full value of my holding that these men are innocent and what I have to speak is the truth."

By all the law he ever knew, every foot and penny of Denby's value was now staked on his oath. Had Aelred ever so willingly perjured himself?

Now the Norman forester stepped forward and gave testimony in his own tongue. His English companions, pressed for corroboration, answered tersely with *Yes* or *No* or *True, my lord*. To Robin's mounting bewilderment, though these men might have offered some explanation of local customs, they carefully volunteered nothing. They spoke as little as possible, wanting no attention on themselves.

"Listen to 'em," he muttered to Will. "Flaming English heroes."

"When there's only one kennel, every dog wants a place," Will said.

"Fermez!" the sheriff silenced them. "You have . . . you will have your time."

The forester-witness droned on and on in Frank. The priest was attentive, but took no written note of the testimony, as would have seemed necessary to Robin. Ralf Fitz-Gerald appeared to have little interest in the proceedings, massaging his right leg now and then.

Wystan stirred with a rattling of his chains. "What's he saying?"

Robin shrugged, feeling helpless. "Who knows?"

At last the damning evidence concluded and Robin was told he might give his testimony. While sternly reminded of his oath, he was given no chance to put forth any fair argument, Huger interrupting at every turn.

"These were my men on my land—"

"The king's land!"

"They had my permission to hunt a roe meant for my table. I explained all this to the king—"

"You had no such right!" Huger thundered at him. "By giving such permission, you are yourself in breech of law."

"But will you hear me?" Robin pressed on doggedly. Their first crops were only just coming in, small game overhunted where deer were plentiful and already grazing in tilled fields. No hungry man with a family to feed was just going to flap his arms and hie the errant animal back to royal forest, nor should he be expected to. There must be some control. . . .

No use. He could see their uninterest. He doubled the force of his arguments while trying to keep his anger in check. Foresters had their place in law, he admitted—with a withering look at them—and they should keep it. The sworn word of a landed thane carried much more authority and should be respected.

"You say my man is tried by English law? That's a lie." Robin pointed at the Norman forester. "This little dog of yours, he testified in Frank. He could've said Wystan raped the mother of Christ for all we know. My man has the right to hear it all, for a start. And you, priest: If this is English law, there's appeal and appeal needs record. You've not put down one flamin' word, no one has. And where and when was the change in laws read in church as is the custom? Not in Blidworth. At what crossroads were they read out so all men had a chance to know the law? Not in Sherwood, by God."

Huger just sat back, visibly bored. "You waste the time of this court. Sire Ralf knows you are lying. He heard from the king's own lips how patiently the law was explained to you."

"*Père Huger, s'il vous plaît.*" The sheriff rose and painfully made his way down from the dais to Robin, who noted how he tried to conceal the shortcoming. "*C'est ennuyeux*, Denby. Stupid. Your man is tried and guilty under the law you hold in your hand. The laws of Canute. Your ignorance is no excuse. If you cannot keep the law, then I must."

"I know the law."

"Then read it!" The sheriff snatched the writ and shook it in Robin's face. "Read."

"I know the laws of Canute," Robin maintained. "I can't read much."

"Learn." Ralf Fitz-Gerald rolled the parchment and thrust it beneath Robin's jerkin. "I do not speak well your tongue, but *I* learn. Bring to me the other man or I must come and take him."

Père Huger began to pronounce the sentence. "All evidence having been heard—"

"We didn't hear it," Robin denied.

No matter. All evidence heard, the villein Wystan was guilty, Denby himself in jeopardy of prosecution if he failed to produce the accomplice. Under crown law the sheriff might hang the felon but Huger counseled leniency: It was ever the wish of the Church, he stated, except in bootless crimes such as murder, that the law mete punishment short of death in order that the guilty might atone in this life rather than suffer in the next. Punishment here would be an example to many. As for Edward of Denby, he was charged to find and return with the other man forthwith.

"You will bring him in three days," the sheriff directed. "Do not hold me light, *Anglais*."

"I wouldn't," said Robin with a tinge of disgust. "No more than I'd count this a court of law."

Ralf Fitz-Gerald turned back to the dais. "Bring the fire."

Two soldiers hurried out and returned quickly with a brazier of hot coals carried on their pikes. The coals had been heating for some time, as if the verdict were a foregone conclusion. Wystan went pale when two long iron rods were shoved into the fire. They were going to scar him. Frightened himself now, Robin knew there was little time for whatever else he could do.

"Lord Sheriff! I claim the right to appeal judgment at the next shire moot. Let sentence wait on the appeal."

Huger regarded him with mild surprise. "Appeal? Guilt is proven."

Desperate, Robin groped for anything now. "Then give him the ordeal. Let God decide."

"Denby." The sheriff rubbed at his leg. "It is finished."

"For the love of mercy, man, all courts abide by ordeal."

"Only if guilt is in doubt." Clearly the court was concluded. The priest gathered up his parchments. Indeed, when he first saw the fire, Robin thought they intended ordeal. Wystan would be required to take a hot coal from the brazier and carry it a certain distance across the hall. His hand would then be bound up. After three days, if the wound had not festered, he would be declared innocent. The two irons, turning red now, told Robin it would be mutilation. Wystan hardly deserved that, couldn't take that. . . .

When two of the soldiers dragged Wystan to the brazier and forced him to his knees, Robin lunged to stop them. He tore their hands from his man before two more burly men at arms restrained him. He struggled against them, appealing frantically to the Saxon foresters.

"You, you're countrymen. Tell them how the law works. This is wrong!"

If they knew that, they only looked away.

"For mercy's sake, speak! What are you afraid of?"

The first iron was lifted from the coals, glowing white now. Wystan wailed as the last of his courage melted away. "Robin, help me!"

"Wait!" Robin shouted. Beyond ordeal one recourse remained to him, one more favored by Normans than his own sensible kind. "I offer trial by combat, Lord Sheriff. Name a champion against me, name yourself if you will, but let God decide between us."

The sheriff needed some translation from Père Huger who flatly denied the right in this case. "Combat is only allowed where guilt can be decided by no other means, Thane. And only in disputes among *noblesse*."

The suggestion frankly puzzled Ralf Fitz-Gerald who gestured negligently at Wystan. "You would die for that?"

The question caught Robin off balance, totally alien to him. "Of course."

"For a serf?"

The incomprehension stopped Robin completely: The man simply could not conceive of what he proposed. "He is my sworn man. What kind of lord are you that you must ask?"

Whatever kind, that was the vast gulf between himself and them. Fitz-Gerald's astonishment slowly resolved to dry amusement. "God would not be with you, *Anglais*. You would die for nothing. Execute the sentence."

One horrified look at the ready irons and Wystan shut his eyes tight, moaning. Only when the guards forced them open did Robin know at last what they meant to do.

15

fATHER BEORN PAUSED between the church and his own house to enjoy
the sweet night air: warm but not too humid. Sherwood folk could get
all their haying done before rain, hopefully. As matters stood they needed
all the luck they could find. Beorn entered the small timbered house and
searched familiarly in the dark for his horn lamp, lighting it from the pan
of glowing peat on the hearth. He poured a cup of warm ale to help him
sleep and was barely two swallows into the libation before the door rattled
with agitated knocking.

"Father, are you there?" Another rattle, more urgent. "Please, it's
Freda."

In the doorway by lamplight, Freda's round face shone white with
anxiety. "Lord Robin's down the Queen's and he needs you now,
Father."

She and her da were closed up and bent for bed, she told him, when
the thane burst through the door mean as east wind in December, calling
for whiskey and his priest and to look sharp about both. Beorn read more
than the facts in Freda's distress.

"Na, he never drinks whiskey, mind, he can't hold the stuff. But more
than that, there's summ'at wrong with him. I can feel." She tugged at
Beorn's sleeve. "Please come."

Carrying the lamp, Beorn hurried down the cart road after Freda. She
sidled in ahead of him and slipped into a shadowed corner from which

she watched her lord with concern. Her father had evidently gone on to bed. Beorn read the situation in the lamplight and one candle burning on the battered table. Robin hunched over his cup, head down. He seemed half asleep. Beorn had seen enough drinkers to judge keenly between them. Some boasted or grew convivial, even maudlin. The still ones were harder to gauge; they might be relaxed or coiled.

"Get me a cup, Freda. A clean one." Beorn sat down opposite Robin, wincing when the young man raised his head. He had been weeping but the tears washed nothing away, only bared a horror. He croaked at Beorn in a reedy voice, "Go to Wystan. He needs you."

The priest downed a nip of whiskey before speaking. "They let him live. Christ is merciful."

"So I've heard."

"Don't blaspheme to me. They might have hanged him."

"No, never that." Robin emptied his cup and placed it on the board in a puddle of spilled liquor. "The sheriff is a merciful man. His fat priest told me so." He pushed one finger through the wet spot, then focused groggily on Beorn's lantern. "Light . . . did you ever think how much a man can see with just a little light?"

"What happened?" Beorn grasped Robin's arm. It was jerked away. "Robin?"

"Don't touch me."

"What happened, man?"

"I feel dirty."

"What of Wystan?"

"Go to him," Robin muttered thickly. "They burned out his eyes."

—carried Wystan all the way home from Nottingham, trying not to jolt the litter, Will behind and himself in front, the poor man screaming with the cloth over his face soaked through now with what they left of his eyes. When Wystan didn't scream he begged them to turn for Papplewick because he needed a priest now and would never live to get one. *You will, man. Lie easy, we'll get you there.*

Hours they toiled, the weight of the litter cramping Robin's arms, his mind seared deep with the memory of what they did to Wystan, the parchment writ rustling against his breast like dry, cruel laughter. They trudged the last weary miles to Denby where Robin somehow couldn't look Marian in the eye and the girl made a sick sound when the cloth was lifted from Wystan's face. Maud hurried off with Judith to mix a balm before they carried the wretched man home to his own croft and Minna. Not Wystan alone on Robin's conscience now as he drank and stared foggily at the horn lamp.

Lie still; I'm off to fetch the priest.

So he was, running down into the dale on the last of his strength. Passing the tavern, everything left him. He hung over the taverner's sty, bringing up what little was left in his stomach. Wystan would never see him again but Minna could. *You are lord and you let this happen?* No, she didn't say as much but Robin read the accusation in her anguish and his own rawed soul. The question loomed over him now, waiting for answer.

There was that he had to say to Beorn but not in front of Freda. "Go to bed, girl."

She looked uncertainly to Father Beorn. "I have to lock up and—"

"Get out!" Robin lurched off the bench, unsteady and brutal now. "I'll close the place and take the skin off anyone who comes, you hear? Who'd want to steal from this sty?" True enough. As much ale and whiskey had been trodden into the earth floor as was ever drunk here, along with scraps of food, chicken droppings and only God knew what else. "The stink of this place will keep them away. Go *on*, I said." Robin lunged at the girl in aimless fury. Freda dodged away and Robin felt Beorn's grip close about his shoulder, the voice low but warning.

"Easy, Rob. Sit down."

Yes, watch it. Easy. Robin relaxed with the quick-shifting mood of the whiskey in him. He blinked stupidly at the frightened girl while drunken compassion flooded through him, recalling a tenderness ages ago before the world rolled over him.

"You're a good girl, Freda. Din' mean to . . . go to bed."

To Freda, Beorn whispered rapid instructions. "Wake up Tuck, tell him to bring my bag with the things for unction. Hurry."

With a pitying glance at Robin, the girl slipped out on her errand. Beorn sat down, refilling Robin's cup. "Here. Get drunk enough to throw it back up."

"I did." Robin wove on his feet. "The way she looked at me."

"No harm. Freda knows you."

"I mean Minna."

Beorn took his whiskey in miserly sips. He would be up all this night until Wystan died or was out of danger, and Minna must be comforted.

"I led him to it, Beorn. Like a goddamned Judas goat, and you know why I had to."

"Yes."

"It was him or all of us." Robin flopped down at the table again, pushing the hair out of his eyes. "They said to bring Much. I can't. Not to that. I had to watch Wystan beg before he screamed . . . taught all my life a man takes his chances with death, and if death's his lot, he goes without a fuss." But they gave Wystan no chance to be ready. That was a painful thing no man should have to see. "Sometimes a man gets to a place where his courage won't reach, just too far, and don't ask for more because y'won't get it."

"I know," said Father Beorn. "I have been there."

"Learned that at York."

"Yes."

"Bad enough to feel your own fear, but to see another man stripped *naked* like that." A sob welled in Robin's throat but he quelled it. Shameful to show such things. Robin rubbed a hand across his eyes to hide the tears, joined them to his own pain and spat them out as anger. "Don't you or any man tell me what's right or wrong. You're just a priest, all you have to do is save their souls. I have to save everything else because you have to be alive to pray, Beorn. You want to give me wisdom, tell me how I can take Much to have that done to him."

Robin's head drooped lower over his drink, speech no more than a rasping whisper now. "Or how I can refuse and keep this place for my folk. If Minna hates me, at least she's still got a roof over her head. Fitz-Gerald taught me good today; taught me how little I am. Uses our own laws against us." He fumbled the rolled parchment out of his jerkin and tossed it to Beorn. "And I can't even read the flamin' thing."

Robin felt sleep coming like a swift mercy. His head dropped on his arms. "Go to Wystan."

Time did not exist in his stupor. Robin heard distant but familiar voices over him: Freda, the deep rumble of Tuck, then nothing. He couldn't move but would sleep here on the hard table much as he needed something softer and yielding to sink into. Marian's arms or even Freda's now—no, that was long ago, but a wise faith to let men pray to female saints now and then, since women had a natural way of caring. . . .

But he must be clearheaded on the morrow. He was still thane. For the little that meant now, how heavy it was.

Denby and Blidworth gave thanks; Wystan would live. Lady Maud and Beorn hardly left his pallet, Judith only to make fresh salve for his eyes. The scorch of his wounds burned them all. Behind every thought lay the knowledge that somehow a dangerous corner had been turned. The women sensed what the men would not utter. Angharad knew it in Will the night he stumbled in from Nottingham, snapping short at his sons, to drink in silence most unlike him. When the boys had pummeled and tusseled themselves to sleep, Angharad sensed the depth of it when Will lay beside her, silent but taut as a drawn bow. She stroked his head lying against her breast. "Nay, husband, you must sleep."

"I cannot."

"What is it that Lord Robin will do?"

"What he must."

And what was that? Angharad feared. What of her own boys? To be fed slaves was better than beggars on the road.

"*Must* is a big word," Will said in the darkness. "But some kind of *must* is coming."

Marian felt the chill of that *must* fall across Robin when he looked at her and somehow through her to a reality he could not go around. She felt part of him gone away when he kissed her. Not that there was that much time for tenderness. There was the haying to finish. Both rose before light each day and were in the fields with the rest of the folk until dark, sweating to get the precious fodder shocked, tied, and into the barn before rain mouldered it.

Then at last the hay was in and dry, one small blessing at least. Robin and Marian were storing it properly in the loft, rain whispering beyond the open barn door when Ethelwold padded in, cloak pulled up over his head. "Lord Robin?"

Robin peered over the lip of the loft. "Aye, up here."

"There's come an oxcart from Grantham. Men of the queen's household."

"For your mother and Judith and me," Marian guessed, wiping the dust and grit from her forehead. "We knew she'd be sending but not so soon."

Sent for they were: Presently the cart was driven into the barn by a Frankish groom—no ordinary conveyance but freshly painted, fitted with stout oaken hoop staves to support a canopy. Inside were cushioned seats for eight passengers, all drawn by four sleek, exquisitely matched white oxen.

Lady Maud would *not* leave on such short notice. While Wystan needed constant care, her place was here, that should be clear even to a Norman. Between her granite refusal to budge and the two foreign chamberers assuming they were not properly understood, Judith was a harried mediator.

"But the cart is rigged for inclement weather as the ladies can see for themselves. It is the express wish of Her Majesty that the ladies depart now."

"Are they bread, these two?" Maud fumed. "Lord, give me patience to suffer fools gladly. They could not be more untimely if they tried. My son has already postponed his wedding once," she declared, standing in her place at the high table. "Judith, you may tell these foreigners they quite put me *out*! No idea or care to how things should be done. My house is in chaos, Minna can barely see to a plain meal for worrying over her husband." Underslept and distracted beyond courtesy, Maud was anything but reasonable now. "In faith I don't know what to say to these people. Let them come again later or when they will or God knows what."

Ethelwold hurried into the hall at that moment, shaking the rain out of his cloak. "My lord, Father Beorn is here."

"Where, then?"

"In the barn giving his old horse a quick rub." Ethelwold glanced at the royal messengers and lowered his voice. "Legal business, he said, and most urgent."

Father Beorn's matter demanded privacy. He had studied the "English" writ of laws and found it of questionable authenticity. They didn't know how much of their language Matilda's chamberers might catch, nor was this the time to find out. Maud could relegate the cart driver to the kitchen house, but it would be a breech of manners to leave royal retainers unattended. Robin had been weighing considerably more than Matilda's inconvenient summons. Now he leaned over the high table to confer with his mother.

"This summons may be for the best, Mum. If you take my meaning."

Maud was not feeling subtle. "I do not."

"Trust me, Mum. We can't afford mistakes now, not a one."

At Robin's urging, Judith thanked the queen's men for providing the richly appointed cart which would bring the ladies to Grantham at the earliest possible time. Meanwhile, in a flourish of the warmest courtesy, the officers were invited to tarry the night and enjoy what cheer Denby could offer. In normal circumstances, they were assured, the ladies would comply upon the instant, but presently they needed a day or two in preparation. Surely the queen would understand. The chamberers were quickly and solicitously served at one end of the hall with a well-sauced venison and lentil soup. Marian would have fetched them ale, but one whiff of Beorn's business fired Robin with more effective intent. To keep them mellow and occupied, Angharad sacrificed the last jug of Scatloch whiskey which Judith graciously presented to their foreign guests.

"A mild Welsh drink, messires. You will find it novel."

Most novel: Within the quarter hour they were gabbling volubly at each other across the low table with increasingly vehement gestures. Judith commended Angharad's sacrifice to the saints. "Nobility in a time of need. They won't mark us now in any tongue. We may proceed."

The family grouped about the high table as far as possible from the Normans. The day was dark enough to need candles in order for Beorn and Judith to compare the two parchment writs spread before them. Beorn had always acted as clerk to Aelred, writing the few necessary letters and filing all writs of forest law handed down by the royal or shire courts. This included the laws of Canute from 1016, of which that given by Fitz-Gerald to Robin was alleged to be a true copy.

Robin shot a look dark as the day outside at the chamberers jabbering over their meal. "You say it's not?"

The priest shook his head. "Hardly. A fool could see that. There are forty-odd articles in the original but only thirty-four in the copy." Most significantly, few customary rights of commoners were listed in the spurious copy which dealt mainly with penalties for offenses against royal foresters.

"Reading is a great good thing," Robin admired earnestly. "Then if I did appeal to shire moot, I'd have a good case?"

"An obvious one in an English court," Beorn conceded with a shrug. "But—"

But nothing. When the time came, Earl Waltheof would surely lend his influence to sway the court. No man had a readier tongue.

Judith had concentrated on the new copy, scanning each line with the eye of a scholar. "This was not even written by an Englishman. I would say by someone trained in our language but not born to it. Look here . . . and here." Her finger jabbed at certain words. "Mistakes of gender in writing nouns that no English clerk would make. Not even an artful deception and about as honest as Satan's sworn oath."

Robin bit off the sentiment. "Telling us by law that we have no law."

Maud's tone made the question into a judgment. "Then you will not turn over Much to them?"

"Not likely, Mum. I'll have straight words with this sheriff first. Father

Beorn, you will write for me." Robin considered the Norman chamberers over their drink. "And Judith, with your fetching eye and honey tongue, do me one more service."

Judith followed her cousin's purposeful glance to the chamberers who had mellowed to a harmony with all the world, quite unaware that a few paces from them, a different way of life had drawn a line and raised a standard. "Of course, Edward. What may I do?"

"Bring them ale to wash down the whiskey. Say they go well together."

"Oh, they'll wake up feeling like death." Marian relished the prospect.

"And praying for it," Robin amended. "So they won't make much haste back to Grantham, will they? Time's our only weapon now. Father Beorn, write for me. To the Lord High Sheriff of Nottingham . . ."

Denby had slipped the time of his summons. Once more Ralf Fitz-Gerald sent men, four this time, to demand the miller. Once more they returned without him.

"Just this letter, Sire Ralf."

Ralf tapped the sealed vellum against one palm. "He refused?"

"He did, sir," the Saxon forester explained. "Polite enough, but I've lived through warmer winters than his courtesy."

As cold, the forester reported, were the Welshman and the priest flanking Lord Edward at Denby's gate. They were given only the letter and the clear impression that to demand more at that time would have been folly.

Ralf had given Denby as much latitude as he could, but no more. And the priest would be Father Beorn, a former carl so one heard. William was as zealous in cleaning house among Saxon clergy as he was among their secular lords. The time had clearly come to take that new broom to Blidworth church. He set the letter before Father Huger, since he himself spoke much more English than he read. The missive was written on worn and much-erased vellum. These people did not write often.

TO THE HIGH SHERIFF OF NOTTINGHAM:
Your men will bear this to you. I demand to appeal the matter of my two tenants to the next shire moot at Papplewick, which is my right by law. The writ under which you punished my fuller is no more English than you are and will be seen so in any fair court. I am the king's sworn man and you his reeve, but surely there must be a just middle way between this ill-writ and dishonest set of laws and the protection I owe my tenants. I will speak with you at any time on this, but send no more

for my miller. I will not deliver him to the unjust doom you laid on Wystan.

EDWARD AELREDSON, THANE OF DENBY

Huger went back to feeding meat from his own silver plate to a brown hawk on its perch. "The mind of a mule."

Ralf tossed the letter on the table. "Sweet Robin of Sherwood."

The priest looked up from under bushy black brows, ruminating through a mouthful of pheasant. "Sweet what?"

"What they call Denby. Droll, isn't it?"

"Curious." Huger paused to belch. "One might devise a falcon on his shield, even a kestrel . . . but a robin?"

"They mean no bird but some sort of old heathen sprite, as I gather." One that couldn't change and wouldn't learn. The felons themselves were unimportant to Ralf now. Denby challenged his authority in Sherwood with this letter.

"*C'est ça.*" Ralf spun around to the waiting foresters. "I want Sire Raimond and twenty men ready to ride tomorrow early. Fully armed."

Time was their small but precious advantage, hours whispering through a glass, melting down a marked candle, shadow creeping around a dial until no more time remained. The queen's chamberers, the worse for drink but wiser, were surely at Grantham now, the weather cleared and the women's packing done. Judith was resigned to the journey, Marian not at all, rebellious in the waiting cart, lower lip jutted in obstinacy. This first visit to Grantham was to be of a fortnight's duration or until Matilda embarked for Rouen. One might as well say a year. The next few hours would likely decide their future.

Robin waited in the open doorway to Maud's bower as his mother drifted about the room in those apparently aimless but deeply instinctive movements that, like a queen bee leaving her hive, went with departing the center of her life.

She searched about distractedly. "My needle and thread?"

Robin tapped the small ivory inlaid box under his arm. "With your jewelry."

"I gave you the ring?"

"Aye, Mum."

"Well." Maud turned with dragging steps to the door. "The sheriff will come today?"

"Or tomorrow for sure. Best be gone."

"Don't rush me out of my own house!"

"No one's happy about this, Mum."

"I certainly hope not." Maud gathered up her second-best dun cloak. "I will not have anyone pestering me today." She took her son's arm and closed the door behind her. "Angharad's been told to put down fresh rushes in the hall, and Minna's to scrub the kitchen, but don't scold if she forgets, poor woman. And see to Wystan every day, whatever he needs."

"No fear, Mum." Robin led Maud toward the cart where Alcuin, the beekeeper of Denby, waited to escort the cart to Grantham. Out of prudence, Robin had ordered Ethelwold to go with them. Only when he helped Maud into the cart did she broach the worry at the bottom of her nervousness. "Robin, if there is any trouble—"

"Now, now, not a bit of that." He stepped up onto the driver's bench to kiss her good-bye.

"You will be reasonable?" Judith fretted at him, noticing the freshly honed ax in Robin's belt. "Not like you were with those knights at the gate?"

"Judith, stop!" Hands white-knuckled in her lap, Marian boiled over. "What do you want of him? He's backed up as far as he can being reasonable. Leave him be."

"Marian's right." Robin kissed Judith and embraced her. "Whatever befalls, I'll not have any of you part of it. Ethelwold, I'll expect you back with Alcuin." He helped the old man up to the bench. "Unless summ'at should delay you. Alcuin!" He waved to the lanky young beekeeper who had never been beyond Denby in his life and was looking forward to adventure and girl-hunting in Grantham. "Lead them out."

"No. Wait." Marian sprang off the wagon seat. "Alcuin, help me down with my chest." Before Robin could stop her, Marian was out of the cart.

"What's this, then?"

"I'm not going. Alcuin, help me with this."

The next few moments were awkward, Alcuin hesitant and confused between Robin's command—"Leave that chest, don't touch it"—and Marian's adamant refusal to get back in the cart. Judith tried to reason with her, Maud did not, only sat gazing back at her hall with the sad vision of a prophet.

"I said *no,* Robin." And Marian meant it. "We're to be married."

"And we will, but—"

"I'll be wife before I go or not at all, and Grantham can wait."

"Girl, don't go thick on me now."

"Don't you!"

"I want you out of this."

"No." Arms folded, feet planted and a tone that ended all argument. "Lying's a poor way to start a marriage." With Alcuin on the other handle, Marian heaved the chest to the ground with a decisive thump. "God be with you, ladies. Whatever's to do, I'll be in the hall. God bring you home soon." Marian took half a dozen determined strides toward the hall, waving Alcuin on. "Hie 'em up!"

As the cart creaked through the gate and away from Denby, Robin watched his family until they disappeared on the track down into the dale. Marian's chest was at his feet, herself apart, facing him. "Jesus, woman."

"I know what I'm doing." However Judith or Maud saw the truth of this day, Marian's sight was sharpened by her own instinct. She came back to grasp the chest by one handle. "You know they'll come today. Will you help me with my chest or leave it here in the dust?"

"Will's spying them out. There's plenty of time."

Marian's head remained bent over the chest until Robin raised her up. "But how much time for us?" she asked.

"You should have gone, Marian."

Her warm brown eyes looked into and through him. "If I must mourn, I'll do it as widow." Marian's arms slid around his neck. "You'll be going, then?"

"The men are waiting."

"Why?" Her voice broke oddly on the question. "Why do they give us so little time?"

When their mouths crushed together, Robin painfully realized the many gifts Marian brought him and that he might be saying farewell to them forever when he walked out of the gate. The light, musky scent of her skin hinting of the herbs she rubbed into it after washing. The wiry life of her body pressed against his own and as tireless when needed. So little time: met in one forest, brought home to another, the pairing of them so natural a man could see all the beautiful design at once. Why did the world take something so simple and make it so impossible?

"I will be back, girl." Yet he held her closer for not being sure. "And listen: When I am back and . . . and there's time, let me try to be a *scyld*-poet just for you."

In a drowsy, unthreatened moment he would find the words to tell her how her mouth felt greeting his, and so much more. Slowly he would string out the words like poetry, giving each hue its full value, of all the colors she brought to his life. So it must have been with Aelred and Maud, but they had years, and for the first time in his life, Robin was jealous of his parents. For Marian and himself, it wasn't fair. He no longer expected fair, but why so little time? Robin felt hollowed out and filled to aching with what it meant to be alive.

"God," Marian breathed against his cheek. "Don't let me lose you too."

"No . . . no, love, it will be well. Just I wish Da had gotten rid of Wystan years ago. I wish Much would run clear away into another shire and get caught where someone else has to deal with him. I wish—"

Passionate, hopeless wishes: that Harold had kept his stupid oath to William or killed him outright so neither left the clutter of their high destinies in his own small life sinking now under their weight.

"Coom, Rob." Marian gave him a last kiss. "Help me carry in my things."

16

A FEW YARDS OFF the cart track, Robin waited in the thicket beside
Father Beorn, telling himself over and over that Fitz-Gerald must be
reasonable, that there'd be no trouble if they could find a compromise.
Until he knew they couldn't, there was no need for the Normans to know
that Tuck, Will, and John were close and ready. Robin prayed matters
would not call for them. What were Wystan and Much to the sheriff,
especially when the evidence of the writs his priest carried would weigh
so clearly for appeal? Fitz-Gerald was not a hothead and Father Beorn a
persuasive speaker.

Just now the priest, clad in an old black monk's robe, fingered the
early blackberry buds, enjoying the muted song of the forest. "I should
spend more time here, Robin. This is a lovely place."

From minute changes in sound, Robin knew someone was approaching
swiftly on the path from Nottingham: The dry, scratching retreat of a
stoat or vole told him that much, then the raucous complaint of a startled
rook high in a tree farther off. "Get ready."

Will Scatloch trotted down the cart track toward them. Robin and
Beorn pushed out of the thicket to meet him.

"Coming at a walk," Will reported. "All mounted, no foot."

"How many?"

"Twenty I counted." Will braced his longbow. "Two knights: the
Fitz-Gerald and a younger pup, the rest men at arms all in mail. Some
with crossbows," he finished significantly.

Crossbows were slower than their own but deadly at short range. "How many bows?"

"Five or six," Will reckoned soberly, setting a shaft to his string. "If anything starts, best finish it quick. Where's John?"

"Just there." Robin pointed some way back down the path. "Stand with him. I want no trouble but John would love some. You understand?"

"I do." Will ran a nervous tongue over his lower lip. "Coming slow, very cautious. Let me get snug with John, count a hundred, and you'll see the first of them."

Will hurried back down the path, slipped soundlessly into the bordering thicket. Standing in plain sight with his priest, Robin counted to eighty-odd before the first horsemen appeared on the track. Cautious they were, keeping good distance between pairs of riders, plenty of room to maneuver if needed. Fitz-Gerald was in the lead; Robin recognized him immediately, helmeted but the nose piece turned up. Sighting Robin and Beorn, he did not slow but barked an order in Frank. Every man in the column raised his shield to ear level so that the column had protection left and right. Robin gave the man grudging respect for his ability. With the same instinct that measured distance in his own bowshot, Fitz-Gerald knew there were more men about beside the two he could see. Robin walked forward with Beorn, hands out and open to show them empty, stopping within three paces of the sheriff and his companion knight. "Welcome to Denby."

Fitz-Gerald's eyes darted left and right. "Why do you meet me here? Why not at your gate?"

"My gate is a different matter. We can talk here."

"Raimond." The sheriff muttered something to the younger knight; whatever was said, the vavasor was hardly reassured by the import.

"Hlaeford gerefa," Robin said evenly, "you must speak English."

Fitz-Gerald leaned over the pommel of his saddle, obviously more composed than the rigid young Raimond. Watching them, Robin was conscious of a slight trembling in his own hands and how utterly still the forest had grown.

"Denby, do you have the miller?"

"We have the law," Father Beorn asserted in a strong voice, holding up two parchments. "The true laws of Canute and this shameful, false copy. Let you compare them."

"And compare well," Robin added. "I will put this case to shire moot and win."

Fitz-Gerald muttered something under his breath. "Hear me well, little forest god, and try me no further. I am done with asking. Give me the other man.''

''I have dealt with forest law for many years,'' Beorn persisted. ''The legality of your action with Wystan is in doubt.''

''In doubt?'' The sheriff spoke rapidly to young Raimond who appeared to take something first as inconceivable, then as personal affront. ''Take care, priest. You are now as close to outlawry as your lord.''

Raimond's right hand twitched toward his sword. Robin casually hooked a thumb in his belt near the throwing ax. Beyond the unnatural stillness about them in these last moments at a brink from which no one would ever step back, Robin's sight was preternaturally clear. The varied greens of Sherwood became brilliant to him, each detail of the mounted men vivid. A horse snorted farther back along the line; somewhere a shield scraped against a mailed thigh.

''It is the miller,'' Fitz-Gerald said, ''or forfeiture of your lands.''

Robin felt his heart begin to thud in his chest and struggled to stay calm. ''The writ you gave me is not even a true copy—''

''Denby, cease!'' the sheriff warned him. ''I am weary of this.''

''And we are not?'' Beorn shot back at him. ''My lord's wish is to obey the law, but you do not stand on good laws. Only compare these writs—''

Suddenly young Raimond exploded in a stream of incomprehensible but peremptory Frank. The sheriff quelled him with a glance and spoke to Robin in a low, controlled voice.

''For the last time, *Anglais*. Will you obey the law?''

Inside himself, Robin seemed to hang over a bottomless pit. He saw with sudden, terrible clarity what was going to happen. Like a *weird*, his sight soared to future and past in the same moment, arrows burying themselves in the center of truth. Robin saw two pictures, each bright and separate, then blurring into one another: a river fording in grey fog, then a doomed line of men at York with another river at their back and nowhere to turn. Fitz-Gerald was no part of law, only of power and death. He knew some of Robin's speech but nothing of the most precious thing behind it, the imperative that placed Aelred in the last shield wall at York and drew another line here, now, in the stilled forest.

''How can I keep the law when the law's a lie? You and your king, you leave us nowhere to turn. You leave us nothing. *You* are the thief!''

Was it him began it? Robin was never sure afterward, as if that mattered a second later. Did the tone of his outburst loose the arrows from the thicket or warn young Raimond's hand to his sword? He remembered only that the knight clawed at his weapon and had it drawn when Robin cleared the ax from his belt and threw. The missile caught Raimond in the unprotected part of his face. He bellowed with the shock of the blow, head jerked back, and reeled in the saddle. In the same instant, one, then another of the men at arms fell from their horses as the air buzzed with arrows like a swarm of angry bees, horsemen milling about, more crying out as the shafts found them.

Father Beorn launched himself at Fitz-Gerald to drag him out of the saddle. Sheer survival took Robin now. He grabbed the sheriff's bridle near the stallion's bit and cut the animal's throat with his hunting knife. The horse screamed; its forelegs buckled. A rider plunged past Robin with an arrow protruding from his side. Somewhere another man shrieked. Father Beorn wrenched the sword from Raimond's numbed grip. Fitz-Gerald was too experienced and far too agile to go down with a dying horse. Feet out of the stirrups before the animal sprawled in its own blood, he leaped clear, shield up and sword drawn. Beorn bore down on him, blade raised—

Robin saw it all in a heartbeat: the sheriff turning on Beorn, flowing into guard, then the mounted soldier bearing down on his priest, sword raised to take Beorn's unprotected head—

"Beorn, behind you!"

—and Beorn whirling fast as he might have in his prime, sword spinning in his grip. But in turning, his back was to Fitz-Gerald and unguarded. Robin shot forward, all his weight in the tackle, and the two of them went down in a heap on the path. Something hit Robin on the side of the head; he saw blinding light and then a blur. The sword hilt drew back in Fitz-Gerald's grip to smash at him again. Robin blocked the blow, slashing savagely at the man's throat, no thought now but to kill and live. The mail coif took the cut, the blade merely grinding against iron rings, but the sweeping backslash left a long red line from the jawbone to the bridge of Fitz-Gerald's nose. Then someone was dragging him off his enemy—"Come away!"—and Robin had only an instant to see the sheriff struggling to rise, blood pouring over his face, before Tuck dragged him away, Father Beorn on his other side with a red-stained sword. The usually ruddy Tuck was pale now. Beorn stared curiously at the sword he held, then let it fall. Tuck pulled at Robin.

"Come away, lord!"

Robin shook his head to clear it. "Get the men out. Get them away."

Riderless horses milled about the cart track now. Someone was screaming, Fitz-Gerald wiping at the blood on his face before lurching toward
one of the mounts, and Tuck's roar boomed over it all.

"Put up! John, Will, put up and away."

Robin ran through the thickets along one of the myriad swine tracks,
Beorn and Tuck hastening after. The blow to his head hurt more now,
but he must put himself between Fitz-Gerald and Denby if the Norman
was determined to go there.

"Anglais!"

Fitz-Gerald's voice—distant, hoarse, tight with pain. "This was your
doing, not mine. Yours!"

"No!" Robin howled back across the forest that separated them. "But
you come to Denby and I'll finish you."

A heavy silence, then the answer, calmer now. "I will come, Robin."

"Haste," Tuck urged his friends. "Will and John know where to
meet us."

"Anyone hurt?" Robin blinked at the two men. "Father?"

Beorn answered in a voice distant as Fitz-Gerald's. "They did not
touch my body."

They hurried on to meet Will and John.

I will come, Robin.

No doubting that now: today, tomorrow, next week—and next time
with a force too large to stop. Denby was forfeit now, lost to him, but
Marian and his folk might be safe. Prized, sweet Denby must be considered no more than an island now, where Sherwood was a vast sea in
which the fish had more chance than the fishermen. They were marked
men, and there would be that each of them needed from home before
leaving, John to close up his forge, Father Beorn to take up again what
weapons he might have kept over the years. This was coming from the
start. When was it not a war since William and Fitz-Gerald set foot in
England? Madmen, all of them, and how could reason live under madness? Who began it? Perhaps John loosed first, or when he himself hurled
the ax at the skittish young knight, what matter? The moment and its act
were foredoomed and himself outlaw since he stood beside Aelred at
York and saw the man's heart break and still have to carry him through
to the end.

Jolting along the swine track toward Denby, alert for any foreign sound,
Robin forced himself to think as his father taught him, the next step and
next after that. He gave thanks to God for the foresight that got Maud
and Judith out of this in time. Marian must follow by morning. When

the three of them halted to breathe, Robin told Beorn and Tuck: "Ring the bell, gather the folk at the church. Marian and I will meet you there."

"Marian?" Tuck went even paler. "God's wounds, is she not gone to Grantham?"

"She wouldn't leave without me. I'll not go without wedding her." Robin regarded the somber Beorn now retreated into his own thoughts. "Marry us today, Father."

Since she heard the clamor in the forest, far and unreal as a ghost-war, Marian had been rooted at Denby's gate, gripping at the post, and breathed deep only when Robin emerged from the trees with Will.

He's not hurt or not that much I can see, and today at least I have something to thank God for.

Will hurried on through the gate to his own bower. When Robin came into Marian's arms, she saw the swelling bruise at his temple, then his grating voice was against her cheek with half a sob in the sound. "There was mail at his throat, else he'd be dead. But I marked him good—oh, God, love. We showed him the laws. We tried to make him see."

Marian touched the swelling lump on his face. There was blood where the skin was broken. *"Ach,* you've a great—"

"It's nowt."

"You're not bad hurt, then?"

"No, nor any of the men." Still she felt the trembling of his body against hers. "But there's sheriff's men down—nine, ten, Will ent sure."

She tried to still her own fear. "What's to be done?"

Robin scrubbed a hand over his eyes. "Will's getting his needfuls. Are you ready?"

Before she could answer, the even tones of Blidworth bell rolled across the dale, calling the people to Mass. Robin turned in the direction of the sound.

"That's Beorn ringing," he said. He tried to smile at her but failed. "You'll have your wish, love. If you mourn me tomorrow, you'll be my wife tonight. Come, help me put up a wallet." When Marian hesitated, Robin took her chin in a hand that shook. "You know I've got to go. There's no turning back now."

"No," Marian affirmed steadily. "Not now."

Angharad's question hung quavering in the air as she watched Will place the arrows carefully in his quiver. "What of thy sons, Will?"

"Is it that I have no care to them? I've told you twice over the way of it.'' Will laid the quiver aside and strapped down the wallet's flap. "I could sing it for you, but it's all one. We'll to Mass and the wedding and then be gone, or the foreigners take me here.''

"They're all foreigners!'' Angharad burst out, gathering her sons to her. Eddain and Gwaun were frightened and solemn, understanding only that their father would be gone because something happened today. They couldn't think beyond that, nor could their mother.

"And because he is your master, you will go.''

"Jesus.'' Will looked at her with wondering disbelief. "Thee think it is no more than that?''

"These are my sons,'' said Angharad, a shelter over them. "That is what I know and no more. What is to become of them without their father?''

The boys were an agony in Will's sight now. They were at Norman mercy if he went. If he stayed, what else but that they could watch him hang, and wherein better for the sight? "Come to me, boys.'' He swept them up in a gentle-fierce embrace. "You mind your mam both. Eddain, you are oldest and the man of this house now. Gwaun-*bach*, you are the spear in his right hand. Take care of your mother.''

"We will, Da,'' Eddain promised gravely. Will squeezed them both tight. "Ah, look you, I will be home before you're that much bigger.''

"Sons, go outside,'' Angharad ordered. "I would speak alone with thy father. Run to the kitchen and help Marian.''

"A part of me runs with them,'' Will grieved when the boys had dutifully gone. He hunched on a stool over the wallet and goatskin bag at his feet. "It is not an easy road I take. Do not make it worse.''

"Worse?'' Angharad's feelings now were stripped to raw instinct. Born free like Will, she'd been brought slave to this place among strangers and even in time come to forget that she and hers were owned. She was not of Maud's blood. Family came first, then other loyalties. In her tongue, one asked not *Are you Briton?* but *Do you have the Blood?* Lady Maud never treated her as a slave nor did Angharad often feel like one, yet the leather collars were there about their necks until the marks became an indelible sign of ownership. Their masters were good folk as Saxons went, but she could not see why Will had to follow Robin to sure death. "He should not ask this of you. Was it you who loosed the first arrow?''

"Who knows?'' Will picked up his bundles and looped them about his shoulders. "Me or John. Someone.''

"John! I well believe that. The man would sooner drink blood than beer.''

"I said I do not know. Am I to answer for all?"

"You leave your sons for no more cause than that he owns you?"

"Woman, leave off," Will groaned, tired and hopeless. "No more of this slave prattle."

"You swore to buy us free whenever you could."

"I did and I *will*. We were born free and free we will be again. Aye, and the boys. Not a day goes by but I promise that. But there's more. When was Robin not more brother than master to me? Count the days when you and the boys went without. Count the nights, when Eddain or Gwaun was ill, that Lady Maud did not forsake her bed to watch with you over theirs. There's more than just freedom, Angharad."

He pulled her close to him, thrusting his fingers into the dark thickness of her hair. "Who owes whom and for what? There are lords who would have sold our boys on the block to any buyer with the price and heed not my pleading or your tears. Nay, you know that is true. And Robin? You think he's no heart because he shows so little of it? Think what it is that *he* walks away from."

Will foundered beneath the enormity of his feelings, just pressed his wife to him. They could talk, yes, and talk was always music between them, loving or fighting, but first and last they always touched, and the loss of this would be a blade through their hearts.

"I love *thee*, Will."

"That's the song I would hear," he whispered into her hair. "That's the strong heart I'd lack else. Fetch the boys and we will go to Mass. Rob's to wed Marian."

"*Dyw*," Angharad relaxed somewhat. "And with all else, I forgot."

"The lass will want your blessing." Will glanced wistfully at their bed. "So would I were there time for that now."

"And I." Angharad wiped at her eyes with both hands. "I am sorry that I fretted you so. I know what has to be, but must I like it?"

No, that would be no part of Will's woman. "Sherwood's that big, and all Robin knows of the place he learned from thy husband. Keep the bed warm, for you've not loved the last of me yet."

Why do I follow him? Did you not mark, Angharad, when I told of the shadow on him in clear sunlight so long ago? Who is to say what spirit whispered to his mother when she called him Robin? Who to say there is not a destiny laid on him for better or ill, gift or curse?

To Will Scatloch the world was a circle. Nothing in that round that did not close again soon or late. Men might not always perceive the shape, but perhaps in the great slow turning Robin had been chosen, balanced as he was between holy cross and an older tree. What else for Will but to follow him while the wheel turned?

John Littlerede cleaned and swept the smithy before leaving the shop he'd owned since his father died. There might be dust and cobwebs where he lived but not where he worked. Today was no different in that much methodical work done one detail at a time. Tuck joked sometimes about the slowness of John's mind but knew the truth of him. He was a man to shape one thought at a time like the steady fall of his hammer on the iron.

For all that happened this day, John felt satisfied and certain of himself. If there were shadows over him, as some said, there were none now on his intent. The world had lightened at last and he saw the straight line to follow. The war was not lost, not ended, never would until Father Beorn prayed over him. John Littlerede felt uplifted, sustained, and secure.

His great, thick body moved with deceptive slowness as he swept the floor. John never wasted more strength on a task than it required, one of the first lessons learned from his father. He wiped the hearth clean and emptied the troughs of standing water, swept every particle of loose dirt and broken nail from between the cobblestones of the traverse where he shoed horses, then oiled each tool and hung it in its proper place. Once he thought his oldest son would learn the smithy in time, but that son was gone now along with his wife and the other children, and after that the notion of an apprentice just didn't appeal to John. Some boy botching his work or talking too much, someone new intruding in this space somehow shrunk now to fit just him. Beorn said he was set in his ways, and John allowed that might be true. After a certain age, a man did not take easily to change. The business with Marian was a disappointment, but John expected he could go to her wedding today and wish her well with a whole heart. Being older made rejection easier to bear, not to mention the prospect of starting a new family at his age. A man should be young for that, green enough not to see too much of what could happen. Complications weren't attractive to John now; he leaned to simplicity.

Freda—if his doings with her were sinful, they were simple as well. Freda didn't ask anything of him beyond what he was willing to share, and that was little enough these late years. Curious how a man got in the habit of closing off parts of himself, showing less and less to visitors. He was almost as old as Freda's father, but Ceolred the taverner wasn't good to his daughter, treated her like a stalled ox and took a strap to her more than needed. So perhaps when Freda got in the habit of passing a word with John at the smithy door—and then quite naturally more than a word—well, John supposed she was just wanting something her da never spared her. No more but no less. They were simple and made each other content if not happy. John was not a sad man, just that he had to think far back, sift through years and faces to remember happiness and then rub the dust away to see it clear. Bargainwise, he wasn't asking more than contentment of Freda, but if a child came of it, he might marry her in his good time. A good healthy girl and for sure easier to be with than Marian, come to that. Marian would have wrinkled her nose at the dust and dirt in his house, and why did he live like a pig when there wasn't a speck where he worked? All his pride had gone into the one after his wife died, leaving the rest to go fallow. Marian would have sensed so many locked rooms in him, dark places where John himself stumbled over shapes he could only guess at, with sharp corners that cut him sometimes. Better this way.

She said no, not with the pity that hurts a man, but like an honor she couldn't accept. The girl has wit enough, but women's wits ent for war, and war is what I've got this day, right enough.

Today the dark rooms in his soul lit up so brightly that even blind Wystan could see what they'd held since Hastings. Wystan would be in the dark until he died, but like a lamp passing from one room to another, that which left him unseeing lit John's way clearly now.

The church bell began to ring for Mass with a mellow, unhurried chime. That would be Father Beorn on the rope, calling his folk perhaps for his last time, putting all the leftover love from other Masses into his arm.

John removed his ancient leather apron. He'd never thought to get a new one, scorched and sour with old sweat though it was, the bottom fringe shiny with filings from years of wiping down the anvil. His apron was as familiar as the rest of his tools, slit just right for shoeing, no more to be discarded than friends like Wystan or Tuck or the memory of Lord Aelred. John folded the leather into a neat square, laid it on the clean hearth, then took up his bow, quiver, and wallet, closing the smithy door behind him. He paused with his hand on the latch, listening to the sound of the bell shimmer in the late afternoon air, remembering bells at Sandwich four summers gone, when the shire fyrd waited with King Harold for the Norman ships that didn't come until summer turned to autumn. . . .

* * *

William did not quite remember me. True, he ent used to recollecting blacksmiths, but you'd think a man big as himself would stay in mind. Last month when he heard Mass in Blidworth, I was in the churchyard passing the time of day with Freda when William came out of the porch with Earl Waltheof and passed me close by, and so I had my second and closer sight of Willy Bastard: fit enough but bandy-legged something fierce from all those years on a horse, and his belly bigger than when we met at Hastings. Well then, he looked at me casual-like in passing —then stops and points me out to the earl, who does the asking for him.

"Fellow, the king wishes to know where he has seen you before."

Well, deep in my heart and my good sense, I knew it wouldn't pay me to say, so I answered very polite and careful. "I do a deal of farriering about the shire, lord, and one man shoeing a horse looks much like another."

William took the measure of me up and down summ'at, then went to his horse and on to Denby. Right shrewd to get around that one so neat. The jest carried Wystan and me through more than one cup down the Queen's that night. But the best of it: Wystan squints at me with his beard full of beer foam and says, "Don't take on, Johnny. Like as not Bastard don't recall me either."

No, he would not; been nigh to four years now. William would remember only the long line of us waiting for his army on the ridge. Eight thousand of us, Lord Aelred reckoned later, the housecarls of Wessex at the center and those of the earls Gyrth and Leofwine to the left and right. Spread out from them on either side, like great war wings, the shire fyrds like ours and a fringe of village men who always come to a battle with no more than pitchforks and clubs and the like. A wall of us eight men deep, eight hundred yards long. Before we closed ranks behind the carls' shields on that clear, cold morning, Wystan and I could see south toward Hastings and the low marsh on our right, sun glinting off the spearheads of the foreign knights as they spread out over the hill south of us, wheeling and trotting this way and that, breaking into three great blocks of men and horses and iron.

That was early in the day before we thought we could lose. Their archers started out for us, but we just laughed at them and ducked under our shields. Then the foot soldiers came charging in and we threw them back too. Once men on foot come that close, it's clumps of little battles all along the line, men running here and there to down someone and grab his weapon, but most commonly there were Wystan and me behind the shield wall, packed in close and thrusting our spears at what we could see, which weren't always that much, I can tell you.

The big horses were the worst, I do think, for we'd never faced their like before. Sometimes our shield wall broke under their charging weight and the knights got in among us to do fearsome damage before getting out or we killed them. With the broad ax of a fallen carl, Wystan did summ'at that day, no mistake.

Thinking back on the matter, we should have held in line, but when you stand in close ranks hour on hour, you get sick of defending and keen to attack. First you're almighty afeared, but when that passes you're madder than a boar hog beset by hounds, mad enough so that when the chance comes, when the enemy makes a mistake and gives you an opening—

Well past noon by then and the slope below us thick as daisies with arrow shafts. They came again, archers first, stepping over their own dead, picking up arrows as they came and loosing at us from close as fifty paces. We were safe enough, but that's a wicked sound, arrows flying in and over you. Then the foot soldiers came through the archers, yelling at us with the knights close behind them, all of them hungry to get at us. That was the rub of it. That was their mistake. Whatever the foot was to do by way of breaking our line, the horsemen didn't give them enough time but came in like thunder, doing more damage among their own than us. The confusion was something terrible before they broke off and ran back. We didn't hear any order, mind, didn't wait for one, just all of a sudden a great host of us were chasing them down the slope, paying them back for a change, cutting them down like barley at harvest. That's when I stopped to pick up the Norman mace and maybe catch a breath, stared around and saw too many things at once. There was Wystan close with the spear in his fist, blood on his face and an eye red as a week on whiskey, pointing across the valley—

"God a-mighty, John—*see!*"

So I did. What frighted me most was that no more than a hundred of us had run out after the foreigners; the rest of our line stood like a wall on the ridge and now there was a river, a proper flood of Norman horse riding out to cut us off, pushing through their own retreating foot soldiers, no mind if they trampled them down.

Then I saw what Wystan pointed at: William himself, riding straight at the two of us through his own men, roaring at them to mark him. He'd stripped the helmet from his head to show them he weren't dead and, like, to put some heart back into them for another go at us. He was that

close to Wystan and me, if we'd had just one good bow and one shaft
between us—but we did not. Just Wystan's spear and me swinging that
Norman mace, a ball of iron on a chain, but the same notion lit on both
of us like the word of God. There was great William kicking his horse
through a clout of men running away, then out in the clear and seeing
us coming at him. He reined up so sharp that the horse's rump dropped
low and the hoofs dug in, dirt flying up in my face. Wystan flung the
spear true as gospel; he'd likely have killed a slower man, but William
took the spear in the center of his shield, too busy to mark me on his off
side. I put all of me behind the mace and blessed that horse of his right
between the eyes. Down went the horse one way and his brains another,
and then everything happened too fast to sort out any one part of it.

Wystan bawled at me: Look sharp or we'd be cut off. By then William
was clear of his late horse and staring around, flustered as myself. I just
yelled at him—"Here, Bastard!"—slung the mace at him and cut along
back up the hill after Wystan, and smartly too, no use to die out there
alone. We had good luck: A few of us got back to the line. Most didn't,
got cut off by the horsemen and had to knot together on a little hillock
down below. They couldn't hold, not the few of them against so many,
but nowt we could do for them except thank God we got back.

The sun moved west while our line shrank but didn't break. No great
matter that Willy Bastard can't quite remember me. When you think on
it—what with having horses knocked out from under him and almost
being speared through by Earl Gyrth himself, I heard, and still liable to
lose the day—well, he had summ'at else to occupy his mind. Come to
that, if a duke is unhorsed by an earl and a smith, he'd sooner remember
the earl, I reckon.

When did the notion take us that we might lose, were losing? Late, I
guess, when the light was going and our lines shrank, the sky red as
half-heated iron in the west and the light on the marshes like blood on
steel and so much blood on the slope below us that horses could hardly
climb the hill for slipping in it. We knew that men were deserting all
around us, trying to get away and home in the dark, but the king's carls
rallied by the two flags to the end. Then it was, I remember, Lord Aelred
strode down the line of the shire fyrd, what was left of us, his mail torn,
helmet gone, and shield split—

"Fall back! We're to form another line before the forest. Shire men,
follow me and fall back."

Growing darker as I ran with the others after Aelred, and the thought took me that I hadn't seen Wystan. When I stopped to look about for him, what with the light nigh gone, back on the ridge I saw nowt but the shape of one flag still standing and under it a knot of shapes struggling like eels in a barrel, and couldn't tell our men from the Normans. Then the last flag wobbled on its staff and went down.

Is King Harold dead then?

I've never had Lord Aelred's wit to know all of what happened that day or what led us so long a road to this one, but looking back toward that ridge, and the shire men running past me, that's when God's shadow fell over part of me and a great light over the rest. I mean—why was *I* there but that Thane Aelred thought it right to follow the king? And why was my own lord there when he'd so often gone against Harold in arms as well as words, but that this time Aelred had pieced it out careful in his mind and decided the king was right?

That's what darkens me, what has fed my anger from Hastings until now. Not that we lost, nor because London and Winchester and the rest gave in so *tame* afterward—all those fat, rich aldermen thinking of themselves—but four shameful years of knowing you've done us a great wrong, William. My wife called the thoughts blasphemy and prayed that God would forgive me. No need, woman. God and I made the same judgment and it was that simple. *I* think you're wrong, William. You've done *me* a great wrong—me, John Littlerede of Blidworth. That's what you'll never understand, you and your Norman lot, that one blacksmith could know you're a bloody thief and write his own warrant on your soul. Robin feels the same, for he saw a bit of my war at York. He might have saved his skin like the tame ones, might have given Much to the sheriff except that the same wrong sticks in his throat as in mine. I wouldn't follow him else. We haven't lost, William, just shifted ground to form a new line as Aelred did.

But then, out of that last struggle on the ridge, a familiar mite of a shape came scurrying down toward me—*John! Hoch, John!*—with something flapping over his shoulder like a cloak too big for the man.

"Wystan, is that you?"

"Who else?" He stumbled up to me, dead for want of breath but grinning like a cat fallen into a bucket of Devonshire cream. Good lord—and then I saw what he carried. "God's holy blood, Wystan, what have y'done?"

He'll never see again, but in that sunset—oh, Wystan's eyes were wild, shining. "I couldn't let them take this."

"But that is the king's—"

"The king's dead," he panted. "And me close to it. Let me breathe. . . ."

For a little space then, before we ran on to stand with Aelred before the forest and that lovely ravine where William lost so many more horses before the end came—I took the grand, rich material in my hands where it furled over Wystan's shoulder. Deep blue it would be in sunlight, but black now in the night falling around us, the fine gold thread and the jewels gleaming in the the last of the light. . . .

17

SINCE HE WAS a boy squire who dreamed of spurs and a sire before his name, Ralf had taken punishment as the price of rank. The accolade of knighthood itself, conferred with a sword, was a symbolic blow, the last he must suffer without redress. He took the scars, endured the broken bones and worse, still counting himself fortunate not to have been disfigured. There were many vavasors with half a nose or half their teeth behind scarred lips, some with half a face. Now there was not even that small vanity to call his own. When they staunched the blood and washed the deep knife wound, Ralf saw the red line that marked him from jaw to the mutilated bridge of his nose. The wound was bone-deep; it would turn white in time but never fade. Robin of Sherwood had marked him for life, an added incentive to hang the outlaw before the year ended.

"Give thanks," Père Huger counseled out of bitter experience and a shoulder rubbled at Hastings. "This is not the worst."

"No." Ralf put away the mirror with the finality of a man who would not often resort to it again. "Sire Raimond endures more pain, to be sure. *Tiens:* we will occupy Denby by the end of this week. The king must know what has happened. You will write for me and see the letter off early tomorrow for Grantham."

The letter sped to the royal residence, a flat and factual report: the sheriff's attempt to enforce William's law, Denby's resistance, good men murdered from ambush, others injured, Ralf's intent to confiscate Denby for the crown. A price on the head of Edward Aelredson, called Robin, equal to twice the value of the outlawed thane's fief:

> —for the outlaw Aelredson and others of unknown number, among whom I cite the slave Scatloch who is ever close to his master, and most particularly one Beorn, priest of Blidworth church, whom the bishop of Nottingham has deemed unfit for holy orders. This priest with his own hand killed at least one officer. . . .

When Father Beorn entered the church, he greeted and gently shouldered his way through most of the folk of Denby and Blidworth. He missed one or two faces but could account for almost all the absent. Alcuin and Ethelwold were in Grantham, Minna tending to Wystan. Beorn would stop to say good-bye and bless the invalid before following Robin into the forest. For the rest they filled the small nave of his church, their worn shoes and coarse woolen foot wrappings, fresh from the fields, muddying the smooth-worn flagstones. Barefooted children, restless and struggling against their mothers' restraint, giggled and poked at each other or escaped briefly to run about before recapture and a smart rap on their ragged rumps—"You mind, now!"

As he stepped up into the small choristry and faced his congregation, he saw John Littlerede enter to stand in the rear of the nave. Robin and Marian waited close to the altar, neither dressed for the celebration their wedding should have been. Close behind each of them, man to man, woman to woman, were Will and Angharad, their boys on either side and solemnly subdued as their parents had strictly warned them to be. Tuck waited near the great lectern from which he usually spoke the responses at every service. For this Mass, possibly his last, Beorn had attired himself in full canonicals. His beefy sexton was turned out in his cleanest and least-patched surplice. On his own, Tuck had troubled some generous householder for a fresh loaf of good wheaten bread which lay on the altar now beside the Communion wine and the freshly burnished silver cup. With a pang of humility, Beorn wondered if he himself were as ready and fit for Mass as his sexton. White rage and the deep, conflicted guilt in his own heart were shabby colors to unfurl in a communion with God.

"*In Nomine Patris.*" Beorn signed the cross. "*Et Filii et Spiritus Sancti.*"

"Amen."

He spoke the *Gratia* in Latin, Tuck answering in English—not the purest form of ritual, but Tuck's Latin was fragmentary and none of the congregation knew any. The unlettered but earnest sexton was taking special care in his office today, mindful of his thick shire accent and overenunciating the responses.

"The grace and peace of God our Father and the Lord Jesus Christ be with you."

"And also with you," intoned Tuck.

As his tongue flowed through the familiar Penitential, the smoldering wrath in Beorn's troubled mind rose up again: Why did he tell his folk to recall their sins when William and his kind should be kneeling here for absolution in their place?

"Kyrie eleison."

"Christe, eleison." Lord have mercy. Christ have mercy.

I will remember this day and all of you—the still, warm air, sun streaming like a benediction through the small, high west windows. His folk mumbling their responses, always uncomfortable to be singled out by God. Robin and Marian hand in hand, tomorrow's shadow already on them today. *But no*, Beorn decided, *I am in no fit state to give Communion.* If he were old Micah or Jeremiah, apt to scorch, scorn, and wither with a word, he would blast every Norman who followed their duke to England, exact every penny in silver and suffering they had cost these folk whom he loved beyond his oath to God, and send every shave-headed one of them to hell. There was his own conflict. The Church was of all nations and none; wherein was he the instrument of vengeance? Yet, try as he might to remember that truth, between the God of William and God weeping for Blidworth flowed an English Channel, and Beorn could not, perhaps would never, reconcile himself to that. To that extent this day he was less of a priest.

So be it.

For the Gospel reading he had chosen a passage well suited to their troubles. Beorn went to the lectern where Tuck had laid open the great iron-clasped book to the passage he wanted.

"I will read today from the book of the prophet Micah who lived in the days of Isaiah. It is a good text for us now because Micah was as angry as I am when he wrote this and for much the same cause. I won't preach obedience to the Church when vavasor-barons become bishops, putting off only their swords but not their avarice. I won't tell you to be meek when foreigners use samite cloth to wipe our blood off their hands. No, God help me, I can't do that."

Beorn bent his head over the text. "Woe to those who plan iniquity and work evil on their couches. They covet fields and seize them; houses, and they take them; they cheat an owner of his house, a man of his inheritance. Therefore, thus says the Lord: 'Behold, I am planning against this race an evil from which you shall not withdraw your necks.' ''

Beorn closed the heavy book and fastened the clasp. "I know that is a short reading, but the best I could choose with so little time and so much confusion in my heart. My people, I ask myself now: Am I fit to speak the word and the promise of God to you?"

"Yes," Robin answered for all of them to hear. "No man better, whatever's happened. They backed us into a corner, Father. We had to fight."

"Edward," the priest reproved gently, "this is God's house and I His porter. Let me say in my own manner what must be said." Looking out over his folk, Beorn searched for the usual homily with which he customarily illustrated for them the meaning of the day's reading in their own terms. Little had occurred to him but two half-remembered tales, only one of them Christian, yet no others so well served his mind and heart now.

"There has always been a moment in the Mass when I ask your special prayers for one of our own in need. Let you then pray for Wystan. Minna requests that those who have clean linen to spare, she is in need of bandage. As well, I have always asked your prayers for myself. This day I beg them. What Lord Edward may not have told you is that I killed a man today."

Little John growled the sentiment from the rear of the nave. "Slowly, I hope."

"It's not a joke!" Beorn flared back at him. "For me it is desecration. What I took up in place of the sword is a thousand-fold heavier—" Beorn checked himself: No, this was not what he wanted to say. "Saving Wystan, there is no soul on Denby land more needful of your prayers than myself. And this first tale will be the picture of it.

"There was a king in ancient Greece who, when an unknown evil blighted his people, heard a message from God that the evil was of his city itself and must be purged before heaven would heed them again. The king was strong and righteous and promised with all his heart to root out the evil wherever it lay, in whatever house high or low—only to find that *he* was the evil and had brought it with him to the throne. His own pride had wrought this evil in the guise of good. Disgraced, blinded by his own hand, the proud king saw then that he had always been blind in believing he could see so far and take so much upon himself. So the wretch went out from his people to wander the road as a beggar.

"I remember the last words of the tale," Beorn said. "Until this day I did not understand them for they held no mirror to my face among others. Something like: Let no man count himself fortunate until he has passed unscathed through all his days."

Father Beorn rested his elbows on the lectern, speaking plainly as one man to friends. "Well, here I am, very like unto that miserable man in his blundering righteousness. Beyond the bald fact, I can't understand what's happened, but when the time came, I found the evil within me. The sword which I thought had been cast aside was still in my hand. A moment came today when Christ rose up before me and asked whom I truly served. I sent him away and made my choice. Pray for me, then. As I stand here before you, the most sinful among you is closer to Grace than I."

"Father, don't take this on yourself."

Marian's gentle admonition startled Beorn. Beneath the chaplet of wild flowers hastily woven by Angharad, the girl's face was sweetly grave. "Remember what we have just asked of God, that He have mercy. Have you not always promised He would?"

"True. That is . . . true, Marian." Beorn was grateful for the simple balm of reassurance, though he would not open all of his fear to Marian who needed happiness now as much as Wystan needed new bandages and comforting. The sword with which he struck today left a deeper wound in Beorn than he dealt. *In the sight of God, I am His always but may be cast out by His Church now. I saw this coming far back but cringed from the question.* Father God, Mother Church: Could a priest or any devout man revere one as the Agamemnon-father of his spiritual being and turn on the mother as compromised Clytemnestra? That conflict laid Orestes and Beorn alike bare to the Furies.

"There is the second tale of which I am minded today," Beorn told his congregation. "In the days of the Danelaw, there was a poor mercer of York who sold good cloth in honest measure and for his virtues suffered Job's trials without Job's steadfast nature."

The mercer tried not to sin but nothing fell right for him. Dishonest competitors drove him to despair and almost to ruin. The Danes, having stolen most of their own wares, sold them in York for less than he could, money-shavers cheated him in exchange. Clearly, to survive he must become a thief himself, or so it seemed to the beset mercer. So out of bitterness and frustration, he yielded to the promptings of Satan. To feed his family, he first cut his cloth to a little less than the legal clothyard. He represented his profit as much smaller than it was, haggled with the moneyers and watched their balances with an eye going sharp as their own, then began to shave silver from the coins he took in. Naturally, the mercer throve in worldly goods, one questionable practice leading ever downward to a sharper one as to the point of a sword, but so gradually that the man never noticed when the wounds from the wrongs done to him had healed and callused over with wrongs done by him to others. Eventually, thriving in avarice now habitual as breathing, the mercer owned nine out of ten pence in York, while the tenth was owed to him or else he was scheming to get it.

The time came when the mercer, now a great merchant, was not young anymore and mindful of Jesus' parable of the rich man and the needle's eye. He prudently resolved to make amends, but the sinful habits of a lifetime were thick on him as dirt on a beggar. No matter what the man did, he made more profit than he could spend or give away. If he wrote off one man's debt, another paid him early. If he gave lavishly to the poor, his shrewd habits in trade recovered threefold the amount. Sickness and then impending death hastened his failing quest. On the day the merchant died, he reckoned he had spent full half of his life buried in sin, the rest in digging out of it with an unfit soul for a spade, and not a day's peace in the lot.

The merchant expected none but Satan to take him on the spot, but the messenger who came appeared no more than a young shire clerk: competent and conscientious, not about to overlook one jot of discrepancy in the merchant's smudged ledger.

"Well, then," the angel allowed, "you've made a proper muck of your life. Can you think of one good reason for God to smile on you?"

The merchant saw for the first time the true state of his spirit—ragged, shoeless as a beggar, hands black with the grime of his avarice. He could feel on his brow, all over him, the dust of the world caked gritty with the sweat of greed. In all honesty he could not find one argument for mercy.

"But I tried," was his sole and feeble defense. "When I found the way again, I did try, but now the dust of the world is so thick on me, God could write His own judgment on my face, it's that black."

The angel considered this. Here was a man who dealt all his life in weights and measures; surely judgment should employ as careful a balance. This merchant flatly failed the test of faith and his virtues came sadly late. On the other hand, he *had* tried to make amends the only way a Saxon knew how, be it commerce or conscience, and that was down to the penny. As his kind legally made nice distinction between free and half-free men, this man was half damned.

"Or half saved," the merchant urged, putting the best face on a sorry truth. He was not altogether fit for paradise, but then again hardly justice to reject him completely. Only half a case, the angel perceived, but if Englishmen could grant him his due by plain reason, certainly God would.

The angel scribe put his finger to the merchant's brow and, in the thick dust that dimmed it, wrote one word: *inasmuch*.

Yes, Beorn felt as his flock sighed in understanding and satisfaction, the tale was a good one for today. God would ever find the clean spot in the grime, the one bright leaf of good intent however thick the forest of error.

"Then let God see through our errors to the justice of our intent and to the good we do," the priest concluded. "And let His angel write upon us, as upon the mercer of York, that one word, *inasmuch*. Amen.

"Before we celebrate the Eucharist, I will ask you all to remain after Mass to witness the marriage of Lord Edward and Godifigu Marian, and to remember that whatever befalls Denby, he is your sworn lord and she your lady. And remember to pray for all of us who must leave you today."

Father Beorn turned to his altar. "Let us worship."

Credo in unum deum, Patrem omnipotentum, factorem caeli et terrae.

At a sign from Tuck, some of the women of Blidworth shyly came forward with small bundles of food and other needfuls donated from every household. Some were for Wystan and Minna. Most were wrapped for traveling to go with Robin, Father Beorn, and all the good men outlawed where good laws existed no longer.

Father Beorn raised his hands over the altar as Tuck rang the small sancting bell.

18

THEY HAD THIS night and after that, since no one knew God's will, there might be nothing else. The light over their wedding day was soft at evening, the sun barely dipping below the horizon to become a long gloaming. To Marian the light and the time were magic and all the more precious for being so brief.

Hand-in-hand they followed the rill through the forest and across open meadow to where Holy Pool rose out of the ground in a natural basin of limestone hidden on all sides by briar and vine that grew almost to the water's edge where a little stone saint, weatherworn beyond recognition, signed the Trinity over the pool. About its base were littered the dried remains of food offerings.

"What saint is this, Robin?"

He couldn't say rightly, no one could. Before his grandfather's time, the older folk of Blidworth remembered, there had been a wooden figure guarding the pool, carved from the heartwood of oak. Heathen or Christian, no one remembered, though offerings were still left. Old god or saint, neither Brihtnoth nor Aelred saw any reason to intrude on custom hallowed by time. When Robin was learning the forest, Holy Pool and its stone guardian were as much a part of Denby faith as the oath tree.

"It belongs here, Marian. As you do."

She nestled her head against his shoulder. "Yes."

Not really dark yet, just a softer light to evening. *Thank you*, she prayed to God and Mary and the little stone saint, *for giving us this much at least, this one night to call our own.* Robin said the oaks and beeches here had never been cut for timber. Most were growing before the Vikings came. They shadowed the eerie light over the pool and made Marian feel as if she were still in church or at least watched over. Heavy, ancient boughs leaning over them like God and His angels warming their happiness with a soft blanket, the silence about them rustling with Robin's clothes as he undressed behind her, and her own beating heart. As Marian slipped out of her gown, she heard Robin splash into the pool.

She was virgin as the forest about her, eager and only a little shy, enough to turn away from him when she undressed. "Is it cold, then?"

Robin thrashed about, sputtering. "Ent that bad once you're in."

Marian dropped her shift and stepped out of her shoes, turning. Robin's back was to her, water up to his narrow hips as he splashed himself vigorously: brown to an abrupt line about his waist from working in the fields, muscles not thick-bunched from violent effort but those of a farmer used to working all day with no wasted effort or leaning for years into a six-foot bowstave. *Mine now, mine by right.* Her hand went out toward the beauty of him—then she gasped aloud.

Robin laughed at her without turning about. "Said it was cold."

Not the shock of the water as she stepped into the pool but the image of another body, whiter, heavier, and scarred like a penitent gone mad with self-mutilation. No—Marian tried to erase the image and the fear. He was outlaw now. That other body would be hunting this smooth one in her keeping, to mark or kill him. Even if Robin lived to come back to her, there might come a day when she tended his dear body in the same bed as the other or on the bare forest earth, when she must cut away bloody linen to see him scarred or bone-broken or—

"Robin!"

Did he hear the terror in her voice? He turned, reaching for her and they came together, the sweet shock of their flesh warm and sudden against the frigid water, Robin's mouth finding hers, then her cheek and shoulder. "You're not half shivering."

"Just the cold," she lied.

"Got to go in all at once. Ready?"

"I am not." Marian squirmed in his arms. "Don't, Rob."

He swooped and caught the slenderness of her up in his arms. "Yes, you are."

"Don't you dare, I hate that—"

"And down we go!"

"No, please, it's ice."

Better to shriek at that than colder fears. Marian whooped as Robin collapsed up to his neck with her in his arms, and the shock of the water tingling their skins as their mouths melted together was warmer than the fear Marian couldn't share with her husband. Not this night, not until fear was in the past and they were safe at Denby again.

They had only this evening that darkened so slowly that a hawk's eye could not mark the change. Marian didn't want to see time passing, sand running down her small glass. Here in the sacred clearing she'd seen only once before, by the small fire in the old wattle hut, they had all the light needed. Beyond the fire the walls of the hut were darkening, a mercy obscuring the spot near the entrance where their two bundles lay ready to go separate ways in the morning.

With Robin bending over her, Marian stirred slightly on the sheepskins that covered their marriage pallet. No, she would not think on morning or of hours left or sands or candles melting down, nothing beyond this moment when they rested after loving, when she looked up into her lover's face and lost herself there willingly. She was not shy with him; that passed at Holy Pool. When they waded out, laughing and shivering, hungry for each other, they clung together, bare and playful as young otters.

She must remember every moment to be treasured later—like this heartbeat passing now, Robin tracing a finger slowly across her brow and down her cheek to the still-damp tangle of hair about her breasts. And the warmth rising, responding to his touch like the drowsy benediction of falling asleep after a day in the sun, and how that warmth, rather than softening to sleep, was rising to heat again. But even that was to come. She caught at *this* moment to be emptied of its sweetness, purring with a kitten's contentment to feel Robin's mouth moving over her breasts and the smooth planes of her stomach.

"Were you pleased when the folk called you *Hlaefdige?*"

"Oh, I was." Another priceless *then* building to magical *now*. Kneeling with Robin while Father Beorn looped the embroidered cord over their clasped hands, then the folk crowding about them, and being dazed by the sudden reality of what she'd dared to do, a bright-burnished surface with fear and desperation eating away at each moment. Small gifts of food pressed upon her, barely spared but not grudged today, and the older wives with sage advice about the night to come, woman-wisdom older than Lilith or Eve. There was the holy relic from Gudrun, a toenail from some saint or other, and the other charm that Angharad pressed into her palm with a shush-and-whisper: "Don't let the good Father be seeing this, but hide it beneath your pillow tonight."

Marian knew what they asked without words in return. She was raised over and apart from them now. Early tomorrow she would make the other vow on the bargain oak with Robin, and then his men would come for him. . . .

No, it's not time yet, not even night.

But it was, Robin no more than a dim shape over her in the firelight, his cheek a flickering profile and mostly darkness under her fingers. Time ran away too fast. She must remember everything about tonight, and afterward regretted being so drowned in each delirious moment that vanished even as she savored it, that she could recall so little out of the whole and that little fading, impossible to choose, as the memory of one flower from a field sewn thick with beauty. Yet sometimes later at Grantham the swirl of impressions cleared and Marian could lift one clear moment from the rush of images and treasure it. Lying still with her head on Robin's shoulder, breathing the male scent of him mixed now with her own. He murmured something in the darkness. Marian stirred and turned on her back, then Robin was over her with a fierce tenderness.

"I feel—"

She traced a finger slowly over his lips. "What?"

"I want to pray to you," he whispered. "No, to pray for you like a grace or a blessing taken from me, and I must beg to have it back. I was frighted enough before, but now that there's us—"

His head was bent over her. Marian felt the tiny, wet spot of warmth fall on her nipple: one tear, and in the firelight the trail of it glistening down Robin's cheek. Something gasped silently in Marian and she reached for him. He needed, and in that need opened himself to her as she to him, as all creatures did when they trusted. The need became their loving prayer, less desperate but more complete this time. Marian cried out sharply once, not because Robin hurt her but because in one moment she pierced him as well, entered and nestled in him. In the middle of it all she was suddenly fiercer than Robin, trembling, raking his back with her nails.

"My mark on you," she gasped against his own mouth. *"Mine."*

It is tomorrow I'll flinch from, when he walks away with Will and the others and I must ride the other way. I won't look back, won't call to him or search him out until I can't tell the green of his cloak from the forest, like a body going into the grave. No, I can't do that. Holy Mary, how brave must I be?

As much as leaving took, then. The day would come and the parting and all that followed. She would kneel to the wise queen and not let Matilda or any outlander see the wound or their guilt smoldering in her eyes. But that wasn't now, not yet. Marian writhed her body against the hardness of Robin's to join inseparably and make them one. She tore at him, the heat and the wonderful trembling rising deep in her, and at last there was no time at all, the magic had defeated time and wiped it all away.

Robin woke when there was still no light at all beyond the hut entrance and only a feeble glow from the small fire. Marian slept on her back beside him, the blanket flung aside in sleep, one hand across her brow. He stretched and sat up, langorous, aching sweetly from the wildness of their lovemaking. His back stung from Marian's nails; he wondered if he'd hurt her, though she never said. They were drunk on each other for hours.

He listened and let the forest tell the time. There always came this hush when all nocturnal creatures were back in nest or burrow. First this heavy silence as the rag-end of night slid by, then a wind whispering through Sherwood as a sleeper inhales and sighs before waking, and then the birds piping from bough to bough before black lightened to grey. When he and Will hunted far from Denby and slept in the forest, this hovering silence, like a missed heartbeat or the world holding its breath, always woke Robin.

A lonely time of day, night dying and day not yet born. Even old Robin Goodfellow could be lonely now. Let him, for he lives beyond time. I'm with her and yet already gone and aching with the loss.

They'd taken each other again and again last night, lord only knew when they finally fell asleep, the wildness as much fear as desire. Robin tried to think beyond tomorrow to an impossible time when they could live with no troubles but children and crops. It would be sweet to love Marian and know that day coming swiftly as it did now meant only sunlight and not a part of her to be torn from him. He'd tried in the night's loving to hold one thing fast and escape from something else. The bright images flashing through his hunger and shuddering release were not all of Marian; there were Aelred and Maud, Father Beorn looming over him and Marian as they knelt to be wed, Will striding beside him—even Fitz-Gerald and that red instant before Beorn pulled him off the Norman, when he could have killed the man, sung over his bleeding, and even taken his scalp.

Death and loving: Strange when you opened up so to join with a woman, how so much else flooded in, pressed from the bowstave of too-swift morning. In the dark Robin could still see the line at Marian's throat and on her arms where sun-browned skin met the whiter rest: the small, delicate breasts, the long body and gangling, coltish legs. There was the morning-gift ready in his wallet—oh, but he meant to find her a cat, promised himself he would.

Already they come between us. What have I married her to and what else could I do?

The skin on his thigh, moist where it lay against Marian's, felt the cool change in the air. Robin heard now the slight rustling among the oaks about the clearing. He slid down beside Marian, pulling the blanket over both of them, staring into the darkness over the soft outline of her hair. When they were home again, when Marian could run once more to welcome him at Denby's gate, he would come singing, by God he would, with a basket, a barrel of cats for her to choose from or keep them all if she pleased, and he would feast on the very sight of her happiness.

There—he heard it now: the first shrill birds challenging each other from bough to bough. Marian's body swelled with a breath like the wind bringing the day. She turned over, still asleep into Robin's arms with a drowsy burrowing against him.

". . . not time yet."

"No." But already there was more light—and thank God for one more day, Robin made bitter prayer. How little a man needed to be happy. All over England, rich or poor, men were waking like this next to their wives, but at day's end luckier men could turn home to croft or hall knowing she would be waiting with the night and so much tenderness to come. No, with all due reverence, God might have managed matters more conveniently.

"Marian?"

She buried her face in the warmth of his throat. "Mmm. . . ."

He tried to blend the magical creature afire in his arms last night and the one he seemed to become in loving her, with the real two of them lying here now, as if today were an ordinary span between cockcrow and Compline, requiring no more of them than any other day. "Where is a word wise enough?"

Her hand moved up his stomach and over his chest. "For what?" she whispered sleepily.

"What I feel. If I said that I love you, that wouldn't half—" Robin checked himself, remembering how she stopped him once from uttering the word they both meant but she feared. Marian helped him now, her mouth breathing close to his.

"I know. I'm afraid yet, but I must say *love* now and believe it because that's all I have for all the days I won't have you." Marian's eyes widened with awareness, roved upward in the growing light. "Like your mum's blue linen, we're out of time."

"Not yet, love." Robin rose from their low pallet and searched out something from his wallet. Marian yawned and turned over to watch him with a smile of pleasure. "Aye, Robin, but you're a fair sight for a woman at morning."

"Time for this." Robin brought the gift to her. To the fourth finger of Marian's left hand he fitted the ring Maud left him. "Aelred gave this to Maud on their first morning."

The ring was a treasure of the goldsmith's art, two perfectly twined serpents, each with the other's tail clamped in a finely articulated mouth. Such rings were given when a man could afford them, not a token of worldly goods endowed but a simple gift to a bride who pleased her husband on their wedding night.

Marian was profoundly touched. "She always wore this. Not a thing in her house she loved more."

Robin kissed the finger and the ring. "That's why she left it for you." Then with a trace of sudden shyness: "You did well please me."

"This is so good of her."

"And not me? I'm the one pleased."

"Mum said this was a magic place."

"Said it often," Robin remembered. "I've known it all my life but never why until now. Come." He kissed her lightly and rose again. "It's time to go to the tree."

Robin pulled on the green linen trews and laced up the cross garters. The trews fitted tight last year but wear and washing had loosened them. He tied his shoes and ducked out of the hut, bare to the waist. Morning was still grey but through the eastern trees the sky was brightening to a clear line of sunlight. Will and the others were on their way or would be soon.

Will, stay away. Sun, stand still, time stop.

Marian knelt by the rill, bare as a fawn, combing the bright gold of her hair over her shoulders in long, graceful strokes. When she stood up, still working the comb, the long line of her body ivory against the deep green of the forest, Robin felt a rush of pleasure and pain that her flesh said and meant so much more to him now than yesterday and in a strange new tongue. *Go away, all of you,* he hated in that unreasonable moment. *I'm not beholden to any of you—just me and Marian, and all I want is to live with her. Don't hang your lives on me. Go away and let us live.*

With the passion of his wish, Robin winced at the impossibility. Life would not allow that clear casting off, nor was he bred to it anymore than Ralf Fitz-Gerald understood the soil he confiscated for his king. Robin forced his mind back to something simple: Marian slipping into the trousers she would wear under her shift for the ride to Grantham on Beorn's old mare. She stood up and dropped the shift over her head in an unconsciously feminine movement that flushed deep beyond desire in Robin. She put on the loose linen kirtle over the shift and came to him where he waited at the bargain oak.

"Just a little sting, no more," he promised tenderly, showing her the knife. "I honed the blade like a razor, it's ever so sharp . . . Marian? What is it?"

She gazed up at him with the bright beginning of tears and a door opened wide in her at last. "No . . . no, I was so busy counting the dear things I've lost, I couldn't let you—not even you—say *love* for fear I'd lose that. Just now by the rill, I knew what a scared little ninny I am, getting ready to be scared to live."

Marian held out her hand to Robin and the knife. "Take my blood with yours. Take it for the bargain. If there's no more than this, I love you. If there are days without you or even years, I love you. Your folk call me lady and I will be that to you and them. I promise, Robin—even though, God knows, I'm scared as a woman can be of what's coming, but I must live with that, and maybe that's what living is."

The rite was simple and as bound to the earth as their lives. Robin didn't know how old it was or the words they should say, only that Guntrada taught them to his grandfather on their first morning.

"You are the people." He drew the knife over the palm of his left hand under the thumb. "I am the land. Together we are the bargain."

Deftly, he made a long shallow cut on Marian's open hand.

"You are the land," she said clearly as the bright-red line welled up and spilled over her palm. "I am the people. Together we are the bargain."

They put their hands together. As the warm blood mingled they held the clasped hands over the bole of the oak. Their blood fell drop by drop on the dark-stained life of the tree.

BOOK III

Robin Hood

19

*F*IVE MEN DANCING all their lives to the beat of one drum, never aware of the rhythm until the drum ceased. Five parts of a natural whole suddenly become five individuals dealing with loss and change as best they could, melting into Sherwood to survive. Travelers from Grantham and Nottingham dropped a word here and there that trickled from Blidworth to Denby and thence to the forest.

"The ladies are stayed at Grantham. They'll not be back."

"Back to what? Best kept lands in the shire and who sits on them now? Fitz-Gerald! A shame to make the angels weep."

"Lady Maud would not want to come back with matters standing as they do."

"True, but what of us and the harvesting?"

"The reeve says we have to harvest for Denby before we do our own."

"Well, quicker done, quicker we get our own in."

"What of a priest for our church?"

"We need a proper lord."

"We need *our* lord, I say, and sod the sheriff."

The men masked their worry in grumbling. The women thought of children and realities, but their refrain was one: What will we do? What will happen to us?

In Sherwood Robin fretted with the same concern. "It's harvest, Beorn: certain things to be done in a certain time. I hear Fitz-Gerald is going to raise flamin' horses on Denby grass. Precious little time he'll give to crops or folk.''

And this in a summer when their corner of the shire was one of the few with good yields while tales of famine were heard everywhere. Normans had no idea of husbandry. The year was a circle dance with precise steps for each season. None knew this better than Alcuin, the lank, loose-jointed beekeeper who never moved hurriedly in that dance nor was ever completely still. Any hall, even Denby, could take schooling in that dance from his wise bees. They knew Alcuin well; he was rarely stung unless careless enough to agitate the workers at their instinctive tasks. They furnished ample honey for the table, mead, and the curing of hams. In return, since their continued efficiency required a full knowledge of everything going on about them, Alcuin never failed to keep his charges informed of current events. Their hives were draped in black on the death of Aelred, told with pride of Robin's succession, his marriage, and now his outlawry. Alcuin didn't think a bee felt sadness as humans did, only a sense of disruption when something wasn't as it should be. With an experienced tongue, he fancied subtle differences in the quality of the honey they produced in different moods.

In the early days of harvest, Alcuin recounted to them the concerns of Blidworth and the last unhappy weeks at Denby, waiting until the last of the workers returned from a find of teasel blossoms, when they were all in the hive and feeling right as they could about conditions.

"Well then," he commenced in the gentle monotone much like their own all's-well buzzing. "If you feel a change, that's the foreigners in the hall. No fear: Our good Ethelwold's still there, and Minna, Angharad, and Gudrun too. Wystan is mending well as he can. I was with Ethelwold when the old man met the sheriff at Denby gate."

Ethelwold and Alcuin stood straight and a little distant as was right with strangers when Fitz-Gerald came to claim Denby in the name of the king.

"And Ethelwold says, very tart, 'Here are the keys to Denby. I will be having them back when the lord returns.' Sad: Ethelwold must now answer to some little Norman reeve, I forget his name but he bites his nails. But I still answer to Ethelwold for your yield, and you to me, so things ent that different in the main."

Fitz-Gerald? That young man didn't have the land born in him like Robin or Aelred, but neither was he any kind of a fool, the beekeeper would be bound. He gave orders for the harvest in a way that showed the man knew what he was about.

"He's to live at our hall, if you please," Alcuin buzzed to his bees. "When he's not lolling about Nottingham, that is, and I am called to the fields myself—scythe, sickle, and the lot. What else? Oh yes. Who showed his face in my doorway last night but Much the miller. God, he was a sorry sight, ragged and more dirt on him than a full hide of arable."

Alcuin gave the forlorn miller a good meal. Freda scurried down with a bit of ale and other folk just happened by with a dib of this, dab of that, so Much didn't fare too badly that day.

"We told him about Wystan and how Robin's in Sherwood where any half of a good man would join him straight. Young as he is, Much is a proper man, and he said to me, 'I'm off to put Wystan's hand in mine, for that's heavy on me.' And I said, making sure he got it clear enough, 'Do y'know your way in Sherwood then?' "

The miller did by Alcuin's guess. Much knew what was right, no more outlaw than Lord Robin or Father Beorn, come to that, but these hard years there'd be better men hanged than walking free. Alcuin would take Much's place at the mill if that was needed and try to make do. He hoped they wouldn't send a Frankish priest to Blidworth church, and that was all the beekeeper had to say on that matter. He praised his bees for their good work: He would be to Grantham honey fair in autumn with the sheriff's permission, a fine great place with a royal manor, and would return to tell them all about his adventures. No fear that he would miss the ladies of Denby; they'd have blessings and good words for all their folk and the bees to boot.

Five men gone back to the forest, Robin and Will as naturally as fish dropped into water, teaching the others how to survive. In late summer the forest was a bounty. Snaring hares was easy, fallow and red deer could be stalked, shot, and dressed out quickly. Lentils, greens, and bread found their way from Blidworth or Denby. Freda's oxcart, creaking toward Denby with a supply of ale demanded by the sheriff's reeve, was set on and robbed of a cask with a parting kiss from a green-hooded bandit.

"Now nip off and tell the reeve you lost but one barrel and nowt of your virtue."

"You've already had more of that than's left," Freda reminisced with pleasure.

"Go on." Robin patted her sturdy bottom, one eye on John shouldering the cask into the bush. "What word from Grantham?"

"None I've heard. The steward will tell us," Freda warranted.

"Let's be off," Will warned. "It's a clear day and no sight dearer to the sheriff than us out in the open."

"God bless, Freda. If the reeve complains, you were robbed and couldn't do a thing about the matter."

"So I was." Freda tugged at the Lincoln-green wool of the cowl that covered Robin's head and shoulders. "By Robin Hood. God be with you, sir."

Five men elusive in the forest as fish in the sea, eating well and building hunters' huts as they had been put up millenia before in Britain. Honing their arrows with grease and sharp sand, ears pricked and watchful for Normans nosing through Sherwood in ever-increasing numbers. Fitz-Gerald hunted often and loved the chase more than the kill since it exercised his beloved horses. Now and then his liveried foresters probed afoot. Men in scarlet and blue were easy to elude by men who looked like the forest itself. They would be as easy to kill but for fear of reprisal against the three ladies at Grantham or Robin's folk in Blidworth.

Beorn kept careful account of the days, saying Mass with Tuck each morning, missing a saint's day here and there when he wasn't sure of the date. All the men had varying skill with the bow, even Tuck and Father Beorn who were better with sword and shield. Under the patient teaching of Will Scatloch and the natural wizardry of Robin—goddamned unnatural if you asked John Littlerede—they began to learn why Normans feared English archers above all other warriors. On a perfect day in August with gentle light under buttermilk clouds, they saw why.

At their shelter, Beorn was boiling water for crayfish; the rest of them were out collecting blackberries so fat and soft-ripe they came half-squashed off the brambles. The berry patch was close to the edge of a Denby wheat field west of the hall. Among the harvesters bending to bunch and sickle the ripe yield, Robin knew every man and woman by sight—and the Norman reeve in his wide-skirted tunic, walking his horse through the stubble in their wake. If the folk saw Robin they were wise enough not to give him away, but none could ignore the figure who burst out of the forest north of the field, a man in ragged linen, yellow hair flying, or the three liveried men in close pursuit—

"God a mercy!" Tuck croaked. "It's Much."

Robin's eye darted from one element of the danger to the other: Much pounding through the uncut wheat, the Norman reeve turning his horse, drawing his sword even as Robin nocked an arrow. The sheriff's men carried crossbows; for range the odds were with Much, but the reeve now spurred to cut him off. Much had a bow and quiver but no decent chance to stand and get a clear shot at any of them even if he were that skilled. Now the field workers were calling to Much, cheering him on. The miller staggered and veered away from the Norman reeve galloping down on him.

"Will with me," Robin ordered. "You lot, back to the hut. Will, give those liveries summ'at to think on."

Fatter and slower than the rest, Tuck it was who turned to catch his breath, see it all, and tell the wonder afterward. There was the field, deadly as that at Stamford Bridge, Lord Robin bounding high as a hound on scent over the stubble after the reeve—

"Run, Much! Run for the wood!"

—and the miller, young and strong but nigh run out, trying to push himself faster but losing ground to the sheriff's men close enough now to stand and take aim on him. The reeve heard Robin shout, reined short, and wheeled his horse about. Robin stopped dead, waving cordially.

"Aye, it's me, little man. Have a go?"

The Norman hesitated for one fatal moment. Tuck saw it all: crossbolts flying and poor Much jerking as one hit him, going down in the wheat. And the reeve deciding one Robin was worth two millers, putting spurs to his horse. Robin took his stand, slow or quick, Tuck couldn't tell for the movement was that smooth, the whole body of the man flowing into the press of his bow—and down out of the saddle went the Norman, pinned neat as a corn doll to a reaper's stack, and Tuck could hear the cheering from the folk in the field, the men's sound deep and dust-raw, the higher voices of the women rising over them sweet as a *sanctus* sung by angels.

Hoch, Robin! A Robin!

And there was Will Scatloch, no less of a marvel, green in the gold of the wheat, deadly as Robin, drawing on the sheriff's men pounding down toward fallen Much. There was one down that fast, then two. The third of them thought twice on the matter and turned round quick as he could, but too late. . . .

Far too late under the unblinking eye of Will Scatloch who sighted on him steady as an adder on a mouse. Tuck saw the Welshman's head lift delicately, sensing distance and wind as he stanced and drew, suddenly still as a man at prayer. The shaft went flashing in the sun, straight as a shriven soul to God.

There was relief and laughter in Sherwood when Tuck panted in, sweating off the first of his fat, Will and Robin supporting the stricken miller between them.

"Feels like I'm hit all over," the casualty moaned. "Pray for me, Father, I'm dying sure."

"Set him down, Will."

"On my front," Much implored them. He was lowered on his belly, face pale as whey. "I can't look. Where's the wound?"

Father Beorn inspected the area of entry. "Impaled through the dignity."

"Lord Robin, before I die—"

"Ah, shut up." Robin cut away the bloody seat of the miller's ragged trews.

"*Ow*—I want to ask forgiveness, for it was me and Wystan brought you to this."

Father Beorn agreed on the guilt, academic as it was. "What penance, Robin?"

"Well then." Robin worked steadily at the bolt in Much's rump. "I find you guilty of poaching my deer."

"*Ow!* Easy, lord, it hurts."

"Steady on, it's coming—and I fine you one crossbolt out of your thievin' arse. There!"

The smooth-headed bolt was wiped clean and returned to Much by his lord. "To keep you honest, mind."

Father Beorn added a just penance. "Three *Pater nosters* each evening for a month."

Much felt gingerly at the devastated area. "Yes, Father. Truly I have been searching you out this last week."

Robin grinned at the prodigal returned to his fold. "Welcome home, Much. There's fish and berries."

The story seeped through Sherwood to other villages. Papplewick buzzed with the tale of how Robin went a-berrying. Edwinstowe heard and then Southwell. At Mansfield Waltheof chuckled privately over the escapade while gravely sympathizing with outraged Normans. From his own purse Ralf Fitz-Gerald put a higher price on the head of Edward Aelredson, known among Saxons as "Robin Hood," for the cold-blooded murder of his reeve and three men at arms. From Southwell, with the first quickening winds of September, the story blew to Grantham and another world.

Both William and Matilda would have much preferred to follow young Adelaide home to summer in Rouen, but the English situation made prolonged absence dangerous. William presently headquartered at Lincoln

Castle, dealing directly with Hereward's rebels in the fens around Ely and Swein's Danish fleet hovering like hungry raptors about the eastern coast. Matilda managed a week at home, then sailed again for Grantham. Lanfranc was to replace Stigand as archbishop of Canterbury and as William's regent in England in his absence, with the close counsel of Queen Matilda.

For Matilda the airy royal manor at Grantham, five minutes' walk from St. Wulfram's Church, was a comfortable second best if she must be away from home. River Witham meandered through the manor grounds, less than ten paces broad near the hall, a placid run for geese and ducks. The hall had long functioned as a royal residence and center of administration, held in dowage by Queen Edith, who visited rarely.

"She is along in years, bless her, but Edith is the best of Godwine's family." Matilda spoke to her visitor in the cool manor hall, empty now save for the two of them. "We thank her for this manor. Lincoln Castle is rather grim in any weather. Edith is the only Saxon within my comprehension, your excellency—with the possible exception of Lady Judith whom you will shortly meet. For the rest, I cannot tell if they are stubborn or merely dense. Please, excellency, sit here by me."

"Your Majesty is kind." The visitor inclined his tonsured head before taking the proffered chair, carefully arranging his canonical vestments.

"No, no, *cher* Lanfranc." Matilda settled herself on a small bench. "Since we must work together, address me as Matilda, your sister in Christ. My royal husband has an instinct for men he can trust. May the English bishops place their faith as well."

There, very neatly done. Matilda was not above using her practiced charm when needed. She well knew Lanfranc's strength and capabilities. The man himself was not that easily sounded. His reputation was enormous: a young monk from Tuscany, already widely known as a teacher when he journeyed to Le Bec to develop a simple monastery into a famous center of learning. A lawyer and supple diplomat but in no man's pocket. The former abbot of Caen was a formidable advocate, intractable in his way as any Saxon. He had vigorously opposed her marriage to Gilly twenty years ago. They needed such a bulwark between themselves and the Vatican, but what were Lanfranc's aims for Canterbury and how much did he want from William in return?

From all her experience with men, Matilda tried to read as much of Lanfranc as she could without appearing gauche. A Tuscan: handsome mix of German and Italian blood warmed in the southern sun. In that beneficent light, wisdom mellowed like good wine. There was a certain

openness in the animated eyes. Possibly deceptive. *So open, he's closed.*
More devious men might trip over their own cleverness in underestimating
Lanfranc, an advantage where crown and Canterbury must act as one.
Sixty-three now, more weathered than aged, Lanfranc still had unmistakable vitality. Despite the thinning salt-and-pepper hair and deeply lined
features, he was a man who glowed in sunlight, opening to it like a flower
with all his senses, loving his art and savoring his wine. These qualities
well balanced the scholarly years in Caen. With Lanfranc their crown
could forge no stronger link with the See of Peter whose banner and
blessing helped them to England. In return they quite practically intended
to pay as nominal a vassalage as they could to Rome, though the archbishop's goodwill need not be strained by that knowledge just now. No
doubt he would guess as much in time.

"Here." Matilda offered Lanfranc a writ copied on fresh parchment. "William's endorsement of your consecration with full particulars
of your regency which will be in force whenever he is absent from
England."

Lanfranc scanned the writ briefly, then rolled it up. "There will be
trouble with the nominated archbishop of York."

Matilda was well informed on the subject of Thomas of York, Aldred's
successor. "The north is always a problem, a door with a damaged lock.
We are keenly concerned with your solution to Thomas."

Lanfranc made a purely Italian gesture of philosophical calm. "Often
the best action is none at all, certainly none in haste. Apparently Thomas
is much like his predecessor."

"Aldred." Matilda's small hands fluttered expressively. "He almost
gave Gilly a seizure at his coronation. All the same"—Matilda frowned—
"even in submission there is a defiance in them. Lady Maud for example,
one of my English guests. Note her when she is presented. Speaks not
a word of Frank and refuses to learn. Perfect manners, no jot one could
object to, and yet . . ." The queen glanced reflectively down the vast
empty hall checkered with sunlight streaming through open casements.
"The other day I touched her arm in friendship. Natural enough, one
woman to another."

Lanfranc prompted her. "And?"

"I felt her . . . stiffen. I saw it in her face, something that told me
quite clearly to keep my distance. *Bien,* what can I expect: Her husband
died at York. They were to be my bridge to the English to know them
better. Now, *hélas* . . ."

Matilda poured watered wine into two silver goblets, offering one to her companion. "They'll be here presently. I've sent for them. The mother, the wife, and the cousin of an English outlaw who has just demonstrated his distaste for our rule by murdering a few of the king's men. I fear my guests must now be my prisoners. So much for impulsive affection." Matilda refreshed herself with a drink from her goblet. "There are days when I could happily dedicate the rest of my life to embroidering in Rouen."

"No. Surely not you," the prelate scoffed politely.

"*Vraiment.* Dull work but it takes so little out of me—ah, here they are."

When the three women of Denby were presented to Lanfranc, the archbishop was delighted to recognize one of them as she bent to kiss his ring. "*Cara* Judith! Surely you remember your old teacher from Caen."

"Your excellency is kind to remember me."

"Kind indeed; as if I could forget. Your Majesty, even as a student Judith had an awesome command of ecclesiastical scholarship. It is very good to see you again."

"By the queen's invitation"—Judith nodded toward Matilda—"and the unfortunate turn of events. We are not exactly guests."

"So you are," Matilda stressed, "by every good wish of mine. However the circumstances fall. Though I must tell you that they have not fallen well."

After a tense exchange, Marian whispered urgently to Judith: "He's not dead. No, he's not, don't say that."

"No, *ma petite,* not at all." Matilda could reassure the girl of that if little else, but four men were dead by her husband's hand and the price on his head risen. While Sire Ralf had himself urged the ladies' return to Denby, the situation made it inadvisable at present. "Meanwhile, we look on you as crown wards to be maintained as ladies in waiting upon ourself."

Judith conveyed the sentiments to Maud and Marian. Maud's reaction was swift and pithy. "This is like telling a slave her collar is now to be of gold. Speak of your cousin."

"My queen, I must say a word in Edward's defense."

"There is no defense of murder, child. The subject is closed."

"Madame, pray you indulge me. The heart of this is the duty of vassal to lord and lord to man. Edward tried to obey the law."

"He did not," Matilda returned with a trace of impatience. "Do not slight my grasp of events."

"Did he not deliver Wystan to Nottingham? Against every rule he lived by, he obeyed his liege lord."

"Delivered one and refused the other. Most forcefully, as I hear."

"Had Edward given his miller to punishment of such unwonted severity, he would not have one freeman left on Denby. They would leave him." In her earnestness Judith's voice had risen. She checked herself to careful respect. Within the perception of any person, high or low, there were blind spots. Robin's led him inevitably beyond the law. The queen's were no less hindering. Folly to argue thus. Laws were always written by the victors. "They . . . would leave him," she concluded lamely.

"This wearies me, Judith," said the queen. "Only the king may pardon his own tenant, who was charged to keep the law and then broke it himself."

"Charged yes," Judith struggled, "but given no real authority. Set on guard like a toothless watchdog, able to bark but not bite."

"Ladies, we regret." Matilda rose, ending the audience. "But we have said. Be at home in our house if you can. It is the wiser course." Her formality melted at the sight of Marian's dejection. She beckoned the girl to her. "You are so young for such sadness. No, he is not dead. Pray God for your sake he will live, *ma chère*. Judith, tell her she is the youth of England I would be close to, the support we look to in future." No, Marian was not yet old enough for that understanding. Only age developed the muscles to deal with sadness. *"Je regrette, m'enfante."*

The English women spoke rapidly among themselves. Matilda could glean their mood only through inflection: Marian's modest but deliberate, Maud's bitten off.

"We obey the queen's will." Judith bowed her head.

But not without comment, Matilda suspected. "One feels the ladies were more explicit, Judith. Be so good."

"Madame?"

"What did they say? Candidly, if you will. I shall not swoon at the literal."

With a propitiating glance at Lanfranc and considerable diplomacy, Judith obliged. "They feel that to be guests in such a manner is not meet; that it is more honorable, Your Majesty's kindness notwithstanding, to consider themselves not wards but prisoners."

"Judith," Lanfranc put in gently, "the hair shirt never became you."

"For Marian," Judith continued, "she takes good care to say that there is nothing personal in her choice."

"Indeed?" Matilda hid the ironic smile behind her goblet. "That warms me a little."

"The queen has been most kind to her, she says, but her loyalty must be to her husband. When the hearth she left is returned to her, Marian will give your Majesty good welcome."

Matilda set down her goblet, indulging a rare vulgarism to Lanfranc in Flemish. "There's Saxon warmth for you: She doesn't hate my guts but please let her go home."

Judith spoke tentatively. "If we may have the queen's permission to withdraw."

"Of course." At Matilda's sign, the three women bowed to her and the archbishop and backed several paces before turning to leave the hall. Matilda watched them out of sight, then sat down again, imploring Lanfranc with soft, helpless laughter. "There, you see? Nothing personal, just a matter of principle."

The archbishop tilted the wine decanter over Matilda's goblet. "They have a better queen than they know."

"*Mon Dieu*." Matilda took a deep drink. "King David grew old and gat no heat. We grew royal and gat no joy. Pray you fare better at Canterbury."

The English women had been given a large, light chamber over the hall. There was one broad bed which Judith and Marian tried to share with a minimum of discomfort—Marian slumbered quietly where Judith tossed—and a smaller one for Maud next to it, beside deep chests for their belongings in addition to those they brought from home, and a carven *prie-dieu* for their devotions. They wanted for nothing but freedom.

"Like the Hebrews in Babylon," Judith remarked when the door closed between them and Norman hearing. "At least she allowed us to withdraw with dignity. We are collared in velvet, manacled with gold."

"A chain is a chain," Maud muttered at the open casement.

"Mum, will they catch Robin, d'you think?"

Maud reassured her with a dubious smile. "Not in Sherwood. Not this year or next."

"Oh-h." Marian sank back on her bed with a little moan. "If I could just see him and know he's safe."

"Meanwhile, like the Hebrews, let us make the most of Babylon." Maud left the casement to sit beside them on the bed. They must take advantage from adversity, she told them. If home was gone, Grantham was the best place for them to help Robin. Tradesmen and farmers were always passing between Grantham and Sherwood. Now that he had a taste of town delights, Alcuin would surely beg permission to come to autumn honey fair and could easily pass news. The queen naturally favored Marian. What was her word?

"Char-mawnt," Marian mangled the term. "I ent sure what it means, but then I was the one who thought Italy was somewhere in Rome."

No matter: Marian would be a charming, pliant willow to shade the dwarfish queen. Both young women would be honey itself to any Norman who addressed them.

"Ah, Mum." Marian pushed off the bed to escape Maud's relentless truth. "All right. I'll be honey to her bread." She went to the open casement, reading the sky over River Witham. Autumn was already leaving its first clear signs for farmers to read. Squirrel pelts were thickening early and they were storing food against the cold months earlier than they did last year. The chill rains would come soon and winter would be hard.

"God keep him warm and dry," she prayed, kneeling at the *prie-dieu*. After her usual prayers to Mary for her continued aid, she entreated Saint Nicholas on Robin's behalf. Her husband was no thief, but since God provided even thieves with a patron saint, Marian asked Saint Nicholas to take care of honest outlaws as well.

20

Six men could build a hunter's hut in an hour, thatched with bracken and impossible to find if one didn't know it was there. Dry enough in the autumn rain, fires lit only after dark and no wisp of smoke to betray the fugitives.

And yet, as Will Scatloch saw the matter, a man needed more than just to sleep safe and dry. When the sun shone a man's soul took in light and warmth as the body did. So the soul went grey and cold as Sherwood's colors faded toward winter. Dreaming into the small fire, the men thought less of their good fortune than their losses now, sadness playing like the firelight over their faces. Tuck swore it was regular ale he missed most, but with a kind of trailing off that told Will the man lacked for much more than that. John grew more silent, morosely arranging his losses in piles and counting them over like a miser. Father Beorn said Mass every day—no excuse for Christian men to lose good habits—but walked alone with God himself, no doubt wondering as he had ever since Hastings how long God and the Church would be truly one master he could serve. Now that he could sit in comfort, young Much relished the adventure of it all and didn't give a damn since he'd left nothing behind of his own. But Robin . . .

I taught him the forest, but there's that he has to learn for himself like any man, heavy as the lessons are. Barely married before he had to leave the lass's bed. Angharad's a painful wanting in my soul, so how must he feel? Worse since Alcuin came back from Grantham.

The young beekeeper came on a gusty day, wicker basket on his back, singing louder than the wind, making sure any Englishman within a mile heard him, greeting Robin's men when they stepped out of the bush onto the cart road. God keep you, one and all! Aye, the ladies are well, guarded, but they found Alcuin quick enough at the honey fair.

"Your lady sends her love, lord, and your mother and cousin as well. They want for nowt but you and pray for you each day. Aye, and look! Here's a bit of honey left from the fair, and some mead."

Those were the best of Alcuin's tidings; there were darker. Denby folk were managing well enough, but had to work more days for the sheriff and less for themselves since they weren't free anymore.

That weighed lighter on Will than on Robin. "Angharad, mun: What of her and my boys?"

"Who works my mill?" Much plied the beekeeper.

"Who's at my forge?" John lowered, dark as October himself.

"My church," Beorn wanted to know. "Has not a priest come from Mansfield even once a week to say Mass?"

"Who sweeps it out and keeps the altar things polished?" Tuck asked.

No one, Alcuin told him. No one at all.

"Clean as a maid's dreams when I left," Tuck despaired. "That is *my* office being neglected."

There was news of the church but Alcuin was sick to repeat it. "I heard at Saint Wulfram's we're to have a Norman priest."

Robin swore under his breath. "The folk won't come."

"Yes, they will," said Beorn. "A priest is of no country when he says Mass."

"That's the worst of it," Alcuin said, hanging his head. "You're excommunicated, Father."

To Will, Father Beorn looked like a man hit in the stomach. Cast out by the Church and cut off from God, who would no longer hear his plea or prayer. Alcuin hastily assured Beorn that Norman priests had to say the damning words and snuff the candles; no English cleric would be part of the rotten business. And what with the *hlaefdiges* Maud and Judith blistering St. Wulfram's in two tongues, the nave of the church was smoking yet. Despite appeal to the queen and the new archbishop of Canterbury, the excommunication stood.

To cheer Beorn, Robin allowed *he* held God to be one thing and the Church of Rome quite another. Heresy be damned, children could not always speak for their father no matter how well they might think they knew him. Cold consolation to Beorn who walked apart and silent as John now, and none of them merrier for the chill October rain.

Six men close about a fire but each alone. Robin poked at the fire with a stick. "Honey fair's past. I'm one and twenty this week."

Will counted on his own. He was two and thirty, Angharad four samhains younger—she thought. The dear, daft woman was never that sure, as if it mattered. *Don't I miss her that much? I hurt for her. Her tongue's sharp over a cup of whiskey, but there's her eye speaking softer, inviting me to bed in the middle of a fight. Oh, God, and the boys I'd cuff when they made too much noise or wouldn't mind. Too often, curse me. There'll be ten kisses each for every time I raised a hand to them, may God forgive me.*

Will felt the same ferment growing in the men about him, spoiling toward a storm. Soon one of them would get a gutful and do something in anger or frustration, take the needless risk that endangered or killed them all. So long as he and Robin kept their wits sharp, the Fitz-Gerald had little chance of snaring them. A hunter might know a great deal about red deer but tasted little of their meat until he learned to think *like* them. The trap of it all was that deer were born wary and men had to learn caution—and often as not forgot the lesson. When the time came, it was Robin himself who took up their anger like a cross, fool enough in one day to last a year. But then one might expect that of Saxons, especially Aelred and his son. Wherever they stood, upon whatever ground, *there* was God and *there* was right. Such could be noble men, Will Scatloch gave them their due. More often they were as much of a pain in the arse as the crossbow dealt Much.

Now, when a man was *dan y cwrw,* under the blessing-curse of drink, he might be able to hold it or might not. Will Scatloch's experience with both kinds was that happy men made for sociable drinkers while a man with a grievance looked for a fight and generally found one. From one good soul or another at Denby or Blidworth, Robin's men always knew when they could approach the hall or village for supplies at least risk. Sven the fletcher sent a parcel of grey goose feathers for arrows. Though terrified of the huge horses snorting and stamping about Denby's stable, Minna teetered precariously on a stall gate in unsung heroism to shear a handy clutch of tail hair from a resentful chestnut stallion for bowstrings. Oh, and on a clear blue-heavened day that was there, nigh on to the feast of Calixtus, with the sheriff's new hogs come rooting in Sherwood for beechmast and acorns—one never to return, alas—Angharad risked flogging to pinch a generous skin of wine from the Black Fitz-Gerald and slipped away to meet Will in a small dip of ground just beyond the point where Denby fields were boarded by beech and silver birch. Will's heart came close to bursting when he saw her, how every part of the woman had grown dearer to him through absence, and he wanted her right there in the bracken. She was always desirable to him without a drop in him and ten times more with one, the way it always was between them: the light in her eyes and the color of them like blue clouded with violet and the set of them he'd seen in no Saxon woman ever. The light-olive of her skin against black hair already streaked with grey when she married him, mere girl that she was then. And the strong, hot body of her that could drive him wild as it did that day. . . .

"Wyti 'n aros," he murmured between kisses, pulling her down into the bracken. "Wilt thou not stay, love?"

"I would but I cannot," she moaned against his cheek, needing him as much, yearning to stay but afraid she'd be missed. Between greedy and delicious kisses, Angharad managed to stave him off long enough to show her gift. "Look what it is that I've brought."

"Ale, is it?"

"No, Will. It is red wine from Normandy. Taste."

He did and found the wine strange but good, warm on his tongue, red and warm on Angharad's lips while he left trails of it on her neck and hands and the tips of her fingers. "And my boys, dearest?"

"Fine and healthy they are . . . Will, stop. I must be back."

"Stay just a little."

She writhed her hips against his, between two fires, needing to go, wanting to lie with him and under him. "Do nothing foolish, Will, that thou come home the sooner."

"I want thee so, it is a fire in my middle. Feel."

"I can, I can, but they will be looking for me."

"And have not I?" Trying to hike her gown up over her thighs. "God, I'm rising like a clan to war."

But she was the wiser of them that day. "Nay, I'll clout thee one." Angharad twisted away, scrambling to her knees, flustered. "I do not leave that easily, but leave I must."

"Angharad—"

"There." She gave him one last kiss that began with his lips and ended with cheeks, neck, and both his eyes. "Do you keep that safe for me."

Will watched her go with hungry eyes, aching for the woman, then unstoppered the wineskin again, wanting to get drunk on the spot. But the dear girl begged him to be sensible and he must for her sake. Besides, the others would be deserving of her gift.

Alone among them Father Beorn knew red wine. He rolled it around his tongue and the roof of his mouth, pronouncing it as fair a pressing as one could expect out of Normandy. Pity they had no cups, for wine was better when it breathed. Breathing or dead, the men gulped it like ale as the skin passed around. Much grew boastful about his adventures in eluding the foreigners. Will eased into gentle melancholy, running a finger over the seasoned yew of his bow, smooth as Angharad's flesh or little Gwaun's cheek that would have an apple blush in this autumn air.

Tuck sang a ballad that pained Will less for its bawdry than the lack of tune. Saxons had no feel for music which truly should go to the head and heart like this red wine. And Father Beorn, fierce eye alight but not softened, gazed away through the forest to—what? There was a frost to the English eye, Will mused; so the priest must have looked standing with the shield wall, sword in hand, waiting as the enemy came to victory or death as the fates would have it. Or saying Mass in his church, breaking the bread of the Eucharist. A hawk always had the look of its kind. In the shield-rank or the church, Beorn's searching eye would go straight to his quarry, be it God or conviction. The hawk lived by his eyesight; so Beorn, even excommunicate, would still spy out God.

Much grew sleepy with the wine, Tuck drowsed. The wineskin passed more slowly among them and stopped more often with Robin. The man took longer drinks, careless of the wine dribbling into his thickening beard and down to stain the sheepskin vest. He hadn't said much for some time, just stared away through the oaks in the direction of home. But . . . not as Will himself had yearned after his wife, not warm and wanting but going darker until his expression reminded Will of John when he would have murdered a Frank or two at Denby gate had not Robin stayed him.

With a casual motion, resting against a tree, Robin drew his throwing ax and tested the edge, then the same with his hunting knife. Without a word, he rose and went into the low hut, emerging with his bow and quiver. He took another drink from the wineskin.

Something twitched in Will's stomach like a warning. "Will you hunt?"

"I will that."

"The red deer are in rut, boyo."

"I know."

"What then?"

Robin braced his bow and slung the quiver. "Sheriff."

Will got quickly to his feet. "Robin, for God's sake—"

"Fitz-Gerald's lived his last night under my roof."

The men had all risen now, exchanging fearful glances. To Denby in broad daylight? Even Little John knew that for mortal folly. "I don't think that's a good idea."

Robin ignored him. "Look after them, Will. That rotten little man's going to Jesus."

"Don't, Robin," Beorn warned. "That's a fool's way."

"Look to your prayers, holy man."

Then Will knew how far gone his lord was. Much stepped forward, arms open, friendly and reasonable. Robin stopped him dead with a leveled knife. "Miller, you touch me—any of you—and you'll bleed for it. I've had enough." And that, to the single-minded Robin, was that. He turned his back on them and strode away toward Denby, leaving a knot of fear in his wake. They lost a few minutes in confusion, none of them ready for this, coming as it did out of nowhere but a wineskin. They conferred quickly. Robin was drunk enough to think he was not. He couldn't think straight now, let alone shoot true. The Franks would cut him down like ripe barley, he wouldn't have a chance.

"Whatever we do, best be quick," Will counseled. "Father?"

Beorn considered, dusting his hands lightly against each other, measuring each of the men about him, pausing on his stout sexton and Little John. "What's best for a man who's drunk too much?"

"Sleep it off," said Tuck from experience.

"Just so," John agreed with a hint of anticipation. "Tuck, my lad, fetch the quarterstaves."

They were ready within minutes, five men to one purpose, electing Will to lead. Much carried his bow, Beorn buckled on his sword. John slapped the formidable ashwood staff against a hard palm. "Right enough: a long sleep."

Will Scatloch judged Robin's long-legged stride from traveling with him over the years. Along the narrow tracks left by centuries of rooting swine, Robin could cover a mile in ten minutes without running. They'd best hurry. They followed Robin's barely readable trail through the brush for a few minutes before second thoughts stopped Will to advise his companions. "He's moving that fast; best we go round."

Will broke into the ground-eating trot that he could maintain all day like a hunting wolf. The others labored behind him as the forest dipped, rose, and rolled away behind them, now and then flushing startled pigs from Denby. Will moved as silently as he could, the others strung out behind him. He prayed Robin would think twice, for it was all of them he might be killing. Perhaps a man could soak up just so much wisdom in a twelvemonth—father dead, land and wife taken from him. He was that young still, didn't really believe he could die, *but he's seen too much in too little time, and it's that he's puking up instead of the wine.*

Their present shelter was less than four miles from Denby. Time was against Will, but this swine track led toward Mansfield, crossing the wider cart path from Annersley which led straight to Denby. Once they struck on the path, they would be close enough to shout at the sheriff and pray his men were occupied elsewhere. Will halted in ck brush, within earshot of the Annersley path. One by one the other men trailed in to group around him, breath steaming in the cold air.

"How much farther?" Tuck panted. "I didn't run so when I was Robin's age."

Will hissed him to silence. "And you, Much."

"Not a word did I—"

"Puffin' like a walrus. Be still."

With a finger on his lips, Will left them and padded forward, careful not to brush against any vine or bramble that might rustle and give him away.

He *had* heard voices, not loud but distinct. Signaling the others to stay back, Will moved forward one deliberate step at a time until only a yard or two separated him from the open cart path. With infinite care he inched forward: three men in the sheriff's livery, two of them Frank by their jabber. The third Will recognized as one of those who'd come to the hall seeking Wystan and Much. The Saxon knelt now, studying something in the loose earth of the path.

"That's him, right enough: tall man with a long stride. Told you I saw him on the road back there. Walking toward the hall bold as a baron."

One of the Franks said something. The Saxon just shook his head. "I know the man. Come on."

Will swallowed as he turned silently to signal Much alone to join him. "Three liveries, two with crossbows," he whispered to the tense miller. "Set a shaft and follow me." Will slid an arrow from his quiver, seeing the fear that young Much couldn't hide. "Three marks in the clear, easy as stealing bread from a blind baker. Don't think, just do it. Ready?"

Much nodded. Will tramped ahead loud as he could out of the brush to take his stand in the middle of the road, flowing into draw as Much trotted to his side. "Hey! You there!"

He loosed even as the three men stopped and swung about in surprise. One man was half turned when Will's shaft took him in the throat. Much's arrow hit the other Norman low in the stomach. The man went over backward with a grunt, writhing on the ground. The big Saxon was reaching for his quiver when he saw Will's redrawn bow bearing on him like poised death.

"Don't, mun."

The forester obviously thought better of it with one companion dead, the other bound that way. He dropped the arrow back into his quiver and lowered his bow.

"Get off the road," Will called over the distance between them. "Out."

"Aye, be off," Much quavered with strained bravado. "We've no time for chat."

The forester unbraced his bow. "I've no quarrel with Robin Hood that he does not push on me."

"I know." Will's arrow was still drawn to the ear against him and unwavering. "Just a plain man with a family. Keep thinking of them and die in bed."

The forester turned and moved off into the bush. Will listened for his receding tred. "Quick, Much. Fetch the lads."

For a sun-browned man, the young miller was now very pale. "I never killed a man before."

"You haven't yet. Hurry."

Much scurried back into the brush. Will stalked forward, blackly cursing Robin for what must be done now. His own target was dead; Much's mark was a stocky little Norman who might linger for days with the arrow pile low in his vitals. He gasped weakly at Will.

"Ai-aidez moi. . . ."

Will nodded sadly. No help for a wound like that. You couldn't draw out the pile without half the man's insides coming with it. Will flowed down on one knee at the forester's back, drawing his knife. *Wee mun, you're a long way from home.*

He was mercifully swift, caught the man under the chinstring of his conical helmet and cut his throat. As he straightened up, Much and the others reappeared. Will waved them forward, kicking loose dirt over the bloodstains in the track.

"We've scant minutes, if that. Get these bodies off the road and come on."

Tuck and Little John dragged the dead men into the bush, then caught up with the others following Will in his loping run toward Denby. Will and Much ran with nocked shafts, Father Beorn hiking up his scabbard and praying under the little breath he had left. John and Tuck panting but grim, carried their staves high for balance as they ran. With every pounding step Will listened for horsemen and doubted the wisdom of letting the third forester go. That bloody flat-faced Saxon would be telling the tale to the first Normans he saw. Before Robin or any of them had time to make half an act of contrition, there'd be more foreigners on this cart road than there were oversea.

Goddamn you, Robin.

Rounding the last bend but one before Denby, the hall almost in sight, there was Robin striding ahead of them, weaving a little, still drunk enough to be a fool and totally unconcerned.

"Robin!"

The tall, hooded figure spun about like a challenge as they panted up. Will wasted few words.

"Master or not, you're a disgrace, you are. Did you not know three of them were following you?"

Robin only shrugged. "I knew that. They got close enough, they'd be dead."

"Two of them are," Beorn said. "You're coming back with us."

"I said I'm going to kill him." Robin gave them his back and strode on.

Will leaped at him, caught Robin by the shoulder and spun him around. "If you've no heed to your own life, think of them—Much and John and Tuck and this good priest, valiant as he is but years past such haste as he's made to save you today." Will yanked exasperatedly at the old leather collar about his throat. "Mary and Joseph, mun! If you weren't my master and son to a better man—"

The words came out of John as a growl: "He's not my master." Even as his staff clattered in the dirt, the mountain mass of him tackled Robin, slamming the lighter man to the ground like a sack of grain. John was massive but Robin quicker. He rolled free and sprang to his feet, stripping the quiver from his back, blood-mad, fists up.

"Come try it, Johnny. You're forgetting your place, you are."

"Hist!" Much leaped between them. "I hear summ'at."

Will searched anxiously in both directions. "Horses?"

"Don't know."

"I hear 'em." Tuck took in the crisis before him: Robin and John squared off with no mind for anything but mayhem. "John!" He tossed the blacksmith his quarterstaff and took a practiced grip on his own. "Let's kiss him goodnight."

With one ear cocked for Normans, Will had to admire the efficiency of John and Tuck. The quarterstaff was natural to their kind, not to kill but apt to make the loser repent of his sins, which was needful in this moment.

"Ha!" Tuck drove the hard ash butt just under Robin's ribs and Will heard the breath whistle out of the boyo's lungs. As Robin doubled over, John's staff landed just over his left ear with a crack! Much later swore he could hear the echo through Sherwood. Robin fell like a pole-axed bull.

"Very neat," judged Father Beorn.

Much was alarmed. Robin didn't even twitch. "You've broke his pate, John."

"Carry him," Will snapped. "I do hear horses. Up with him and let's be gone."

Only moments off the path they were when the horsemen clattered past from Denby. Robin slumbered over John's broad shoulder with the welt along one temple rising in a formidable lump. Will felt that John could have put Robin to sleep with half the force, but the lesson salted down better this way. Robin could be thick for sure.

"I think he's dead," Much mourned when they laid the inert form in the bracken by their hut.

Will thoughtfully covered Robin with a blanket, then rested against a tree beside his errant master. One by one the men drifted away, tired and glad to be alive, until only Will and the priest remained by the unmoving form beneath the blanket.

"First peace he's known since Lammas," Will reckoned. "How is it with you, Father?"

With the spare movements of a man who had no strength left, Beorn unbuckled the sword belt and dropped it at his feet. "I'm past this, Will."

"Not a bit of it," Will denied with as much cheer as he could muster. "Yourself's the best man here. Is there any of that devil's wine left? I need it now."

"So do I." Beorn went to fetch the wine.

Resting against the oak, they sipped the last of the drink. Nigh on to sunset, when Beorn listened out of habit for Blidworth bell that would not sound now, Robin groaned and sat up with bloodshot sight. He felt gingerly at the lump on his skull and fell back like the dead resigned to burial. After a few moments he rolled painfully on his side and was sick in the bracken.

So he brings up the wine, Will sympathized tenderly, *and some of the rage with it. One and twenty, is it, and his lady no more than a girl, full of woes that should yet have been years in the coming. Either lucky today or God does not mean him to die yet. For sure there's no room or time for any one of us to be fools now.*

Among Will Scatloch's ancient race, heroes were god-touched, all their lives determined by fate. If there was a doom on Robin it was written by no god but his moment in time and the nature of his own kind. Say that he dreamed as Wystan once did, looking up from his fetters to envy the freedom of a bird and marvel at the liberating power of its wings. Robin groped and stumbled toward a soaring for which he yet had no word or shape, only felt wings beat in his soul, imprisoned but born to fly.

21

RALF FITZ-GERALD HAD business at Grantham in November, but waited
out the fierce seasonal gales. On the first calm day, he started with an
escort of five soldiers to present his revised shire tax rolls to Geoffrey
de Coutance, reeve of the royal manor. Neither William nor Matilda was
in residence, the king yet at Lincoln, the queen visiting her infant Henry
at Winchester. Ralf was frankly relieved at their absence, not prepared
to explain beyond the obvious why Robin Hood was still at large. Still,
like any hunter, Ralf began to discern patterns in Robin's movements.
The track east toward Trent River and on to Grantham was fairly open
country. The outlaws kept to the densely wooded tracts, so there would
be little danger of surprise today. Ralf rode at ease but alert, indulging
a personal whim. Where other knights like Raimond de Beaumont might
travel with a hawk on their wrist, Ralf considered Perdu better company,
and so the three-legged tortoiseshell cat had seen much of the shire from
Ralf's open saddlebag. Now and then as he rode, Ralf reached down to
stroke Perdu under her chin, which she loved, always lifting her head to
receive his tribute.

More and more Ralf disliked being away from Denby. Though the
Saxons there regarded him as affliction to be suffered stoically, he drew
his own pleasure from a wonderful sense of *old* about the steading, the
very rustic smell of the place. He got on well enough with Ethelwold,
through whom he passed his will to the household and the serfs of Blidworth. Ralf respected Ethelwold, who had never lost the bearing of a

soldier. In this respect the old man could school Raimond and a few others in dignity and reserve. Sweet Robin's ax had left a deep trench in Raimond's cheek and taken a few teeth. Now the youngest of the powerful Beaumonts swaggered about Denby with the air of a veteran even though he'd seen little of real battle.

Raimond and a few others quartered on Denby might be trouble, but Ralf drew a clear line from the beginning, knowing William's aims and policies. They could boil out of his sudden, savage rage as in Northumbria; more often they emanated from his shrewdness. This England was bridled but not yet broken. The Isle of Ely was still in Saxon hands, surrounded by impassable fens where Hereward laughed at the notion of surrender. William was a king with a wild beast gripped in each hand, England and his home suzerains. Maine was rebellious, Brittany treacherous, his eldest son, Robert, already proving more liability than heir. The last *contretemps* needed was one more insurrection. One kept a firm hand on the chain, but did not needlessly taunt the collared beast. There would be no undue friction anywhere Ralf was in authority. At Denby and Blidworth that included the safety of the women. The slave Angharad would speak no English at all when provoked, though comely in her odd Welsh way. As for the over-ripe tavern girl, Freda—*bien,* what she bartered or sold to Ralf's men was her own business. He would provide no grounds for trouble of any sort. To the lustier men under him, he repeated the king's penalties for rape, which included castration. The English placed an inordinately high value on a woman's chastity; adultresses were publicly shamed. Ralf himself invested less admiration in this pedestaled virtue but wanted no grievance out of these sullen folk. He closed his eyes to certain facts. The tavern girl was no nun, Angharad filched trifles whenever she could. Though nothing could be proved, any missing supplies probably found their way to Robin. If Ralf ever caught anyone at this . . . but of course he had not. Yet.

More, the new men coming from Normandy knew last year's Northumbrian campaign only from tales, not how it was to live in iron for weeks until your skin crawled with its own filth, face black from the smoke of the burnings, until the worst brutes among them sickened of destruction. Ralf's attitudes had less of sentiment than stultification about them beside being practical. Order served all, chaos none. There was nothing for him in Normandy. For all purposes England was now his country as much as Robin's—there was a droll thought—and any sane man must see that the savaging had to end.

No, there was much more to the matter than that. From his first day

242 · PARKE GODWIN

at Denby, Ralf sensed an element he needed like cool water to thirst. Compared to Normandy, England was an ancient and civilized land. Monks spoke of a great chronicle begun centuries past among these people, not only the deeds of heroes but a year-by-year history of the realm, factual and prosaic as the men who wrote it. Their illuminated gospels were painstaking glories to God—yet at sunset on the Eve of All Souls, Ralf saw fires on distant hilltops and heard Angharad praying in her own tongue, invocations probably older than Christ to keep the vindictive spirits of the dead from her door. In the customs of Saxon and Welsh alike, when his own kind paused in scrambling for money and place, a man saw everywhere the impossible hybrid of gods and God, ignorance and learning, genius and wooden stupidity.

For all that contradiction and perversity, Ralf Fitz-Gerald would not change one tree, flower, meadow, or heath. No, sweep Hereward from his fens, Robin from Sherwood, lay down fresh rushes in the tidy hall, then get on with building.

They were in sight of St. Wulfram's bell tower when Perdu leaped from her saddlebag to a purchase on Ralf's leg and thence to his shoulder. Minus a foreleg, Perdu had yet grown from clumsy kitten to agile young cat since Ralf acquired her, balancing on his shoulder and kneading at his cloak before settling down to take the air in regal manner.

"Voilà!" one of the men jested. *"Sire Ralf de le chat."*

Why not? Ralf contended. Life was hard enough. One needed something to be kind to. They rode through the ancient town and past St. Wulfram's churchyard toward the large manor complex to the east. When Ralf drew up at the stables, dropped his reins to the waiting groom, and dismounted, Perdu sprang from his shoulder and made off on some quest of her own. No matter, she always returned.

"See the queen's chamberlain," Ralf advised his men. "We will sleep here tonight and leave in the morning. Stay close, stay out of trouble. No need to search for cheer. Sire Geoffrey de Coutance sets an admirable board."

He waited for the queen's officer in the great hall, warming himself at the roaring fire pit. Only a short delay before Geoffrey de Coutance strode into the hall in his long English gown, keys jangling at his belt, left sleeve pinned up where he'd lost half an arm at Chester. The knight advanced with a quick, vital step, hand extended to Ralf in greeting.

"Good time of day, lord sheriff."

"And to you, Sire Geoffrey. I have the tax rolls you requested."

As the supper hour was at hand, trestles had been set up along both sides of the hall. Coutance and Ralf took seats opposite one another at a point near the fire.

"How goes your new office, Ralf?"

"Like this, like that." Ralf turned his hand over and back. "Better than Chester, eh?" Far better for Geoffrey de Coutance. Just verging on middle age, the man had the initial advantage of prominent family connections, though those carried one just so far. Under William a man rose rapidly only if he could administrate. Geoffrey had abilities to support his ambitions. He dealt daily with the English but never acquired the subtlety of a Waltheof, a blessing to Ralf who found such lords suspicious and faintly effete. Geoffrey waved the stump of his left arm in its sleeve, smirking at Ralf.

"I swear by Saint Gervaise: There are days when I can still feel my hand at the end of this buggering remnant. And you?" The queen's reeve noted the new long scar across the sheriff's face. "That is new."

"A few more like it and I may well decorate a church corbel: Nottingham's own gargoyle. *De rien*. Here are the tax rolls for the shire."

They worked through the fading late afternoon light, calling for candles when servants came into the hall to light wall sconces for supper. The candle was brought by a small, self-effacing woman who hastened away after the reeve spoke to her in English.

"Have to learn something of their tongue," he explained. "Never get anything done without it. "Now, *attends:* There is an important detail for you from Osmund, bishop of Nottingham. I understand his brother, Père Huger, has acted as your clerk."

"Yes."

"Lovely man." Geoffrey's expression contradicted the sentiment. "Without a parish until now."

Ralf remained neutral in his observations on Huger, though certain realities were well known among William's vavasors and clergy. After being crippled at Hastings, Osmund's younger brother had no recourse but to take orders in the church. He was an efficient clerk, but Huger missed the sword he could no longer wield more than he did any altar. Bishop Osmund had sent word to Ralf earlier that Huger would assume the post and livings of Blidworth's priest.

The Englishwoman returned with wine and goblets on a salver.

"How did Huger receive the news?" Geoffrey inquired delicately.

Ralf only spread his hands: He couldn't say.

"Come, Ralf: Be candid."

"Not the lightest spirit I've known."

"Nor always the best policy to make priests of former vavasors." Geoffrey paused while the woman filled their goblets. "In any event, Osmund will journey to Blidworth beginning on the seventeenth to install Huger and reconsecrate the church. On Saint Cecilia's Day as I understand. That is fitting."

Ralf kneaded at his bad leg. Dampness in the air always bothered the scar tissue. The Englishwoman brought them a plate of sliced apple and pork. She wiped meticulously at a small wine spill, then retired a few paces from them, ready to respond to any further need they might have of her.

"The bishop will be collecting his own rents in south Sherwood." Geoffrey offered the plate to Ralf, who waved it away. "He suggests you meet him at Papplewick with an escort."

Ralf turned the logistics in his mind. Better to escort from Nottingham. He elided mention of the few outlaws in northern Sherwood, grateful that Geoffrey did not raise the point which might be embarrassing just then.

But now—surely Sire Geoffrey would pardon him—he'd ridden much of the day and had been sitting too long. His leg bothered him. If their business was concluded, Ralf needed a walk before supper. Geoffrey rose with him as the woman inquired deferentially, "Will my lord reeve have further need of me?"

"No, you may go."

The woman bowed slightly and withdrew. She was unremarkable in every way. Ralf had barely glanced at her.

Marian's heart went out to protect the tortoiseshell cat from the instant she saw it on the larder shelf nibbling at a platter of fish bound for the oven. The Norman butler would have made short work of the marauder. When Marian came in, the cat was still eluding the butler's grasp with insolent ease.

"Wait, man." Marian passed her hand lightly over the uncooked fish. "Don't you know how to fetch a cat?"

She knelt reaching for her quarry. Scenting fish and no danger, the cat hesitated, then came to Marian, who scooped her up with a soft purring sound to put the animal at ease. "Eh, you're a young one, you are."

The butler took up the platter of fish, grumbling. "You'll have fleas in your shift. That's a stray."

"No, too clean for a stray. She's eaten regular." There weren't that many cats in Grantham to begin with. Cuddling her prize, Marian inquired of the kitchen staff who the owner might be. None of them had seen the damned thing before: probably from a barn litter somewhere, and keep it away from food about to go to the reeve's table. Cats as pets were rare to country folk. They wondered why the girl bothered to ask.

"Then you're mine," Marian declared, nose-to-nose with the tortoiseshell. She climbed the stairs to her own chamber to fetch her heavy cloak for the walk to St. Wulfram's before supper. There'd be a wait for confession. Merchants bound for Nottingham goose fair would be having a care to their souls before commencing such a journey. When she entered her chamber, Maud was folding a scrap of parchment into a leather purse which she hung at her girdle. The room was fairly dark, only one candle burning on the *prie-Dieu*.

"Look, Mum, what I've found. Got a spot of white like chin whiskers."

Maud took up her cloak and swept it about her. "Robin always meant to find you one."

"He would, the dear man."

"Will you go to confession?"

"If I can find Father Cedric. I wouldn't tell a Frank what I had for breakfast."

"Father Cedric is not hearing confessions today. Nor tomorrow," Maud added significantly. "Nor henceforth."

"Why ever not?"

Maud stroked the cat at Marian's bosom. "Because when they rang the bell, closed the book, and snuffed the candles at Beorn's excommunication, Cedric would have no part of it."

Not surprising therefore that the bishop of Lincoln straightway relieved Father Cedric of his parish livings, summarily offering him to Earl Waltheof (and obscurity) as clerk of Mansfield's *scriptorium*.

"A shame." Marian went to get her winter cloak out of a chest. "I'll go with you anyway."

"No, I must speak with the good father alone. We'll be guarded outside the manor grounds and two guards will be twice the bother to them." Maud's smile was tart with purpose. Any measure that inconvenienced Normans suited her well. "Wait a bit."

When Maud left, Marian removed the candle from the *prie-Dieu* along with the ink-daubed quill left there. She wondered what in the world

Maud needed to write. She set the candle near her bed and had just settled on it to enjoy the company of her cat when someone tapped softly at the door.

"Judith? Come in, the latch is out."

The cloaked figure in the doorway was not Judith. "Lady Marian. May I enter?"

Marian caught her breath. She had heard he was here on shire matters but hardly expected to see him and not at all sure she should allow it. His face was shadowed under the cloak's hood, but she remembered the lure of him. Among a hundred men her eyes would go to him and not know why, only that they must. That was shameful: He was Robin's enemy, sat in her husband's hall, ate off Denby plate and Denby livings. He was the symbol of their defeat, yet her own unfit feelings for the image of him made Marian feel like a whore. Oh, nonsense—she rapped her own spiritual knuckles—if she were older and more experienced with men, she wouldn't be quaking like a ninny . . . but she was.

Ralf came into the chamber, tactfully leaving the door open. "You do not remember me?"

Her throat felt tight. "Yes."

The cat meowed and squirmed to be set down, but Marian held her close, very much needing a barrier between herself and his invasive presence.

"May I to sit?"

"If you're seeking Lady Judith, she's not about."

"No. You are modest," he said.

"What?"

"To think I would naturally be seeking someone else." Ralf unbuckled his sword belt and settled himself in the room's single backed chair. Like many of the Normans, he found English clothes more suited to English winter, dressed in a long blue robe over loose red trousers cross-gartered to the calf. Still, he seemed stronger, more relaxed. His English was better too, Marian noticed, though he still spoke in the back of his throat. "What does the *scir-gerefa* wish of me?"

"I was looking for my . . ." Ralf's expression shifted slightly; he seemed to revise his intent on the spot. "For my chance to thank you for ministering to my sickness at Denby."

"No more than Christian, that."

"No less than the greatest kindness."

Just then the cat writhed out of Marian's grip, hit the floor in its off-balanced but confident way and sprang into Ralf's lap, meowing volubly.

For the first time, Marian heard him laugh as the cat pushed her head against his chest for affection. His head went back; the hood slipped away from his face. He'd let his hair grow against the cold, black as Angharad's. When he turned slightly toward the candlelight, Marian saw the long, trenched line across the cheek with no other mark on it. Her hand went out inadvertently. "What . . . ?"

His eyes lifted from the cat to her. "Yes?"

"You were hurt."

"This?" He dismissed it. "Well, my luck has held too long."

"Was it mischance?" Not an accident, not that, couldn't be.

Ralf stroked the cat once more, then rose and returned it to Marian's arms. "Your husband, madame."

Marian's stomach knotted. So that was why he'd come, to tell her Robin was caught. Hanged. Dead. Wretched, she could only shake her head mutely against the fear coursing through her like poison. Ralf Fitz-Gerald still stood too close to her; she ducked her head over the ridiculous cat. Then he answered the question she lacked Maud's cold courage to ask.

"He lives, Marian."

Alive. Thank God. Yet alive. She forced her lips to form the word. "Where?"

"I do not know. In his forest."

Mary Virgin would have a hundred ave marias tonight. She hadn't thought it possible for a woman to age so in a single instant. Lived today, perhaps dead tomorrow by this man's hand. Robin might elude Ralf or even kill him, but others would come, and one day there would be another knock at her door and Matilda would summon her with deep regret. . . .

"Why in God's name won't you go and leave us alone?"

The question and the verbal blow did not appear to discomfort him. "*Parce que*—it is the way of things, Marian. I follow my king." Ralf struggled visibly with something beyond an alien tongue. "But if something should befall your husband—"

"Shut up, man. Don't say that . . . please."

"No, it is only that I wish . . . I would you should not mourn too long. You are welcome always at Denby."

With feminine instinct, Marian knew what he meant and feared the truth of it in herself as well as him. Dreams were truth of their kind, and she had dreamed of this man before he came. She gripped the cat in her arms to keep her hands from trembling, wanting to sound proper. "*Hlae-ford cnecht,* you know right well that can't be. When Denby is ours again, when my husband welcomes you in his own hall, then I will present the cup to you.''

Ralf pressed one hand against his right leg. He winced furtively though the sound of him was gentle. She wouldn't have thought gentleness went with this battered, beautiful, alien glamour. "You are very young, Marian. I hate to see sadness in you. Do you know what is . . . of the most beautiful in you?"

Beautiful? "You should not speak so, it is not meet."

"I am called Ralf."

"I know."

"It is the peace of you that I admire. The . . . stillness. Out of a thousand faces a man finds one in which, somehow, he cannot bear to see pain. Yet I have brought you nothing else." He might have said more, searching for some response in her but finding none. He picked up the sword belt. "*Quelle pitié, Marianne.* I am only the king's arm, not his conscience."

"No." Marian desperately needed him to go now. "That's for men like my husband."

"Robin the conscience of the king?" Ralf tasted the thought and found it wry. "No, lady, that is too much."

"If it's so damned much, why does the king need to silence him?"

"You have a good wit, Marian," he conceded, politely swerving from the subject. "What is the name of your cat?"

"I thought she might be yours, the way she went to you."

"No."

"I only just found her. Ent got a name yet."

"Why not call her Perdu?"

"Per-doo?"

"The name for all lost things." Ralf gave the cat a final caress under her chin. "And if I know aught of cats, she might take to a little baked fish this evening. Good rest to you, Marianne."

Marian remained motionless when the door closed behind him, trying to take comfort from the cat purring against her body. *I love you, Robin. I love you!*

She wondered why she swore it so fiercely where Robin would never doubt her. Oh, then: There was more to this wonder of loving than a country girl knew.

At Marian's age, far more than she would have guessed. She had been given the one creature in the world beside herself whom Ralf Fitz-Gerald allowed close to him. The gift, even had she known, would have been offered as a trifle, large sacrifice made into simple grace, a feat his king never managed. Marian had learned the primary colors of love but not yet the delicate shades.

* * *

Maud knew the three of them were watched closely whenever they left the manor grounds. The guards always kept a discreet distance, undoubtedly by Matilda's express order. Truly, the queen meant them no harm. For Maud's part, the good intent was entirely one-sided. She intended as much harm as she could inflict. At the moment she hoped to shield Robin as well as she could.

Vespers Mass was over at St. Wulfram's and the light near gone when Maud passed through the churchyard, mingling with farmers and tradesmen making their way to and from the north entrance of the church. In the gloom she was only one small cloaked woman among many. Doubtless a guard was following. Let him work at keeping her in sight.

The great nave of the old Saxon church was clamorous with the babble of folk still hanging about after the service—Norman knights and clergy, tradesmen, parti-colored mountebanks and *jongleurs* bound for Nottingham with their entire household and substance rolled on their backs. The line for confession queued patiently before the several stalls along the west wall. Maud crossed herself at the font, genuflected to the altar and then melted into the press of people about her. Turning casually as if someone had called to her, she quickly singled out the earnest young Norman soldier who had been near the manor gate when she passed through. She didn't let her gaze pause on him but scanned further around the great, noisy open space before making for a sunny-faced priest ringed about by leaping, importunate children. Father Cedric was rumored to have more children of his own than many local householders. Middle-aged but still vital, to Maud he had the same qualities that burnished Lanfranc's nature and made the Italian tolerable, a man who loved life.

"Lady Maud—*ach,* give me a moment. Away, you heathens," he growled good-naturedly at the children. "Away with you, I've business." The process of disentangling himself from their sleeve-tugging siege took some moments, but finally Father Cedric dispatched the last of them with a kiss. "Give you good day, *Hlaefdige.*"

"And you, Father. Keep smiling at me. Give me your hand." Maud bent to kiss his fingers, for all the world one of those tremulous women to whom all clerics were exalted. "You will notice over my shoulder—casually—a Norman man at arms trying to be inconspicuous."

Cedric did. "He tries too hard."

Maud turned earnest, imploring, a supplicating hand on the sleeve of his priestly gown. "Now I will earnestly beseech you, seeing that the other priests are so occupied with confession, to hear mine in the consistory. You will say yes."

"Of course." Cedric was struck off the list for the sacrament, though not strictly forbidden to hear confession. "But why in the—?"

"One last favor before you depart for Mansfield. We will enter the consistory, leaving the door quite open. You will take a chair. I will kneel beside you where the soldier can see me."

Admiring her cool presence but somewhat bewildered, the priest walked with her toward the consistory to one side of the apse, Maud for all the world a helpless female on his arm. "It is barely four days since your last confession."

"I have only two matters on my soul, Cedric."

"And they are?"

"A purse of alms for the poor of Mansfield."

"Most generous. And . . . ?"

"A grey goose feather for Sherwood."

"Oh, yes." He understood her now.

"Leave the door open, Father. I must look devout for the soldier."

In the consistory, Cedric sat down at one end of a long bench, shading his eyes. "While we're on the subject," he inquired softly, "do you have any instructions for God?"

Maud sank demurely to her knees and crossed herself. Beyond the door, the guard was trying to be invisible and within earshot all at once. "Bless me, Father, and listen closely. This purse contains the feather, the alms, and a letter. . . ."

22

*F*ROM THE CHURCH Maud returned to help serve supper in the hall and thence to pick up her knitting where she left it—to all appearances a modest, obedient, and unassuming woman. In truth she had far better assets for intrigue than Judith who never escaped notice in any company of men. Maud's retiring demeanor, when she wished, could render her unremarkable as faded tapestry. Judith was not shy about her accomplishments or those of her kin and might well have blurted Maud's fluent knowledge of Frank had she suspected it. Hence Maud's white lie to her niece. At first a defense to keep the Normans at a distance, the ploy became more serious when Robin was outlawed and a weapon now. The sheriff had been ill when he first came to Denby and did not take close note of her, nor did he remember her today. Thus she marked Geoffrey's instructions to Fitz-Gerald when she served them, and transmitted them to Robin when Father Cedric journeyed through Sherwood to Mansfield. Maud's letter was brief and precise. Whatever the Church decreed as the properly subordinate place of women, they often made the best spies.

Two days later in regard to Osmund, bishop of Nottingham, Robin knew where, when, who, why, and approximately how many. Maud's motive was merely to inform her son of men and movement to be avoided. However, there were other unhappy men in Sherwood, and the sequel to her letter hinged on one of them, Alan of Linby Dale.

. . . leaving Nottingham on the 17th to install Huger at Blidworth and reconsecrate the church most like on the 22nd, the day of Cecilia Martyr. He will not come directly but will collect his overdue rents along the way. Fitz-Gerald will escort, possibly from Nottingham, surely from Papplewick. We want for nothing save you, beloved son, and pray hourly for your safety. All our love comes to you from Judith and myself and Marian, who wakes to think of you and ceases only to sleep.

Joyeux Noël/M

Robin squinted at the closing. "There's Mum being playful. What's this *joy-ooks* at the end?"

"Frankish," said Father Cedric as he embraced Beorn and mounted his mule to go on toward Mansfield. "Merry Christmas."

Martinmas had come and the fall slaughtering of hogs, and naturally a fat haunch cured by Alcuin found its way to Sherwood. Over their meal, Robin's men considered it Yule gift enough to be fed and warm and where not to be in Sherwood for the next few days.

"Or," Robin speculated, "where we might be to some profit. Carve our guest some more of this fine pig. Alan, have you ever pondered on the magic of changes?" He held up his knife with a chunk of steaming ham impaled thereon. "When we raise the beast, it's pig. On a Norman table it becomes pork."

"Ah, they're great ones for magic." Alan took the fresh slice offered to him. "I steal William's pig, he calls me thief. He steals my land and I must call him king."

"They do make good—what d'you call this brown stuff?" Much slathered his ham generously with the foreign delicacy out of a clay pot.

"Mustard," Alan said, adding that King William had much to answer for when his time came. "I do not think the man was raised up right."

"Alan of Linby Dale," Robin reproved him with a twinkle, "you are my guest, but hardly the man to sit in judgment on thieves."

"True, Thane Alan," Will purred over his ale. "Lord Robin never held with theft among landowners. Sets a bad example for a man's tenants."

"I tried to explain that." Young Alan hung his head and got on with living down his too-recent disgrace with the men of Sherwood. "I was desperate."

Robin winked at Will. He might have eased Alan's humiliation but considered it medicinal. As he regarded his peer across the peat cooking fire that warmed and sweetened their hut, he balanced a number of elements in his mind. The last few days had mixed rain with snow. His men would be easier for Fitz-Gerald to track. No margin now for the foolhardiness that earned him a good whack from John's staff. The blow hammered better sense into Robin. If he appeared less tightly coiled now, there was deeper seriousness within. Few beyond Will and Beorn noted that he had grown quieter, showing less of anger and more of his innate good sense, exposing neither himself nor his men to needless danger. Nor would he now for Marian's sake, *who wakes to think of you and ceases only to sleep*. There would be nothing foolhardy this time. Maud's letter, meant to caution, could inspire as well. Alan was a friend and in trouble.

Alan of Linby Dale found the boldness to rob but lacked true facility. A seven-night past, with no snow yet on the ground to mark their trail, Will and John were on an errand any good forester would undertake without hesitation. Northwest of Papplewick, Robin's band had come on a blood-trail, a great red buck by the signs. Some huntsman had put a shaft into him. The buck was wounded and would surely die a lingering death if not dispatched by a better bowman. They never found the ill-fated animal but were accosted themselves, brought up short by an arrow that buried itself in the ground at their feet—

"Hold!"

A man in helm and mail, sword belted at his side, bow drawn on them. Will and John had a horrible sick moment thinking he was one of the sheriff's men and more close by—but the helm was Saxon with a face-piece that masked most of the man's visage, and he stanced the bow like a native.

"Drop your weapons. Down."

Down they went. The stranger stepped over the fallen log that had been his place of ambush and stalked closer. "Your silver."

John blinked at the apparition. "My *what*?"

"Your purse, hind. Yours too," the brigand snarled at Will.

Will touched his leather collar. "It is a slave I am and this a blacksmith of Blidworth. What wealth would we be hoarding between us?"

The bow bent on them wavered. "Of Blidworth?"

"And Denby," John added. "When Denby was Lord Robin's to call his own."

"Denby." The erstwhile robber sank down on the log. "God, if that's not my luck all over." He tore the helmet off to reveal yellow hair and a face English as blood pudding. "The poor robbing the paupers."

"And I don't take kindly to that," John informed him as Will put the ox horn to his lips and blew two quick notes. The young man was faintly familiar to John, wearing arms as if he were long used to them.

"If it is of any comfort, sir"—Will tried to cheer the dejected youth—"there's not a false penny between us."

"I don't care about that. I . . . I am sorry, in faith I am."

"You wear the arms of a thane," John observed. Arms without a speck of rust, hair and beard well trimmed, good leather shoes without much wear. "You're not a poor man."

The response issued from an abyss of misery. "Look again next week."

Will heard the others approaching in answer to his horn. "We thought you a Norman."

"I thought you had money." The young man's despair turned tart. "But you needn't insult me."

"Hullo, Rob," Will greeted his lord as Robin, Tuck, and Much appeared through the trees.

"Heard the horn; what's amiss?"

"Only a good man trying to worsen himself," Will told him.

Robin's countenance lit up with a sudden broad grin. "By Dunstan's Lock—Alan! Merry meet." He pumped the man's hand vigorously.

Alan rose to meet him with a bedraggled courtesy. "And to you, Edward."

Robin threw a fraternal arm around Alan's shoulder. "His da and mine were good friends ever. Six good hides at Linby. Why are you armed, man?"

"Robbin' us," John declared. "Or trying to."

"Wha-at?" The word drew out with Robin's disbelief. A landowner stealing from commoners and his own countrymen to boot? "Your father would've skinned the man who said so."

Alan of Linby Dale tried to look his boyhood friend in the face, then around at the confounded men of Sherwood. He sank wordlessly onto the log in confusion. Robin sat beside him in the grey November light. No one spoke for a time, no sound but the oaks and brambles dripping recent rain. A general air of embarrassment hovered over the men.

Robin said at length, "Well, I just don't know."

Alan writhed in his disgrace. "I am sorry, Edward."

"Alan—shame on you."

"Never heard of such a thing," Tuck humphed.

"And us with not half our own troubles." Suddenly Robin laughed at the absurdity of the situation. "But I'll warrant you've heard of them."

"Who in the shire has not? You have ill fortune, Edward, but don't compound my disgrace by laughing at me."

"Well, then." For Alan's benefit, Robin named his men all around. "My forester, Will Scatloch. My blacksmith, John Littlerede, and Tuck, the sexton of Blidworth church. There's our priest back north a piece, Father Beorn. Good men all: This is Thane Alan of Linby Dale, as fine a farmer as his da was,'' Robin commended with a brotherly arm about the shoulders of his unhappy friend. "But I don't think thievin's his bent."

In truth, as Alan explained his plight, he was no more thief than Robin, but in circumstances nigh as bleak. His lands at Linby were now within the huge estate of Osmund, bishop of Nottingham. He had been delinquent in his rent since Michaelmas, five pounds in all, and no way to raise such a sum with a poor harvest. All his folk had been close to famine this year. When Alan thought of his lady and small daughter, he went plain mad with the worry, desperate enough to try anything. The bishop would be coming soon for his money, the matter was pay or be evicted, and what was a man to do? He wished Will and John had been Normans. Rich ones.

"First you'll eat with us," Robin invited. "Then you'll sleep warm and dry. No trouble was ever the worse for food and rest."

But what *was* a man to do? Robin pondered now as he ruminated over his meat. He put down the knife, wiped his hands on his trews and took out Maud's letter, passing it to Beorn. "Read slowly, Father. Especially about Marian."

He listened to the priest read, hands folded over his mouth and chin, the way he used to at chess with Ethelwold on winter nights. The steward always won until Robin learned to think many moves ahead. The same logical concentration forged his successful ambush at Tadcaster. One word issued from behind his clasped hands: "chess."

"What of chess?" Tuck wondered with a soft belch.

"Papplewick." Robin took the letter from Beorn, leaving the hut and a huddle of men no more enlightened than before.

Outside, Robin scanned the clearing sky and smelled the air. Not that cold. They might have more rain but no snow. Deep in thought, he was still careful to avoid well-traveled paths, moving deliberately along a barely visible swine run through the underbrush. A brilliant blue-green kingfisher swooped ahead of him, making for the rill to feed beneath the thawed waters, while a garrulous band of starlings had found firethorn berries to feast on. Part of Robin's mind stayed on the problem at hand and its evolving solution, part read the forest around him. A red squirrel spiraled down a tree trunk. The long, black-tipped ears of a hare shot away into thicket. The wind from the north carried the acrid smell of salt and smoke. Alcuin would be laboring long hours now at curing and smoking hams for the sheriff. The stronger odor would be from the tanning vats, the stink of pig and chicken dung from the tanner's bating troughs. Fitz-Gerald was battened on Robin's land but not interrupting the natural order of tasks except for the great horses stalled in the barn.

Down on one knee, Robin cleared a patch of earth. With his knife he drew several lines for the cart routes between Denby, Papplewick, and Nottingham, then the only horse route north from Nottingham toward Edwinstowe. There was no direct route for horsemen from Denby to Linby Dale unless they rode cross-country through heath and wood. By the established tracks, they must travel to Papplewick and turn west.

In his mind Robin moved pieces, elements, forming a picture. Six miles north of Nottingham the single route forked like a tree trunk: northwest to Papplewick, northeast toward Edwinstowe. The knife point hovered over the Y formed by the division of routes, then descended near the fork.

"Me to move and that's where."

If one were hunting a bishop, that was. The problem was the knight. There were great open stretches of open heath in south Sherwood where men had no chance on foot against mounted knights. On the other hand, men on foot could move faster through the thickets, and Normans considered walking a degradation.

Robin pored over his earth map, planning one move and the next and next. The why of all this—why he contemplated risking himself and his men for Alan—went beyond friendship. There were precious few Saxon peers left to whom the folk could turn. If Alan lost his land, the bishop would surely snap up the holding and there'd be even more foreigners in Sherwood. Aside from that remained the honor involved in an unpaid debt. The spring before he marched to York, Aelred had borrowed a fine team of eight oxen from Alan's father to clear new bookland for cultivation, proposing to return them after harvest. By then both Aelred and Robin were hastening north with the rebel force. Hard on their heels, the Normans swept through Denby and commandeered every draft animal in sight to pull their supply wagons. In the hard times that winter, Alan never called the debt in kind or cash, nor did he remind Robin of it in his present dire need. But the debt remained outstanding.

"Get ready to move. We're for Linby Dale," Robin announced when he returned to his men. "Tear down the hut, scatter the bits, hide our moveables. Alan, your rents will be paid."

Because Alan couldn't see how, Robin obligingly redrew his map in the dirt and described the plan for all of them, no less than larceny on an admirable scale. Alan would return to his lady and none grieving but the bishop and the sheriff. His companions applauded the conception. The bilking of a Norman was not without allure, but Father Beorn saw the flaw: what of Fitz-Gerald?

"If he's delayed, he won't be meeting Osmund at Nottingham," Robin argued.

Delay him with what? Will posed. "Riddle me that."

John had a direct method, daring as Robin's. "Burn the barn and his horses inside."

Robin was appalled. "That's *my* barn you'd make free with."

"How else?" John challenged. What with unarmed common folk and Norman guards everywhere—how else? "Fire's the best way."

"And someone to scatter the beasts out of the barn," Beorn amended.

Robin detested the idea of destroying his own property; he would be going back to that barn someday, God willing and luck holding firm. Still, aside from the sheriff being summarily called to God in his sleep, nothing practical presented itself.

"Just a small fire?" John wheedled. A small fire at the right time among horses already restive with the stink from tanning hides. Alan had several good mounts himself and knew their feelings on the smell of tanning.

"We'll need one of your horses," Robin concluded. "Your fastest. And one good liar."

Alan was impressed with Robin's cool confidence, going about robbery systematically as ploughing a furlong. But what need of a liar?

"A great need, one to swear black is white while wearing both and make you believe him."

An unusual request, but Alan had a woodcutter-tenant whom he had never caught red-handed in veracity. "Mark, Edward, I appreciate your efforts." But there were limits to what one peer could ask of another. If caught he'd be hanged on the spot.

"I'm for hanging now," Robin reminded him, "and all these here with me, but there's a beauty to the matter as well. You will be snug at home, innocent as a lamb, paid what Denby owes you—for the bishop will be carrying a deal more than five pounds."

* * *

In the early morning of the sixteenth, Sven the fletcher had barely opened his eyes and turned over when his stolid wife crawled from their pallet and stepped over the sleeping children to answer an insistent pounding at their door. Little John it was, with a message to be passed with speed to certain folk at Denby. Later that same day, with Norman men at arms everywhere about the steading, one person or another—Angharad, Minna, or Ethelwold—went to the barn on some errand or other throughout the daylight hours, each concealing a small amount of flammable substance which they left in a shadowed corner of the unused wool room: oily rags, seasoned kindling, or dry straw. Toward evening, someone thoughtfully left flint, steel, and a tinder box by the inconspicuous pile and covered them with rags.

The fire broke out in the early hours of the seventeenth, long before the men detailed for the bishop's escort were stirring. Sentries heard the milling, screaming horses first, then smelled smoke and saw the flickering lights through spaces between barn timbers. The stable doors burst open even as a sentry ran to cry the alarm, and forth poured a torrent of terrified, white-eyed horses that no one man or six like him could halt in their plunging need to escape the flames. They galloped headlong for the low steading wall, following the stallions, jumped it and vanished neighing and snorting into the dark. The barn was seriously damaged before men could control the flames. The arsonist Little John had tried to keep the blaze local but the Normans took so much time putting the damned thing out. And what with unlatching the stalls one by one, unbarring the barn door, frighting the horses good with a burning splinter, and then making off in dark and confusion, his hands had been full. He apologized to his lord for the miscalculation.

"Truly, John, I can hear your grief," Robin understood sourly as they jogged south toward Linby. "A wonder I've a barn left at all."

Ralf Fitz-Gerald knew the burning was deliberate, but the sentry was a reliable man and swore he had seen no living soul beside himself before giving the alarm, not even one innocently bound for the latrine house. Yet the horses had not kicked free of their stalls. The barn door, always barred at night, was inconveniently open. They lost more than an hour putting out the fire, several more waiting for enough light to find, calm, and collect the runaway horses.

The escort was five hours late starting for Nottingham. Bishop Osmund expected them by nine at the latest. When they did not appear, Osmund assumed delay, planned to meet them at Papplewick, and set out on the north route with his brother Huger and a small escort to collect the first of his overdue rents along the way.

On that chilly morning, Bishop Osmund dealt with a gloomy series of negatives. He did not relish winter travel through Sherwood. There was no good road north from Nottingham. His train must follow a mere cart track toward Papplewick with detours to collect his rents from delinquent tenants, and the same tedious, quagmired route afterward into Blidworth to rededicate the two-penny church and install his brother as priest.

The train lumbered north toward Papplewick with Osmund's steward, his cook, Huger and his new sexton, a handful of soldiers, and all of Huger's moveables packed on three mules. Thirteen men in all, an inauspicious number when Osmund rued the whole business later.

North of Nottingham Osmund's tenants mixed in a patchwork of fiefs with those of Ralf Fitz-Gerald. By noon and blunt insistence, the bishop had collected much of what was owed him. To those unable to pay, his steward sternly promised eviction at the Christmas quarter before the train moved on toward Papplewick and the last of the debtor-tenants, including Thane Alan. In Osmund's present mood Alan could be counted as another negative: not openly rebellious like the Denby fellow but sullen and stiffish. One of those Saxons who would stand aloof in the company of Normans but refuse to sit with them unless commanded.

This stretch of Sherwood was checkered with open heath and worked fields. Sheep wandered the cleared lands, nibbling away imperceptibly at the coverts of deer. Osmund's train came to the fork in the cart road where they must bear northwest. They plodded on as the muddy track crossed broad heath bordered east and west by forest. Riding beside his brother, Osmund saw Huger's lips part in sudden pleasure. Out of the treetops west of the heath, two rooks flapped into the sky. Foresters would have known from their agitated cawing that something disturbed them in the nest. Huger saw only the soaring kestrel that veered toward the rooks from high above. The canny rooks shot down again into tree cover.

"There is beauty," Huger vowed, following the kestrel's graceful sweep across open sky. "There is the only true freedom."

"Help! My lords, help me!"

They heard his voice before the ragged man staggered out of the trees west of them, clutching his head and running as fast as he could. Riding ahead of the bishop, the men at arms turned toward the piteous figure, then looked back, silently seeking their lord's will in the matter.

The man had a head wound, still bleating for aid as he stumbled up to them. "In the name of Jesu, protect me."

The train had halted at Osmund's signal. "Fellow, what is the matter?"

"The villein's hurt," Huger said.

Nastily hurt; as the grizzled peasant dropped on his knees in the mud before Osmund, they saw the bright fresh blood trickling from his crown and down over his forehead. He raised clasped hands in supplication. "Truly, my lord, God sent you this day to my aid."

"Aid in what, man?"

"Robin Hood," the peasant gasped. "Him it is and no other. Robbed me of my best young ewe he did, even now back in the forest." He pointed shakily whence he'd come. "Nay, he demanded my purse." He dug dirty, callused fingers into the leather bag at his belt and produced a single tarnished coin. "By Saint Werburgh: one penny to it, no more, and this penny promised to the poor box, but he'd have that too had I not run away. Help me," he implored, "for I think he pursues me still."

"There!" one of the soldiers shouted as the rider in green cantered out of the woods and reined short, apparently as surprised as the Normans. The wounded peasant emitted a dolorous wail—"It's him! Robin Hood"—and scurried to shelter behind the bishop's horse. Before anyone could collect their wits, the outlaw launched a shaft at the train, booming out his challenge: "GREYFEATHER!"

The bishop's mount shied as the arrow drove into the mud near his hoof. Huger snapped a command at the soldiers. "Jean, remain with us. The rest of you after him. Ride him down. *Allez.*"

The green-clad outlaw threw one last defiance over his shoulder— "God bless the soul of King Harold!"—turned his clean-limbed chestnut horse and galloped back into the forest with seven Norman soldiers in full cry after him. In a few moments the forest swallowed up both quarry and hunters.

"Broad daylight. The man's mad. Well, no fear," Huger assured his brother, "our men will run him to—"

He was still speaking when the first arrow hit the horse under their remaining guard. The animal reared and went over on its side, pinning the startled rider under a writhing flank. Then Huger's palfrey mare was hit twice in the neck and flank, buckling at the knees into the mud. Years of training yanked Huger's feet from the stirrups before the dying animal could roll on him.

In another instant, the bishop's mount was pierced through the shoulder. Osmund managed to clear the saddle awkwardly, lost his balance and sprawled his length in cold mud. "After the men," he bawled at his steward. "Call them back, it's a trap."

Five men in faded Lincoln green broke at a run out of the trees to the east. The steward raked spurs over the stallion's flanks; before the obedient grey could stretch into full gallop, two of the marauders halted and loosed at the steward. One arrow struck the grey in its flank, the other took the rider full in the back. The horse stumbled but kept its footing, the steward slumped to one side and dropped heavily from the saddle, one foot caught in the stirrup. Within a few seconds, Osmund and Huger stood on the muddy cart track surrounded by downed horses, a terrified cook, a peasant gibbering incoherent pleas to Jesus and Mary Virgin, the phlegmatic but confused sexton, a profane mule driver trying to quiet pack animals with the smell of blood in their flared nostrils—and five grinning Englishmen all with arrows nocked to their longbows.

"John and Tuck: the bags."

Huger gaped when he recognized Edward of Denby. The outlawed thane booted the wounded peasant in his rear and gave him a shove to encourage retreat. "Out, scut. You've hindered me enough this day."

The Saxon scurried away across the heath, still holding his bloodied pate. While John and Tuck looted the packsaddles, Robin indicated the dead steward hanging grotesquely from his saddle. "I am sorry for that man. I was aiming at the horse."

"Do I not keep telling you?" Will Scatloch deftly severed the bishop's purse from his *cingulum*. "Never hurry. Haste makes waste."

"No one move." Much menaced the Normans with his bow, fierceness jittery with nerves. "Hurry, then, they'll be coomin' back."

"Found 'em." John and Tuck hauled the heaviest bags free of the packsaddle.

"The former Thane Edward, brother," Huger remarked with cold disgust. "Whom we will shortly hang as Robin Hood. Mark his face."

"As I mark yours, Huger," Robin answered levelly. "If you're to be priest at Blidworth, pray your Mass has more mercy than your justice. That's my village. Tend them well."

"And have the place cleaned out," Tuck admonished, heaving the money pouch to his shoulder. "There's broom and lye soap in the sacristy. Are you the sexton?"

"That I am," the slow-moving, thick-bodied Saxon told him. "Been such in Nottingham for ten years."

Tuck gave him a professional inspection up and down, evidently concluding he was better than no sexton at all. "You may have my house, then. The fireplace and the door hinges want mending. I never got to them.''

"Done." The moneybag swung over Little John's shoulder with the solid *chink* of silver within. Without another word, he and Tuck toiled away toward the forest under their burdens.

"That is my money," Huger fumed. "And the rightful rents of the bishop of Nottingham."

Will raised his bow slightly. "I would not press the point, mun."

"Indeed I would not," young Much agreed with some venom. "John was for taking your eyes, priest. He says they're owed to Wystan."

Huger was never a fearful man, notwithstanding the weapons trained on him. "God help you, Denby. When the rope goes around your neck, the Devil will be waiting for you to drop."

"Heed him." Osmund was firm as his brother. "I know something of you. Rebels are not without honor, perhaps, but a common thief is damned anywhere."

Robin returned the bishop's empty purse. "When you hang me for theft, at least admit I was apt to the trade as you. Will, Much—go."

They sprinted away to help John and Tuck with their load. Robin covered their retreat with his bow. Aside from the inconvenience to his priest-employer, the English sexton could not quite bring himself to curse Englishmen, neither did he wish to be robbed of the few pence in his purse. Robin's eye was on him and seemed full of enterprise. "I'm a poor man," he attempted. "I hope you do not think of taking my lean purse."

"Take from Englishmen? I'll leave that to William," Robin saluted him cheerfully, backing away from them. "Mind Tuck's house and mend his fireplace. There's crayfish and trout in the rill for a fisherman. Freda down the Queen's Rest is a wizard with a roast, but her fish just comes out leather. Cooks it to death."

To Huger's rising irritation, his placid sexton was actually cordial. "I do thank you for that."

"And there's rare good apples for the taking north of the village." Robin broke into a run, trailing a last warning to Huger. "Tend my church well, Norman."

Half an hour later the hot pursuers of "Robin Hood" rode reluctantly back to their lord on winded horses. The outlaw was riding a *destrier* from hell—*vraiment*, the very look of the beast was strange—that outdistanced them through forest, over broken ground and open heath alike.

The sight of the unhappy bishop and the general mayhem urged them to postpone lengthy excuses.

"He was here," Osmund informed them icily.

"Who . . . ?" Then whom or what did they follow?

"No matter, you oafs," Huger raged. "Robin Hood was here."

Taking up the steward's body and their suffering, leg-broken companion from under his dead horse, several of the men continued to wonder at the man they followed, even more at his tireless horse. Actually the rider was Father Beorn, Robin's only experienced horseman. The stallion was hardly diabolic but an Arabian. There were few of the breed in England: relatively light for war use, but incredibly durable and far swifter than the Flemish breed. Beorn could have lost the soldiers easily but his task was to give Robin time. The prize Arabian had been won at dice from a Frankish trader less nimble at calculating odds than Alan of Linby Dale, descended from five hundred years of avid gamblers.

That week at least, neither Osmund nor Huger would have appreciated fine equestrian points or the undeniable finesse of the venture, though legions of English roared over the jest, beginning with Alan's woodcutter wailing danger, fear, and loss while dramatically daubed with pig's blood. Not to mention Alan himself, aggrieved but paying his rent in cash, and feeding his Arabian an extra helping of grain for noble service.

On a night when there were no Normans in his hall at Mansfield, Waltheof regaled his guests with the story. "Which my harper has but late put to music. Come," he summoned the musician to take his place before the high table. "Sing, harper, and the more sweetly that we remember. My lords and ladies"—Waltheof raised his drinking horn to the company—"the lay of Robin and the bishop."

Ralf Fitz-Gerald came in for a generous share of the bishop's wrath; the king would hear of this and presently, have no doubt. The price on Robin's head rose to a staggering twenty pounds, equal to the value of a rich manor or a thriving town, cried out in churches and at every crossroad in the shire. Heroic ballads aside, Ralf knew, sooner or later someone would hearken to the music of money and hear the persistent question beneath the music: How much is loyalty worth? Put that loyalty in the scale against a rising price. Sooner or later one dish would sink.

At Christmas, churches in Papplewick, Southwell, Blidworth, and Edwinstowe found their poor boxes full to bursting. At Blidworth, had Father Huger troubled to notice, the folk of the village were modestly comfortable this Yule season, though the sheriff was not wrong in his instinct for the English urge to profit. At the Queen's Rest, the few coins dropped heavily from Ceolred's one hand to his other. They felt substantial. They hinted of more, like twenty pounds. The man was instantly shamed and thrust the thought into a dusty corner of his mind where it remained like a mute guest, unobtrusive but there.

23

*I*F YULETIDE WAS not festive, the men were stunned by sudden riches. The greater part was given out through the shire, but each of Robin's men received three pounds for his share in the venture. Father Beorn deemed it more reclamation than robbery—and, marry, that was well said. An honest man could not call it theft. When called before God and English saints, Osmund and Huger would have a raw time of it explaining how they came by such pelf.

Three pounds each, a staggering sum for country fellows, much more than Little John could cup in his broad hands together. Such amounts had no real meaning to them, save perhaps Will Scatloch, who was almost captured before the money and a remembered promise fused together in his mind. For the rest, they dreamed impractical ends.

Tuck salivated with his prospects. "I will buy ten barrels of ale from Ceolred and a tun of that red Norman wine. Then I'll be to Grantham for the finest relics to set into our altar when I'm home. And what will you do, John?"

Littlerede ruminated on the question. Such dreams weren't as simple for him as they might be for Tuck or young Much, who was feverishly building opulence from this promising start. When their troubles were done and the king pardoned them (as surely he must, Much reasoned), he would go up Nottingham dight in the best apparel a man could order, knock on the door of some wealthy merchant, and speak of investment. And if the merchant chanced to have a comely daughter, Much would dicker for a wife and so have rich in-laws. By God, he'd get on in this world. John pointed out that Much was only half free, bound to the land under Robin as ever he'd be under Normans, but Much accounted that no obstacle to a man of means.

John Littlerede allowed that was well and good for a stripling with young ambitions. He didn't rightly know what he would do with his three pounds beyond firing up his hearth at Blidworth again someday. His personal wishes and wants had more to do with memories than silver.

Robin was more concerned that Christmastide with the consequences of the robbery. He hoped the sheriff would not take it out on Blidworth. While he hardly regretted the act—a grand lark in a good cause—he reckoned he might have planned a mite further ahead. What of Marian at Grantham? What of Maud and Judith? He must survive for their sakes. Survival took more and more caution this winter. The colors of the sheriff's foresters no longer announced them from a safe distance. They went now in dull Lincoln green, as hard to spy out in the forest as his own men. As for the money, Robin was no more accustomed to large sums than his friends were. He gave some of his share to Minna and Wystan, slipping into their croft one midnight with whispered Yule greetings, hugs all round, and the silver slipped into astounded Minna's hand.

With motives and desires of his own, Father Beorn found a fitting use for his share, and Will Scatloch discovered there was nothing to clear a man's mind like a touch of near-death.

On a January day when the mist lay thick over Sherwood, Will judged it time and safe enough to inspect his snares. He left early, purposing to return by noon, but the midday bell rang through the fog from Blidworth church with no sign of him. Hours later when the brief winter light began to fade from the day, Will stumbled out of the fog flanked by worried Tuck and John and clutching his bloody right arm.

"Careless just once," he seethed in self-disgust. "Both eyes seeing family and not what was in front of me."

The arrow came out of nowhere, he said. If the archer were a mite more skillful, Will would not be telling the tale. "But I am and there's a lesson learned." The Welshman searched Robin's face with an intensity his friend had never seen before; naked fright was there but something under the fear, a determination. "Tuck, be a good man and fetch my moneybag."

The sexton inspected the tear in Will's sleeve and the wound beneath. "That wants tending."

They all saw it: Will Scatloch snapped at Tuck like a distempered dog. "Devil the hurt, fetch my money."

Strange. Petulance was no part of Will Scatloch, nor temper unless he was drunk. A more potent motive drove him now, muttering to himelf while Beorn boiled dried woundwort with honey for a healing poultice and wrapped the arm round with a length of their hoarded clean linen.

A harrowing tale Will told them. By a tree near the thicket where he always set his most productive snares, Will had let his thoughts drift to Angharad and the boys. A moment only; he was warning himself to stop dreaming and stay alert when the long arrow pinned his right sleeve and a good piece of his hide to the grey beech bark.

Stand in the name of the king!

He tore himself loose, feeling the sting and the hot blood running down his arm, bounding away to put a deal of Sherwood and fog between himself and the law.

"I heard them coming after me, two or three by the sound. Tuck, where's my money? Did I not ask? Then *get* it, you goddamned fool Englishman!"

None of them knew what to make of him, harsh manner worse than his wound. An easy-going man turned suddenly mean, shivering against a tree in their midst but not from the cold, even though his wool tunic and trousers were soaked through.

"Easy on, Will." Robin put a reassuring hand to his friend's shoulder only to have it shaken off.

"Leave me alone. They're good, those boyos of the sheriff. Hard to see now. Tried to lose them. . . ." Will led them away from the camp but could not shake off his trackers. He left a blood trail leading south, doubled back, and went to ground in the thickest cover he could find, a cave of tangled vine long used by does when the time came to give birth to fawns. Lying still as the doe he heard the nearing, unhurried tred of the hunters. They paused, went on, and then returned.

He's gone on right enough.

Maybe he has, maybe he ent.

You saw the blood up there.

I know what I saw.

Dead still he lay while the minutes and then the hours crept by. His clothes grew sodden while the blood clotted on his wound, teeth chattering with cold, body one unending shudder of fear, cold, and wound shock. The sheriff's men crossed and recrossed the area around him before going away. Will prayed all the while to Saint David, who took pity on him and excused his near-fatal lapse of alertness this time. Perhaps for the last time.

When Tuck put the moneybag in the Welshman's hand, Will looked up at the concerned friends over him—serious, not to be denied. "I've been almost killed today and the shadow is still on me. You lads go on. I would speak alone with my lord and priest. And look sharp," he warned them in parting. "Have a dove's eye to danger. The hawks are out and hunting."

Vespers bell came to them faintly with the early twilight of winter. Robin could no longer see Will clearly in the gloom, but the sound of the man was flat, gritty, weighted with resolve. "All those hours shivering and bleeding in that thicket, I thought to be dead with every breath. The truth was so clear it was a pain in my head."

Never in his life had Will thought so lucidly, mind lit bright as Beltane fire. In one terrible sense the arrow didn't miss at all but went clear through him, impaling Angharad, Eddain, and Gwaun as well. "Do you know what it is that I am saying, Robin? They're my blood like that running out of my arm. They are a charge on my soul, and what happens to them if I die?"

"You needn't ask," Robin said, kneeling beside him. "So long as I'm lord, they have a home."

"Listen to him. Wake, Puck-Robin. You have no home, and when will you? They might kill you tomorrow, kill us all."

Beorn said, "I never saw my Will lose heart before."

Will glared at the priest. "Will you listen? Listen and be witness, Father. I want my dear ones free of Denby and I'll have it so."

Robin could see no future in that. "That's folly."

"Devil that!"

"Dangerous."

"And today was not?"

"Hard enough for us to move now. What'll you do with Angharad and the boys mucking about and having to be watched every minute? Where's your wits, man?"

Will cursed softly in Welsh. "God, you're a thick one. I said free: of you as well as the bloody Franks." The moneybag chinked solidly as Will dropped it at Robin's foot. "If I have to die, let me die free."

Robin might not have understood. He did not pick up the moneybag, only nudged at it curiously with one foot as if it were something alien.

* * *

Strange to the men: Will's steely new purpose and Robin's mute resistance. When Beorn broached the subject, Robin very quickly ended the conversation.

"Plague me no more in this." And there it was.

Robin was confused, not thinking clearly. The near-death of his closest friend jarred him more than he showed. The offer and demand from Will shook him even more deeply in a place where words and reasons couldn't reach, laying bare the inconsistency in Robin's purely English character: an instinct for progress side by side with a fear of any change come too suddenly. A love of justice part of a way of life in which slavery was accepted without question by honorable men. What Robin was used to and comfortable with he perceived as right and good. Only Beorn came close to understanding his turmoil. He knew the bastion of Robin's "right and good," since every man needed one. First the conquest took his country, then stripped him of title, land, family, and home. Will Scatloch was only the barbed point of a long, sharp sword cutting that already sundered world into smaller and smaller pieces. Not Will alone but all the shattered pieces disappearing day by day.

Something must be done. The other men puzzled uncomfortably while two days passed wherein the two pillars of their fellowship barely spoke to one another. Finally, as arbiter for them all, Father Beorn saw his duty clear. Will needed an answer as much for his state of mind and that of the rest of them as anything else.

These last few days they'd had to move again because of the relentless patrols—north this time within the sound of Edwinstowe church bells. Beorn found Robin moodily washing his face in a small stream, and noted how long and unkempt the man's hair and beard had grown. They'd all gone to seed this winter. Hogs would not give them houseroom. Beorn sat down on a fallen log.

Robin dried his face on one sleeve. "Well, what? If you've come about Will—"

"Well, I have."

"Weeping Jesus, I don't—"

"Don't fly off but heed me. The men are wondering at you in this."

"Let them. There's more to think on than Will Scatloch. I'm dealing with the lot as best I can."

"Best indeed," Beorn scoffed. "Not dealing at all. The man's made a legal offer and deserves an answer."

"When I give him one." Robin scanned and listened to the forest for any sign of disturbance: quiet but not unnaturally so. He settled himself beside his priest, rubbing at his overgrown beard. He was yet loath to speak of the matter. Beorn helped him a little.

"What is the heart of this? More than Will, I'm bound."

"I never treated him like a slave. He's family to me, like my own."

"Like your hall," Beorn interpreted. "Your barn, your sheep. Yours."

"Not like that at all. You heard him. He'd be free of me and Denby. What's Will to do with freedom? Where would he go with a wife and children? Welsh foreigner, known and wanted; he'd not get a mile before they caught him."

"Foreigner?" Beorn's smile was faintly ironic. "We're the foreigners to Will. Normans are just more of the same. It's a quandary, Robin—and we are the paradox at its core."

The word was new to unlettered Robin. "What's paradox?"

"Two things that can't possibly be yoked together but are."

"Don't come scholars' words to me," Robin said. "I know nowt of 'em."

"But you have heard poets sing in Denby hall." Beorn himself had seen men of honor weep over poetry that lauded honor, loyalty, and high motives, then rise next day to herd manacled slaves to the block. "With no more thought to the wrong of it than you, Robin. Paradox? You put your lands and life on the block to defend Wystan. You lost them because you wouldn't deliver Much. You'd do as much, you'd go on the block yourself for Will. But you'll turn about without so much as a blink or a blush and insist you own him."

"Well, I do. The records of sale are in your church."

Beorn opened his hand and let the grass drift to earth. The man was thick indeed. "You don't see my point."

"I do not." So much change had battered at Robin this last year. Within a few minutes yesternight he saw his best friend stripped bare with fright, no longer wise but nakedly mortal, demanding from a place where Robin couldn't reach him. He wasn't ready for any of this, pushed into one more corner. He felt Will deserting him and went stubborn, arguing from every reason but the one most painful. "I don't make the laws. They were well provided. I'm owed summ'at."

"You are." Beorn rose and waved to someone back in the trees. Will Scatloch came into view, the moneybag in his hand. Robin grimaced at his priest.

"Just happened to walk this way you'll tell me."

"No, but I thought to have a word first."

"Well, then." Robin confronted Will, arms akimbo on his hips. "How does the arm?"

"Tolerable. Master, I come again to ask for my freedom."

" 'Master'?" Robin's expression curdled with exaggerated surprise. "There was none of that between us."

"Only yesterday did I see the truth of it. Will you sell me my freedom?"

Robin tried the course of patient reasonableness. "More than the matter of *will I* or the price. There's your safety. What will you do?"

"I'll see to that when I'm free," said implacable Will. "Three pounds and here it is."

"Damn you," Robin erupted. "You're a mule, Will Scatloch."

"*I'm* a mule?"

"Keep your voices down, keep soft," Beorn warned. "They'll hear you in Grantham."

Robin understood stubbornness. He dug in his heels and stood on law. Three pounds would manumit Will and his wife—"Provided I'm willing, but there's Eddain and Gwaun." The boys were born at Denby, the result of Aelred's investment in their parents. Any owner was justified in valuing them at ten shillings apiece.

"You're shy a pound." Yet Robin would not look at his friend when he said it.

"A pound. Is that the law, Father?"

"Yes, Will." Beorn showed his open reproach to Robin. "A shameful law for a hateful practice."

"A pound more . . . well, I don't have that much." Will flung the bag to the ground, his voice breaking in terrible Celtic despair against the stone of hopelessness. "It's a curse, this money. To put dreams in my head and not the reach to grasp them. Damn you back, Robin! A friend you called me—"

"You are." Robin turned his back on Will, throwing the pain to Sherwood at large. "This talk of money. To me—"

"Robin," Beorn tried to mediate. "Be a fair man. Be the just lord you are."

"Fair? Damn it all, what he comes buying I would have given once we're home again. *Given.*"

"And when's that, Robin?" Will challenged, inexorable. "You could be dead tomorrow and myself lying next to you. Do you have any hint of my meaning?"

"Do you of mine?" Robin sank down on the log, head in his hands. "The law is all that's left to us. They took our crown, our lands, changed everything—"

"It's not your land on the block now but me and mine. Given is it? No. I thank you for that, Robin of Denby, but I'll have my own by law."

"Then by law you owe me four pounds," Robin shot at him belligerently. He needn't have clubbed Will over the head with the truth, but understanding both men, Beorn knew there was no meanness so small or cruel as that sprung from love.

"That's my last word, Scatloch. Four pounds or go to hell."

"I'll get it," Will flared back, nasty as Robin.

"You'll put it in my hand first."

"Done." Will scooped up the moneybag and flung it at Robin.

"And the rest? Your blood wouldn't have a roof over their heads but for me."

"By God and Saint David," Will vowed. "I will be finding a bishop of my own."

"Will, stay. No need." Beorn slapped his knee and rose. "Robin will have his pound from my purse this day. The price is met, sale done, and myself the witness."

Robin only stared at the moneybag like something he did not want in his hand. "Yes. Done."

Will drew his hunting knife and sawed vigorously at the leather collar worn for thirteen years, sliced it through. Hurled it away with all his force. "Bless you, Father, it is a pound I owe you."

"Forget the pound, and bishops as well," Beorn advised. "Sets a bad example for the commons, eh, Robin? Come, take Will's hand."

They clasped hands awkwardly on a bargain struck and a falling out healed. "'Tweren't money, Will. Money was no part of the matter."

"Nor for me," Will agreed. "But I must do this."

"Don't leave until tomorrow. It's a far piece to Denby and nigh on to dark now. Will you wait?"

"Until tomorrow's light," his friend promised.

That was how Will Scatloch spent his gain and Father Beorn part of his, both in a good cause. As for Robin, he was often as much of a quandary to Will as ever he was to William or his sheriff. Next morning Will said farewell all round, knelt to Beorn for blessing, and went lastly to Robin who leaned against an oak tree with eyes cloudy as the day and troubled as history. He tried to make light of the parting.

"What a free man you'll make, Will. You couldn't buy thread to patch the seat of your trousers. Do you not know the world costs money?"

Robin thrust into Will's hand a purse containing almost four pounds. Will never knew what to make of that, nor did Robin in truth, only that he felt vastly better when he embraced Will and sent him on his way.

Father Beorn, that thoughtful man, did not expect to see Will soon again. Will set out for Denby with determination in his gait, to give the good news somehow to Angharad. Concerned for his safety, Beorn consoled himself: No one knew Sherwood better than Will who was not about to be caught napping twice by any man.

Oh—but to feel as rich as Will when Robin put the money-gift in his hand; to feel the man's victory when he cut the collar from his neck and went to remove them from his loved ones and say like any free man: *This I have done. This is mine. . . .*

Would it were that easy for me to buy *my* freedom with pence, cut away the collar of my oath, and say to Holy Church, "There, I am free."

That's not like us. God holds my vow as an unpaid debt. We put collars on our slaves and other chains on ourselves. Before we came to this island our deepest bond was that between lord and man, and our old poets sang of the unhappy man separated from his oath-lord: he was *wraecca*, the lost wretch. He was wanderer over the earth, whose freedom lay only in keeping faith with his master.

Where's freedom for me, then, who laid my head upon my Lord's knee and swore to be his priest beyond life? I am the wretch now, cut off from my Lord's hall, yet forever His man. The Church that cast me out is like a stern mother guarding her daughter from a suitor who will not be denied, but creeps nightly under his love's window, pleading to be heard. So I beg God to open once more to me and hear my suit, my love.

Holy Church may doom me, but I'm a Saxon like Robin and can't believe God does not hear my prayers. If I heard a man's confession when I was distracted or indisposed, did God not mark all the same? When Tuck said chantry prayers for the dead after drinking too much the night before, was his voice muffled in heaven?

No, I think she takes too much on herself, this Mother Church of ours. Like well-marrying women who forget humble beginnings, she has become less the temple of Christ and ever more the fortress of Peter, Paul, and pride of place. I think God leaves too much of spiritual governance to her unreliable mercy. There's tyranny in her kindness. Tuck saw that plain enough—

"Christ's vicar or not, it ent right for a man to sit on purple in Rome and condemn us here. No, by rutting Jesus Christ—forgive me, Father —but it is not *right*."

Not right at all, my rough-minded, clean-hearted Tuck. We have always been men to look heresy in the eye and call it truth if need be. The time may come when we must leave one loved parent and cleave to the other, yet I would not have it so. I miss my Church as keenly as Robin and Will long for their wives.

And yet it was no Church but a Spirit that I bonded to. To us the mead-halls of lord and Lord are much the same, but where the lord's will is not clear, the lady's word will sway men while she swears she speaks in his name. I think there be in England many lord-lost men like myself, remembering the cheer of the hall, unready to take another oath or lesser place.

Will Scatloch, your life is blessed with simplicity. I wish I stood as clearly on right as you did with Robin. I wish God would embrace me as Robin did you and say, "Go with my blessing, seek out the right, but come home again to my hall. . . ."

Meditating on his place in the cosmos, Beorn differed little from other middle-aged men who considered themselves tolerably wise. Every so often God delivered a surprise just to keep him humble. Will Scatloch returned to Robin's band two days later without Angharad or his boys, without anything but a great confusion.

24

Denby was now a Norman barracks, looked and smelled like one. Several dozen rough men and their horses could very quickly do that to the tidiest of steadings. Ethelwold always had to step over horse-droppings in the courtyard. Minna, Gudrun, and Angharad moved silently in their duties and tried to be invisible. There were hawk perches in Robin's hall now and a confusion of dogs added to the nightly uproar at supper.

Righteous old Ethelwold did not blame the sheriff entirely for this: He was the best-governed of the lot. Life could be far worse if Fitz-Gerald let his men treat servants and villagers as they pleased. They were trash to Robin's steward, even the high-born knights like Raimond de Beaumont. Knight indeed: Not many generations back the Beaumonts were Norse pirates beaching their longships on the Seine to see what could be plundered from France. A land-gift from the Frankish king did not make them honorable in Ethelwold's reckoning. Denby's venerable steward was not the least surprised that Sire Raimond incited the Plough Monday trouble.

In early January, the men of Blidworth had always kept the lighthearted custom of Plough Monday. Dragging a light plow, they went from door to door collecting gifts of food and cider. If a householder gave generously they scratched a line before his door and he was safe from mischief. If he proved mean, the ground was plowed up before his house where rain frequently turned it to mire. More than once young Robin did the plowing himself for a lark.

Their feast collected, the men would tramp on to the Queen's Rest where Ceolred had a fire and spit ready to prepare their feast without charge, and always to set aside a tithe of the mild extortion for Father Beorn and Tuck, who usually joined in the cheer to roar *Was hael* with the lustiest of them.

The pickings were lean this year and not that many men with time or inclination, but Alcuin joined with Anlaf the cooper and Sven the fletcher to collect a trifle from one house and another, though no man's doorway was vandalized. They felt secure, having gotten the sheriff's permission to hold their feast. Since the patrols now made it worth a man's life to meet or be "robbed" by outlaws, the Plough Monday revelers debated whether to tithe to Father Huger.

Anlaf was outraged. "A foreigner?"

"His sexton's not," Sven reasoned.

"The notion's ill," Alcuin prevailed. "We will tithe to Wystan."

No one objected to that, little as there was. They went on to the tavern. With Freda turning the spit and cider warming by the fire, the Queen's Rest could have been merry that one night. But Raimond de Beaumont stalked in with three men at arms and insisted on being served. None of them was in a good mood. They'd been hunting all day without success when Raimond's horse shied and threw him. The young knight was bruised and shaken, mostly in his dignity, glaring at the silent peasants about the tavern.

"My lord," Ceolred explained carefully, "this is Plough Monday feast. They do not eat from my larder but from their own. I am closed for trade."

The Normans knew nothing of the custom and cared less. They went to the feast table, meager as it was, and helped themselves, calling for ale. Nothing for it; to avoid trouble, Ceolred served them.

The trouble began when he brought his reckoning—not that much but Raimond refused to pay, considering himself a guest like the others. "You said you were closed, did you not?"

Still rankling from his fruitless hunting and the humiliation of being thrown, he argued and shouted at Ceolred who could be touchy himself. To Raimond's vehement insults, he responded with a stream of gutteral Saxon contempt. Raimond backhanded him across the face. Then while his men kept Alcuin and his companions at bay with drawn swords, the hardy young knight beat Ceolred so ruthlessly that the taverner suffered injury to his spine. So ended the feast of Plough Monday.

On Tuesday, Freda told Ethelwold, who informed Ralf Fitz-Gerald just before supper was laid. The sheriff was still brooding over the robbery of Osmund with small tolerance for new difficulties.

"Raimond, you say?"

"Men have been punished on Denby, my lord sheriff, but never mistreated. Everyone here depends on everyone else."

Ralf slapped a fist into his palm. "Raimond."

"You must call him to account."

The fist ground again into Ralf's palm. "Yes. And a little of that *must* for Blidworth. Is Sire Raimond in the hall?"

"Not yet, sir."

"I would have him there."

Ethelwold knew Raimond would make a point of coming in his good time. When supper was laid in the hall, several dogs were baying about the fire pit as they were thrown bits from the tables. Dogs and men had much in common in Ethelwold's view. Some were all noise. Some didn't bark at all, just went for your throat. The steward had no particular concern for any Norman knight, but he accounted Raimond de Beaumont no match for the sheriff in a confrontation. And yet the pup would bark until someone spanked him out of the habit.

These latter months, supper in the hall made Ethelwold want to weep for shame. Beside the clamor of the dogs, tonight there was a clanging contest of sword and shield in progress between two rowdy young squires below the fire pit, encouraged noisily from the tables. In high spirits, two dozen raucous knights and men at arms cheered on the friendly match which ever threatened to turn mean as one or the other gave or took a lusty whack. The men at the tables reached across each other for this bowl and that viand, and usually threw at each other as much as they stuffed down.

From Ethelwold's viewpoint near the door, the hall seethed with movement and uproar—except for Ralf Fitz-Gerald, a motionless figure in black and gold at the high table. Amid the riotous soldiers, his stillness was eloquent. One hand rested on the board near his untouched trencher. Not entirely still. One finger tapped steadily on the board in a slow, expectant cadence.

Someone hammered at the hall door. Ethelwold pushed it open and Sire Raimond swaggered in. The young knight wasn't drunk but had obviously taken a drop before answering the sheriff's summons. He advanced down the middle of the hall, bellowing cheer to the gladiators flailing away at each other. Fitz-Gerald's head moved. No more, just that. He nodded to Ethelwold who pounded his staff on the floor. "Peace there. Quiet for the lord sheriff."

He had to go on pounding; the tables subsided raggedly. Ralf Fitz-Gerald stood up in his place. "Be *still!*"

When the thoughtless men at the tables saw the purpose in Ralf, they quieted until the crackling logs could be heard clearly in the fire pit and the snuffling of a hound near the spit. Raimond stood between the tables, the two sweating, embattled squires paused. Raimond gave the sheriff a sardonic obeisance.

"Sire Fitz-Gerald."

"Beaumont." Ralf resumed his seat slowly. "I will not greet you as knight. You are recreant."

The tables lapsed from respectful quiet to shocked hush. Terms like this between knights could end only one way. The smirk vanished from Raimond's lips as if slapped away. "I need not take insult from you."

"But you'll serve it out, you will," Ralf lashed at him. "When you're home at Beaumont, you can be the terror of your papa's serfs. Blidworth is my charge. You owe Ceolred the taverner the price of your entertainment last night."

Raimond's mouth dropped open. He was nakedly astonished. He gazed around at his brother knights, wondering if he'd heard aright. "I *what?*"

"Which will include compensation for the beating you inflicted on an unarmed man. A Saxon lord would be thus bound to pay. By God, so will you."

Raimond stiffened visibly. More than one vavasor in the hall knew the young man's best interest lay in obedience. They also knew the differences of birth between Raimond and Ralf. Like the other great houses—Tosny, Vernon, and Montfort, the Beaumonts were not known for humility. He retreated as far as a Beaumont could. "I cry you pardon, Sire Ralf. If this hog-wallow is so dear to you, *mon vieux*, I will spare them in the future."

"I had not finished," Ralf went on in a deliberate manner. "You will apologize to Ceolred."

"NO!"

Ralf's finger lifted and fell again. Tap . . . tap. The hall around him now had a silence Ethelwold could feel until Raimond broke it, the puppy yapping when he should have shut his muzzle tight. "You exceed yourself, Fitz-Gerald. I do not apologize to serfs." He turned to find a seat at the low table, but Ralf's voice covered him like a shower of fire.

"You will not sit with honorable men, Raimond."

Raimond whirled on him, hand gripping his sword belt. "I have served and suffered in this miserable place. I will take my orders from you, Fitz-Gerald, but not humiliation." He addressed the men near him with derision. "See how his office has puffed him up. You're a village brat yourself, sheriff."

Ralf's forefinger froze in its movement.

"The king's creature, first to last," Raimond said. "And you dare chastise me for . . . why this puny English Robin who robs bishops under your nose and laughs at you, even he is better born than a castellan's bastard."

Ralf shot from the high, carved chair like a missile from a catapult. The savage burst of energy propelled him in one clean bound onto the table, scattering bowls; with the second he was off the dais, facing the sword-drawn young knight.

"Sire!" One of the two squires who'd been at swordplay tossed his blade to Ralf who caught it and crouched at guard. All around the tables the men were standing now, no sound but tense mutterings. The matter should not have come to this pass. Raimond needed a lesson perhaps, but not bloodshed. Neither of them was shielded, circling each other, the heavy swords spinning light as willow wands in their grip. Then, faster than the old steward's eye could follow, Ralf took two steps toward his opponent like a dancer, swinging in an overhead cut that Raimond parried, but the unbelievable force of the blow broke his sword clean across with a shriek of metal. Ralf's open left hand came up catching Raimond under the chin. The knight staggered back, off balance. Ralf kicked him once in the groin; the young man's eyes went dull with shock. He collapsed on his knees, clutching his privates.

Ethelwold heard the snarl of a predator as Ralf raised the sword two-handed to take the man's head. So quick, so vicious no one had time to intervene.

"My lord," Ethelwold sent the words like a command. "Hold."

Ralf hovered over Raimond, literal death. The sword quivered.

"Enough, my lord," Ethelwold suggested in an easier tone, coming down the hall to Ralf's side. Firmly Ethelwold stepped between the sheriff and the stricken Raimond. "Some acts dishonor a fine sword. He is done. Put up."

He saw the man's eyes come back from cold murder. Fury unclenched and slowly relaxed. Ralf lowered the blade, glaring about the hall, grown terrible. "The castellan's brat still serves his king. So do you all. To-

morrow the steward will summon all Blidworth." He bent to the an-
guished Raimond. "And before that company, you will make restitution
and apologize to the taverner."

Raimond could barely speak. His tears were not of pain but frustrated
rage. "When the king hears of this . . . when my father hears . . ."

Ralf ignored him. "Tomorrow, Ethelwold. Early. The whole village.
Here." He threw the sword to its owner and stalked out of the hall. The
heavy door boomed shut thunderously behind him.

Ethelwold put out a hand to help the young knight unbend. He couldn't
yet, just stared at the expensive broken sword at the steward's feet.
Ethelwold's consolation was softly spoken for the young knight's ear
alone. "Someone had to beat sense into me once. The best of men need
a good kick now and then."

"Shut up," the boy groaned, still squeezing his testicles. "I'm done
with all of you. As for that creature, we will meet."

Angharad saw the public humbling of Sire Raimond next morning and
had the full tale behind it from Ethelwold in his matter-of-fact way. Some
men's rage was white-hot iron and this sort Will's wife could comprehend.
The Fitz-Gerald was none of that, but ice. Ethelwold said he was for
flogging the knight like an unruly boy before apologizing to Ceolred.
The steward talked him out of one extremity and the older Norman
vavasors out of the apology. None of them, they argued, should be shamed
that far in front of the peasants. Considerations of discipline were all
very well, but the precedent might be dangerous.

Possibly. A chieftain of Gwent would have the young spawn's head
on a pole. That he lived said much for the forbearance of the Fitz-Gerald,
a quality none of them would now mistake for weakness.

So that cold January morning, all Blidworth was forcibly summoned
to Denby courtyard where young Raimond, pale and furious, paid a
generous reckoning into Ceolred's hand. The sheriff gave Raimond no
more note, just grasped the pommel of his saddle and leaped astride the
stallion without touching the stirrup. They were said to be able to do
this, Norman knights, and that in full iron. Angharad saw it for herself:
Like an arrow from Will's bow he was, a sudden expulsion of energy
where the whole cat-coiled body of the man shot into the air, forking the
big grey clean and jerking its head about. Angharad felt that savage
energy as much a part of the man as the control that curbed it. Around
the rough square formed by Normans and villagers, he trotted the snorting
stallion, standing straight up in the stirrups.

"Hear me, Normans and English alike. I keep the king's law in Sherwood. That law will punish where it must. You of Blidworth and Denby, heed me well." The sheriff pointed to Raimond. "If I punish my own, do not hope I will pause on you. Your former lord, the murderer and thief Robin Hood, still lives in Sherwood."

Angharad fancied that Fitz-Gerald's eye, commanding all of them, fell on her and paused briefly. "I am not concerned with your love or loyalty to him or his men." The sheriff held up his gauntleted right hand. "To any who aid him: if a woman or child, a flogging; if a man, the forfeit of his right hand. Think on the serf Wystan and remember well."

In her love for Will, Angharad could be a foolish girl, in anger a violent storm with the sun slow to shine again. Toward her children, she was pure instinct. No one, not even Will, came before them. When Alcuin passed the word that Will awaited her in a certain dusk where the birch grew hard by Denby fields—yes, Angharad would risk flogging or worse to go to him. Other risks were another matter. She knew clearly the sheriff's bent and responded not as a wife but a mother. Black Fitz-Gerald he might be, but with the clan chief's bearing and iron hand.

The day Will Scatloch returned to his friends, Robin had spent a risky hour or two culling an older ewe from Denby's flock, Much and John guarding in case of trouble.

Butchering was the simpler part. He and Beorn were skinning the carcass, Tuck firing the last of their hoarded peat in the pan as darkness fell, when a dejected Will trailed into camp, hopefully the only soul in the shire able to track them so unerringly. Without a word he laid aside bow and quiver, took the knife from Robin, and went at the skinning with a bare nod to Father Beorn. Not usually taciturn, Will showed no inclination to chat now. Enormously relieved to see him, Robin had to speak first.

"Well, then."

"Well."

"Where's Angharad and the boys?"

"Not coming."

There were times when a man more needed occupation for his hands than his mouth. So for Will now. He plied the skinning knife in silence, pulling the fleece free. Robin hovered near.

"What happened?"

"Nothing."

More silence.

"Well, I was worried. You might have said you'd be back."

"Never said I would not."

There was Will for you, at least of late. A man to test patience. Yet there was that about him as he worked with ferocious concentration that did not invite closeness. Not until next day when patrols crisscrossed Sherwood and all save Robin and Will remained in the shelter, eating cold mutton and daring no fire for warmth.

Will stepped warily out of the brush to examine footprints in the muddy cart track while Robin watched both ways over his nocked bow.

"Not an hour old," Will judged. He moved back to cover. "Three or four of them." They walked on, drab shadows sliding through the grey-brown and black of the forest in winter. "Too many now and too close. North Sherwood's not safe for us anymore."

"I've thought on that. We'll go to Linby," Robin decided. "Alan's folk won't betray us."

"Won't they now?" Will touched his arrow-torn sleeve. "As fine a piece of Saxon arrowsmith's work as ever near killed me."

"What's that mean?" Robin knew all too well what it might but balked at admission. Will made it plain.

"Three pounds heavy in my hand did wonders for ambition. But twenty? Twenty pounds would set a poor man up for life and ease the conscience that went with it. Put it to sleep, if you take my meaning."

They hardly relaxed from alertness when pausing to rest, searching continually about them in all directions for human sound or movement, no matter how slight. Will spoke barely above a whisper. "And I thought cutting their collars would make them free. She would not come, Rob."

They were turned away from each other, scanning the terrain about them. Robin said nothing.

"I told her she was free—*hist!*" Will went feral. "Hear something?"

"No."

"Well, it meant a deal to herself, but not all."

Hardly all. Will showed her the money to make freedom an easy road. Angharad only said *slave or serf, what difference?* She would not have her bairn wandering the roads. At least Denby meant a dry roof, a warm fire, and food for Eddain and Gwaun. Sherwood? Angharad would not see her boys growing wild as hogs turned out to forage. *Look at you, Will,* she pitied; not a bath or a razor to his beard since God alone knew when. *And I love thee, Will, but the Fitz-Gerald is a strong man, Norman or not. I've seen him hard and I know him just. My boys need safety.*

Robin kept silent and let Will ease the pain out of him, a little wiser than last year. Would he ask Marian to live like this, winter-hungry, full of wood lice, and danger ever close as the shaft that grazed Will?

"She knew how much that hurt me, that another man could keep my bairn better than me. I almost gave her my right hand in a good one, shamed as I was and angry. She said . . . she said loving had no place in the matter."

Will was weeping silently out of a deep wound. No part in the matter. She put herself beyond the man, who reached for her naturally since the day they met. "I thought I knew her, Rob."

"Will, I'm sorry." Robin put a hand on his friend's shoulder. That was all he could do. Nothing to say.

"I cut the collar from her dear white throat, that much I did." And she was pleased and would take the collars from Eddain and Gwaun and tell them proudly of their father's gift.

They tensed. Both heard the sound: the muffled steady tred of men moving not too far away, not crashing through the brush but stepping carefully with no more sound than they could muffle. A bare twenty paces away, Robin and Will lowered their hooded heads and eased slowly down to one knee, unmoving as stones until the sounds faded.

The strong, just Fitz-Gerald was still reaching for them. They must go south today.

25

WILLIAM, WHOSE ENERGY and determination increased rather than waned with time, was bound for Ely this spring to scour Hereward and his rebels finally from the fens. He paused briefly at Grantham to greet and confer with Matilda and make plans for the future. One of the officers summoned to audience was Ralf Fitz-Gerald.

Sire Raimond had left Denby in a temper, presumably to complain to William. Ralf felt he handled that well enough. Let the Beaumonts rage as they might, the king would hardly upbraid an officer for maintaining order. Far more serious was the robbery of Bishop Osmund and Huger, humiliating in its efficiency. The waylaying of Osmund was as swift and precise as the ambush at Tadcaster, and Robin Hood was still untaken in Sherwood. Six men had eluded, out-guessed, and out-manuevered Ralf for the better part of a year. In no gentle terms, put off by no excuses, the king would demand to know why.

Yet there were compensations. He might see Marian at Grantham. The April rain ceased suddenly, the sun came out, and the countryside blushed like a plain woman paid a devastating compliment. In the fields along the way peasants were spreading manure. Deywomen would be busy in every byre. On days like this the whole of the midlands had the sweet-sour smell of milk and dung.

At the manor, Ralf no sooner announced himself than he was summoned into the royal presence—not in the great hall but to Geoffrey's small scriptorium where the reeve's records were compiled and kept. The chamber was chilly. In one corner a Norman monk copied a writ, stopping often to blow on his fingers. There was a small refectory table in the middle of the room and a smoky brazier close by. William loomed glowering at the head of the table. On his left, a cushioned box giving her added elevation on the refectory bench, tiny Matilda worked at embroidery.

"Sire." Ralf knelt to the king.

William acknowledged him brusquely. "Good day."

"My lady."

"Lord sheriff," the queen nodded. "We have looked forward to your visit."

William motioned Ralf to sit, allowing the young knight a meager smile. "We are pleased with your results in the tax rolls. Very thorough." The smile clouded over and William turned aside with a sigh. "And you need not concern yourself in the matter of the Beaumonts."

"They owe us a great deal." Matilda inspected her last stitches. "*De plus importance,* they owe us money."

"Osmund is another matter." The king leaned forward, hands folded together on the table, the bench groaning under his formidable weight. He spoke with deceptive patience: "The former Thane Hereward is a danger soon to be eliminated because he has been a rallying point for Saxon resistance. Denby is a small man, a gnat's sting on a horse's rump, but already one hears of him beyond Sherwood. He could become a Hereward. You have been admirable in all other respects, Ralf. Why is he still free?"

There was the bald question. Ralf regarded his hands and answered carefully. "My lord king, I have enlarged the price on his head from my own estate. Bishop Osmund has also put up a goodly sum."

"Quite," said Matilida to her plying needle.

"Any man who aids him risks losing his right hand. But my lord king, if I hanged every friend he has, there would be no right-handed men left in Sherwood."

"You recite the obvious. There's a price on Hereward but I'm going in after him myself. 'Go thou and do likewise.' How many men are with him?"

"Five, my lord, so I believe."

"Five!"

"Sire, the task would be easier had he fifty."

Matilda laid down her emboidery. "We do not question your competence, Ralf, but you may have underestimated Denby. The king himself was impressed with him."

"I will freely tell him so when he hangs," William declared.

"Though not to the point of indulging his women any further," the queen continued. "His mother, wife, and cousin have been moved out of the hall and into markedly less gracious accommodations."

William's sentiments in that regard were open and blunt. "I'll not keep them in comfort while he's running free and laughing at us."

Ralf thought of Marian. "I did not know that."

"They are my prisoners. Mewed up. They move nowhere without a guard or permission. They live on what we allow them. See that Denby knows of it. If he must be free, I want him miserable. And I want you to go in and *get* him."

Their house within the manor grounds was once a huntsman's hut. The man must have been a lifelong bachelor, Maud decided with distaste, for the years of dirt. The bed spaces were no more than low stone shelves about the fire pit with ragged featherbeds on them. They ate at the lowest place in the hall, among the servants and under guard. The hut was drafty, the roof leaked, and they had to warm the place on a miserly ration of firewood. But even as they hunched about the small fire, warming their hands over the tea steaming in clay cups, the women of Denby found some measure of defiant cheer.

"A bishop," Marian giggled nose to nose with Perdu. "You hear that, you good English cat?"

Judith savored the thought like a vintage wine. "A rich, fat, greedy, money-minded, bloody sod of a bishop."

"Judith. Bite your tongue."

"By your leave, Aunt, it's too funny."

Like her son, Lady Maud could be quite adaptable in practical matters while thoroughly old-fashioned in others. She never tolerated crude language. "The house is cold, the tea is insipid, and we are living in the king's gutter. That is no reason to speak as if we were born there."

"But a *bishop*," said Judith with a wondering shake of her head. "Edward was always such a one for the law. Wherever did he find such a flair for the outrageous?"

"I don't know." In all honesty, or most of it, Maud did not. "Certainly not from my side of the family."

Judith sputtered into her tea—"That will cost him Hail Marys"—

caught Marian's eye and they both ignited again because it *was* so deliciously outrageous, utterly fine, served the bishop no more than his Norman desserts, and they were young enough to believe misery never lasted.

The following Sunday in Blidworth, Father Huger made two announcements after Mass. The ladies of Denby, blood kin to the outlaw Robin Hood, were now confined in strict durance at Grantham and would continue so until his capture. The priest reminded his sparse congregation of the sheriff's penalties for giving aid to any of the felons.

On a more agreeable note of general interest, by royal proclamation a grand tournament was to be held at Grantham early in May on the Feast of Philip and John. Blidworth was not aroused at the tidings; there'd never been such in England. The very word was foreign. But Queen Matilda decreed, from the love she bore her English subjects, that Grantham might hold its traditional May celebrations, and the last day of the tournament would include a contest of archers, open to all. To the best of them would go the prize of a golden arrow.

News of the tournament was a catalyst in England. The conquered nation shook with another eruption of Norman high spirits as with the stamping of a noisy tenant in an overhead room. Every bachelor vavasor with a horse and armor prepared for it. Very young knights never blooded in war saw splendor and glory in the spectacle of the grand *mêlée*. More experienced warriors saw an outlet for their winter-mewed energies plus opportunity for profit. As in actual war, opponents defeated in tournament forfeited expensive mounts and armor and had to ransom them for cash. Enterprise was not only free but rampant. Ralf Fitz-Gerald chose from among his best horses. At Mansfield, nursing grudge and a bruised pride, Raimond de Beaumont prepared to ride in Waltheof's retinue. Whatever side Fitz-Gerald took in the *mêlée,* he would take the opposite, seek out *le bâtard* on the field and pay him back. Waltheof declared, in his pleasant but condescending way, that he was the superior of any Norman on any horse or field. Native and Norman foresters from as far as Chester and York bundled their bowstaves and best arrows, counted their money and joined the caravans of cheapmen, jugglers, knights, and cutpurses roistering their way along the muddy roads toward Grantham.

In Sherwood, Robin cared little for the tournament or the lure of a golden arrow. The sorry condition of his family reached him from Blidworth: They were barely maintained by the crown, guarded in a mean house, little better than felons. Their own money must be gone by now. He rubbed a forefinger over the scar at the base of his thumb and felt thoroughly frustrated. "You'd think Willy Bastard had enough of war, mock or real."

Quite true; his king would rather have built and endowed five cathedrals than see another battlefield. Certainly his queen felt so. The tournament they decreed at Grantham, to be presided over by Matilda and Lanfranc, reflected more careful policy than martial enthusiasm.

Like an old sailor sniffing the wind for a storm, William suspected trouble even where he saw none. A tournament would draw his vassals from every part of the island and some from Normandy. His queen and archbishop would take note of which notables came, which declined, and the reasons scrutinized. Important men would be studied for the company they kept on the field or at table. In some cases fealties would be resworn. While William marched against Hereward at Ely, most of the potential troublemakers would be neatly contained in one place, feasting and profitably breaking each other's bones to no political harm.

The archery contest was Matilda's innovation, a concession of goodwill toward the English to include them in the spirit of the event with the lure of a rich prize to the best. For comparative skill, she had no doubt the arrow would go to a Saxon. This too was part of policy. William was about to extract Hereward like a bad tooth from his watery stronghold. Depriving the nation of their last hero, he deemed it wise to give them at least temporary godlings in return, including an English Queen of the May and the traditional Beltane festivities added to the saints' day.

Lanfranc and the clergy resisted in the matter of the May festival. Pagan holidays had been universally damned by the Church, if with discouraging results. William had no time to parse motives with the archbishop. "*Pardi*, Lanfranc, I have entrusted you with my seal. You will appreciate the honor and trust me with one day."

A small point which Lanfranc ceded with Latin subtlety. His Church was in the process of shedding the influence of kings. This was not the year to scuttle a ship still a-building.

"Then surely, Gilly, you will trust me with two days," Matilda gently turned her husband's logic on him. Her more sinuous reasoning suggested that Lady Judith be chosen at a suitable moment as Queen of the May. She was charming, lovely, and a double symbol to the English: peer to the nobles, however distant, and cousin to a local hero, however felonious. The status of the Denby women was awkward in terms of the goodwill William needed this month. For Mora's sake he relented in the same way he spent money—reluctantly and as little as possible.

"Oh, be it so, Mora. Be it so. Let them out, put a gilt bauble on this . . . Judith? But the day after Philip and John, back to prison."

In the last days of April, Grantham swelled to bursting with folk of every condition. Fair stalls went up on the fringe of the tournament meadow. At midnight on the thirtieth, young lads and adventurous girls went a-Maying in the nearby woods for garlands. In the rollicking spirit of misrule, a clubfooted beggar, slouching into Grantham for alms on Beltane morning, volunteered to be Jack in the Green.

Light rain washed the morning fresh before dawn and let the sun rise to sparkle on Grantham. Marian's winter cloak would be too heavy when the sun was full up, but she had no lighter garment. This glorious day, even with a guard at her elbow—nice enough young Fleming named Gunstal without a word of English—Marian felt marvelous just strolling toward the main streets of Grantham. She would have left off her veil but that wasn't proper in public. Her clothes were threadbare enough. With the Fleming guard over her shoulder, she did not intend to be taken for an apprehended prostitute.

Behind her, distant in the broad tournament meadow, there was the sound of hammering and fainter noise from folk setting up stalls for their wares. The noise of real gaiety was before her in the narrow lanes of Grantham where the folk were gathering to whoop and follow the May dance that would wend through the alleys, in and out of houses, and end at the churchyard. She'd seen such dances and Jackys up Tadcaster, but nothing big as this. She turned an ear to listen: A shout went up in Beer Lane. The dancers were coming.

"Listen, Gunstal!"

Her guard raised his black brows. *"Comment?"*

Marian tried descriptive gestures, then gave it up. "Ah, come on with me."

Beer Lane was at the western end of Grantham near the fragrant brewery. Elbowing through the crowds, Marian watched as the procession appeared in the winding lane.

"Oh! They've got a Jacky!"

The crowd sent up a roar when Jack in the Green appeared leading the garlanded parade. *Jacky! Jacky! A Jack!* And such a Jack: in a grotesque, beribboned mask from which his beard bushed out on all sides, oddly hunched with the wicker pyramid that encased him from shoulder to thigh and so thick woven with holly and ivy that he looked like a dancing bush. Lurching but nimble, the man's left foot was deformed, severely twisted inward toward his right giving him a clumsy, spiderish gait. To add to the clamor, dogs circled the Jacky in his wicker bastion, barking and *owooing* at the alien sight of him as he capered and whirled to the chanting of his raucous followers. Out of Beer Lane he led his youths and girls, dancing into wider Manor Gate with the holiday crowds, dogs, and the odd chicken or goose fleeing to avoid being trampled— singing, bawling, clucking, and quacking in a riotous escort. Every door stood open today and most were decorated during the previous night with bits of greenery by way of the revelers' comments on the householder. Marian hummed the old tune from home: "She that's fair, she'll have pear/He that's glum shall find a plum/But them that's scorned shall find a thorn."

She always wondered what apple would mean. Something good: Apple was in full sweet bloom now, many of the spiraling dancers bedighted in chaplets of the small white blossoms. The procession wove like a snake into one house and out the back with townsfolk like a floodtide washing around and after them, cheering on the snake's tail: two hardy boys bearing the new-cut top of a fir tree ten feet in length to be set up in St. Wulfram's churchyard.

The happy insurrection invaded house after house. Marian in their wake could hear the dancers as they entered, roared through, and out again. Here and there a woman's high-pitched laugh rode over the ca- cophony, or the crash of something heavy overturned within a house. No harm done and all in fun. It was spring again, the sun coming home and sod the frosty-eyed priest who said they were wrong to dance. Frost was winter to be cast aside now. Jack in the Green's coat of holly and ivy was the green of life, the tree its very spirit.

When at last the dancers turned from Manor Gate into the churchyard, a bevy of little girls and boys, their arms full of bright ribbon streamers, were waiting near a freshly dug post hole. The procession snake-coiled about them, then broke up as the tree-bearers advanced and laid the May pole reverently on the earth. The children rushed forward, shrieking and busy to tie their ribbons near the top. Then the youths thrust the tree upright into the post hole while others filled in the earth and drove thick wooden wedges around the base.

By now the children jostled and giggled themselves into two circles, one inside the other, each child clutching a ribbon end. As the circles began to move in opposite directions in the weaving dance, their high, sweet voices rose in a carol, jerky with their skipping steps. In and out of each other the circles wove, intricately plaiting the ribbons about the fir until all the streamers were woven tight.

All through the pole dance Jack in the Green cavorted just beyond the children. Very limber with his feet despite the deformity, Marian admired. When the dance was done, the older boys charged down on Jack in a rush and roar, tore away the mask, and lifted the wicker frame from him to reveal the grimiest, flee-bearded beggar ever to curdle Marian's sight: a leather cap originally brown but black with dirt now, a face that might have been washed in dung for soap, and a distorted, idiotic grin from which more teeth were missing than not. Under the filthy sackcloth smock his upper body was slightly hunched with deformity. He lurched about the crowd, scrofulous hand outstretched, droning his plea for alms in a thick Yorkshire drawl:

"Alms f'Jacky? Alms, goodwi-ife?"

Parish orphan, Marian decided with some sympathy. Born in a ditch or a stable, probably to die there had not some Christian taken him to the church to be baptized and raised on scraps in castoff clothing. Old before his time from hunger and hardship. He approached Marian now but before he could make his plea, the guard Gunstal fetched him a smart rap and warning.

"Va t'en, fou. Je dit va t'en!"

The beggar cringed and retreated beyond the guard's reach, still holding out his grimy hand to Marian. "Alms for Jacky?"

Gunstal went to hit him again, but Marian stayed his hand. "Don't. It's good fortune to be kind to Jacky today. Kind. *Gentil. Comprennee?"*

"Kind t'Jackeh," the beggar wheedled, inching closer. "Alms, *Hlaefdige?"*

Lord, she wished she could. "Bless you, Jacky, there's not a penny to my purse or it would be yours. But bless you and the good green spring."

"Alms?" Jacky croaked from more habit than hope. Beside the remains of unpleasant teeth, there seemed to Marian a hint of lewdness in his distorted leer. He tugged at his ragged cap in deference to Marian and spidered away to greener fields. "Alms for Jacky 'n good Philip 'n John . . . ?"

A sudden blare of trumpets startled Marian. Just outside the churchyard in Manor Gate, three riders were halted amid the crowd—trumpeter, one horseman with a drum slung across his saddle, one holding aloft a broad parchment.

"Hear the king's will!"

The trumpet spoke again, the drum rumbled.

"Hear the king's will, all folk of Nottingham and Lincoln shires."

No one was dancing now, more folk milling about the richly dressed herald. He unrolled the parchment and barked his proclamation in a loud Frank-accented English.

"Whereas the outlaw Edward of Denby known as Robin Hood be yet not taken, be it known that any man who shelters or gives him succor shall suffer the loss of his right hand. Be it further known that any man revealing the whereabouts of Robin Hood, thief and murderer, and the outlaw be taken in consequence, shall receive a bounty of twenty pounds silver from Ralf Fitz-Gerald, Lord High Sheriff of Nottingham—"

Marian and her guard drifted closer in a press of villagers to hear the writ.

"—or from Ivo Taillebois, Sheriff of Lincoln. For the following named felons, each, ten pounds in silver."

Marian listened as names she knew, names that went with dear faces, were droned out with no sense of the life or soul behind them. She never thought the crowd would turn ugly but somewhere in the crowd pressing close about the heralds, someone shouted "A Robin!" Then another voice took it up with the high squealing voices of the children near the May pole.

"Robin! A Robin!"

And from another quarter a great bull-bass roar. "Greyfeather!"

The crowd began to chant, "Robin! A Robin!" Here and there *Greyfeather,* the Norman slang scooped up in English and flung back at the conquerors. Then someone threw a stone that struck one of the horses on the head. The animal shied and reared, frightened by the blow and the crowd pressing too close. The rider fought to keep his seat. Suddenly the plunging animal screamed and went down on its haunches. The Normans shouted for the villagers to give ground but they were a single dangerous animal now, smelling blood, surging closer as they chanted.

Marian's Flemish guard swiveled about, gauging the trouble and how much help was at hand if matters became ugly: not much. With a stern gesture to Marian not to move, he swung his pike high and dashed forward to aid the heralds. He was scarcely gone when Marian felt something pressed into her hand from behind: a leather bag that clinked. There at her side, grinning, hunched and unsanitary, was Jack in the Green.

"What's this, then?"

"Weepin' Jesus, Marian, what's it look like? I've not got till Saint Michael's—*hide* it."

Marian's heart actually skipped a beat, dove into her shoes and bounded high as heaven. "Robin!"

The grotesque Jacky bobbed his head in loutish respect. "When they ring the bell for Nones, lose your guard and find Father John at the church." He covered the rest with the thick north country burr, limping away. "And he'll bring you to bless poor Jacky, loovely woman."

When she could breathe again, Marian fumbled the purse inside her cloak with a shaking hand. Fear, wonder, and joy rioted through her. She must tell Mum and Judith, must get to the church. Not now, but at Nones, he said. Lord, that was hours still. Father John. Yes.

Eventually the disturbance in the street dissipated as more soldiers pushed back the holiday crowds with pikes. None of the king's men were hurt but someone had hamstrung the downed horse. When young Gunstal returned, red-faced and swearing in his foreign tongue, Marian felt giddy, light-headed. She beamed at him. The sun was warm, the day the most beautiful ever to come from God. Indeed, as the two of them made for the fairgrounds, Marian took his arm and managed to look feminine and helpless.

26

*M*ARIAN BURST OPEN the door to their prison house, hovered quivering in the entranceway, and her joy lit up the squalid chamber like a dozen candles.

"Mum! Oh—wonderful!" She caught Maud up and spun her about. "Wonderful, wonderful-er, wonderful-*est*." No, not enough for the way she felt. She pounced on flabbergasted Judith in an avalanche of affection that tumbled the pair of them to the floor. "And I love you, dear Judy, yes I do."

"Stop, you mad woman!" Judith tried to keep her composure, rather difficult while rolling on the floor. "You'll have us both filthy."

"Then up, my girl." Marian bounced up, lifted the bag of coins from an inner pocket of her cloak and spilled the hoard jingling over their small table. "Look."

They did, but belief lagged behind sight. Maud put a hand to the shining miracle but did not touch it. Like Faerie gold, the hoard might simply melt away.

"Marian, where—?" Judith made a rapid estimate, splaying coins this way and that. "Why there's almost a pound here. Where on earth did you get it?"

"From Jack in the Green," Marian brimmed. She couldn't keep still any longer. She tossed her cloak aside and hugged both women to her, tremulous with joy to share and more to come. "Go to the fair, get our needfuls. Don't carry too much silver, there's thieves all over this day. Well, my sweet Gunstal's waiting and I'm off." With an impulsive kiss for each of them, Marian tripped to the door. No: she had to tell, too much happiness to hold alone. Marian hugged herself for pure happiness. "It is a gift from the world's dirtiest thief and the best and the dearest. He's *here*, Mum."

Maud uttered two soft syllables like prayer. "Robin."

"What hour's it now?" Marian jiggled to be away. "Oh, I'm off. Hide the silver—wait." Marian scooped up a few coins for her own purse. "And tell no one."

"Robin." Maud visibly swelled with pride. For a moment Robin's mother looked as if she might dance a bit herself. "Well." One hand flew to her lips. "For once I can look at Grantham without wanting to spit."

"Where's Robin?" Judith worried. "They'll take him."

"Oh no, Judith," Marian denied at the door. "You wouldn't believe. Oh, you wouldn't believe a word of it—but I'm off!" And she was, leaving Maud and Judith solvent but utterly mystified.

The broad tournament meadow just east of the manor grounds was a delicious feast of smell and sound to Marian. On the north side, workmen hammered in the last timbers of the covered pavilion for tomorrow's royal and noble spectators. On the eastern edge, hastily constructed but sturdy pens swarmed with bawling cattle, while sharp-eyed drovers marked their quality and haggled down their price. On the south side, a long line of bright ribboned stalls burgeoned from wagons, laying forth all a buyer could possibly need. Tomorrow the smell would be that of horses, the sound of iron, but today belonged to the people. Jugglers, acrobats, and fire-eaters tossed, tumbled, and magically consumed. From the back of a garishly painted wagon, ferocious puppets portrayed Man torn between God and Satan with the latter getting his due lumps from a paddle. From every stall the dealers proclaimed their wares: horse-bread, salt fish, new-tanned leather, bags of lentils and bolts of cloth, new pottery fresh from the kiln, beeswax candles and plump bags of tallow hung in rows and hawked as the purest. Here and there corn-badgers speculating in grain plunged critical hands into open bags, judged what spilled back from between their fingers, frowned professionally, and allowed they might buy in bulk if the price was reasonable.

And marvelous, warm, thick beer to be drawn from a great tun in a wagon and served in a good generous-bellied bowl. Marian drank half of it down with gusto, offering the rest to her sandy-haired Gunstal from Bruges, who made sure no officers were about before draining the bowl.

"Let's have another," Marian ventured. "No? Well, I will."

They strolled together through the crowds, Marian close to her Fleming's elbow all the time, enjoying herself, chatting effusively, but with an eye on the shadows shrinking, drawing in at her feet, listening for a bell as the morning sun climbed toward midday. She took Gunstal's arm and smiled at him until the muscles of her face hurt, told him the story of her life in tranquil Tadcaster. She bought more beer and urged his share on him. With Gunstal catching one word in five, Marian talked his head off.

"Look here." She opened a small wooden box displayed at a mercer's stall. "*Ach,* Mum will be wanting these when she comes to the fair. Needles we call 'em. Nee-dles. No matter, they're ever so dear. Now where was I? Yes, there I was, fourteen and growing taller than my folk expected but *tired* all the time, if you know what I mean, because my humors could not keep up with the growing bones, and . . ."

Mellowed by the good beer, Marian reveled in the color and movement around her, feeling the moments and minutes pass and her shadow tending to a mere blob at her feet. She talked on; she invaded Gunstal's full attention, demanded it.

Earnest young Gunstal from Bruges honestly liked Marian. Until today he found guarding her not unpleasant, but she jabbered so this morning. The clearest English was difficult for Gunstal. The soft-voweled, choppy sound of Marian broke on his ear like surf on a rock. He went from polite to strained attention, to boredom, then restiveness. When the time neared midday, Gunstal evinced the aspect of a fox in a trap. He yearned for silence and the beer cart again.

St. Wulfram's bell sounded clear over the noise of the crowds. Marian gave Gunstal her hundredth intimate smile in the last hour. "Why, I do believe that's Nones bell."

So it was, midday and the fair meadow packed with most of the population of Grantham. "And here's the beer wagon again." Marian bought another bowl, drank a little, and offered the rest to her guard. "No, you rest here." She pointed to the mercer's stall not far away. "Don't stir, I'll be back."

With no haste Marian moved the few steps to the next stall, fingering broad swaths of dyed linen, nodding back to Gunstal enjoying his beer and respite. A poorly dressed young woman edged in beside Marian to ogle the fresh colors of new linen, caressing the material with the hope-lessness of one who would serve an extra year in purgatory for the price of a few yards.

"Ent half lovely," she yearned in soft rapture, "but too dear for me."

Marian shot a furtive glance at Gunstal whose snout was deep in the bowl of beer. She clinked the silver in her hand where the woman could see it. "Would you earn sixpence toward the price for a minute's work?"

"Sixpence?" The ragged woman gave Marian her full attention. Six-pence was not to be sniffed at, a day's wage for a male servant in the royal household. "I would that."

Marian instructed her. "Just there, see him? A soldier named Gunstal. Go to him—his far side, mind—tug at his sleeve and ask him the way to the corn-badgers or what you will."

"No more than that?" No more; the money changed hands.

"Just turn him for the trice, that's all I ask."

The henchwoman did not have an expressive face but managed a sly comprehension, complicity, and even a glint of enjoyment. Silver clutched in a fist that would not open until she got home, she sidled away to her task. Marian found a moment to admire her own ingenuity. If Robin could fleece a bishop, she could certainly distract a guard. Now her decoy was at Gunstal's elbow, casually moving to his other side. Now she was speaking and—now!

Marian slipped nimbly between two stalls, hiked up her skirts, and fairly flew down the line of cheapmen's wagons. She must be well out of sight, one dull brown veil among a hundred before the guard noticed she was gone, putting more distance between them with each second. Now the stalls and wagons were behind her as she ducked in and out of the press of townfolk, passed the west exit of the field where industrious squires were already setting up tents for their knights. Marian dodged through them, out into teeming Manor Gate and into St. Wulfram's churchyard. Only a few steps more. Pure joy squeezed her heart tight, because at last she was no longer waiting or running from but *to*. . . .

She found short, rotund Father John halfway down the nave of the church. A whispered word and he led her out again through the north entrance of the church to his own small house across the yard, halting at the door. His instructions were brief.

"Bolt the door. There was water inside. I think he's washed." The priest's eyes glimmered with dry amusement. "Let us hope he has. Bless you both."

And Father John left her.

Everything happened too fast then. When Marian opened the door, the room's single occupant whirled around, one hand to a dagger, before they came together in a rush of needing. Robin barred the door quickly and caught Marian in his arms, carrying her to the bed.

"Jack in the Green," she whispered into his bushy beard. "Oh, sweet Jacky, where have you been so long?"

No time for talk then. Beneath the hunger for him, part of Marian's mind whispered *how thin he's grown* before they threw back the covers to reveal the most beautiful bed in the world: soft blankets and clean linen sheets, luxury piled high on the luxury of each other. They talked little stripping out of their clothes and that nonsense, too eager to come together. This moment couldn't be gentle, couldn't be lost. There would be time later for gentleness. Robin's mouth ravaged hers, wolf-hungry for the essence of her. He was in her, bursting with a cry within a few moments, his great silly beard chafing her cheek and Marian didn't care. She felt him start to withdraw from her and held him tight with arms and legs. "Don't . . . no. We don't have time to be apart."

"No." He kissed her less hungrily now. "Not a bit."

Marian gazed up into the dear face so close over her, searching for what she left half a year ago. Robin was still there, all that she loved, only the mildness was gone. "Robin Goodfellow, how goes the wood?"

His body moved over hers less urgently now. "Don't talk."

When at last they lay apart for the time, Robin could take neither his gaze nor his hands from her. He needed to remember what he loved to begin with and sought to find it now. Her cheeks were chafed from his beard grinding into them. He could hardly believe they were there together. "Strange. . . ."

Marian nestled to him, one leg between his. "What's strange?"

"You: here with me after so long. And walls. A roof over my head."

"Good?"

"Good but like I'm in a box."

"Robin Goodfellow." Marian ran her tongue over his lips. "And the men?"

"They're fine. They won't give up. Fitz-Gerald won't either."

"He's here."

"I saw him."

"Did he see you?"

"Who looks at a beggar?"

Marian raised up on one elbow stroking Robin's chest. "I heard of the bishop."

"Heard you were in prison. That's why I came."

"Oh, sweeting: Mum and Judith, when they saw all that *money*."

"You've not told them?"

"Not all. Not yet. *Ach* love, but how did you manage to look so—" Adjectives failed Marian. "—so splendid dirty?"

Robin chuckled, his breath warm against her breast. He moved ovei her again but in a different need. The hunted, haunted thing in him fled to her from something. "Say you love me, girl."

"You know I do."

"I need to hear you say it," he urged with a fierce tenderness. "Remember and take it back with me."

"Then I love you—yesterday, today, and all our tomorrows. When was there a time when I did not? Before we came home to Denby, I knew I could love you, Robin."

"And I. For sure, it was the same with me. You'd think God would let life be simple just once."

Marian stretched her arms above her head, body writhing like a contented cat waking from a nap. "Years off my life when I left you, but you gave them back today." She giggled into his beard. "What a Jacky! How in the God-loving world—?"

"Penny here and there among the Grantham boyos," Robin admitted. "And five shillings to Father John for the poor box."

"Five!"

"Disgraceful, ent it? The price of charity's going up."

"Dear love." Marian stroked his overgrown hair. He darkened it with some kind of berry dye. "We'll be home soon. We will."

When?

Will's flat question haunted Robin's mind. When would home be possible reality? Safer to lie close together, and let this single room be the world, let Marian talk of her days in this place. Mum was Mum, never changed. They were officially out of favor now and sometimes called to work as scullions in the manor kitchen—the king's doing, not Matilda's. Mum didn't mind that, she'd lived through harder falls. She could manage a few pots, but Judith was clumsy and knew nowt of kitchens. Oh, and Marian had a cat of her own again, a dear thing, and what of Will and Angharad?

Robin flopped over on his stomach, face half-buried in the pillow. "I've freed them."

Marian rose up over him, stroking his back. The ribs showed plainly now. "*Ach,* you didn't."

"Will wanted it. Surprised me. I don't know how Da would've dealt with it, but I was almighty surprised. So much change . . . but we'll put it right, Marian, I swear to you we will."

"How? You said the sheriff won't give up."

"Did I say I would?"

"Robin, you must leave Sherwood before he finds you."

"Leave?" The notion was utterly foreign to Robin. "Why? It's mine. My father's and his father's."

"What good if you're dead?"

"Will said that," he answered cloudily, "but the land might be my son's."

"Aye, it might, if the king gives it back. Someday. Somehow. Can I put my arms about that, Robin? And you just lie there, thick as ever Will said you were, and tell me you can't leave even to save your own life and the men's as well?"

They both started at the sound of a footstep outside the door. Robin reached for his dagger where it lay on the floor. The footsteps faded. They relaxed slowly as the tension drained out of them.

"Marian." Robin turned over to her, and she saw plainly the stamp of too much fear and strain in his thinned face.

"I don't even know what or why anymore, girl. We do what we can. We try to stay alive. Twenty flamin' pounds on my head: Jesus, there've been days I'd turn myself in and die rich."

"Can't you go north, husband? Nay, just for the time?"

"Sherwood's *mine*. If I go I'll never get back. You think I don't know that every waking hour?" Robin lay back, one arm flung over his eyes. Marian heard the fatigue and desperation hardened into a permanent set. "I hear they're singing songs about me. How would you rhyme the truth? I've got a boar by the tail. He can't get at me, but I can't let go."

Stroking his face, Marian spoke before thinking. "I saw how you marked him."

No, she shouldn't have told that. Robin uncovered his eyes and searched her face.

"You saw Fitz-Gerald? When?"

"He—well then, he came to my chamber once."

Robin sat up, serious. "Why? What did he want?" Marian felt she'd said too much. She couldn't explain and now wasn't the time, but Robin persisted.

"What did he want with you? Were Mum and Judith there?"

"No." She shouldn't tell, shouldn't have mentioned Ralf at all, more ill served than good. But Robin was her husband. There would be no lies between them ever, because ever might be tomorrow or even today. "He came to see me."

Robin swung his legs over the side of the bed, his back to her. "Did he touch you?"

"No. What do you think of me, husband?"

He said it heavily. "What do you think of me?"

Marian stretched across the bed to his side, holding up her hand with the scar under the thumb. "Does that answer? Don't be bread."

"Well, then, what did he want?"

"I'd never have thought as much." Of Ralf Fitz-Gerald, that formidable man, the truth sounded pathetic. "He's lonely, Robin. I tended him at Denby when he was sick, remember? Oh, it's nowt. He could've felt the same for Judith."

"So he just pranced in and let you know his mind."

"Not like that. He was . . . kind. What they call *gentil*."

"Don't talk Frank to me."

"No help for that; I hear it all the time." Marian was wise enough not to tell him all. The rest was idle dreams and foolishness, at worst the kind of wish-demon visiting young women in their sleep. Marian promised herself the notions would be confessed to Father John at the earliest moment and penance paid to the last jot.

Her husband still stared at the floor. "Nigh killed him that once. Next time I will."

"Come back to me," she invited from the pillow. "Don't be foolish."

Robin lay down again beside Marian—troubled, not looking at her. "He takes my home, my lands, but that's not enough, he wants you. I will kill him next time."

"Stop growling and hold me." Marian pulled the covers over them. "And mark what I spoke me to the Lord. High. Fitz. Gerald"—punctuating each word with a kiss—"when Denby was yours again, when my own good husband opened the gate to him, then I might give him the cheer in your hall."

Robin slid his arms about her. "And a little foxglove in his beer."

He shifted over her again. Her body welcomed his and this time loving took delicious forever.

When they dared stay no longer, Robin dressed quickly in his rags again, the tattered breeches more holes than wool, ruined shoes, and sackcloth leggings. He opened the door, peering about before he went outside, returning with a handful of earth which he deposited carefully beside Father John's washbasin. Marian left off dressing to watch him. Warped, unpleasant Jacky literally grew before her: an earth-saturated lump of beeswax altered the shape of his nose, charcoal darkened and bushed out his brows. Robin moistened the dirt and rubbed it evenly over his face. Then a twist of raw wool wedged between gum and upper lip, teeth blacked out with tar and the rest dulled with earth. The coarsened mouth of Jacky leered at Marian. He shrugged into the sackcloth smock, the left shoulder padded with wool for a small but noticeable deformity. Robin turned his left foot inward toward the instep of his right and sidled to Marian in the odd crouch the twisted gait gave him, the clean, straight line of him corrupted into a gnomish lump.

Except herself. She hugged herself to him. "You're a rare smelly old pig."

"Alms, goodwife?"

"I didn't know you could be a player."

"Didn't know I could rob a bishop until I tried." Robin tilted up Marian's chin to him. "Be passing the time of day with no more lonely Franks, mind."

She kissed the twisted but very dear mouth. "When will I see you again?" *Ever?*

"You will that."

"I mean here at Grantham."

"Oh yes. My love to Mum and Judith."

"Where will you be?"

"Oh," he evaded with another kiss. "Here and there."

"*Robin*—where?"

"You'll see me."

"Nay, if you'll not answer I'm off straight."

But he held her prisoned in his arms. "We'll go home, Marian."

"I know, love."

"We will."

Only a few seconds left together, far too precious to waste. Marian clung to him. "I want to know where you are."

"Best you don't, any of you."

"Tell." She gripped his augmented nose. "Or I'll tear the silly wax from your nose and the wool from your mouth. I *will*."

"Ah, leave off, I'll have to set it again."

"Tell then."

"Leave off. I'll tell," Robin relented, whispering close to her ear. "I heard summ'at about a golden arrow." He turned Marian firmly toward the door. "Go on, now. Look for me."

"Tell me to go while everything in both of us says stay. Yet my guard's running mad by now."

"There will be Denby again," Robin promised her. "Somehow. I swear it, love."

What a day! Marian sang to herself, hurrying back to the fair. Not a day but a lifetime in small. The stir and color of a fair, losing Gunstal like a proper fox, loving Robin and for some painful time lying worlds apart from him in the same bed with the shadow of Ralf between them. Loving again, seeing new sides to the man she thought she knew. *There will be Denby again. A lifetime in a day, and all of it looks better on a full meal*—of any sort, Marian purred to herself.

The afternoon light was soft over the meadow as Marian mingled with the crowds, rising up on tiptoe to spy out Gunstal. She would be innocent but contrite when they found each other—*Oh, I did look for you, but so many people and someone said you went to church. Well, here I am. Where else would I go, dear Gunstal?*

The sun was warm on her back, the crowd's noise pure music—*and I can still feel you in me, Robin.*

She had to believe a time would come when happiness need not be crammed into hours, when there would be leisurely days to spend like a prodigal. For now, as on her wedding night, each moment must be known and drained of its sweet like the juice from a ripe pear.

She caught sight of Gunstal: the red-faced lowlander hurried here and there, peering about the crowd, more than worried, a man under a doom. Coutance would be taking some hide off him for losing her.

"Hey, Gunstal!" Marian stopped and waved furiously. "*Here* I am."

Now he saw her, bore down on her with the full weight of authority, and for all the hiding she got in his outland tongue, Marian was hard put not to laugh aloud. She was a dangerous woman these days, wife of a desperate man with twenty pounds on his beautiful head. Right here under the nose of Normandy, loving her until she felt she could relish a nap after dinner—and talking of a golden arrow.

Oh, that made the bread rise. That was honey-sweet, that was plain, flaming fine! And Gunstal, dressing her down in anger and relief, would wonder no doubt why Marian beamed through his jeremiad and suddenly leaped at him like a playful kitten with a totally unexpected kiss.

27

$\mathcal{E}$ARLY NEXT MORNING the fair crowds were cordoned behind ropes on the south side of the meadow while workmen hurried to set up wicker and straw targets for spear hurling. The temporary village of tents at the western end of the field bustled now with boisterous vavasors greeting each other, squires laying out armor and weapons, hanging shields on the poles before the owners' tents. Beer and wine sellers cannily shifted their wagons closer to this new source of income. A steady stream of younger squires, the fetch-and-carry boys of bare fourteen, plied between the tents and wagons. Young Henri had just hung out Ralf's shield and returned to the tent, piping his question in a voice lately undecided between alto and baritone.

"Lord sheriff, shall I bring some beer?"

Ralf laid aside the spear thoroughly inspected for the smallest crack in its shaft. He rumpled the new squire's light-brown curls. "No. I drink afterward, never before. *Mais regarde.*" Ralf lifted the mail shirt he would wear under scale armor in the *mêlée.* The boy had to squint closely to see the few clots of rust. "See what you missed?"

"*Hélas,* messire."

"You are negligent, Henri."

"Just a little, sire."

"Little is the beginning of much. You know what one calls a careless vavasor? Dead. Clean it out, rub a bit of oil on the job, and I'll bring you a quintain ring tomorrow."

The squire fell to his task as a handsome and convivial head ducked inside the tent entrance. "Sire Ralf. *Bonjour et bonne chance.*" The rest of Earl Waltheof thrust into the tent. He was not yet armed, clad only in breeches and a splendid padded undertunic. "What's this of the queen?"

"I would have come to my lord's tent," Ralf said. "Her Majesty wishes to speak with you before the hurling begins."

"We are both of the lady's green tomorrow, companions in the *mêlée.*" Waltheof rattled a pair of dice invitingly and cast them out on Ralf's cot. "Will you hazard for five prisoners?"

Ralf scooped up the ivory cubes and dropped them in the earl's hand. Waltheof had claimed he would put Norman knights to shame in this tournament, stated with the good-natured charm Ralf distrusted. Everyone was drawn to the nimbus of glamour around this young Saxon lord. Ralf often wondered why he was immune. Perhaps it was the hard-shell peasant in his own blood.

"I'll throw with you when I have ransoms to wager."

"Modest."

"Merely cautious, my lord."

Behind the earl's faintly condescending congeniality, Ralf sensed a man weighing him for something more than a potential adversary.

"The king himself has said you are formidable," Waltheof admitted. "Well for me we're on the same side tomorrow."

"My lord is kind."

"And you are cautious. Yes. The greater part of valor, as they say. Yet such as de Gael and Breteuil have mentioned you. I wish always to have the best men about me."

"*Votre serviteur.*"

To Ralf, Waltheof's manner always carried a dollop of amusement at the world in general. *Unwise, Saxon. Such as you laugh at majesty and trip over mole hills.*

"By the by." Waltheof paused in leave taking. "Young Beaumont is with the king's reds tomorrow. One hears he has a quarrel *à outrance* with you."

"He thinks so. *N'importe.*"

"Be that as it may," Waltheof advised, "employ that caution you confess. Blunted or not, a spear or sword in the right place can do great harm. Again, good luck."

* * *

The competing knights waited at the western end of the meadow, trumpeters alert for the queen's signal. So far, so good, Matilda reckoned. The English attendance for the first day was gratifying. There'd be this many and more tomorrow. What else? At the moment the queen felt like a master chef who might have omitted one vital ingredient from a superb dish. Judith? That business was accomplished in a few words with Earl Waltheof. The earl was sure to distinguish himself in the lists, but distinguished or not, he would choose Lady Judith as Queen of the May.

Judith sat in the royal box behind Matilda, who was ensconced between Lanfranc of Canterbury and Geoffrey de Coutance. Spread out from herself throughout the pavilion (like political wings, Matilda conceived with some amusement) were the greater and lesser lords and chatelaines, some journeyed from Normandy for the occasion. Beyond the queen's earshot but no doubt venomous, the Countess of Beaumont whispered to the Countess de Tosny. The Countess of Hereford chatted with Judith of her daughter, for whom she had high hopes of a good marriage in the near future

Prisoner or not, Judith shone forth among the Norman *dames des choisies,* dressed and veiled wholly in white, which gave her the aspect of a subtly erotic nun. Matilda realized with a tinge of envy that the young woman simply did not have a bad angle to her face. Would her own daughters had been so blessed. In her well-worn and quite old-fashioned gown, with its full supertunica, Judith still managed to make the more stylish Norman women look dowdy.

"My queen." Geoffrey de Coutance leaned in to Matilda. "The heralds wait only your signal."

"Then we begin." The green samite kerchief fluttered in Matilda's hand.

The trumpeters pierced the air with their massed call, their extended flourish underscored with drums. A great *Oh!* went up from the pavilion as the horsemen advanced down the field, destriers governed superbly to a high-stepping walk. Eight abreast they rode, peers of the realm in the first rank: Earl Roger de Breteuil of Hereford, Waltheof of Huntingdon, de Mowbray of Northumbria, lesser barons flanking and following them. In the second and third ranks came the king's principal officers, the reeves of his suzerain like Ivo Taillebois of Lincoln and Fitz-Gerald of Nottingham. Then the peacock-proud scions of Normandy's greater houses, finally the "shirttail" bachelor knights of little or no estate. Their formation pivoted on Earl Waltheof and wheeled into line before the royal box, eighty-odd men in mail with bright-colored surcoats over their armor. The spears dipped in salute to Matilda. The horsemen wheeled again and proceeded to the eastern end of the meadow, waiting while the wicker targets were positioned.

Waltheof was among the first four riders to tilt at the red circle painted on linen. As he trotted his horse out to begin, a huge shout went up from the commons crowded along the south side of the meadow. The earl doffed his helmet and held it out to the people in dedication: This was to be for them and in their honor. He set himself in the stirrups and dashed forward, spear aloft.

Ralf judged the performance with a professional eye. The earl had a good seat on a fine black, not too tall at the shoulder, but chosen obviously for speed and steadiness. His cast was true; as he flashed by the target the spear went home, centered in the red circle. Another great roar went up from the Saxons, and this was to be the tenor of the day. Their Waltheof could do no wrong. His first cast was not matched until Ralf Fitz-Gerald on his favorite grey spurred forward, allowing the destrier to find its gait, a trot flowing into canter and then gallop, horse and man one missile with the spear its point. Right arm cocked high—back—and the shaft centered in the target.

From spear-hurling to the quintain, Normandy and England were two men alone that day; others were simply not in the same class. For hoarse-shouting England, Waltheof was the sun at noon. For Normandy, Ralf Fitz-Gerald brought the *noblesse* to their feet again and again and even won a flash of Saxon approval when he cantered to his squire with the captured quintain ring and tossed the promised prize to young Henri.

Waltheof's last sortie was unlucky from the moment he touched spurs to flank. Watching, Ralf felt the earl's seat was not right, nor his couch with the spear. Waltheof missed the quintain ring and struck awry. The crossbeam swung about and hit him in the back of the head. The blow sprawled Waltheof out of the saddle. He fell heavily with one foot caught in a stirrup and was cruelly dragged until squires halted the black.

Ralf would have called out of courtesy at the surgeon's tent in any case, but the earl sent for him. Ralf found him supine on a cot, leg in the air, while the Breton surgeon cautiously worked the swollen ankle back and forth.

"Best brace and wrap it," was the Breton's medical opinion.

"Ah, Ralf." Waltheof raised his head, presenting the sheriff to his two visiting companions. Ralf recognized Roger, earl of Hereford and young Rolph de Gael who was something of a favorite of the king. "My friends, this is Sire Ralf Fitz-Gerald."

"Lord High Sheriff of Nottingham." De Gael was little more than a boy, possibly all of nineteen. His acknowledgment of Ralf was audibly worshipful. "I am very honored."

"And I, of course." The grey, blunt Roger de Breteuil gave Ralf a small nod. "With a hundred like you and Waltheof, the king would wear every crown in Europe."

"Anyone might," Waltheof attested. "Would Arthur have prevailed without Lancelot and Gawain? You are splendid, Ralf."

"Thank you, my lord."

"Not at—*ow!*" Waltheof jerked when the surgeon too roughly handled the swelling ankle. "My dear fellow, your last patient may have been a mule, but do you think you could manage to do whatever it is you do without amputation? Ralf, *attendez.*" Waltheof could not ride more today, possibly not tomorrow. Meanwhile the queen had a ceremonial chore. "Do you know Lady Judith of Denby?"

Ralf did, the other face through the haze of his fever. "Robin's cousin."

"Quite. I was to crown her Queen of the May. I've already sent word to Matilda that you'll do it for me. There's a good fellow."

"Delighted, my lord."

"You'll find the gilt whatnot in my tent. And will you come dine at Mansfield at your earliest convenience? I should like your grey to stud."

When Ralf took his leave of them, Waltheof bent a baleful eye on the surgeon binding his ankle. "*Mon vieux,* leave us for the nonce. You will find the air infinitely fresher outside."

Alone with Hereford and the eager Rolph, Waltheof inquired of the earl, "What do you think?"

Young Rolph leaped in effusively. "My lord, Ralf is a Roland. Rides like a god, commands the greatest respect, yet modest as a monk."

"I quite agree." Waltheof winced at a twinge in his ankle, then covered it with the sort of observation these men expected from a Saxon. "One might almost think him English."

"Ah, my lord, you know what I mean."

"I do. And you, Roger?"

Hereford had more experience, which showed in his reserve. "Says little and does much. Put us all to shame at quintain, but could he take the more difficult ring?"

"Why not?" Waltheof gingerly wriggled the toes of his injured foot. "He did so once for a shire. He might again for, say, an earldom."

When de Breteuil made a dubious face, Waltheof modified slightly. "Or a barony. Let us watch him. Dine with him and introduce him easily to our friends."

Who had real friends in such a venture? Waltheof wondered skeptically, looking from one to the other. One has followers with vested interests. The middle-aged and quite realistic Roger would want much for his support. Young Rolph de Gael would probably want more than he was worth; the same could be said of the others. A man of loyalty and ideals would be worth much. Who had friends? Waltheof would dearly love to ask them, heart-to-heart: Do you have any idea of what we do?

No profit there. He masked his concern in lightness. "This ankle feels wretched. Help me up, the pair of you. Surgeon!"

Tiny Matilda stepped up onto a low box to make her proclamation from the pavilion. Such elevations were always ready and in place for her when needed. Now she stood beside Archbishop Lanfranc, speaking in Frank, and depending on the herald to bruit her sentiment to the English.

At her signal, the trumpets flourished.

"Nos enfants d'Angleterre!"

"Our children of England: We decree through our love for our subjects, that in keeping with your own ancient custom, the fairest of your own most fair shall be crowned Queen of the May. And tomorrow the very best of archers will receive from your queen's hand the arrow of gold. But now—let your queen be crowned."

Another flourish from the trumpets and the horseman on the grey advanced down the middle of the meadow with the gilt crown on the end of his spear. At sight of him the commons gave only a moderate response to the pavilion's salute: not their Waltheof but the foreign favorite in his place. The rider walked the grey to a halt before Matilda who waited with Lady Judith at her side.

"Sire knight," Matilda called to him. "Why do you come here?"

Ralf uncovered his head to the queen. "Lady, I come to honor the Queen of the May."

"Name the lady."

"Lady Judith of Denby." Ralf dipped his spear to put the gilt crown within Matilda's grasp. The small queen held it high, out to the commons, then settled it on Judith's white-veiled head as the hoarse cheering rose from the English commons, now swelled by the *noblesse*.

"Here is your Queen of the May!"

Judith descended from the royal box. Grooms hurried to place a wooden mounting block by Ralf's horse. Judith extended her hand to him. "Well, Lord Sheriff, it is a fair day for England."

He took her hand to help her mount. "The fairer for your presence, *demoiselle*. Have you ever ridden croup before?"

"No, but royalty is obliged."

"Take good hold of me."

"Sire Ralf, you may depend on that."

Ralf walked the horse the length of the pavilion while Judith kept one hand raised to the Norman ladies and wondered, behind her fixed smile, if Ralf Fitz-Gerald didn't feel the least bit awkward about this, considering his rather intense relationship with Robin. As Ralf paraded her before the commons, Judith caught sight of the scrofulous beggar bobbing through the crowd abreast of her. Shouldering his way closer to the ropes, then under them as the peasants close by pointed and cheered.

"Jack in the Green! Look, it's Jacky!"

The crowd guffawed at crippled but nimble Jacky as he went down on one knee by Ralf's stirrup.

"Blessin', leddy. Blessin' on the Queen of the May."

Ralf would have ignored him and ridden on, but Judith asked him to stop. "This is the people's day, sir knight. 'The last shall be first,' remember?" Judith extended a white hand to touch the beggar's grubby paw. "Blessing on you and all of yours, Jacky."

The misshappen mouth twisted in a parody of reverence. "And one for me old mother and good wife."

You impossible scamp. Get away before he knows you. But Jacky still waited for her benediction. "Jacky, any woman wife to you needs blessing, and I give it. Ride on, sir."

Another burst of laughter from the crowd as Jacky scurried back behind the ropes, dodging this way and that to avoid being cuffed by soldiers.

"There's one or two like him in every village," Ralf tossed over his shoulder. "Even in Le Thiel, where I was born."

"Yes. Unfortunate," Judith agreed soberly. *You need the quarry's scent freshened in your nostrils, Ralf. You did not know Robin Hood when he knelt before you.*

She caught sight of Marian and Maud in the crowd and waved to them—then spied the ubiquitous Jacky inching closer to the two women—

"God bless, Aunt!"

—and almost forgot riding under the sun like this that they were a beaten people. Oh, she felt good this day. The sun shone, English voices cheered her, Robin made outlawry into honor, and though she might gladly tarry many evenings with a man like Ralf Fitz-Gerald, this one marvelous day Judith could not manage to feel conquered in the least, thanks just the same.

28

By NOON OF May third, Ralf found himself sharing the victory of Matilda's greens, warmed in the reflected sunlight of English enthusiasm for having fought at Waltheof's side, owed a tidy sum in ransoms, and possessed of a little more wisdom if only in the form of questions. If Robin was a thorn in his shoe, the man certainly had beautiful relatives. Between Marian and Judith one could reflect for a year on the mysteries of beauty. If Judith was without doubt the fairer, why did the lesser draw him so?

Once he prayed to see his death. God or the Norns answered him, showed him death but didn't take him. In Marian they held out life and joy but denied him the reach to grasp them. So much for philosophy: Whatever the alleged consolations, Ralf Fitz-Gerald would not reckon them worth a damn.

He sat on a low stool in the surgeon's tent, naked except for his breeches, awaiting ointment for a rankling collection of cuts and bruises, smelling his own sweat and that of the injured men around him. He was lucky to have no hurts worth mentioning, thanks mostly to Waltheof. Others fared far worse with broken arms and ribs. On a cot nearby a young knight of the reds kept spitting blood from a lung punctured by a splintered rib. The smell of blood mixed with sweat and the sound of men dealing with pain, boasting of their victories or the steadiness of a good horse, others cursing the ill-fortune of ransoms owed but ill-afforded.

"Ah, Sire Ralf, there you are."

A number of wounded greens sat up to bellow or croak greetings to Waltheof as he hobbled into the tent on a crutch to loom over Ralf.

"You are not seriously hurt, Ralf?"

"Cat scratches, that's all."

There was solicitude and respect in the earl's manner. "That is good."

"And you, my lord, should not have taken the field today." Waltheof's right ankle had been seriously wrenched in yesterday's fall. He should not have stood at all; nevertheless he rode and fought afoot throughout the *mêlée* at Ralf's side. Now he merely made a comic face at the notion of disability.

"Nonsense. Annoying, that's all. Young Raimond is in greater discomfort. I waived his ransom."

"You *what?*" Ralf was surprised beyond manners. "What in hell for?" Raimond lost horse, armor, and weapons to Waltheof under the strict rules of the *mêlée* but could certainly afford to redeem them. "You gave him the drubbing he deserved. Let it cost him."

Waltheof beamed. "You address me at last as *tu*. Good. I pride myself on good taste in friends. Promise me you will come to Mansfield soon. My chef sets the best table in the Midlands."

This Englishman was clearly courting his favor, Ralf knew, quite plainly offering new vistas of prestige to a plain officer of the king. Only his reasons were obscure—and why let Raimond out of paying ransom?

"Beaumont is a capable knight," Waltheof explained casually, "but not yet a large soul. There is nothing more galling to a bad-tempered boy than generosity added to humiliation. Defeat is total: one of the more gracious forms of cruelty."

Yes, savage or subtle, Saxons were crueler in their way than his own kind. A man who slighted his own pain gave little note to pain in others. The insight prompted a long-deferred question. "My lord?"

A bandaged vavasor vacated his stool just then. Waltheof eased himself down onto it, stretching out his injured leg. "Let's not stand on rank. My name is Waltheof."

"Why do your people take scalps?"

"Scalps?" There it was again, the bland mask of bemused innocence. Waltheof appeared to be searching memory for an answer of small importance. "Oh, that's old-fashioned."

"Not entirely," said Ralf.

"From the days of the heptarchy and the Danes."

"At Tadcaster, one of my companions had his scalp ripped away."

"Indeed? Probably a Northumbrian," Waltheof surmised, offhanded as a man speculating on the weather. "They're a rough lot. But really, that's from the old *berserker* days. Considered showy now."

The English term escaped Ralf. "Showy?"

"Excessive. *De trop.*" Waltheof rose and set his crutch. "In any case, you might ask Robin Hood. He planned Tadcaster, hadn't you heard? His father was very proud of him. Well, I must be off. Come to Mansfield, then. We'll have a proper visit."

And the hero of the *mêlée* went pegging off on his crutch; he even limped glamorously. If Ralf hadn't seen for himself that day, he might have doubted Waltheof mortal enough to sweat.

Still, Ralf indulged in a snort of dry, vindictive humor. Robin at Tadcaster. Robin and the bishop; by God, he might have guessed. That must indeed be heaven's punishment for praying to know his death when it came. God granted his wish too clearly and too close, binding Ralph's destiny so tightly with that of Robin and Marian that like a bee he could not sting without some death to himself.

This somber thought occupied him while the surgeon's apprentice smeared salve over his bruises. Ralf cut the process short, calling for his clothes. "Enough. I need to get out of here. This place stinks."

He wished heartily that he could as readily fathom Earl Waltheof's motives. Sure as his own seat on a horse, the man had an instinct for people. Blunt William could take schooling in that much, the sense of his own charisma, the instinct to know exactly where and when he shone most brilliantly in men's eyes. And yet Ralf would sooner trust William.

Waltheof rode knee to knee with him in the first charges of the *mêlée*, splintering two lances but never unhorsed, while the Norman ladies squealed and shrieked. When they fought on foot, Waltheof was back to back with Ralf, using a round, bossed Saxon shield. They were beginning to be outnumbered as the opposing side pressed in on them. Time after time as the sun climbed toward noon, two and sometimes three men beset the earl. Waltheof's sword was good, but not the stuff of fables; it was his use of the shield that set him off. When they came overhand at his head, he was under the shield while the sword guarded. Never a moment when one hand did not work with the other. And he saved Ralf from serious injury. Beleaguered as he was, thinking the contest already lost, Ralf failed to see Raimond de Beaumont, still mounted, guiding the stallion closer through the press of men while he covered himself with the long oval shield, sword arm ready, raised, tensed as a bowstring to lose.

"Ralf! Guard!"

Ralf whirled in the thick of bodies around him—one man down, blood streaming from a split scalp, another spitting fragments of broken teeth —to see in one red instant the vindictive triumph in Raimond's scarred face as the sword came down. Before he could move to guard, Waltheof's shield caught the blow. As Raimond drew back to strike again, Waltheof flung his shield square into Raimond's face, launching his whole body after to grasp the young knight around the neck and drag him from the saddle, a prisoner.

"That will do for you, laddy. Do you yield?"

Raimond had no choice, leading his horse off the now thinned-out field. Ralf listened for Nones bell as he fought. Only a few men left on either side, then somehow more of their greens than reds—and the boy Rolph de Gael actually chanting a laud for pure joy as he scythed forward through a knot of opponents to reach Ralf and Waltheof and become the third side of an invincible bastion.

"Glorious!" he roared. "Just glorious. For God and Waltheof!"

De Gael fought with the passionate, wasteful, limitless energy that came with being nineteen but never again. They were pressed hard. Ralf could see no other greens about them. They would be taken in a moment, no help for that. Then, under the metal shriek of his hacked sword parrying another, Ralf heard the Nones bell from St. Wulfram's. In a moment the trumpet would sound the end of the *mêlée*. One thought went through the surrounded three of them, one volcanic surge of outward thrust. Waltheof battered one opponent to the ground, ducked another and disarmed him. De Gael's swing tore the helmet from one man and sent him to the trampled grass with a bleeding pate. Ralf locked hilts, hooked a leg behind his opponent's, and let the man's laboring weight do the rest. As he touched the point of his sword to the man's chest—"Yield you now"—the heralds' trumpets called them to cease.

When Ralf looked about, he and Waltheof and de Gael were still a fortress in the middle of the field, sweat clammy in their armor, swords bent and shields battered, but untaken.

"What we could not do." De Gael clasped Waltheof's shoulder in pure adoration. "My lord, what such as we *will* not do!"

Only now did Waltheof show any hint of discomfort, favoring his right leg. "Cursed inconvenient, this silly foot. Help me, Ralf."

Ralf could barely hear him over the thunderous applause and bellowing from both sides of the field. The earl held out an arm; Ralf slipped under it to support him. Waltheof could barely hobble now.

"You should not have fought."

"What's that? Can't hear you."

"You should not have entered the *mêlée*."

"No, I daresay." Waltheof halted to look back at young de Gael who had simply collapsed on his rump like a puppy whose body had quit before his brain got the news—one hand bruised and the other bleeding, face sheened with perspiration, no doubt feeling marvelous. Waltheof winced with the pain in his ankle. "There are days when life is pure annoyance. One just has to get on with it. Here. Set me here."

The pair of them planted themselves between Matilda's box and the English commons straining against the ropes. Supported by Ralf, the earl raised his sword in salute to the queen, then turned about to his countrymen as their roar settled into a chant of victory made out of his name.

Wal-theof! Wal-theof! Wal-theof!

Cyn-ing! Cyn-ing! Cyn-ing!

"My lord," Ralf bawled in his ear. "Are they calling you king?"

"Oh, they get carried away."

And yet Ralf felt the earl straighten against him. *Something* coursed through the man, shaped the pain on the anvil of personal pride. Waltheof raised the sword again in a sweeping salute to his own people.

Wal-theof!

Cyn-ing!

Close to two in the afternoon the archers assembled at the western end of the field while their covered straw targets were set a hundred paces away at the eastern end. Young Henri, Ralf's squire, had packed the tent and equipment on a mule, bound for the manor where Ralf would sup and stay the night at court before returning to Denby in the morning. Knight and squire guided their mounts behind the archers busy inspecting arrows, sticking them in the ground in groups of six. Some of them had the dark, unmistakable Welsh features: small, compact men with broad shoulders and disproportionately long arms. There were a few Normans. Most were English foresters given leave by their lords or the peasant-wizards who defied rope and branding iron every day to feed their families. Henri was amazed at the length of most of the arrows.

"They're called clothyard arrows," Ralf told him from visceral experience with the missile. "Do you know what you're seeing, Henri?"

"What, sire?"

"The only weapon able to bring down a line of knights in a matter of seconds."

"Look!"

With a great rush the first missiles flew up like a swarm of lethal wasps—up, riding the air, flexing, curving downward toward their marks.

"I have seen them before, Henri." Ralf urged the grey onward toward Manor Gate. "I hate the buggering things."

Like Robin, who waited once on the walls at York and never knew that what advanced on him was the future, Ralf turned away from the whining, hated shafts and couldn't know, in the very morning of his kind, that he was seeing a death vaster than his own.

29

W<small>HEN HIS FIRST</small> six arrows were shot at a hundred paces, five of them in the target and the last two close to the center of the clout, Robin knew the negligible wind down to the lightest puff. A beautiful day for shooting, sun at their backs, and the rest of this day belonged to England. He hunched inside his ragged smock and grinned at his arrows with Jacky's obscene mouth.

He'd never shot in competition before but couldn't see much difficulty where distance was known, crosswind slight and himself taught by the best archer in the isle. Will made the bow he carried today, two inches beyond six feet in length, cut from the trunk of a churchyard yew, sand-smoothed and supple from years of tallow rubbed into the grain, its hundred-weight pull able to cast an arrow accurately half again the length of this meadow.

There were fine archers around him today as, rank by rank, they stood up to the shooting line. None was easily eliminated at a hundred paces. Robin carefully kept his shooting just accurate enough not to be ruled out at the distance. After eighteen arrows apiece, the competition narrowed to a dozen odd archers who advanced to the eighty-pace mark.

He was not bothered at all that many nobles left the pavilion, uninterested in a contest of louts. Judith was still there by the queen, the sun glinting on her gilt crown. Jesus, what a fine moment when he knelt to her, not failing to relish the scar he cut on Fitz-Gerald's face. Marian and Maud were still watching him from behind the ropes, but now, like

Will Scatloch's hand on his shoulder, something stern disciplined his
attention to the contest. *You can lose today,* Will's voice warned in his
mind. *Watch the Welshman.*

That was well bethought. The Welshman, Morgan of Powys, was
another Scatloch: the same stance, anchor, and release flowing together
smoothly as water over a stone. At a hundred paces, Robin barely equaled
him. At eighty, Morgan bested him by one arrow and a clean inch closer
to the center of the clout. Not even second to Morgan, he was bettered
at the range by a Norman who'd fought at Hastings.

Fie on you, ghost-Will jeered in his brain. *You'll never match a Briton,
but a bloody Frank?*

Something was wrong where nothing should be. His stance was perfect,
his shafts the handpicked best, each one painstakingly measured to his
arm and fletched with feather from same wing of the grey goose for
perfect spin. What, then? As the remaining half dozen of them moved
to the sixty-pace mark, Robin flexed his fingers in the leather shooting
tab and worried. Two of the dearest women in the world were watching
him. He'd had a fleeting moment with them before the guards pushed
him away.

"Marian, love."

"Aye, be careful, you impossible man."

"Hello, Mum. Do y'loov poor Jacky?"

"Dearly, but get away. They're watching us."

"Oh, it's a lark. God bless. . . ."

The Saxon men followed the contest closely as the Norman nobles had
the finer points of the *mêlée*. They knew nothing of cavalry and little of
sword, but all of them were bred to the bow and knew to a man every
nuance of performance, perfection, and flaw in the dwindling line of
archers and whom to cheer for.

A Morgan! A Morgan!

A Jacky! A Jack!

Only twelve arrows were allowed at this ridiculous range. Robin placed
second after his first six. Three men dropped out, then the Norman when
he failed to allow for a sudden puff of wind. Morgan and himself now,
with the Welshman clearly ahead. Robin nocked the first of his last six
arrows as the noise from the crowd smothered down to an expectant hush.

What was he doing here? He'd got the money to Marian and loved
her as they both needed, touched hands and hearts with his mum, even
sparkled in a moment of secret fun with Judith. But now his aim was
hopelessly off, second-best, and he had no chance against Morgan who

was not a human man at all but a war machine, a lethal catapult. The Welshman placed his final shafts all within the clout. As the judges ran out to study the grouping, Robin set himself and waited.

Six centered for Morgan, five of them clustered so close together that were there a smaller ring within the clout, they'd be inside. The sixth was low by no more than the width of two fingers.

Robin stanced, drew, and loosed his first shaft.

Center. *That's better. Help me, Will.*

What was it made champions? Earl Waltheof had the quality, and damn him, so did Fitz-Gerald. Robin could almost cheer the man when he helped the earl hobble out to receive the homage of his people.

Second shaft—there! Centered again as the English crowd roared for him.

Mum's right. I'm daft to be here.

Could he Jacky-slouch to the middle of the field, doff to the queen, and then his own people? Was that why he was here, for a formless thing called England? He felt proud that they cheered him, his mind full of Marian, family, the image of Fitz-Gerald.

Third shaft, fourth, fifth. All clustered thick as hedgehog's quills in the center. A roar like surf grew louder in his consciousness. The folk were screaming now, even some of the Normans.

That felt wrong, that last shot. Summ'at low.

He raised a hand to the judges for time, spider-scurrying down the field to inspect his last shot. A good two inches low: bowstring creeping away from true anchor. Change that simple enough, but "creeping" was a beginner's flaw. Whatever threw him off today, thank God he wasn't shooting for his life, or even fresh meat. Will would be ashamed of him.

Once more he bobbled back to his mark and set himself for the last shot—seeing and hearing everything about him: Norman women in bright colors, Judith in white. The dun and black of his own people behind the ropes, Marian and Maud with their eyes on him. *And me in the center, Will. Midway betwixt them all, halfway between honor and ordinary. I said that once to Marian, but I'll lose today. The Welshman's too good.*

His sixth shaft sped home into the center of the clout. He heard a smattering of applause and approval in Frank, drowned out by a great wave of shouting from the English.

Robin and Morgan waited on their marks while the judges inspected both targets not once but twice, puzzled, gesticulated over them, argued heatedly. Then one of them, a shire man by his accent, trudged up the field to announce the decision.

"Too close. One more shaft apiece."

There was a tense, murmuring wait while Robin and Morgan retrieved their shafts and new targets were fitted over the straw hurdles. Robin fingered through his arrows, inspecting each minutely from pile to nock for any new flaw. He finally selected one: not a full clothyard length, but the shaft *felt* right. He wished the rest of him did; suddenly and passionately wanted Marian and Maud, Judith and all of flaming England, to cheer him as they did Waltheof.

Then Will helped him.

That's what's wrong. My body's right but my head's not. There's no crowd, no family, nowt but me and the mark.

Steady down, steady on.

A few paces away, dark Morgan nocked his final arrow. Before taking his stance, he raised one hand in salute to Robin. "I've not seen finer than yourself even in Powys, Jacky."

Robin heard the sincerity in the man's respect. Such was an honor to return. "I've seen only one man your equal, and he is from Gwent."

"That is natural." Morgan winked at him, stancing. "Come, boyo: Let's show these horse-lovers what a man can do on his own two feet."

Satisfying, beautiful to watch the wee man flow into it, one with bow and shaft alike as he stanced, anchored, and loosed, the arrow singing through sunlight and going home so close to center that Robin could detect no drift to left or right at all.

Steady down, Will whispered, *steady on.*

Robin took a deep breath and set himself, feeling only the nock and waxed bowstring between his fingers, seeing only the tiny center of the red circle, that invisible O all of his reality now. Heard nothing, thought nothing. Marian did not exist here, nor Fitz-Gerald, nor the muted, meaningless crowds. He was the center, part of bow, shaft, and target alike. All were one and would come together natural as fingers closing, and—

Loose.

Jacky it was, misshapen Jacky who won for England over the Welsh wizard Morgan, and the two had a dizzy moment together before the crowds poured past the ropes to descend on them.

"By Saint Davy, it is no shame that I lose to such as you," Morgan acknowledged.

"Nor I to you." Robin wrung his hand, one eye on the avalanche of folk surging toward them over the field. "If you fancy living free and eating the king's deer, seek me in Sherwood where I go by the name of Robin. Tell the queen I can't tarry, but will send to her. God bless.''

Morgan had bare time to gape at the bowman hobbling toward the line of cheapmen's wagons before the tide of people surged about him. Jacky was engulfed, but not stayed. The last Morgan saw was the hunched back darting behind a wagon.

In the royal box, Judith waited with the queen as the English folk rolled toward them in one roaring mass. She couldn't make out Robin in their midst, but she felt their marvelous pride as when Waltheof saluted his own people with Ralf beside him. Ralf and Robin: that two such men should be enemies. She imagined what they could accomplish together, but no one harnessed stallions side by side or yoked two bulls to a plow.

Like racing surf, the English mob surged against the pavilion timbers and fell back, parting to let swarthy Morgan kneel before Queen Matilda. "Long live the queen, Marm."

"This is your day," Matilda said to Judith. "Speak to your people."

Speak what to whom? "Archer, where is our Jack in the Green who shot so well today?"

Bewildered as the ladies, Morgan couldn't say precisely. "All I did see was his back in leaving. Marm, it is a coil to be the best and then see myself bested yet. God and the Devil if they worked together, is it, could not fashion a better eye or arm than his. *Glorious* he was, and yet himself saying he could not tarry."

Judith might have shrewdly guessed. *Wise, Robin. You've already bent your luck to breaking and should be gone. Sweet cousin, God bless.*

"Could not tarry?" Matilda pressed. "How annoying."

"Please you, Marm," Morgan explained. "He said he would send word as to the golden arrow. From Sherwood, he said."

"Sherwood." Chill understanding settled on the queen and colored her answer. She tossed a small purse to Morgan. "We thank you for your skill and pains. Lady Judith, did you know of this?"

Holding the golden prize, Judith managed to look blank and angelically innocent. "Madam?"

The queen sighed, having in any case to accept a *fait accompli*. "No, I suppose not and we doubt not we shall hear from this Jacky."

Morgan piped up helpfully: "The name he gave was Robin, Marm."

While Judith struggled to keep her expression opaque, Matilda nodded with strained cordiality to the Welshman. "Thank you. We know the man well."

Robin? Aye, Robin. The name murmured through the English crowd, later to spread far beyond Grantham like sparkling ripples in a pool of defeat.

One night at Mansfield soon after, Waltheof interrupted serious debate with Roger de Breteuil and Rolph de Gael to bathe his two guests in a winning smile. "Have you heard who took the golden arrow? Robin Hood, none else. My harper will be devising a new ballad to entertain you."

The burly Breteuil, Earl of Hereford, voiced a cautious consideration. "You should not so openly tweak the king in the name of Saxons. He will suspect your loyalty."

Waltheof blithely disagreed. "Dear Roger, not a whit. He would suspect the more if I did not occasionally glow with native pride. In these dark days, who will grudge us a candle-end for light? Where were we?"

"Speaking of Fitz-Gerald," young de Gael prompted.

Just so. Waltheof need not impress them with the sheriff's obvious worth. "We must have him with us when the time comes."

De Gael saw no reason against it, but Breteuil was unsure in this dangerous area where there could be no margin for doubt. "What if we disclose to him and he will not stand with us?"

Waltheof pared a sliver of cheese from the wheel before him and munched it. "Obviously, we would then make sure he cannot stand against us." He washed down the morsel with a swallow of wine. "And if we could keep them from each other's throats, I would have Robin Hood as well."

Rolph de Gael agreed after a moment of thought. Though not yet a Hereward, the outlaw thane would jump at their cause.

Hereford dismissed the nomination out of hand. "He has no name. He is not noble, not even a knight."

"But like Hereward, his name is growing," Waltheof countered. "Say that England is a flower, my lords. We may be the blossoms, but Robin is the root that goes deep in the earth. You grew in different soil, Roger. It is difficult for you to conceive, but Robin *is* England."

For the Norman earl, quite difficult. There were times when Waltheof's English cast of thought eluded him completely.

* * *

When Judith answered Matilda's summons from her prison house, the queen handed her a scrap of well-worn vellum to read. Judith recognized Father Beorn's handwriting.

TO MATILDA, LADY OF ENGLAND—

I would liefer have received the golden arrow from my dear cousin's hand, but that seemed unwise. The queen would show herself kind to deliver the prize to St. Wulfram's to be melted down as alms for the poor of Grantham. I ask the queen's further kindness in speeding my love to my wife and dearest family.

EDWARD AELREDSON, THANE OF DENBY

"What does he want, this cousin of yours?" The bit of embroidery jerked in Matilda's hand; she closed her eyes and sucked in a relieving breath. *"Mon Dieu."*

"My queen, are you ill?"

Ill enough to be snappish while the sudden pain in her vitals eased too slowly. "Of course I am. Who would not be, always traveling, never enough rest."

"May I fetch you some comfrey?"

"I asked you a question young woman."

"My queen?"

"Lord, what an ambassador you would make, even to Rome. What does Robin *want*?"

Judith sat back, regarding her hands.

"Child, I house a number of pains. Your family is only one of them. Answer."

"May I be candid, madam?"

"Please. We have no dearth of liars."

"His own lands returned for a start, and perhaps . . . his country."

The presumption was for a moment quite beyond the Norman queen. *"His* country?"

"As he loves it, my queen. He'd like it back."

Matilda bent her head over the embroidery work. "You have a barbed wit, Judith. Only the Church or grand tragedy has room for such ideals. You see, my dear, England is no longer an island but part of a larger and better-managed kingdom from which the last obstacles will soon be cleared away. Ely will be taken, Hereward killed or neutralized, your Robin snared. Accept that. It is the will of God. And yes, now I will take some tea."

Part of every English soul knew Hereward and Ely could not hold out forever. They braced themselves for the inevitable while crowing over the magnificent, brazen gall of Robin and the golden arrow.

Marian mourned the dark truth and glowed with the brighter in the afternoons when the morning sickness of early pregnancy let her feel human.

BOOK IV

The Matter of England

30

$\mathcal{A}$s SUMMER CAME on, conflicting news seeped outward from fen-girt Ely. The isle was finally taken. Was not taken. Would fall in a week. Would never surrender. Saxon folk hung on every meager word from Ely, weaving the slightest deed of Hereward and the defenders into the whole cloth of legend.

While England waited and hoped, Marian quickened. When she missed her courses in June, she suspected and hoped. When again in July with the new soreness in her breasts and unmistakable morning sickness, she was sure. Robin must be told somehow, must know before Ralf ran him to ground. While Judith counted their money and reckoned in linen and fresh wool to be spun into swaddling for the child and new garments for Marian, Maud took charge of passing the news to the father. When Marian was permitted to go to Mass, Maud pressed five goose feathers into her hand with precise instructions. "Give these to Father John for the five most reliable travelers bound west. One of them will find Robin."

With Perdu riding jauntily on her shoulder, Marian sought out the priest and passed her message.

She ever hoped for a word in return. Sometimes the priest had news for her. Robin was south, for her own sake not saying exactly where. He was well, the men throve in good spirits and more silver would reach the ladies, don't ask whence.

"And what from Ely, Father?"

"Ely stands, child. Go and pray for me."

329

Through the summer "Ely stands" became an English refrain to the persisting Norman chant of purpose. Ely stood and defied William with every exaggerated exploit. Tales of Robin Hood went round tavern and hearth. Robin was here, there, two places at once. Robin stopped a monk and a knight and invited them to dine. When the meal of fine venison was done, each was asked to pay his share. The monk said he had but tenpence, the knight declared three pounds in his purse.

"So Will—Scarlet? Aye, Scarlet's the name—turns out one purse and Little John the other. The knight spoke true, but the monk had much more than he said."

"Right thieving bastard."

Because the knight was honest, as the story went, Robin charged him nothing for his supper, but the monk went penniless on his way and Robin laughing at him. No fear they'd capture that one. If the sheriff hunted him north, he was south, or the other way around. Ralf Fitz-Gerald patrolled Sherwood personally when he could, questioned and weighed the men of Blidworth. The news from Ely interested him little. He had seen the fens. Knights hungry for reputation and plunder were welcome to the adventure.

Lammas came and August nights gradually cooled. Marian flushed to radiance with the child, marvelously healthy when the morning sickness let up. But no word from Robin, only the dear tales folk heard about. Marian recounted what she gleaned as the tea steeped, Maud and Judith spun out the raw new wool onto the bobbin, and Perdu purred contentedly against the warm mound of her belly.

"Oh, this one's a rare fancy, you'll never guess. Robin was to a wedding in Edwinstowe."

"Ach, he wasn't!"

"He *was*, Mum, and in a monk's robe if you please, beard shaved off smooth. I'd love to see that, prickly as it was—oh!"

The tortoiseshell cat sprang down from Marian's lap, glowering at her former place, tail twitching in consternation. Offering tea to Marian, Judith asked, "How is it? A pain?"

Marian patted her belly. "His lordship kicked me again. Aye, and kicked the cat fair off my lap, there's a shire lad for you. Come feel, mayhap he'll fetch me another."

Perdu returned warily to her lap as Marian went on with the tale which must be true. Young Alcuin had it from Angharad who nipped out to lie with Will one moonless night and heard it from his own lips. A young farmer, once free and of three good hides, came lamenting through Sherwood and stopped with Robin's band. Frightened at first that he'd be robbed of the few pennies his Norman landlord left him, he accepted the skin of ale from Tuck and when he'd drunk enough to ease his tongue, the young man poured out his grief. At Edwinstowe in three days' time, his true love would be wed to a rich Norman more than twice her age, and no help for it where his own lands had been seized and himself left a pauper.

The men all agreed the matter was a shame, especially Will Scatloch who put much store by a good woman. Robin did not say much, just shaved his beard and borrowed a dun robe from Tuck. He went straight to the church at Edwinstowe, arranging with the English priest to be the one to confess the bride, not an easy task since it required some bruising of the sacraments. A donation to the poor box swayed the priest who admired Robin though not to the point of indulgence. When the girl came blushing to the closed confessional booth, Robin told her quickly through the lattice that there was a fast horse waiting to carry her to her true lad.

"And off they went," Marian concluded with a flourish, "leaving the old groom brideless and the Norman guests confounded and all."

"And that is how Puck-Robin went a-praying," said Maud as she spun out the long strand of dark wool with sure fingers.

A summer for heroes, right enough. Hereward shook a fist from the fens while in Sherwood Robin thumbed his nose, robbed or entertained passing Normans, or stole a bride with the best intent. At Mansfield Waltheof heard the tale from his larderer who gleaned it in Grantham. Listening with him, young Rolph de Gael, half Breton but the other half English, thrilled to the tale which he pronounced dashing as any sung in Provence.

"Upon my faith, this Robin is gallant. You choose men well, Waltheof."

Robin himself spoke little of the adventure since truth was sadder than legend. The lovelorn young farmer indeed shared his heartbreak with Robin, who even put a shilling in his purse. True, Robin went in monk-cowled secret to Edwinstowe to rescue the supposedly despairing girl and arranged with the priest to hear her prenuptial confession. From there out, truth was shabby fabric for the weaving of myth. Only to Will Scatloch did Robin confide the ridiculous end of it.

"The Normans were thick about the church as fleas on a hound. I whispered through the lattice of the confessional who I was and that I'd come to take her back to her true lad, riding double on Alan's fast Arab, and we had to nip off quick, so was she ready?"

Hot in the confessional, Robin sweating in the monk's robe, puzzling silence from beyond the lattice. Then the girl answered politely enough but to the point, more practical than most as it turned out. "Her" lad was not a provident farmer and never would be now, she said, whereas her bridegroom settled a handsome dowry on her. She would be a good wife to him while he lived, which wouldn't be that long, and well provided thereafter. Robin should not think her ungrateful. She knew him for a worthy lord with troubles of his own and thanked him for his pains but was *not* about to leave plenty for a pauper however young and comely. There was the future and her blood to think of. Fare Robin well, she must be going now.

"And go she did"—Robin sighed—"and there sat I in that flamin' hot box feeling foolish and most like looking every bit of it. Nowt to do but slip out, blessing and smiling my way through the bastards to where I left the horse and off fast as I could. Makes you think, Will."

"Think what?"

"I don't know." Truly Robin did not.

"The least she could send," reckoned sentimental Will, "was that her heart would be his forever."

"She did not, for it weren't," Robin reported with no sentiment at all. "Like dogs, some folk will go with whoever feeds 'em. Makes you think."

About Lammas day when blackberries were thick in Sherwood and the living that easy for forest men, Ralf Fitz-Gerald sat in the Queen's Rest drinking beer and contemplating Ceolred the taverner. While no overt informer, Ceolred was already in Ralf's debt to some extent and therefore a valuable pawn. Ralf bought a round for his host, was courteous to Freda, and talked amiably with them to improve his English. He mentioned casually that many of his men at Denby were being drawn off by the king for the Ely campaign, confident that the news would reach Robin.

Meanwhile the grey feathers went out from Grantham, with one messenger after another. The last was carried by Morgan of Powys. After the May tournament, he'd hung about Grantham thinking to take service with Sire Geoffrey. In truth Morgan had little to go home to in Powys, an independent sort who didn't fancy the arbitrary ways of his own chieftain any more than those of the outlanders, including Saxons. As time went on and his purse went lean, something—Morgan couldn't say what—began to gall him about Grantham. He never liked the stink of

Saxon towns or Norman stables or walls and roofs that cramped him. He couldn't sleep well under such and said as much to Father John.

"Why not go to Sherwood?" the priest suggested. "There is a lady with a message for a certain Jacky who would make it worth a man's effort."

Jacky, was it? That would not be the same Jacky that Morgan shot against and almost won over in the tournament? No, it would? Fair bargain, then, especially with a few new pence to nourish Morgan's starveling purse. Of Will Scatloch's age but hardly as responsible, Morgan blithely left tavern reckonings unpaid, swore eternal faith to several women of Grantham, including two lonely widows, kissed and sang to each, and was off with a full quiver and two good bowstaves on his back. As a forester he could easily elude the wrong sort of company while crossing Sherwood. Finding the right sort proved more difficult. He was two days in the forest without seeing any but sheriff's men and those at a safe distance, trudging south toward Papplewick, singing softly to himself when two men glided onto the path in front of him and another behind, silent as spirits and better armed.

Little John made a quick decision. "Looks a Breton. Sheriff's man."

Much challenged the traveler. "What do you in Sherwood?"

Morgan framed his answer carefully, one eye over his shoulder on the man behind him. He produced the feather from his jerkin. "The truth of it is, I seek a certain Jack in the Green."

Much snorted. "Don't he just?"

"This Jack would know Morgan of Powys."

The Lincoln-clad man at his back came closer. "Powys, is it? *Pwy sy'n fel Cymri?*"

Morgan lighted up like a soul redeemed. "*Neb,* countryman. No one is like the Britons whose deeds are those of heroes and whose song is the tongue of angels."

Will eased his bowstring forward. "Is it from Grantham you come?"

"It is." Morgan ventured a tentative smile at his fellow Welshman. "Would you be a certain man of Gwent?" The smile waxed ingratiating as Morgan presented his credentials to the still-dubious Much and John. "Thruppence from Lady Marian, this feather, and a message to Lord Robin from his wife."

"Come with us," Will said.

They walked south for a quarter of an hour, veered off the path, then Will put horn to lips and blew two quick muted notes.

Robin appeared within moments; he recognized Morgan immediately with a hardy handshake. "Will, here's the best bowman in England—saving yourself, of course."

Morgan allowed that Robin's health and appearance had much improved since Grantham.

"He's come from Lady Marian," Will declared.

"Good man! How does my wife?"

Morgan dutifully delivered his tidings. About Candlemass in February or perhaps a little earlier, Lady Marian would bear a child, alive if it pleased God. If a boy, he would carry his father's name. Edward Edwardson.

The men pounded Robin's back in congratulations and Will regretted there was no drink for proper marking of the occasion. Robin looked slightly dazed, at a loss for words. He finally managed something coherent. "All of you, take Morgan to camp and stuff him with all he can eat. Morgan, thank you. Yes, in faith, thank you. I'll . . . be in later."

Robin had to be alone now to sort out the riot of his feelings. A child, then. By the ridiculous swelling in his chest the thing might never have happened before. He wanted everyone to know, including Fitz-Gerald. Robin felt giddy with wonder and happiness for a full hour, shaking his head continually: "Well . . . well, what do you think of that?"

They would go home. He promised her that and swore it again now while the afternoon light turned to soft gloaming. So much more than themselves to look after now. A son to Denby or a daughter.

Candlemass, Morgan said. Then Marian was in her fourth month. They'd money enough, thank God, but Marian was still mewed in that mean little house without even a dry floor.

Yet Will must school me. What's a man do for a wife with child? I'm that ignorant.

Ignorant and suddenly frightened in a new way. That wouldn't do at all. Robin tried to think clearly: If he were caught, that would be like a death to Marian. And what future for their child? God's gift, the dear and priceless best of both of them, out of their joined bodies like their blood on the bargain oak. What hope for that best but a bowed-down life as William's serf? No, Robin struck out the thought. God would not allow that.

Oh? Why not, when God had said yes to so much cruelty? Even Father Beorn, when he grew discouraged, said that God seemed to be sleeping. No way out and the candle burning down, the child growing in Marian's womb even as he brooded here, coming sure as Resurrection and a deal sooner. What sort of provider was he?

Robin lifted his head to the ancient trees about him. *Pray for me, Beorn. I've never bent my back to anyone, could not even when they left me no other way. I'm for a rope by any road and I can see my child's back already bent in the womb. Help me. I'm an ignorant man, poor as your wisdom reckons riches, and the world's too big for me.*

Grantham turned umber with autumn while Marian's body thickened with the child. Strange to be such a lump; she'd always moved lightly, able to run fast as a boy. She waddled comically now, feet splayed like a goose.

In early October, William sent confidential word to Matilda at Grantham:

> It is only a matter of time, Mora. The monks of Ely have rich holdings beyond the island which I will seize unless they are reasonable and aid me. If Lanfranc cavils, that is tomorrow's problem when Ely is secured. I have lost far too many men against these rebels and patience wears thin. Very thin: Therefore do not clutter your letters to me with the bitches of Denby, pregnant or otherwise. Marry off the comely one if you wish. Otherwise, prisoned they are and by the Face of God, prisoned they stay. How does little Henry? Well, I hope.

William conquered Ely more with ultimatum than force, finding men's vices always more reliable than their virtues. The monks of the island, fearing for the confiscation of Church and personal wealth outside Ely, were persuaded to bargain privately with the king.

Ely fell on October 27. Hereward and his few faithful escaped through the trackless mere in boats kept ready for the purpose. Once the isle was taken, William proceeded with his wonted efficiency, punishing some rebels with mutilation, pardoning others. Some were thrown into dungeons and died there. The perfidious monks lost their treasures anyway when William levied a crippling tax on them, scooping up what they had selfishly tried to hoard. After Ely the tales of Hereward continued to multiply with the need for native heroes. The deeds of a young farmer thane in Sherwood grew with them—thin, gay strains over the dirge of defeat.

Morgan of Powys saw no difference between Saxon and Norman when it came to taking a purse and could not bring himself to lament the fall of any foreigner. Will Scatloch put the matter clearly for him: To Robin outlaw was one thing and common thief another. He would have none of the latter at his fire—and do you mark that, Morgan? Would you steal from a Briton?

"Not from my own trev nor from my own clan, I would not."

"But from any other, I suppose."

"Why not? Took our herds and our blood too, often enough."

"Look you, Morgan," Will reasoned as they straightened ashwood rods for arrows. "It is much like the passing of great Arthur at Camlann and afterward when the Saxons pushed us west and west into the last mountains and darkened the beauty of our songs with sadness. Now you see their world die in the same turning. These English, they are not for sad songs, but in their own way and tongue that is what you are hearing."

Sadness perhaps for old folk who'd seen the past repeat often enough to look like the future, but Marian was young. Hope and the future were natural and gay to her as heather on a heath. The child grew and kicked in her. Her child and Robin's must know it was valuable and wanted. God willing, a day would come when the babe was old enough to understand and Marian would sit at spinning new wool with the child listening and she would tell the stories again. . . .

I'll tell my child about this year, tell it often since for him or her it will be long ago. How we were prisoners to the foreign king with almost the last of England gone down at Ely but the best still free and proud in Sherwood. Your own da, sweeting.

It's chill and dark without sun, and I couldn't read my name if you wrote it large for me, but I don't need that to read God's lesson for England. Without the sun we slept and waited, wrapped tight about the future like yourself inside me before you were born, and if we're waiting still, don't count us dead. Don't ever do that. The sun will come again, my baby, and up we'll spring like flowers, beautiful as God made us and tough as weed.

31

On a bright windy day in September Ralf Fitz-Gerald was crossing
the manor yard at Grantham when the sight of a small Saxon woman,
plainly dressed but sword-straight in her carriage, struck him with sudden
déjà vu. She was guarded by a pikeman whom she ignored insofar as
she could like something unpleasant stuck to the sole of her shoe that
she couldn't scrape off.

She had emerged from the small house where Marian was kept with
her kin.

The connection was a thunderclap. *That* was where he first saw the
woman: at Denby, kneeling formally to William and Matilda. He was ill
that day, but it was she . . . and *she* it was who served him in the manor
hall when Coutance gave directions for Osmund's escort. Maud of Denby.
Sweet Robin's lady mother.

Maud entered the kitchen house. Ralph continued toward the hall,
spinning out a particular thought in his mind. Matilda said the woman
spoke no Frank and apparently refused to learn. What more natural? Most
of his own peers dismissed English as too difficult and not worth the
effort in any case.

Yet obviously Robin knew of Osmund's route and purpose beforehand.
Why else the barn at Denby burned and horses scattered only hours before
he was to meet the bishop? The further Ralph pursued the sequence of
events the more they led him on. Osmund was waylaid at just the right
time and place to give Ralph the least chance at prevention. As at Tad-

337

caster, Robin had to know where and when. How? Ralph addressed his enlightened disgust to the clouds over Grantham. "Perfect."

Say that Maud dissembled and well understood Frank. She was the only one who could have overheard him and Coutance in the hall that day. Possible.

No, probable. Ralph halted before entering the hall. *Suppose. What if?*

Judith was Maud's blood niece, daughter to a thane, highly placed before the ravaging of the north. So the queen told him, adding that Judith's parents spent much time at King Edward's court, where more Frank was spoken than English. With little war to distract them, the English nobles inclined to education. Surely Judith's mother was tutored early in Frankish. Was it reasonable that her sister Maud was not?

"Too perfect."

If he were right, if Maud was an industrious spider spinning her web in Matilda's house, that could be dealt with summarily. Bring the woman before Coutance and hammer the truth out of—

No. Wait. Assume he was right, the mother guilty as her son. The same weapon in his own hand, why snare Maud alone? That would only make Robin harder to catch. Obviously she had a way to inform him and he would trust any message she sent. The right information convincingly obtained could net them both.

Go in and get him, William said. *Or bring him to me.*

Ralf took no time to admire his own cleverness. Marian could be harmed in this. *She avoids me but she's growing big with the child, more and more helpless.* What of her? William's rage was vindictive and unpredictable, tending to sweep the innocent along with the guilty from his path. Throw Maud into the dungeon she deserved, Marian might well be caged with her and lose the child and perhaps her own life in the clammy filth of a cell. No. His suspicions took him to Maud and no further. He would not look beyond her until fact screamed at him.

Be innocent, Marian. Be innocent or let me forget you.

If he must be William's arm, let there be no hesitation in his sword. He had one loyalty, whatever feelings else. Ralf entered the hall and asked for Sire Geoffrey. He was directed to the scriptorium off the hall where he found the reeve with Tancarville, William's traveling steward. A great many records were strewn over the table between them, while at his desk in one corner a monk-scribe searched and muttered through even more in hopeless resignation.

"Good day, Ralf," Coutance greeted the knight. "You catch us in *contretemps*. I think you know messire Tancarville?"

"You've come from Ely, Sire de Tancarville?"

"Only this morning." Tancarville lifted a clutch of papers and dropped them in disgust. "Where the fen themselves are better organized than this manor. Damn that—what was his name?"

"Brother Mauger," said Coutance, obviously embarrassed at the state of the manor records. "Kept the accounts well enough before he vanished this summer, God knows where. Just made off. It now appears he had no system at all, found everything by memory. We'll be weeks sorting this out."

"If we are lucky," the Norman monk commented.

Ralf eased himself down at the table. "I'm damnably dry and scratchy in the throat. Would you send your scribe for a drink?"—adding in a whisper to Coutance—"I need him gone for a minute."

Urged to enjoy some refreshment himself, no hurry, the scribe left on his errand. Ralf spoke quickly to the royal officers. He'd come with his regular report, but there was a more pressing matter in which he needed their help. Let Geoffrey have wine and food brought to them in the hall, some viand that required preparation at the table by a servant woman; a particular woman though selected as if by chance. The one called Maud.

"Maud?" Coutance could not place her among the serving women, but then there were so many.

"I know," said Ralf. "We can better describe our horses than those who serve our tables. We barely look at them. They don't exist." The Saxon woman's headdress showed no more of her face than a nun's. For that matter who would notice a shabby young monk in Edwinstowe or a stinking beggar who just happened to be Grantham's Jack in the Green?

"Or his mother in his kitchen. The retiring Maud."

"Good God." Coutance tapped a fist against his skull. "Of course. I knew she was a prisoner and just did not—"

"Just so," said Ralf. "I was as careless when we spoke of Osmund and she just happened to serve us."

Coutance shook his head. "The butler has charge of the serving women. That little mouse, she barely opens her mouth. Almost invisible."

"So is an adder most of the time. Come with me in this," Ralf urged. "Let's see what players we ourselves can prove."

* * *

Maud had no reason to suspect a trap. Sire Geoffrey came into the kitchen, ordered pears and a cold leg of mutton to be sliced and served at table. He chose a woman helping the cooks, saw she was busy, and singled out Maud. When she brought the food to the high table, Tancarville and Fitz-Gerald were arguing rapidly back and forth across Geoffrey de Coutance who was trying to keep the discussion amicable despite rising tempers. They'd been drinking wine, Fitz-Gerald perhaps a bit too much. Maud well remembered Tancarville from Denby; he accused Robin of impertinence when her son spoke plain truth. The steward snuffled continually with a cold. Small wonder; he still wore his hair far too short for English autumn. None of them took note of her. She had ample time to eavesdrop, pleased that the usurper of Denby was on the coals himself today. The king's steward was in an abrasive and demanding mood: William was very displeased with the situation in Sherwood which should be remedied before he came himself to heat up the fire under Fitz-Gerald—who could easily be replaced.

The sheriff's replies were defensive and irritable. No one realized his problems, especially now when most of his men and horses had been requisitioned to Ely. What remained was a sad joke, half a dozen knights past their prime and all with chronic wounds or sickness, the rest squires or plain men at arms. Of a need he doubted if he could even mount them adequately.

Tancarville was not impressed. "Then what intend you in the matter of this farmer and his half dozen serfs?"

Ralf drank. The words slurred when he spoke. "I will get him."

But when? Next year? "The king sees only that he is dancing rings about you, playing with you. Obviously you have not your former zeal. Have you lost your courage as well?"

Fitz-Gerald lurched to his feet, spilling his wine. "Watch your tongue, clerk."

Tancarville bounded up to meet the challenge, Coutance a hasty barrier between them, arguing for amity and common sense. "This does no one any good. It is from our purpose which is the treasure train from Doncaster."

Beckoned to wipe up the spilled wine, Maud listened intently and tried to remember every detail. A Saxon estate near Doncaster confiscated when the thane went into voluntary exile like so many others. Apparently the movables and treasure were considerable, needing wagons and a number of mules. More important, there were holy relics from several churches within the thane's holding which the king wished to donate to Canterbury. Mules and wagons would be provided. As for men, Fitz-Gerald must manage with those he had.

"Invalids and boys," the sheriff mumbled. "Marvelous."

"See that it is," Tancarville warned. "The king does not like to look a fool. He dislikes even more being robbed. As for the relics, you know his devotion to the Church."

To Maud, William's piety was no greater than it should be, considering the probable state of his conscience. She was not allowed to go to Mass that day or the next, closely guarded to and from her duties. When she finally secured permission, she passed a letter to Father John in the confessional, word to Robin of the train—whence, where bound, cargo, and the probable time, to be escorted by Fitz-Gerald with the few men left him. Maud did not see the snare loop into which she stepped, did not think consciously of traps, yet maternal instinct shaded her letter with caution.

> The people hail you, but those who truly love you would sooner see you alive than the idol of any folk. Marian and the child do well. For their sakes, Puck-Robin, be wise and live, even to the quitting of Sherwood if best safety lies elsewhere. Fitz-Gerald has declined in the king's favor due to your continued freedom and the brave use you make of it. From this letter you will know where he is and how employed, but be wary, son. Sew confusion if you must, but no undue danger to yourself. /M.

Before Maud's letter could reach Robin, two events occurred in summer that affected him profoundly. One was tragic, the other simple fate that lifted Robin's eyes beyond Denby and Sherwood and set him on the long road to Norwich and beyond. Into Sherwood one day came the self-willed young monk named Mauger, truant from Coutance's scriptorium, carrying with him the damaged but priceless copy of an old book.

32

W**HEN** FATHER BEORN compared himself to the lord-lost wretch of the old poems, he might have pointed as well to Father Huger, the Norman priest who replaced him at Blidworth. Huger was not cut out for holy orders and bitterly resented the fate that left them the only hope of advancement befitting his birth. He filled the office to the letter but far short of the spirit and spent as much time as possible at Denby in the more compatible company of vavasors and horses. He found Beorn's house cramped and barely adequate after his spacious quarters at Nottingham. Without this resentment and frustration, he might have drunk less and found the celibacy urged by the Church and his brother Osmund a more bearable burden. He still kept his armor and sword in keen condition as if part of him could not let go of the snapped-short end of a future never to be.

One warm afternoon in August two months before the fall of Ely, he was grateful for a visit from Sire Ralf, who asked confession and then shared a cup of ale in Huger's house. When the vavasor took his leave and walked away to his horse, Huger envied everything about him: the sword-symbol of his class and pride swinging against his leg, the warrior's body and carriage at home in iron as a falcon in feathers. Huger looked after Ralf's whole life with naked yearning. A wiser or stronger man might have accepted and come to terms with reality. Huger only turned back to his house and went on hungering.

He stood for a moment glowering at the wooden rack that held his

342

armor and the scabbarded sword set upright against one wall. Huger
gingerly flexed his ruined right shoulder, then held the arm straight out
in front of him. Not too much stiffness. He drew the heavy blade from
its silver-mounted scabbard. The wrist and arm were not used to the
weight anymore, but years of training left some strength. Huger held the
sword out straight at shoulder height. The weapon wavered but did not
fall. He spun it once with a smooth motion of the powerful wrist, again,
then swung from the shoulder with his whole body behind it—

"Ah!"

The pain shot through the shattered collar bone and upper arm, telling
him he was a fool to try. He dropped the sword, kneading at his shoulder
and cursing softly.

"You pathetic, useless fool."

"Père Huger?"

He hadn't heard the soft knock at his open door where a pleasant-
faced young monk waited with his traveling staff and a heavy wallet on
his back. "Your sexton said I would find you at home. May I enter?"

"Yes." Huger sheathed the sword, hiding his embarrassment under a
show of courtesy. "Yes, of course. You are—?"

"Brother Mauger, late of Saint Wulfram's." The monk put down his
wallet with a thump, accepting the offered chair and cup of ale. About
Fitz-Gerald's age, Huger would have said, but slight of build, speaking
excellent Frank with an East Anglian accent. To the priest, gravid with
his own sorrows, the youthful monk had an airy manner and a confident
cheerfulness that occasionally bordered on impudence. His conversation
smacked more of the library than the cloister.

"Born here, traveled in Normandy on abbey affairs. My father—so
I'm told—was a passing Norman who couldn't tarry. I was raised by the
monks at Peterborough."

"Near Ely, then. Where the king campaigns." Huger refilled their
cups. "I was at Hastings with him," he added, weighting the words with
all the significance they could bear. "I was a vavasor myself and know
what such men and mounts can do. Why, I ask? Where is the difficulty
in scouring a few rebels from one small island?"

"One small island and very determined rebels." Mauger regarded
Huger with satirical eyes over the brim of his cup. "Courage is a great
virtue in a vavasor, I must admit."

"Greatest of all! You imply our men lack it?"

"Oh, not at all, not a whit," Mauger assured him hastily. "Far from
my point. Still, at Ely the king fights not only men but terrain. Courage

does not impress a swamp. You cannot challenge a sinkhole. It just sits there and waits for you to take the wrong step and then it kills you. Nothing subversive; the place has been drowning Saxons for centuries. Obviously the king's men have difficulty in comprehending that.''

There it was again, that offhanded levity that discomfited the humorless Huger. He didn't know if Mauger was laughing with him or at him. "*Bien,* they cannot resist forever,'' he dismissed the subject. "What brings you from Saint Wulfram's?''

Bound to Nottingham, Mauger said, bearing a general letter to the clergy at large on liturgical questions and the observance of saints' days for the coming year. When Mauger opened his wallet to produce the letter, Huger saw what made the pack so heavy: a thick bundle of parchment, hundreds of folio leaves.

"What is all that?''

"Scrap,'' Mauger answered casually, strapping up the wallet. "Waste, old scribblings. My teachers at Peterborough ever lectured me on a light disposition. I carry this to remind me of Christ's burden. Of course, some prefer the hair shirt—hello, lass.''

The plump apple-cheeked girl hovered respectfully in the doorway waiting to be noticed. She carried a large dish covered with a cloth, and a jug. "It's a good supper tonight, Father,'' she promised warmly, "and it's hot.''

At the sight of her, Huger's expression lost its habitual bitterness. "You are good, *ma chère.* Will you join me, Brother Mauger? Freda will bring another portion.''

"No trouble there,'' Freda assured the monk. "Back in a blink. I always stay and talk to Father Huger.''

So the young monk might gather from the air of intimacy between them. When the girl set the dish on the table, Huger let his hand linger on hers.

Among Brother Mauger's attributes was a diplomat's sense of selective truth. He did carry the liturgical letter, one copy out of dozens deliverable by anyone, but it usually got him supper and a bed on his way which was more or less toward Nottingham. Actually he sought something becoming ever rarer, a church or abbey still in English hands with whom he could safely leave the "old scribblings" salvaged from the library at St. Wulfram's. Mauger had come to call these pages the Matter of England, an incomplete copy of the Great Chronicle. More complete manuscripts of the work existed, but not so many that one brittle, brown sheet could be spared. However, four days since, the Norman brother superior in charge of the lay monks of St. Wulfram's had puffed and grumbled into the scriptorium and dropped the tattered lot of parchment pages on Mauger's writing desk.

"Just taking up space," he grunted. "Use it for scrap or wrappings or get rid of it."

To the intellectually defiant young Mauger that was the last straw and a clarion call. He was bored with keeping manor accounts, flat entries, and dull numbers with no grandeur or sweep of language, fed up to the teeth with the brother superior's ignorant arrogance toward English writings as unworthy of study or space in the library. Mauger's rebellion was of the cool sort that did not seethe or howl. He simply laid down his quill, bundled the manuscript with his few possessions, and set out totally without permission to find more enlightened English clerics who would cherish and preserve the Chronicle.

Perhaps a wandering foot had something to do with his decision. That foot had taken him in sixty-six to Stamford Bridge to stand against the Norwegians with Harold's levies. He did not mention this to the military-minded Huger; in truth Mauger was never clear why he went except that he'd never seen a war or his king. Père Huger was clearly not interested in anything English. The priest droned on through the evening about Hastings, the girl hanging over his shoulder and departing only briefly for her father's tavern then returning, clearly to stay. Mauger had hoped for an invitation to stay the night which was not forthcoming. He was advised to walk the mile or so across the vale to Denby. The monk did this and enjoyed a second supper, jesting with the Norman knights and conversing more soberly with Ethelwold. The next day, he met a number of the sheriff's foresters in Sherwood, who greeted him fair and warned of outlaws. *Prenez garde.* Robin Hood was no respecter of clergy high or low.

In the afternoon, Mauger turned off the Annersley path to enjoy the bread, cheese, and beer provided him at Denby. He thought he was alone, not all of his alert mind on the meal, but would have heard anyone approaching.

"Who are you?"

Mauger's head swiveled about, quite startled to find himself observed by three silent men. For all his confusion, he did not have to ask the same of them, not by now. They were obviously foresters but their clothes were far too worn for well-kept sheriff's warders. They did not have the look of house-dwelling men about them. The big one with the wintry mien of a berserker would be Little John, the older man might be the excommunicate Father Beorn of the songs. As for the slim younger man, there was nothing bluff or threatening in his manner, only open curiosity. Considering his reputed deeds, the literary monk expected someone more imposing.

He inquired politely. "Am I in the presence of Robin Hood?"

He was quietly corrected. "Lord Robin of Denby."

"Brother Mauger from Saint Wulfram's, and I've very little in my pack."

"We'll see. John, the wallet."

Mauger's pack was turned out. "Just odds and ends and a great lot of parchment." John set an arrow to his bow. "I'd best have a look about. They might have followed him."

"Oh, I shouldn't think so," Mauger hazarded as John glided away into the bush, silent for all his size. "That would be the one they call Little John. I've heard of him in the stories."

"John has many friends," Robin allowed with a little more cordiality. "As for his enemies, you wouldn't want to be one." When he found Mauger had been at Denby, he questioned the monk closely about the place while Beorn fingered avidly through the parchment sheets, muttering his astonishment and appreciation. The ancient, dog-eared pages crackled to his touch.

"Robin, do you know what he has here? The Great Chronicle. Part of it at least. I've read in this book. Not many copies left." Beorn reverently replaced the pages in the leather wallet.

"Not half enough," Mauger agreed, "and those in danger of being thrown out like this one had I not snatched it up and tucked it away, the past saved from the present as you might say."

"Good for you, lad." Beorn clapped him on the shoulder. "But what of your post? This will cost you at Grantham."

No help for that as Mauger saw the matter. He considered himself absent merely from an office, not from God.

"My sentiments too," said Beorn. "Come Judgment, we may have a strong case."

John returned from his look-about: all quiet. The four men rested, well hidden in the bracken. Mauger passed his ale skin around while they plied him for news of the outside world. What of Robin's family at Grantham? Alas, the monk could say nothing of them. Of Ely then?

"Stands like a rock," Mauger gasped after a gulp of pungent ale. "They fair laugh at William."

Sitting against a tree, shaggy head down on his arms, John asked, "What of Blidworth, man?"

Mauger could only report the village peaceful, what little he saw. He had stopped at Father Huger's house—

"That's Beorn's house," Robin caught him up.

—to chat over a cup. The priest was apparently respected and even popular if the girl was any measure of the rest.

John's head came up. "What girl?"

"Stout lass from the tavern. She brought the priest's supper."

"Freda."

"Freda, yes. That was her name. She seemed quite attached to Father Huger."

Beyond Beorn's recollection that Freda never brought his supper unless he was ill, the subject passed although Mauger did glean the impression they were displeased. Not with him personally; nothing would do but he sup with them that evening. Robin had more questions about Norman dispositions at Denby and his own folk in the hall, Beorn about the village. But John said no more, head lowered again on his thick arms. Never a garrulous man, none of them noticed that he spoke very little more the rest of that day.

This summer, Robin's men quartered on Thane Alan's land around Linby without undo worry. The sheriff's patrols were thinly manned and irregular and Alan's tenants quick to warn of any strangers close by. On a cool, dark day of heavy rain when none from Nottingham would be abroad if not necessary, there was a gathering in the house of Wulf Edricson, one of Alan's larger freeholders. Formerly free, that was. Wulf's family had owned their two hundred acres for a century under Alan's forefathers.

All of them wanted to hear of those times once more. So this meeting in the main room of Wulf's house. There was his fat wife and five sturdy, grubby-faced children. There was Alan and his wife, Lady Algive, for whom Robin felt a flush of warmth because she was a country girl like Marian. While they gathered, he dandled Wulf's youngest boy on his ragged knee, seeing in the five-year-old a son of his own. The child was shy but curious, bursting to ask and finally did:

"You Robin 'ood?"

"I am that."

The child peered at him and made his own bald judgment. "Said you was eight foot tall. You ent."

"If I were big as that, where'd I find trousers to fit? Riddle me that."

"Don't know."

"Well," Robin concluded with crisp country logic, "nor would I, if I were eight foot tall."

The cottagers and bordars tracking mud into the house to hang about the edges of the group were as eager and shy. There was a boy they knew once, the son of Aelred, but this was Robin Hood. People talked of him like Hereward. They peered closely to see the tawny hints to his hide that would mark him half red deer like his old gran, Guntrada.

"Scarce more'n a lad."

"Nor he ent that big."

Lady Algive saw in the man a quiet gravity missing in the overconfident friend of Alan's youth.

They crowded into the main room of Wulf's house, warm and sweet-smelling with the peat turves glowing in the fire pit. Father Beorn sat at one end of the long table, flanked by Robin and Mauger, the rest of the band along the benches. Years ago Beorn had read in the unique history now before him. Robin knew of it from his father. The rest of them knew only that there was a wondrous tale of their own folk to be told. Like the day outside, a great cloud hung over their race. They wanted to hear of the sun again.

Father Beorn and Mauger took turns at the reading, wetting their throats with beer. Beorn read in the calm, stately cadence polished from a thousand Masses, Mauger with the intense conviction and anger of a young man robbed of his past and future. The words spun out with the strength of one and the passion of the other. The folk listened to the stride of their own language across unimaginable years, sometimes prosaic, often colored with the writer's own indignation or approval. As the reading went on, the farmers lost their diffidence, pressing closer, even venturing personal comment.

"That's the truth, that is. I heard from my da how Godwine killed King Edward's own brother. Right butcher he was."

"But a smart one. He always knew where to cut."

"Aye, but my da said—"

"Ah, stuff your da. Shut up and listen."

Mauger read of the brief, black reign of Harthacnut when England was Dane-ruled, and of his unlamented death which was surely God's design.

"So that's how it was," Much marveled at the words that bore out what he'd heard since childhood. "My grandfather told me that when he worked the mill for yours, Robin."

"Edward was half Norman," Alan disapproved flatly, "and there's the start of our troubles."

Not all of the men agreed. There had to be a strong king over a country or the earls and that lot ran wild.

"And what if the king runs wild like Willy Bastard?" Robin posed. "A king, yes, but you've got to have bars and checks on him as well."

"Oh, wisely said," John sniped. "And who's to do the barring and checking, you? And if that's to be, Robin, then who's the bar on you?"

Robin heard the knife-edge in the query but answered levelly. "That was always you, John. You and Much and Anlaf and any man who could come into my hallmoot and complain, and by God, complain you did every flamin' month I can remember."

"Did I ever come without right?"

"And never went without your due."

"Bloody *hell* I never. I had to fight your da and you for every—"

"Master Littlerede, hear me." Mauger rose in his place. "Don't you see where both of you are right? There *was* a hallmoot where you *could* come and complain. And where's the bar and check on you? It is here." Mauger's forefinger stabbed down forcefully on the parchment. Men died, Mauger told them, their voices faded and were forgotten, but writing lasted and reminded men of what they could be, this testament no less than those of Christ.

"That's true," Robin reflected quietly. Mauger put truth in better words than ever he could manage. Like *nation*, which was fuzzy to him as an idea but not the deep feelings that went with it. "Look you now: You put a clout of us together and we're summ'at more than a country. I don't know how but much more." Robin floundered, appealing to Father Beorn. "Read that bit again where my da went out with the king's levies against Godwine. Read it, Father."

1052. The king had great land levies on his side in addition to his shipmen, but it was hateful to almost all of them to have to fight against men of their own race . . . they were unwilling to increase the danger of leaving this land wide open to the invasion of foreigners.

"There!" Robin's open hand slapped down on the page. " 'The danger of foreign invasion.' Plain as bread. There's men like Fitz-Gerald who'll follow a king because he wears the crown. But there's men like us—all over England and mayhap nowhere else—who chose him because he was right and held with laws *they* thought out, and they flamin' well spoke up or rose up when he did not.'' Robin grinned sourly at his big black-smith. ''Like you, Johnny: a noisy lot just like you, and there's my point.''

Robin looked about at the faces of his folk and Alan's, men, women, and children. ''What you're hearing is what we've lost. That's what they stole, not just Denby or Linby Dale.''

When they came to the last pages, Mauger was reading again, the broken-off account of Harold's battle at Stamford Bridge where he stopped the Norwegian invasion only weeks before William landed at Pevensey.

'' 'And there were slain the king of Norway and Earl Tostig and countless numbers of men with them. The Norwegians—' ''

Robin looked up expectantly in Mauger's pause. ''Go on, then.''

''That's all there is except this.'' Mauger showed him the defaced and unreadable last sheet, blotted out and covered with idle scribblings. The men had been leaning forward, hanging on every word, frustrated at such a stop right in the middle. No more? Cut off in the midst of the grandest licking Saxons ever gave to thieving foreigners? *Je*sus!

''I was there,'' Wulf Edricson maintained. ''Men ran in full armor so far and fast to reach the field in time, some gave out and even died before striking a blow.''

''I know.'' Mauger broke off a bit of bread to dip in his soup. ''I tended some of them.''

Wulf found that hard to believe. ''What would a mite of a monk like you do in a battle?''

''Get terribly frightened, mostly. Pulled a few wounded men out of harm's way and that.''

''Whoever writ,'' one old cottager complained, ''why in hell did he leave 't undone?''

''That's why we must find a proper place for the book,'' Mauger insisted, ''and scribes to make more copies.''

Beorn had stacked the pages neatly and now wrapped them in their linen cover. ''Mauger is right. There must be a proper place found. This is the last of us and the best.''

''Easily said,'' Will commented, ''but we're a bit hemmed in.''

Yet the need hung in the air. Robin felt it as a living thing and the realization as something of a shock though true for all of that. ''Ideas—''

''Eh?'' Will prompted. ''What say, Rob?''

"I said ideas live longer than men."

John belched over his soup. "Saving they don't have to eat and breathe."

"Johnny, I feel it in my bones," Tuck snorted ruefully. "Someday you're going to agree with someone and by God the strain will be the death of you."

Robin had risen in his place. "No, but it's true. Look at us, look at all of you. We can't read but we heard and I don't think I'm the only man here who felt proud. I'll do it, Brother Mauger. If Fitz-Gerald is to get me, I'll be got doing summ'at more than running and hiding. By Saint Dunstan and the holy lock of his hair in our church, I will see this book into proper hands."

"Lord Robin, don't swear," Much implored him, impressed but fearful. "I beg you, do not."

"Why not, Much?"

"You say there's men like us all over. There ent, not men like you to stand between us and great Norman lords who don't care a shaved penny for common folk. We need you more'n any book."

"You don't," Robin contradicted gently. "You need this writing and what it says as you need the gospel at Father Beorn's Mass. I—I don't have the words to tell you why, Much. But that's gospel truth itself."

"I can tell them," Beorn said quietly, one hand resting on the bundle of manuscript. He spoke to all of them as he did in his church, choosing simple words and images to touch their understanding. "We are like to the Hebrews of the Old Testament. They were riven of their rights and lands, but even scattered over the world they remained one living folk." And why? With their Ark they took their books of law and the *idea* of a people whom the Lord named a peculiar treasure in His own house. "This is our treasure, Much, the essence of us. Lord Robin's oath is far from foolish; it is necessary."

Robin raised his right hand. "I swear it again. By Saint Dunstan I will find a place."

Father Beorn sealed the oath. "So be it."

"I stand witness to that," said Alan.

Welsh Morgan was struck by the solemnity, which he understood not at all. When the murmurs of conversation lapped again about the table, Will explained the significance to his countryman. Robin had sworn before men of God and his peer. By Saxon custom he was bound to the oath by God and honor and would be accounted less if he shirked the charge.

The oath was given, the deed to be done, but neither history nor a man's life ever resolved so simply. Events never stood alone but leaned with others in intricate balance. Other facts and motives already tipped Robin's scale. Simply put, the Norman priest Huger was all too human and Freda had more urgency than common sense in the matter of men. Then of course Little John was not one to see any side of a problem but his own.

33

JOHN WAS GUILTY in what he did, the man himself would not argue that. He was not a Robin, a seed unfolding to thrust a shoot up into sunlight toward flowering. His mind was not fluid and could not weigh one fact against another in the light of a mutable common sense. In the perpetual shadow over him, he knew loss, vindictiveness, and retribution. In a different world where wife, children, and living were left to him, he might have spun out his life a stubborn man contending no more than the quarterly rents owed his thane. But he lived in William's reality that told him to take loss and swallow it, left him on the outside looking in, with no choice but to be against. Every loss stood out clearly and some were not to be borne. Mauger's casual remark about Huger and Freda set him to brooding.

He knew priests were only men; as many had wives or lemans as did not. If Huger forced his will on Freda, that was one crime for which even Normans had hard penalties. But if Freda was a willing party, that was shame and disgrace. She was a comforting sort but no common dox for all of that. The trouble was, the girl smiled too easily and never thought to say no. If that were the case, someone in Blidworth might think to put the matter right and harm her. John could not allow that. The priest had to go.

John's motives were that simple. Crime was no part of the matter. As with most men, he had a clearer idea of the good he intended than the tragedy he wrought.

Perhaps Huger's motives could be easiest understood: bitter and wasting, trained for a battlefield he could no longer ride, able to fill his present office but not to grace it. What compensations for such a man? Each day he said several Masses for an impassive congregation in Latin they could not understand, heard confessions in their tongue which he comprehended imperfectly. If the sexton joined them for ale and idle talk, Huger could not because of the impassable bar between their class and his. He had no common meeting place with villeins and sought none. Buried in this living grave, Huger felt less and less like a man, inert and unable to escape. Such men hunger for any salve; whatever their feelings the plainest to an instinctive woman was their need and vulnerability.

Freda would have been married before this, possibly to John had not the troubles come. Ready and ripe as she was, a moment came when she sensed and responded to a man's open need. There was no thinking the matter out. Perhaps a smile, a tone of voice that lowered guard and invited, asked. A mutual yielding to no apparent harm and no one's business but theirs, a moment that lengthened into a habit. For a little while a man made her feel wanted. Freda never thought to ask for more. She helped Huger to sleep better and to wake with less reluctance. Thus the facts and motives. If the event was ever woven into a tale to be told or sung, it was changed beyond recognition.

John left the other men sleeping in Wulf's house, departing well before light. He had made his preparations unobtrusively the night before, needing only to pick up his bow and quiver before closing the door behind him. Only five or six miles to Blidworth along the now-familiar swine tracks. He could be there in little more than an hour, but John was in no hurry. Robin and Will had taught him the value of caution and a year in the forest salted the lesson well. Wary lived, careless died. He stopped often to watch and listen for any sound, even the unnatural silence that warned of some intruder on the small animal lives of Sherwood.

Twice he spied men without being seen: a char-burner clumping to or from his hut, muttering to himself as men will when solitude was their whole life, and once three of Fitz-Gerald's foresters passed close enough for him to hear them speaking softly. Moving south they were. John waited well after they were out of sight. Right clever ones, they were: two or three ahead and as many behind. Sure enough, two more came stalking along the same path, with knocked arrows to their strings. They moved more quietly than last year, having learned the same hard lessons as himself. But not well enough, John judged grimly. He could have done both were that his business, and another day perhaps he would.

His progress toward Blidworth was slow but deliberate. By now he knew the favorite thickets of red deer and how to spy out the entrances to them where certain bushes were bent aside from the animal's movement to water at dawn and evening. He chose one with no signs of recent use and settled down to munch dark bread and a pear. By all signs no rain was promised, the moon nearing full last night. Good weather for harvesters, good visibility across the vale when John took up his next chosen waiting place where tree cover opened into the vale midway between the church and the western rise leading to Denby. From this spot he could see the harvesters returning from the fields, the Queen's Rest, his smithy, the church, and the priest's house. That was important. After dark, he would move to his final position, selected as carefully as that of a deer hunter schooled in the habits of his quarry. The priest's door would be barred with a stout beam. At Beorn's need John replaced the bolts for the iron rests last year. No way to force the door and too noisy in any event. Too slow and chancy trying a window. The doing required time and patience. Brother Mauger was a sharp-eyed fellow, noting that Father Huger had a fondness for ale and beer. Such a man would be rising sometime in the night to visit the wattle latrine pit outside his house. He would die quickly then and Freda would be safe.

Little John finished his meal and stretched out in the thicket to nap. Awaking several hours later, he felt thirsty. He hadn't provided water or beer; Robin might have seen him filling the pouch and guessed he was for traveling. Any road, he could drink from the rill after dark. He knew the time by the degree of light filtering into his hiding place. The harvesters in the fields would have eaten their noon meal and returned to work by now. John waited until deeper shadow filled the deer close and the forest sounds nearby were normal, then cautiously emerged, braced his bow with a shaft to the string and went on.

His next hiding place was connected with a clear memory. He was at his forge at a day lovely as this but warmer. His door was open; he saw Marian pass by with Lady Judith on their way to the church. John remembered envying Robin for the warmth and light the girl would bring into his life. The thought wasn't as painful as it might have been to him younger. His troughs needed more water. He shouldered the yoke with its buckets and went down to the rill.

Here it was—from where he stood by the stream—just about here that he saw Much come running out of the trees, dash straight for him, gasping part of the story and lurching on, leaving him and the rest of Blidworth to know the sorry end of it.

Late afternoon by the sun now. Still and silent, John could have told the time by sound alone. Up the rise to the east, he heard the Vespers bell. From the west, faintly came the cheery voices of men and women encouraged that the day's work was almost done. Those harvesting their own strips began to straggle down the hill and across the vale toward home. Most were still afield, sweating to cut and sheave the sheriff's crop. Across the vale, Anlaf's old bossy cow was lowing and leading the rest of them home, heavy-uddered and ready for milking. The cattle plodded slowly, grazing broom buds as they moved. Beyond Anlaf's house, John saw the tall figure of Alcuin come out of his croft and putter among his hives. Not half daft for a young one, the beekeeper, the way he talked to them more than he did to folk. John wondered how much a bee understood. He reckoned not much, but that wasn't material to Alcuin who claimed he could understand their mood from the sound of them.

Sven the fletcher came down the slope, homeward bound, sickle stuck in his belt, then Anlaf himself. The afternoon light softened to dusky gold. Freda came out of the tavern to empty a bucket of slops and scatter feed to the chickens. John saw Huger emerge from the church and enter his house. He hoped the priest was shriven this night. The matter would sort better if he were.

A few minutes later, Freda came out of the Queen's with a covered dish and a jug, stepping smartly up the hill toward Huger's house. She turned at the unbarred door and pushed it in with her rump, disappearing inside. Dark now, the priest's door harder to see. John rose from his place beside the thick gorse bush, stretching his legs, then strode out into the twilight vale, keeping his eyes on the slope to the east. He stopped, seeing the dim figure come down the hill toward the tavern: Aye, there she was and long enough with the Norman to spoon-feed him every bite. He saw her open the tavern door, spilling brief light in the yard before it closed again. He flattened out by the rill to drink and then waited. The few lights he could see winked out one by one. The sexton's house went dark. The sheriff's curfew was not that much of a hardship to Blidworth folk. Few stayed alight after dark anyway. Only one light now, a tiny gleam from the priest's house. John stood in the darkening vale under God and the stars, smiling at the house. Then he moved forward, his shadow pouring over the upward slope, sharp in moonlight before cloud closed over the orb like a drowsy eyelid.

Treading softly, John slipped into the shadow of the priest's house. Dim light still flickered from the single casement propped slightly open within a few feet of him. Not near wide enough for a sure arrow shot. John eased along the wall to spy inside. The Norman priest sat at his table drinking by the light of one tallow candle. John frowned at the waste. Father Beorn would have used a rush-light for thrift. Nothing about the priest moved except his arm with the cup. He seemed to be staring vacantly, a man drinking himself to sleep because there was nothing else to do. John left the casement, returned to his hiding place and made himself comfortable. He had never been an impatient man at any task. Huger would come out to the latrine now or in a hour or perhaps when he woke, but he would come.

Within the house, the sharp scrape of a chair leg on the plank floor. The casement banged shut and was barred.

The moon stared at him. *I see you, John.*

"I know," he whispered back. There would be sore matter in confession when he got round to that, but then none of what brought him here could be laid on his doorstep. *Blame the foreign king, moon, and go your way. Go to sleep.*

Huger had been drinking; possibly enough to forget to bar the door. John skirted the long way around the house to see, staying in shadow as long as he could. He lifted the latch slowly, knowing just where it might make protesting noise, since he fitted it for Father Beorn himself. Barred. John returned to his place. He had been thorough at least, which was enough for the time. He was about to settle down when something alerted him, he didn't know precisely what, but the hackles of instinct rose before his conscious mind could think. A sound?

Yes. The faint distant squeak of a door hinge. There was clear moonlight now. In a moment John made out the plump woman's figure hurrying up the hill. He recognized Freda. For the first time since setting out his mind went muddy with confusion and anger. He'd planned it all but not this. *Go back you little fool. Get out of this.*

Purpose cleared; he had to move now. John waited until Freda reached the priest's door then moved quickly to the near corner of the house, only a pace or two from her. If this was how the matter fell out, so be it. Freda would knock. Huger would open the door.

John waited for the first furtive knocking then moved quickly. Freda didn't hear him step up behind her. His broad right hand went around her neck and over her mouth. Freda stiffened with sudden fright. John held her close against him.

"Just me, love. Johnny," he whispered. "I didn't want you in this, but in you are."

She didn't struggle against him. Too smart or too frightened. There was yet no sound from within the house. John was sorry she had to see, but Freda would understand. He hoped she did. Her head twisted slightly in his grip. He could see one eye wide and staring with terror or something else.

"You've got careless where you lie down, girl. Knock again."

Her hand went out, hesitant. She knocked again a little harder. From inside John heard a soft thump and then the scrape of wood against wood as if someone had lurched into a chair or table in the dark. Then the sound of the bar being lifted. The door started to open. Freda twisted suddenly in John's grip. Her strength and speed surprised him. She bit hard on his fingers—

"Jesus, girl—"

"Huger, look out—"

The thing happened all at once. John caught Freda by the throat; in the same instant Huger pushed hard to shut the door against him. Too late now. Why in hell did she have to be here? He slammed her hard against the door frame then bunched all his strength against the door. It gave before him. He let go of Freda. His hand flowed down, came up with the knife as he plunged into the dark chamber. The priest's night-shirted figure was clear enough. John launched at him, the knife in an upward thrust with all his power behind it. The first stab caught Huger in the abdomen. He grunted with shock and pain, going over backward with John on top of him. The second thrust went into his heart.

When the body ceased twitching, John went methodically to work. He never worked with an imperfect tool. Fastidiously he wiped the blade clean on Huger's nightshirt then made the first incision from ear to ear high across the forehead. That done, he took a bit of wrapping brought along for the purpose, unfolded it, and laid it by. There was a deal of blood. He expected that, wiping away as much as he could on Huger's shirt. Then he wrapped the result of his labor in the sheet of parchment and tucked it in the scrip at his belt.

Only then in his stolid way did he think of Freda. He didn't want to hurt her and hoped he hadn't been too rough pushing her out of the way, but she shouldn't have cried out. He hadn't counted on that.

She lay with one foot across the door sill, half on her side. John paused in the darkened doorway, hands braced against the frame, looking down at her. Oh, then, he guessed he did hurt her summ'at.

His shadow fell over her as John knelt beside the inert girl. "Freda?

Girl? Don't be angry, the thing had to be done. You never know what's right, so I couldn't let him be at you. The folk would shame you for what he did. Freda . . . ?''

He lifted her into his arms cradling her against his chest. Her head lolled. As with his own infants long ago, he put a hand behind Freda's head to support it. Except that her skull felt too soft there, warm and sticky with blood.

Regret flowed slowly through John as he sat in the moonlight rocking her gently in his arms and whispering to her. *You should not have been here. I swear to you the matter was not supposed to be like this.*

The Norman was the wicked one. John explained that to her over and over, but she'd be marked in Blidworth for it. At the very least none would come to her wedding, no mind if she married John himself, which he'd thought on often. They might even whip her. Ceolred was mean enough for that, but Johnny meant her no harm.

His mind worked as ever on one thing at a time. There was the regret and the sorrow. John spoke his reasons to death in his arms, then accepted that death. He rose with the girl against his chest like one of his own children fallen asleep by the fire and needing to be carried to bed. In the cold moonlight, he strode slowly down the hill to the Queen's Rest and chose a place beside the door untrodden and still soft with grass. He laid Freda on her back and crossed her arms over her breast, then returned to pick up his bow and quiver. Before striking out across the vale, he stood a moment huge with his shadow sharp across the priest's yard.

Freda would understand. When they met again, John was sure she would forgive him. Robin was a different matter, his family the word of law for years. Aelred would have hanged him speedily and Robin would be like to hang him now. It was the foreigners' fault. Not a sorrow in Sherwood a man couldn't lay to their door.

"I know," John softly answered the unforgiving eye of the moon. "Damn me to hell if you must, where's the news in that? I've felt your shadow cold on me for years. Ask me why I did so, I'll bloody well ask back where were you when we cried out?''

He was a long shadow in the vale, moving north away from Blidworth, away from Robin and all he knew. Robin would never have him back, not now. He must go north. Beyond Doncaster there weren't many people at all now. A man could hide alone. John didn't want to be alone, but that seemed to be how his *wyrd*-fate spun out. He drifted slowly through the moonlit vale toward the dark line of the forest, surprised to feel the tears warm on his face. Strange; so long a time since he'd wept for anything.

34

$\mathcal{M}$URDER IN BLIDWORTH? Robin couldn't believe it at first, but all of them heard the stir from Nottingham. Bishop Osmund himself would be involved in the search for the culprit. Fitz-Gerald had already hanged two men of Blidworth in reprisal for Freda and the priest.

"Your beekeeper Alcuin was one of them," Sven reported.

"Alcuin?" Robin was still numb with the senselessness of the deed. "The man never picked up a weapon in his life."

"And old Frith the cordwainer. Nor that ent the worst." Stout Sven was weary from his too-swift journey through Sherwood and at high risk for leaving his village without permission, but someone had to pass the word along with the letter secreted from Grantham in a peddler's pack. He'd hurried all the way, starting before light. He didn't know exactly where Robin was, no one did, but Sven suspected Thane Alan might know. He was taken to Wulf Edricson's house and given breakfast, the men crowding about as Sven dropped the hard facts like stones on the table.

"No, not the worst. Lord Robin, the sheriff's give out that you did it."

Only a year before, Robin might have erupted in anger. Now he merely passed Maud's unread letter to Beorn. "Murdered my own? He's a hard one. He'll have it all: my land, my life, and now my honor. What say my folk?"

The fletcher was quick to assure Robin no one believed such a lie. No

360

difference to the sheriff. "His men herded everyone in the village—men, women, chick, and child—up the hill to the church and made 'em watch while they hanged the men from the tree nearest. You know how Frith had the misery in his bones," Sven recalled sadly. "Poor old man could hardly get up the ladder."

But the folk of Blidworth, they had a notion who was guilty. With John missing for days, neither did Robin or any of his men need to speculate.

"Johnny could be mean," Tuck avowed, "but I did not think he would do such a thing."

"He's dirtied all of us," Much mourned.

Of all of them Beorn felt John's sin most sharply. The man had been his parishioner, often confessed but not often enough. "Let God help him, for we can no more."

"Save your pity," Robin said in a voice devoid of friendship or mercy. "My father would have hanged him. If Fitz-Gerald doesn't, I will."

John's act was one blow that left them reeling. The next was not long in coming. Later that same morning, Thane Alan rode home from Nottingham. Bishop Osmund was collecting his men and paying others to join the search for Robin Hood. In a day or two they'd be pouring through Sherwood like ants. The men were no longer safe at Linby.

"I've been your friend and you mine." Alan took Robin's hand. "But there's my family and Wulf's and the others I must think of."

"I know. As I would." Robin embraced his friend and gave orders to be ready to move. He wasn't sure where, but for the sake of the men he felt he must go. "Do you see what they do, these Normans? What they make of us? Little John was in a trap and did what any animal will that only knows it's caught and has to get free. They are the trap. They make us tear at ourselves, gnaw through our very lives, even kill each other. They make all of us sick as John."

He took up his hooded green cloak against the rain falling outside. "Will, get the lads ready. Father Beorn and Mauger, come with me."

Their margin of safety had never been wide, now it was gone. In Wulf's barn Robin paced slowly back and forth as Beorn read Maud's letter, coming to rest against a post with folded arms. Beorn read through the letter twice.

"The lady gives good counsel," the priest judged. "We must quit Sherwood."

"But not all together," Robin considered. "Alone or by twos by different routes."

"Not much chance without you, Rob."

"No fear. *I* couldn't find Will Scatloch if he didn't want me to."

"Will, yes," Beorn conceded. "Or wild Morgan perhaps, but Tuck and Much? They're not used to making their own decisions."

"Then when will they be, Beorn?"

"Or me. I'm not that young anymore. I passed fifty last month," Beorn admitted. "There's aches here and there. I'd be a sorry sight trying the open roads. We need you, Robin."

"Marian needs me too and what can I do for her?" Robin pushed the damp hair back from his forehead. "Got to scatter, that's the only way. Weeping Jesus, they heard you read from the book. They're what the damn book's about, men choosing for themselves."

"I'll stay for one," Mauger volunteered casually. "You might need a few thinking men."

"Are you daft, little monk? You think it's games this sheriff is playing?"

No, Mauger did not. He scratched vigorously at the short hairs on top of his head where his tonsure was growing out again. "I've always been a curious sort, never gone to war so I found one. Never thought to be outlaw but I must confess there's a certain dignity in the occupation."

Robin turned away hopelessly: a wise precaution for God to put special watch over men and fools.

"Mauger, be out of this," Beorn earnestly advised the young monk. "Your name's not linked with ours. You have a future somewhere."

"Some nice clean spot on the national dung heap? No, Father. Grant I'm not entirely frivolous. What's left of honor in England is right here."

Robin wouldn't hear of it. Mauger was educated, valuable. He could read their history and laws.

"But you feel them, Robin. *You're* what they're about. They're in you like bone and blood, what King Alfred meant when he started the Great Chronicle and founded schools. Did he fight the Danes for years, freeze in a marsh with a few men like you in Sherwood, through a mindless need to dominate and rule? You swore an oath; I'll warrant you never swore better. And I need you to help preserve this book," Mauger concluded, rather pleased with his logic and eloquence.

"Then we have to think and plan. We have to . . ." Robin's head fell back against the post. "God's wounds, I just hope Fitz-Gerald is tired as I am."

Beorn and Mauger would have to go with him, then. And Will as well that they had two good bows for protection. The rest into Northumbria where folk were few since the destruction, or west with Morgan. But first, just a little confusion for Ralf Fitz-Gerald to keep the bastard's life miserable.

"Beorn, read Mum's letter again."

Listening to the words, Robin stood in the open barn doorway, studying the sky beyond. Wind from the southeast and not too cold; a good chance of fog from the North Sea and the Wash. Fog was his best friend at Tadcaster and would be excellent for hunting treasure.

35

YELLOW AND RED. Yellow and red.

"There's nowt, just dirt—"

Of course. Robin cursed his carelessness as he ran. Too simple from the first, too easy.

Yellow and red, pale-yellow hair like flax. Swirl of flax and then the sudden red of blood from Much's lung staining the yellow.

"—just dirt and rocks!"

Much the miller had blue eyes, cornflower blue that always looked surprised somehow. Three pounds was a fortune to him. He wanted to invest, marry well, and be a broker.

Swirl of flaxen yellow flecked with deep red as he swung about from the mule so fast that his long hair whipped over his mouth when the clothyard arrow hit him—

"Robin, it's a tri—"

—spearing through the word in a red-spraying rush of air punched out of his pierced lung, and the yellow hair lashing in his agony, Robin whirling about to see the dozen and more riders dash out of the forest at them.

"Scatter! Cover!" Robin had time to get off one arrow at the nearest horseman, time to see Will, Morgan, and Tuck running through rags of fog toward the dark cover of the wood before bolting himself. From the sounds, at least one of them was coming after him. His legs stretched out in great, bounding strides but the hoofbeats were closer. One rider.

Robin clawed an arrow from the quiver, setting it as he ran. Once he turned or if he missed—Christ, there was no *if*.

When his right foot landed firmly, Robin swiveled on it, left foot set and the bow pressed in one unbroken movement. The mailed rider was too close to miss but his right arm was raised, the spear cocked to fly and someone bellowed in Frank. The arrow sped. Robin heard it *chunk!* home through scale and ring mail, padding, flesh, and bone. The rider reeled backward and fell, one foot dragging in the stirrup. Robin sprinted on into the cover of the ancient oaks.

His instincts scathed him as he plunged through the trees. He should have known from first sight of the slow-creaking train that something was wrong. Ten laden mules all strung together, followed by two ox-drawn wagons. Only six guards for escort, none of them well mounted. Swift and easy, no need for anyone to die unless Fitz-Gerald was among them. Bows in tandem, two and two. Will and he hit one of the lead pair of mules, Morgan and Much did for one of the first pair of oxen, Tuck's bow covering where needed. The guards gave in too quickly. The sheriff was not anywhere to be seen.

Robin, it's a tri—

He tried to think as he ran. Tuck wasn't quick on his feet as the others, did they cut him off? They'd not do for Tuck without a fight.

They were still coming after him, crashing through the thick under-brush. He slowed to a loping walk, sucking huge gulps of air into his lungs. The odds were with him here. He'd been careful to choose this spot, thick with bramble and ivy under foot, the holly trees among the oaks drooping long fronds of spikey leaves to the ground forming an impenetrable screen laced with the last of drifting fog. However many pursued him, they couldn't see far.

Robin broke out of the brambles onto a stretch of open ground, running swift and silent on a carpet of leaf mold centuries deep, making for the next stretch of brambles. He chose his stand where a holly screen was dimmed by a low-lying swatch of mist and slid noiselessly behind it, nocking a shaft to his string. Over the muted thrashing through brambles, there were voices now.

"This way."

"No, here."

Steady down, he willed the slight trembling in his hands. *Steady on. No more than targets at Grantham.*

Ralf must be with them. Someone was smart enough not to come in after him on horseback, though the advantage was still his. Normans were not used to going afoot. He could run the heart out of such men before they caught him. From the sounds he reckoned four of them, perhaps five. *Be one of them, Ralf. You or me, the game ends today.*

Robin waited while his breathing slowed to ease, silently mouthing the act of contrition. He quelled that. Not himself today, but Ralf.

He was feral now, all eyes and ears and fingers hooked about a lethal string, a green man blending with his green hiding place, waiting. There: There was the first of them. Looked a Saxon, blond as Much. Nigh as young but not as cautious. Robin felt faintly sick. Now it came to killing his own kind like John had. His fingers hesitated on the string. A man young as himself, mayhap alike with a wife and a child coming. He might pause over that but not the cocked crossbow the man carried.

Your wife's home, mine's in prison.

Robin pressed into the bow.

We tear at ourselves. Now we kill each other just to live.

Loose.

The man went over backward, arms flailing. Robin eased away behind the screen, moving faster, breaking into a run only where he could go silently. When he stopped again, they were still coming on. He'd cut his left hand coming through the last patch of brambles. Robin squeezed more blood from the laceration, then ripped a piece from the ragged sleeve of his dark-green tunic, squeezing as much blood onto it as he could. He couldn't help leaving footprints in the soft loam carpet; they'd come straight here to his close. He deepened the cut with his knife to eke out as much blood as he could, staining the tatter of cloth and the holly leaves to which he stuck it as if the sleeve had torn in his flight.

They weren't in sight yet, moving carefully but not so quiet a man couldn't hear them who'd grown up matching his stillness to that of deer. Robin rustled his holly screen enough to be heard, then slipped away dragging one foot through the loam as if hurt. He kept that up for perhaps fifty paces, moving in a gradual turn to his right. Ralf would see what was happening or one of them would if they were forestwise but by then he would be behind them.

At the end of his turn he chose his cover, set an arrow, and waited.

The oaks in the fog were ghosts looming about Robin like the old *scin-laeca* appearing at a warrior's death to tell him his skein was spun out. No bird sounds, no furtive passage of a stoat or hare. Only the blood in his ears, the whisper of his own breath. Nothing moved.

Robin heard before he saw: the deliberate, barely perceptible tred of the hunter. He strained his eyes into the mist. *Where you think he is, look a mite to the side, you'll see better.*

The forester moved cautiously out of cover, dogging Robin's drag-footed trail. A small, compact crossbowman, weapon held at the ready. Robin's bow was lifting, the press already willed to his muscles when the man suddenly turned and trotted back into tree cover without making a sound.

Robin relaxed the bowstring and waited. Dimly among the trees he saw a movement: two of them but he hadn't arrows to waste without a clear shot. In a moment, a second man emerged from cover studying Robin's false trail. He pointed ahead. Robin divined his meaning from the gesture: no, straight ahead, not circling. You can see he's hurt.

Robin pressed into the bow and loosed.

Two down.

Slow as a wood spider spinning its web to the ground, Robin reached for the second arrow stuck upright before him, plucked it delicately from the soft loam, fitted nock to string.

No, you won't come straight, you're not that thick. You'll wait like me. Show yourself once, Ralf, that's all I need.

Ralf and the man at arms, Waldemar, lay along the lip of a shallow, bramble-choked depression, well screened by hanging holly and mist. They dared not move or talk above a whisper. Two men were dead. The second to die insisted Robin was wounded and moving in a straight line. *Le petit* Daniel knew differently, but he'd been gone a good hour now.

Ralf's clothes were soaked through from the damp loam. Beside him cradling the cocked crossbow, Waldemar felt the damp and squirmed with chill discomfort.

Ralf hissed his order, "Don't move."

Waldemar strained his eyes into the mist. Just beyond their hiding place was a clearing beneath the oaks perhaps twenty paces wide bordered by a wall of bramble. Waldemar did not share the sheriff's conviction that Robin was still near, but he was concerned about Daniel. The other searchers could be miles away by now.

"I would say Daniel is dead," Ralf guessed without interrupting his back-and-forth search of the terrain to their front and flanks.

"We are from the same village. He is my friend," Waldemar appealed as strongly as a whisper could. "We must look for him."

And you've never lost a friend here? Ralf thought grimly. *You're yet a virgin, friend.* "Robin is close."

"Why? Why would he stay?"

"I know how he thinks. He wants me. I owe him the man-price on those I hanged and his friend we took today."

No time to lecture a Norman villager on the two-sided thinking of Saxons. They valued honor and admired craft in the same breath. If Robin could satisfy one through the other, he would, knowing that in cover like this wood the contest was tipped in his favor. Ralf wondered if the rest of his men had run Scatloch to ground. Not likely; when he gave the order to pursue on foot and without armor some vavasors wasted precious time stripping it off, others refused. Damned fools: Ring mail and scale-iron coats did nothing in a wood but slow a man and make noise, no protection at all against arrows. Ralf had dressed in thick English homespun himself with leg wrappings and light shoes.

Waldemar nudged him. "Nothing out there. He's gone."

"Then perhaps you will be alive tomorrow. If you're wrong, I will miss you at table."

Waldemar started to answer but Ralf stilled him with warning eyes and a touch on his arm. He heard something, a faint rustling in the brambles across the clearing. Not quick and darting like an animal but slow and deliberate, a man bellying along.

"Straight to your front," he directed Waldemar's vision. "No, a little to the left. See anything?"

Waldemar's left hand eased forward along the crossbow's stock. "I hear."

The dragging sound came closer; faintly now they could perceive movement in the brambles. Ralf took a second bolt from the quiver slung at Waldemar's hip and stuck the short, smooth-headed missile where the bowman could grasp it quickly.

Waldemar's head came up, slightly turned to one side listening. "Hear that?"

"What?"

"A man. Close. Listen."

Ralf heard it now: very close to the limit of the brambles in front of them, over the rustle of movement. The sound of breath expelled from painful effort. And then the outline of a body emerged, dim in the mist, from the underbrush. Waldemar grinned in cold satisfaction. "I told you. Daniel got him."

"I said don't move."

"Why?"

"Look." Ralf remained utterly still, concentrating on the half-visible figure. "Daniel carried a crossbow."

Waldemar saw what he meant. The shaft protruding from the wounded man's back was the length of a man's arm and hand. Waldemar swallowed hard. "Mother of God, he got—"

"Be still."

"But—"

"Shut your buggering mouth."

Quite clearly now they could hear the moaning, almost see Daniel's face as he pulled himself forward tortuously on his arms. Waldemar tried to obey the order of silence. He couldn't.

"You hear? He's calling me."

"Don't move if you want to live."

"Let go of me. I am tired of this." Waldemar twisted around to Ralf. "Your Robin is long gone."

Ralf tried to restrain his man at arms but Waldemar was already up, thrusting the crossbow aside, making for his wounded friend in a crouching run. Ralf's lips went back in sick disgust. *Merde.* No time. He grasped the crossbow, desperately trying to see everywhere at once. No time to tell Waldemar why he shouldn't expose himself, that a wounded man who could still move was a stalking horse for Greyfeathers. If he tried to reach his friends for help, the Saxons would just move with him and find the rest. The experience was a pang in Ralf: Waldemar down on one knee beside his friend, a chicken on the block with the ax already coming down if Robin was out there. Movement, Ralf told himself. Look for movement anywhere, look for—

The arrow hit Waldemar in the neck. The man made a wet, gurgling sound that became a kind of hog-squeal as he tumbled away from Daniel. But Ralf had seen the telltale movement off to his right.

I know where you are. From here you look like a bulge on that tree trunk. You won't come out, Robin, you're not a fool like Waldemar.

Turtle-slow, Ralf slid his left arm under the bow stock, sighting on the dim perpendicular line of the oak trunk. The upper end of the horn-notched longbow was just visible. Robin would move away slowly as he came, deliberately as he flanked Daniel, looking to get another of them or even two. Waiting to make sure there wasn't a third.

Then as Ralf watched, the dark bulge became a head and torso and Robin moved out into the open. Ralf's mouth dropped open in amazement at the uncharacteristic carelessness. Then he saw why. Robin's quiver was empty. He'd spend his last shaft on Waldemar. He needed at least one of them back, felt it safe enough to try.

The tall figure stepped lightly across the clearing, face obscured by the dark-green hood. Ralf's forefinger curled around the bow's trigger. *You fooled me at Tadcaster and with Osmund. You flirted within the length of my sword at Grantham. Twice out of three chances the deer may elude the hunter.*

In the last second as Robin knelt by Daniel, Ralf decided to go for a better shot erect. He gathered his legs under him. He made no sound he himself could hear, but as he brought the bow up to sight, something feral in Robin must have alerted him. His head swiveled about, body turning as he rose in the same instant that Ralf loosed the bolt.

Ralf heard the shock and pain, the grunting gasp as Robin doubled over and fell backward, both hands clutched around the bolt in his guts. He tried to rise; the pain was too much. Ralf had his foot on the cross brace to wind the weapon again, but paused. Robin was done. Ralf drew his sword instead, walking forward into the clearing.

Robin lay half turned on his right side, both hands still pawing numbly at the bolt. It hadn't been centered true, but struck him just over his hipbone. Impossibly, he was trying to draw it out. He looked up at Ralf, eyes dulled with shock. A year and more since they met face to face; to Ralf's surprise after all this time, he'd forgotten how young his enemy was. But stubborn, still trying to pull the bolt out of his vitals.

"Don't, Robin. It is only pain to no purpose and you have no more arrows."

"You've no more men."

"No. You have cost me."

"I want . . . to stand up."

"Why?" Now that the moment was come and the simple last stroke of his sword all that remained to end it, Ralf was strangely reluctant. He would not hesitate. There would be pride perhaps, but no pleasure. "Well run, Robin. Do not try to get up. I will be quick."

"No." Robin labored clumsily to one knee, groaning with the effort. "*Scin-laeca* is coming for me," he gasped through his teeth. "Old ghost warrior. I should die on my feet . . . where he can see me."

Every breath of the man was the sound of a saw through wood. He rose, wavering, right hand still gripping the bolt, but Ralf could see the sheen of blood spreading over his thigh below the jerkin's lower edge.

"I prayed once to see my death," Ralf said. "He looked like you."

With one fumbling hand about the bolt, Robin seemed to gather himself for some final effort. "You think God has a Valhalla . . . a Woden's hall? Or just someplace full of stinkin' pious Franks?"

"What are you doing?" Ralf could barely believe his eyes. Robin was still trying to pull the missile from his flesh.

"Oh . . . oh, this'll be a mean one. But I want to die in one piece."

Ralf saw the blood drain out of the weather-browned face. The mouth went tight and livid as Robin inexorably drew the bolt from the wound. He held it up in front of him with curious contempt, then let it drop. "Rotten little beggar. Well then, get on with it."

"You fool." Even as his grip tightened on the sword pommel, Ralf had to say it. "All you had to do was obey the king's law."

The bloodstain was spreading rapidly. Robin tottered, barely able to stand. His lips moved but no sound emerged. Ralf gripped the sword in both hands to sheer the man's head off clean.

"I promise you before God if it is in my power, Marian and her child will live."

The drooping head came up. With his last life, Robin was laughing at him.

"They will, Ralf." Robin flung the loose dirt concealed in his fist into Ralf's eyes. Blinded, the sword raised to one side, Ralf had no time to swing before Robin's body smashed into his and took him over backward. The man was weak with shock and loss of blood, but Ralf could not see. He lashed out with his fists, trying to blink some sight back into his eyes. Robin was on top of him, embracing him like a lover, gasping at his ear.

"You know they will."

Ralf jerked at the shock and sting as the knife broke the skin of his lower back, not stabbing but boring into flesh searching for his vitals. But Robin didn't have the strength to finish him. Ralf felt the body pressed against him bunch and gather once more. With a roar of rage that broke in a scream, Robin put his last strength behind the knife. While some power remained to him, Ralf drove his fist again and again into Robin's wet wounded flesh.

Robin went limp. Weakly, Ralf pushed the weight of the man off him. The knife was still embedded low in his back—not through a lung, Christ, not that. Even if he lived he'd spit blood through the few years left him. Grasping at the blade in his back, he could see a little now. The blur of Robin was trying to crawl away, unable to stand but moving. He somehow managed to rise into a stumbling crouch for a few faltering steps. Ralf groped about for his sword hilt, found it, the other hand trying to grip the handle of the knife in his back. The blade came out in a crimson wave of pain and took his consciousness with it.

When Ralf opened his eyes he was lying curled on his side, face in the earth and his mouth gritty with loam. His back was wet. No telling how much blood he'd lost but he didn't think the wound was that deep. He was cold. That always happened with shock. He blinked the last dirt out of his eyes. Waldemar and Daniel lay where they had fallen, but there was no sign of Robin. Ralf managed to get on all fours and tried to rise. After one effort that brought a rush of blood from his wound, he gave that up. He couldn't straighten up without bleeding to death. Like Robin. He wondered how far the man would get with so little blood left in him before the canny ravens found him and knew it was only a matter of waiting.

Someone ought to look, find the body that couldn't be far off, not with that bad a wound. Someone must take Robin's head and show it to the king.

Gradually, Ralf became conscious of a tedious sound: his own rhythmic whimpering that broke into a grotesque chuckle.

"Find Robin?" he rasped to the no longer concerned corpses of his men. "Who will find me?"

. . . not going to die, can't, not yet. Thank you for shriving me, Father Beorn, but I'm not going to die today. Just keep saying that. Will, be waiting. Marian be waiting somewhere, some time. I promise you I'll look on our child.

Got to get up and move. Got to get up or die.

I see you there, old ghost-warrior. Go away. If I can go ten feet, I can go a hundred, and a hundred after that. Find some mud and lady's mantle to pack this wound. Nay, don't argue, old soul collector. Didn't you hear me, then? I'm not for dying today. . . .

Over and over Robin told himself that, staggering out of the cover of the wood and across the open heath through rags of fog toward the blessed murmur of running water. *By holy Jesus, I'm going home.* Just that his legs wouldn't go any farther and sprawled out from under him. He lay in the mist-sodden grass, tried to rise but couldn't. Robin began to crawl slowly as a crab, pulling himself along on his arms. When he could crawl no more and lay exhausted with one ear against the ground, he felt the faint thudding of feet hurrying, coming closer. Robin tried to lift his head but it weighed far too much.

Fog over the riverbank and somehow his eyes were blurred. God, let it be Will; if not, there wasn't that much he could do now. He tried to move again, willed it clearly, but his arms were too far away.

Two shapes came out of the fog toward him.

Something squeezed tight in Robin's chest. His heart sent a soaring *gratia* to the mercy of God. Here! he cried. Here I am! Only a pitiful bleat emerged from his throat. The last thing he heard against the breast of the mothering earth was Will Scatloch calling his name.

Robin opened his eyes to shadow and light that meant nothing, but he'd heard someone speak of life. He felt far distant from life now.

"Of course he's alive. Lived through the night, but there's high fever. The danger's not past."

He was lying on a low pallet. Hanging from walls and low roof beams overhead, bundles of dried leaves swayed gently in a draft. The shallow fire pit in the center of the hut gave off the aroma of peat, warming a leather cooking bag hung over it on an iron tripod. Robin smelled pease porridge. He'd eaten the stuff all his life and loved it, but now the smell made him sick.

Barely alive. He stirred feebly on the pallet, tried to call out to someone. Too much of an effort. In a moment, then. He'd just close his eyes for a little. . . .

The hut of Wytha, the char-burner's widow, was a ruin of mud-daubed wattle long in need of fresh thatching to the roof. The hut stood in a tiny clearing naturally curtained by holly trees so old they no longer grew straight but twisted slantwise as their ancient roots sought water.

Wytha herself might have grown with the trees. Her hair was white and thin with the pink scalp showing clearly through but her pale grey eyes, buried in a maze of wrinkles and sags, were clear of rheum and still bright. Impossible for Will or Morgan to tell the *wicca* woman's age. She said she came to this forest in the time of Canute and Will for one believed her.

"Good you brought him to me," she snuffled, counting nimbly over the silver Will put in her hand, "and better you brought him now when the moon is a-waxing. My power to heal grows with it." She squinted at Will Scatloch with a gleam of calculation. "Now, for a spell upon the man who wounded him—well, that must wait for waning and will cost you more."

Will's fingers drummed on his bowstave. "I've got spell enough for him. Don't haggle, woman. Just see him well." He and Morgan were worn to the bone themselves. Their quivers were empty and they'd left a trail of dead or wounded sheriff's men between Ancaster and Witham River. "Tend him well. It is a man of honor in your house."

The old woman turned away with bored impatience. "Welshman, I know who he is."

Will caught her sleeve. "If you know that, then you've been paid enough to forget." He glanced at Morgan of Powys sprawled against the hut wall, fallen asleep from plain fatigue. "I mean that, woman. All the charity's wrung out of us. You never saw him."

"No fear." Wytha peered closely at Will. "You have the Sight."

Will was startled; this had nothing to do with their problems. "Sometimes. A little."

"Sight knows itself in others. But trade is trade." Wytha jingled the coins in her dry old palm before they vanished into some recess of her shapeless woolen smock. "And art is art. That is Guntrada's grandson. I saw the scar on his hand. He is married to the oak."

These were matters Will would not speak of. "His wife is Lady Marian."

Wytha turned back into the hut with a shrug. There were marriages and marriages. Guntrada had been a *wicca* of great powers when her eye fell on Brihtnoth of Denby. Certainly those powers did not lessen afterward. The grandson lying within the hut was a mystery to Wytha though she would never admit as much to Will Scatloch. Anyone but a forest-bred man would be dead from such a wound. Robin had done precisely the right thing to give himself what chance there was: drawn the bolt, bled the wound clean, and packed it with the right healing herbs. That was not what confused Wytha. When others were spreading the tales of Hereward, she threw the rune bones to devine the hero's future. Long before Robin was carried to her she had cast for him. All very well for men to say and history write, but Wytha traced the strands of a more elusive web. The earth was a living body. As stones rose to its surface naturally and bits of iron would in time work out of wounded flesh, so certain men rose above their birth to be seen and sung while great kings faded from memory. All part of the pattern whether men perceived or not.

Hereward's destiny was completed, the runes told her; there was nothing more for him to do. Those refugees from Ely who trailed through Wytha's clearing to accept a bit of rest and broth before moving on seemed to know that much. Whoever was king, they were going home to get on with life. In the pattern of runes on Wytha's dirt floor Hereward's fire was burned out.

But this one, the blood of Guntrada—

The man stirred on the pallet. Wytha left off tending the porridge and went to restrain him gently so the wound dressing would not be disturbed. His sleep was still the oblivion of sickness. She would feel easier when that gave way to normal rest.

The runes for this one were incomplete, no full pattern to them. All beginnings, all becoming, opening out beyond sight or understanding. A life like an arrow just loosed from a bow, flying up, not yet pulled toward earth. The few clear images only teased Wytha's understanding: all moving toward the east and the sun, a roil of running men and a flag among them, toward a high place which was still not an end for this man but only another beginning.

He muttered with the fever she had to break. Wytha squatted by the pallet, troubled by questions. It was not good for a wise woman to be unsure.

Bowman, what are you? Where does your arrow aim that not even gods can see where it will fall?

36

That NOVEMBER REQUIEM bells tolled throughout England and Normandy for the premature death of William's second son, Richard, killed in a hunting accident in the forest of Ytena near Winchester. Norman ladies of the nobility donned white in formal sorrow, though few English mourned one more foreigner who would have been king over them when Bastard went inevitably to hell.

Matilda was at Winchester when Richard died. She came to visit infant Henry but remained to make wake over another son. She rode to Grantham, physical exhaustion adding to the weight of her grief. She was granted little time for the cleansing balm of tears.

Almost three decades later when William II was killed in the same forest, Englishmen called it singularly poetic justice. Their narrow dislike of foreigners saw no difference in Norman princes though they might have had a less rapacious king in the eighteen-year-old boy laid out among tall candles at Winchester. His mother rode to Grantham through freezing November rain and towns whose church bells tolled her son along the way, while Matilda remembered her bitter joke to Lanfranc: Royal she grew but joyless. She had borne nine living children in twenty years, still spending more time in the saddle than under a roof and suffering the chronic ailments of that life, constipation and painful hemorrhoids. She was ever dosing with rhubarb, elm, and cinnamon, and being "purged of necessity" as her physicians delicately put her condition.

The English were less euphemistic. "Willy's been shitting on us for years. Nice to know she can't."

Matilda confided once to Lanfranc after one of these rigorous purgings, "I am not even allowed the modesty of dignified ills."

Nine children and never to know the rest which was the best healer of all. What grew last in her fecund womb was malignant and would kill her.

On entering the hall at Grantham, she was greeted by Geoffrey de Coutance, who knelt in respect and sorrow, tendering news from William. The king was entrained from Ely with prisoners and would be with his queen on the morrow. From Dover to the Welsh marches and the Scottish border the king's will held unchallenged sway at last.

Matilda removed her wet mantle, pale and shivering, seeing only a waxen face on a bier, dead flesh once come living from her own. "I do not wish to hear of England now. I am weary of the subject. I am going to bed."

She gave directions for hot comfrey and chamomile to be brought to her chamber. When her waiting woman Jehanne brought the simple to her mistress, Matilda lay like pathetic wreckage across the huge bed, silent tears streaming from her eyes. To Jehanne she looked like a wounded animal.

The rain had stopped but low clouds still scudded west before the wind. From the doorway of their prison house Judith saw the long procession begin to enter the manor gate with William at its head.

"He brings the prisoners from Ely," Gunstal informed her.

Judith ducked her head back into the house. "Aunt! Marian! Our men are coming."

Marian levered herself off the bed and went outside with Maud. Wrapped in their shabby cloaks the three women watched the long worm of English defeat inch through the gate. First came the king followed by Tancarville and William's chief steward Fitz-Osbern, then a cortege of bedraggled knights in wet rusted mail on horses worn spiritless as their riders. Then, flanked by mounted men at arms, came the English prisoners on foot, yoked two by two like oxen and linked by heavy chains that rattled in cadence with their still-vital stride. Some wore ring shirts over their tunics but all were bareheaded. From their bearing, these were men of carl rank, military retainers more used to battle than working their lands, ruddy-faced men who looked far less worn than their captors.

But in chains. "It is true then," Judith said. "The isle is taken."

Marian compared the prisoners to the Normans guarding them. "They don't hardly look surrendered."

"A battle is not the whole war," Maud told her. "We will win next time."

William and his high officers proceeded to the stables. The long line of prisoners waited in the courtyard. Whole chained groups simply sat down in the mud, grinning defiantly at their guards.

"Come, we will go to them," Maud declared in her settled-and-done manner. "Not you, Marian. Go back in the house."

"No, Mum. I want to talk to them."

"Not fitting in your condition," Maud decreed with iron convention. "And the air is chill. Come Judith."

With Gunstal their shadow, Maud and Judith went down the line of men, greeting them: "Hail to the sons of Hengist!" Maud saluted them. Judith added, "God shield the heirs of Alfred."

The prisoners were glad to see women of their own kind. At closer inspection, they showed clearly the weariness of men who had walked and slept in the open for three days with little to eat and less to drink. Judith asked permission of the guards to bring them water. In a rush of generosity and pity Maud offered the last of their own beer.

"We've but two jugs, Aunt."

"Bring them. Hurry."

"No need, Mum." Just behind them, Perdu on her shoulder and wide-eyed at the chained men, Marian waited with both jugs of their last, precious beer. She offered them to the men with shy pride. "My husband is Thane Edward of Denby."

The men were grateful for the drink but the name meant nothing to them until Marian added, "He is called Robin Hood by the folk."

Yes, some of them had heard that name and good to know he was still free. There was an undertone more of bitterness than defeat about these men. They hadn't been beaten. No, by God, never that, but sold out by their own monks. The Judas-price could still buy traitors.

There was one older man with an overgrown mane of red hair fading to rust and hands callused from a lifetime of grasping sword and shield who was less boastful than his companions. "I was to Stamford Bridge and Hastings after that." His hoarse voice tolled the names like the bells mourning the Norman prince. "I saw York and I was to Chester with Edric the Wild. Now Ely." He passed the empty jug to Maud. "Not beaten, lady, but I'm fought out. When we're sold by our own, it's time to quit.''

He made to spit in disgust but thought better of it in front of women of quality. He thanked them for the beer then stared away at the grey horizon as if it were the future. ''Don't matter who wins what now. We're done.''

Matilda welcomed her husband in their private chambers, wretchedly ill but doing her best to mask it from him. William was more exhausted than she'd ever seen him. Every line of his massive body sagged. Matilda eased him into a chair and removed his ruined shoes and the damp-rotted wool wrappings beneath, wrinkling her nose at the smell.

''Nothing's dry at Ely,'' William grumbled. ''Everything rusts or rots. I feel old, Mora.''

''Nonsense. You're a great, strong bear.''

William shifted his aches in the cushioned chair that felt like heaven. ''The sickest bear you'll ever see. You could bait me with sparrows.''

He'd been luckier than most of his men at Ely. Fever and flux ran riot through them. Blessed good fortune that England was quiet for the time since few were fit for major campaigning this winter. William opened his heavy arms. ''Come be close to me. I need you.''

Matilda curled gratefully against his chest and presented her homecoming gift, meager as it might be. ''To speak of birds: There is one less robin in Sherwood.''

''Eh, what?''

''Ralf Fitz-Gerald lured Robin Hood with a ruse. Killed one man outright, hanged another. Robin he gave a mortal wound.''

With an effort he hardly wanted to make, William recalled a very young man forcing himself to kneel in fealty. ''Then Denby's dead?''

''Ralf thinks so. They fought and he was sore hurt himself. He will report when he can ride. There were never as many of them as one thought. Nothing runs free in Sherwood now but the king's deer.''

That at least was good news. ''I will enjoy riding to hunt with no one shooting back at me . . . lord, Mora, I am so tired.''

''And you're congested. I hear it in your breathing.''

He held her, relishing the silence and the little privacy they were ever allowed. They did not speak immediately of the grief at Winchester but of how young Robert must now be groomed for the crown and the changes that would mean. The boy needed tutoring to temper judgment and broaden wisdom. Above all they must consider an advantageous betrothal.

Matilda whispered her thoughts against her husband's massive chest, speaking reasonably, speaking of all but the unbearable hurt at the center. Finally, worn as William, the tears broke through that she could show to no one else.

"Perhaps . . . I wouldn't cry so if I felt stronger."

"There now, it is all right, Mora. But you must get in bed this instant."

Someone knocked at the door then, polite but insistent, with unsettling news from the Scottish border where King Malcolm had begun raiding again. William did not even have time to bathe or change his clothes before he was needed in the hall.

Ralf had recovered from worse wounds than Robin gave him. When he was able to travel painfully to Grantham in December, he requested before the hearing that no word of his intent be vented beyond the royal couple. William agreed curtly. Deeply concerned for Matilda's health and sick with grief over Richard's death, he regarded the prosecution of Lady Maud a minor matter to be allowed scant time and less charity.

The trestles were cleared of the noon meal and the hall emptied before Maud was sent for. Only two hours past noon, but in this bleak December the hall sconces were already lighted. William and Matilda sat at the high table flanked by Coutance and Tancarville, Ralf standing to one side. Maud and Judith were brought from the kitchen. Gunstal fetched Marian from the prison house. The three women were placed before the blazing fire pit and the dais. Ralf was alarmed to see Marian involved in this matter. She was hugely pregnant now. He had not expected this and feared for her, hurrying to the king.

"My lord, there is some misunderstanding. I make no accusation against Marian or Judith. There is no evidence of their guilt in this affair."

"I will judge who is guilty," William snapped at him. "State your case and be done. The queen is ill and should be abed."

In a flash of ironic memory as he turned to the women, Ralf pictured an equally foregone trial at Nottingham and Robin pleading for Wystan. Ralf convicted the peasant for the sake of authority. He wished he could be as detached now. Marian answered his silent concern with an opaque stare from the other side of the wall that ever sundered them. If God was just, He also had a taste for cruel laughter.

For Marian's sake Ralf would have softened the blow, but Maud was subtler. He dared not allow her the advantage of her cool self-possession.

He loomed over her abruptly, his voice harsh as a blow. *"Madame, votre fil est mort."*

Intent on Maud, Ralf did not see Marian flinch and go white. Judith's lips moved but she stared impassively before her. *Your son is dead—* and Ralf detected what he sought: that death reflected as the shock widened Maud's eyes, the pain of the knife going in and the enormous effort to bear it silently.

"Yes, you comprehend well enough." Ralf pulled Maud forward, spitting his accusation in rapid Frank. "You were the one who betrayed Osmund to Robin. You were the one who told him of the treasure train. Sire de Coutance, give your evidence."

Coutance verified the statement and the ploy. The woman was suspect and allowed to hear false information. The train was no more than bait.

"But only you could have sent word to your son. Lord king, here is your spy. Through her Robin Hood knew every move made in Grantham. I make no charge against the other women."

"Three dogs in a small kennel?" Tancarville doubted. "Which of them will escape fleas?"

"They are all guilty," William said. "No, Matilda, do not rise."

But she had, leaning on the table for support.

"Lady Maud, is this true? You sent such treasonous letters to your son?"

"Treasonous, madame? A million would call it patriotism. You would do as much."

"The perfect spy," Ralf concluded. "She speaks Frankish as well as we do."

Maud found cold amusement in that. "In your case, vavasor, far better. But the girls had no part in this. The queen may look no further than her country cow."

"I was never your enemy, Maud. I had nothing but goodwill toward you. I . . ." Matilda trailed off, wilting over the table. Quickly supported by Coutance and her husband she sank back into her chair. "Be brief, Gilly. I have no heart for this today."

"Trust me for that, Mora." William turned on Maud, a volcano ready to erupt. God had taken Mora's dearest son. He could do nothing to ease that agony, but the Saxon bitch was fair game and guilty as Lucifer. "You sow. By God's Face, you breed treason in the very womb."

For all his girth William sprang onto and over the table, descending on Maud, seizing her, slapping her viciously back and forth across the face. "You pass it in rutting, like original sin! You lost a son? So have we. Pardon if I don't weep. *How* did you pass the letters? Who helped you? Speak!''

Coutance had considered all possibilities. "Most like through a Saxon priest at Saint Wulfram's. That would be the most convenient route.''

William bellowed in Maud's face. "Was it so? Which priest? Which one?''

He raised his hand to strike her again but suddenly Judith put up her arm to fend against him, and—"Stop!''—awkward as she was, Marian moved to put herself between the king and Maud, but Ralf pulled her to one side.

"Marian, stay out of this. God knows, I don't want you—''

She turned on him, savage as the king. "Get your hands off me, Norman.''

William pushed Judith aside and grabbed Maud again. His next blow struck her to the floor. He quivered over the woman, ready to kill her. "Do you see that the queen is ill? You knew her kindness even as prisoners. But for her you would have been in irons long ago, the pack of you. And so you will. Guards!''

With Judith helping her, Maud got to her feet. Her lips bled from the blows and her voice trembled. *"C'était un grand plaisir, Guillaume.* More than pleasure, it was an honor.''

"Put them in irons. I want them at Hough Castle tonight.'' William lunged away to the dais, Ralf hastening after him.

Ralf went beyond caution now and knew it. "My lord, Lady Marian and Judith are innocent. I swear to that. There is no need—''

William swung around to the younger man with pure murder in every line of him. He bunched Ralf's tunic in an iron grip and lifted him off his feet. "You think I will make distinction between these vermin? Get away!'' He dismissed Ralf with a shove, pushing past Coutance to sweep up the tiny queen in thick arms against her protest.

"This is ridiculous, Gilly. I am not a cripple.''

"Be still now. I have you.'' He carried Matilda from the hall and up the stairs to their chamber, hurling orders at servants left and right. Bring hot comfrey, summon the queen's physician. Turn down her bed. Now leave them alone, out. With vast tenderness, William laid his wife in the readied bed and tucked the covers about her. "Now rest. Rest and you will be well again.''

"Why not call a priest? You'd think I was dying.''

William pressed her hands to his lips. "Those women gave you pain. I could kill them for that.''

"Not the girls," Matilda resisted. "You don't think when you're angry."

"You are too fond, Mora. You would forgive anyone. You'd mother every child and stray cat in the world if I let you."

Matilda nestled her cheek into his broad palm. "Why else would I love a brute like you? Oh, I know," she sighed. "Maud did cozen me. Well, I brought them here. Pity. I could have learned much from them."

"Bitches."

"Gilly, don't send the girls to Hough. Even Ralf says they are innocent."

"Will you for once not think with your heart?"

"Whatever Marian might have done, her child is innocent. Is it too much of a mercy for her to bear it in a warm room?"

"Oh, I don't care." William bent over her tenderly. "Just be well again."

There were few things he feared and Matilda knew them all. "But for you I've always been alone. If the English hate me, I can laugh. If God is against me, I can deal with that. But to be without you—"

Just then the physician knocked and entered, bowing to the king who reluctantly gave place at the bedside. Later William sat by his wife as she slept. Messengers, most of them from the northern border, were intercepted at the barred chamber door where they collected anxiously, waiting until the king saw fit to see them. His queen was ill. Finally the business of the kingdom could wait no longer and William had to leave her.

Not so . . . not so. She didn't see Robin dead, wouldn't believe until then. Marian had not cried out in the hall when she heard what she'd feared since her wedding night. She screamed but no one heard what pierced down and inward, searing her like a scar on the vitals. If Robin died, a part of herself died with him. Like the old prisoner from Ely, she would be fought out and done.

Not so, then—but why no word from Robin as the weeks dragged by one after another like dirty footprints through the snow? Not even Father John for comfort now; all the Saxon priests were gone from St. Wulfram's, swept out by the king. Epiphany passed under a foot of snow as Marian and Judith trudged day after day between prison house and scullery. The work was hardest on Judith. The peasant cooks, coarse as barley dough, delighted in ordering "Lady" Judith about and always gave her the worst tasks, scouring scummy pans or hauling slops to the hog pens. *There—*

Marian could read their petty satisfaction—*that will learn you to put on fine airs with us*. Judith could cheerfully murder every overbearing one of them, though she tried to be philosophical. "We're luckier than Aunt; they spared us the dungeon. Marian, will you sit down? The way you fling yourself about. What *are* you doing?"

"Tidying."

In the last days of January, Marian was siezed by a sudden and fierce nesting instinct. Fighting to believe Robin still lived and touched her, she swept and dusted relentlessly about their dingey house, counted baby linens over and over and wouldn't hear of lighting to rest. The child would come naturally and the queen had been kind enough to make some provision for the event.

"No fear, Judy girl. We don't grow delicate up Tadcaster. My mum was born in a barn on the winnowing floor."

"Good God." Judith warmed her hands over the small fire before departing for the loathed kitchen. "No, don't get up again. I can fetch my cloak."

Marian brought it anyway, draping the garment over Judith's shoulders. "I know the kitchen's hard on you. Won't be forever. Robin's not dead."

"So I tell myself, so I pray." Judith turned up her hood and laced it tight. "But with all their erudition, the convent never explained how life can be nine tenths pure frustration and the rest mislaid. I suppose one just has to last it out."

Which Judith would, Marian was sure: proud as Maud but young as herself and wanting all the things should go with youth, watching the days of her life fall like dead leaves from a tree with no spring or budding in sight.

Ralf came one day only minutes after Judith left for the scullery. Marian thought he might have planned it so. She'd been resting by the meager fire with her hands buried in Perdu's fur for warmth. Ralf entered followed by a strapping young village boy with cheeks cold-rosy over his muffler, bent under a wicker basket loaded with seasoned firewood. The porter stacked his load neatly in a corner before he left. Ralf chose three split pieces from the pile and arranged them carefully on the fire.

"The steward sent the wood," he said.

Not Coutance, Marian knew better. Beyond guarding them Coutance was totally indifferent to Judith and herself. The wood was Ralf's gift. She wished he hadn't come, put off by his presence and nothing to say to him.

"You are not working today?"

"They've let me off until the child is born. It's that soon."

"May I sit down, Marian?"

She didn't feel well enough for good manners. "I'm the king's prisoner. His sheriff will do as he likes."

Ralf removed his cloak and threw it over his shoulder, settling on one of their rickety stools. "I would not trouble you, but there are serious matters to speak of. I see you are not in mourning."

"No death I know of. For sure not my husband."

"Marian—"

"Not until I see his body. Not until Father Beorn tells me so."

"Very well." Ralf accepted her stubbornness. "But your child comes soon and there are realities."

"The queen's seen to that. I'll bear the babe in the manor house."

There the point, Ralf told her. The queen was a kind woman but could work only so much. Here or somewhere else, Marian was likely to remain prisoner. If released she would be no more than a serf, bound to one lord or another. "To the king you are nothing. You know you are much more to me."

"Is that what you came to say, Ralf? I asked you once not to speak of that."

"I must speak now. As your time comes, in a way time runs out for me as well." Ralf spoke quietly but in complete earnest. "*Chère Marianne*, there are marriages of convenience. Indeed, most that I know of are little else. There is such a match being considered for me. For all the king's convenience, I would rather choose for myself. My choice will not surprise you, I think."

"No, I'm past blushing." Marian settled herself on her bed-shelf. The burden in her belly, carried high so long, had dropped low and the vague discomfort of the morning was now more pronounced. No contractions yet, but they must come soon. At least this kept Ralf and the matter he pressed at some distance. "But my husband lives."

"Name of—Marian, will you wake? Please wake," he beseeched. "Robin . . . we fought. He might have killed me and near did. But he couldn't be alive, not . . . not like that. *Bon Dieu*." Ralf glanced aside in frustration. "Do you think I am not sick of this? As good men go, I would rather kill ten less worthy. What Robin aims at I cannot see, but at least he is true to it. I had a duty. Once I thought I would take pride in ending it. When the time came I did not. But I swore to him that you and your child would not want. Why do you look at me like that?"

"Seeing your realities," Marian answered. "Seeing the world and knowing it for a sad place. Growing up."

"I am not a murderer."

"No. You're lucky to be alive, you are."

"Just that—*je ne sais pas*—I am sorry."

Yes, she heard the tangled, incoherent regret in the man. "I believe you."

Ralf might have thought he heard encouragement in her admission. "I will ask the king to give you to me in marriage."

"I'll refuse," she shook her head firmly. "With the whole Church behind me for a start if they don't know for flat truth Robin's dead."

"Marian, you are deaf and not thinking! Consider the child."

"You're the child to think this way! God, what do you expect? You trap Mum because she loves her son, and then ask . . . *child* indeed. Please go, Ralf. I don't feel well."

He refused gently. "I ask pardon but an answer as well."

How when she just gave it? The discomfort in her body made Marian sharp. "Impossible."

"I think not." Ralf rose and came to stand close over her. "There is much you have not said. I have been honest. I love you. Give me honesty in return."

If there was anything once, that was a moment a lifetime past. He talked of realities but knew nothing of them. "You're the king's officer and England's full of your own women now."

That wrung a hard smile from Ralf. "Yes, many. Daughters of high houses, *dames des choisies*. Do you know whom the king is considering for me? Lady Judith."

That did shock Marian. "Mary and Joseph!"

"Well invoked. The Queen of the May, well connected to dead kings and no land or money, yet suitable to a man born to a mother with no name at all and a father with little more. I was luckier than most bastards. And smarter by the time I was ten. I would have done anything to rise."

So would you all. Why, I'm tenfold freer in prison than you out of it. Until your lot came, Robin and I were contented with what was ours. In Willy Bastard's kennel, the big hounds kill the little ones, so one must grow big in a hurry. "Good dog, Ralf."

"Yes!" He flashed back, stung, gripping her arms. "Now you have it. Now you are learning the world. *Good dog.* How else does the dog get his bone when the king is all and nothing else for such as me? People like you and Robin, you have no idea, never did.''

He spun away from her, too urgent for stillness, the central ache of his life driving him about the cramped chamber. "Denby, it is a dream. You all live in a dream, in a mirror that shows everything backward. Please, Marian. Will you for once not be Maud? Pride with an empty belly?''

This time, he told her, the good dog had earned more than a bone if less than a highborn virgin, and thank God for that. "They speak of a *vicomté*: all Nottingham and Sherwood in fief. It is more than a chance, Marian. It is just the beginning, I warrant you. Your child could share in my inheritance.''

And more, he promised. As diligently as he worked to trap Robin and Maud, so he would sue to the king for all of them to be released to Denby. He offered himself and all he had or could do. "So let us be honest. You have some feeling for me.''

"You read me wrongly.''

"You have. I knew that the first time I saw you. The last time we talked.''

"I—''

"No, don't turn from me. Is it so hard for you to say? God, you are a strange, cold people. And cruel. Do you think it is easy to stand naked like this?''

"Let go of me. Please, I want to stand up.''

He went instantly tender and anxious, genuine fear and concern in his eyes. Some part of her, pitying the life of him so hard won and so strangely wasted, was touched.

"You have pain?'' he worried.

"Just uncomfortable.''

Ralf started away to the door. "I will fetch someone. Tell me whom you want.''

"No. Wait. It isn't time. Soon but not yet. And there's that would be spoken, and when it's said I want you to go and never come again.''

"That is hard to promise but I knew you could be cruel.''

"Was it true, then? You swore to Robin for me and my baby?''

True, though Ralf couldn't clearly say why but that swearing seemed right.

She believed him in this too. A strong man who commanded others, gave and took orders, hurried about at the king's whim. There was always a beauty to him, something clean compared to others of his kind, even an honor; yet the life the driven man could call his own a woman might tuck into a needlecase. He'd given her honesty. She would repay in the same coin, cancel the debt and be quit.

"Yes, I'm growing up quick this year." Marian spoke with a grave deliberation from a distance beyond the child moving through her toward life. "I wanted you once, when you first came. I was a country girl with a country charm under her pillow who dreamed a shape like yours. Then there you were in front of me, ill and in need of tending. Beautiful and helpless all at once and I reached for you as any child will reach for something bright."

"I wouldn't know," Ralf said with an arid bitterness. "I spent very little time as a child."

Marian caught her breath: not pain, but the sudden wet rush of warmth between her legs. She sat down quickly, filled with tingling anticipation and a little fear. *Soon. Today. Just hours now.* "It's nigh time. They've broke."

"Broke? What?"

"The waters."

Suddenly Ralf Fitz-Gerald was no more effective than any other male at such a moment, instinctively rattled and nervous. He fumbled the cloak about him. "Stay. Rest. I will go for someone."

"Not yet." She wanted him gone but not before ending for good and all what could never properly begin. "What I said: that I wanted you."

"Please let me help you. If you knew how much—"

"Shut up! And listen!" More than the child would leave her today, something else fiercer and darker would come first, hard and tearing as the child. "Aye, take that much for gift. But for all the rest, Ralf: What you are and what your filthy kind's done to us and stolen from us; for the hungry months I've been penned up in this dirty sty where my husband had to come to me like a thief and live like an animal on his own land; for Judith who's got nowt but the like of you for help, and Mum in a dungeon where *you* put her, with no help at all—for all that, Ralf, if I had a knife I'd cut your Norman throat. Take that for a curse and leave me."

She hurt him; she saw him flinch. The man was no brute, but when you trampled people's lives you came away with blood on your boots.

He said at length, "You do hate me."

Christ, what a sad, lost lamb he was. Marian felt a tinge of pitying contempt. "What do you want, forgiveness? What need? You've won it all, you've got it all. You'll damn well die rich, Ralf. Rich"—she gave the word all the meager value it held for her—"and noble. Now leave me alone. I've a baby coomin'. Let me get on with it."

He hesitated with his hand on the door latch, bending to stroke his fingers once along Perdu's back. "Good-bye, Marian."

Ralf closed the door behind him. Marian heard his muffled exchange with her guard, then feet clumping rapidly away through the snow. She sat on her stool, trembling with what was out of her at last and what must still be born.

"Perdu. Here, cat."

The three-legged cat bobbed to her and hopped into Marian's arms, purring against her body, tilting her head back to be scratched under the chin. "Fair enough, kitten," she whispered tremulously. "You purr away and I'll shake and between us we'll manage, won't we?"

Holding Perdu, she waited for the first contractions to start.

Marian gathered herself for the last effort, only a rawed animal panting for a voice. Someplace she must get to, she and the child. The midwife was murmuring soft encouragement out of her wrinkled and toothless mouth: Rest easy, she could deliver on her back after all. Marian was glad of that. After the hours of walking about and squatting and turning this way and that, there wasn't much fight left in her. Strength and will belonged now to the cruel contractions pushing the child toward birth.

Matilda swabbed at her forehead with a cool cloth. "Not long, dear. Not long now." The tiny but strong-willed queen would allow no assistant but herself to the midwife which the peasant woman must have resented during the labor, but she could hardly take professional umbrage at the crown.

"But, lady, it is always done—"

"Stuff and enough! None of your sauce, woman. I've had nine of my own."

"Peace, I beg you both," Marian gasped. "Hold my hand."

The pains weren't separated at all now, just one red agony. Marian set herself to endure, but this one coming was too much, beyond bearing. The very hands of God reached down, reached in and tore her asunder—

"JESUS—"

She went white. Long, hard fingers vised cruelly around Matilda's. No mercy in her now, only a primordial purpose not even part of herself. Little queen, little enemy: Something in Marian wanted to crush the woman, grip and twist anything or anyone against the torture. Her mouth distorted, carving a prayer out of pain. *"He's not dead. He's—"* The hoarse remnant of her voice rose suddenly too high on the final wave. "Alive!"

And the child came red and wet from her body to be spanked into squalling life and washed by the midwife, swaddled, and placed again in her arms by a queen. When Marian thought back on the time later, why, infant Jesus with his three kings and frankincense and that didn't do much better.

"Mais certainment he is alive." Matilda eased the baby into the natural curve of his mother's arm. "Look, *petite*. You have a man child."

37

At FIRST, THERE were only periods of darkness and light, no sense of time at all. Then nights and days Robin could count, filling out to weeks and months. Inching toward recovery like an army fighting uphill, his body warred against fever and the wound that closed so slowly. Death had come close and been sent away and must be bored with him now, throwing up ghostly hands in exasperation: Live and to hell with you, Aelredson.

I was too weak to kill you, Ralf, but by God let you be sick as me.

He was never as bull powerful as Ralf but healthier from birth. His constitution gained over the wound. The fever sweated out of him, soaked him night after night until Robin was soul-weary of the pressure of the bed against his back, dreamless half-sleep where lights danced behind his eyelids, and the flat, alkaline smell of poisons expelled from his embattled body. He had no appetite at first. Food nauseated him but he forced down the broth Wytha prepared.

He fought to live as Marian must fight to bring his child into the world. Frail and vulnerable now, soul as well as flesh bruised with pain, Robin sometimes felt closer to her agonies than his own and prayed of God an untroubled birthing for his lady. He sensed now both the toughness and the fragility of human life. The lump called Robin was not impervious or immortal. It could die and would someday. And a man had other limits. He had reached his and should not be henceforth careless of what God saw fit to leave him.

"Have we passed Candlemas, then?"

"A week gone," Will Scatloch told him.

Then his child was born.

Sometimes in his weakness, with no strength to resist, guilt bore in on Robin. Marian was not the only one who suffered pain for him. How many other lives had he wasted or killed with the arrow of his own purpose? Living with pain himself, the vivid memories made him wince physically and curl his body in a ball on the pallet. The family prisoned because of him, Wystan given to the iron, Much drowning in his blood at Ancaster, loyal Tuck twisting on a rope. There were terrible days when the best Robin could call himself was a selfish fool.

"All of them, Morgan. What have I gained?"

Morgan held the spoon close to Robin's mouth. "Eat the soup."

The only positive good was his oath to see the Chronicle to a safe place, a debt unpaid.

"Eat, you daft Englishman."

"Promised Mauger and Beorn."

"Will has gone for them." Morgan slurped at the soup, wiping the spill from his ragged black beard, spooning up more for the invalid. "If they are in Sherwood and alive, they will come."

The scarecrow turned great hollow eyes on Morgan. "Like chess. I've wasted moves and people, wasted the whole game."

"Soup, Robin. Have I not been thatching the old woman's roof all this morning and hungry myself? Eat."

Now that the worst sickness was past, Robin's mind worked with a still clarity, showing him shapes, moves, mistakes in his motives. Like learning chess from Ethelwold. Before he realized the object and nature of the game, he went greedily for pieces one by one while Ethelwold built his defenses a move at a time until attack was impossible and his own defeat assured. Robin had gone at the Normans the same way, fox-clever but ultimately snared. He took a piece here and there but never reached William secure in his last row behind pawns, knights, and castles.

He couldn't make a future out of running, not with Marian and a child. The last mistake almost killed the fox; on odds the next would do for him proper. How much could any of them live without before life ceased to be living? For Marian and the babe, for Will and Beorn and so many more who took his hand and his oath, he had to believe in some kind of a future. Not just buckling under or giving in to the foreigners, but . . . something.

Not pieces but the long game.

He reckoned the hours by light in the forest, the passing weeks and coming spring by the warmth in that light spilling across the threshold and by the busy caw of nesting rooks. Now, with Morgan helping, he could falter a few steps from the bed and back. By May Day, he could sit outside breathing in the wood-scented air of coming summer like young wine. Then a marvelous day when, sitting by Wytha's door, Robin heard something. Morgan caught the sound as well, ready with Wytha's firewood hatchet in his hand. The holly screen rustled and parted and Will Scatloch emerged into the clearing followed by Father Beorn and Mauger. They both carried worn leather wallets with all they owned. Not much left to them, but Mauger's wallet still bulked with his precious Great Book. Robin rose unsteadily to embrace his priest.

"I prayed for you, Robin. I hoped God had not called you yet."

"Almost, Father. I did the like for you."

"The sheriff's given out that you're dead," Beorn told him as they gathered about Wytha's small hearth that evening.

To which Mauger added over his porridge, "He's so sure of it, Normans take their ladies larking through Sherwood now."

Thane Alan told them there was talk in Nottingham: The sheriff was to be made a vicomte.

"Fitz-Gerald of Nottingham, no less," Will humphed.

Robin had put aside his bowl to peruse several pages of Mauger's book, turning them to the firelight, lips moving with his word by word effort. "Mauger?"

"Aye, shall I read to you?"

"How long will it take me to learn to read this book?"

The question took Mauger by surprise; he couldn't say. "How much do you read now?"

"Not enough." Robin glanced up from the parchment. "Can you make ink?"

Mauger appealed to God above. "Now he wants ink. To what purpose?"

"Until I can travel, you and Beorn will teach me to read and write." For the sake of their astonishment, he added, "Truly I am apt and wish it. Frank as well as English."

Will Scatloch whistled. "There's ambition."

"No, Will. Survival."

"You've always survived, mun."

"I don't mean just me."

To Wytha the wisdom of the world had little to do with writing. "You are of Guntrada's line. Your *wyrd* is written in the forest. What need of writing?''

Robin stroked her withered cheek. ''For all your Sight, can't you see the answer? Feel the earth turning a new way?''

Like a sleeper turning from one side to another as day broke. Robin did not truly know all of his reasons except that old peoples like Will's read meaning in the earth and sky while his own conceived in the different permanence of words on parchment. He was ignorant. To have any place in this changed new world, any chance in play against the Normans, he must be able to read the law. Fitz-Gerald told him that much once—scornfully, but with much truth in that scathing. While he healed he would begin to learn and go on learning after that. As when he shot against Morgan for the golden arrow, he concentrated. Nothing existed for him beyond purpose and what Mauger and Beorn taught him day by day. They made him ink from charcoal and woad, quills from the pinions of a fallen hawk.

''Copy,'' Beorn dictated: '' 'We will preserve this book.' ''

Robin labored dutifully. WE WILL PRESERVE THIS BOOK. IN THIS YEAR OF GOD'S GRACE. . . .

''Write,'' Beorn commanded. ''What are the four pillars of English justice?''

THE FOLK MOOT, THE HUNDRED COURT, SHIRE COURT, AND WITAN.

Forms and customs of law when he had the words to comprehend them. The history of his own land and people as expounded by Mauger. ''The throne established on power alone must maintain itself by the same means. Alfred envisioned something else: the throne based on law and principle. That is England, Robin. Power checked by principle. We are unique,'' the little monk enlarged on his theme. ''You said once that ideas were bigger than men. King Alfred knew that was true.''

The rudiments of Frank.

''In the best Frank you have little more than bastard Latin.'' Mauger spoke slowly in that tongue, repeating the lessons over and over for Robin. ''There are several ways to pronounce vowels depending on how they're used. To speak of bastards, you habitually refer to Fitz-Gerald as one. *Un bâtard.* Get it right or he'll miss the whole point, don't you think? Again.''

They taught him without glimpsing his ultimate purpose. Robin was no longer playing for pieces but position in a game so ponderous, stretching so far ahead that not even Father Beorn could discern the distant end. William had left the apparatus of English law intact; that was the vast playing board. Possibly Robin had a short life ahead as an outlaw, but perhaps more. As he labored to spell *survival* and as he defined it now, he must believe in a future.

THE POWER OF ENGLISH IS ITS—

"Ability," Mauger prompted.

ABILITY TO MOVE AND PERSUADE AND TO—

"What was that word?"

"Illumine."

"That ent English."

"It's Frank, but we'll borrow. I-l-l-u-m-i-n-e."

TO ILLUMINE THE MAJESTY OF THOUGHT. "Mauger, you're a flamin' poet."

Day by day Wytha cast the runes which stubbornly refused to yield their secrets. Robin told her of the turning of the earth; nothing turned that Wytha could perceive, only spring to summer. She had done her task well, healed him while he seized on this fool learning like a hermit monk finding the White Christ at his very own table. Guntrada's grandson was silent and concentrated over his studies, but a silence that brimmed with birth and questions.

One day Wytha was alone in the hut with Robin. To save his parchments, he often scratched words in the dirt beside his pallet. The sickness had left him gaunt, all bone, shaggy mane and beard, shadows under his eyes and a taciturn reserve like the priest.

"Wytha, look."

He pulled at her sleeve to show what he'd done. For the moment under all that book learning and thoughts Wytha couldn't follow and future she could not read, there was something clear and simple: happiness and pride and all of it suddenly very young.

"My wife's name." He drew a line under the letters. "The first I ever wrote it. MARIAN."

He had covered the dirt floor with his useless letters, a whole history so far as Wytha could see. "What's all the rest?"

With his knife Robin obliterated all but the name. "A letter. Someday I will send a real one that Judith can read to her."

Robin took up a page of the Chronicle to read. From marking words he wanted explained, he'd acquired the habit of reading with a quill in his hand. He took it up now, tapping the feathered end against his front teeth. "And perhaps someday my child will read as well. I told you. The earth turns."

"Your grandmother never needed such," Wytha grumbled. "Nor did I in giving you back your life."

But Robin had felt a turning of the times as with the subtle tang in the air as summer drifted toward fall. Like Wytha muttering over her rune bones now, he groped in the dark for the shape of change.

As he went silent over his parchment, Wytha cast the runes once more—and caught her breath. For the first time, there was a clear pattern. The rising arrow of Robin's life arced over at last toward a resolution she could read. The first cast showed her a bird, the second a wing. In the potent third cast, she perceived a single feather.

Like that in Robin's hand. He dipped into the ink pot and wrote a word. "We'll be leaving you soon, wise woman."

Late one afternoon in mid-September when the air was on the turn between harvest and autumn, Ralf stopped at Blidworth church while riding home to Denby. He tethered his mare in the churchyard and entered through the open porch door. Bishop Osmund had not bothered to appoint a new priest after Huger's death. Now and then, still courting Ralf's favor, Earl Waltheof sent Father Cedric from Mansfield to say Mass and hear confessions. Ralf wished the Saxon cleric would come more often. Since the hangings, especially the execution of Tuck, a priest of their own would keep the village more manageable.

The sun was low and the nave in deep shadow. No one inside but the dullard sexton whose long Saxon name Ralf could never remember. The sexton grunted in recognition over his task. By the light of two rush candles on the altar, the man scraped his broom lazily across the ancient flagstones, pushing dust and blown leaves toward the porch. Ralf went to the altar and sank to his knees, crossing himself, needing more than prayer to sort out his thoughts in the presence of God. Behind him the sexton's broom swished and scratched across the church floor.

At this turn of his own seasons, Ralf's life was too similar to Robin's, however much or little he relished the irony: A simple man did not always draw a simple fortune, let alone control it. The world herded him this way and that like dust before the sexton's broom.

Six years in England this month, almost a quarter of his life. As that life shaped, clearly this was to be his country henceforth for good or ill. When Denby was no longer a barracks, he meant to restore the steading to its former peace for his children, and there the worm in the apple. William brandished a gift before him: Look! Here are honors, titles, success. Why will my good dog not wag his tail? *Because the garment no longer fits well but pinches here and sags there.*

She did say she wanted him once, laid that much of a feast before Tantalus but ever out of his reach.

If I had a knife I'd cut your throat. No girl said that but a bitter woman in her sorrow. Surprising that he was still vulnerable enough to hurt so much. *The knife went in, Marian. You don't need another.*

A title for his loyalty, a door opened at last to his ambition, and for his life an exquisite empty casket. Pray God in time a philosopher could teach Tantalus to be happy with those morsels he could reach, else rise and walk away. He would seek that wisdom.

And Judith is fine after all.

Beautiful, accomplished, and clearly grateful for parole from a world in which she was lost and alien, returned to the scope she knew. Beyond the family loyalty she bore toward Robin, Judith found Ralf pleasing in person. He had some instinct for these things beyond vanity. When Matilda placed the woman's hand in his, Ralf sensed in Judith a ready acceptance.

To our loyal knight we give in betrothal our kinswoman Judith.

Late a prisoner, now a pride. The king's generosity smacked more of Matilda's in this. Well, Judith would grace his table and give him children connected by that kinship to William himself.

So in time the king might say, "Come, Ralf, take place at table beside me. Be my steward, be my earl. Send me your sons in fosterage. They will never need to know of Le Thiel or your mother's hovel, only the ripe, sweet fruits of your labor."

Farewell in love and peace, Marian. Tantalus will be wise and walk away. So much is worth a marriage and Judith's bed. That is how men advance. You and Robin and your misty forest are yesterday, but I am now.

Five soundless shadows spilled across the rear of the nave. To the startled sexton, a finger laid across bearded lips urged his silence. The four other armed foresters insured it. He was to go on sweeping, they signed. The broom was taken from his hands with barely a break in motion, but toward the altar now. Head bowed over his clasped hands, Ralf's arms were suddenly pinioned tight, his head jerked far back. He was totally helpless. The knife edge kissed his throat and held there.

"*Bonsoir, mon seigneur.*" The intimate whisper greeted his ear. "I wouldn't want to go without saying good-bye."

First the shock of recognition, then the sickening fear. No stranger to death, Ralf was surprised to find how much he wanted to live.

"Once you told me to learn. So I have, even some of your tongue."

Ralf braced himself for the knife. "You can do nothing gracefully, not even die." The knife did not move. "Why do you wait? I have prayed."

Another voice with the lilt of Wales. "Don't tempt him, mun."

Ralf gagged with his throat stretched so tightly. "Killing me will change nothing."

"If it would, you'd be dead," the soft, flat voice told him. "I know you've seen her."

"Who?"

"Don't waste my time. Did she bear son or daughter?"

"I heard a son."

The hand holding the knife moved slightly. "His name?"

"Edward."

The deep tones of an older man now. "Good, Rob. We will pray for them both."

A snap of fingers, the rustle of movement. Ralf felt the strings of his purse jerked taut and severed. Unable to see much at that awkward angle in the gloom, he still recognized the excommunicated priest relieving him of his sword belt. But the blade pressed again into his flesh, nicking him.

"How do Marian and my son?"

"Well, I heard."

"My mother?"

"Alive at Castle Hough."

"While they live, you do. And you see how easily that can change. What of Judith?"

"She is freed. I am to marry her." Once uttered, Ralf regretted the words. Full truth now could be as dangerous as lying. But he heard a low, dry chuckle at his ear.

"Beorn, didn't I say the times changed? Well, 'cousin' Ralf, I'll consider your purse and sword groom-gifts to the family."

Surer now that today wasn't his last, Ralf breathed a little easier. "You take it well enough."

"We were ever folk for bargains and the middle way, remember? You get a woman worth three of you. She gets to live like a human being for a change. Not the best trade but a start." The voice at his ear hesitated;

Ralf heard a note of curiosity. "You troubled before raising your sword to swear provision for Marian and my child."

"I did."

"A man looking his own death in the face has marvelous clear sight. You took no pleasure in what you did."

"I thought of Marian."

"That's all?"

"All you would understand. I am sick of killing."

"I did wonder at that. So am I. Whilst we speak of killing, I never did your rotten little priest. That was John."

"One might have guessed from the scalping."

Something like a sigh at his ear. "There's Johnny for you, an unforgiving man. Huger was *nithing*, without honor. John sent him to hell with that mark on him."

"You are savages!"

"Easy. Don't move. You could go the same way. Will, snuff the sheriff's candles."

The knife lifted from Ralf's throat and settled again just under his hairline. His scalp prickled. "Very simple. The first cut is made . . . so."

Cold iron went stinging hot, biting into his forehead, burning from left to right. Ralf felt the blood rise and flow from the shallow wound, then a stunning blow at the base of his skull sprawled him face down at the base of the altar. When he could think again, he couldn't see and feared for one sick instant that they'd blinded him. He felt at his eyes: no, only full of blood from the streaming cut across his forehead. Ralf wiped futilely at them, groping to his feet.

"You, sexton! Where are you? Bring me water."

The damned peasant took his time coming with a bucket to wash away the blood. There was enough of it. Head wounds never seemed to stop bleeding.

"There were five of them, my lord," the sexton defended himself abjectly. "Nowt I could do the whole time."

"Never mind." Ralf still could see very little and the nave was dark now. "Help me to my horse."

He stumbled out of the church guided by the loutish Saxon, blinking through a sticky mess of blood, trying to focus his sight. "I left my horse here. Where is it?"

Ralf found his mare by tripping over her. As he fell his outflung hands landed in a pool of sticky warmth. Robin had left his throat whole but cut the mare's.

Helpfully swabbing at Ralf's face, the sexton waxed even more apologetic. "Nay, was nowt I could do there either, my lord. They said they did not want you following." The sexton was confused and thoroughly shaken, offering what assistance he could. He regretted his lord was robbed while omitting mention of the three silver pence passed to him for his inconvenience.

"Follow where? They said nothing, not a word? You're a fat Saxon liar!"

"My lord, I am not." But the sexton was far past his prime and never aggressive. With Ralf shoving him backward, raging through a mask of blood, he did manage to remember something they said. "A book, sir."

"Book? What book?"

"I don't know, sir. Just summ'at about a great book."

38

Not even the king could deny the Mass to Christians, especially on a feast day like Saint Michael's. Marian wrapped little Edward in his softest blanket, kissed his button nose and told him, "Now we're off to church."

The baby gurgled at her. Edward had her eyes and was a sturdy babe. That was all she could tell at eight months. She wondered would he be light-complected like herself or if his flaxen fuzz would darken to Robin's chestnut. She did the best she could; he took well to her breast and no milk troubles, thank God, but Marian wished he were fatter with winter coming on.

"Come, Gunstal," she summoned her laconic but dutiful guard. "To Mass."

Judith lived in the manor now but came every day. She'd been allowed to church earlier—to pray for what? Marian wondered. Poor Judith: For all her high blood and education, life tossed her this way and that like a ball, prisoner to Queen of the May and back. Now from jail to marriage. Marian knew Ralf's private feelings in the matter and tried to imagine Maud's. Better Mum didn't know for the time. As for Judith, she was composed enough in the telling of it and, to Marian's eye, scarcely heartbroken.

No, you ent sorry, and I'll not blame you for that. Ralf's far from the worst and off my back and conscience now, and the rest none of my affair.

"I bless you, Judith."

"Do you?" Judith searched anxiously for approval. "I'm sick of living like this, sick enough to be selfish. Tired of fetching and carrying for those common bitches in the scullery. I know Aunt will call me traitor, but I'm not, Marian. And once married, I can work to free you and Aunt. Ralf will help; he offered as much himself."

Marian stopped her with a kiss. "Peace, Judy girl. I know."

No date had been set for the wedding. Ralf was not yet invested and there was the ancient tangle of Judith's bloodline to be traced by the ferret-scribes.

You'd think she was a prize horse. "Hell, hell, hell," Marian muttered, walking beside Gunstal up Manor Gate toward St. Wulfram's. She guessed Mum would be years accepting the marriage, if ever, too old-fashioned and stone-blind about any way different from Denby. England wouldn't be rid of Normans this year or next. If not Ralf for Judith, who or what else? *With love or without, they'll have children like Robin and me. A long, strange road to look down, but there's been so much change already. Well, Judith's child will be Edward's cousin, and who knows but they won't be playing together someday? Eh, my Robin, won't you roar at that?*

She chatted with Gunstal, pausing as a gang of laborers streamed down Manor Gate from the west: farmers impressed for the new ditching east of the manor grounds. Marian waited, jogging little Edward in her arms in the bright, crisp sunlight of late September. As she observed the shuffling line of workers, a tall man with a pick on his shoulder stepped casually out of the line perhaps thirty paces away and halted, looking directly at her.

She had stifled the cry when she heard of his death; she would not cry out now in joy to give him away for all she wanted to. The ancient sheepskin vest and ragged farmer's tunic hung loose on him. He was thin, hair and beard so uncombed wild that even Maud wouldn't know him at once, certainly no sheriff's man. But he was there, still as a couching deer in the sunlit street, arrow-straight in the shoulders as she remembered, unquenchable life in every line of him.

He slid the pick casually from his shoulder to lean on it, never taking his eyes from her or the child.

To Gunstal, who was leaning on his pike, Marian said, "We'll wait 'til they pass. Look, Edward.'' She carefully peeled back the baby's blanket and held him up. "Look at all the men." Her hands trembled under the warm weight of her baby. "See?"

I knew you would come. My lord, here is your true son.

Yes, she saw him.

Robin watched hungrily, soul-starved as Marian uncovered the tiny face.

God bless you both. Is he healthy? Does he thrive?

He dared not come closer or even appear to be looking directly at them, but sent his reaching spirit to embrace the woman and child. As on their wedding night, let time stop. Let him stand here, stepped aside from the moment as he left the moving line of men to feast on the sight of them. Will warned him against coming, but the risk was his alone and worth it. Worth the months on Wytha's pallet, worth all of his promise about the book, repaid the hard effort to learn. He could spell out *tyranny* with his pen and knew time for one that ate into his moment. The last of the workmen would be passing soon. He'd be standing alone, staring enough to make her guard suspicious. Yet he wanted to go on gazing at Marian and the future in her arms.

The passing ranks thinned out; now the end of the line straggled past him. Robin got in step with the last man, clapping him on the shoulder. "G'day then. And a fine day it is!"

"Fine to be home," the farmer grumbled, "not working for foreigners."

As he passed her Marian turned with him, casually enough but making sure he saw the baby clear. Robin caught a brief, heart-filling glimpse of the small face cowled in the blanket, round cheeks apple-reddened in the brisk air. *Oh, he's your eyes. I'm glad of that.* He looked as long as he could; he must look away the next instant for her own safety.

With her back briefly to the guard, Marian's lips sent him a small, secret kiss.

Robin tore himself away and walked on, ox-lumbering and stoic as the big peasant in front of him. He wanted to shout in triumph, weep in frustration. He shouldn't have come—no, he was glad, too close for too long to death and endings. If only for the space of a few heartbeats, Marian held out life to him like water to thirst.

Truly, Robin marveled as he dropped away from the line and slipped west again through Grantham—truly, and with no prejudice whatsoever, no more beautiful babe was ever born in England or the world. Nor any touch of God's hand made a man feel so complete, so proud, or so shivering scared.

Look on my son, William. If Marian and I are the last to put our blood into the tree, he's the future you can't stop. Do what you will: Steal the land, burn our cities and our books, sew our very souls with salt, no matter. By God, we'll grow again, you son of a bitch. Right under your Norman nose and beautiful to boot.

BOOK V

The Fighting Man

39

*T*HAT SPRING, WILLIAM went north with levies and ships against Malcolm of Scotland, but England knew internal peace. The Midlands drowsed through sun and gentle rains. Quiet as the situation appeared, to Ralf Fitz-Gerald there was a vast difference between couched and crouched enemies. One lay at ease, the other prepared to charge.

Coutance scoffed at his worries. "You've been too long a watchdog, seeing peril everywhere."

"That's my office. Did you ever have the feeling of being watched when no one was there? If someone wanted to make trouble, what better time than now?"

Now when the king was so far north, totally committed beyond the edge of the tactical map. Reign and government rested with Lanfranc at Canterbury and Matilda wherever she rode between Grantham and Winchester, two of the three pillars of peace. The third, the loyalty of vassals, was what Ralf doubted.

The vague malaise did not afflict the sheriff alone. Matilda and her archbishop were troubled by similar presentiments, a nagging sum of little things. The normal correspondence from Flanders and France had turned unusually bland and noncommittal in recent weeks, the same from Anjou and Brittany from whose counts Matilda was used to continual squabbling, complaint, and sword-rattling arrogance.

"One could yawn through their dispatches these days," she commented to Lanfranc. "It's as if they were waiting for something to happen."

Minor things, nothing substantial one could point to. Waltheof of Huntingdon and Roger de Breteuil, earl of Hereford, had been close for years, young Rolph de Gael invariably a third in their company. In March Rolph married Hereford's daughter Agatha and was invested by William as earl of Norfolk. Though born there and half English, Rolph had strong family ties and vast holdings in Brittany. Since the marriage his correspondence to his vassals across the Channel had markedly increased. Some of the couriers were in the secret employ of the archbishop. As a matter of course a number of Rolph's letters were intercepted by Matilda and Lanfranc. They contained nothing overtly suspicious from the ebullient youth who as one of the three victors of a May Day *mêlée* simply collapsed on his rump, grinning while Waltheof acknowledged the cheers of the English peasants. Huntingdon was a darling of the commons, true, and Rolph was popular: enthusiastic and voluble but not terribly literate. Like most of his peers he dictated his letters to a scribe, yet some of these missives fell with a subtler resonance on the delicate ear of Lanfranc than he would ascribe to de Gael.

"No cause for alarm," the archbishop considered with one of those shrugging gestures which the Italians rendered eloquent. "However—"

Matilda understood precisely. "Quite. We will watch him."

At Wytha's forest hut near Ancaster, Robin's companions staged a more overt rebellion. No, they would not disperse. If Robin wouldn't allow them to go with him, they would wait him here and safe enough, far safer than he would be riding alone.

"Then stay and there's an end." Robin looped the quiver over his shoulder and buckled on the sword belt taken from Ralf. "I'm enough by myself to win or fail."

But why, they pressed him, when the five of them gave as many chances of success? Don't be bread, man. But Robin's will was firm. They were the best and truest friends, they'd helped him to survive as much as Wytha, but this he must do alone.

"That's rare gratitude," Mauger seethed. "I was the one who brought you the book, my quest from the start. Why should I not see it through?"

Ungenerous indeed, a meanness unlike Robin. Nay, come, could he give them one *good* reason to go alone?

"Aye, good enough!" Robin burst out finally. "Tuck was my man. They hanged him. Much was my man. I was that close to him when he died. I *saw* . . . I still see him." Robin met each man eye for eye. "And I tell you by the rood I don't want to look on such loss again. I'm not so reckless bold as before Fitz-Gerald put a hole in me. There's pain I'll face and that I need not. Tell Angharad of your death, Will? Call me coward first, I shrink from that. You, Father? Christ, are we not poor enough? And you, Morgan. You'd be a treasure to Wales, shortening life for the bloody marcher barons."

"I've done that already, mun. That's why I'm here."

"Brother Mauger, wherever I bestow your book, they'll know what man saved it. Your name will be in their prayers. There, you have my reasons; give me your hands. For the rest I can think but one thought at a time now, so leave me be. God bless and farewell."

"Do you think we'll see him again?" Mauger worried to Beorn as Robin vanished beyond the holly screen.

"Of a surety." Beorn forced the ring of confidence into his words. *But perhaps not in this life.*

At Linby Dale, Thane Alan had the same reservations but still felt indebted to Robin, presenting him with a parting gift of the Arabian stallion Hratha. Fussing with the saddle straps, he declared the horse a temporary loan like the team of oxen years past.

"Ride him well," Alan urged. "There's few like him yet in England. He's tough but sensitive. A bad rider could ruin him. Be firm but gentle. Don't saw his mouth with the bit—there, Hratha, easy." Alan stroked the fine, small eared head and tapering muzzle. "He's a desert breed. He can graze on scrub and still outrun anything a Norman rides. Legs of iron, feet like rocks."

"I only asked a horse." Robin was overwhelmed with the lavish gift. He'd ridden Hratha before in the business of the wedding at Edwinstowe and knew the stallion's worth. "Not the best in your stable."

Alan shook hands with his friend. "Where will you go, Robin?"

"God knows." Robin mounted and gathered the reins. "Where I need to. Merry part, Alan!"

He rode through the winter, a seedy, shabby man in an old black mantle mounted on a regal horse so much more presentable than himself that English monks from Whitby to Worcester joked that the horse should be fed in the refectory and the tattered man stabled. Wherever Robin went English abbots seemed to have vanished. All the responsible offices were now held by Normans. The worst of winter slowed and sometimes snowed him in. Hratha grew used to Robin's seat and rein as spring came on, tireless as Alan boasted. More than once he lost Norman patrols with ridiculous ease when they would have detained his rider.

One drizzly day in April, Robin rode up to the Galilee Porch of Abingdon Abbey, nestled in a turn of the western Thames river near Dorchester. He let Hratha's rein hang loose and entered the church with his precious bundle of the Chronicle, crossing himself at the font in the lay brothers' choir. He'd heard only the past week that Abingdon still had a Saxon abbot, a respected library, and no Normans at all yet. Perhaps he'd come to the end of his quest. If not, there might still be a meal, bed, and a dry stall for Hratha. Robin shambled wearily down the choir to the rood screen and the great carved crucifix, sinking to his knees.

"Lord Christ, I thank you for bringing me safely this far. If I must go on, let the saints Dunstan and Werberga watch over me, my lady, and son and the good men who would not leave me."

If he survived his first year, Edward would be walking and making his first attempt to talk. A time to share gone forever now, never to be found again. Perhaps that one heart-piercing glimpse of the child in Grantham would be all—

"You, fellow!"

Robin's hand slid toward the sword hilt. He turned to see a stern-visaged old man in black habit just emerged from behind the rood screen.

"Are you a barbarian that you come to God with a sword?"

Robin got up, reassured by the native accent. "With so many foreigners in church now, sometimes a sword is wise. I seek the lord abbot."

"I am Abbot Wilfred." Robin was inspected from wind tangled hair to ruined shoes. "Whose man are you?"

"My own. My father held his lands of a king." At other abbeys Robin had encountered English clerics more interested in their own welfare than the English cause, venal enough to whisper suspiciously of him to Norman prelates. Others gave more helpful advice in private. From the inner pocket of his muddy cloak, Robin produced a bedraggled goose feather. "Some at Worcester said this might signify to the right man of God."

Abbot Wilfred took the feather; his stony expression softened slightly. "Perhaps."

"And this." Robin opened the bundle and held out a few parchment sheets. The abbot scanned them perfunctorily at first, then with avid interest.

"Where . . . where did you get this?"

"Saint Wulfram's. The Normans would have thrown it out. Brother Mauger took himself and the book from Grantham, for he thought it worth saving."

Wilfred's pale eyes ravaged the pages. "Come with me."

Willingly, but first Robin asked to stall his horse. No, he could not leave the task to a lay brother. The horse was testy with strangers. When the stallion was watered and generously grained, Abbot Wilfred hovering close with endless questions about the prize Robin carried, they passed up the day stairs to the Abbey's library. Wilfred peremptorily summoned every monk in sight to follow them. "Come! See what God has sent us!" The monks swirled into the library and gathered about the writing desk where Wilfred laid out the manuscript like a feast to their incredulity. From the vestry just beyond and from the chapter house more monks and priests crowded in to gasp at the miracle, to flutter and coo like doves over the delicate red and blue tinted letters and numerals that illuminated each year's entry. Robin was quite forgotten on the fringe of their excitement until a faintly familiar voice asked of Wilfred: "My Lord, who brought this?"

Robin brightened when the priest turned to him. "Father Cedric! Well met, but how in the world—?"

Maud's erstwhile confessor embraced her son. He was on leave from Waltheof's library at Mansfield to read in the penitentials of Dunstan. Abingdon's copy was nearest. And what of Lady Maud and the rest, and where did Robin get the treasure of this Chronicle? Mauger? Oh, indeed, Cedric knew that precocious young scamp.

"Bright as a penny but in need of humility as you are of a hot meal. Come, look at this with us." Cedric dragged Robin through the crowd of clerics about the desk who were comparing the gift with another manuscript less worn. "There will be another copy commenced at once," Cedric vouched wistfully. "Would I could take up the pen myself. My Lord Abbot and brothers, let me present you to your benefactor."

"My name is Edward." Robin quickly explained that the real benefactor was Brother Mauger, that he was only a messenger himself but one who would thank them deeply for a meal and a bed.

The pale, elfish little monk who kissed Robin's hand in gratitude had far too little hair before the tonsure took most of the remainder. His intelligent scholar's eyes glistened with zealous tears. "If I could tell you, good Edward. The Normans plundered us as soon as they got this far west. Our golden reliquaries, the great silver cross. Our copy of this book is almost all they left to Abingdon. So few exist. Now you bring us one more. I do not think you know the magnitude of what you have done. May you be blessed.''

Abingdon's library had never seen such bibliophilic passion. They would *all* share in copying the manuscript, each a section and that forthwith. Brother This would prepare new parchment, Brother That fresh ink and quills, Brother Else would illustrate the pages with his best washes. As for Edward, the nobles from nearby Dorchester and Bampton should come to feast and honor him.

"I think not," Father Cedric delicately advised Wilfred. "The less noise there the better."

No matter, the book was the prize. They palpitated over it, reading aloud, turning leaves with white hands long and lovingly stained with ink and scholarship. Smothered exclamations rose like mist from them. Never mind that it was defaced and incomplete. Truly, as in Exodus, God lit the Children's dark way with miracle when needed. Cedric drew Robin and Wilfred apart from the fervor. Not wise, he enlarged tactfully, to let anyone know of Edward's presence, especially the Norman lords. Certain men of Sherwood were of high interest and higher reward to them, if the Abbot took his meaning.

Wilfred did. What he assumed remained tacit. "Then Brother Edward will need tonsure and habit, will he not?"

Out of the bee-buzzing excitement around the writing desk there suddenly rose a squeal of utter shock. "What is *this*?"

Abbot Wilfred asked mildly, "What is *what*, Brother Egbert?"

"The . . . the backs, Lord Abbot. Someone has scribbled and—and pothooked all over the backs. Page after page!"

"Oh," Robin confessed with major embarrassment, "that was me."

"You?" Brother Egbert uttered the pronoun as if it were soiled beyond laundering or even belief. "*You* wrote on the Great Book?"

Sacrilege. Robin felt distinctly uncomfortable. "Mauger was teaching me and I'd nowt else to write on."

"Well, really." Brother Egbert might have expired with the profanation. "I must say!"

"Under the circumstances," Abbot Wilfred suggested, "let us count our blessings several fold. And do be quiet."

Egbert subsided like a summer storm. Once again Robin was forgotten in the majesty of his gift. Yet he couldn't help being touched by their passion, the more learned image of his own. They cared to the point of tears, even Egbert's outrage, about something he'd groped and fumbled toward long before he could read a page of Mauger's book. This was where England would be saved, in this little room, not by great lords but common men.

"Where will you go now?" Cedric asked out of concern.

Robin didn't know. If his oath was filled, the future was blank for the time. He would return to his waiting men. But where after that?

None of indecision for Father Cedric. "Nonsense. You'll come with me where you're not only welcome but honored. To Mansfield. Why, the earl's harper's composed songs about you—and Hereward of course, but yours are more fun."

Songs about him. Marian would be proud, and if the harper remembered for a few years, little Edward might hear them. Earl Waltheof had invited him more than once. To Mansfield, then.

Ten nights later in the Queen's Rest at Blidworth, long after curfew, Ralf Fitz-Gerald instructed Ceolred to relight a rush candle: They had business. Ceolred set the holder with its single small light on the battered table between them. He wondered what the sheriff wanted of him now, but became more interested when the Norman undid a fat purse from his belt and set it open on the table.

"Ceolred, I have stood for your rights, have I not?" The sheriff scooped a handful of silver from the purse. The coins gleamed in the rushlight. "You know my word is good."

"Aye, lord." Ceolred had no doubts about the sheriff's efficiency in helping or hanging. But there was money in the man's hand, and as the taverner watched, he idly spilled a few pence on the table with the solid ring of true silver weight.

"Two men rode through Blidworth last night. Two robed as priests or monks. Don't waste time in denial. I know they stopped here. My men are watchful and you are not the only Saxon amenable where money is concerned."

Five more coins rang on the table. The sheriff stacked them neatly. "One of them could be Robin Hood. True?"

Ceolred dropped his gaze to the table. In his mottled motives, fear and dull anger mixed with the need for money. More was due him than he ever got. In his gruff, incoherent way, he mourned his murdered daughter and missed her. Though never gentle with Freda, the girl was all fate left him after his wife died. He was owed for her. The sharp-eyed sheriff probably read his thoughts.

"You know he is responsible for Freda."

"Heard it was John."

"What matter?" Fitz-Gerald brought more coins from the purse, adding them to the neat piles before him. "By your own laws, Robin would be bound for what his sworn man did."

"He would." Ceolred watched the stacks of silver grow. A full pound in front of him, now two. Jesus in Heaven, he *was* loyal to Robin, had been to the man's father, but he was owed as well. Now the sheriff was offering more than money, speaking persuasively of a new life elsewhere.

"I will release you from the land. Robin never did as much."

Three pounds on the table and still the coins spilled jingling from Fitz-Gerald's hand. Four pounds, five, a full quarter of the price on Robin's head. Loyalty was all very well for them as could afford it, but Robin was responsible for John.

"A new post in Nottingham, perhaps in my own service. I could use a cellarer at one estate or another."

The silver shimmered in the rush light like moonlight, more money than Ceolred had ever seen at one time, a myriad good reasons clear in its substance and luster. He reached to touch the miracle but Fitz-Gerald caught his hand. "*If* Robin spoke to you."

"He did."

"And if you know where he went."

"He was with a priest, a Father Cedric."

"Cedric of Mansfield." That might follow. "And bound there?"

Ceolred's soul, never magnanimous, held summary court between conscience and need. If Robin was fool enough to stop here in the first place, that was not the taverner's worry. But the thane had the habit of concern for Blidworth, three generations of caring in his blood. He simply could not pass by or stay away, asking after everyone in the village and hall. That was honorable: Ceolred never grudged the virtue to any of Denby blood. But Freda was murdered and cold in an early grave. Robin should have prevented that. The whole world gone to hell as far as Ceolred could see and none of it his fault. Guilty and liable, the verdict returned. Guilty! roared the fortune on the table. Yet Ceolred could not bring himself to say the word. He turned aside, nodding quickly to be done with it.

"Mansfield." Ralf Fitz-Gerald pushed half of the money across the table, and scooped the rest back into the purse. "Yours when I get him. Well done, taverner. Now put out the light and go to bed."

40

THE GREAT SPRAWL of Mansfield manor loomed up before Robin and Cedric near midnight. As they crossed the courtyard to stable their horses, Robin, never used to towns or crowds, gleaned the nervous impression of many more men than even a great earl's manor required. Torchlit details of armed soldiers marched about the grounds, others ringed around watchfires.

The household was abed and all accommodations crammed with guests, they were told by a sleepy chamberlain. Father Cedric's quarters were available but nothing for his monk companion. Cedric mentioned a name and suggested the earl should be informed immediately. The chamberlain padded indifferently to inform the more alert steward who hurried to Earl Waltheof's bower.

"Denby? Robin Hood?" Waltheof bolted out of bed, leaving his wife to return to sleep while he held a hurried conference with the steward. "Don't tell me there are no available chambers. Denby is my friend. Let him share with Cedric tonight, but find the best for him tomorrow morning. Dressed as a monk? Then *evict* a monk. A priest if you have to; God knows we've enough of them."

And then Waltheof himself went to wake and inform several other guests of unexpected good fortune.

Robin shared Cedric's bed that night, a fleece mattress and down pillows, fantastic luxury to him. He rose before first light as Cedric left to attend chapel prayers at Prime. As a farmer he never wasted daylight;

as an outlaw morning meant Fitz-Gerald's men abroad. He was just finished dressing in his monk's habit, regretting the tonsure that left the top of his head naked to every wayward draft, when Waltheof knocked briskly and gusted in full of welcome, followed by a very young man who apparently could not wait out the morning Mass but must meet Robin now.

"Traveling as Brother Edward," Waltheof instructed his youthful companion. "But allow me to present my good friend Robin of Denby."

"Robin Hood." Rolph de Gael eagerly siezed and pumped Robin's hand. "I am honored."

"And this importunate young fellow is Earl Rolph of Norfolk, Vicomte de Montauban in Brittany and God knows what else, and—if your memory fails, my glorious companion in the lists at Grantham."

Robin bowed formally from the waist. "Respects, your grace."

"Oh, leave off gracing." Norfolk went on wringing Robin's hand, his English lilted with the Breton sound not unlike Will Scatloch's. "My name is Rolph. Greet me as equal, for so we are and shall be."

"You are very kind . . . Rolph."

"Look at him, so modest," Rolph deplored. "You have none but friends in this court."

"I'm afeared it's habit, sir," Robin confessed. "Whenever king's men got this close they were trying to kill me."

"Nonsense." The young earl clapped him affably on the back. "Here in Mansfield we have a saying: We have no king but—"

"Excuse me," Waltheof interjected politely. "Perhaps Robin desires fresh clothing."

"No, I'd better stay monked."

"With a sword?" Waltheof indicated the sheathed weapon standing against the wall by Robin's long bow and quiver. "Fine blade but a bit unmonkish, wouldn't you say?"

"Borrowed of a need, sir."

The earl's brows elevated in elegant amusement. "Marvelous hilt work. Someone of note, I imagine."

"Sheriff of Nottingham."

De Gael hooted. "Ralf? Of all knights. *Ma foi*, he'll be disgraced."

"Never at my table," Waltheof decreed. "But as you see, Rolph, in England even outlaws have style, which requires some talent for the outrageous. Come, Robin, let me show you Mansfield. You've not been here for years."

In the spring sunlight, Mansfield was a continual bustle, stir, and rattle of activity. Robin's nocturnal impression was confirmed. There were many more soldiers about than normal security would dictate even at Grantham.

"The king may soon call my levies against Malcolm," Waltheof explained.

Levies indeed, a proper army from what Robin saw. The manor grounds swarmed like an agitated colony of ants. Some of the troops were English but as many Norman and dark, voluble Bretons. Breteuil of Hereford was pointed out to him at a distance, and Count Hoël of Brittany. In several places the old timber stockade walls were being uprooted; in others troops of masons were rebuilding the wall in stone. Ox-drawn wagons unloaded provisions at the kitchen house door, others bundles of arrows and spears at the earl's armory house.

"One must be ready when the king calls," Waltheof said.

Whatever the need, Mansfield was more than ready for anything. Not only soldiers but Norman ladies were everywhere, exercising their gilt-harnessed palfreys about the manor yard in a bright profusion of colors: the Countess of Huntingdon in scarlet trimmed with miniver, Rolph's bride, Agatha, Breteuil's daughter, resplendent in a green kirtle piped with gold and daringly laced behind in the latest continental fashion. Used to the properly modest drape of Saxon women's clothing, Robin was scandalized by the sight of a noble woman's bosom so revealingly outlined in public. Agatha dismounted on Rolph's arm and offered her hand to Robin with self-possessed courtesy. Barely eighteen, Agatha's palm was already callused from riding but she could turn a compliment deftly as Waltheof. "Brother Robin indeed. They say the king finds you a most expensive cleric."

"Not half so dear as I'd wish, lady."

"*Là*, husband, I do not usually find Saxons comely, yet I think this robin's mate must worry when he is from the nest."

Robin breasted the compliments with his barely learned Frank. "Very worried, madam. She is the king's prisoner."

"*Oh, quel dommage. La pauvre.*" The petite Agatha appealed to her husband, Norfolk. "Something should be done about that. The wife of an absolutely irresistible man must be as much herself. Ah! *Magnifique,* Waltheof!" And Agatha was off in a flurry in rapid Frank, lavishing her host with admiration for the rich tabard of marten fur worn over his yellow pelisse.

In all, Robin found himself praised to heaven by everyone he encountered that morning, men savoring his exploits, women openly declaring him far too manly for a monk's habit. Sharing the bathhouse with Father Cedric before the noon meal, Robin confessed it all very unsettling. Norman men had always been enemies, and as for their women—

"Bold as men!" he sputtered, scrubbing vigorously with a brush. "Flatter a man to his face with their husbands standing by, and plain *shameless* in dress."

"All in light jest; that's the way of Waltheof's court," Cedric assured him. "You're a country lad like me, Robin; they're all wanton to you."

"Tell you flat, a good thing Marian ent here. She'd set them straight in a hurry, to speak nowt of the hiding *I'd* get for letting my head be turned by such high-flown muck . . . here now, what's that damn smell?" He sniffed like a hound encountering an alien scent. "It's the water."

"The bath's perfumed," Cedric informed him. "Essence of roses. Waltheof always orders it for his high guests."

"Jesu defend." Robin hauled himself dripping from the large tub, grabbing for a towel. "I'll reek like a Nottingham dox."

When he returned to his quarters, a soldier waited to escort him to his new accommodations: a grizzled English carl with a west country drawl and sad eyes over drooping, stained mustaches. Robin's weapons were missing.

"The earl, he wanted his armorer to copy the hiltwork on that fine sword of yours."

"Copying of my bow as well?"

"Wouldn't know, sir. I'm to show you your new chamber now."

A fine, freshly swept closet all to himself. "I'll be close, sir," the carl assured him from the door. "Earl's orders."

Robin sat down on the richly quilted bed. If this morning augured the rest of his stay in Mansfield, there was no danger but growing fat at table and conceited from the women. "Why?"

The soldier tugged at one of his food-darkened yellow mustaches, turning confidential. "The earl trusts Englishmen, but we ent all English here, are we?" Later when Robin left his room for the latrine, the carl was not far away there and back. However luxurious, his situation began to appear decidedly odd.

Dinner in the great hall brought no more ease. Robin was unnerved by the jostling crowds and noise echoing from the high, shadowed rafters. Directed by the portly steward to a place of honor with Cedric at the central of three tables running the length of the hall, Robin winced at the babble. He covered his ears, long used to silence and comparative solitude.

"I've not seen so many noisy foreigners since York."

Nor so much food or overwhelming favor. The large bowl of lumpy salt was presented to him personally before being set out on the table amid great steaming bowls of frumenty, blancmange, boiled eels, platters of fresh venison, salt pork, and pastries of poached capon and dove. Servants ran continually between kitchen, tap, and tables, pouring a river of ale while pipe and fiddle whined and squealed through the clamor.

"I saw—" Against the noise Robin had virtually to bellow in Cedric's ear. "I say, I saw wagons coming in all morning. Waltheof must be stripping his hides bare."

"Mansfield has become an armed camp, but I couldn't tell you why."

No small reason. That was plain. As a farmer Robin disapproved of such extravagance. Far too early in the year to be feasting so with new crops barely in the ground. And the gathering at the high table—Waltheof flanked by Norfolk and Breteuil of Hereford and Hoël of Brittany—smacked more of a council than ordinary dining. "Do you know what all this bodes, Father?"

Cedric didn't follow. "What bodes what?"

"I don't rightly know, but they've taken my arms and there's a guard on me. Down the table a bit, keeps me in sight."

Cedric's calm clouded. "Pray I've not brought you to trouble."

Robin couldn't yet say he had, but under the courtesies and favors heaped on him, his danger-honed senses registered something strange as the goddamned perfumed bath.

Toward the end of the dinner, Waltheof's fat steward pounded on the dais floor for silence. When the cavernous, echoing hall subsided to a murmur, Earl Waltheof stood up in his place. "Rise, Robin Hood, and let your countrymen honor their own. Let Norman and Breton alike see what men we breed in this island. I pray you, stand."

Robin obliged to a spatter of applause and cheers from the lower table filtered through food-crammed mouths.

"Gentles, I present Robin Hood—who, but for royal villainy, would yet be lord of his own lands at Denby and worthy as his father. If he has stolen since, there are churches and folk in Sherwood who bless him, for they saw the profits thereof. If we in England have one more record of our past it is because he rode the length and width of our land to bring the book to the good monks of Abingdon. Is this what the king calls an outlaw?"

"No!"

"Never!" Rolph de Gael bellowed, pounding the high table. "Let him be restored, raised."

"My lords," Robin protested when the clamor subsided, "I never left the law until England's law turned against me." He cast a nervous glance at the Norman soldiery along the tables. "Give me leave to sit again."

"But why?" Waltheof demanded in high good spirits. "Will you not stand while my harper sings his lay of your adventures?"

His grace be thanked, but Robin would sit, explaining with some embarrassment that the last time he'd been so obvious a target he'd paid dear for it. The wispy little harper came forward, bowed to the high table and to Robin, nestled the small Welsh harp into his shoulder, and began to sing. Robin needed some time to recognize the matter from the harper's high nasal voice and all the flourishes added to a plain tale.

The song recounted (more or less) his exploit with Bishop Osmund, though the harper's flowery version served more trimmings than meat. All courage and courtesy, rough laughter and escaping unscathed, the Bishop undone and fuming in Robin's wake. The ballad ended and was followed by one about the golden arrow. Robin's mind wandered from the performance.

Not like that at all. Not all bright moments and winning. So much of it was being lonely for Marian or scared for my life or Will's when he risked it for an hour with Angharad. Trying not to bleed to death. Fine to sing of golden arrows but that seems so long ago. More than months, years now, and less than a full day spent with my wife, none at all with my son. I wonder if Hereward feels like singing wherever he is or if he's just sick of it all like me. Finish your silly tune, I'm tired of it.

For all his private disillusionment, for all the honor and cheers, ale cups pounded on the board and the kerchiefs fluttered by the ladies from the high table, Robin's discomfort increased. If so damned honorable, why was he disarmed and watched? His mind, schooled by Mauger and Beorn, put a keen edge to the question now. Where once there was uncritical reverence, now Robin had precise terms for Waltheof. Where once he looked to the man as a kind of godling and by the custom of his people ranked Woden among his ancestors, now Waltheof seemed contrived, awash in charm and glamor. Nothing the man did was excessive or even spontaneous like young Norfolk. An open man would be awkward sometimes, would stumble or blurt, give offense from clumsiness if not intent. Waltheof never said or did the wrong thing, probably never put one foot before the other without planning. Ungrateful to think thus of a man so bent on showing him favor, but . . . nevertheless.

Necessity made him as contrived now. Robin smiled at Waltheof and his guests, accepted sweetmeats sent down from the high table and the purse with them, nodded to Waltheof when the earl left the hall with Hereford and Norfolk. Now the steward came down to tell Robin that Waltheof desired present and private conference with him.

Robin excused himself to Father Cedric just as the hall doors opened to admit Ralf Fitz-Gerald and a detail of five men, all in mail and armed. Robin hastily turned up the cowl of his habit and followed to a side door indicated by the steward. When he glanced back, there was disturbance centering about the sheriff. Fitz-Gerald was arguing vehemently with one of the earl's carls, very like about entering the hall armed where weapons were forbidden. The sheriff's determination was eloquent in pantomime: He was on the king's business and would stay armed. Speak of filthy luck, or was it bad luck? If that business was himself, how did Fitz-Gerald know he was at Mansfield?

Father Beorn would call that academic. Robin ducked out after the steward who beckoned him toward the earl's private bower. Unarmed, the sheriff too close behind and uncertainty ahead, Robin could only follow.

"Come in, Robin!" Waltheof waved his jeweled goblet in invitation. "Steward, leave us."

Only the three of them waited him in the richly appointed bower. Winter and summer: the suspicious, surly Breteuil, open-hearted young Norfolk and Waltheof lounging in a massive gilt chair. "Some wine?" the earl inquired.

"No, your grace." Robin knelt to him, urgent. "Fitz-Gerald's in the hall."

"We've just heard," Waltheof acknowledged sanguinely. "Our good fortune."

"None of mine. I must ask my arms back, at least my bow."

"Bow?" Waltheof was apparently at a loss. "They took that too? Can they do nothing right, these churls of mine? I sent only to borrow the sword."

"Look, Saxon, you're safe here," Breteuil asserted bluntly. "We've seen to that."

"Safe as ourselves," de Gael expanded. "Once more, let me say there is no man more honored in England, none more—"

"Indeed not, Rolph," Waltheof abbreviated him politely. "But allow me to put our purpose."

Rolph flushed a little, aware of his haste. "Of course. Your pardon."

A boy, Robin judged. Of equal rank but defers to the others. None of them seemed at all concerned about the proximity of Fitz-Gerald. "My lord, what of the sheriff?"

"He will be welcome," Waltheof averred. Mansfield's gate was ever open to the man, who would do nothing untoward. Coming in the king's name, Fitz-Gerald was still under Waltheof's peace and would bear no weapon in the hall. "I'll see him presently. But to the matter. With his usual passion, Rolph has only voiced a respect we all share, Robin."

"Talk!" Breteuil broke in with little grace and less patience. "We'll know your bent, Denby. You knelt to Waltheof as earl. Would you swear to him as king?"

"And lend your help to that end?" de Gael prompted.

Robin looked from Breteuil to Norfolk, finally to Waltheof, utterly stunned. The earl did not gainsay them but clearly waited for his answer. Once Robin might have thrown himself at the man's feet and sworn fealty then and there in any honest endeavor. Now something told him to hold back, feel his way, make cautious or no answer among men who disarmed while flattering him to the skies.

"King Waltheof."

"Of the House of Northumbria, the son of Siward," Waltheof reminded him as if Robin needed refreshing.

"King Waltheof . . . it has a nobler ring than William."

"Robin, I give you no empty flattery, I'll add no idle dream. By winter I will be crowned at Winchester. As far west as Wales, as far east as Brittany, we are ready to rise. Rise with me."

What's in that wine of his that I'm reeling with it myself? Caution, boyo. "England has waited many years for a true king."

"There." Waltheof rose to swing an arm around Robin's shoulder. "I said he'd be one of us."

"You're easily convinced," Breteuil observed. "He states a fact and you take it for fealty. Don't bandy, Saxon. We want your oath sworn on relics."

"You press me too quickly, sir."

"Plain question, you dolt. Huntingdon has always wanted you with us, seeing some value in a gamekeeper that I cannot. Whatever, you are here, he's asked and you'll answer."

Robin was aware of the disparity of their mix. One too smooth and affable, one an impetuous boy, the last an overbearing bully and possibly the dominant one among them. "How answer, my lord?" he parried. "I think you should not demand of me until you have my oath."

"Oh, come." Rolph's hands spread wide with the obvious. "What lord more fit for the crown?"

"I don't argue that, but hasty bargains are not wise for a farmer. I never bought a cow without knowing what bull sired the calf she carried, or a horse without a look at its teeth. A king's a greater matter than a cow, but the principle's the same."

"So it is!" Waltheof slapped his knee jovially. "He says true. Speak out, Robin. Count my teeth if you will. What do you want?"

To know more for a start, he hedged. They were all high men. Where did an outlawed farmer fit their destiny? They could pick and choose among better known and revered than himself. Why not Hereward?

"Hereward is tamed," Waltheof said with quiet contempt. "A mastiff with his fangs drawn and few followers now, for all his repute. He is content to sit at home. He is beaten."

"I have only four men. Never had more than five."

"So few? An industrious half-dozen. No matter." Waltheof brushed the fact aside. "You are no mere outlaw, as Hereward for a time was no mere thane. You are Robin Hood. If William's foot is on the people's necks, you are in their hearts. Who would not follow you if you sent a call through the Midlands? Every good bowman, every freeman cheated of his lands by William, every honest landowner forced into outlawry or close to it in his heart would flock to you. The commons, the heart of the land," Waltheof described with rising warmth. "Men like yourself. Mine to pardon, yours to command. A company of archers the like of which no army has ever seen. I want the folk to see you at my side. For that loyalty whatever reward our gratitude can furnish."

Robin was clearly over his head. As decisive as the dangers were the profits of this chance, but still his instincts plucked at common sense. *You're a farmer, think like one. No good husbandman risks foolishly either against the weather or politics.* "I . . . would need assurances."

"Now we're down to it," Breteuil grunted, picking his teeth. "How much?"

"My family freed."

"Instantly." Waltheof's righteousness was very likely sincere in that, Robin gauged. "There was a crime in itself."

Right, then. Robin knew his market better now. "Hostages set aside. Men of baron's rank—no less, mark—impawned against their release."

"You hardly needed to ask that. The first such captured are yours." Waltheof gripped Robin's hand. "And what else?"

"Only what was mine before. My home and hides in Sherwood."

Waltheof laughed deprecatingly. "So little?"

"So much, your grace, and so long missed."

The earl beamed. "Norfolk, did I not say him aright? They'll follow us from loyalty, but this man from love."

Fine words, but the jaded Breteuil had obviously bargained for higher stakes with greater men. "Then let him swear. We take the field soon. Do you come with us? You're Waltheof's darling, not mine. Kiss him if you want, but I'll have your oath."

The man was a bully for sure. There'd been the time to be supple and hesitant, now a little stiffness might be the better gambit. Robin frowned at the foreigner and allowed a chilly moment to pass before answering. "I think you will not, Hereford."

"What?" Breteuil's brows went up in surprise. He was not used to being discarded so lightly. "What did you say? You trifle with me?"

Now, quickly, a little salve on the wound. "For your own assurance, sir. An oath on ten minutes' knowledge is only ten minutes deep and so you would hold it."

"I think he's caught you there." Rolph winked playfully at his father-in-law. "*Touché.*"

Still Robin played for time, plying them with questions. Swear what? And to where, when, and with what confederates? What assurance of success?

"The map will tell you that," Rolph warranted. "Earl Roger in the west, Waltheof and yourself in the Midlands, myself in the east. Fitz-Gerald too, if—"

"No," Robin denied bluntly. "The sheriff is my blood enemy."

"Say he were not," Waltheof posited smoothly. "We cannot afford dissension."

So they want him, too. A grey fear skittered down Robin's spine. He could stall and hedge just so long and so far. They'd already disclosed enough to make him dangerous. Against that his only guarantee now was Waltheof's goodwill which wouldn't last forever. If he joined them, well and good; if not, the alternatives were grim. He hadn't been in this much trouble when Ralf shot him. "Earl Waltheof, let me ponder this."

Breteuil pressed him. "How long?"

"My lord of Hereford, I will be open with you. My family's prisoned, my mother in chains. If we should fail, they could well be dead. To be plain, I know full well I will not leave here until I answer that question."

"Robin," Waltheof protested as if the very suggestion wounded. "Give way, Roger. This young farmer's more statesman than the lot of us and you never understood our ways. He won't leap without looking first. That is only prudent. I would not trust a hasty oath any more than you, nor one coerced. Be my guest, Robin, and by our ancient custom piece out our purpose sober, feel it out in drink if you will, and find good reason between the two. Come." Waltheof gathered them all in his characteristically expansive gesture. "Let's pacify the militant Fitz-Gerald. I tell you both, Denby's word is hard money. You should have known Robin's father. There was a man."

"No slight to your peace," Robin fretted as the four of them made for the hall again, "but I'd feel better with my bow."

"Your arms will be returned forthwith," Waltheof promised, but let the matter drop without saying precisely when.

When they entered the still-crowded hall, Robin quickly estimated the situation. There was Fitz-Gerald and his detail, confounded but stubborn, encircled by thrice their number of courteous but insistent pikemen. Waltheof cleaved through the circle to embrace the sheriff warmly.

"My dear Ralf, marvelous you've come! And here's Norfolk, the third of our triumvirate at Grantham. You are well come in time for dinner."

"Your grace, I'm here on royal business. Stand, Robin!" Ralf's arm shot out at him. "Arrest that man in the name of the king."

Now young de Gael descended on him, affable as Waltheof. "My treasured friend, Robin's a guest as you are. Don't be gauche." He offered his hand which Ralf took with some awkwardness.

"My lord of Norfolk."

"And in the name of my peace"—Waltheof's glance flicked to his pikemen who moved unobtrusively into a closer knot about the sheriff and his men—"I will ask you to disarm." The earl lowered his voice, which lost no warmth of welcome while assuming a note of authority. "As a guest and a friend, let asking be enough."

Enough if he knows what's good for him. Robin relished the sight of his enemy effectively checked by a few pikes and an avalanche of courtesy. *Let him shake awhile. I'm wrung out being scared all alone.*

41

HE WOULD THINK on it sober and leave the drink, thank his grace the same. Between earl and sheriff a careless man could go to God well before his time. Robin sat on his bed and pondered his predicament. The guard outside, neither too close nor ever far away, inspired concentration.

So that was the game: Rise up against William, crush all opposition, and crown the beloved Waltheof. Not the worst time for it, nor the least prepared from what Robin noted, and he was wise enough to know he couldn't forestall Waltheof much further. Lithe as a cat the man was, never at a loss for the right word.

On the other hand, they asked him only to be with them what he'd been for years, and no king needed ousting so much as Willy Bastard. Why should he not join them, free his family, and take them home? Waltheof had every chance of winning and himself the repute to sway the commons. If the folk loved him to the point of ballads, he had earned that love every day. But just what did he join?

I'd quicker trust Norfolk than the others. He's a friendly pup with his heart in his hand. Hereford's a mean old wolf. Waltheof trusts me just so far, belting up Norfolk when the lad said more than he should. From the Welsh border to Brittany: Then the Breton Hoël must be in this with them. Ambitious, but would such a tomorrow be so bad?

A line of rebels across England as Aelred hoped before York was doomed. His family released and every chance of winning. . . .

If.

A great many *ifs*. Robin wrestled with them back and forth across his chamber. When put to *if,* those chances were not without doubts. In war or weather, something always went wrong. One necessary element might be late, another lost through one mischance or another. When Robin shaded his mind's eye from Waltheof's light, the man had his weaknesses. He relied too much on his power to persuade and other men's constancy, lolled in confidence. More than one pretender had gone to the block when fewer men followed to war than flocked to their halls.

Aelred laid down his life for Waltheof; what froze a son's trust now? Yet, if it *could* come to be. Waltheof crowned, an English king again, Norfolk in his pocket, Brittany a comfortable Channel away . . . aye, but what of hard old Hereford and others like him? As men went, and Robin knew them better now, Roger de Breteuil was no more than a shave-penny miser like Ceolred, biting every coin for fear of being handed lead for silver.

When the fat boiled down, they didn't trust him worth a damn. For his taken weapons, all soft assurance but no hard iron. Whenever Robin's mind went forward with them, his instincts pulled him back to the forest and Will's teaching. No great buck worth his points gave the hunter much time for a clear shot. He could decide more surely and certainly breathe easier with a forest between himself and Mansfield.

Robin carried these thoughts through the afternoon and the seething courtyard. His bow had still not been returned and somewhere behind him would be the stolid west country carl. Cowled in his monk's habit Robin strolled in a leisurely circuit of the manor grounds, memorizing those open or incomplete sections of the wall a man might slip through by darkness. His walk threaded him through groups of Norman and Breton soldiers and between wagons. One was laden with bundled spears and arrows, another smelled of dried fish.

Standing by the wagon, he sighted Ralf Fitz-Gerald coming from Waltheof's bower. From long habit Robin went alert. The sheriff was unarmed, out of mail and alone, but making straight for him. Robin quickly spied the Norman soldier following at some distance. He turned and walked toward the chapel; with problems enough he didn't need the sheriff to compound them.

Still a long hour to Vespers and the chapel was empty. He'd heard Mass that morning but not yet said his daily prayers for the welfare of his family. Kneeling halfway down the small nave, he was not at all surprised to hear the scrape of a shoe at the entrance. That was his heavy-footed guard trying to be discreet. Then a lighter step came down the

nave behind him. Robin turned in a sudden surge of irritation. Watch if
they must but give him leave to pray.

Ralf Fitz-Gerald was almost on top of him. From pure reflex he sprang
up at guard—

"Robin, hold." Ralf held out empty hands, extending the right to him
and speaking in a voice louder than needed between them. "The earl's
peace binds me. And he has given me every reason to hold friends with
you for the nonce."

Robin glared at the outstretched hand. "What's that for?"

"Take it, fool." The warning barely moved Ralf's lips. "Every good
reason," he repeated for other ears than Robin's. "The earl bade me
take your hand and let us pray together. So I promised him."

Hare took the hand of hound, then Ralf flowed to his knees and crossed
himself. They were being watched; Robin knelt beside his enemy, unable
to resist the comment. "Well, here's new and different."

The response was a sibilant hiss. "Bow your head and pray. Have
you joined them?"

So they'd been at Ralf too. Robin wondered how much the man knew
and how far allied or against. "Not yet."

"They took my weapons." More, they separated Ralf from his men,
got them drunk and tumbling whores, talked at him for an hour. "You
know how much trouble we're in?"

"We?"

"Keep your voice down, idiot. Will you join them?"

"Against you and the king, why shouldn't I?"

"Leave cleverness to the earl, Robin. He's better at it. Are you one
of them?"

Robin would hardly be less cautious with a known enemy than a
potential one. "Think of me. Remember where Marian is and where you
put my mother. What have you and your king got for me but a rope?
Waltheof was my father's friend."

He heard the short, dry chuckle. "Friend? Who do you think sold your
father?"

What?

"What's that you say?"

"Waltheof sold York to William."

"You're a goddamned Norman liar."

"Look, I was there. William was willing to bargain for a quick victory
at York. Waltheof paid the Danes to go back to their ships, kept his title,

a place in the council, and sweetmeats like Mansfield for being a good boy.''

No, Robin couldn't believe that. ''He never!''

''Wouldn't he? You never wondered how Waltheof stayed in power when other earls died or went to prison?''

Robin's throat constricted; he felt physically sick. Someone had paid off the Danes. Aelred naturally thought it was William. Standing in the shield wall and going down under that last brutal charge that Robin still saw in dreams, outnumbered and without hope, his father never thought the traitor was one of his own. *None of us did. Jesus, Waltheof. . . .*

Ralf was whispering again, insistent. ''We've been enemies but you're an honorable man. Insane but honorable. Count me no less so because I am loyal to my king. Do you want to get out of here alive?''

Through a fever of rage, Robin hissed, ''What in hell do you think I've been praying for?''

''And I.'' Out of the corner of his eye Robin saw the man's shoulders shake with silent laughter. *''C'est drôle.* That I must trust my life to Robin Hood.''

''I ent got much love for you either.'' But at least both of the man's hands were fisted against him, not friendship in one and a knife in the other. Ralf wouldn't sell him. Yet. One move at a time, but think out the next five. ''Right, then. We'll get out.''

''How?''

''Leave that to me.''

''Need horses.''

''No, forget that.''

''Can't go on foot. They'll have us in an hour.''

Robin's turn to be amused. ''I've gone on foot for years and you've been that long catching me.''

That shaft went home in the clout. Robin heard the rancor: ''Not one to hide your light, are you?''

''Never knew the half of that light until you came.'' Robin raised his head and crossed himself, loosing a last sardonic bolt at Ralf in parting. ''Alms for Jacky?''

He'd left recklessness behind in Sherwood, in his own blood and that of friends or men who'd tried to kill him. Left worshipful ardor and most of belief to the like of Rolph de Gael and with them the impulsiveness of youth and open honor. Earlier that day Robin felt shamed and confused by his own distrust of a national idol like Waltheof. Now his motives and conscience were unclouded as Little John's and as ancient.

"You should have known Robin's father. There was a man." Oh, you're a wonder, Waltheof, you're solid gold. Ralf called us savages? In the old days when we were half Dane and wild as good hounds bred with wolves, there would be a death for you deserving of that term. I'd break out your ribs one by one, peel them back, and take your heart. We're civilized now and have the law, even a genius for it, as Mauger taught me, but we still write blood debts in the old ledger. You owe me, Waltheof.

But I'll let the king do for you, and when they set your head on a pole, I'll turn it with my own hands toward York. Toward your treachery, that you must look a better ghost in the face when my father judges you—

"Your grace! Good afternoon. And to you, my lord of Norfolk. No, no business, just taking the air before supper."

Meeting Waltheof and de Gael by chance, Robin showed them every warmth, not laid on thick but just enough. He had thought deeply on their course. Yes, he understood their purposes, agreed with their reasons, but—they must bear with him—there were doubts and reservations. About Fitz-Gerald since they would have truth. He would put his quarrel aside for the general good, but they could hardly expect Robin to embrace the man. Yes, the sheriff took his hand in the chapel and Robin would be as large. He'd seek the man at supper, try for amity, but could not promise. God keep their graces until then.

Robin did not ask again about his weapons but reflected the image they would readiest believe, a simple man dared to greatness, passionate but naturally hesitant at the brink. They didn't trust him yet and might not fully even sworn—unless he could sell them tonight as blithely as Waltheof sold Aelred. Robin took the earl's hand in parting. And smiled. *There's for my da.*

As the great hall filled for supper, Robin kept an eye out for Ralf. From years of eluding the man, he knew how nerve-racking constant danger could be and wondered how Ralf was dealing with the problem. Badly, he hoped. Servants and minor officers were taking places at the lower ends of the three long trestle tables when the steward entered with his white wand of office held before him. He was followed by a regal swirl of color amid the dun and black homespun of commoners: Waltheof and his Norman countess, Norfolk with pretty Agatha on his arm, the lowering Hereford who seemed to carry his own bad weather like a cloud overhead, then Count Hoël of Brittany, and Mansfield's chaplain. Robin spied Ralf Fitz-Gerald in their wake.

There was no special ceremony at the supper. The steward rapped for silence, the chaplain read a few verses of scripture, then a battery of servants scurried in, setting out dishes along the high and low tables. Waltheof seated his wife, then descended to Robin with his arm through Ralf's, directing them to the head of the central table.

"You here, Ralf. Robin there," Waltheof set them opposite one another. "Now be good as your word, son of Aelred, and take this man's hand."

Robin complied with a reluctance matched by the sheriff. Waltheof placed his hand over theirs. "And let me seal it so." He beckoned in a flash of gold-embroidered sleeve: Instantly two manservants were at his side, one with a covered dish, the other bearing two silver goblets and a generous flagon of white wine which the earl poured himself.

"From the Aquitaine," he flourished as if airing the pedigree of a fine horse. "The best of their vinyards. And the dish"—as it was set between their wooden trenchers—"bream and eels sautéed in the same vintage." Waltheof tore a bit of bread from a nearby loaf, dipped into the sizzling sauce and sampled it. *"Merveilleux!* A good sauce is like a good marriage: flavored with both ingredients plus the indefinable something more. *Bon appétit."*

He left them, wafting a faint trace of perfume in his wake. Robin broke off some bread and pointed to the delicacy. "After you."

"Pas de tout," Ralf demurred politely. "After you."

"Ta." In the midst of their peril, which was understated as one of Waltheof's jests, Robin could still feel a certain curiosity about his enemy now that they were for the moment at least not trying to kill each other. The man had a strong face, albeit trenched with the marks of their enmity: the pale scar from his jaw to his nose, the newer mark across his forehead. And the other from Ancaster. "How's your back?" he inquired with cordial malice.

"Well, thank you. How's your belly?"

"Still there—easy, man."

"What?"

"Don't relax, they're watching every move we make. You're my enemy; be a little stiff, not too eager to break bread with me. You can read a man's meaning from his body, and Waltheof's reading right now." Robin drank and refilled his goblet, casually setting the flagon out of

Ralf's reach. "You want it, reach for it and don't look straight at me yet. That's too friendly."

Ralf stretched across the table for the flagon. "God defend, I would not give that impression."

"What have you learned?"

"Not much. Just—"

"Don't *relax,* fool. You don't enjoy sitting this close to me, remember? And you ent a farmer."

"God be thanked." Ralf dipped into the eels and bream with a chunk of bread.

"Mayhap, but that don't teach you when to plant barley."

"As usual, you are incomprehensible."

"Never mind, just thinking out loud. Meet me at the chapel when the bell rings for Compline." Robin stretched far forward over the table for the wine, whispering quickly to Ralf. There was an unfinished gap in the new wall hard by the chapel which was their best and perhaps only chance. Surely guarded at night. Compline would ring at nine. The wall side of the chapel would be in shadow then. Clear on that?

"Clear." Ralf picked at the fruit on his trencher. "You're a good little Jacky."

"When I'm this scared, I'm that good." Robin lifted his goblet in a wry toast. "To my cousin Judith. I almost hope you live long enough to see her again."

"*Merci.* Almost the same to you."

"If we get that far. We could be dead before then if they don't believe us." Robin paused with the goblet halfway to his lips. A quick glance at Waltheof showed him attentively turned toward them. The earl greeted him with a wave of his hand. "And from here out, you little bastard, they've got to believe us."

Robin saw the reaction in Ralf's eyes and the stiffened shoulders. "Even in our purpose, I don't like that term. You're a foul-mouthed man from a foul-mouthed people."

"Now you're learning. That's the style. Am I indeed?" Anyone watching Robin then would believe him insulted past apology. He slammed the goblet too hard on the board and rose, tense and cold, leaning across the table to Ralf. "That's right, I've just insulted you. Up, Ralf . . . slowly, that's the way. Two dogs about to tear each other apart—*don't look away*. It's me you're about to dismember, nowt else in your mind."

"With pleasure," Ralf swore under his breath. "The last man who called me that—"

"Aye, they're watching. Now we'll give 'em summ'at to believe."

The men nearest them at table had stopped munching, alarmed by the murderous physical tension between Robin and Ralf. They were committed now, but escape was only part of Robin's strategy. As crucial was the information he must take with him. "And here's the easiest part of all, wee sheriff. Think how you'd love to piss on my grave and bed my wife."

Robin dashed his wine in Ralf's face; in the next instant the back of his hand lashed across the man's cheek. The nearest diners erupted from their places to get clear of fist or knife range as Robin, clearly demented with rage, launched himself at Ralf. They rolled in a heap on the floor, snarling and punching at each other. In a moment they were circled by Normans and Saxons alike, encouraging one or the other.

"*Bon! Encore!*"

"Pay him a good one, Robin!"

Waltheof and several men at arms broke through the hooting crowd and tore the combatants asunder, Ralf restrained by two beefy Saxons, Robin pinned by the earl himself and frothing to get at his enemy.

"Leave off, let me go. I'll kill him—"

"You will not. Stay, I say you will not."

"Let him," Ralf spat, wine dripping from his contorted features, blood from his nose. "Give me a sword. A knife. Anything. My bare hands."

"Hold him," Waltheof commanded. "And you, Robin, I'll break your head before you break my peace. I say *hold*."

"By holy Dunstan," Robin raged. "Don't ask me to make one with that. Steals my land, kills my men, that's not enough. He looks to bed my own wife."

"Liar!" Ralf shot back, struggling against restraint. "How many good men have you done for?"

"Take Ralf away," Waltheof ordered curtly. "Cool his temper. And you, Robin—"

"Aye, what? What? You'll give me reasons to hold peace with such as that. A *rat* has more honor."

"Come with me. Nay, come!" Still quivering Robin was dragged by Waltheof toward the small butler's pantry behind the high table. The earl slammed the door behind them and barred it. They were alone in the twilight from a single rush candle fluttering in the draft. Elegance had vanished from Waltheof's manner. As he measured Robin now, he looked like a merchant caught between impatient creditors. "You utter fool. I expected better of you."

"Expected what?"

"Patience and trust."

"Oh, indeed," Robin trembled. " 'Come with us, good Robin. Swear to us, son of my old friend.' Put my hand in that snake's—"

"Still yourself and listen. This is a great thing we do and dangerous as all such ventures must be." Waltheof paused on a note of despair. "Breteuil and Brittany: Even before I wear the crown their balance is delicate. A time will come when England is ours again, all the Midlands yours if you wish, but you must wait and hold faith."

"Then trust *me*." Robin countered flatly over folded arms. "Give me my weapons."

"When you make a peace with Fitz-Gerald I can count on."

"I'll raise the dead first. My lord, you don't need him."

"Listen to me. I've always needed him."

Yes, there was command and strength in Waltheof. He said listen and one did. Robin subsided a little. "Then for the love you bore my father, I would know why. Every wrong, every sorrow to my blood comes from him."

"Very simple. He commands a large force at Nottingham and through Sherwood."

"You tell me what any cowherd knows." Not entirely, but the picture came clearer now. A belt across England they said. Himself the popular ornament and Ralf the assurance that the belt was firmly buckled.

"No cowherd has my problems." Waltheof sank down on a barrelhead. "You're a farmer. Would you plow with bulls? That's what I've been doing for two years. Breteuil a bull in the west, Norfolk the too-eager bullock in the east—attack now, let us go now!—Count Hoël already asking more for his support than one can wisely promise. Once I told you I wanted to save what I could of England." Waltheof was not dissembling now, a man still young but aging rapidly from the ravages of his own ambition and their cost. "That's neither cheap nor always clean. I have had to make sacrifices."

Aye, you have that.

The earl peered at Robin through the gloom, hesitated then apparently decided. "In a month or six weeks, as soon as they can count on forage as they go, de Gael will march from Norwich and Breteuil from the west to join me. Beyond that you will know when you swear fealty to me. Which I must have tonight."

Therefore Robin must appreciate the value of Fitz-Gerald as an ally. As an obstacle he was too dangerously close to Mansfield. As the earl put forth his reasons, Robin appeared to be satisfied, but there was the matter of lands parceled out in the Midlands when Waltheof was crowned. "What's your grace promised him?"

"Enough." Waltheof grimaced dismissively, rising. "As promises to foreigners go. Once I'm crowned, such debts are less urgent. We are English and necessary. The sheriff is neither." He laid the hand of confidence on Robin's shoulder. "Are you with us?"

Robin frowned as if weighing all he'd heard while quelling his own confusion and anger. "My father taught me to be sparing of oaths."

"Rightly. They are what a man is measured by."

"Will you have mine here and now?"

"In the pantry? Oh, I think not." Waltheof's lightness returned. "I'd receive it in the latrine if need be, but we can afford some little solemnity. I am very glad, Robin. From this minute we build England again." He flung open the pantry door. The hubbub of the hall swelled in Robin's ears. "Come, Thane—or shall I say Baron?"

Robin managed to look both overwhelmed and ambitious. He allowed the earl to shepherd him through the hall. Waltheof had looked dingy in the pantry shadows; perhaps that light flattered himself no more. His skin crawled when the man touched him, but by way of survival he'd convinced Waltheof he could be bought in the man's own coin. Pray Ralf could dissemble as well.

A scant few minutes later, in Waltheof's bower, Robin swore total allegiance to the rebellion.

Ralf was nowhere to be seen. When Robin asked casually, the time had just gone eight.

42

ROBIN CROUCHED IN the shadow of the chapel's west wall. Compline
bell had rung. By twos and threes the clerics of Mansfield hurried to the
final devotions of the day. Not much moon and that as often clouded as
clear. Just as well for Ralf and himself. Robin anxiously scanned as much
as he could see of the manor grounds: And where *was* the Lord High
flaming Fitz-Gerald? With his life at stake, quick or dead, you'd think
the wee man might be prompt.

A light footstep behind him: Robin whirled with the small fruit knife
in his hand. Ralf glided closer in the darkness. "*C'est moi.* I avoided
the light."

"Were you followed?"

"No, I've sworn to Breteuil, had to. You?"

"Sworn tight," Robin said. "Candles, casket of relics, the lot."

"Did they believe you?"

"Ah, you'd have wept. *I* almost believed me."

Ralf felt gingerly at his nose. "*Vraiment,* you were too convincing at
supper."

"My heart was in it, Sire Ralf."

"But we've still no weapons." Waltheof promised them in the morning
which helped the present need not at all. Ralf glanced nervously toward
the gap in the unfinished masonry of the new wall, and the sentry crossing
it now. "We're not out yet."

"Quiet, I'm counting." How many sentries and where? One man was moving across the gap, now a second met him from the opposite direction. They paused to exchange a few words, one of them laughed, then they moved apart, each toward the shadowed limits of his post. Without arms they might manage one guard but two were chancy and time was against them now. "Took the carl off me but most like I'm already missed."

Ralf thought that probable. "Hereford took me aside and cautioned me to watch you."

"Lovely man. Search his own mum for a knife in her shift, he would. Get ready."

The sentries met and passed each other again. About fifty paces each from the gap before they turned back. Robin touched Ralf's arm. "When we go, move fast but stay behind me. I know where we're going. You don't."

They measured the wait in heartbeats, every moment and sound like Breteuil finding them out. The guards took forever reaching the far end of their rounds.

"Now." Robin sprinted toward the opening in the wall, Ralf close behind. They broke out of shadow into hazardous light, with each stride expecting a challenge or a man blocking their way with leveled pike. Now. They must have been seen by now. The guards weren't blind—

"Halt! *Arrêtez!*"

Robin dashed through the unfinished wall, urging Ralf over his shoulder. "Run!"

He hadn't allowed for a guard outside the wall. With his head half-turned he might have run himself onto the Saxon's leveled spear— "Robin, look out!"—but swerved as the man lunged at him, lost his balance, and sprawled. The guard shifted his grip on the spear haft to skewer him—as the scream and the shape behind it hurtled out of darkness like a stooping hawk. Ralf's feet hit the sentry in the soft midriff. The man doubled over with a bellow of exploded breath. Robin leaped on him. He plunged the small knife into the sentry's neck and was running again before the man fell. More shouting behind them. The two guards appeared at the wall opening.

"*Va,* go!" Ralf snatched up the fallen spear and launched it at their pursuers, then dashed after the dim figure of Robin streaking for the village beyond the manor grounds.

They dodged and swerved between houses, Robin surefooted in the meager light, Ralf tripping constantly over obstacles—

"*Merde!*"

—to be hauled erect and pulled onward. Laboring after Robin, Ralf lost all sense of time and most of his wind. Once clear of the village Robin crossed the meadow beyond in a tireless jog, slowing to a rapid walk only when Sherwood closed around them. When they stopped at last for too brief a rest, Ralf wanted to sit down but Robin denied him.

"Rest on your feet or you'll stiffen up."

"This is the wrong way," Ralf protested. "We should go east toward Denby. At this pace we could be there in an hour."

"And Waltheof sooner. There's likely horsemen bent there now."

"We need horses," Ralf labored out of his raw throat. "And a weapon or two would be advisable."

"No, Grantham's only twenty-five miles."

"On foot?" The high cliffs of impossibility rose up sheer before Ralf who had never walked more than five miles at one time in an otherwise hardy life. "Nottingham is only half that far and my garrison's there."

Robin was only too aware of that. "Once you're safe in Nottingham, where am I?"

"*Nom de Dieu,* you can be dense," Ralf breathed. "We need each other."

"In Sherwood you need me. Forget Nottingham."

"Half the distance means half the risk. Beyond needing you so much, you might consider it a point of honor."

"Ralf." Robin expelled his breath looking up at the pale moonlight filtering through tree tops. "If I weren't so scared, that would be funny."

"Laugh then. You'd be hanging on a spear right now if not for me. Look, we can go by way of Linby," Ralf argued. "You have loyal friends there, I've learned that much."

True, Alan and all his tenants and Ralf had a valid point. Twelve miles were less risk than twenty-five. "Nottingham, then, but if there's trouble, if we're cut off, we've got to run east for Grantham. Sherwood's going to be dangerous come light."

"Always the middle way."

"Tried to tell you that once, before all our troubles started." The sweat of exertion was drying clammy on Robin's skin. He wiped at his face. "Any road, thanks for back there."

Ralf shrugged. "Not at all, *Anglais.*" They stood in the near total dark amid overhanging trees, each a dim shape to the other. "There is something else while we touch on honor and needing." Though Robin could barely see the Norman's face paler than the dark around it, Ralf was suddenly diffident, turned a little away from him. "I did ask Marian to marry me."

No sound but their breathing and ghosts between them, Wystan and a woman.

"To be my *vicomtesse*. I thought you were dead and by God I hoped you were. She refused me, sent me away. That is the truth and the end of it."

"Thank you for that," said Robin. "You could have saved yourself the trouble."

In the gloom Ralf's reaction was inaudible but intense. Robin touched his arm. "Time to move before we catch a chill. Keep up with me."

"A moment." Ralf shook off his hand. "While we pause there are other truths you might add to your vast wisdom. First, never again call me bastard. A fact of life can still be insult. Secondly, never call any Norman a Frank. That also is an insult."

"You're all one to us, boyo."

"And that is my very point, 'boyo.' If there's one word for your people, every damned mother's son and daughter among you, it's *smug*. Save myself the trouble. Middle way. There is no middle way, just *your* way and nothing else exists because you are the *smuggest*—" Ralf gave it up. "Name of a saint. Let us go."

They struck out in a wide circle through the forest, veering south toward Linby.

They dared not stop again until near dawn. By then Ralf was shivering and soaked with dew from plodding along tracks he never knew existed but which Robin found in the dark. No wonder the man had eluded him for so long. He knew the forest like his own bower at Denby.

The moon was long down when Robin halted. "Light's coming soon."

None Ralf could detect. Black as pitch.

"You don't see it. More what you don't hear. Silence, then a breeze with a different smell."

They were not far from Alan's land now, in the last thick cover for a mile or so. Here they should rest until Robin knew they were safe. The morning wind came, then the first piping of small birds. With the first hint of light, Robin searched about them for something, found it and pointed. "There."

Where the hazel grew thickest, a doe's lair. Robin crawled into it with Ralf after him. The doe had pushed and rubbed an ample hollow space in the brush big enough for more than herself.

"She's carrying a fawn this time a year. Gone for water now. She'll know we're here and stay away. Better rest."

Ralf's head dropped on one sodden sleeve. He fell asleep almost immediately. When he opened his eyes pale daylight filtered into the thicket. Robin was thoughtfully stropping his fruit knife on a slab of tree fungus. "Good thing you don't snore," he noted, bent over his task. "The doe came back. Alan and the Bretons did not."

Ralf yawned, then sat bolt upright as the meaning sank home. "Bretons?"

Sure enough. Men in Hoël's livery scouring the wood, some mounted, others on foot. Alan and Wulf Edricson were with them plus a few other English from Linby, all with nocked bows.

Ralf rubbed at his eyes. They felt gritty, his whole body cramped and stiff. "But he's a friend of yours. He was always loyal to you."

"Always." The blade slid and turned, slid and turned over the fungus. "I've been pondering words like *traitor*."

"I see." With the knife in Robin's hand, Ralf thought he did. "Second thoughts? Have I become an inconvenience?"

"No." Robin slid the blade into the small sheath hung from his rope cingulum. "But we've no chance at Nottingham now." He seemed absorbed with a private problem that baffled him to some degree. "I didn't think of that. Alan would side with Waltheof and why not?" Waltheof had been as much of a hero to Alan as to Robin once, and the view from Linby Dale was not clouded with knowledge or complexity. To Alan, Waltheof would be England's hope. Any impediment to that was enemy to Alan, old friend or no. Robin rested on one elbow, searching the filagreed light overhead as if it held answers. "Waltheof doesn't see the long game. He's shrewd but not wise. You say you were there. Why did he sell us at York?"

Ralf massaged his aching feet that sent plaintive messages far up his stiffened legs. "Because he's a shit of a peddler like Hereford."

"Don't tell me that. There was more, had to be. He had honor once. He was a man." Robin struggled with a conflict clear to Ralf only in its smothered intensity. He saw Robin's profile, gaunt, the youthful roundness chiseled to planes. Once there'd been a deal of boy in that face, earnest and open as de Gael, who challenged him to trial by combat for a peasant as if that would have solved anything. The boy was gone, burned away.

Ralf rubbed at his punished feet and told the truth as he knew it. "William planned to make an example of all Northumbria. He couldn't afford a long siege before a walled city with his back exposed. As for Waltheof, you overestimate his virtues. He always waited to see which way the wind blew before hoisting sail. As you have pointed out so tiresomely, you are a race of bargainers."

The time was ripe for rebellion when the Midlands and Northumbria flocked to Waltheof in 1068. Add Danes and Scots and victory appeared certain. But William continued to advance. The inconstant Waltheof began to doubt. Was this the time to fight or bargain? Was this the way to retain power? He distrusted Danes and Scots alike and, in short, lost faith.

"Waltheof sent in secret to bargain with the king. He didn't count on Aelred and the other thanes moving north so quickly . . . or William's supply wagons being stopped dead at Tadcaster by a company of archers acting on their own. You recall that, I'm sure."

Robin lay back staring up at the twined branches overhead. "Yes."

The motives were clear. A bargain was cheaper to William. Waltheof wanted to retain power at any price. He sent money to the Danes, whiskey to the Scots, and the Saxons took the brunt. York was lost before the first arrow flew.

"Was it so?" Robin did not look at Ralf. "Don't lie to me."

"It is no lie," Ralf said doggedly. There were many things in this Englishman he would never understand. Waltheof was more of a realist; he knew how survival was managed in high places. "I carried the word between the earl's messenger and the king."

Robin lay silent a long time as the light grew a little brighter in their hiding place. "You've bred horses at Denby."

"Yes. I admire them." Loved them, really. In his present situation Ralf readily admitted horses more reliable than men.

"Then you may understand how I was raised to feel about the land. You have to care about it," Robin avowed. "While I healed from the wound you gave me, I learned to read. Did you know that?"

"My compliments."

"Learning's a fine thing: clothes your thoughts and puts shoes and even wings to their feet." One learned words and the different ways they could lean by way of meaning. "Traitor is a word. Patriot's another. Alan's a patriot, so is my mother. Waltheof will take so many patriots down with him before this is done."

Like Marian's last words to him, Ralf heard Robin speaking now from a far place in his soul. He touched the man's arm. "I understand."

"Do you, Norman?"

"You have not erred in this. For what it is worth, you will have my voice before the king."

"Ta for that but I want more out of this." Far more than family or blood feud as Robin laid it out in a farmer's terms. No matter who won, the common folk would bear the cost. Did Ralf ever see a whole village disappear from starvation? Or the few survivors selling themselves, free-men becoming *laet*-slaves just to feed their families? Crops burned or taken for forage, lives torn up. To such people either side in a war meant ruin. Even if Waltheof took the crown and managed to hold it against William and his sons, how long before Hereford convinced Norfolk and Brittany and all their hungry dogs following at heel that they didn't need Waltheof any more than William? What then? Years of war, years of hunger and misery, the people choking the roads, looking for someplace without a war, as Marian was doing when Robin found her.

"Do you follow, Ralf? Anarchy: There's a word. And English is a word, no more. Wherein's this an English rebellion? It ent that at all. Just power. I ask you, is this a way to plant barley or breed horses? Fields trampled or bad riders breaking the spirit out of good animals or making them brutes too mean to manage? If we wouldn't farm or breed so for one minute, is it a way to rule a country? *Is* it?"

Ralf might labor at comprehension, but there were leaps in Robin's thinking one could not follow. "You can't compare husbandry to rule."

"No." Robin shifted restlessly with bitter disgust. "Such as you never would. The men who fight don't sit next to the men who work. God made you for war and told you it was flaming glorious. Grab what you can, follow the king if he's strong enough, kill the poor sod if he ent, and to hell with the rest. Well, *I'm* the rest, Fitz-Gerald. Marian's the rest, and Will and Beorn and Tuck and Little John. Maybe Johnny more than all of us, goddamn his murdering soul. It's our lives you tear and worry between you, and we don't take kindly to that notion of husbandry."

"There are things a king must do to maintain power."

"Stuff your king. Let's have a look at your feet."

Ralf removed the wet wool wrappings. His feet were swollen and blistered, but he had refrained from complaint out of pride.

Robin clucked over the sight of them. "Small as Marian's. No wonder you ent much for walking."

Not much, Ralf admitted ruefully to himself. The narrow foot had always been the status mark of the knight who rode all his life, though a few calluses would be more useful now.

"Well, there it is," Robin shook his head over the martyred extremities. "Bleeding feet or no blood at all. We'd better move on."

Robin raised his head listening to the forest beyond their shelter. Satisfied at length, he crawled past Ralf to the entrance of the lair. He waited a long time before inching through the last of the hazel screen, then crouched, listening again. Finally he beckoned Ralf to follow. The sun was still not high and south Sherwood hazed with mist. That was their good fortune but they'd lose the advantage when the sun burned it off. From where they were was as far to Grantham as from Mansfield. A full day's walk for a man on foot. If they weren't stopped or forced to hide again, they might reach the royal manor by Vespers.

If they weren't stopped.

They crossed River Trent by an ancient foot bridge, unopposed. Once they had to lay soaked and chilled in a vine-choked rill while Bretons and Wulf Edricson's men clumped by and lingered interminably within a few yards. Toward noon they were almost caught. Thinking themselves well east of the searchers, Robin had kept up that wolf-trot pace of his until, crossing a stand of silver birch, Ralf collapsed on his stomach, panting.

"Got to rest. . . ."

"Not here. Too open."

Robin started to pull him up but Ralf shook him off. "Get away, damn you. I can't go any farther without catching my breath."

Even as Ralf gasped out the words, Robin's body tensed with a sense of danger. Ralf heard the distinctive whine and flinched as the long arrow buried itself in the earth a hand's span from his ribs. Robin sprinted away, the wet monk's robe slapping heavily about his long legs.

"Run!"

Ralf heaved himself up, running with no wind left, only fear. Another arrow whined past him as he dodged through the birches after Robin. A third grazed his sleeve and inspired him to double his effort. He forgot the agony in his feet and lungs, legs pumping as he thought they never could. Churning at the limit of his speed and strength, he dogged the bounding figure ahead of him into deeper forest. He ran until his heart must burst. When they broke out onto a barely defined footpath, Robin eased down to a trot again, then to a loping walk for the best part of an hour, finally to a heavy-breathing halt. Ralf's knees went out from under him, every muscle quivering. He felt nauseous; his stomach heaved up its meager contents, spattering in the bracken under him. When he raised his head, Robin was looking at him with a kind of pity and that eternal, maddening superiority that must allow for the inadequacies of outlanders.

"Don't . . . don't worry about me," Ralf rasped. "I'll last while you do.'' Robin held out a hand to help him up but Ralf struck it away. "Go to hell. Just go to hell.''

"You are a strong one, I'll give you that.''

"Damned right!''

Robin wilted down in the bracken, kneading his leg muscles. "Me, now, I'm a bit run out.''

Ralf glared murderously at him. The man was impossible. Robin had deliberately skirted villages. At least one of them was within Ralf's own holdings, another belonging to Bishop Osmund. "We might have gotten something to eat or even a horse.''

"Throats cut more likely,'' Robin said matter-of-factly. "Waltheof's on the move, has to be the minute he reckons we've got away. No telling who's with who among the nobles, but in the villages Waltheof's the hero and you're the enemy. We're the enemy. Ready to go?''

"I said so, didn't I?'' Ralf struggled up with an effort heroic in itself. Just standing tortured his feet. He disdained to wince. Robin himself, thank God, was no longer moving with his usual ease. That gave Ralf something to believe in. They lurched on as the eastern limits of Sherwood thinned and straggled out into open meadows. The horizon about them was smudged with smoke rising lazily from distant villages. Somewhere, faintly, the placid chime of a church bell lifted with the smoke as if rebellion and danger were distant chimeras and men had time to pray in peace.

Compline bell was ringing from St. Wulfram's when sentries on the manor parapet caught sight of two figures hobbling toward the barred gate. They moved slowly, like old men long miseried in every joint.

"Halt! *Qui va là?*''

The answer wheezed out of the night. "Open in the king's name.''

Now the two sentries came together over the gate, peering down at the strangers. "Whose men are you?''

A second voice came back in English, pallid as the first. "King's men, you silly sod. Open.''

Still unsure, the guards challenged again. The authority, when they could make it out, was no more than a slurred mumble. "Sheriff of Nottingham.''

With a third guard bearing a torch they descended to unbar the heavy timber portals. In the wavering torch light, the two men sat slumped against the gate posts, unmoving as the wood itself.

"It is the sheriff. Come in, my lord.''

Ralf made no move, not even the lifting of his head. "Presently. If you will, ask Sire de Coutance to come to the gate."

"Come? But—"

"S'il vous plaît," Ralf entreated in a reedy voice with the last of his strength. "You see it is that I cannot rise."

"And on your way," Robin croaked at the guard, "the lady in the small house yonder? Ask the guard to bring her and my son to the gate."

"Son . . . ?" The Norman knew Marian and the circumstances of her incarceration. He held the torch closer over the gaunt lump of exhaustion sprawled against the gate timbers. "Name of Jesus! Look who's caught in the catchpole at last."

"Just bring her, man."

43

A DRUMBEAT IN GRANTHAM, a stir of purpose felt like swift river current around one's feet under the tranquil sun of early May. Messengers dashed in and out of the manor gates at all hours to the creak of incoming supply wagons and a litany of armorers' hammers. Lanfranc arrived from Canterbury with his entourage, Matilda from Lincoln, constantly together now in the scriptorium or receiving an unbroken stream of postriders.

"From Nottingham, *ma reine*. The garrison stands loyal and ready. Bishop Osmund's levies as well."

The first bad news might have been predicted. Less than six miles from Mansfield, little Denby was overrun. Fortunately the troops were English, commanded by Thane Alan. None of Robin's folk was harmed, but the horses were confiscated. The sheriff's men had to flee for their lives.

"My queen, the messenger from Lincoln. Deliver your tidings, man. We are pressed for time."

"Your Majesty, de Gael and his wife and companions were sighted south of Lincoln. They've fled to Norwich. Skirted south of our city and took ship across the Wash."

"That boy did indeed bear watching," Matilda muttered to her imperturbable archbishop. "We will not advise William's return. The Scots would like nothing better. We will deal with this ourselves."

A skirl of preparate movement, a red stroke inching across the green

446

of spring. The pawns crouched as power pieces aligned. A dozen reins gathered in her small hands, Matilda could still be amazed at the appearance of Robin Hood in tandem with Ralf Fitz-Gerald and not prisoner.

"Wonders apparently never cease," she commented as the two enemies, now inconceivable allies, limped into her presence. "One could wish they occasionally paused."

Matilda surveyed the black-monk figure of Robin kneeling before her. She spared far more affection for Marian than her outlaw husband and had been privately relieved at the first news of his death. Naturally he disappointed her.

"My lady, vantage is ours," Robin urged. "The rebels must move now or lose everything, and there's no forage yet for them to count on." He nudged Ralf kneeling beside him. "Said you didn't know when to plant barley."

Matilda experienced some bewilderment. Somewhere this English Jacky-monk-chameleon had learned to speak functional if atrocious Frank. "Rise, messires. Well managed, Sire Ralf. As for you, Denby, you've flouted our authority for years. Now you insult the Church and the cloth. Why should we give you credence?"

"Allow me, madam." Ralf raised his head to her. "Neither of us would have escaped Mansfield without the other. I gave Robin good reasons to join with us and I know his own. They were freely arrived at and far more intelligent than Waltheof's."

"Sufficient for us to hazard on them?" Lanfranc inquired shrewdly. "What does this brigand ask for changing his flag?"

The price, yes. Matilda was on familiar ground now, the erstwhile outlaw in no position to haggle. "Pardon aside and parole conditional, what consideration does the thorn ask now that it is drawn from our foot?"

"My mother," Robin pleaded. "If she could at least be taken from the dungeon to better lodging."

Matilda could give him no assurance in this, having no authority to free William's prisoners of any stamp. "We will wait to taste the fruits of your loyalty first."

"Lady, I am here of my own will. I will be loyal."

And yet the queen did not quite understand why such a man would not align with the earl who was a native hero much like himself.

"Had I gone with him, madam, I might have been a baron," Robin told her. "When the queen reckons my loyalty, let her write that in the ledger for a start."

Perhaps. For the moment Denby might return to his wife and son, Ralf to the ministrations of the surgeon for his feet. "Come, Lanfranc. We have yet another full day's labor before us."

In the scriptorium several monk-scribes were at work on the ceaseless royal correspondence. Matilda dismissed them for the moment, desiring private conference with Lanfranc.

"What is the matter, good sister?"

Matilda fretted about the chamber, riffling aimlessly through sheets of ready parchment. "We thought England was secure. Obviously it is not. The thorn in our shoe becomes the spur to our horse. What do you think of Denby?"

"Behold the man: Robin Hood." Lanfranc spread his hands in absence of opinion. "I trust the sheriff who trusts him."

For that reason, Robin Hood would henceforth be in Fitz-Gerald's charge. "But at the first sign, one hint of defection or wavering loyalty"—Matilda drew a finger across her throat, a graceful depiction of violence—"*finis*. Meanwhile what he knows will be useful."

To Lanfranc, quite accustomed to interpreting the moods of this capable woman, something else nagged at his queen. "You are scrupled to some degree? The mother?"

"No—though perhaps, when weighed, there are worse felons. I was ill that day and Gilly full of spleen. No, merely that I have been unobservant."

"You? Never."

Matilda examined a batch of fresh quills for their points, wishing her awareness as sharp. "I am fond of Marian and Judith. They are so different. One loves as easily as her absurd cat purrs. The other, for all her acumen, is so maladroit at simple things. Did you note them all together in the hall this morning? Ralf's hand went to Judith but all too often his eyes went elsewhere." Matilda had noted the inconsistency before but never connected the occurrences or thoughts. "I offered him the wrong woman."

The Italian caught her nuance immediately. Judith was his former pupil; he knew her well. "Oh, I would say not, though the vavasor may be some time in coming to assess his good fortune."

That barely satisfied Matilda of Flanders. "How unperceptive of me." Her shoulders rose and fell in a resignation that accepted the tragicomic, wholly ridiculous nature of human passion. "*Bien*, to work. Scribes!"

* * *

For the fourth time in as many days, Judith endured the tale over, stitching new clothes for Robin who could not be torn away from his son.

"Oh, it was just *loovely*," Marian savored over her needle. "On our way to church and there on a sudden was Robin in the middle of Manor Gate like Jesus come again. Oh, Rob, I tell you my heart stopped then. Now, Edward"—as the boy let out a plaintive whine and struggled in his father's arms—"nay, love, give him to me."

"But I want to hold him," Robin protested. "What's wrong now?"

"Wants to get down."

"But—"

"He's that shy of you yet. Give him time."

Edward had been told over and over that this was his father but did not believe it on his own terms. In the little house, Mum and Judith and Perdu were his trinity. Beyond that were Gunstal and occasionally a small Tilda-somebody who smelled sweet and sent good things for him to eat. This huge stranger who came and went these last few days was a disruption and not accepted yet. He smelled and felt strange and held a body too close and tight. Edward endured captivity but kept his head resolutely turned away toward Perdu who was far more interesting, especially when he ruffled her fur the wrong way.

Robin reluctantly surrendered the boy to Marian. He shouldn't be too eager but let Edward's curiosity draw him back in the natural way of things. Released, the child staggered a few steps toward the cat, lost his balance and flopped on his bottom. Hardened by experience, Perdu moved warily to the other side of the hearth.

"And here are your new breeches." Judith tossed the garment to her cousin. "Put them on. I'll turn my back."

As Robin tied them at the ankles, Marian brought the new blue robe with gold piping just added to neck and sleeves. New fashions were seeping in from France, but Robin would none of their Flanders foolery or Paris-foppish nonsense. In court or hall, a man's robe should be loose, long, and dignified.

Turned away in decorous modesty while he shed the monk's robe, Judith hadn't looked directly at Robin much at all since he returned. He puzzled at the diffidence. Now she took her Psalter from the chemise case at her girdle and gave herself to reading.

"Because of Ralf," Marian had explained earlier in Judith's absence.

That was understandable. Robin slipped the robe over his head while

Marian tugged and smoothed the garment about his shoulders and slack waist. "It's loose on you. You're down nigh a stone of weight, I'm bound." Then with a whispering glance at Judith over her book: "Be gentle, Robin. She needs you to approve."

"Take Edward out for a turn," he whispered back. "Go on, the cat will thank you."

Marian quickly gathered up the child. "Judith, I'm just off to the market and back."

When they were alone, Robin bent over Judith's shoulder, reading from the open page. " 'For he hath not despised nor ab . . .' "

"Abhorred."

"—'nor abhorred the affliction of the afflicted; neither hath he hid his face from him; but when he cried out unto him, he heard.' "

Judith turned to him in admiration. "You astonish me, Robin."

"From the Chronicle and Beorn's memory, that's how I learned. You could tell he loved the Psalms the way he spun them out, every word tasted and not a one forgot." Robin poured some tea and sat on the floor beside Judith's stool. "One day I will make arrows from such words. I feel them sure in me like a grip on the bow."

Judith returned her attention to the Psalter. Robin let a few moments go by in silence. He was long past the brash bluntness that would have confronted her head on about Ralf. With a wisdom gentler than when he donned the coronet, he thought it better to come sideways at the matter, aligning himself not against Judith but with her in the face of more formidable opposition. This might put her at ease. "Here," he offered her the tea. "Drink while's hot."

"Thank you, cousin. Marian tells that story over and over, you know. About seeing you in the street. It was a miracle."

"Well, then, I have traveled, seen all England. Those Norman women at Mansfield—I tell you, Judith, when all women dress shameless as that, there'll be fires lit in every pulpit up and down the land."

"Speaking of Mansfield and miracles," Judith reminded him, "you and Ralf were the sly ones getting out of there neatly as you did."

"Since we're touching on Ralf . . ."

Judith closed her book. "I wondered at your mind in that."

"Well, we're not sworn companions yet." Nowhere near that but the world no longer wore the simple colors of old Denby or Sherwood. Someday he and Ralf would face each other again across another line drawn between his conviction and the sheriff's duty. That would be as it fell out; Robin wouldn't burden Judith with such now. "Years I've fought them and no more love for them now than when I started. They're a bad lot but Ralf is the best of them. That ent the coil, cousin." As Judith turned to him with the beginnings of relief, Robin presented the image of innocent consternation. "What in the world will we tell Mum?"

Judith flushed, returning her book to its case. "I have lain awake over that."

"I will speak reason to her."

"And I think you will need a whole witan for that."

But Robin saw the tension had faded from her eyes and the gratitude that replaced it. "Girl, you heard me argue reason with the king. Surely I can bring my own mother around."

"Just that I thought you would be ashamed of me."

"Because Ralf was not forced on you but a match you want?"

"More than want."

"There, you have my blessing." He reached for her hand. "As the world goes, we may profit by a vicomtess in the family. None of us are what we were when I came back from York. You've learned to scrub pots and I've learned to read. So we meet in the middle and Mum is yesterday." Robin fell silent over the cup and his cloudy thoughts. Yesterday: That was like putting a headstone to his mother, true as the fact might be.

Judith bent to him. "What is it, Robin?"

"Thinking of what you said long ago when I turned the knights from our door. It's their world now and a hard one, an ugly place. Mother has to live in it like the rest of us. Oh, enough of that. While Marian's out, there's summ'at else."

He rose and went to the new wallet bought for traveling. Robin rummaged in its depth and brought a folded square of parchment to his cousin. He handed it to Judith, suddenly diffident himself. "A letter to Marian. I wrote her every day while I was mending."

Judith didn't quite understand. "Every day?"

"In the dirt by my bed. No parchment to spare. This I wrote in the hall last night. Something I want her to have later."

He'd be leaving soon, he said, going to find Will and Morgan and others like them for the queen. Marian would have word of him with every postrider sent to Grantham. So he intended, but the only constant in an army was that nothing worked right or the way one expected.

"Riders are delayed or lost or never come at all. You get one of those dry spells, a week or so, break the seal and read this to Marian. No,'' he scoffed at her, ''don't pull a long face at me, girl. No fear: I'll be safe enough when we come to it.''

Letters galloped westward to men known to be loyal: Aethelwig, the abbot of Evesham, and to Wulfstan, Bishop of Worcester. The English prelates had no great love for William, Matilda knew, but even less for the chaos of revolt.

It is our wish that you contain Breteuil by any means. You need not engage unless pressed, merely prevent his power from joining with that of Waltheof. *Delay* is your ally, your object, and Hereford's enemy.

The stress on *delay* was Lanfranc's, who wanted no more bloodshed than needed. The postscript smacked of Sherwood.

Make all good use of bowmen if attacked.

The king was not to be distracted from the Scottish crisis. To Lanfranc's reassurances that the situation was in hand, Matilda added her own wifely comments.

You must not fear the matter will run loose, Gilly. This plot, when examined, is too clumsily conceived. More Saxons align with us than with these renegades. Among our unlooked-for allies, if you can survive astonishment, is the former Thane of Denby, Robin Hood, whose purpose to thwart Huntingdon approaches obsession. Your first instincts about Denby were precise as usual. He is impressive but do not ask me to tell how. For his fealty, which we trust only so far as we must, he has asked no more than the release of his mother. To this I will add my personal urging.

William's reply contained meanings in a code often employed between them. He would return secretly as soon as possible. Meanwhile he retained a firm and intractable grasp of the situation.

I will pause on the release of any prisoner, man or woman. Use Denby but keep him on Fitz-Gerald's rein. In the matter of Norfolk and the Danes, use your discretion which I trust implicitly. You know what to do.

With his Breton connections, Rolph de Gael was the key. The rebellion was not so poorly planned as Matilda first thought, but forced to engage before its elements were securely joined. Cut off in the west before he could fully mobilize, Hereford could only wonder how Waltheof fared. In Mansfield, Waltheof found himself effectively checked by the Nottingham garrison. There were a few skirmishes; he marched his men this way and that only to find himself frustrated at each attempt and with few supplies beyond those he began with. For the first time in his charmed life, Waltheof was conscious of a grave error in judgment.

"Error? I would call it disaster to have counted on Fitz-Gerald," his wife chided him. "That nobody! You think because you take such a creature to your heart, you win him to your side?"

"No," Waltheof worried over his wine and the map. "The wrong nobody was Robin."

"The rustic? Ridiculous!"

"You did not see him then, lady. There might have been a very demon in him playing at monks and modesty, playing at rage so well that he *sweated* choler. The man has no scruples at all."

Waltheof concentrated on his map, trying to guess where Norfolk would be now and in what state of readiness. Rolph was unimpeded so far. The cause was not yet lost. If he could move west fast enough, the two of them would still be a formidable threat to William. Brittany was still with them, only Hereford was cut off. The earl stared at the picture of England until his eyes ached from trying to foresee royal strategy. Who would they unleash to stop Rolph de Gael and where?

A similar map was spread over a table in the scriptorium at Grantham, lit by rush lights. Matilda, Lanfranc, and the readiest assistants to hand, Ralf and Robin, stood about it. Since the queen wanted him here, Ralf's forces at Nottingham were commanded now by capable lieutenants. If the west and Midlands were contained, the east could still ignite the whole country, and there was an element of which Robin was ignorant until Ralf mentioned it over the map.

"Danes?" Robin stared across the table at him. "Swein Estrithson?"

"Swein is dead, but his son Cnut still asserts Danish sovereignty in England."

Neither the queen nor Lanfranc appeared surprised by the intelligence. "They're leagued with Danes," Robin said heavily. "Why didn't you tell me?"

"Breteuil informed me when I swore to him. After that," Ralf recalled, "we were more occupied in getting out with whole skins. Cnut will land on the Norfolk coast. You know what will follow."

"That is why Norfolk's defeat must be total and swift," Matilda said. "The coast will be burned before the Danes land. Every field, every mouthful of food and handful of grain. Nothing will be left for raiders. Denby? You have some comment?"

"Nothing, madam."

But there was something. Even Lanfranc noticed the distaste like a flinching in the Englishman. "A very heavy nothing I would say."

Robin dropped his eyes to the map, seeing beyond the lines of march and attack to burning fields. "The sheriff knows my mind in this. It begins, doesn't it, Ralf? Why didn't you tell me?"

"Why didn't Waltheof?" Ralf countered. "That's how much they trusted you. They knew you'd be against it, might even turn round at the wrong time and fight the Danes."

So he would, but that was aside from the present need. Robin forced himself back to the tactics of advance and countermove. If he were de Gael, how would he move and where?

Matilda pulled her shawl closer about her shoulders. This long past midnight the air was cool. "Where may we best confront him?"

Poring over the map, Robin read more than was drawn there; matters like soft soil, the likelihood of rain to slow progress. His finger came down at a point halfway between Ely and Cambridge. "Here. The first chance Norfolk has of swinging north on firm ground."

Matilda reflected on the advice and position. "Lord sheriff, do you think what I think?"

Ralf did. "Richard de Guilbert."

"Who's that?" Robin asked.

"Baron of Buckden and Newmarket."

Baron Richard de Guilbert—young, competent, no doubt of his loyalty. His holdings lay just north of Cambridge where he commanded some of the best cavalry in the east. With no further hesitation, Matilda went to the scriptorium door, threw it open, and snapped an order that echoed through the silent empty hall. "Geoffrey? Anyone? Messenger!"

44

*A*BOVE ALL ROBIN wanted to join the forces keeping Waltheof at bay.
When he thought of the earl's smooth treachery, how he'd killed Aelred
and nigh seduced himself, Robin wanted to burn Mansfield with Waltheof
inside and sow his hides end to end with salt. Every day he haunted the
hall and scriptorium. The "long belt across England" was severed in
three parts, Breteuil ineffective in his western keeps, Waltheof unable to
move. *Go in and get him!* Robin raged, discarding the folly in the next
breath. That was playing for pieces again. The long way was shortest.
*You can't move, my lord, and it's enough for now that I scotched you
myself.*

His heart and purposes were composed. He knew the measure of what
he did when he knelt to the queen and swore his oath of fealty. "Edward
of Denby, you gain everything in this," Matilda told him after her re-
ciprocal oath. "You lose nothing."

Not quite nothing. There was his innocence, which had only proved
an impediment. For gain, he'd just begun, though in no coin a Norman
would reckon.

Once sworn, the guard was removed from Marian's door and life.
On Robin's parole she had the freedom of Grantham, and the erstwhile
prison house became more like a home. Judith once more resided in
the manor house. As often as opportunity presented itself, Robin pressed
for his mother's release. Now and then Robin and Marian took dinner in

455

the hall—below the salt to be sure, but enjoying the sight of Judith at the high table with her intended husband.

"I could feel spiteful," Marian admitted. "She's that beautiful."

Munching his dinner, Robin allowed they were a handsome enough couple. Many things were dead and past. Even Maud would see that in time after she came up out of captivity, God willing. If the sun didn't shine as brightly on her world as before, well, Mum must like or lump because that world was changed. In that much she could learn from Ralf and Judith.

He doesn't love her and she knows it. I'm sorry for that, but in the way she takes his arm you can see that ent the abiding matter with them. She's glad of it, going to be Lady of Nottingham, get flowers handed to her by tradesmen's children on feast days, and by God she'll be a flower to the town itself.

Robin went on eating, remarking casually to Marian, "Wonder if she's good in bed."

"Who?"

"Judith."

"You rotten old pig." Marian kicked him under the table. "Your own cousin!"

"Ow! I was just speculating. When they come down to it."

"For all I know, you talk the same about me."

"No, I never!"

"Mind your mouth, then. Ought to wash it out with the linen."

The manor gates stayed open after dark now as messengers came and went with orders and reports between the crown and Richard de Guilbert.

. . . must assume de Gael on the march from Norwich within ten days. Dear Richard, as we repose all trust in you, do not engage on the first hasty reconnaissance but choose carefully both time and ground.

Ralf had studied de Guilbert's intended battle array with some reservations. He didn't doubt the baron's competence but the few archers he proposed to field seemed hardly adequate to any engagement or siege. Ralf brought the matter to Matilda's attention one afternoon while she rested between letters and orders. "It is clear, *ma reine,* that the baron does not share my respect for bowmen. I strongly suggest he add more."

"Ralf, my embroidery is there by you. Give it to me." Matilda took up the fine intricate work that so relaxed her. She hoped someday to do something truly creative in the vein. "Lanfranc and I do not drowse at our charge. Why do you think we have kept yourself and the best archer in England here with us instead of loosing you to reek havoc on Waltheof, as indeed Denby longs to do? Your orders were writ this day.''

We direct that Ralf Fitz-Gerald, Lord High Sheriff of Nottingham, form and command a company of one hundred English archers to be attached at the earliest date to the levies of Richard de Guilbert, Baron of Buckden. It is our further pleasure that Edward of Denby, having renewed his fealty to us, be appointed captain of archers subject to the commands of our trusted Fitz-Gerald.

"Now, that's a delicate matter,'' Robin stressed as he and Ralf dodged across the manor grounds between armed horsemen clattering toward the gate in twos and threes. "I can find you the best in the world, boyo, but every other man's a price on his head for taking the king's deer and not likely to come skipping out of the forest for me or anyone else without some surety. Hallo, Marian!''

They halted amid the jingle and clatter of the passing knights. Marian had just emerged from their house to walk Edward a few steps before the noise and size of the horses convinced him life was safer in her arms.

"Mind out the horses!'' Robin shouted to her over the passing din. "I'll not—here, you!'' he warned a knight, jumping out of the huge horse's way. "Ride that bloody beast or eat it, one or the other. Marian, stay back. I'll not have these great lummoxes running you down.''

"No fear, love,'' she flashed back gaily. "I'm used to 'em.''

"You mind me and take care!''

She stepped back to safety but there was a sight for a man to nourish on: his son wrapped in her arms and the silly three-legged cat perched on her shoulder, wary as the child. Not much time left before he must ride away from them. The queen and Lanfranc demanded his every other hour, it seemed. The two were sensible folk for foreigners, when you came to it. The Eye-talian it was who speedily amended Ralf's commission.

Such men enlisted by Sire Fitz-Gerald shall enjoy royal amnesty saving they commit no further offense against the king's forest laws.

The first would be Will Scatloch and Morgan of Powys. Mauger would clamor to be there, of course, to see the adventure and likely write of it someday, and Father Beorn because Robin could not imagine life without that steadying strength beside him. Tuck and Much should have been there; they'd have paid Norfolk a good one or three. *And where are you, John Littlerede? Not that I'd have you.*

Daily the forces assembled at Grantham, poised to be sent where needed. On the fourth of May a servant knocked on the door of Marian's small house, a young page bearing the news that Queen Matilda would inspect Castle Hough next morning. *Le maître* Robin should be ready to ride in her appanage. Robin had already heard the rest of the news.

"Ralf and I, we'll be leaving from Hough."

"So you won't be coming back?"

"Not for long if we do. There's my men to gather." Robin poked in the ashes of the fire pit with a kindling stick. "Form the company, you know."

Marian asked, "You'll see Mum at Hough?"

"The queen intends that much at least. And as soon as we're done with little de Gael. . . ."

"Yes." Marian lifted the lid from the soup she was warming for their supper. "Judith knows. She sent us some wine for tonight."

Robin observed his son and Perdu in one of their brief truces. The cat touched her nose to Edward's, then washed his face with her rough tongue. Robin refused to dwell on chances and brevities. They'd go to Mass before supper and Robin prayed the boy wouldn't pull away when his father wanted to hold him. After supper they'd drink the wine and make love, and Robin would have the memory of Marian beside him and the boy bundled in his blankets.

"We'll need to be quiet," Marian suggested tactfully. "Wake him up, he's the devil to put to sleep again."

Robin embraced her from behind. "Quiet as wanting you can be, though I'll not make a secret of the matter."

"Ach, he'll be all eyes." For something to busy her hands Marian stirred the spoon through the thick soup. "God in heaven, Rob, but I'm weary of saying good-bye to you."

They went to Mass and later drank the strong red wine with supper. They sang softly together with Edward cranky and at last dropping off in his mother's arms.

"I'll put him to bed," she said.

"You put his bed. I'll hold him." It was a plea. Robin eased the boy against his chest, devouring everything about his son, glad the child was too near sleep to be shy. The soft hair was darkening and smelled sweet from fresh rainwater washing. *You'll be a big shire lad when you're grown. One day when I'm an old da by the fire, you'll stand taller than me. I'll never look to any man's son hereafter without seeing you. To think I was put off when Will wanted to buy his own free and I put a price on them. I'll tell this to you because you're a man and we'll keep it privy between us. Your mother gave me tomorrow in the gift of you. Now I must go give the same to folk like us. Right enough, loving teaches a man.*

Morning was already lightening between Matins bell and Prime when Ralf awoke. His needfuls were bound up last night and ready for the pack mules, since he'd be traveling on with Robin from Hough. May was warm for riding in armor; the mail and scale-iron coat would be left off until needed. He dressed in sturdy new linen trousers and long English tunic, choosing the lightest mantle he owned for the journey. When he enlisted men with Robin, Ralf wanted as little as possible about him to proclaim Norman to them. The sun was barely over the treetops when one of the female manor servants knocked on his door to announce that Lady Judith waited him below in the hall. She would take breakfast with him before hearing Mass, if that was the sheriff's pleasure.

"Tell the lady I will join her presently."

A pleasurable surprise and one to bring a smile. Since Judith's liberation from the tyranny of the manor kitchen, she never left her bed a minute before necessary and sometimes forwent breakfast altogether. She had risen specially today to see him off.

When Ralf descended to the hall, two yawning male servants were setting the last of the trestles in place for the household breakfast. Judith sat alone at one table, striking against the background of her drab surroundings, in yellow linen kirtle over which her new blue mantle was draped casually. She was not veiled, but the raven-black hair had been done up in ivory combs with meticulous care. The thought occurred to Ralf that considerable art had gone into the appearance of artlessness.

"Good day, Ralf."

"Lady, this is charming." He seated himself on the bench opposite her. Judith had procured hot bannock cakes from the kitchen and was covering some with butter, others with sweet pork fat. "You are kind to see me off."

"I planned to. Don't take that one"—as Ralf reached for a bannock to one side of the dish. "Emilie left a dead fly in the batter." As Judith had suffered beyond measure under the cook, she was saving the evidence. "She is an abominable cook and a slovenly bitch in the bargain. I will be morally delighted to bring this to the notice of the chief butler."

Her conversation pleased as well as her person. Ralf took the mug of spiced tea she poured for him and pretended not to notice when Judith covered a small yawn.

"In certain light, Judith, there is violet in your eyes."

"I haven't thought of that for years." But his notice obviously pleased her.

"I've spoken to the queen. When I return from duty with de Guilbert, there's no further reason to delay our marriage."

She wanted to know if the matter of the rebels would mean a long campaign. Ralf sensed she meant a severe one. "I think not."

"Good," she said. "We need peace as a wound needs bandage."

"Now you sound like Robin."

"He would know. He was virtually born in the forest; knew the fields by the time he was ten." Judith put down the bannock she'd been nibbling daintily. "When we were children there was always dirt ground into his knees. One needed armed force to tub and scrub him down. A part of him died when he had to leave Denby. And Aunt—" Judith tactfully changed the drift of her conversation. "They have an almost mystical feeling for Denby. The Church is their religion but Denby is their faith."

And he himself had sundered them from it. "There are those things I have had to do and many I regret, Judith."

"*De rien, mon cher,*" she absolved him gracefully. "I simply wished, once we are married and you invested, that they be given every reasonable consideration." Her violet-hinted eyes flicked up at him and down again. "In so far as you can within the law."

"The law and Robin: That is telling the deer to be considerate of the arrow. Thank God you have lived in Normandy; we meet easier in understanding. I have heard Robin's thoughts but still cannot fathom what the man means or wants. You might call us respectful enemies. But I will do what I can. You have been humiliated enough."

"Mine was least," Judith shrugged. "Only a slaver of a cook over me. But for Aunt and Robin—because you see no tears, do not think there's been no weeping."

Ralf would never assume that about any of the English now. He took a third bannock cake from the plate. Judith was studying him, chin on her hands. "You have a cool way of appraising a man, Judith."

"That disconcerts you?"

"Should it?"

"Many men find it uncomfortable for a woman to think at all. I was putting you next to my cousin, contrasting your colors. Yours are more complex."

"God shrive me of that. You do not know how I yearn for the simple. Thank you for breakfast."

"Don't go yet."

"I have a little time still."

"I have been working on my trousseau. The queen's women help when they can."

"Good, demoiselle."

"Of our marriage." Judith spoke with audible hesitation now, a marked departure from her usual confidence. "I will not pretend the arrangement does not make me happy."

To Ralf's surprise, she had suddenly become shy and stiff, as if she were unsure of herself.

"I will not expect to hear the conventional perjuries of courtship. Such things as declarations. Words have always been too easy for me and as lightly held. It is the simple that eludes me. But arranged or not, I knew from the first day at Denby that such an alliance would please me."

Ralf said quietly, "Thank you."

"However, I am not blind."

Ralf apprehended her meaning, and perhaps that strain made discord through the words she wanted to hear from him despite her rather studied protest. He knew her better for the insight, this oddly fragile woman who always kept feeling at bay with facile intellect but tried to face the fact of Marian with a candor that touched him. He reached for her hand. "Lady, will you look at me? No, you are not blind, nor I a liar. Grant that, grant as well that if I once dreamed, I woke. Did you know—no, don't look away, Judith. Please."

"I am shy," she resisted. "This is strange to me."

"Lovely as you are?"

"Don't tease me!"

"I swear I—"

"Shy is not stupid," Judith flared suddenly. "Put to it, I dare say my mind is quicker than yours."

"*Sans doute:* far quicker."

"Simply that there are questions I will not ask. Ever."

"You need not. As for the conventions, shall I tell you something?" Ralf tilted up her chin so that Judith must meet his gaze. "There are legions of women who can be beautiful by candlelight, but by Saint Gervais, you are the first I've ever known to enchant in the early morning. That is a gift.''

Judith flushed and typically deflected the compliment. "If somewhat assisted. *Merci, Ralf. Et bonne chance.*''

"To you also, my lady. And for the rest"—Ralf lifted the offending bannock—"let the cook stand accountable for her villainous cakes.''

"She'd profit from a flogging,'' Judith judged on a note of anticipation, rising to take his arm. "Until you return.''

"Will you come to the stable with me?''

"In the old days I would have come to the very battle,'' Judith asserted. "Verily, and stood where you could see me with my breast bared that you fought the harder to hold what was yours.''

As they passed down the hall toward the pantry, Ralf conceded that would be inspiration of a heroic mold.

"Robin said you called us savages once. To the contrary, we've become too civil,'' Judith reflected. "The Church has endowed me with too much modesty for such display and Dame Nature too little to inspire you with. Ah, Master Butler, there you are.''

Judith held the tainted cake at arm's length for the butler's inspection, an indictment before his eyes. "Our Emilie will be better at scrubbing pots than poisoning the queen's household. Regard the insect here entombed and see to it.''

The sun, still low, sent long slant shadows over the queen's train forming at the stables. Ralf heard the familiar jingle of harness and clatter of shuffling hooves, mail, and weapons with no eagerness at all. Once he'd trained his life to this with the passion of a priest; now he prayed with equal fervor that this setting out would be the end of it. Wounds became scars that healed white and tough, but there must be an end to scarring.

Judith watched the grooms cinching saddles and stowing gear. "There will be your folk and mine on both sides. No, this will not be clean at all.''

To Marian, with the stretch marks of birth on her stomach, no one got even a little way through the world but its marks were on them. She recalled an old *wicca* woman up Tadcaster who owned a human leg bone with regular lines that showed where the mortal rested a bit in growing and then got to it again. So with life, Marian judged. So with Ralf and now the deeply indented scar on Robin's stomach from the wound that nigh killed him. She kissed the scar often that night. Not to wake the child, their lovemaking was tender and quiet, like hands joined over the oak or placed together in prayer.

She slept in the crook of Robin's arm and came reluctantly awake with the growing dawn sounds from the courtyard, knowing it a fault to lie abed now when she must ready oatmeal for her husband and son. Her head was no longer on Robin's shoulder. Marian rubbed the sleep out of her eyes and turned over. The house was already warm, the peat cooking fire started. Robin was dressed for traveling in his short Lincoln tunic and trews, the leather jerkin hanging with his wallet on a peg by the door. He was seated on the floor by Edward's pallet.

Marian started to speak, shaped her lips to his name, but something stilled the sound. She could see only the top of Edward's tousled head but knew he was wide awake as surely as she did when he was too quiet and she looked to see that he wasn't in trouble or swallowing something he shouldn't.

No—lying awake and very still, answering his father's grave watch over him with fascinated silence. They were speaking without words and Marian would not intrude if they went on so for hours. They didn't have hours.

Robin raised his eyes and smiled at her. "I made the breakfast fire."

"Ta, love." Marian pushed back her hair and got up to make the meal before he went. They didn't speak of leaving or where or why. A gap had been bridged, since Edward allowed himself to be kissed this morning. Then a knocking at the door and waiting men and horses beyond it. Ralf saluted her from the saddle and there were the queen's horsemen strung out behind him.

Robin squeezed the boy once more and put his arms about Marian. "God bless, girl."

"God bless. You'll tell Will I asked after him?"

Easier to kiss him and take the boy inside than to tell the man how much of dying this held for her. Not a full month of nights together since they were wed and still more of good-bye than meeting. How desperation could turn bitter and even prayers cloy on a wife's lips. Kings and great lords gave commands, great actions moved forward and something called history got writ down in a great book Robin told her about. But why him? Why her? *Why us? damn you,* Marian prayed and flayed at her God fiercely. *Ent there marring enough on us? You set things to right and stop this . . . please stop. How strong are we supposed to be, you careless, wasteful old man?*

45

THE TINY VILLAGE of Hough lay only seven miles north of Grantham, a pleasant morning's ride in good May weather. The new motte and bailey castle, commanding the highest ground, was one of a line of timber fortifications rapidly erected by William on his march against York and Northumbria. Such forts were as uniform as Roman camps. A huge circular ditch was dug, as much as three hundred and seventy paces in circumference, and the dirt piled in the middle to form the high mound on which the square or round two-storeyed timber keep was built. A retractable bridge connected the keep to the stockaded bailey below which was crammed with barracks, stables, cook house, armory, and all activities necessary to maintenance. Hough had not proved strategic after the fall of Northumbria but might be a liability now if Waltheof broke out of Mansfield. The castle-fort, under the command of the castellan Sire Stephen Baudreux, required inspection for readiness in case of attack, or might be razed at William's order rather than fall into rebel hands.

A dungeon had been dug out of the mound under the floor of the keep. Several English thanes had languished or died in it since Hastings. Now the primitive earthen chamber housed Maud of Denby. For reasons of her own, not the least of which was compassion, Matilda would allow a brief visit between Maud and her son.

Once inside the bailey, the queen left inspection to the knights of her appanage. She gave her palfrey to the grooms and called for Sire Stephen, who hurried down from the parapet, a squat, battered stump of a man in his fifties, scarred and with few teeth, the dependable sort of knight William preferred for guarding his back.

After greetings, Matilda inquired of the castellan, "How does your prisoner? We would see her."

The woman? Baudreux could not say precisely. He had not seen her personally for several months.

Something turned over in Robin's stomach. *Months?*

"We will see her now. Be so good as to accompany us, Sire Stephen."

From bailey to keep was a considerable climb, more than fifty wooden steps which the small queen managed with a firm grip on the castellan's arm. Robin, Ralf, and the queen's attendants followed in her wake. This was Robin's first close look at the inside of a Norman bailey. He shivered entering the keep. The lower floor was no more than an ill-kept guard-room, the floor planks covered only here and there with old rushes like the hair on a mangey dog. There was little furniture: a large, backed chair with heavy arms, two stools, and a rough table warped and stained from years of spilled food and wine carelessly wiped away or not at all. And somewhere in this filth they kept his mother.

At a snap of Matilda's fingers, one of her chamberers tugged a cushion from its velvet bag, placed it on the seat of the backed chair, and bowed the queen to take her place. Matilda drew her blue mantle closer against the draft, a perfumed handkerchief to her nose to ward off the pervading sour smell of ingrained dirt. "Bring out Lady Maud."

Baudreux motioned to the guard waiting at the door. "*Ouvrez.*"

The sentry grasped an iron ring that lifted a trap built into the floor. He brought a ladder from one wall and lowered it into the pit below. "Woman, come up. You there, woman!" He called again. "You are to come out."

Robin stepped to the open trapdoor, appealing to the man. "Let me. I will help her."

As he knelt over the square of darkness, a sharp, acrid stench struck his nostrils as from an opened grave: poisonous air, dampness, and human waste. A dead-white hand grasped a rung of the ladder. The woman made her slow, stiff way up the ladder, reaching for Robin's outstretched hand; as she did, Robin heard the muffled, pulpy ripping of a damp-rotted seam.

"Mother. . . ."

"Close the trap after her," Baudreux ordered. "The place stinks enough."

Robin gagged back the cry in his throat as Maud stepped out onto the floor. She wove on her feet, a starved, scrofulous ruin blinking against the light not often seen in a year and a half. Her veil was gone. The linen might have been used for a wash cloth until it fell apart or simply been discarded as too filthy to bear against her skin. She had lived in the clothes worn when brought in irons to this place. They were rotting away from her. The once lustrous chestnut hair had gone dull and mostly grey, damp-matted over the blotchy parchment-white skin of her face.

Robin put his arm around the wraith of her, torn at the heart by the clammy smell of her clothes and skin. "Mum, it's me."

She might have seen him, a point beyond him, or nothing at all. Her eyes kept closing against painful light. One mottled hand lifted again and again to shade them but forgot its errand before touching her brow and returned to the compulsive motion of scrubbing the other. Robin led her to a stool by the table, glancing at the queen. Matilda's expression was difficult to interpret. Robin knelt by Maud, prisoning one hand in his. "Mum, look at me."

Her ghost-pale features shadowed slightly with recognition. There was a congested, phlegmy sound to her voice. "The light hurts. I can't see you well. Puck-Robin?"

"Aye, Mum."

"Oh." She bent toward him slightly and said in a rasping whisper, "They told me you were dead, but I wouldn't believe it."

"Not me. No good fox leaves himself only one way out of his den."

Maud blinked at him. "And Marian?"

"Has a son. A boy named after me."

More accustomed to the light now, Maud's sunken eyes lit with a flicker of awareness. She seemed to recognize Matilda and the dark man who usurped her home and tricked her into this place. Her lips writhed back from discolored teeth. "What are *they* doing here?" The grimy hands scrubbed at each other. "Oh, you are taken, then?"

"No, Mum. I'm free."

"Be wise then. You must . . ." The thought merely evaporated while another returned. "You have a son? Then he will make the bargain. We must school him to be ready." Maud bent her head closer, as if strangers had come unbidden into Denby's hall and she would know why. "Robin, why are these people here?"

He told her again: no fear, he was a free man. Maud surrendered to a fit of deep, hollow coughing. She clutched her son's hand with no more strength than infant Edward. "You must go to Earl Waltheof and place yourself under his protection. There was none your father trusted more.

It is just that I am so dirty. They hardly give me enough water even to drink and . . . and they do not change the other bucket often enough.''

Ralf caught Robin's eye. The sheriff had remained respectfully silent but now canted his head slightly toward the door: They must be riding on.

"Wait, Mum," Robin said. "I'll speak to the queen about that."

He rose from Maud's futile hand washing and approached Matilda whose embroidered handkerchief was now balled tight in one hand. A tiny doll of a woman whose feet did not even touch the floor where she sat, yet the full power of William here in this dirty place. Robin knelt by her chair, keeping his voice low. "Lady, this was all I asked. Now I beg you. My mother is dying. Let her die in the light."

Matilda extended her hand that Robin help her rise. He thought he heard some constriction in her voice. "It does much amaze me that one insignificant family could be so much—you have your orders, Denby. Go carry them out."

"My mother would ask—"

Maud screeched suddenly. *"Robin!"*

She had risen from the stool, clear-focused for one searing moment. "Don't speak to her. I would not have you show honor to that woman."

"Woman, hold your tongue." Baudreux approached the queen deferentially. "Madam, I will send her down again."

"She'll go on my arm if she must," Robin warned, stepping in front of the castellan. "What kind of a man are you? She said she doesn't get enough water to drink, let alone wash with. Look at her." His eyes begged Matilda beyond words. "Lady, for the love of God."

"Baudreux!" The command snapped the chunky castellan to instinctive attention. "I will take dinner at this table. Considering the state of this keep, say rather I will suffer it. Lady Maud will join me. Wash the table first." Matilda suddenly turned her back on all of them with an eloquent disgust that went far beyond her orders. "Fitz-Gerald! Take your captain of archers and be about your duties. Denby, you are an ignorant peasant troublemaker, born and bred between insolence and treason. But do as you have sworn and I will be just. Now get out of here."

Robin embraced Maud in farewell. She could barely lift her arms about his neck, asking with the secret urgency of a child, "Did you ask about the water?"

Robin shut his eyes tight against the pity that blurred them. "I did. The queen will put it right."

"I heard you. You're wrong. I'm not dying. Just a little water to wash."

"Mother, I have to go. Got to see to this for all of us."

"Get to the earl," she whispered. "He will help you."

"God be with you, Mum."

"I'm *not* ill," Maud insisted with feeble irritation. "I'm—" She might have been asleep before and come suddenly awake. Maud gazed at the Normans about her with hostile awareness. "Why are you with these?"

"I must go, Mum."

"Why, Robin?"

He kissed her again. "The queen will tell you. She wants you to dine with her. Good-bye, Mother."

Robin wanted to weep or scream, but Ralf waited at the top of the steps to the lower bailey. He would be shamed to show the torment to a foreigner. Though it rose and filled his throat like bile, Robin shut his mouth tight around anguish, let it sink back into his guts and darken there. Helplessness did that to a man.

"Robin?"

He came back to the present and the sheriff waiting on him, hoping the man was as sickened by this as himself. "What?"

"Nothing." Ralf turned away. "We do what we must."

"Yes, what we must. And long live the king, ent that how it goes? Come on." Robin brushed past Ralf, descending the steps heavily toward his waiting horse. "Let's go clean up his goddamned mess."

Baron Richard de Guilbert, assigned to suppress Norfolk, was loyal to William whom he considered first among equals. His quandary lay in the fact that there were now so many equals on both sides of the rebellion. Many present opponents, like Rolph de Gael, were friends to him and more than a few others kin by blood or marriage. From the first de Guilbert knew the war could go either way, especially in Brittany. Where would he find himself then? As a consequence, the baron followed a cautious road between self-interest and duty, did everything right but reluctantly, did not lose the encounter at Thetford but fell short of winning.

No blame fell on him then or afterward. Richard de Guilbert had all the virtues of his caste and the accepted vices, including his mode of thought. He was a large man in the mold that later characterized the Plantagenets: reddish-blond hair worn long since Hastings, clear-blue eyes, and ruddy complexion. Hale and bluff, he cut a marvelous figure riding before his levies, armor and weapons polished and gilt harness jingling, the conical helmet always left off until absolutely needed since his wife once commented that his hair shone in sunlight.

When they were sure de Gael was on the march, de Guilbert's scouts estimated the enemy's best route and speed: south along the Roman road from Norwich, veering west as soon as they could count on firm ground south of the Fens. On their second reconnaissance, de Gael appeared to be moving toward the little hamlet of Thetford.

"About three hundred knights," the sweating messenger panted at de Guilbert's stirrup. "Baggage train but no foot or siege engines."

The baron's back was to Thetford forest northeast of the small town when the two forces arrayed against each other. The conventions of honorable warfare were scrupulously observed. Earl and baron, each with an escort of knights and squires, rode out from their lines to meet in an open meadow. Rolph de Gael knew he was outnumbered but noted the baron's few archers. Their lack of preparation did not escape him. He greeted his friend with generous affection and inquired after the baroness who was his own distant kinswoman. As the lines waited, perspiring in full armor under a hot sun, the commanders came with delicate courtesy to the matter at hand. De Guilbert would accept their surrender in the king's name which he hoped Norfolk still honored sufficiently to heed. Otherwise there would be battle.

"I have no wish to try against you, kinsman, but the dice are thrown," Rolph responded with gay determination as he wheeled his horse about. "I am committed, and God defend the right of my cause."

De Guilbert underestimated Norfolk's determination and possibly his desperation. In the first sortie the baron sustained more casualties than his opponent who generously withdrew to let de Guilbert's men recover their wounded. De Guilbert tardily advanced his archers against a second sally but without cover. They volleyed at Norfolk's charging squadrons, were hit, broke and ran, becoming an obstacle to their own advancing knights who trampled many of them under the heavy warhorses. A truce was called until morning.

That last charge cost Norfolk too many of his best. He could not get around the enemy. Under cover of night he left a few watchfires burning for diversion and slipped away in retreat to Norwich. Next morning de Guilbert weighed pursuit against the casualties sustained. He must still take Norwich and detach a substantial force to gut the Norfolk coast of food and supplies before the Danes landed. For this he would need more men, fresh remounts, and siege equipment. He marched back to Newmarket to refit.

Norfolk had been prevented, and no one publicly rebuked the loyal baron with such charges as indecision or the criminal, needless waste of good archers. At Newmarket de Guilbert estimated for Matilda and Lanfranc that the siege of Norwich would only put a period to what was already concluded in England.

"Dusting and wiping," he joked to his knights. "Cleaning up, that's all."

Of scant interest to him or any of his knights was that a shirttail vavasor come to prominence as a sheriff would join him shortly with more English archers. The baron knew Fitz-Gerald and would welcome him, but cared little about the bowmen. Regarded as scantly more useful than camp followers, the deaths among his own bowmen were not even counted in the casualty rolls.

46

From ANCASTER TO Newark and on through the tiny villages of Sherwood, Robin led an incongruous troop that lengthened as he went. From Wytha's forest den came his own—Father Beorn, Will and Morgan, and Mauger who would not miss one more chance to peer over history's shoulder. From Nottingham came a mounted escort of ten men at arms plus Ralf's sometime-squire, young Henri, who served him in the lists at Grantham. Henri had grown and his voice settled and deepened since then. As with most folk when they experienced the "bold and unholden men" at close quarters, the squire was disappointed at how ordinary and shabby they were. Until Robin, Will and Morgan shot against one another in practice—*then* they became part of the bow and grew wings.

From Edwinstowe to Southwell, Papplewick, and Annersley, at each village church in Sherwood or wherever the forest paths crossed, Robin exhorted the men to join him.

"Full amnesty to any man who puts his name or mark on our roll. That and a bounty of five pence," Robin declared.

Some gaped and tried to get close to the walking legends; others were more cautious: the tattered nut-brown men in faded Lincoln, rarely under a roof, who lived on the king's deer but paid for survival in broken families and long-missed homes. These leaned on long bowstaves in the rear of the crowd, as far as possible from a sheriff they had good reason to avoid since less peaceful meetings. None made up their minds on the spot; that was not their way. Most were grateful for the Nottingham garrison picketed between themselves and Mansfield, but thanks the same, they'd go home to their fields. Not without shy curiosity however.

"You must be Will Scarlet."

"*Scarlet* again? The name is Scatloch." Nothing so rubbed Will against his grain, weary of his good name taken in vain. "And don't be gawping at me. Listen to Robin when he speaks to you."

Blunt men asked blunt questions. "Why are you with Normans?"

"Fair question, fellow. What's your name?"

"That's for me to give when I will."

More often than not Ralf knew the name and the price on the man's head, which Robin promised would be canceled if the outlaw joined their company.

North again at last, wending toward Denby. Men appeared on the forest paths now, showing themselves to the Normans because Robin Hood rode before them. Some joined, others doubted, but all questioned with the shrewd profit-and-loss sensibility of farmers. Many had already gone with Thane Alan to serve Waltheof. They never rode. A man on horseback meant Norman to them, and for this reason Robin always dismounted to address them. They heard what he said and the Norman sheriff promised, but ever they asked why Robin Hood rode for a foreign king against his own kind.

"Against my own?" Robin challenged finally. "Who says that? Who thinks that? Most of you have weedhooks in your hands and well you should. This is the time of year for them, though it's a poor planter who can't tell weed from crop. I'm a farmer like you and my own blood back to Alfred."

Striding among them, recognizing a man here and there. "From Plough Monday to Yule next, I know the land like you. When to plow and when to harrow. When to drive cattle to graze and when to keep them from the grass. There's shepherds among you. I've sheered my own sheep in June and boiled the wool for oil myself. I've carried scrip and tar box like you and sweated to rid my ewes of fly-blow and maggot sores. I've worked with my own wife beside me at haying, stunk of blood for a week at Martinmas slaughtering and my hands stung as long from the salting. I've lived on thin cabbage soup as you have at the end of winter, and the meat on my table, when there was meat at all, was not venison but deer; not pork but pig.

"Against my own? *You* are my own. Waltheof's a weed and I go to step on his head as you would, to root him out with my hook. He's not my own nor yours, not even England's, but the false painting of her on cheap linen. And what's behind that picture he'd have you weep over and swear to? Nowt but Normans and Bretons, foreigners as far as you can see. Waltheof ent us or for us. He's for Waltheof alone and no mistake. 'I'll have mine and to hell with you.' That's his catechism.''

To Ralf Fitz-Gerald listening, Robin might be recruiting for the king, but his sentiments were subversive as ever. Born a hereditary landowner and half rooted in what he warred against, the man transcended himself when he spoke like this, ignited with an almost religious intensity the English churls recognized. To Ralf, there were alien and dangerous strains in Robin.

You're a man with a cause, a secular saint, born to trouble the sleep of kings. No man can be his own master, no man wants to be. We were not made for such loneliness and if you dare them so far, God help you, Robin.

"Waltheof and his rebel earls are hounds. Hounds on a leash serve a purpose; loose they're harder to heel. You can't tell them the land needs such a labor at such a time. All they want to know is where their bone is buried. You go with the hounds now, or stand silent by, and you'll see the worst kind of war, *civil* war season after season that leaves your fields fallow for years while one dog turns on another.

"Against my own? Because I know Waltheof for a dog, I turned on him. Because I turned in time, he can't run loose and you'll be harvesting between Lammas and Saint Michaels instead of boiling roots and acorns for hungry children.''

To Ralf's perception, Robin only damned one breed of cur to another. These would turn on him one day and heel to the hand that held the whip or fed them.

"I'm no friend to William but at least he's for that peace and balance Waltheof would destroy for his own gain, not for you lot. Never for you. You pull the mask off good Huntingdon, wipe the seeming from worthy Huntingdon, look on the true face of *noble* Huntingdon as I have—you'll see his love for England clear. He sold her cheap at York and left me and my da to go down with her. You'll see it marvelous plain in the Danes he plans to loose on East Anglia this summer. You all remember Danes and how little they leave. I'll tell you straight: Nor in contending now nor winning later will any of them give a fiddler's fart for you men, only what's their lordly due from your labor. Nay, don't ask me why I ride for the king, not when there's such weeding to do.''

Morgan of Powys for one was impressed. "*Dyw* but that man's a wicked silver-smooth tongue to him. Give him a harp and a cause, I'm thinking, and he might well be a Briton. Was it you, Will, who put the music into him?''

No, that Will did not though he'd heard the notes far and faint from years back.

Those men who joined the company were instructed to meet Robin at the sheriff's house in Nottingham in two days' time. When Mauger had listed the volunteers and Ralf paid out the king's silver to each, they turned at last toward Denby. Beorn longed to see the church so long denied him, Will to see his family. For Robin the yearning was simpler. He wanted to walk on the earth where he was born.

Denby's fields were trampled by rebels and loyalists alike. Much of the new crop was lost and the steading itself a pathetic sight—refuse in the courtyard, the barn doors torn off their hinges for watch fires, not one of Ralf's horses left nor any other livestock visible. No one appeared immediately when their cortege reined in at the gate. Then a door creaked open cautiously in one bower.

Robin called, then Will Scatloch in Welsh. "Angharad! It is me! Your own man come home."

She came running out of the bower then with Eddain and Gwaun outstripping her to reach their father and hug him. In minutes the familiar, loved handful of Robin's folk followed. Stately Ethelwold strode out, his joy barely squeezed into suitable dignity when he greeted his lord and priest. Old Gudrun hobbled after from the kitchen, cooking ladle still in her grip, and then Minna, wiping large red hands on her apron.

Lord Robin come home! They hardly noticed the sheriff or the men at arms. *Look* how thin they were, Will and his lord alike, and a shame to Angharad that there was not that to make a feast of welcome for heroes. Minna could tell to the crumb what the filthy marauders on both sides left in the larder, for there was indeed no more than crumbs. But see, Will, how big your boys are now! Eddain thirteen and Gwaun all of eleven.

"And you, Father Beorn." Angharad fluttered over her priest, wanting him to bless her be he excommunicated or not. "Will you not go to Blidworth where the folk can warm themselves at the sight of you?"

"Come, Father," Mauger urged, "and I'll go with you. I want to see your church."

"My church." The very sound of it was strange to Beorn after all this time. But fine.

"Look at them all," Robin glowed to Ethelwold as Will, Angharad, and Morgan chattered away in Welsh, the boys skipping and yipping about them. "Does a heart good, my friend."

"It does," the steward agreed. "I wish Aelred were here."

They said no more, the young man and the old, content to watch their folk in a communion that needed no words. Ralf understood a little of their narrow pride now. A place like Denby became more than timber, more even than the people, taking on a soul of its own from everything and everyone gone into it. Robin turned slowly about, a fixed point in his own world, to see again the horizons known from birth.

Minna had heard from one or another good man passing through that Robin had a son who would be the fourth generation on the land. She warranted she and Wystan prayed every night for them—and mentioning her husband, there was a matter the lord could help with. So long, that was, as he was staying the night. Minna seemed hesitant, darting timid glances at Ralf.

"No fear, Minna." Robin took her hands to draw the woman out. "What can I do?"

"Well, he doesn't go much beyond the croft now." Minna was quick to add that Wystan did for himself quite well at home; but with so many of his friends gone, the tavern closed so no one could even bring him a cup of cheer, her man had a lonely time of it all day. "He always talks of your last visit, sir. Would you be good enough to look in?"

"I'm off straight," Robin promised, hugging Minna impulsively. "You smell wonderful."

"Sir!"

"You do. You smell of my own hall and kitchen. It's good to be back."

Ralf cleared his throat. "I'll go with you." His tone quite clearly made it insistence.

Robin looked doubtful, Minna dismayed, but Ralf knew it only good sense. "Huntingdon might have bowmen slipping through our pickets in these woods. We'll take the whole detail."

"Well enough." Robin put one foot in the stirrup and swung up. "But you ent what he'd call close to him. Stay by the door until you're asked in."

"You would think I came to England yesterday," Ralf muttered as he mounted. "I can look on what I had to do. *Allons.*"

Wystan's croft lay to the north of Denby hall through a stand of massive old beeches, across a neat ash coppice, and along a century-worn footpath that ended in a small clearing and Wystan's thatched, rough-planked house. To one side was a smaller hovel for storage and an open wicker-screened latrine pit. Two scrawny hens foraged futilely in the bare earth about the door. There would be none at all, Minna stated with outraged pride, had she not managed to hide the pair from the Nottingham garrison who liberated the rest of their poultry.

Young Henri sniffed distastefully. "Whole place stinks."

Ralf vouchsafed him a tight smile that required tolerance to maintain. "You don't know what stink is." *Good little vavasor's son that you are. I was born in a hut like this.* "Dismount the detail and wait. The rill from Holy Pool should be just over there." Ralf pointed through the woods to the east. "The men can water their horses. Not too much; we may have to ride quickly."

As Ralf and Robin approached the house the door opened. With some relief Ralf saw that Wystan's eyes were covered with a clean linen bandage.

"Who's there? Who's come?"

"It's me to see my friend."

"Lord Robin?"

"May I come in?"

Wystan broke into a wide grin. "Come in and welcome! Two visits in a month: getting to be a proper pilgrims' road through here. Who's with you? I heard a deal of horses."

"King's men." Robin gripped the outstretched hand.

The welcoming grin faded to wariness. "You're not taken?" The fuller's head cocked to one side. "There's one beside you."

"The sheriff," said Robin. "You've sharp ears."

"I've come to that. Got so I can hear the birds yawn before they sing of a morning." Wystan waved Robin through his door. "You come in, my lord."

The invitation clearly excluded Ralf. He took a position in the open doorway as Robin entered the shadowed hut. But for minor differences Ralf knew the hut well from the first eight years of his own life, a memory brought sharply back by sight and smell. There was almost no furniture: a low stool, a straw mattress laid over the sunken dirt floor in one corner and covered with a frayed blanket. A low dry stone wall divided the interior of the croft between human habitat and a byre reeking pungently of recent animal occupation. These people had few metal implements of their own. The iron tripod over the small central fire pit was unusual, probably fashioned by Littlerede, suspending the leather cooking bag over live wood embers. The rank smell of pig and old dung was enriched with overtones of onion and cabbage simmering in the bag of pease porridge.

Wystan knew precisely where everything was to be reached in his own house. With no groping about, he took a wooden dipper from its hook on the tripod and offered some broth from the porridge to Robin who accepted it with polite thanks. They chatted familiarly in a country dialect from which Ralf caught only their general drift. Wystan had been frightened when the war came so close. The king's side took the sheriff's pig and two chickens of their own. The rebels made off with the horses, and wasn't that a shame? Wystan knew none of the reasons for all this, but found it difficult to imagine Robin fighting for the Norman king.

"Good business, Wystan: March now so we won't be marching for years to come and more strangers mucking about and stealing your chickens."

Wystan could see the sense of that. "Thatch the roof before it rains. If you've had your fill, will you dip me some porridge?"

Ralf watched the lank man fill the dipper and place it carefully in Wystan's hands. In the simple act Ralf perceived what he himself was not, at least not yet. Robin possessed a common touch with his own peasants, generations of respect given and earned in the hall, fields, and crofts like these, in simple words and actions between men who needed no more to understand each other.

Wystan settled on the pallet, smacking his lips over the porridge and offering Robin the one stool as honored guest. "Heard about Tuck and Much."

With a furtive glance at Ralf, Robin said only, "Yes."

"John was here."

"No—when?"

"That was—oh, a good two weeks gone. Said he was to the north but there weren't any work for a smith. Hardly any folk after Willy Bastard got done. Proper graveyard one end to the other."

Robin pronounced the words like a verdict. "Let John not look to me."

"He ent," Wystan mumbled over his porridge. "Johnny says no mind, we're all dead as the north now."

The two men fell silent for a space, now and then sharing the dipper of porridge between them. Ralf rested against the door jamb. Some of his men had taken their mounts to the brook. Henri sat cross-legged on the ground, stroking his horse's lowered head.

"So you'll be marching soon," Wystan said after a time. "Wish I could go, wherever it is. A man gets tired of nowt to do but sit and think,'' he sighed on a wistful fall. And that would be a glorious sight when Robin and his shire lads set out their banner against . . . who was it?

"Foreigners mostly. Knights and such.''

"No sin there.'' Just that folk *were* puzzled Robin didn't go with the other side.

Not that they weren't asked, himself and the sheriff, Robin declared, but neither of them judged that good bargaining.

"Better trade to side with him?'' The blind man challenged bluntly, acknowledging Ralf's presence for the first time. "I'd look first to see Christ come again.''

"There's poor friends and good enemies, Wystan.''

"He blinded me. He drove you off your land.''

"Aye, he's a hard one but a man of his word. And he asks the cheer of your house.''

"Oh, then?'' The curtained face inclined slightly toward the doorway. "Let him ask for himself.''

Robin urged Ralf with his eyes: *You heard him. Ask.*

"May I enter your house, Wystan?''

"Come,'' said the fuller with cool courtesy. "There's porridge hot.''

Robin handed the dipper to Ralf. *Take some.*

The cabbage-rank mess held not only the pulpy end of their winter vegetables along with early radishes and comfrey greens; there were also shreds of rabbit and generous chunks of fresh venison. Littlerede probably brought it to his friend with no concern for the felony. As he politely swallowed a little, praising the taste when there was little, Ralf realized the truth of what Robin had so desperately tried to impress on him. These people could not survive without breaking one law or another. "Thank you, fuller.''

"May it well become you,'' Wystan answered formally. "Robin, will you carry your father's banner in this war?''

No, he could not. The flag with its device of an oak tree had been lost at York with Aelred's shield.

Wystan thought that a deep pity. A lord should have a standard all men recognized in the field.

"There'll be the baron's flag or whatever.''

"A Norman flag?'' Wystan's stress eloquently conveyed the inadequacy.

"What matter, man?''

"It does matter!" Robin might have offended the man; he almost bristled. "It is a great matter. I was there, Aelredson. You were not."

"Where?"

"Hastings." The blind man raised his head as if listening to distant echoes. "That was a day to remember, but you weren't there."

Ralf ventured quietly: "I was."

"You?" The bandaged face raised toward him. "Then you know the truth of it."

"As you say, a day to remember. I try not to."

"Well you might try," Wystan chuckled dryly. "I almost killed your king myself that day. If he carries the same shield still, you'll find the mark of my spear on it. Y'did not take our ridge easy." Again Wystan lapsed into that peculiar, listening silence. "A man in the dark has time to remember, Fitz-Gerald. There was you stealing a whole country and you called me thief for one deer and put out my eyes." Wystan added flatly: "May God damn yours."

"Wystan." There was an odd note of primness in Robin's reproof. "The man is a guest in your house."

"So he is, so he is." Wystan paused a moment then slapped his knee, a man come to decision. "Since the matter's come up, I'll show him thieving. And you, Aelredson."

Wystan rose and stepped over the low stone partition between house and byre. He moved surely to the far wall and rummaged under a pile of old sheepskins for what they covered, a bulky square parcel wrapped in unbleached linen and tied with hempen cord. Wystan brought the heavy bundle to Robin and placed it in his hands.

"Your father never knew I had this, none did but John and Minna. Don't say no mind or no matter to me. It was a great matter to us then. Open it."

Before the contents were fully unfolded, Robin knew what he held. Not a man in England would not. Ralf Fitz-Gerald had lost good friends charging up a blood-slippery hill to take it.

The banner was of heavy wool needleworked on canvas, a deep blue field on which a warrior, richly devised in gold wire thread, stood with battle-ax upraised to strike. About the four borders, like the stars over the stilled field on that October night, the jewels gleamed against the faded wool. Wystan reached to caress the material. "I saved this."

Robin held in his hands the Fighting Man, the personal standard of King Harold himself. Ralf stared at the magnificent symbol, remembering. *William put a rich bounty on this flag and we hunted the thing all over the field. He wanted it burned or in the grave with Harold and it was here all these years.*

Wystan was speaking to him again with the formal distance in his voice these island folk employed with outlanders. "I took this when your lot came up the hill for the last time. Nigh dark then, but I saw my king fall and his standard bearer go down. *I* saved this, foreigner. Didn't think on why, just grabbed and ran. You remember the second battle back by the other hill? The ravine where we caught so many of you?"

Only too well Ralf recalled that efficient, peculiarly English slaughter, the archers crying out *Rood!* and *Holy Cross!* while they butchered calmly as carving at table.

"That was Robin's father who rallied us to cost you a deal more before we went home, rest his soul." Wystan crossed himself carefully and kissed his fingers. "Robin, hold up the standard before this Norman. Go on, man, shake it out. Let me show him summ'at."

The blind fuller grasped one edge of the heavy banner. "Count the stones, Sheriff. Sixteen there were when I took it from the ridge and sixteen yet. Minna helped keep me honest, said we might not sell a single stone. I wouldn't, not without sore need. Never came to that somehow. *Close*, Robin, but I could not bring myself to take out the smallest one. And this Norman calls me a thief? Well, curse me, I was the start of all your troubles, Lord Robin," Wystan conceded sorrowfully. "I did poach now and again—aye, and repented and said the penance prayers Father Beorn laid on me until I'm fair lily-white through the soul by now. Well, past is past, ent it? Seeing you've no proper standard, I thought: What a fine sight that would be to shake this flag in their face one battle more. Take it, my lord, and this time beat the bastards *good*."

Ralf emerged first from Wystan's house, leaving Robin to his farewells. He did not join Henri and the others but waited alone a little way from the door.

The Fighting Man. The last, troublesome ghost of England buried in a byre and furled in darkness, the opulent jewels lightless as Wystan's eyes. William would never allow it to fly again anywhere. Ralf recognized Wystan's feeling and the sentiment, but the notion was mad. More than mad, it was dangerous.

"Ralf."

Robin came out of the croft carrying the flag bundled and tied again. "When we group in Nottingham, have your people fashion a staff and case for this."

"Do you know what you ask, man? Need I tell you how unwise this is?"

Robin might not have heard him at all. He hefted the bundle. "You might say heavy as a king's conscience. Needs a strong lad to bear it."

"Name of Christ, you are difficult."

"Vavasor, you've asked Saxons to fight with you. You command but they follow me. The king won't care why we serve him, but we just might. Don't say anything, Ralf. Not just now."

Ralf Fitz-Gerald might have said much, whole books by way of prudent objection. Something stilled them. He did not.

47

*L*ATER THAT MONTH William departed south from Solway, breaking his journey at several castles. The barons who entertained the king observed him to be in unusually high spirits, but when he departed Hough for Grantham his good humor had abruptly vanished. Simply put, William was an exasperated husband bent on a few pointed words with his consort.

The queen greeted her royal husband in the hall with Lanfranc. William dismissed the officers of his train and beckoned wife and regent to the scriptorium, unceremoniously banishing the scribes from the small chamber. Mud-spattered and saddle-weary, he stumped his huge bulk up and down the chamber before his two confidants in a brusque summary of the Scottish campaign.

"Malcolm came and submitted. I have his sworn fealty, for what it's worth. And hostages of course," added the king who never ceased to marvel at the disillusionment still to be found in a skeptical lifetime. "Which means we may have a season or two without hindrance from the north."

"Gilly, do sit down," Matilda entreated. "You're worn to the bone."

"I've been in the saddle for days. I need to move. Give me the news. Not all mixed," he snapped peevishly at Lanfranc. "Day by day; I want to see the development."

The situation was static and contained, at least this side of the Channel. Breteuil and Waltheof immobilized, de Gael's castle at Norwich presently under siege by Baron de Guilbert. Earl Rolph was no longer at Norwich but had taken ship, leaving the castle under the command of his chatelaine, Countess Agatha. There was yet no reliable information as to de Gael's destination. Lanfranc thought he might have gone to rally his Danish allies. "Or to Brittany, my lord. Possibly to Philip of France."

"Who daily wafts protestations of love to us as his vassals in Normandy," Matilda remarked acidly, "while sending more tangible support to Scotland."

"Dear Philip," William sighed heavily. "How I love that cousin of yours. Who's his food taster? Perhaps we could poison him . . . Lanfranc?" For the first time since greeting his archbishop, William noticed the cleric's formal garb. "Why are you in full canonicals?"

"My lord, I celebrate Mass at Saint Wulfram's this afternoon."

"Oh, yes. Yes." William sat down at last, bestowing a meager smile on his queen and cleric. "The thoroughness of your intelligence, your preparations and dispositions: I commend them all. Your grace, I will not keep you from holy offices." His inflection turned statement into suggestion. The Italian courteously withdrew.

"Mora, you sit down," William bade her crisply. "There is something we must have clear between us."

Matilda took a chair. "Whatever is that?"

"I broke my journey at Hough last night," William announced significantly.

"Is Baudreux ready? I certainly impressed the need on him."

"He is prepared for any chance. Far readier than I was when I saw that Denby woman wandering free about the bailey yard. Baudreux told me you gave orders to that effect."

"Did you observe the woman?"

William had not, nor was that his point. "Do you know what I am this year, dear wife? A frantic carpenter dashing about my own house with hammer and nails to keep this or that piece of the roof from falling on us. It heartens me not at all to find that my own queen, an otherwise impeccable lieutenant of state, is pulling out the nails in my wake."

Matilda only shook her head. "You did not see her."

"Mora, please stay on the point. You gainsaid my direct order. Denby—my God, I am sick of stubbing my toe on that brood! That damned woman—"

"No need to bellow, Gilly. Why are you such a bear today?"

William subsided somewhat. "The woman was in league with her son against me. She sent letters, spied, she's hangable as Denby himself."

"You did not return her to the dungeon?" Matilda's question carried its own poignant concern. "Please say you didn't."

"No, and for better reasons than you employed in letting her out. Lanfranc is regent but you are the crown in my absence. You undermined my authority, madam. I will not confuse my castellan by countermanding yours, but don't ever do it again."

"You should have smelled that keep when I was there. Denby lifted his mother out of that foul pit like something from a grave."

Her husband smiled ruefully. "Saint Matilda."

"Don't blaspheme, Gilly."

"Patroness of stray cats and forlorn Saxons."

"And don't employ that tone with me, sir! The woman was dying."

"*Quel dommage.* I will not grieve."

"Gilly." Matilda composed herself and took a more reasonable tack. "Maud is unimportant, a small woman with a narrow life, narrowly perceived. I consider she has paid for what she did."

William regarded his wife from under a raised eyebrow. "You consider?"

"Your queen considers," the tiny woman answered firmly. "My sentiment is as restrained as yours. Not drawing out your nails but occasionally straightening those poorly hammered. And touching on stray cats, were you more prudent trusting Waltheof or bestowing the earldom of Norfolk on de Gael? Admit that and recall it was Denby who came with Ralf Fitz-Gerald with the first word of Waltheof's treason."

Matilda knew she was right—humanely if not politically. Remembering Maud across the table at Hough: a bag of bones and damp filth, her feeble, dull-eyed attention drifting away again and again. She asked continually for water to wash, rubbing one fish-white claw over the other. "You did not see her, Gilly."

Matilda went to stand behind her husband, massaging his shoulder muscles. She laid her cheek against his. "My love, you are the bravest, strongest king in the world. You were angry that day. You were ill yourself and worried for me. You bent a nail and threw your hammer like any cranky carpenter."

"Perhaps." William's shoulders moved gratefully under her ministering hands. "After this I will be a miser with my trust."

"Clearly indicated."

"And earldoms."

"*Certainement.*"

"Where did you put Denby? At Huntingdon's throat?"

"He'd love that, but no. I sent Sire Ralf and the ineffable Denby to de Guilbert. Here: I'll show."

Matilda found her new diagram of the fortifications and positions at Norwich. Placing the map before William she drew one finger north to south across the bight of River Wensum to show the siege dispositions. "Norwich is in the barrel and the bung tight."

William looked over his shoulder at her. "Are they discussing surrender?"

"Not precisely, but you know Agatha." Matilda did. "In faith, I don't know whether that arrogant little bitch should be hanged or just spanked."

William might have commented on the choice of de Guilbert to conduct the campaign. In his private opinion, the baron lacked decisiveness. At the moment he decided not to speculate.

Jesus, Mary, and Joseph!—Robin deplored every day, sweating in the hot June sun—the silly baron should have gone for Rolph de Gael after Thetford, let his bowmen range the earl's flanks like a wolf pack and whittle him down to nothing before he even reached Norwich. These Normans had a split mind when it came to war: one half for winning and devil any Saxons in the way, the other prancing about in a foolish but rigid dance of courtesies between brothers in arms.

"Never in my life have I heard so many *apray-voozes, jonteel-homs,* and *silvoo-plates!* By God if you didn't know they were at war you'd think they were getting married."

"They are knights," Ralf patiently tried to explain. More than soldiers, they were a fraternity, a caste of men raised above others, with values different from Robin's and rules hallowed by long custom.

"Custom! Damn it, you fight a war to win so you can get home to what matters." Three of his men had already deserted, gone back to Sherwood—and curse Robin if he could blame them. They went home to care for their crops. And here the rest of them sat before Norwich, looking foolish. "We'll have to starve 'em out now, and they don't hardly look hungry yet."

Because of the stalemate, they sat on their backsides getting flux and camp lice while summer bloomed and good husbanding weather wasted. Norwich keep and bailey loomed on a high natural hump in the middle of the Norfolk lowlands, nestling in a bight-loop of Wensum River. The old city walls had been breached with hardly any resistance. De Guilbert's cavalry deployed and set up their tents in a long crescent across the open neck of the loop within the city walls. Catapults hurled stones and balls of flaming pitch into the bailey. Now and again siege towers drawn by oxen and sweating men rumbled to the bailey ditch bearing shielded archers who volleyed flight after flight at the defenders within. At such times they cost Norwich dearly, mostly in their English equals, but essentially the situation remained unchanged. Even Father Beorn was moved to scorn: "War was different when I bore ax and shield."

"And not so long ago," said Mauger who had plugged his fingers into a man's chest at Stamford Bridge to keep him from bleeding to death, scornful as Beorn of the endless and fruitless parleying back and forth. "If those ladies aren't careful, they're going to hurt themselves."

The men spent much idle time gazing up at the formidable heights of Norwich keep. "We ent ever going to take that place."

"Devil we ent," said Robin of Denby.

The vast stockaded bailey spread out to the south of the high keep, fronted by its own bank and ditch. To the northeast on the banks of Wensum lay the old Saxon village called Tombland. After weeks of siege and intermittent rain, the southern and western meadows beyond the bailey were a quagmire of mud and sodden tents where Robin's men did their best to keep clothing and equipment dry. Decent lodging was confiscated by the higher lords. For the sake of respect and example, Ralf quartered in a small tent with Robin and Henri.

Such orders as the baron relayed to his little-regarded bowmen were passed through Ralf to Robin, who was not popular at first, especially among demoralized veterans of Thetford like Dickon Blue. He personally inspected each of his ninety-odd archers' huke-bags. Most carried the requisite two bowstrings; Robin made sure each man left Newmarket with three beside a horn of beeswax to keep them supple. Worn shooting tabs were replaced. Every man's leather arm brace must be ready to hand at all times. Going down the lines in Robin's wake, Will Scatloch listened to each braced bow for the slightest cracking. Then came Morgan running fingers sensitive as blind Wystan's over each bow surface for the minute irregularities that might mean the start of splintering.

Robin drilled them daily to break their ranks into files if knights needed to come through. They might never be used by the baron as they should be, but after meeting Dickon Blue, Robin determined they would not be useless casualties. He detailed a husky little Manxman as standard-bearer but gave the flag into his hands with the case sewn tight and not to be opened without his express order.

"Our own colors," Dickon snickered. "They'll surrender on the spot."

Dickon Blue looked, sounded, and smelled like every unwilling soldier since Egypt warred with the Hittites. He had commanded the baron's archers at Thetford. He would much rather be somewhere else now, but hardly dwelt in hope, expecting the worst from de Guilbert and seldom surprised. This molded his features into a perpetual grimace of disgust. In Dickon, *Why us?* had long left off asking and had become, *Who else?*

Through the dreary march to Norwich and the stalemate of siege, the difference between Robin's men and Dickon's was obvious. The Sherwood men were ready to fight if they must and get home. The others were sullen and disspirited. Ralf contemptuously called them the "buggaralls." If the baron wasted them, they'd grab what they could and run. They were survivors who stole when and what they could and always knew how to avoid work or find the best available food, drink, or whores. They would sit out the siege and go home richer.

"The same in Normandy," Ralf told Robin. "Rats can live anywhere."

"They don't want to die for nothing and neither do I," Robin summed the problem to Ralf. "I'm going to the baron and speak some reason to the man."

"Then I'd best go with you. Unless I am there, he won't even see you. He'll think you a malingerer sneaking behind my back."

The baron's quarters lay just northeast of the bailey in the spacious wool hall near an old Saxon church. Robin and Ralf presented themselves early in the morning. They were told the baron had just risen but would see Sire Ralf within the hour. They waited longer than that before he appeared in a rumpled nightgown, fondling a Saxon woman who had obviously seen better days. Richard de Guilbert gave the dox a pat on the rear to speed her home and greeted Ralf with yawning cordiality.

"Baron: my captain of archers, Edward of Denby. He wished to speak to you."

"At this hour?" De Guilbert dropped into a chair, one leg draped over the arm rest. "Something of consequence, I hope."

"Sir." Robin labored with his faulty Frankish. "I have trained my bowmen to cooperate with your knights in the event of battle. We have—help me, Ralf."

"With every fifth man as a pivot, the ranks become files through which the cavalry can pass."

"Admirable." The baron yawned and scratched his scalp. "*Excusez-moi*, Sire Ralf. I am not fully awake. Well?"

"Sir, it's a matter of efficiency and—what is the word, Ralf?"

"Morale."

"Just so: morale. My men will fight better if they don't have to fear injury from their own horse."

Yes, of course, the baron recalled the incident at Thetford. Regrettable but hardly his knights' fault. In any case, the baron had no plans to employ bowmen beyond the siege towers.

"Regrettable? It's a disgrace!" How large a disgrace quickly ran beyond Robin's Frank and boiled over in English to make Ralf wince. Fortunately the baron caught little of it and could only infer from the Saxon's suddenly stiffish manner.

"Baron," Ralf interceded, "he wishes you to give a cautionary order to your knights in this regard. The which I second, my lord. These are men, not cattle."

Richard de Guilbert could hardly believe a vavasor would put forth such a request, no matter how respectfully worded. Certainly Sire Ralf knew what horsemen had to contend with on the field. "Ask them to step nicely around a chaos of footmen? *Ma foi*, knight."

Robin spoke rapidly to Ralf, bowed stiff as a lance to the baron—*à votre service*—and walked abruptly out of the hall.

De Guilbert yawned again. "What was that about beside Saxon bad manners?"

"Richard, the matter is serious."

"What did the fellow say? Seemed absolutely livid."

"He is a passionate man and often blunt. He said to inform you that if any of your knights injures one of his men in the field, the rest will take it personally."

"Personally?" The audacity brought the baron to his feet to loom over Ralf. "That peasant threatens me?"

"No, my lord. He promises." Ralf met the larger man eye for eye to impress his point. "We are old friends, Richard. I know your sentiments and your present position. I too have friends in that castle. Reluctance is understandable."

"I follow my orders. Do you imply that I shirk my duty?"

"My lord, I do not."

"The crown saddled us with these Greyfeathers. For yourself, I am sorry to see a fine knight so wasted."

That was Robin's point and his own, Ralf argued. "I have fought them and know what they can do. I will not presume to tell my lord how to employ such men, but I beg you not to waste them. In all humility, bowing my service to your will: Use them, Richard."

Beneath consideration. "No."

"Use them. They can win for you."

"Out of the question."

"Good God, why? The crown order is clear enough. They won't care how you go about it."

Richard de Guilbert was genuinely astonished that a knight soon to enter the peerage would need to ask. "You have been too long in your forest, Lord Sheriff. In that castle is the best blood of Normandy. Breteuil's daughter. Beaumont, the nephews of Tosny, men of the highest houses. Comrades . . . friends. I will follow the king's order. Beyond that, do you think I will brutalize, that I will insult such men by allowing a rabble of vicious cowards to loose on them? *Jamais*. Good morning, Sire Ralf."

Countess Agatha and Raimond de Beaumont strolled along the west parapet of the bailey wall, observing de Guilbert's tents and the desultory movement of men among them. Through the interminable and indecisive parleys they had gleaned a clear picture of the enemy's strength. When the baron's standard of a leopard *couchant* rose over his field tent, they would bargain again today with a marked difference.

Barely nineteen, Agatha had qualities beside her acknowledged beauty that only older men and other women measured accurately. Breteuil's daughter was as cool and hard as her sire. She knew exactly with whom she contended and what she would have from this situation, facts she now laid before her fiery young knight commander with clipped precision. Her husband, Rolph, had probed de Guilbert's reluctance at Thetford. Before departing to continue the war in Brittany, he urged Agatha to exploit the advantage: to delay, haggle, and demand, ultimately to fight if need be with a strong chance of victory through greater determination.

Agatha must do that now. Supplies were running low. They could not be sure the enemy would not be reinforced. Though de Guilbert had not assaulted their walls, her castle could withstand siege just so long before surrender or a profitable armistice.

"We will require, all of us, safe conduct to ship," Agatha stated. "With all baggage and movables. We surrender nothing but the keep."

"And if he refuses?" Raimond responded with open eagerness. "My men are spoiling to be at them."

"Then we fight, Raimond." Agatha awarded her knight the sudden bright smile that disarmed more experienced men without effort. They never saw its calculation until too late. "I have treasure here, gold and silver plate. They will meet our terms or you will sortie against them. We're ready to risk all, the baron is not. He thinks he has won by the mere fact of siege."

Thus the static game verged on movement. There would be prisoners and ransoms back and forth, but now victory would go to those who needed it most.

When Agatha's mounted procession issued from the bailey's south gate to a sally of horns, Robin and his men were just returning from the field stoves after a breakfast of hard bread, ale, and fish going bad in the heat.

"More talk," Robin seethed at the distant line of rebel knights. "More sitting on our arses."

"Not my worry," Dickon philosophized, tearing at a chunk of bread with strong teeth. "Sod 'em all."

Will and Morgan cheerfully agreed, having a vested interest in life, though at this rate the lice, flux, and bad food might kill them anyway.

Robin looked about for his company surgeons. "Where's Beorn and Mauger? They'll miss breakfast."

"Ah, they've ate," Morgan told him. "Gone down to the riverbank for herbs."

After inspecting the men for battle readiness, pointless as it seemed, Robin returned to the tent he shared with Ralf, to find the man stripped to the waist and scratching himself furiously.

"I'm lousy! Itching all yesterday but never thought—ah, *merde*." Ralf put on his last almost-clean skirted tunic and buckled his sword over it. "God knows where I caught them."

"Where I did," Robin supposed. "Whole camp's alive with 'em. Four men down with flux, Beorn says." Another week like this and the rebels could walk out of Norwich unopposed over a carpet of invalids. "Ta for putting in a word with the baron. I don't suppose he's any orders for us."

By way of answer only a negative grunt. Ralf had to return to the parley which went worse by the hour, tempers rising with the gritty heat.

The sun climbed higher and hotter through the morning. Rather than remove their mail, the parley moved out of the tent to the open air. Robin hovered about them to catch what he could of their questionable progress. He caught the drift: Agatha would not leave without her valuables. No knights would surrender to be ransomed. Men grew irritable in the heat; courtesy frayed and broke. Personal challenges were hurled, everyone gabbling at once. To Robin, for all their efficiency in fighting Saxons, these Normans turned bread simple against each other. Each man's personal honor must be upheld before all else. Gauntlets were thrown down to be snatched up by an equally hotheaded adversary. A flaming wonder they ever carved a duchy out of France. No more than outlaws, the pack of them. Robin grew bored and let his mind drift to Marian.

Suddenly Countess Agatha shot to her feet raising an imperious arm for silence. "Suffice, de Guilbert! Prepare yourselves. We will array against you."

The shouting and the insults trailed off. A division appeared in the crowd, one side moving back from the other. Baron de Guilbert bowed formally to the countess.

"So be it, madam."

The knights on both sides shouldered past Robin, their eyes newly alight with purpose and excitement. Regardless of outcome this was what they wanted, understood, believed in, and lived for.

"So it's fight at last," he called to Ralf as the knight strode past him moodily. Lately Ralf's disgust rivaled Dickon's; now it was classic.

"Yes, but of course we are out of it. The good baron won't insult his peers with common bowmen." Ralf slapped his gauntlets against one palm and stalked away to his horse like a man mortally offended himself.

Raimond de Beaumont was not the most experienced commander Agatha could wish, but the prominence of his family plus his raw aggressiveness precluded any other choice in leading her cavalry. Shortly after midday, the south gate opened and Raimond rode out followed by his full compliment of a hundred and fifty knights.

Dickon Blue jeered at the sight: "Another bleedin' May dance."

"It is a shame to weep over," said Morgan of Powys, not sorry for what he was excused but nagged by a depressing sense of uselessness. "Give us enough shafts, could we not end this and be home in a week?"

Shading his eyes from the sun's glare, Robin followed the preparate maneuverings of the two opposed forces. A dance, but a deadly one. The shifting about of horsemen on either side of the meadow gradually subsided. Two long bristling lines faced each other across the mud between the bailey gate and siege tents. From his position to the north, the image came unbidden to Robin: a chess board, the decisive move always more obvious to the uninvolved observer. So damned simple. His sight swept to the unattended bridge across the deep ditch at the gate, then over the lines of horse and the two hundred yards of trodden mud between them.

Go in, de Guilbert. Do something right. Charge them first.

Now there was a taut, crouching stillness in both lines like tight-wound catapults needing only a touch to loose them. Baron de Guilbert and Beaumont walked their horses to the center of their forward ranks to face each other. Standing among his bedraggled men, Ralf Fitz-Gerald duplicated every move on the field in his spirit and experience. Feet setting more surely in stirrups, left hand gripping shield and reins, the right finding the spear's best balance for the cast. In his own terms he saw more than Robin did. *Take the advantage*, he silently beseeched de Guilbert. *At him now, don't wait.*

"HOLD!"

The command thundered over the field with the power and authority of an intervening god never for an instant doubting he would be obeyed on earth. The sheer imperative of the sound and its advancing source shocked both sides off balance for a moment. Standing beside Robin, Beorn squinted through the sun at the approaching figure.

"Your eyes are better than mine, Robin. Am I wrong?"

A number of feelings mixed in Robin's soft reply. "No, Father. I can't believe it either. But it's him."

If war was different things to different men—horror, honor, life itself—the leaven of absurdity was one of them. The huge man with the broad-headed battle-ax on his shoulder came on like a ship under full sail, striding down the lethal alley between the lines of cavalry as if oblivious to both. Coming abreast of the baron and Beaumont, he swung about, walking backward as he shouted.

"Ta for the wait. Just hold 'til I'm past and I'll be obliged. Easy, lad." This to Beaumont steadying his skittish horse. "Easy," the calm voice boomed out over the killing-field with sublime detachment. A Leviathan in worn Lincoln and leather, the ax riding light as a kindling stick on his shoulder. Ripples of laughter played over both lines, the release of tension among men turned for one outrageous moment from the deadly to the ridiculous, like Death himself with scythe already raised, slipping and landing on his rump.

Clear at last of the lines, the intruder wheeled again, waving his thanks. "Right then. Get on with it."

He turned again and strode toward the straggling clumps of archers, toward Robin and his own purpose. Behind him the lines tensed again. Then, spurred by a piercing trumpet they rumbled forward toward each other. Their charge, their collision, the screaming of horses and stricken men did not concern the solitary traveler. He walked placidly to Robin and halted, grounding the great ax.

"Wystan said you have the standard. That's his and mine to carry." He glanced casually at the roiling mass of horsemen on the field. "We can speak of the other matter in its time."

So Little John returned to his personal war like a man coming home.

48

With the shock of colliding metal and flesh, the startled birds wheeling in the hot, cloudless sky, scattered and flew away. They fled the contended field for quieter air where men disputed a different honor in a different tongue. Men to whom the screaming combat on the meadow beyond them was slighter and far remote from their own.

Robin stared coldly at his former friend. "I'll have nowt to do with you since Freda."

John searched for a sign of acceptance from the other men of Sherwood. In Will's silence he might have read a forgiveness, in Beorn's sad eyes at least an understanding. "It was an accident, Father. I never meant . . ."

The excommunicate Beorn said only, "I know. We will talk, but it is between you and God."

"It is that, and so I'll answer. Wystan wanted to be here. Give me the flag and say I carry it for him."

"Lord Robin, what difference?" Between unforgiving Robin and silent Fitz-Gerald, Mauger felt impelled to speak. He jerked his thumb at the clangorous field where Normans were killing each other with no need of assistance. "Forgive his one sin, remember more virtues, and let him carry the flag."

Little John shifted from one foot to the other before Robin. "You and Aelred, you were always so quick to judge a man. So goddamned . . ." Whatever, the word eluded him.

"Self-righteous?" Ralf supplied with a slight but convinced smile. "Will that serve?"

"Close enough. Both of you judge me afterward as you will." What he needed now, John managed only with difficulty. "Thane, I'm asking. Please."

Beyond their stillness, the foolish battle roared too loudly that it also mattered. It did not. Robin moved from his folded-arms stance of denial, walked a few steps away from John. He noted Will and Morgan with their unspoken *yes*, and young Henri yearning toward glory on the field.

"John," he said finally, "you try a man's faith."

But Beorn was at his elbow speaking softly, a man much concerned with forgiveness on his own the last few years. "I've known you all your life, Rob. I've wiped your nose and heard your troubles and watched you grow into the best of Aelred and far beyond him. But carry your own cross, not the world's. Leave a little for God to do on his own."

"What are you saying, Father?"

"Think how far he's come to ask, all those miles, knowing what he needs and what it will probably cost him. He needs to be here. He's always needed to be here, and John isn't an asking man. Think on that."

"It's hard, Father," Robin ground through his teeth. Then he looked around impatiently. "Standard bearer!"

He took the cased flag from the little Manxman who was glad to be relieved. "Was an honor to be sure," the retired ensign from the Isle of Man admitted, "but a great burden as well."

"Come here, John. I'll not put myself out for the like of you. You want this, come take it."

When the blacksmith faced him, Robin shoved the Fighting Man standard into his hands. "There's your honor for what it's worth. Sire Ralf, do you mark me?"

"I do, Captain."

"When the baron sounds recall, when we fall in to march home, Littlerede has one hour to quit my sight. After that you may hang him from anything that will hold a rope."

John's shaggy head chopped up and down once. "Fair bargain."

Morgan sang out: "There's a bounty for volunteering, John."

"Right," said Robin. "Sire Ralf, give this son of a bitch his five pence."

"And tuppence I've long owed you." Will Scatloch gladly dropped the silver in John's hand. "Welcome home, Johnny lad."

John retrieved his ax, and rested the flagstaff on the ground. In his eyes as he turned toward the disputed field, Robin might have seen a justice harder than his own.

Raimond de Beaumont and his knights cantered across the bridge and into their bailey, roaring their exultant victory. Some were hurt and a few had to be lifted from the saddle, but all were drunk with the pure joy of war. Countess Agatha had judged correctly: The balance tipped and fell now in favor of Raimond's raw will to fight. She hurried down from the walls, pushing her way through lathered horses and staggering knights to reach Beaumont. He swayed on his feet, holding on to his slimy bridle, wild-eyed and trembling with blood hot as the searing sun.

"There's blood on your mail, Raimond."

"Not mine, lady. None of mine."

"You were splendid! One more sortie and we have them."

They had torn huge rents in de Guilbert's mounted lines. The next fierce charge would see a total rout. By Vespers bell Agatha could dictate her own terms for the evacuation of Norwich. Ringed about by her perspiring, jubilant knights, Agatha lifted herself up in Beaumont's stirrup, searching for her usual messengers. "Nuncio to me now! Give me a herald here!"

Ralf swung down from his saddle before waiting Robin, Henri close behind. "The heralds say they will sortie again."

"And us?"

"Out of it," mourned Henri, disgruntled as his knight.

To Robin, this baron strained belief with sentiments verging on treason. "No orders at all, just stand down?"

"But stand ready." Ralf scanned the company lounging about in small groups, some lolling against the wagons loaded with their extra arrows. "I got that much out of the idiot."

"Been ready from the start."

"*Bien,* that is something at least. The men should be kept busy."

The physical attitudes of the men betrayed their feelings in a kind of slump. Excused, out of the fight again. They knew how little they were valued. Even to the malingering worst of them the order carried an indefinable sting. Good to be safe, but still—*we are here and ready and men ourselves. A shame, as the Welsh Morgan said, and a blind waste beside.*

Stand ready. They heard the order from Robin and obeyed with glum efficiency. When the bailey gate opened, de Guilbert's knights mounted and walked their horses into line against the coming assault. Each of Robin's archers slung a full quiver and laid by as many fifteen-arrow bundles as he could carry. Some bore stakes to be hammered into the ground if they took up a position. They shuffled into ranks now, knowing they would not be called to move forward, irrelevant as crows on a fence. Robin stood between Ralf and Little John in the forerank as Beaumont crossed the bailey bridge at the head of his squadrons.

Ralf remarked casually, "Since we approach the trivial, Beaumont sent me a personal challenge. I kicked him in his mentality once."

"Ethelwold told me. Good for you."

"*Merci.* I felt better for days afterward."

Now Robin's attention was on the rebel squadrons moving into battle array, and on something beyond it. "Do you play chess?"

To Ralf an odd question at the moment. "Very well. What has that to do with castles in Norwich?"

"Knights on the board. Powerful but clumsy. Easier to get them into trouble than out."

They waited. Men shuffled about in place, wondering when the damn thing would begin. Sweating in the humid heat, one man prayed aloud that the knights were as uncomfortable. "Must be hot in all that iron."

"Hotter if we had a go. One good flight, that's all we need. Go through 'em like butter."

Two piercing notes from a horn quivered on the still air. De Guilbert's lines moved forward at a walk. The rebel lines advanced at the same leisurely pace. The ponderous warhorses gained momentum only with agonizing slowness, heaving at last into a gallop. The riders raised their spears to ready as the gap narrowed between sides.

Tensed, leaning into the distant battle, Robin's men flinched in empathy as the two lines struck each other and became a confused mass. Spears flew, swords flashed out. Horses wheeled, screamed high and went down. For an instant only clashing chaos, then out of it charged Richard de Guilbert crouched behind his shield, sword high, guiding the horse superbly with knees alone as he chose his opponent and plunged back into the fray.

"*Pour de Guilbert!*" hooted the admiring Henri in spite of himself. "*Encore, bon chevalier!* Oh, do you see him?"

Ralf saw more than Henri did, more than the embattled baron himself: the gradual turning of his flank under the savage onslaught of Beaumont's wing squadrons. Then Robin yanked at Ralf's arm.

"Do you see there?" He pointed to the bridge across the bailey ditch.

"That's where we should be and should have been from the start." Robin spun about to face his men. "Anyone sick of this beside me? Anyone want to be done today and get home for the haying?"

One man in the rear piped up: "Why not?"

"Robin, what—what is this?"

Robin only shook Ralf off, set on his own course now that infected first one, then another, and yet more of the men around him. "Dickon, what say you? Follow me to the bridge?"

"If there ent no way around it, aye."

"Not from here there ent. Brace!" Robin steadied the bowstave against his calf and braced his string, calling for the squire Henri. "Good lad, you heard Sire Ralf give the order to stand down?"

Confused but with growing excitement the boy bobbed his head.

"Then you can swear to the baron with a clear conscience that I disobeyed."

Ralf caught his arm and would not be shaken off. "Are you mad? He could hang you and every man who follows you."

"Get away, Ralf. I'm going in."

"You will not."

"There before the bridge." Committed now, alive with the clear thing to be done, Robin grasped Ralf by the breast of his mail coat and pulled him close. "The baron didn't want to win, now he can't. Not without us. Ride to him. When we're in place, Beaumont will be caught between us. Tell de Guilbert to re-form and then hit them hard."

Ralf knew what was happening. Command had been taken from him, but the baron was losing the field and possibly the campaign. Only a lifetime of discipline enabled Ralf to resist a moment longer. "I gave you an order, all of you. You will stand."

"No one's asking you to go, little Frank," John reminded him serenely. "You're not needed."

"Dickon to me!" Robin called as he pointed out his intention to Ralf. "We'll throw ourselves out there, three ranks in front of the bridge. Stop 'em up tight. They can't get back inside, not past us. Take the boy and ride." He gripped Ralf's hand. "Good luck."

Dickon Blue stumped up to them, braced bow slung over one shoulder. "Well, what's the word?"

Robin's arm shot out toward the parapets of Norwich castle. "Those bowmen on the walls: We'll be well in their range. Can you keep their heads down?"

Dickon turned aside to spit at his feet but did not seem at all sour just then. "All day if we've shafts enough."

Henri brought the horses, quavering a little as he worried to Ralf, "Would the baron really hang them?"

"He would. I've seen it done." Ralf put one foot in the stirrup, then paused. He threw one conflicted glance back at the Saxons preparing to move, every one of them sharp and vital with purpose now. "But he can't hang me, not with a commission from the king's regent and the queen's own will. *Montez.*"

Robin had laid an insubordinate blessing in de Guilbert's vacillating hands. He must use it now. Ralf urged his horse out in front of the company, holding his sword aloft. "Robin! All of you! By the Good God, you will not carry this alone nor deny my share in it. By my order, Robin: Advance the company and block that bridge. Littlerede!" Ralf found his hands shaking on reins and sword. "It's your flag. You wanted to carry it. Shake out the colors. Let them see who comes against them."

As John tore the cover from the rich blue folds glinting with gold, Robin couldn't help grinning up at Ralf Fitz-Gerald and what he'd taken on himself. "God bless, boyo."

"Bless yourself, *Anglais*. I'll be back." Ralf spurred toward the baron's lines, Henri shouting with pure excitement close behind.

"*Aïe! Va, bébé.* Go!"

On the walls Agatha's soldiers saw the surge of men running toward the bridge. Saxons among them stared at the blue and gold standard rippling on the human tide; saw it clear but hardly believed. Yet no mistake. There weren't two such flags in the world.

Robin reached the bridge, bellowing at his men to form three lines of thirty each. "Cover the walls, Dickon! First two ranks, get those stakes in quick."

And Little John, content in a cosmos at last set to rights, raised the Fighting Man high to jam the staff deep into the ground with all of a savage-joyous heart in his arms.

"And—*there!*"

That afternoon, even as the men ran toward the bridge, Judith was reading Robin's deferred letter to Marian in the small house at Grantham. The same heat simmered the air beyond their open door and Perdu curled, napping, in the coolest corner of the earthen floor. Marian listened with Edward on her lap as Judith read in her soft, cadenced voice. There hadn't been any word in days. Marian loved Robin that he'd made provision like a secret gift before leaving her.

> . . . keep this as remembrance of my memory of you. Last night I watched you and the boy asleep. Against the peace of you, I saw all the anger boiling in me and wondered how I could still all down to that simple serenaty. Not sure I spell aright, but watching over you both, I knew that if there were such peace in me, how could I go off to any killing? How leave it now save I must?
>
> Who was ever so married as we, girl? Our blood in the tree, our boy in his bed so beeutyful asleep. Whatever happens, I will never be away from you, not for one breath or beat of your heart. I will be the wind that kisses your cheek, the rain that washes your tears and the sun that dries them warm. When Edward feels Sherwood alive about him, when he hears old Robin Goodfellow stride like thunder through the green—as I did once and ran afeared—say it is only his own da walking Denby to see all is right.
>
> You know what I try to say, Marian. You have always known. No fear, girl. Against what I have to come home to, this Norwich is naught to fret a man.
>
> ROBIN.

Judith folded the bit of parchment and placed it apologetically in Marian's hand. "My cousin ever surprises me. Perhaps it is the curse of education. I have lost the grace to be so simple."

Marian set Edward down and went to the open door, holding the letter and breathing the air of this still, hot afternoon. "They'll come back." She was sure of it. "Just ent right not to."

—as Raimond de Beaumont, plunging out of the *mêlée* to reform and charge the baron's knights once more, saw three lines of bowmen blocking any return to the castle. He was not dismayed, only surprised. Beyond the dishonor, the thing was absurd, even incongruous. Over the rumble of hooves on the field, two men's voices rose harmonizing in a melody old when their Arthur was young. In the center of the bowmen planted still as gravestones before the bridge, a Lazarus banner curled in a freshet of breeze, risen from the dead and impossible as the men themselves.

49

"FOUL!"

"Recreant! Dishonorable!"

The outraged accusations went up from Beaumont's knights, hurled at Baron de Guilbert. Use of bowmen had been expressly ruled out by parley. Surely the baron would not break word to his fellow knights. The bastard Fitz-Gerald perhaps, though it was not the sheriff advancing from the archers' ranks but a lean Saxon in battered leather and grimy linen.

On the bailey parapet a veteran serjeant at arms, a Wessex man himself, strongly advised Countess Agatha to leave off cursing and stay under cover. He yanked her down abruptly before arrows cleaved the air precisely where she had been.

"Cover, lady. They'll kill you quick as me."

More startled than frightened, Agatha refused to believe him. "They would not dare."

The old soldier knew otherwise. "They'd bloody love it. Stay down."

"Send out pikemen to break them up," Agatha ordered.

"Pikes? They won't have a chance against—"

"Do it. Sire Raimond must have a clear way in."

On the field, Raimond de Beaumont could be faintly amused at the presumptuous peasants aspiring to block his return to the bailey; even more that one of them approached to parley like an equal. A moment then, while his knights and horses breathed. Accompanied by his squire, Raimond walked his horse forward to the shabby, unarmed man waiting with hands on hips. The Saxon stated his business without bothering to identify himself.

"Last parley, Norman. My men have your range. Either one of you touches sword or tries to run me down, there's two Welshmen drawn and glad to kill you, *compris?*"

"Whose man are you?" Beaumont demanded. "By what command do you do this? Fitz-Gerald's?"

"Mine." Robin's eyes did not waver from the Norman's face. "I'm tired of you."

Beaumont's scrutiny narrowed. The man was dimly familiar. "Are you indeed?"

"Shut up and don't waste my time. We ent much for this polite foolery you call war, and we don't take prisoners. Look about you. You can't get out and you can't get back. So I'll accept your surrender in the name of the king," Robin concluded as if the matter were too evident to argue.

"I have seen you before, fellow."

Robin ignored him, a man with a point to make. "Unless you want to have a go. Make up your mind. I've had a gutful of you lot and I want to go home." He turned abruptly and strode away toward his own lines.

Raimond reined his horse about, assessing de Guilbert's strength and the changed situation. He had the advantage against the baron's cavalry, much less with his back exposed to bowmen. He called after the Saxon: "Die if you wish. We cross that bridge."

"You tried that at Denby," Robin threw over his shoulder. "Remember? I took it out of your face."

Beaumont twisted around in the saddle. One hand went to the broad scar on his cheek. *Denby. Yes.*

Robin's two front ranks were staggered among and behind the sharpened stakes, the men placing arrows upright before them in the mud and trampled turf. Will Scatloch sang out as Robin approached, "What said the sweet boy? Wise or dead?"

"He's coming," Robin answered for all to hear. He drew his dagger, knelt, and kissed the cross hilt. *God defend me.* Every man in the ranks did the same, making a cross of dagger or short sword in a brief prayer. Some placed small stones or bits of turf in their mouths, born of earth and prepared to return to it if God willed.

"Dickon! They'll have to open the gates for him. You know what to do."

"I do." When he scowled, Dickon was homely. Grinning now with sheer vindictive gusto, he was grotesque. He set out his shafts meticulously, fitting one to his string while searching the parapet above. They were keeping their heads down. "Show yourself, witch," he crooned to the place where he'd last seen Agatha. "Put up your pretty head. There's lots of accidents."

De Guilbert and Ralf Fitz-Gerald glared at each other from their saddles. Beyond in the middle of the meadow, Beaumont's hundred and forty-odd knights trotted smartly into two long lines facing the bridge. The baron trembled with rage and shame.

"You ordered this?"

"I did," Ralf answered distinctly and loud enough to be heard by many of the baron's knights.

"You hear what they call us?"

Ralf nodded resignedly. "Boys throwing boys' insults. You are here to prosecute the king's campaign."

"Within the rules of warfare which you seem to have thrown to the winds. And that flag? You know what it is."

"And flown by my order," Ralf confirmed levelly. "Since you refuse any pride to my men, they brought their own."

They faced each other sweating beneath their mail in the hot glare of the sun, de Guilbert near incoherent with the blasphemy of a situation rapidly escaping his control. "Your order is mutiny and that flag is treason."

"No more than you to sit here maundering on honor while Beaumont and Agatha act. They are *using* your absurd honor against you and still you cannot see." Ralf twitched reins and moved to the baron's knee, lowering his voice. "Richard, no one accuses victory of treason or anything else. Take the moment. Hit them from behind. Robin expects you to come in. End it."

With a physical twinge of empathy, Ralf perceived his friend's courageous but vacillating soul stretch on the rack of all he was and believed: bidden by a king who wanted results but inevitably to be judged by the hard code of his peers. Then a trumpet cleaved the air and the cry went up from the vavasors around them.

"They go!"

"Please, Richard. You can't stop it now and there's not much time."

"No." When de Guilbert turned to Ralf friendship was dead. Buried. "Get away. I will prevent their escape, that is all. Since you ordered this disgrace, share in it."

Ralf backed his horse. "So I will. Tell the king, tell God if you will, the order was mine and I am proud of what my men have done with it. Not one hesitated. If they have soiled your honor, they just may have saved your backside." Ralf kicked his horse into a run toward their supply wagons.

Mounted as his knight on a horse too light for war but swift, Henri followed pell-mell, throwing a fearful glance at the bridge. If Beaumont was trapped, so was Robin, who lacked the force or the arrows to sustain his position without support.

The low thunder of rebel cavalry gained speed as they closed on the waiting archers. In the first rank Robin watched them come. "Ready!"

Far too slow: He perceived that flaw at York and Grantham. The field half gone beneath those heavy horses and still not at gallop. *Steady. Don't give the order to press too soon, their strings will creep. Frightened . . . scared as Johnny's mad. Saw it in his eyes when he took the flag from me. All those miles, Beorn said. Bent here since Hastings like the rest of us. Maud, Marian, Freda, me—all come here to this moment.*

"Press!"

Yards behind Robin, John set himself with his ax before the Fighting Man. "Open your heart's eye, Wystan, and see the glory of this. Come on, you Frank bastards. Come on. . . ."

"Steady on," Robin cautioned his men. "Just like practice but with bigger targets." He felt the diminishing distance as they rushed at him. Nothing existed but himself and the target and the line that bound them together. "Loose!"

The air tore with a harsh, deep *whirr!* The wide center of the first line of horse seemed to trip over an invisible barrier and crumple. Unable to slow, the second wave bounded or stumbled over the confusion of downed men and horses, then faltered alike as the second flight hit them and then a third—

—as Dickon Blue and one other man, hacking furiously, severed the final rope that retracted the bailey bridge and scurried back to their own rank. Let who would cross against them. No one would be pulling the damn thing up.

Robin's men let out a hoarse cheer as the remnant of Beaumont's charge limped back, many on foot and far too many others lying on the field behind them. A few bowmen started out from habit to take spoils but were halted by Robin's cold promise.

"Any man goes beyond these stakes, I'll kill him myself."

"Stand fast," Little John rumbled. "Men who did that at Hastings never heard Vesper's bell and neither will you."

"Stand ready. Look to your shafts. Dickon, cover the walls."

"Ah, belt up. We're doing it," Dickon shot back sourly. "Where's the baron? Comin' any time this week?"

Ralf and Henri galloped up in a spray of mud and flying turf, hurling bundles of arrows without dismounting. "Give them out. We'll go back for more."

"I don't think so." Robin's chilled attention was far across the meadow. "Not now."

Ralf turned to see the detail of seven knights circling their wagons with torches. One of them spurred on toward the bridge. Ralf swallowed, feeling the effort rasp in his dry throat. "God no, he wouldn't."

Ninety-odd men marooned between castle and cavalry. No one spoke; the thing was too brutal and impossible for that. The men watched as de Guilbert's own knights set fire to the wagons and the rest of their arrows.

His horse dead on the field behind him, Raimond de Beaumont kept blinking the blur of shock from his eyes as he limped toward his men. He had never faced massed English archers before nor believed the tales of them. He was enough of a commander to assess his pitifully thinned vavasors and how their manage on reins was far less assured and quick than before. A wall. They had run headlong against a wall. He would not have believed it. From predictable victory they had moved into the shadow of possible defeat. Beaumont stumbled to his white-faced squire and grabbed the man's bridle.

"How . . . how many lost?"

Stunned himself by the slaughter, the squire looked about with barely focused eyes. "By those here, almost half."

"Give me your horse. Down, I say."

Whatever he did, it must be quick. De Guilbert's knights heavily outnumbered him now and were maneuvering in a long crescent line denying him escape—as if Raimond would try. Before him the horns of the crescent; behind, only three drab lines of English. To the north, the wagons burned by de Guilbert, perhaps a fool but blessedly a man of honor.

The English waited him. With a limited supply of shafts they had no more choice than himself now.

Beaumont hailed a companion slumped forward in his saddle. As he rode around the ashen vavasor, he saw that the man's right leg was arrow-pinned to the hard leather of his saddle. The point must have penetrated the horse's flank to some degree, mingling animal and human blood on the rich blue lambswool of the saddle blanket. Beaumont clapped the knight on the shoulder as his squire called out:

"Sire, the baron comes to parley."

Flanked by the squire striding on foot and the wounded knight managing his horse only with difficulty, Beaumont met de Guilbert midway between the mounted lines. He was hardly in a receptive mood, boiling to be at the bridge, to run over Fitz-Gerald, Denby, and their peasants out of pure pleasure.

"Raimond, I—I have done what I could short of riding them down myself." De Guilbert was painfully apologetic. "That I will not do. You have acquitted yourself with honor in the face of Fitz-Gerald's shame which is none of my doing. Give me your sword. Surrender."

He held out his hand but Beaumont struck it away. "Be damned! Have we not been more than equal to you? You think we cannot break through that scum at the bridge?"

De Guilbert frankly did not. "*C'est impossible.* You know you have not the power now."

"Power?" The leg-shot knight wheezed through his pain. "We have the heart. See where I am locked to my saddle by this shaft? Well enough, for I do not quit horse yet."

Beaumont swung his destrier about. From the tossing of its head and snorting, the animal had fight left in him. "You hear, Richard? Come against me if you will. We go. *Allons, mes coeurs!*"

Sitting his horse as Beaumont moved away, de Guilbert knew he had discharged himself insofar as he could to brother knights, enemy though they were. Gone further than he should in burning the wagons. He experienced a bleak, bottomless moment of sickness in his soul: Nothing was right anymore. Fitz-Gerald was in the wrong but saved the day, Denby was probably mad. And yet . . . Richard de Guilbert hovered over a dark chasm of the spirit before becoming aware of the older knight at his knee. "Yes?"

"My lord, whatever stain on the bastard of Nottingham, let the victory be not his but yours."

As it should be, the baron reckoned riding back to his lines. Whatever scruples, he must be decisive. He had seen that storm hit Beaumont's charge like the angered hand of God, seen the pikemen run from the open gate to the bridge only to falter, go down or retreat. The battle was being taken away from him.

A hundred yards away in the middle of the torn field, a trumpet summoned Beaumont's men to prepare.

Behind the wide nose-guard of his helm, Sire Jean du Plessy's expression was remote and glacial as he delivered de Guilbert's will to Ralf Fitz-Gerald. He ignored the tall Saxon standing beside the knight who had put himself beyond the pale. The shame was his; the archers did not exist. And yet, *pardi,* Fitz-Gerald did not even blush.

"Greetings, Jean. What from our lord beside incompetence?"

"Embarrassment at your recreance, vavasor. He arrays against the rebels so far as honor allows but will no more. You will strike that insulting flag and quit this position, or keep both at your own peril."

"I see." Ralf lowered his face to hide an irreverent smile at du Plessy's indignation which surely must reflect the baron's. *He looks shocked as a buggered bride.* "Alas, the flag is not mine but belongs to the bearer, John of Blidworth. One would advise you not to insist."

The knight-herald turned his heavy Flemish mount about, adding more mud to Ralf's already spattered armor. "What answer shall I take to the baron? Will you retire?"

Neither Ralf nor Robin seemed inclined to say or quit anything. The Englishman's placid blue eyes, fixed on du Plessy, glimmered with mild humor. Ralf's reply was brief and pointed.

"Say that my duty is here. For the baron's duty and what he has done to us--you must pardon me." Ralf turned his back on the knight and walked away to Henri.

Robin took a purposeful step toward the herald's horse. "Hear me well—"

"Lord Robin." Mauger had come closer to hear the exchange and now touched his friend's shoulder. "May I? My Frank is the more fluent."

"And your charity," Robin admitted, stepping aside. "Tell him good. We ent moving."

"No fear." Mauger shifted the bag of rolled fresh bandage on his shoulder, moving to the knight's stirrup. "*Bon seigneur,* tell your baron since he seems loathe to touch a soiled war, we have borrowed it for the nonce. If he prates of honor, say it is here. Let him share the feast or not keep us from the table. Enough, Robin?"

"Enough. Now get your fat horse out of here," Robin growled at du

Plessy. "We ent dined. To you that nag's an honor. To us it's a meal. *Va t'en.* Go."

The knight rode away, curving wide around Beaumont's lines that were forming into a wedge. A detail of five of Robin's men had dashed forward to salvage shields and spears from the carnage of fallen knights. Remaining arrows were hastily shared out among the archers. Dickon's men had swept the walls and driven the pikemen back within the bailey at a heavy expense of shafts. The order went through the ranks: controlled volleys to be loosed only on command.

In the first rank Will Scatloch took four arrows from a bundle and passed four to Morgan of Powys. "Waste not, want not. Don't miss."

Morgan placed the arrows upright in the turf by his right foot. "I have not missed since I was fifteen."

"Listen to him," Will deplored with a deep sigh. "Greed and boasting, boasting and greed. It is a flaw in thee, mun."

A blast from Beaumont's trumpeter brought Robin and his men to alertness. The rebel wedge formation gathered in on itself like muscle bunching to exertion. At Ralf's side with drawn sword and shield, young Henri became absurdly aware of a single drop of sweat rolling down his cheek. He flicked a nervous tongue over dry lips, suddenly glad he hadn't eaten. "I've never seen a charge from this side."

"Nor I," Ralf admitted, adding with a touch of lightness he did not feel: "We become almost English, Henri. I think the word is immigrants."

Henri gripped his weapon. His teeth wanted to chatter. He clamped his lips tight around them.

From the rear rank: "Gates opening again."

"Let 'em," Dickon Blue said, low and tight. "Right wing cover the gate, left watch the walls."

With the second trumpet, Beaumont's wedge came on at a brisk walk which moved rapidly into a trot. Robin measured their advance as mere objects, targets. If his men had few arrows, there were at least shields to cover Dickon's rank from the walls and spears for close defense if the bastards got that close.

Not if but when. They will this time, got to.

"Ready."

Every archer stanced, advancing his left foot, three fingers on the bowstring, waiting, sweating with more than the heat. Robin prayed. *God, I've so much to live for. I wish I could just run away to Marian and the boy.*

—as the forward surge stretched into gallop, the drumroll of their hooves a deepening thunder in the earth. This was Beaumont's idea of life, not Robin's. *He lives for it. I've got to live through it.*

"Press!"

The deadly bows raised and bent.

"Pikemen coming out the gate."

"Hold them!" Dickon bellowed, pressing into his bow. "Drive them back! Loo—"

He went down with the crossbolt from the wall in his chest. The last Dickon saw in this world were thick legs bounding over him as John left his standard and charged the pikemen, ax swinging like a reaper's sickle.

"Loose! Press. Loose."

In a staccato rush, two concentrated flights struck the juggernaut wedge, most aimed at the horses' massive chests. As the point of the attacking wedge blunted and went down, four knights from either side swept out, crouching low behind their shields. They swept inward again at an oblique angle through the stakes to hurl their spears. Three bowmen were hit but none of the knights got out. Two of them went down under arrows. Two fell to Ralf and Henri, the boy maneuvering with his shield for cover as Ralf hurled a fallen spear at one and himself at a second. Henri took the knight's head off with his sword. The body jolted away still mounted as if horse and corpse still had purpose. Henri swallowed hard through a queasy sound.

Ralf pulled him back to now. "Don't be sick. You don't have time."

Robin, with only three arrows left, saw Beaumont erupt from the confusion of knights milling about in the foundered attack. The man bellowed an order: Like birds following the commands of instinct, his knights broke left and right, lumbering back up the field.

Nocking his last arrow, Will wondered, "Look you, Robin: Are they quit?"

Will's sight answered for him. Some forty of the knights had survived their withering accuracy and were quickly re-forming to come again— came again even as the Welshman stanced. No formation, controlled as a windstorm, but coming on and over the sound of them a clear distant trumpet—

"Loose!"

As the last arrows flew and took their toll, Ralf heard the baron's signal. He saw the crescent lines move forward and gather speed in the last instant before Beaumont's men battered through the few remaining stakes against Robin's archers who had nothing to stop them now but spears. Ralf crouched beside Henri as a spear hit and skidded off his oval shield. *Thank God. He's coming. We may be dead when he gets here, but the fool is committed at last.*

Their arrows gone, the bowmen were bared to the fury that broke over them like a hurricane. Robin fell back with Will and Morgan, defending himself with a spear alone, and the battle became unequal hand-to-hand. Robin slipped and fell, barely scrambling aside from trampling hooves. John ran in to cover him, shouting and waving his arms to shy the horse, then buried the ax in the animal's neck. Blood on his hands, blood on the haft. Dimly John realized some of it was his own.

Fighting back-to-back with Henri, Ralf had one red vision of Hastings and the final moments on the ridge. John's ax stuck deep in the wound; the blacksmith lost his blood-slippery grip on it as Beaumont bore down on him from behind. Ralf and Robin saw the rebel leader in the same instant, cried the same warning—

"Behind, Johnny!"

"Littlerede, guard!"

Ralf lunged to help John, but had to dodge a horse which plunged between. Instinctively he ducked under his shield. The rider slashed at him but pushed on toward the bridge where, with no more arrows, men were now struggling shortsword against pike. His view cleared in time to see Robin hurl his spear at Beaumont who caught it on his shield. Propelled by long legs, Robin sprang at the knight and dragged him from the saddle. Ralf caught a blurred impression of John crawling weakly toward the Fighting Man, stubbornly dragging his ax and spitting blood.

Then Henri's shrill warning: "Guard, Ralf!"

His body reacted before his brain, bringing up sword and shield together, and someone was shouting *HOLD!* Something struck him a glancing blow on the helmet. A fleeting blur of color as knights dashed by to the left and right of him jostling him apart from his squire and carrying the fight away from Ralf like swift-eddying surf. Ralf rubbed at his eyes. His stumbling progress had brought him close to Robin whose eyes lifted with his murdering fists over a broken thing he straddled. The eyes for an instant touched Ralf like icy hands, opaque with madness. The long body flexed, loosed like a catapult driving the cudgel fists down again and again. Tearing the mail from the blood-mask of the face. Going for the throat with a dagger in a sweep with the whole lunatic body behind it.

Something was wrong with Ralf's vision. He couldn't see much, only heard that spine-crawling sound he knew was Robin. By mere shape he recognized Henri close by. He heard the boy grunt with pain and shock and then fall. And always that damned silly voice bellowing *HOLD!* as if there were reason and order anywhere in this red acre before the bridge.

He was shouldered off balance by a reeking horse and fell over his squire. Ralf pulled his shield over him as the victorious litany went up.

"They cry quarter, Baron!"

"Hold in the name of the king!"

"Put up. They cry quarter!"

Down the years as often as he had come to this darkness in death's antechamber, Ralf was always amazed. *My God, I am alive.* He still couldn't see; his eyes were glued half-shut. They felt warm and sticky and so did his mind. Moments or minutes later he felt Henri's body jostled against him and recognized Mauger's voice.

"Easy on, boy. Sire Ralf, here's water."

Ralf pushed the shield off him and rose on one elbow. The noise of war was distant now, inside the bailey. He groped for the bucket of water.

"From the bailey well," Mauger told him, working at Henri's lacerated shoulder. "Can you move it, Henri?"

Ralf remembered his first injury as a squire. He had been as white and weak-voiced as this one. Henri quavered: "A little. Hurts awfully."

Mauger knew the bone was whole. "Broken you wouldn't feel it yet."

Clumsily Ralf wiped at the drying blood that hindered his sight. "De Guilbert finally moved."

"He did." Mauger ripped the scale-iron coat away from Henri's shoulder and smeared the wound with herb ointment. "But not soon enough."

The feeble cries for a surgeon wailed around them like unavenged spirits. "All right, I'm coming," Mauger promised them hurriedly. He was white as Henri, not a man to relish days like this, never to boast of them, revulsion choked tight under a kind of courage Raimond de Beaumont would never know. He bandaged Henri's shoulder, then handed a wad of clean linen to Ralf. "This will wash you quicker."

"How many did we—?"

Mauger cut him off with a look. "Don't count, Ralf. I can't." He picked up his bag and moved on to the next wounded.

"I can't look," Morgan muttered, grey with shock and fear. "Tell me truly, Will Scatloch: what is it that I need, bandage or priest?"

"It is a scratch that you have taken." Will knelt over his friend, quivering himself, licking at the wide laceration on his own right hand. Morgan had a deep spear wound high in his leg. Will had pulled the

blade out himself. "Will you have Lord Robin see you vanquished?"
You will not die nor dance again, not pierced so.

Will shifted to sit beside his friend. His shaking limbs told him the price of exertion and that he was not that spry anymore. Not old, mind, but neither young though his soul was timeless and gave him more Sight sometimes than even a Celt would wish. Here were he and Morgan, Britons following a Saxon to a Norman's war. *There's confusion.* Or perhaps not if that was the fate of Britons. Broken from their seed-home, scattered like chaff down the wind of time itself ever to fight under flags never their own, but always knowing it for the same ancient war.

"Mauger?" he called. "Here when you come to us. Morgan's down."

50

 f ORTY MEN TOO numbed by violent effort to stand unless they had to, sitting in the mud to one side of a captured bridge. Heads hunched over their knees and flies buzzing about them. The conflict had broken over their heads and swept past, resolved somewhere else. Some of their dead were already taken up; the rest waited with the limitless patience of that condition.

Young Henri had energy left to move about and had gone into the bailey to see how the baron disposed in the matter of prisoners. Ralf had no desire to move. In the mud before him someone had dropped a new azure ribbon. Ralf contemplated the incongruity for long moments before reaching to pick it up. He wound the sky-blue strip of samite around his filthy gauntlet. The material was utterly immaculate. It seemed illogical in that place. Ralf's dull attention fumbled at the puzzle then gave it up.

In the midst of war there was always absurdity. Without doubt even in hell one laughed now and again at the utterly ridiculous or ironic. When Countess Agatha was escorted across the bridge and through the remnant of Ralf's company she did not apparently recognize him.

Looked right through me, probably Robin as well. We're not very well turned-out today. Judith and Marian might glance once, see beggars and walk by.

Ralf turned his head with considerable effort as it seemed to weigh more than usual and smarted from the wound in his scalp that had bled so freely. "Robin?"

Robin sat in the mud beside something incomplete in expensive armor. Ralf thought at first he was badly wounded, blood from head to waist. His left hand gripped a large red lump by its stiff-matted dark hair. As Ralf called his name, the Englishman raised his head slightly, the eyes met his. They were saner now but Ralf could read where they had been.

An approaching horse rode into the periphery of Ralf's dull consciousness and halted close by. "Fitz-Gerald."

Ralf rose clumsily as a crippled bear to gaze up at Richard de Guilbert with the bleary focus of a drunk.

"As would have followed in any case, we have taken Norwich. Do not compound the charges against you, Sire Ralf." De Guilbert pointed peremptorily at the Fighting Man. Father Beorn was tending to John who even wounded refused to move from his position before the bridge unless his flag went with him. Father Beorn planted the standard to one side of the bridge. John was carried to lie under it.

"You will surrender that illegal flag now," the baron demanded.

Not much of it left to surrender: partially torn from the staff, pierced by spears, sword-rent, more mud than blue in the field dulling the jewels and golden figure.

"No, Richard. It will come down but not to you."

"Once more you disobey."

Ralf wanted to bathe for a full day and sleep a week. He bent to pick up his sword and shield. "You will have prisoners and ransoms enough. You do not deserve that flag."

When de Guilbert twitched the reins to move his horse forward, Ralf stepped between him and the standard, pointedly raising his sword but not his voice. "Stay back."

"I would, Baron." Robin lurched past Ralf to confront de Guilbert, still carrying the obscene fruit of his labor. "The flag belongs to John and will go with him. This is yours." Robin lifted the head he had sawed with dagger and battered with bare hands from Beaumont's body. He dropped it by de Guilbert's stirrup and walked away to the Fighting Man.

"Take your victory, my lord," Ralf bade him. "I must see to my men."

"Stay!" the baron snapped with less authority than he would have wished. The sight of Beaumont's head was a shock. "This matter is not concluded. When the king hears of your conduct—when he hears of that standard you allowed to fly—"

"Allowed? I *commanded* it!"

"Of course," the baron said, now at a loss beyond bare insult. "I might expect that of the Bastard of Nottingham."

"The king will hear," Ralf answered, wearied of the silly, irrelevant man. "The king shares the awkward condition of my birth. I have his confidence and his ear as one bastard to another. Shall I tell him how you burned your own wagons and left us to die?"

He pointed with his sword to Beaumont's head. "Would you remove the rubbish as you go? Raimond and I were not close. Go away, Richard. I am very tired."

He watched the baron ride away toward his tent where Agatha and other prisoners waited the usual and costly courtesies of war. He'd made an enemy of de Guilbert with this day's work and probably more to come. This would no doubt concern him in the future but at the moment Ralf couldn't bring himself to care.

Father Beorn could do nothing for John. Beaumont's sword thrust went through his unprotected back and punctured a lung. Blood came with every gurgling breath. The man's eyes were unfocused. Nothing for the priest but to give him the last rites. John lay beneath the torn Fighting Man with his priest, Robin, Will, and Mauger about him. Every so often he tried to speak.

"Get away. Get away from this hill. . . ."

Not his friends he was seeing, Beorn realized, not this place nor this year. John had been returning a long time to a lost ridge in his soul.

After a time he seemed to recognize them and know where he was. John was content. Beorn guessed he would leave his life swept and tidied as his forge.

But will I, then? Beorn questioned as he bent over John. *Do you hear me, God? You've got to hear me.*

"Can you hear me, John? Follow me. In the name of Almighty God, I release you—"

Robin broke in stubbornly, John's hand clamped between both of his own. "He's not going to die."

Will restrained him gently. "Let be. Let the good father do his office."

"—release you from all punishments in this life and the life to come."
God, turn and heed me now. Listen to Johnny, take him clear and free even if it's through Your postern gate. I take his sins on me. The worst of them was unintended, the least passion and belief. They stole his country. If that's a sin in John, it's worse in me and a wound in Robin. Lay John's sins on me.

"Do you renounce Satan and all his works?"

The wet whisper was barely audible: ". . . do."

"Can you make a good act of contrition?"

John struggled. His lips formed the words several times before Beorn heard them. ". . . heartily sorry for having offended thee and I—I forget the words. Robin?"

"Aye, man. I'm here."

"You know that Freda was mischance."

"I know. I couldn't forgive you because—for Christ's sake, Mauger or somebody! Keep the flies off him! Because I cared about Freda that much. I'm a pig-headed man, John."

That brought a faint smile to the crimsoned lips. "You are that."

"Jesus, fight it Johnny," Robin begged. "Don't let it happen. I was wounded worse and here I am."

Beorn gently tried to push him away; John didn't have much time, but Robin wouldn't give up. "*Fight* it."

But John was always one for doing everything in order. With Mauger wiping the blood from his lips and Beorn prompting the words, he went on sweeping clean the last cobbles of his life. "I firmly resolve with your grace to sin no more, to do penance and amend my life."

I will pay. I will amend, Beorn secretly underwrote the debt. *Go in peace.* No holy water but what Mauger had fetched from the well. Beorn blessed it and anointed John's brow, eyes, and lips.

"Robin?" The voice was clear but faint, already begun a long journey. "You ent said you forgive me."

"Freely, John. God witness."

"Well then, I forgive you, too," John allowed in gracious parting—then added with a sigh, "Were y'not such a land-proud son of a bitch, we might've got on better."

The dead were given decent enough burial in makeshift graves in Tombland, but that wouldn't quite do for Johnny. Robin cut the torn standard from the staff and gave it to Will and Mauger, who shrouded John's body in the thick folds. Then they waited for the oxcart to come around for him.

Robin drifted to stand near Ralf Fitz-Gerald. Neither of them spoke for a time, Ralf watching with dull disinterest the movement of horsemen about the field, hearing the noise of victory from within the bailey. De Guilbert's knights had found the wine stores. He guessed some of Dickon

Blue's men, the bugger-alls, were stealing whatever they could tear loose and carry away.

"You win, Ralf."

"What?" When the Norman looked up he was surprised to see fresh tears washing over the mud and dried blood beneath Robin's eyes. "I thought you were wounded."

"No. You?"

"Nothing much. I am very good at staying alive."

"Ent you just. We'll have to live with your kind from here out, I reckon. God . . ."

Ralf thought to get up but that required effort. In a moment. "Self-righteous, yes, but I must deny you self-pity. Is there so little waiting for you? So little done here? You took Norwich, you and your damned Greyfeathers. You won."

"Not yet." Through the grime and tears, Robin glowered up at the hated Norman mass of Norwich Castle. "Not yet, Ralf. But we will."

As he took Robin's hand to rise, Ralf could interpret nothing in the man's expression. Like most Normans, he could read English faces no better than the future.

51

fOR THE REST of that year, William was absorbed with the rebellion in Brittany and relied on Matilda and Lanfranc to sift and resolve English affairs. Breteuil was imprisoned, Waltheof fled to Flanders. The kingdom was healed but not yet hale. Less important matters received briefer attention, such as the inflammatory letter from Richard de Guilbert accusing Ralf Fitz-Gerald of disobedience, treason, and flying a battle flag that should not have existed after Hastings. The screeching diatribe impugned the new vicomte's honor, crown loyalty, fitness for elevation, everything but his questionable birth. The baron was not incensed that far beyond caution.

William was more of a realist. Victory was a fact and wounded pride incidental. The matter of the Fighting Man struck him closer to home. From Normandy, the king demanded a full accounting of Ralf. The damned flag should have been burned or buried with Harold. Wherefore did it still exist and with whom?

The response from Nottingham was closely perused in Grantham and Rouen. Here and there Lanfranc discerned subtleties of phrasing that smacked more of his prized pupil Judith than her husband.

Nor I nor Denby knew of the flag until immediately before the Norwich campaign. It was taken from Hastings and preserved by John Littlerede who died at Norwich in the king's service. Whatever ensign my English

518

followed, no other men of any rank or condition were clearer in their duty to the king, none more direct in its conclusion. In the matter of Baron de Guilbert, it is this very determination of which he complains. . . .

Hard facts outweighed emotional charges. William knew the rebellion divided friends and loyalties. Of his own disposition he would not have sent de Guilbert to Norwich. Obviously, the man prolonged and then nearly lost a campaign which Ralf Fitz-Gerald, Denby, and a handful of English plucked out of the flames for him.

The whole business? Lamentable but academic. The pragmatic king knew a practical sheriff on sight and preferred him to the prejudices of ancient blood. As for Robin and the Fighting Man, Judith's fine hand was even more evident to the Italian archbishop.

. . . after weeks of waste, they won Norwich in a terrible hour. Their treason, if such it was, showed as in a mirror the glowing opposite of that shame. Of ninety-five men, I lost fifty including the standard-bearer John Littlerede who, lacking a proper shroud, was wrapped for burial in the flag he carried. The grave is marked by a stone hard by the church in Norwich Tombland.

Superstition and pained conscience were part of William's character. Sentimentality and largeness of heart were not. The flag was dangerous. He gave secret orders to open the grave and verify the truth of Fitz-Gerald's statements.

His messengers wished to be precise: And if the flag was indeed a shroud?

"Then leave it one," William decreed. "So it should have been since England was ours."

As with John's grave, the matter of Norwich was closed.

The rest of Ralf's courteous letter dealt with matters secondary to the crown, save perhaps William's passion for hunting which Sherwood satisfied above all other royal preserves.

My lady wife Judith adds her thanks to my lord and the queen for the gracious pardon of her cousin Edward and the release of Lady Maud. My enlarged honors now requiring a number of stewards and delegation, let my king not be displeased that I have sworn Edward of Denby as my vassal to hold of me those lands once owned of his family. He is not ambitious. This is all he has ever wanted.

In her scriptorium, Matilda mused over the letter with Lanfranc. "Extraordinary man. The whole brood in fact. Would you ascribe ambition to that pastoral brigand?"

The archbishop's hands shaped a reaction untranslatable as his smile. He had more synonyms for ambition than Matilda had. "As time will better define. I know him far less well than you."

Matilda laid the letter aside and took up her embroidery, lips pursed reflectively over intricate stitches and the equally involved English character. At her age and position, simplicity became attractive. "Oh, Marian is an angel. But with Robin I share Gilly's feelings: a sort of political indigestion. Let us speak of more pleasant things. I am weary of England. How I would adore to be home now, but as usual there are matters of state. Pass me the green floss there?"

Putting aside old enmity and newer respect, time would indeed better define Robin of Denby to Ralf Fitz-Gerald. Much of the man was plain, antique, and even quaint. Much else was not. As a vassal Robin would have a voice in the forest courts at Papplewick. Between one's duty to crown and the other's passionate notions of law, they would inevitably clash again.

"Though God keep us from that. I would not have it so," Ralf protested to Judith as he blew out the candle by their wide bed and lay beside his wife listening to the muted sounds of Nottingham settling for the night beyond their window.

"God keep us all." Judith nestled her dark head on Ralf's shoulder. "It was a goodly letter, Ralf. You said he was not ambitious."

"I know. All the same . . ."

"What?"

"*Rien.* Nothing."

Nothing tangible one could point to and say: Here is ambition. Not as most men defined the term.

Yet I heard him when he rallied the men to march, heard him speak of realities and now, while I felt he reached far beyond now. The king is my world, Judith. Robin's aims I cannot understand. Honor is lettered differently on his page. I gave him Denby for Marian's sake, gave him his forest and pray he will stay there. Sweet Robin's dangerous as flame in dry straw.

But I am tired, you are warm against me and I am more for sleep now than philosophy.

* * *

Sunlight over Denby land never glared, more mellow gold than dazzle. The oxcart creaked up the rise from the vale and Robin saw beyond Denby gate to the rye fields, where Blidworth reapers cut and stacked the yield. Not a generous harvest; the war left its mark. They must all eke and ration again, but surely next year would be better.

On the bench behind Robin, Marian and Maud swayed and jounced with the movement of the cart. Solemn and wide-eyed between them, Edward absorbed the quiet and deep-green of this new world. His mother savored deeply the sight of the reapers, humming a harvest song learned from her grandmother. She loved it all, especially the familiar-strange sight of a dark colt of a boy running to open the gate.

"Look, Mum. It's Eddain, and see how he's grown." *Has it been so long, then?* Marian clasped Maud's pale hand where it lay listlessly in the woman's lap. "You're home. And so are you," she informed Perdu peering from the new wicker traveling box, a gift from Queen Matilda.

Framed in her new linen veil, Maud's cheeks were gradually losing their pallor with the blessing of light and air. More silent than before, she would never again be the sure mistress who bound up all of Denby in the plying stitches of her needle, nor the picture Robin remembered with a pang: galloping swiftly across the vale to Blidworth with the news of Aelred's return, the bright laughter of her happiness floating back to her son. She would never lose the compulsive habit of scrubbing at her hands when they were not occupied and would wear brighter colors always, as if warming her soul through her senses. There would be light again, even sparkle in the deep-set eyes but always as well the shadow of where she had been.

"Lord, but this place is a havoc," she pronounced with distaste. "Wants a good straightening."

"Greetings, Lord Robin!" Eddain called in a voice breaking on man-hood as he swung the gate wide. He loped to the side of the wagon, bobbed his head to the ladies, grinned at little Edward. "*Och*, there's a *man* his mother has brought home."

"Where are my folk?" Robin wanted to know. "Have they all come?"

"In your very own hall, my lord," Eddain announced with a bardic flourish. "All who have awaited you, all who have come on before. *Dyw*, it is grand!"

Grand it was to Robin as Eddain ran before them to open the hall door. Lady Maud went first on Robin's arm. Marian followed with Edward clutching one hand, Perdu's wicker box in the other. As family now,

Perdu would mouse to her heart's content in hall and bower. Marian let Edward walk beside her that he enter his father's hall on his own two feet.

As Eddain said, they were all waiting in a formal line on the south side of the hall as was proper for retainers and guests. Robin breathed deeply the familiar air of this center to his life. Angharad, Minna, and Gudrun had scrubbed it clean of foreign trespass and strewn fresh rushes and herbs, yet to Robin there was the bothersome sense of a personal space used by outsiders and not quite the same. His mother straightened her back from old habit as Ethelwold, bearing his white wand of office, presented himself and bowed his head.

"My lord and lady."

Robin took the old man's hand. "No longer *lord,* Ethelwold."

"Perhaps not at Grantham," his steward temporized, "but this is Sherwood."

So it was and all of them there: Will and Angharad, Mauger and Beorn, Minna and Gudrun wringing work-rosy hands in their aprons, tremulous but happy. Even Wystan, turned out by his wife in blue linen Sunday best with an immaculate bandage over his eyes. Robin stopped by him.

Wystan had only one question. "Where is the flag, Thane?"

"With John. He carried it well and in your name. Did he not, Will Scatloch?"

"He did," Will swore, "in such a glory as Taliesin himself might sing."

"John's at King Harold's board tonight. Be you at mine."

All of you be with me, Robin wished to his people. This night was the feast of the Assumption. They would pray to Saint Mary. *Brother Mauger, stay with me until the world and your restless heart dance you away. School me more for the battles to come. Teach me to think.*

Robin moved down the line to Gwaun standing taller now beside tearful Angharad. "Eh, you've grown like your brother."

To Morgan, favoring his left leg at Will's side: "I will have a need for good foresters now."

"Lawful ones, Morgan of Powys," Will reminded him out of the side of his mouth. "We shoot for the sheriff now, not at him."

"Christ, Scatloch. It is a burden you are when a man wants to feel free."

And finally, Father Beorn, greyer now but still a hawk. "Well, Beorn. We've been a way together."

"And I think much changed, Robin."

True. In the forest was one need, here another. The dear man was still cast out by his faith, forbidden even to enter his own church. There was a waste. Beorn eased John from one life to another in the mud at Norwich, and though Robin privately guessed how, Beorn would never speak of the matter. Like himself the man was used to shepherding the lives of his folk. God was beyond Robin's reach, but churches were made up of mortal, mutable men. Surely Ralf could help. Judith knew the archbishop-regent. There'd be a middle way somewhere.

Lady Maud spoke for the first time when she embraced Angharad. "Are my keys to hand?"

"Lady, the good steward has them."

Ethelwold presented the heavy iron ring laden with keys to Maud, who paused a moment, perhaps relishing the solid, safe weight of them.

"Lady Marian?"

The world Maud knew was lost and gone but not her proprieties or sense of what was just. She passed the ring of keys to Marian, each an iron finger on the hand that held firmly what belonged to it. "Be so good, *Hlaefdige*. Hear me all. Henceforth Lady Marian will head the table and the prayers as mistress of this house. And here is Edward, the son of Edward, who is the son of Aelred, who was the son of Brihtnoth. . . ."

And here's me and Robin and our life and my cat, Marian savored as she walked beside Robin next morning through the high, green arcade of oaks. *More than a place, a faith and a way. Even Ralf knew that.*

They strolled at ease, Edward astride his father's shoulders, Perdu draped over Marian's left shoulder and fascinated as the child with this new world to roam and hunt.

It was early still; some of the mist not burned away by morning sun helped the soft loam underfoot to mute their footfalls to a silence where only blood could be heard singing in the ear.

Unless one were truly listening. Robin lifted Edward down and set him on his feet, kneeling behind the boy and close to the small ear. "Listen. There's much it's telling you."

Marian knelt beside them. "He's a young one for that, love."

"He is not. No younger than I when my da bade me so." Now, before words and names came to clutter hearing.

"Over yonder." Marian pointed a way through the columns of the great old trees to cleared land beyond. "That was to be John's bookland."

"Hush." At Edward's shoulder Robin delighted in the lifting of the boy's head: He did hear something perhaps, the first of myriad voices that would always tell him where and who and what he was while out-landers heard nothing.

"Yes, that was John's," Robin murmured after a time. "Would have been by law. Law is the arrow they've left me, love. Every law is a bow, every line of them a shaft with a sharp pile. And I'm the best archer in England."

Marian said nothing, accepting what she did not understand. Like his forest there were places in Robin she had never seen: in his way as private a man as the blacksmith he spoke of.

"I buried John's flag, not ours."

Edward child-shrugged off his father's arms, wanting to stand on his own, unhindered even by love now. Robin stood back with Marian, knowing the boy's concentration and fresh wonder. On a branch overhead a bird tick-ticked, a red squirrel darted up a nearby tree trunk. The slight scratching of its claws caught the boy's attention with the same feral intensity, following the sound and movement.

"Hear it," Robin whispered.

The boy listened to his forest.

Author's Afterword

*F*OR INTERESTED READERS, a few definitions might be helpful regarding terms, customs, and motivations described in *Sherwood*. Robin Hood as legend needs no explanation. As possible fact, he is very likely a composite of a number of men run afoul of forest laws over several centuries. The essence of the legend is common men defying unjust laws and the abuse of power. The tradition of placing Robin in the twelfth century seems to have begun with Scott's *Ivanhoe* and continued via Hollywood and television. Beyond pure romance, this has always bothered me from the standpoint of historical truth. "Good" King Richard spent no more than four months of his ten-year reign in England and regarded it mainly as a source of revenue for his wars. I chose to set the story a hundred years earlier at the time of the Norman Conquest, where the dramatic elements would not be changed but only intensified.

The Normans conquered and imposed feudalism on a people much more socially complex than themselves. Among the Saxons a man's place in society was measured for legal purposes by the money value of his holdings. The title of *thane* designated a man who owned at least five hides of land. A *hide* consisted of between a hundred and a hundred and twenty acres, varying in different parts of England. With seven hides Robin would be a small but substantial landowner.

To call such people democratic would be inaccurate, but they were what democracy evolved from, an instinctively legalistic, contentious, profit-minded folk who already had a massive body of written law and civil custom where their Norman conquerors had none. A contradictory people with precise social gradations from king through half-free cottagers like Much to slaves like Will Scatloch.

There was little hard money in general circulation, since most rents and exchanges were made in food or personal service. The silver penny and half-penny were the only actual coins current, shilling, pound, and mark being terms of account. By modern standards, the buying power of a penny would be huge. A windfall of three pounds to each of Robin's men as their share in a robbery would be unimaginable wealth to peasants.

The Normans transformed England, probably for the better. They had an energetic genius for organization and efficiency, the English for law and political progress. William, probably illiterate himself, wondered at and ultimately left the unique Saxon legal machinery intact. His purposes may have been ruthless; he could more efficiently collect taxes with the system than without it, but in the hands of Englishmen and the later Anglo-Normans, the precedents of this cumbersome machinery churned inevitably toward Magna Charta and beyond. If men like Robin had no word, they nevertheless had a sure instinct for the justice toward which they groped.

Seen in this light, Robin and Marian, Tuck, Wystan, and Little John would not have been out of place on Boston Common, Bunker Hill, or at Valley Forge, where their direct descendants stood up and, in the matter of taxes, told another king, "That ent right."

About the Author

PARKE GODWIN SOLD his first short story in 1952, but tried a number of careers before returning to writing. He has been a radio operator, research technician, maître d'hôtel, short-order cook, and an actor—which he considers by far his best training as a novelist.

Always eclectic in subject matter, his works include *Firelord* and *Beloved Exile,* which are novels of Arthur and Guinevere, as well as modern satirical novels, *Waiting for the Galactic Bus* and *The Snake Oil Wars.* One of his short stories was dramatized on the new *Twilight Zone* series as "Time and Teresa Golowitz," starring Gene Barry.

Mr. Godwin now lives in California, where he is at work on *Conscience of the King,* the concluding volume of the life of Robin Hood.